Edward L. Blanchard

The Life and Reminiscences

Edward L. Blanchard

The Life and Reminiscences

ISBN/EAN: 9783337057473

Printed in Europe, USA, Canada, Australia, Japan

Cover: Foto ©Raphael Reischuk / pixelio.de

More available books at **www.hansebooks.com**

THE

LIFE AND REMINISCENCES

OF

E. L. BLANCHARD,

WITH

NOTES FROM THE DIARY OF WM. BLANCHARD.

BY

CLEMENT SCOTT AND CECIL HOWARD.

With Portraits and Illustrations.

IN TWO VOLUMES.

VOL. I.

LONDON:

HUTCHINSON & CO.,

25, PATERNOSTER SQUARE.

1891.

PREFACE.

" At the midnight in the silence of the sleeptime,
When you set your fancies free,
Will they pass to where—by death, fools think—imprisoned
Low he lies who once so loved you, whom you loved so,
Pity me ? "

ROBERT BROWNING.

UNLESS I am very much mistaken, few people will be more astonished at the details of the busy, painstaking, perplexing, honourable, and affectionate life contained in these interesting pages, than the most intimate friends of Edward Litt Leman Blanchard. I claim to be one of them. I knew him intimately, from the time that I changed from boyhood to manhood until the hour of his death. I was for many years his constant companion in business and in pleasure also. Although far older than myself, I looked upon E. L. B. as a brother rather than a father, for as long as I knew him he never lost the heartiness, the impulse, and the energy of a boy. Night after night I have sat by his side at the theatre, spring after spring I have walked by his side about his beloved Gravesend district, round and about the Kentish villages, over the sandhills between Sandwich and Deal, by sea and meadow,

by lake and stream—ever finding him the dearest
of companions, the most amusing of *raconteurs*;
and yet I, of all others, as I read, and read on,
the pages of the record of a life's endeavour, feel
that in reality I never knew the man at all.

I am certain at any rate of this, that I did
not know the suffering man. I did not know
what intense disappointment and perplexity he
was concealing under the mask of his sunny
garrulity. I did not see the fox gnawing at the
vitals of this brave and honest gentleman.

Blanchard's early life as I knew it, or as I
thought I knew it, his daily toil and drudgery,
and his heart-breaking exertions, before God
lightened the burden and gave him his life's
sunrise with the well-beloved Carina, seem to me
like the record of some extraordinary martyrdom.
How nobly, how loyally, how honourably it was
all endured! He might have said, and said truly,
as he does say in the private pages of this diary,—

> "Once I said, almost despairing,
>   This must break my spirit now;
> But I bore it, and am bearing—
>   Only do not ask me how!"

There are very few men who can keep the dark
secret of their life's sorrow so closely hidden as
Blanchard did. He had the tenderest of hearts;
but he did not wear it on his sleeve for daws to
peck at. In all our walks, in all our rambles, in
all our confidences, he never once alluded to his
sorrows, or his privations, or his domestic anguish,

or the terrible pulls that were being made at his
slender purse-strings, nor did he even distantly
allude to the love of his life miles and miles away.
That was too sacred a chapter in his life's history
even for his familiar friends. I knew nothing, and
I don't believe that any other of his intimate
friends knew more. His nature was so lovable
and sunny that he did not care to bring his
wretchedness outside his own four walls. Friendship, nature, and tobacco were the solace and
so to speak the reaction of his life. His heart
might bleed when at work in his own lonely
chambers; but he did not bring his misery outside his own street door.

I first met E. L. Blanchard at.the old Arundel
Club, in Salisbury Street, Strand, at the time when
I first started, quite as a boy, on the thorny path
of journalism. I was at the time in Government
employment; but I occupied my evenings in
going to the play, and was lucky enough to be
able to make a little money in addition to the
enjoyment of my personal pleasure. In those
days the Arundel Club was a delightful society,
and, in fact, it was a liberal education for a
young journalist. Here I met Blanchard, and
Robertson, and Byron, and Leicester Buckingham,
and Frederick Guest Tomlins, and Bayle Bernard,
and Stirling Coyne, all connected in one way
or other with dramatic journalism; and these
men, some of them old enough to be my father,
held out to me, from the outset, the cordial hand
of good-fellowship.

But it was Blanchard who specially attached himself to me, and gave me the benefit of his encouragement, advice, and experience. I count among the happiest days of my life those on which, after office hours in Pall Mall, we used to meet at the " Edinburgh Castle," or Carr's, in the Strand, or at the Arundel Club house dinner, and repair afterwards to the play. The whole journey to the play-house was enlivened with anecdotes or reminiscences. The far-off journeys we loved best. If business took us to Sadlers Wells, or Highbury Barn, or Cremorne, or the Surrey, Blanchard would be sure to know some wonderful tavern noted for some remarkable commodity. In we had to go, following at his heels as if he were the Pied Piper of Hamelin, to taste this or that, and to hear stories of the wonderful actors and literary men who had frequented the house. Blanchard was a walking encyclopædia. With him at your side there was no need to consult Peter Cunningham or John Timbs. He had a delightful way of elaborating fact and of hanging round it a garland of fancy. If exaggeration it may be called, it was very charming exaggeration. His imagination was so keen that he could not always keep it in restraint.

And so it came about that in the destiny of time I came to be appointed the deputy to Blanchard on the great daily newspaper on which he had worked incessantly almost from its inauguration. As dramatic critic of *The Sunday Times,* of *The Weekly Despatch,* of *The Illustrated*

Times, of *The London Figaro*, of *The Observer*, and
of many other papers, I had sat by Blanchard's
side, always receiving from him encouragement,
sympathy, and advice. When the time came for
me to be associated with him in the dramatic
department of *The Daily Telegraph*, he was the
very first to pat me on the back; indeed, I am
not at all sure that he was not instrumental in
securing me the coveted post. There was not a
trace of jealousy or envy in Blanchard's nature,
and from the time I joined *The Daily Telegraph*
our friendship increased rather than waned. He
knew better than any man the value of applause,
and recognised what a small amount of it ever falls
to the anonymous critic. Often he used to say to
me, "When we write we do not write for the
public, but for the esteem of the two or three
friends who love us";—and so he never failed, even
up to a few months before his death, to send me
a line or a post-card when any article of mine had
particularly pleased him. It was this encouragement that did me more good than anything else
in the world. Molière used to read his plays to
his cook. I have a friend—a poet, dramatist, and
journalist of our own time—who insists upon
giving his tit-bits in verse or prose to a confi-
dential housekeeper. I know myself that, when
I have written in hot haste a poem or an article,
I feel I must read it to somebody. It may be
very vain, and in the eyes of some contemptible,
but it is a fact. Blanchard recognised the journal-
istic failing, for he knew that the word of honest

praise would produce better work by-and-by. He was right. We do not write for the public, but for the one or two who love us, and who understand us.

Almost cradled as he was in the theatre, the son of a celebrated actor, with his child-life spent among members of the profession, it was natural that Blanchard should have had a greater knowledge of the subject on which he wrote than any man of his time. He was gifted with a marvellous memory, and was scrupulously accurate. His library was not a very extensive one, and yet he never failed in names or dates. In fact, he had two memories, and, as many cynics insisted, could recall things that occurred before he was born—because he was the companion of his father, and was the transmitter, as it were, of his father's recollections. This was the reason that E. L. Blanchard was supposed to be so old. He remembered what his father told him, and the general impression was that everything he told his friends had occurred to him. In his best days my old friend was a lucid, comprehensive, and admirable critic of stage plays. He belonged to the old school of journalism, and adopted the rigidly impersonal style. It was the paper that spoke, not the writer. If he ever erred, he erred on the side of kindliness and charity. He could not bear giving pain to any one. His love and care for children and dumb animals were pathetic. I don't think he would have tolerated the destruction of a black beetle, and if he were bothered by a wasp he would coax it out of the window. His gentle, considerate, kindly nature animated all his work; and though he loved the art to which he devoted much of his life, he loved the feelings of the artist better. Yet at times he could be righteously severe, and sometimes astonished us all with what is now known as a "slating" criticism. His notice of *The Pink Dominos*, when first brought out at the Criterion, was one of the strongest things of the kind I ever read. But, in addition to his dramatic work, he was a facile journalist and a graceful poet. For years and years he contributed special descriptive articles to *The Daily Telegraph*, by whose kind-hearted proprietors he was held, from first to last, in affectionate esteem. At one period of his life his impressionable nature led him into the study of spiritualism. From his infancy he was an admirable conjurer, a bit of a necromancer; and, as we see, he once edited *The Astrologer*. He liked his friends to believe that he had mysterious powers. In the heat of the movement, about 1860, he was in the thick of the spiritualistic mania, and honestly believed what he was told to believe. But the exposure of the Davenport Brothers, the downfall of D. D. Home, and the discredit that attached to the *séances* of Mrs. Marshall and others, somewhat shook his confidence. He did not declare himself a pervert from the faith; but he quietly renounced the active part of spiritualism. You see, he was a conjurer, and knew the tricks of the trade. At that time the discussions at the

Arundel Club between Tom Robertson, a confirmed sceptic, and both Blanchard and Leicester Buckingham, avowed spiritualists, were lively enough, and led to many a scene. In after years Blanchard was able to separate hypnotic influence from charlatanism: he knew that there was a border land between will and stage trickery.

I have seldom met a man so mentally and physically active as E. L. Blanchard. He was a great pedestrian, and never seemed to tire. His tastes were simple, and his habits healthy. He loved to get out of London and to run down to his beloved Gravesend, where, in half an hour, he would forget the cares of London life, and be cheerfully smoking his pipe in the cosy garden or wainscoted parlour of some village inn, and delighting in the conversation of mine host and the rustics. It was here that he picked up characters for his plays and poems and stories. He knew the value of reaction—no one better. And small wonder that such a man should be beloved by the children! They literally adored him. It did not matter where he was—on the outskirts of Cobham or in Drury Lane—the children were always tugging at Blanchard's pockets, where they would be sure to find either sweets or some stray pennies for goodies in the future.

Who would have dreamed that the man as we knew him, the sunny, light-hearted, affectionate companion, full of anecdotes, apparently without a care in the world, left us at night to return to a home to face despair such as would have crushed the strongest of us? Who could conceive that this generous creature was supporting out of his slender earnings innumerable relations, and restoring again and again the ruins of a shattered home?

But it is a long lane that has no turning. The sorrows allotted in life to some of us do not last for ever; and Blanchard, after years of patient fidelity, won the joy for which he had longed in vain. His romance of a life had a most dramatic moment, which he once confided to me. Far away in the wilds of New Zealand the beloved Carina, so often referred to in the diary, was taken suddenly ill. She was quartered in a rough but homely hut, which, as so often happens in the colonies, was papered with scraps of newspapers from home. Opening her eyes after the delirium of fever, when tossing on her restless couch, the eyes of Carina fell on some verses signed "E. L. B." In this heartfelt poem was the wail of a constant but almost broken-hearted man, " Come back to me ! " That poetic prayer was answered, for she did come back. The child-lovers were reunited, and Carina gave to this lonely, dispirited, and forlorn man the happiest hours of his honourable but desperate life. I, who knew the old Southampton Street days, the old Gravesend days, the lonely birthdays and Christmastides, can safely say that with the happy home in Adelphi Terrace and the love contained in it, came the crown of a long and trying life,—E. L. B. was happy at last. He smiled with his heart as well as his face. He lived just long enough to be spared the miseries attendant on old age that verges into second childishness. He was released from toil; and though he never had an opportunity of continuing the history of the stage from where Geneste left off, down to the nineties, still I would hope that his exhaustive diary here given to the public contains matter and reference enough to guide the future historian. It certainly bridges over the blank period of unwritten history between Macready and Henry Irving.

It is not my fault that these recollections are in diary form. Although it may not be the most convenient shape for a book that is history and autobiography at the same time, still thus the material was handed to me and thus it was bound to remain. But there was one way that even the rough notes of a private diary could be improved upon and made valuable to the dramatic student. I am deeply indebted to my friend and colleague Mr. Cecil Howard for his industry, accuracy, and patient research in illustrating this volume with those notes and comments which cannot fail to be of the greatest assistance to the dramatic student and historian. With laudable patience Mr. Howard has added, wherever he could, to Blanchard's store of facts. Practically such a labour is inexhaustible; but a line had to be drawn somewhere, and it was drawn at the publication of this book. I do not say it is complete;

but it is the best we could do in the time, and the credit of the compilation belongs to Mr. Cecil Howard, dramatic critic, and patient editor of *Dramatic Notes*.

I have also to acknowledge the generous assistance and co-operation of Messrs. W. E. Church, Harry Plowman, J. T. Foard, Lionel Brough, Dr. Lomas, and my thanks to Mr. Harrington Baily for the kind loan of the picture of the members of the Urban Club.

CLEMENT SCOTT.

EDWARD LEMAN BLANCHARD.

EDWARD LEMAN BLANCHARD was born at No. 28, originally 31, Great Queen Street, London, December 11th, 1820. From his possessing such a marvellous memory, and being enabled to speak of events that happened when he must have been quite a child, it was generally supposed by those who knew him intimately later in life that he must have " put back the clock," and was really much older than he declared himself to be. The exact date is, however, proved by his father's diaries, which are in the possession of E. L. B.'s widow. William Blanchard,[1] his father,

[1] The following was found among William Blanchard's papers, and would lead one to believe that he had the intention of writing his autobiography :—" *Life of William Blanchard, comedian, nearly thirty-five years an actor of some reputation at the Theatre Royal, Covent Garden written by himself.* I was born on the 2nd of January, 1769, at three, o'clock in the morning, at my father's house in Nessgate, York, where he had carried on the business of staymaker and hosier. My mother was a native of Leeds, and her name, as I have heard, was Ann, or, as she was generally called, ' Nancy,' Bowzer. She had one son before me, who died young. I was the second, and survived ; but when I was only a year and a half my mother had a daughter ; she died in child-bed, the infant died also, so that I never had the happiness of knowing my dear maternal parent. After her death my father had no pleasure in home, and he at length placed me with an old couple in Tanner Row, of the name of John and Nurse Hassell, and he himself went to Helmsley Blackmore to manage . . . . "

In the graveyard of Chelsea New Church, dedicated to St. Luke,

was twice married; his first wife, Susan, died on May 15th, 1807, leaving him with four children, John, Charlotte, Mary, and Betsy. On October 15th, 1808, he married Sarah Harrold,[1] and she

repose the remains of Blanchard and Egerton, two actors of established character, side by side. William Blanchard was what is termed " a useful comedian ; " whatever part was assigned to him he made the most of it. At the age of seventeen he joined a provincial theatrical company at York, his native city ; and in 1800, after fourteen years of laborious country practice, appeared at Covent Garden as Bob Acres, in *The Rivals*, and Crack, in *The Turnpike Gate*. At the time of his death, May 9th, 1835, he resided at No. 1, Camera Square, Chelsea. Blanchard had dined with a friend at Hammersmith, and left him to return home about six in the evening of Tuesday. On the following morning, at three o'clock, poor Blanchard was found lying in a ditch by the roadside, having been, as is supposed, seized by a fit ; in the course of the evening he was visited by another attack, which was succeeded by one more violent on the Thursday, and on the following day he expired.

[1] Mrs. E. L. Blanchard gives the following amusing account of how William Blanchard the elder first became acquainted with his second wife :— " E. L. B. derived much of his inventive talent from his clever mother, who used to illustrate by *doll models* all the nursery stories on which he afterwards founded his pantomimes; and, at a very early age, he used to invent words for Little Boy Blue to speak, for the Old Woman who lived in the Shoe, Bluebeard's family, etc., etc., which year by year he enlarged and improved until his true talent developed itself for stage purposes. The circumstances under which William Blanchard, his father, first met this charming little lady, then Miss Sarah Harrold, were very amusing and romantic. He was a widower with four daughters, all considerably older than she was ; they were schoolfellows. One Christmas they begged their father to let them invite her to stay with them for the holidays. He consented, never having seen her. At the same time was expected a relative, a young middy ; his portmanteau had arrived the day before himself, and un-locked. The schoolfellows, full of animal spirits, peeped into the trunk, pulled out the uniform, and in a merry humour Miss Harrold must please to dress up in it, and caper about pretending to make love to one of the Miss Blanchards. Papa, hearing some screaming and noise, opened the door suddenly to enquire the cause, and saw the supposed middy embracing one of his daughters in her bedroom. He was about to hurl the impudent intruder downstairs, when the girls screamed out, 'Oh papa, papa, it is only our schoolfellow, Miss Harrold, having fun !' Then his wrath turned in another direction, and he ex-claimed she could be no modest girl who would dress up in male attire,

became the mother of William, the first born in 1811, and Edward. The following are taken (fully quoted) from William Blanchard's diaries; the entry of December 11th, 1831, should completely set at rest any question as to E. L. B.'s age.

"*May 2nd*, 1825.—Mrs. B. took Ned to see the pantomime, and wisely took her reticule, with about £5 in it, which a thief cut off and stole from her."

"*Oct. 8th*, 1827.—Dear Ned went to school at Brixton for the first time."

Before this, the elder brother William had gone to school in Brixton, and the address there given was at Mr. Smith's, 4, Clarmont Place, Brixton. This was in January 1826. William appears to have gone as a day-scholar, and to have lived with his grandmother, who resided at Brixton.

"*Feb. 2nd*, 1829.—Saw my darling Ned off for Lichfield, under the care of Mr. Henry. *8th*.—Heard our darling Ned had arrived safe."

in a private house, and no fit companion for his daughters. The poor little supposed middy had hidden in shame behind the bed-curtains till he was gone, then she made them promise to say she had left, afraid to see him again ; and knowing there was to be a dance in the evening, she prevailed on them to let her be announced by another name, as an outside visitor, and to get their father to ask her to dance with him. She was very pretty, and charmingly dressed, and the papa was nothing loth to lead such a partner to the head of the room to open the ball. She threw out all her allurements, made herself agreeable, and quite won his heart,—so much so, indeed, that, though only seventeen, she became his wife, and the stepmother of four daughters, two of whom were already married and had children ; and I have often heard E. L. B. tell the amusing story of one of these children (of course, his niece) being eighteen years older than himself, having taken him as a little boy to see an old gentleman friend, and with much suppressed fun presented him thus : ' Sir, allow me to introduce to you my uncle,' and dear E. L. B., appreciating the situation, made a most condescending bow."

In September of the same year Blanchard Senior went into Lichfield, and then he writes :—

"*Sept.* 21*st.*—Drove over to see Ned at Noxall, and found the dear boy quite hearty. Brought him back with us. 22*nd.*—Took my darling boy a long walk. 23*rd.*— Ned and I went with Mr. Taylor to the farm. 24*th.*—Took leave of my dearest Ned this morning—bless him ! "

E. L. B. seems to have remained at Lichfield —except that he came home for the holidays— until 1831. In that year he left England with his father [1] and mother for New York. They left Liverpool on board the *Marion* " on October 11th, 1831, and reached New York on December 21st, after seventy-one days at sea, the weather having been dreadfully stormy ; " and during the latter part of the voyage they had been almost as badly off for food as the seamen on board.

On December 11th (while at sea) W. B. writes:

"*My dear Edward's birthday ; completed his eleventh year.* God preserve him."

[1] Mr. William Blanchard had a tempting engagement offered him by his son-in-law, Thomas Hamblin, to appear at the Bowery Theatre, New York. At the same time were engaged E. J. Parsloe for clown (one who had made a reputation as the Nondescript in *Peter Wilkins* at Covent Garden), Gay was harlequin, and Louisa Johnson (also known at Covent Garden) columbine. The pantaloon was one by Sonas, Hamblin's nephew, and they all appeared in *Mother Goose*, but the venture was a disastrous one. The New Yorkers did not quite understand this, the first pantomime ever played in America. Parsloe had hurt his spine on the voyage ; he could not do his best ; the third night he was very ill, and was dead in the morning. Gay, E. L. B. relates, wandered on to the West, after vainly endeavouring to establish himself in Boston and Baltimore ; and, appearing one night at an Indian encampment in his harlequin's dress, was taken by the red men for a great medicine man, and lived with them a year, till he had parted with all his spangles. He eventually found his way back to England and Whitechapel.

At the end of 1831 Blanchard Senior is still acting in New York.

E. L. B. was sub-editor in 1836 of Pinnock's *Guide to Knowledge*, as will be found mentioned in his diary, November 18th, 1885 ; and, as sub-editor, to use his own words, received " the princely remuneration of ten shillings per week, paid at first by Whitaker & Co., Ave Maria Lane."

In the year 1839 private theatricals were given, of which two playbills are reproduced (*see* pp. 6-9), and a pantomime was also performed at a large school in the Old Kent Road, called Rodney House. It was produced by a number of young men, assisted by the choir boys of St. Paul's and the Chapel Royal.[1]

This pantomime was written by E. L. B., who also constructed the tricks, played Harlequin, and generally superintended the whole performance.

It was called *The Old Woman and Her Three Sons ;* or, *Harlequin and the Wizard of Wokey Hole.* Owing to the large amount of vocal talent the music was made a prominent feature, and the choruses were most efficiently rendered. This pantomime was so successful that it was repeated for several evenings, and it was at one of these subsequent productions that Blanchard, in consequence of the indisposition of the lady (or gentleman) who played Columbine, had to relinquish his duties as Harlequin, leaving them to his under-study, and play the part himself.

---

[1] On this subject he wrote the following in after years :—" People who are extremely curious in such matters may like to know that the

Judging from a contemporaneous criticism, his assumption must have been more vigorous than graceful ; as a lady in the front of the house, who was not in the secret, remarked that the " girl " who played columbine was positively immodest.

THEATRE ROYAL.

In consequence of the unprecedented demand for places to witness the Performances that have astonished and delighted such crowded audiences during the past week, the Committee of Management feel it incumbent upon them to state that the Royal Belvidere Theatre will open for

TWO NIGHTS MORE,

Being Positively the Last Nights of the Season.

Upon this occasion will be presented Mayhew's laughable Burletta of

"THE WANDERING MINSTREL."

Mr. Crincum, Mr. Blanchard ; Herbert Carol, Mr. Cottrell ; Tweedle, Mr. Holcroft ; Jem Bags, Mr. Howe ; Mrs. Crincum, Miss Ellen Best ; Julia, Miss Fortescue ; Peggy, Miss Bland.

---

first amateur pantomimes ever represented were given in the years 1838, 1839, and 1840, at a large theatre, specially fitted up for the occasion each succeeding Christmas and Easter, at a spacious mansion then known as Rodney House, in the Old Kent Road. Admission was, of course, only by tickets gratuitously issued, and the performances were so successful that they were repeated several nights in succession. Original music was composed for these remarkable entertainments by the late Mr. J. Howe, an accomplished musician ; and the vocal portions were rendered by the well-trained choristers of St. Paul's and Westminster Abbey, under the direction of Mr. John L. Hopkins, afterwards organist of Trinity College, Cambridge. The elaborate scenery, properties, tricks, changes, and transformations were all of home manufacture, and attracted considerable admiration at the time, and out of the thirty merry-hearted youths who combined to produce these notable entertainments, about three survive. One is Mr. James Coward, the Crystal Palace organist ; another is Mr. Withall, a grave solicitor, who married the once popular singer, Miss Kathleen Fitzwilliam ; and the third is the writer of these lines, who wrote the three pantomimes, respectively entitled, *The Three Men of Thessaly, The Old Woman and Her Three Sons,* and *Harlequin Pat-a-Cake.*"

After which,

"CAPTAIN STEVENS."

Captain Stevens, Mr. Edgar Mills ; Splashton, Mr. Perkins ; Tom Stag,
Mr. Howe ; Tim, Mr. Blanchard ; Podger, Mr. Holdfast ; Colonel Rochfort,
Mr. Phillpots ; Snipperwell, Mr. Forrest ; Felton, Mr. Pelham ;
Miss Rochfort, Miss Bland ; Blonde, Miss Best.

In the course of the evening a professional gentleman will perform several
favourite pieces of music upon the newly invented and much-admired
Instrument,

THE CHERUBINE,

Sole Inventor and Patentee, James Braby, Esq.
The whole to conclude with the
new grand and never-to-have-been-sufficiently-laughed-at comic pantomime,
entitled,

"THE OLD WOMAN and HER THREE SONS,

or,

Harlequin and the Wizard of Wokey Hole."

With new Music, new Scenery, new Dresses, and new Decorations.
Jerry, *alias* Robbin the Bobbin, with an Appetite and a Song,
Mynheer Perkin.

THE TWO PRETTY MEN.

James and John, afterwards Harlequin and Clown—Signor Spangleletti and
Herr Howsch.

Grimgramgromgrumblegloom (the Wizard) - M. Giggaggogmagog.
Flimflamflostikos (his Spright-ly attendant) - Benjamin Brimstone.
Elves and Villagers by an efficient *corps* of Supernumeraries.
Dame Wrinkletwinkle, the Old Woman (afterwards Pantaloon), M. Hillini.
Florinda, the Rose of the Village (afterwards Columbine),
M. Blanchardini (who will have the honour of again bewitching the audience
in the above character).
Curtain rises at Seven precisely, after which time seats cannot be kept upon
ANY *consideration.*
VIVANT BELVIDERE THEATRICALS.

The following lines were sung by the choir,
and to them an interesting reminiscence is
attached :—

    "There was an old woman had three sons,
        Three sons, three sons, three sons ;
    There was Jerry and James and John,
    There was Jerry and James and John.

> " Jerry was hanged, and James was drowned,
>   And Johnny was lost, and he never was found ;
>   And that was the end of the three sons—
>   Jerry and James and John."

Five-and-thirty years after this, Blanchard was the guest of Mr. Bevan, the banker, at his residence near Barnet, and as they were smoking their cigars in the garden after dinner, close to an open window of the house, the sound of a piano was heard, and a voice singing, " There was an old woman had three sons," etc.

This voice turned out to belong to a gentleman who occupied a responsible position in Messrs. Barclay & Bevan's establishment, but who had been one of the actors in this pantomime, and who had never met the talented author and harlequin during the thirty odd years which had elapsed since its production.

To this playbill there is yet another interest attached. Years after, when *The Wandering Minstrel* was revived at the Olympic, little Robson made a great success as Jem Bags.

The theatricals were repeated the following year, as shown by the reprint of the playbill.

THEATRE ROYAL.

On Monday, Tuesday, Wednesday, and Thursday,
The 13th, 14th, 15th, and 16th of January, 1840,
Will be performed at the above attractive place of Private Amusement, the popular Farce of

THE QUEER SUBJECT!

Dr. Bingo......Mr. SELWYN.	Ned Snatch......Mr. HOPKINS.
Charles Markham......Mr. PERKINS.	Tom Darking......Mr. DIGHTON.
Sammy Spectre......Mr. BLANCHARD.	Bill Mattock......Mr. HOWE.
Giles......Mr. HILL.	Hodge......Mr. HOWARD.
Countryman......Mr. WILLIAMS.	Julian......Miss BLAND.

After which, the celebrated Burletta of

THE UNFINISHED GENTLEMAN!

Lord Totterly......Mr. SELWYN.　　　Frisk Flammer......Mr. PERKINS.
Charles Danvers....Mr. FAULKLAND.
Bill Downey......Mr. HOWE.　　　James Miller......Mr. BLANCHARD.
Catch......Mr. HILL.　　　Nibble......Mr. DIGHTON.
Robert......Mr. NELSON.　　　Thomas......Mr. Williams.
Louisa Bloomfield......Miss E. JAMES.　　　Mary Chintz......Miss BLAND.

The whole to conclude with a new, grand, original, peculiar, pastoral, periodical, parodiacal, pathetical, paradoxical, phantasmagorical, physiological, physiognomical, philosophical, performable, practicable, preternatural, powerfully-picturesque, potentially-punning, and pre-eminently-pantomimical Pantomime, entitled

PAT-A-CAKE PAT-A-CAKE,

Or, Harlequin and

THE BAKER'S MAN!

The dresses, decorations, machinery, tricks, changes and transformations entirely new.　The scenic department under the able superintendence of the Miller and his Men.

The music composed and dis-composed expressly for this occasion, and the Pantomime written and invented by Francisco Frost, Esq., Gent., Author of *The Three Men of Thessaly, The Old Woman and Her Three Sons*, etc., etc., etc.　The Harlequinade scenes under the especial direction of Mr. E. L. Blanchard and Mr. James Howe.

Prince Pattypan......SIGNOR ALBERT SAUSSAGEO.
Piecrust (*the Baker*)......Mr. FLOURDOUGH.
Pudding and Pie......Messrs. PASTRY and PATTYPAN.

Lightcrust......Mr. MEALYMOUTH.　　　Thickcrust......Mr. NIGHTMARE.
Pastrypantile (*the genius of the cake*)......Mr. GAGGEGGIGGOGGUGMAGOG.
Poohpooh and Peppercorn (*his attendant sprites, working as bakers under the names of Longcrust and Shortcrust*)......Mr. PERKINS and Mr. CROSS.
Pierre Pattycake (*the baker's man, afterwards Harlequin*)......M. BLANCHARDINI.
Peregrine Pepper'em (*afterwards Pantaloon*)......M. HILLINI.
Demons, Imps, Villagers, etc.
Mrs. Priscilla Pepper'em (*afterwards Clown*)......M. HOWANI.
Patty Pancake (*the pretty pride of the Province, afterwards Columbine*)......Madlle. E. JAMES.

Doors open at a Quarter to Seven, commence at a Quarter past Seven.

Stage Manager......Mr. JAMES HOWE.　　　Chorus Master......Mr. HOPKINS.

Vivat Regina.

Almost immediately after his father's death in 1835, which took place when E. L. B. was at a good school at Ealing, he travelled with an entertainer who was exhibiting the oxy-hydrogen microscope, the sort of thing that was afterwards shown at the Polytechnic, magnifying the drop of water, etc. Young as he was, E. L. B. used often to take the place of the lecturer, and acquitted himself well. However, the affair did not pay, and E. L. B. was left stranded in the West of England. He borrowed half-a-crown from a scene-painter whom he met at Bristol that he knew, and with only these funds walked to London, taking three days over the journey. He then turned his attention to writing. In the next four years his pen produced thirty dramas, farces, and burlesques, and a number of pantomimes, under the name of Francisco Frost. In 1841 he was editing Chambers's *London Journal.* He edited Dugdale's "England and Wales Delineated," and also Willoughby's Shakespeare. He was twenty-four years of age when he started *The Astrologer and Oracle of Destiny.* The title-page bore the representation of a long-bearded, ancient man, with the stars around him. This must have been congenial work for E. L. B., this supposed reading of the stars, for he always had a leaning for the mystic and occult—witness the great interest that he took in later years in spirit-rapping. At twenty-five E. L. B. edited *The New London Magazine,* and amongst the works to which reference is made in the course of his diary should be mentioned " Brad-

shaw's Descriptive Railway Guide," "Adams' Illus-
trated Descriptive Guide to the Watering-places
of England, and Companion to the Coast " (1848;
second edition, 1855); 1855, " Adams' Illustrated
Guide to the English Lakes," also "Adams'
Descriptive Guide to the Environs of the Metro-
polis;" 1851, "The Stranger's and Visitor's
Conductor through London;" 1859, "Adams'
Descriptive Guide to the Channel Islands, the
Isle of Wight, and the Isle of Man." Besides
these, the " Carpet Bag crammed full of Light
Articles for Shortening Long Faces and Long
Journeys," and a " Handy Book on Dinners and
Diners at Home and Abroad, with Piquant Plates
and Choice Cuts." His *Carpet Bag and Sketch-
book*, which he wrote for W. S. Woodin, and the
Seven Ages of Woman, for Miss Emma Stanley,
were the two cleverest of their style, and made
a world-wide reputation, though he wrote many
others. He also wrote a drawing-room play, *The
Three Temptations*, and was the author of "Flights
of Fancy," a medley of quips and cranks in prose
and verse; it was a comic encyclopædia, full of
puns and witticisms.

When quite a lad, E. L. B. travelled with a well-
known conjuror named Blitz, and being on one
occasion at Lichfield at the period of an election,
Blitz, who was manipulating a vanishing doll,
made a bet that the doll would fly up to the
belfry of the cathedral and be found there.
Blanchard, to whom the accomplishment of the
trick was relegated, went to the lodge, where,

finding the porter asleep, he took the keys and ran up to the belfry, where he affixed the doll to the great bell with the election colours (which afterwards proved the winning ones) attached to it. The experience he gained with this conjuror enabled him to take part in the entertainment which he described in a story, contributed to the *Theatre Annual* for 1886, under the title of " Ten Terrible Minutes : "—

" Possibly few among us have arrived at maturity without being able to recall some period of their lives when they had felt an agony of suspense in a position of extreme peril. I have had my experience with the rest, and I now place it for the first time on record, accompanied by the solemn asseveration that every moment of those terrible ten minutes, to which I shall afterwards have to allude, comes back to me, with what I may call the responsive tingle of a tick of time, though the hour to which they belonged is associated with a memorable day included in a year that passed away nearly half a century since. This seems a long time to look back upon, but to the present remembrancer the event might have happened yesterday, so vividly are the details of a very peculiar predicament impressed upon his mind. How the writer of these lines found himself placed in the awkward and dangerous position to be afterwards described, will assuredly need a few explanatory paragraphs beforehand.

" In the autumn of the year 1833, the most attractive exhibition in the Metropolis was that of the Oxy-hydrogen Gas Microscope, shown at a large saloon in New Bond Street, Piccadilly, and as one of the youthful spectators invited to witness the ' wonders of the invisible world,' I remember to have been greatly astonished even as a tolerably experienced sight-seer, though still at an early age. It was curious to observe that so many remarkable revelations of the marvels of the miniature universe passed altogether unnoticed, whilst the skeleton of that objectionable insect, the flea, magnified on the disc to the dimensions of a camel,

invariably elicited from the company such a curious compliment as three distinct rounds of applause. It was not for me
any longer to cling to the old proverb that familiarity bred
contempt; and the general admiration expressed on the
appearance of this awfully enlarged object led to some quiet
rebukes, which would have, perchance, become more audible
had I not been gently reminded that no charge had been
made for my admission. It was, however, something quite
new in the world of science. Everybody was talking about the
novel discovery, and when I went back to my old school at
Ealing, I used to surprise my playfellows by relating what I
had witnessed, and showing them, through a sixpenny con-
vex lens, then sold at toy-shops as a ' burning glass,' the
exaggerated forms of small flies on a leaf, after the learned
oratorical manner of the lecturer in New Bond Street.

"It so came about that my entomological studies in very
early life attracted the attention of a sanguine speculator
with whom our family had a rather close relationship. To
be possessor of such a powerful microscope was the height of
his ambition, and, after various negotiations had been set
afoot, it was arranged, in May 1835, that I should accompany him on a tour through the country to introduce the
latest London scientific exhibition to the provinces. The
enterprising capitalist, whom I will call, for the sake of dis-
tinguishing his prominent characteristic, Mr. Solomon
Sanguine, had a profound belief in the speculation resulting
in a large fortune. Though on the sunny side of thirty, he
had been speculating with disastrous results from the days of
his boyhood, and finding that a business he had purchased
as an ' oil and Italian warehouse ' in Old Compton Street,
Soho, was not likely to answer his expectations, he sold the
shop, bought a horse and gig with the proceeds, and cheerily
embarked in a fresh enterprise. Tangible security being
proffered and accepted, Messrs. Cutter & Clarke, opticians,
of Reading, undertook to supply the microscope with all the
necessary appliances ; and one of the partners agreed, for a
consideration, to accompany the ' show ' and keep it in good
working order. Mr. Solomon Sanguine, carefully coached in
his descriptive details, was to be the lecturer, and, though I
had not completed my fifteenth year, I was engaged at a

nominal salary to fill the office of a kind of secretary, read up subjects for illustration, and make out alluring programmes of the entertainment to be given. I remember that I was rather proud of seeing in print a particular paragraph I had written, setting forth that this 'Revelation of the Wonders of the Invisible World would amuse the young, delight the old, please the gay, and gratify the grave.' The elaborate lecture I had prepared, chiefly from a familiar volume recording the study of insect life, by Messrs. Kirby & Spence, was read with enthusiastic approval by the light of a bright sunset in spring, under the grove of elm trees then forming a picturesque avenue leading to the grounds of an establishment at that time known as 'The Stadium,' of which my eccentric acquaintance, the Baron de Beranger, was the proprietor. The place, situated on the northern bank of the Thames beyond Battersea Bridge, was afterwards destined to have a wider popularity under the title of Cremorne Gardens.

"It was then arranged that the marvels of the 'Oxy-hydrogen Gas Microscope' should be first exhibited at Winchester in the course of the following fortnight, and that a tour through Somerset and Devonshire might advantageously occupy succeeding months. The working partner, Mr. Clarke, was to precede us to the old cathedral city with the microscope and huge gasometers, that all might be in readiness. The enterprising capitalist was to drive down in style with his horse and gig, and I was to start at eight o'clock in the morning, on the day after his departure, by the Andover coach, commencing its journey from the old Knightsbridge booking-office, under the shadow of the Cannon Brewery. On my arrival, after a long, wearisome journey, which seems curious to recall in these days of rapid transit by railway, I found the enterprising capitalist had smashed his gig and killed his horse by driving too furiously into the inn-yard of the tavern where he was to take up his quarters; and a particular lens, magnifying, as was asserted in my highly-coloured prospectus, 'thirteen millions of times,' had been shivered into fragments. However, though we could not at once develop our fullest resources, faith was kept with the public, and at the appointed date we opened in the capacious Exhibition Room, at that period called St. John's Hall. The living objects which I had industriously collected a few hours previously from all the stagnant ponds in the neighbourhood, and which were shown as the remarkable organisms to be found in a drop of pure water, did not tend, I fear, to encourage the growth of those teetotal principles then beginning to find advocates; but the apparition of the Flea, occupying the whole dimensions of the disc, proved a stupendous success, and the poor dried husk of the departed tormentor, rendered transparent through being steeped in Canada balsam, brought down his three rounds of applause as he had done before. He was evidently regarded as the comic actor in our seriously scientific entertainment, and was greeted with shouts of laughter and peals of plaudits whenever he appeared.

" Our powerful illumination was produced by the combustion of two gases uniting on a cylinder of lime. This cylinder was fixed on a spindle, and had to be turned by the finger whenever a fresh surface was required. Besides a rather alarming ' fizzing,' which, as the room was always kept in perfect darkness, could not be readily accounted for by the audience, an occasional cry of pain or groan of despair coming from the interior of the apparatus when the hot cylinder was wanted to revolve, had no reassuring influence. We had to carry about with us two large metallic gasometers, from which the microscope received its supply of light through tubes. The hydrogen was produced by mixing diluted sulphuric acid with granulated zinc, and huge glass carboys for the purpose had to be constantly emptied and replenished, with disastrous effects upon the wardrobe during their conveyance. The oxygen was evolved from black oxide of manganese heated in an iron retort—an interesting chemical experiment confided to my care some time before the company assembled. When the exhibition commenced the hydrogen was allowed to play upon the cylinder for a few minutes so as to heat the lime gradually and expel all the moisture it might have gained from the atmosphere; and then the oxygen was cautiously introduced, when the brilliant illumination of the large white calico disc followed. Before this happened I had, however, frequent occasion to observe that many who had paid for front seats deemed it prudent to change their positions and get nearer the door of exit.

"It was then that I had to explain there was not the slightest occasion for alarm, and that the powerful lime-light used for the oxy-hydrogen gas microscope was the invention of Captain Thomas Drummond, of the Royal Engineers, who, with a view to its ultimate employment for the illumination of lighthouses along the coast, had first exhibited the 'Drummond Lime-Light' in 1830 at Purfleet, with such startling effect that shadows had been thrown at Blackwall, a distance of ten miles.

"How, with fluctuating receipts, the 'Scientific Entertainment' was introduced to the inhabitants of all the principal towns and cities of Wiltshire, Hampshire, Dorsetshire, and Somersetshire need not be minutely recorded. It will suffice to say that the enterprising capitalist, having no resources whatever, and failing to discover any probable chance of profit, abandoned the speculation in despair. His working partner prudently took back to Reading what remained of his apparatus; and a youth, scarcely fifteen, and unaccustomed to a vagrant life, found himself one evening in August, with only two shillings in his pocket, left in a remote country district one hundred and seventy miles from home, only to be reached by a weary walk to London.

"Youth has a happy knack of making light of difficulties, and though this was not the issue I had foreseen of my first tour as an entomological lecturer, there was something like an adventure in making the bold experiment of walking back and practically acquiring a topographical knowledge of the high roads leading through the southern counties towards the Metropolis.

"The August of 1835 was a remarkably fine month; the harvest was early, the nights were warm and pleasant, huge sheaves of bronzed wheat met the eye in nearly every direction, and all the Somersetshire lanes were overshadowed by apple-trees bearing fruit in rich profusion. Thus, for some miles at least, bed and breakfast could be obtained without the expenditure of more than a penny for a morning roll. There was enough exhilaration in the atmosphere, and sufficient prospect of picturesque landscapes along the route, to render the possibility of crossing the Mendip Hills and reaching London by way of Bristol and Bath, places I had long desired to visit, easy of attainment, and productive of, at least, mental enjoyment. Resting myself on a stile that came in my way during a long walk from Ilminster, I was pondering over the peculiarity of my position when a jolly-looking gentleman, driving a well-caparisoned horse and gig, came within sight, and paused for a few minutes at the wayside. There was a strap to be fastened, which— though I knew nothing of equestrian appliances, except those coming under my notice during Ducrow's summer season at Astley's—I managed to fix at last in the proper place. I was then asked would I like a lift along the road, and the assistance proffered was readily accepted. During our drive mutual confidences were exchanged, and my jovial acquaintance informed me that his name was Harvey, and that he was the landlord of the 'Red Lion' at Somerton, to which market town he was returning. Incidentally I learnt that he had married an actress, who had acquired some provincial celebrity in her day, that he had always a great sympathy with the 'show folk,' as he termed them, and that on this very evening he had thought of amusing the members of the Farmers' Club—who would have their annual dinner in the large room of his tavern—by showing them a few tricks in conjuring, of which he had been an amateur professor. A few weeks previously he had bought from an itinerant illusionist passing through the town, and unable to discharge a small private account through lack of public patronage, a supply of apparatus which would make a sufficient show for the occasion ; but, as all the tricks required confederacy, he could not possibly perform any of them without obtaining the aid of a competent assistant.

"As it so happened, I had rendered, in a friendly fashion, to Signor Blitz, the expert plate-dancer and professor of legerdemain, similar services some years before, during my schooldays in Staffordshire, and thus I could confidently undertake the very responsible duties of an invisible confederate. In another hour we arrived at that extensive establishment known as the 'Red Lion,' at Somerton, and, after some substantial refreshment, the landlord and myself arranged two capacious chambers on the first floor, communicating with folding-doors, and rather ostentatiously known by the title of 'Assembly Rooms,' as an improvised 'Temple of Magic.'

"No charge was to be made for admission, this being a supplementary entertainment given by the landlord in consideration of the many years the 'Farmers' Club' had honoured him with their support; but the glittering display of gilt cups, canisters and candlesticks would have been worthy of a strictly professional exhibition famous for this kind of paraphernalia. A large kitchen table, placed in front of the fireplace, and covered by a gigantic coloured tablecloth, of an ornamental pattern, looked exceedingly imposing when profusely decorated after this fashion, and a huge shelf underneath, upon which I could comfortably rest, removed all suspicion from the company that anybody was concealed beneath, as several inches of the flooring were still clearly perceptible. I soon discovered that the genial landlord, Mr. Harvey, was a clever manipulator of cards and coins, and that he was thoroughly delighting his audience by the revelation of an utterly unsuspected talent. I had made the 'dancing half-crowns' very successfully tell the number of pips on spades, hearts, clubs, and diamonds, respectively chosen from the pack by members of the company, and had astonished a young bachelor agriculturist by tinkling on the rim of a goblet the alarming number of children he would have when he would be married to the lady of his choice.

"The great trick, which was to crown the performance of the evening, was now to come. A bank-note, inscribed with the name and address of any individual present, was to be burned before the eyes of everybody in a wax candle on the table, and when this candle was cut up into three pieces, whichever one was chosen would be found to have, instead of the wick, the rolled-up bank-note, previously supposed to have been consumed. A merry Somersetshire yeoman unhesitatingly lent for the purpose a Bank of England note for ten pounds, with his name and address pencilled on the back, so that the identity of the note could not be possibly called into question. It is not here necessary for me to reveal the secrets of the conjuror's craft, but I may be allowed to explain in a rather indefinite manner that this trick, which was one of the most surprising of those performed by Signor Blitz, had to be accomplished after this fashion. With the aid of some dexterity in what is technically known as 'passing,' a false note, frequently no more than a folded piece of tissue paper, is consumed in the flame of the candle, and the ashes are carefully collected. In the meantime, the conjurer, passing behind the table to obtain a suitable tray, contrives to drop on the ground the real note so carefully annotated, which the confederate, with the aid of a piece of wire, twists into the smallest compass, inserts in a fragment of wax candle, from which the wick has been extracted, and places ready for the hand of the exhibitor as he comes round.

"From my place of concealment I hear all that has taken place previous to the dropping of the note; but, to my inexpressible horror, I find that the note has been dropped open, that a fresh visitor arriving at that moment has caused a strong current of air to enter the room, and that the draught has sent the note, which ought immediately to have been inserted in the prepared fragment of candle, fluttering along the floor, and finally up the chimney. Thus did the ten terrible minutes begin. The horrible suspicion that, under the circumstances, I might have been unable to resist temptation, and have feloniously appropriated the money, was the first idea that occurred as likely to be entertained by the kind host of the 'Red Lion,' now so generously entertaining his guests. To render myself visible, and search for the fugitive flimsy up the flue, would have been to destroy the mystery of the hour's entertainment. If the note went up the chimney, and was blown away into space at the summit, my character would be irretrievably ruined. Never did ten minutes pass so slowly. The conjurer had to pass and repass the table in vain, without receiving that coveted fragment of wax candle with the ten-pound Bank of England note carefully tucked up inside; and, in the meantime, filled up the interval by talking with the chief constable, who happened to be present, about a recent robbery that had taken place in the town.

" Rescue, happily, came at last, in the form of a little black kitten, which had been sleeping unobserved on the warm hob of the fireplace. Hearing something rustling by, it had started up to capture a supposed mouse. The friendly paw of puss, after a short chase, brought the coveted possession within my reach. The bank-note was restored to its owner in the accustomed manner, to his great astonishment, though not without some misgivings, as it had been necessary to perform extra illusions by way of interlude ; and the climax of borrowing the yeoman's hat, and sending up from beneath the table that very black kitten, whose existence had been previously unsuspected, brought our entertainment to a triumphant close ; and thus ended those terrible ten minutes."

It must have been somewhere about the year 1838-9 that E. L. B. was for a time manager of a theatre of which he gave a description in the *Theatre Annual* for 1886 under the head of " Some Managerial Memories : "—

" Fifty years ago, when I was a juvenile resident in that once picturesque suburb of the Metropolis then fondly described by all the elderly inhabitants as ' Old Chelsea,' there stood a lonely mansion in the King's Road, on the left-hand side as you walked westward, that few belated youthful travellers cared to pass after dark. It was a large, but not lofty, villa, standing in its own grounds, and fenced in by some rusty broken railings from the main thoroughfare. This building, which had been long unoccupied, was known as ' The Old Manor House.' The dilapidated structure by daylight was not particularly cheerful to look at, for most of the windows were broken, and there was a rank luxuriance of weeds in the front garden, which seemed to be the especial resort of all the cats in the neighbourhood, who had long appropriated the place as their happy hunting-ground. When night approached, unearthly sounds would be heard about the precincts, and phantom forms would be seen to dart from the doorway and flitter over the gravelled and grassy pathway leading to the extensive orchard at the back. Matter-of-fact people ascribed these mysterious occurrences to a mundane origin. It was popularly known that in the rear of the old Manor House there were groves of fruit trees from which luscious mulberries and toothsome apples and pears might be surreptitiously abstracted without any objection being urged by the legal proprietor of the estate—whoever he might be; and some went so far as to assert that what the superstitious took to be the clanking of chains by some imprisoned ghost was only the metallic chink caused by certain unlawful trespassers actively engaged in knocking off the tops of ornamental railings, which would be sold next morning as fragments of old iron at a marine-store shop near the river. Nevertheless, to an earnest student of Mrs. Radcliffe's novels and an eager devourer of the gruesome stories related in a penny periodical called *The Calendar of Horrors*, published about that time, the dismal edifice seemed to possess every feature of a haunted house which the most exacting ghost-hunter would require.

" After a long period of neglect, workmen at last began to appear about the premises, and in the autumn of 1837 pedestrians who had missed the last omnibus, began to walk about midnight for the first time on that side of the way, deriving courage and consolation from the knowledge that they had seen with their own eyes, in their morning progress towards the City, painters, plumbers, and carpenters, at work putting the old house in repair.

" Early in the following year, to the great gratification of the most nervous dwellers in the vicinity, the Old Manor House became occupied; but to the surprise of some, and perhaps to the horror of more, it was announced to be opened as a place of public entertainment. The new proprietor was Mr. Richard Smith, a pleasant, portly gentleman, who was said to have derived much pecuniary advantage from his connection in an official capacity with Crockford's Club in St. James's Street. He erected a capacious building for hot and cold baths—luxuries then unknown to dwellers in the suburbs—and, opening the capacious grounds to the public at an admission fee of one shilling, boldly proclaimed, by advertisement, that the Old Manor House in the King's Road, Chelsea, was henceforth to be known as 'The New Vauxhall and Royal Bath Gardens.'   Vocal and instrumental concerts were given on three evenings each week; and, in humble imitation of the Surrey Zoological Gardens, then at the height of their popularity, a panoramic painting was prepared, representing Fort Bhurtpore, behind which fire-works, manufactured by 'Professor' Turnour, son of a well-known theatrical agent of that name, were let off in a series of squibs and crackers, to realize the daring capture of the Indian fortress by the English forces.   It was a pleasant promenade enough among the fruit trees, from which the visitors chiefly obtained their refreshment—for only wines were sold on the premises, under a free vintner's licence—and the company, consisting chiefly of local sweethearts, preferred to treat each other to apples and pears, snatched off the branches above them, rather than expend superfluous cash in shilling goblets of hot negus.   As the expenses were great, and the profits, under these circumstances, were ex-ceedingly small, the proprietor decided on discontinuing the concerts and erecting a theatre on the ground occupied by a portion of this unprofitable orchard.   Architectural plans for such an edifice met with due approval; and in a short space of time arose 'The Royal Manor House Theatre,' capable of containing an audience of about five hundred persons, paying respectively one shilling and two shillings for back and front seats.

"The first lessees of the newly erected building were Mr. Charles Poole, previously manager of the Chichester Theatre, and a Mr. Fleming.   It was understood between the two speculators that one found the experience and the other the capital.   There is reason to believe that in the course of a few months the partners exchanged their qualifications. Light one-act pieces were creditably represented, but the audiences were more appreciative than remunerative, and, with an abruptness that was, at least, inconvenient to the members of the company, if not surprising to the habitual frequenters of the establishment, an announcement was one night posted up in the greenroom—which was the emptied tank of the tepid and now disused swimming-bath—that the season would close on the following evening.

" In this dilemma Mr. Richard Smith, the proprietor, appealed to my sympathies, and besought my assistance as the only person he knew who had the slightest knowledge of theatrical matters. I was to have no pecuniary responsibility of any kind whatever, but was only asked to keep the theatre open until a new lessee, who was daily expected, could arrange preliminary negotiations. In a weak moment I consented, under these circumstances, to become manager. I conferred with the few remaining members of the company, explaining to them the position of affairs, and impressing upon them that the receipts every evening would be equally divided among them, without any deduction for my own share in the transaction, as I had the advantage of a small income derived from a novel I was then writing, published as an illustrated serial in penny numbers. The proposal met with a general concurrence, and for a fortnight the performances of the Royal Manor House Theatre were continued, the light comedian, Mr. A. Sidney, even undertaking to strengthen the attraction by singing sentimental songs in evening dress between the pieces. It is pleasant to record that this affable gentleman afterwards became more distinguished by his developed talents as Mr. Alfred Wigan, one of the most accomplished actors who ever adorned the British stage.

" As was reasonably to be expected, the company diminished in number as more eligible engagements presented themselves ; and at last two alone remained—Signor Plimmeri, a clever posturer, whose reputation was chiefly identified with the playbill announcement that he was the ' celebrated manmonkey,' and Mr. Richard Flexmore, a very agile youthful dancer, who lived to become well known as a popular clown and pantomimist. To represent even the lightest forms of dramatic entertainment with such limited assistance was a manifest managerial difficulty, but it was surmounted for a while by devising new versions of pantomimical burlettas in which a monkey was the prominent character, and a comic dance could be introduced with some faint show of probability. The small members of the Smith family, when dressed up and placed in the background, formed an imposing group of four supernumeraries, and the present writer contrived, by coming on at one entrance as the chivalrous hero of the piece, and entering at another as the indispensable comic countryman, to delude the few spectators in front into the belief that something like *Jack Robinson and His Monkey* was being acted according to the prompt-book, though we all of us extemporised dialogue and action according to the fancy of the moment.

" To give something like substantiality to the playbill, I produced a farce I had written called *Angels and Lucifers*, representing myself the character of the itinerant vendor of Congreve matches, Benjamin Brimstone, afterwards rendered so popular at the Olympic Theatre by Mr. George Wild. Strange to say, an unexpected success was obtained, and a continuous run of thirty-one representations was the result, enabling the company to be reinforced by three additions, male and female. Our costumier at that period was Mr. Moss Cantor, of Whitechapel, who undertook, for the moderate stipend of half a crown per night, to furnish all fancy dresses required. In his wardrobe, nightly conveyed and returned in a small bundle, tied up in a blue-and-white pocket-handkerchief, a policeman's uniform could not be included; and as such an attire was indispensable for one portion of the impersonation, recourse was had to a daring expedient. The policeman on duty in the King's Road at nine o'clock was always accustomed to turn into the grounds of the Manor House to see that proper order was being preserved. At such a time a light frugal repast of beer and bread and cheese was regularly provided in a certain dressing-room detached from the theatre, and once used in connection with the old baths. As a curious coincidence, it may be recorded that at the very time the inexpensive supper was placed before the guardian of the peace, his coat, hat, and truncheon were invariably required on the stage; and the temporary usurper of the uniform, encouraged by the laughter he produced through a grotesque exaggeration of the authoritative demeanour of the awe-inspiring functionary, sometimes forgot that the important official he had invited to an economical banquet might be shivering in his shirt-sleeves, anxiously awaiting the return of his warm coat. On Monday, January 25, 1841, the impersonator of Benjamin Brimstone celebrated the lengthy career of his farce by a special programme identified with the 'author's night.' He was hurrying across the gardens, at the end of the performance, to return to the rightful owner the borrowed garments of authority, when he was intercepted by a sergeant of police, who directed him at once to go forth and quell a pugilistic disturbance taking place in front of the White Hart Tavern, at the corner of Smith Street. Before any explanation could be given he was hurried into the midst of a quarrelsome crowd, to deal alone with a turbulent throng as best he could. Seizing the smallest of the combatants, he took him round the corner, and suggested instant flight. 'Thank you, policeman; this is a generous deed, and never shall I forget it!' came from the lips of the released captive.

"The supposed policeman, with pantomimic flourishes of his staff, easily dispersed the lingering crowd, and then returned to a dimly lighted dressing-room attached to the Manor House Theatre. Here, in a very few minutes, he restored coat, hat, and appendages to an individual who had just finished the contents of the tankard before him. Years elapsed, and the sequel of a story that might have furnished the ground-work of a romantic novel was thus told :—A young journeyman baker was in love with his master's daughter, and on the night in question had resented some disparaging remarks on her character. Had he been locked up for assault, his own reputation might have been seriously affected. To the policeman who so quickly took him into custody and so generously liberated him immediately afterwards, he believed a deep debt of gratitude was due. The baker's journeyman, marrying his employer's daughter, became a master baker himself, and carried on a large business. He made instant inquiries respecting the name and number of the policeman on duty in the King's Road that night when he found himself so perilously involved in a personal quarrel. It was discovered that the said policeman was married, and had a large and increasing family. By an unknown hand four quartern loaves were left at that policeman's door every day, and no payment was ever demanded. Every Good Friday morning, moreover, pyramids of hot cross-buns were always found mysteriously deposited on the threshold.

"In a few more years—here the story begins to read like a fairy tale—the grateful baker emigrated from Chelsea to Canada, and rose to be a man high in position. He had the opportunity of appointing the chief of the constabulary for the district, and he nominated the kindly Chelsea policeman, who accordingly went out with his large family, all being placed in good positions at high salaries for the respective posts they filled. Sitting by my fireside of a winter's night, and falling into a reverie connected with the past, I often wonder whether the good-natured policeman of the King's Road, who used to eat my bread-and-cheese suppers in his shirt-sleeves, and so obtained vicarious honours, and acquired possession of diverted benefactions, ever became aware of the odd method by which he rose to unexpected prosperity and colonial distinction.

"My managerial experiences of the Royal Manor House Theatre comprised on a small scale all the inflictions that the lessees of larger houses have to undergo. Unimportant as was the establishment, and remote as was the locality, not a day passed but some aspiring dramatist would leave a five-act tragedy at the gate called by courtesy the stage-door, and beseech its due consideration with a view to its early production. What strange interviews did I have with histrionic students who only wanted to be told how they could come upon the boards to take the London stage by storm! Among the most eager for an appearance in a Shakespearean character was a retired prize-fighter, whose name lives in my recollection as Tom Oliver, and who then was held in high estimation as an umpire at pugilistic contests. He was very anxious to take the theatre for one night, guaranteeing a full house, if he could only play Hamlet or Richard the Third—it was immaterial which, as either part would have to be studied for the occasion—but for the sake of his friends who would support him, he stipulated that in the course of the tragedy there should be a scene representing *Tom Cribb's Parlour.* The only satisfactory trial I was enabled to give an amateur at this period was afforded an unassuming young gentleman who made a marked success by his performance in the farce of *Shocking Events,* and whose rapid advance in the profession he had adopted I afterwards marked with great interest.

That amateur was Mr. Nye Chart, at once recognized as an excellent Shakespearean comedian when he made, in 1849, his professional *début* at Sadlers Wells, and who afterwards gained a well-deserved position as the respected lessee of the Brighton Theatre. There is little more to be told. Mr. Richard Smith, finding the theatre was an unprofitable speculation, and obtaining a licence to sell spirits, built Rodney Street on the site of the grounds, with a public-house at the corner, and soon after 'The Royal Manor House Theatre, King's Road, Chelsea,' became absorbed in a building known as 'The Commercial Rooms.' One at least among the many passengers along the King's Road sees more spectres arise out of the pavement as he passes the modern building than ever stirred the imagination of belated pedestrians fifty years ago."

It was well known that E. L. Blanchard had for years determined to write the reminiscences of his life. The work was put off from time to time till too late, though some preparation for it had been made in his keeping, during forty-five years, a daily record of his doings, his work, and even his inmost thoughts. He had evidently had the task in view when he inscribed the following, found among his papers:—"All facts, however microscopic, are important in the building of real history. I am about to lead you into the byeways and the high-ways of literature, which have been well trodden. The bridle-paths through which I am going to ask you to accompany me are known only to those who have in their adventurous youth struck across some very thorny and uneven tracks."

When almost in his teens E. L. B. was a most prolific dramatist. He thought he had discovered a short road to wealth when he found that managers were liberal enough to give him 10*s.* an act; he used to buy some paper and retire to a coffee-house, where, over a roll and butter and a cup of coffee, he would pour out the most powerful dramas. What a contrast to the present period, when a successful dramatist may realize £20,000 from one piece alone !

The managers for whom he chiefly worked were George Wild[1] of the Olympic; B. O. Conquest, then of the Garrick Theatre in Leman Street, Whitechapel; and at a later date C. J. James, of the Queen's Theatre in Tottenham Street, to be afterwards better known as the Prince of Wales's, when Mrs. Bancroft inaugurated her memorable management.

The following were also found amongst his papers after his decease :—

(1) " 1 fancy I might for my own reminiscences write 'an anticipative review' by way of a novel Preface—'The Small Notes of a Small Author.'—E. L. B."

(2) "Title for book—'My Recollections and some other Trifles,' by E. L. Blanchard, the 'other trifles' to be the lyrics added to the end of the volume."

(3) "Motto, possibly for my 'Memoirs:' 'I am sorry to be threescore and ten because so very much is expected nowadays from men of that time of life.'—*Sayings of a Statesman.*"

The Astrologer was started by a man of the name of Haddock, who, like a good many of those who employed E. L. B., was short of money.

---

[1] For Wild he wrote *Angels and Lucifers The Artful Dodge, Jack Nokes and Tom Styles, Pork Chops, Babes in the Wood, The Road of Life,* and *Game and Game.*

E. L. B., who did all the work, was a little knocked up, and Haddock, who happened to be, or appeared to be, in funds, proposed that they should go to Folkestone, and that he would stand the expense. Accordingly they went, and stayed there the next day. Haddock seemed wild and excited, and said he must return to town; he did so, but E. L. B. remained for a day or two longer. When he got back to town he went to *The Astrologer* office, and found that the door was locked *from the inside.* Being unable to make any one hear E. L. B. became alarmed, and with assistance broke open the door. *The ink was wet on the last sheet of the current number, but there was no Haddock, and he was never heard of again, in London at least.*

Malicious tongues said that there was a parapet running outside the top floor in which *The Astrologer* was got ready for press; that Haddock had creditors, and that it was to escape them, and not to accompany his Satanic Majesty, with whom *The Astrologer* was supposed to have dealings, that Haddock so completely effaced himself. It was whispered that years later he was seen in Jamaica. The *Astrologer* office was at the corner of Wellington and Burleigh Streets. Strange to say, a species of revival of the work took place last year, for in August 1890 appeared the first number of *The Astrologer's Magazine,* published by W. Foulsham & Co.

At this time he was living in the Blackfriars Road, but early in July he removed to Southampton Street, Camberwell. He was then writing much for John Cleave [1] and Stiff and Landells.[2]

To follow the diary day by day would be too great a tax upon the reader; from it, therefore, will be drawn extracts showing the inner life of the writer, and recording the names of those with whom he was brought in contact, with anecdotes relating to them, etc.

In his twenty-fourth year he appears to have first conceived the idea of keeping a diary, in June 1844, and commences thus :—

" *Thursday, June 27th.*—I this day took it into my head to keep a diary, having got half through the year without one. What I shall do with it remains to be seen. I fancy there will be little use for the red ink divisions, except on the expense side. *28th.*—Blackfriars Road. Smoked a pipe after breakfast (surely a diary should contain chronicles of pleasure as well as of pain). Went to Grafton Street to see my brother; he was out. Sauntered home thinking of love, doubt, despair, disease, and death. Mysteries altogether."

[1] John Cleave, a publisher of Shoe Lane, Fleet Street, became notorious for his contests with the Government in floating unstamped news sheets—for they could scarcely be called newspapers. Cleave's *Gazette of Varieties* was one of these publications, ultra-Radical in politics, and adorned with coarse caricatures, designed by an artist named Jack Wright, scene-painter subsequently to Brading, of the Albert Saloon. E. L. B. wrote for Cleave in the publication above-named, and there is an imperfect copy in the British Museum Library. Cleave suffered imprisonment in Coldbath Fields Prison, and his daughter married Henry Vincent, a Chartist orator, but in after years a popular lecturer and preacher of the Gospel.

[2] Stiff was proprietor of the *London Journal*, Landells an engraver on the *Illustrated London News* and *Punch*, of which he was one of the four original proprietors. Landells was also a publisher, and, at one time, connected with Stiff. He also wrote much for Masters, or some of his family, and developed into a successful theological publisher for the Ritualistic school. For him E. L. B. wrote *Ice.*

He wrote a good deal for *Parley's Library,*[1] and was busily engaged on Kent's *Almanack.*[2] To enable him to do this properly, he had to pay constant visits to the British Museum, reading up astrology and logarithms, old black-letter books of two centuries back, etc.

Leigh Hunt was then a constant associate of his, and he commenced his business intercourse with Albert Smith, sending him two articles. On July 5th, " Olympic Theatre advertised to be let.[3] Think it ought to be let—alone. Not bad t hat ! *awfully antique.*"

On 19th he wrote an article for Cleave entitled " A Walk for an Article."

On July 23rd he mentions a fatal accident on the Blackfriars Pier,[4] and his illness " from the

---

[1] *Parley's Library* then was a popular penny " mag.," famous for E. L. B.'s potting down three-volume novels, to wit, Bulwer's " Eugene Aram," " Last Days of Pompeii," and " Last of the Barons," with clever elucidation of plot and illustrative extracts verbatim, for the charge of 3*d.* (three numbers) ; and also Dickens's " Old Curiosity Shop " and " Barnaby Rudge," by Hewitt, a Manchester sub-editor. The illustrations on wood were excellent. E. L. B. used to get about 10*s.* for " potting " down these famous works. No copy in Museum. Cleave was a type of the practical printer who elevated himself to a proprietary by industry and practical knowledge. E. L. B. thought highly of Cleave, although my old friend smilingly told me that Cleave was never flush of money.

[2] W. Kent, of Paternoster Row, for several years brought out a *Shakespeare Almanack,* with a chronicle of events for 365 days, and a quotation, of course very pertinent, for each from the poet's works. Some of the almanacks were illustrated by Kenny Meadows.

[3] The Olympic closed on Wednesday the 3rd inst. with the First Part of *King Henry the Fourth,* for the benefit of Mr. Laws ; but no Falstaff was forthcoming till nine o'clock, when an amateur took up the part at the third scene. The Olympic had been under the lesseeship of Mr. G. Wild.

[4] The accident referred to occurred through the breaking down of the floating pier belonging to the Watermen's Steamboats. Too

constant annoyance in my domestic arrangements. Some change must be made. Endeavoured to write, but energies crushed and crippled by home troubles."

On the 24th "met Britton Jones, who showed me over his Blacking Warehouse!" This was an eccentric mercantile character who, it is said, parted with a horse and chaise for a marvellous blacking recipe, which, practically worked, was to suppress Day & Martin, and so create for its owner a colossal fortune. It was to be specially used in polishing military harness at "a minimum of elbow grease with a maximum of lustre." E. L. B. wrote advertisements for it both in verse and prose.

On July 25th "heard of Miss Forde's death.[1] Remember her first playing for me was as Phillis in my *Arcadia* at the Grecian."[2]

great a crowd congregated on the pier to witness the Bankside Boat-race. The temporary bridge gave way; some twenty people were precipitated into the water, of whom seven lost their lives.

[1] A charming ballad-singer, whose duet with Billy Williams at Vauxhall—"Pretty Polly Hopkins"—for a time was quite the rage. As her voice and personal charms waned, she was glad to sing at Bagnigge Wells, White Conduit, and, even, the Albert Saloon. "Sally" Forde attained eminence as a ballad-singer in her early days.

[2] Of this *Arcadia* the following will prove of interest:— Between 8 and 9 o'clock one evening in 1843, E. L. B. paced anxiously between the Canal Bridge and the old "Eagle" in the City Road. He was to receive the opinion of "Bravo Rouse's" dramatic reader on the *libretto* of an operetta entitled *Arcadia*. If the estimate proved favourable, Mr. Rouse's company and conductor would be turned on to furnish the music. A half-hour later, E. L. B. was in the seventh heaven of ecstasy, for the reader expressed himself in terms of warm commendation of the book, which meant the possibility of earning a £5 note. The dramatic reader of the establishment turned out to be no other than Mr.

GRECIAN SALOON AND OLYMPIC TEMPLE, EAGLE TAVERN, CITY ROAD.

Sole Manager, Mr. Campbell.

On Wednesday, April 18th, 1841,

ARCADIA; OR, THE SHEPHERD AND SHEPHERDESS.

New and Original Operatic Spectacle. Overture and Music by Mr. Harroway, R.A.M.

Justice Jumble (*an amorous Justice in love with Phillis's money*)......
Mr. ADAMS.

Sylvias (*the gentle Shepherd, passionately fond of Phillis*)......
Mr. E. TAYLOR.

Damon (*a Bacchanalian Shepherd, friend to Sylvias*)......Mr. BALDWIN.

Colin (*a Woodman in love with Daphne*)......Mr. GLINDON.

Strephon......Mr. ISMAY. Pan (*a Sylvan God*)......Mr. G. HERBERT.

Glaucus......Mr. WOOLLIDGE. Hymen......Mons. SCHMIDT.

Shepherds and Satyrs......Messrs. WALBOURN, GRIFFITH, BOWDEN, ROCHEZ, HULINE, and LEMAN.

Apollo (*the God of Music disguised as a Shepherd*)......Miss COVENEY.

Phillis (*the Shepherdess who sang, " But if thy purse be empty come not to me a-wooing "*)......Miss FORDE.

Daphne (*a Shepherdess in love with Colin*)......Mrs. YOUNG.

Venus......Miss LANE. Diana......Madame SCHMIDT.

Shepherds, etc. ......Messrs. RAYMOND, GLINDON, and BOWDEN; Misses FREEMAN, RAYMOND, and H. COVENEY.

The piece will commence with an Arcadian Ballet, arranged by M. Schmidt.

Jonas Levy, who, with his delightful memories of old playhouses and players, happily remains amongst us. When Rouse joined the majority he bequeathed Mr. Levy his dramatic MSS., enough to fill a tea-chest. Doubtless *Arcadia* is among the treasures.

Miss Harriet Coveney played one of the characters. The Grecian Theatre was owned and constructed by a Mr. Rouse, who having been a bricklayer took a very practical share in its erection. This gentleman used to occupy a prominent private box, and on his appearance there used to be saluted by his friends and admirers with cries of " Brayvo Rouse." On one occasion he went to sleep in the box, and on waking up said that the performance must be stopped, as he had been robbed of his watch and chain. However, the next minute, finding it on the floor, he obligingly said the performance might be resumed. Capillaire was a favourite drink at this establishment. I believe that it was some sort of syrup, but as a beverage it has faded out.

Rouse ceased to be lessee of the Grecian Saloon March 21st, 1851 ; then taken by Conquest.

On Thursday, August 6th, he started for Brighton to collect materials for the "Descriptive Guide of the Watering-places of England, and Companion to the Coast," published by W. J. Adams, of 59, Fleet Street, and in which E. L. B., in a bright and lively yet instructive style, gave particulars of the Isle of Man, the New Forest and South Coast, Weymouth, Dawlish, Plymouth and West Coast, Exmouth, Sidmouth, Torquay, Brighton, Hastings, Dover, Margate, Ramsgate, Gravesend, Sheerness, Southend, Herne Bay, Walton, Harwich, Yarmouth, Lowestoft, Cromer, Tynemouth, Warkworth, Alnmouth, the watering-places of Wales and the Western Coast, etc., Scarborough, Irish spas and watering-places, the Channel Islands, and the Isle of Man. Engaged by Osbaldiston, of the Victoria, to write the opening burlesque (*Jack and the Beanstalk*), he calls on Miss Vincent.[1] *Jack and the Beanstalk* was produced August 26th, and was a success.

The daily round of work told upon him severely, and we find an entry towards the end of August :—

" Weather magnificent. Still pant for the shady green of rural localities, and would give a trifle to be now beside some streamlet, where the rustling branches—pshaw ! "

[1] Called, forty-five years ago, at the Victoria, " the only acknowledged heroine of domestic drama." Her performances of Susan Hopley in *The Vicissitudes of a Servant Girl*, and Mary Ann in *The Child of Charity*, used to bathe a Lambeth audience in tears. She succeeded Clara Fisher as Albert in Knowles's *William Tell*, with Macready in the title *rôle*, soon after its first production at Covent Garden. Miss Vincent was a very clever melodramatic actress.

"30*th.*—Began Almanack calculations, and stay in all day to execute them."

"*Monday, Sept. 2nd.*—Hudson Kirby[1] made his first appearance as Sir Giles Overreach in *New Way to Pay Old Debts* at the Victoria. House crammed; Kirby well received."

He met Bruton[2] the next day.

Now and then we come across such entries as the following :—

"4*th.*—More dreamy than usual. I scarce know why, but the past seems to come more vividly back than ever. Oh if I could but more follow the dictates of my heart!—no matter, *nous verrons.* 12*th.*—Though hard at work again correcting proofs and writing *Toilette of the Work Table,* packed off two packets, one for *Illuminated Magazine* and the other (*Puck*[3] matter) for Railway Bill. 'Nothing venture, nothing

[1] A young American melodramatic actor, who achieved a high position in the chief character in a piece called *The Carpenter of Rouen,* which he acted many times at the Surrey, Victoria, Marylebone, Standard, and Britannia Theatres. He was only twenty-nine at death.

[2] James Bruton was a comic vocalist, song-writer, and journalist; originally a silversmith, but who came out as a writer in Mrs. C. B. Wilson's *La Belle Assembly* in 1831. He first sang at Bagnigge Wells and White Conduit Gardens, and afterwards at Vauxhall. When Offley's in Henrietta Street, Covent Garden, became a regular concert room, Bruton became its director. His singing of his own song, " I'm for Freedom of Opinion," supposed to be a vulgar dogmatic vestryman laying down the law, was very funny, and its author's talk bristled with puns and quaint sayings. He was a Bohemian, and passed his evenings at clubs. His two best pieces of authorship are the farce of *Bathing* and a sentimental song, "Happy Land," written about 1842.

[3] *Puck* (Howe & Parsons, Fleet Street). The Shakespearean Goblin on a mushroom conspicuous on the heading, and by six successive wood blocks the Goblin was made to appear rotating with every day. In two months it was resolved to change the form of publication and bring it out twice a week. Albert Smith editor, Tom Taylor, E. L. B., etc. Mode of advertising borrowed from Marriott's notion

have.' 19*th.*—Row with Kirby at the Victoria Theatre.[1]
20*th.*—Otway engaged to supersede Kirby at Victoria.
Placards and bills for paper warfare issued on both sides.
23*rd.*—Heard from Leigh Hunt, who writes from Dover.
Looked in at Victoria. Capital house. Otway and *Othello,
Dead Shot,* and *Giovanni in London.* Louisa Lyons[2] the
heroine. 24*th.*—Went with Alderton to the Baron de
Beranger, who recognized me, though six years have elapsed
since we met.[3] 27*th.*—Wrote some little pars for Alderton
about ' Screw Penholder.' "

" *Oct.* 4*th.*—Saw *Babes* ' barbarously murdered.' Got
copy of ' Bradshaw's Railway Guide to Brighton.' Came

with *Illustrated London News*—four men, each bearing a cut, made out,
each letter richly gilt, on a board before them :

" In an entirely new form,

For Twopence :

Every Wednesday and Saturday."

Puck merged into *The Great Gun,* price 3*d.* ; first number published
in Fleet Street, Saturday, November 16th, 1844. F. W. N. Bayley at
first editor. He was in great difficulties at the time, and only went
out on Sundays. " *Quod est scriptum est scriptum* " [" *What is writ is
writ :* " two writs]. Bayley left the publication at the third number.
Albert Smith wrote in this his amusing *Memoirs of a Latch-key.*

[1] This row arose through Osbaldiston coming forward and stating
that Kirby, who was playing *Othello,* was drunk. Opinions appear to
have been in Kirby's favour.

[2] A comedy actress five-and-forty years since at the Strand,
Olympic, Lyceum, and Victoria Theatres. The daughter of a woman
who kept a glove-shop in Carlton Street, Regent Street, Louisa
when a young girl was beautiful enough to sit for the Madonna
to Stephenoff and Chalon for their *quasi*-religious pictures. Afterwards a Royal Academy of Music pupil, and a chorus-singer at the
Italian Opera under Lumley, she subsequently turned actress, being
brought out by Hammond at the Strand. In after years she was
known as Miss Louisa Turner, and lived in splendid style at Bayswater, giving wonderful parties. After this she made a first-rate
matrimonial match.

[3] Baron de Beranger was an eccentric foreign nobleman, who for
several years was proprietor of Cremorne Gardens, and under his
management it became famous for balloon ascents, associated with
the well-known aerial voyager Green, who, having some dispute
with Gye at Vauxhall, betook himself to the wing of Beranger.
He died about thirty-five years ago.

home for quiet read. Domestic matters; all money again; heart-sickening, very! *5th.*—Spent pleasant evening with De la Motte[1] and Alderton. *7th.*—Met Aubrey, 'Charles,' I think. Had a glorious stroll to Dulwich. Graham appeared at the moderately successful City of London, opened with Mrs. Walter Lacy manageress, Wilson lessee.[2] *8th.*— Rambled over to Nunhead. Saw the cemetery. Splendid prospect from the hill beyond Peckham Rye. Seized with a crushing fit of the miserables; blues awfully. Sunshiny weather nevertheless. *9th.*—Couldn't stand it any longer;

[1] De la Motte was a water-colour artist of clever powers, who used to attend a pipe-smoking coterie calling themselves " The Club of the Comfortables," meeting at a tavern whose windows were above the north-western corner of Westminster Bridge. Whether E. L. B. was a member I am ignorant, but amongst those on the roll were his close friends, Robert Cruikshank and Richardson of the *Times*. Other members were Captain Medwin (associated with Byron), Warren the *aquarellist*, Diddear the actor, and Teddy Colman, son of the author of *Broad Grins* and *The Heir-at-Law*.

[2] Cockerton proprietor, Wilson lessee. *School for Scandal*—Mrs. Walter Lacy, Lady Teazle; W. H. Williams, Sir Peter; James Brown, Charles Surface. Miss Daley and Mr. Radford sang National Anthem. À'Beckett's *Alauddin* followed. Hit of the evening, " Real Bohemian Polka," danced by Mdlle. Louise, of Her Majesty's Theatre, and Mdlle. Adèle, from the San Carlo, Naples. House crammed.

When the first theatre of this name in Norton Folgate was burnt down, several melodramas by E. L. B. in MS. were consumed. Its lessees were Cockerton, an oilman of Islington, and " Jem Crow " Dunn (an imitator of Rice), an American comedian, who used to act niggers on his native stage, and who appeared with immense success at our Adelphi. Among E. L. B.'s consumed dramatic treasures was one dealing with the sins and sufferings of the lamented Jane Shore, and the prowess of the Duke of Shoreditch, a hero amongst the Finsbury Archers. When the new theatre was built, E. L. B. still had some connection with it. One of its after lessees, T. P. Taylor, son of the celebrated English Platonist, author of *The Bottle* (from Cruikshank's pictures), and a wonderful version of *Vanderdecken*, was a friend of E. L. B.'s, and the latter wrote a piece or two for him; but it was only paid for in good fellowship, Taylor being quite impecunious, the usual characteristic of those for whom the generous Blanchard worked the hardest. There was always "a good time coming," so these paupers, and sometimes " sponges," declared; but E. L. B.'s pocket never bore witness that the " good time " had chronological fixing. Taylor, however, was not a sponge, but his " revenue " was only " good spirits."

rushed off on a ramble. Crossed Surrey hills, back by New Cross. Met Edward Miller. Told me he was going away to Cornwall. Lucky dog!"

Some idea of his working and walking powers may be gathered from the following entries:—

"On the 11*th* started for Portsmouth. Delightful journey. Got to Gosport same night, and crossed the ferry for Portsmouth. Stopped at the 'King's Head,' and went to the Landport Theatre—Hagg the lessee. Good piece, fairly represented. 12*th*.—Crossed over to Ryde, Isle of Wight. Walked to Newport, had tea at the 'Bugle.' Visited Carisbrook Castle, and at 7 p.m. started for Brixton, through Shorewell. Altogether, fourteen miles. Snug bed, and to sleep. 13*th*.—Strolled all through the Undercliff to Ventnor, where I slept. 14*th*.—Rainy weather. This day walked back to Ryde, then re-crossed to Portsmouth. Louis Philippe just started back to Dover. Went on to South-ampton, and slept at the 'Red Lion,' in High Street. Very old house. 15*th*.—Strolled to Netley Abbey. Glorious ruins; quite in ecstasies. Caught in heavy shower return-ing. Read the papers at a place called 'The Canal Coffee House,' in 'the Ditche.' Met old enemy, crusty landlord at 'Red Lion.' 16*th*.—Started on a glorious walk to Win-chester. Stopped on my way at the 'New Hat.' Capital ale, like sherry. Got into Winchester, stopped at Barton's Coffee-house. The town dull, dirty, and dreary. Cathedral, however still fine; like St. George's Hall, Windsor. 17*th*.— Walked to Twyford in morning. Smoked pipes galore. Got to a station (Bishopstoke), and left for Basingstoke by six. Slept at 'Wheatsheafe;' read and to bed. Town flat and dull."

His little tour ended on the 18*th*.

" Rambled to adjacent ruins of Holy Ghost Chapel; then, taking the train, went on to Woking. Got out here and had a five mile walk to Chertsey, thence to Weybridge; again train and arrived home by night. 25*th*.—So busy with

Guide that I stopped again within over 'mine own fire-side;' a phrase of one who—no matter. This fire sets one dreaming—very. Why cannot I think of the future, not *the past ?*"

"*Monday, Nov. 4th.*—In all day getting on with *Guide*; rather tedious work. Went to Vic. in evening with sketches of masks. 9*th.*—Alderman Gibbs initiated by the ceremony of rotten eggs into the Mayoralty![1] 12*th.*—Perpetrated pipeology with De la Motte at the *Leo Vermillio.* 13*th.*—Terrific explosion at Blackwall. Samuda, the engineer, and six others killed.[2] 16*th.*—*Great Gun* out this day, first number. See *Puck.* Felt really very ill. 17*th.*—Stopped in all day reading and writing *Poetry of Gruels.* 18*th.*—At home till evening writing, but wanted at Victoria in the evening. Bourcicaults have comedy of *Young Hearts, and Old Heads* produced at Haymarket, and met with great and deserved success.[3] 19*th.*—To town early with another crushing attack of the blues ; cause as usual. Collins appears at the Haymarket. Still desponding. 22*nd.*—Second number of *Great Gun* published. As far as it has yet gone, a decided failure."

"*Dec. 11th.*—Birthday. Just twenty-four. Spent evening with my mother. 17*th.*—Melancholy death, by burning, of Clara Webster."[4]

---

[1] The Lord Mayor seems to have been much disliked by his fellow-citizens, and his progress was anything but a happy one—more groans than cheers. At Gresham Street the horses became restive, and a wheel got locked in one of the posts of the barrier.

[2] This accident occurred at five o'clock p.m., on Tuesday the 12th, through the bursting of the main steampipe of the *Gipsy Queen,* 500 tons burden and 150 horse-power. Jacob Samuda, aged thirty-one years, senior partner in the firm of Jacob and Joseph Samuda, and six other men, were killed.

[3] *Young Hearts and Old Heads* (produced under Webster's manage-ment): Littleton Coke, Charles Mathews ; Bob (his servant), J. B. Buckstone ; Lord Charles Roebuck, Holl ; Countess of Pompion, Mrs. Clifford ; Miss Rocket, Miss Julia Bennett ; Colonel Rocket, Strick-land ; Lady Alice Hawthorn, Mme. Vestris ; Tom Coke, Webster ; Jesse Rural, Farren. A great success indeed ; author and company called, etc.

[4] Miss Webster was filling the *rôle* of Zulica, the royal slave, in the ballet of *The Revolt of the Harem,* on Saturday, December 14th, at

Here the first volume of the diary ends, covering only five months and eighteen days, but a painful record of hard work and struggles for daily bread, without any kind sympathy or comfort in his domestic life.

Whether the diary for 1845 was lost in some of E. L. B.'s removals cannot be ascertained, but there appears to be no detailed record of his doings during that year. In 1846 he begins with: "The curse of fame, the ban that levels the poet with his fellows, is the keen susceptibility of his emotions. The writer who has most musically expressed his griefs has felt them himself most keenly. It is from the greenest laurels we distil the deadliest poisons."

"*Jan. 8th.*—In town all day. Went to the Bower[1] with

Drury Lane, when her dress caught fire. She rushed round the stage, and the flames were ultimately extinguished by Daniel Coyle, a carpenter, who was severely burned. Miss Webster lingered till the following Tuesday morning. She was twenty-one, and a niece of Benjamin Webster.

[1] The Bower Saloon was a minor theatre in Stangate, Westminster, and was cleared away on the removal of St. Thomas's Hospital to that locality. The theatre was opened in 1838; Phil Phillips, the scenic artist of the Surrey Theatre, having, in 1837, taken a tavern with some land, on it he built this place of entertainment. The venture was not too successful, but had its palmy days, especially when managed by George Hodson, who became the lessee. He had conducted the "Yorkshire Stingo," where in those days a variety entertainment was carried on. George Hodson was the grandfather of Mrs. Labouchere, who was born on the premises of "the little theatre in Stangate," commemorated by Robertson in *Caste.* The old proprietor's son, George Hodson, married Miss Noel, sister of the late Mrs. Henry Marston, the fruit of the union being Henrietta Hodson. The late E. H. Tully, afterwards leader of the orchestra at Drury Lane, was at one time the musical director, and Phillips himself (during his occupancy) painted the scenery. J. B. Howe, of the Britannia, James Fernandez and other good living actors, came out at the Bower. The house changed hands many times, but ultimately became little better than a penny gaff.

F. G. D. *Cricket on the Hearth*, very fairly-played pantomime. 12*th*.—Went to see Kent. Introduced to E. E. U.
K. Called at Olympic in returning about *Cricket on the
Hearth* to Ventry. 14*th*.—Attended meeting of contributors
to Mephys (*Mephistopheles*)[1] at Healey's. Wooler[2] called.
15*th*.—*Cricket* burlesque at the Olympic, failure.[3] 16*th*.—
Had a very pleasant evening with W. L. Phillips. Music,
etc. Only Lewis the artist present."

[1] Mr. Blanchard was one of the chief contributors. Amongst the
numerous comic papers coming into existence after *Punch* had attained
success was one called *Joe Miller the Younger*, with which Albert Smith
closely associated himself. Soon after being started it became the property
of Healey, owner of *The Medical Times*, an individual who was nothing if
not original. So he at once changed the name of the humorous journal
he had purchased to that of *Mephistopheles*,—not altogether a happy
selection, as in the mouths of the newsvendors it became corrupted
into "Tophy ; " and they used to go into the dealers' with requests for
"Sixpen'orth of Tophy." Mr. Healey's proposed method of getting
material for his paper was, furthermore, a very original one. He
invited all the contributors to his residence, plied them with oysters
and champagne and cigars, so that they might be stimulated to say all
sorts of good things, which the editor, Mr. Richard Brinsley Knowles
(son of the dramatist, Sheridan Knowles), was to take down, and afterwards reproduce. Novel, however, as was the plan, it did not work.
The authors and artists met. They consumed dozens of delicious
bivalves and magnums of Cliquot, and they let off a prodigious
number of jokes. At the end of the sitting every one expected that
enough copy had been supplied for at least a number and a half. But
when the editor was asked how much he had got, the answer was that
he had laughed so much he was not able to take a single note. This
plan, therefore, was abandoned, and very soon *Mephistopheles* made a
final exit.

[2] T. P. Wooler, son of Wooler, editor and proprietor of *The Black
Dwarf*, a scurrilous Radical print of 1820, and a solicitor for some
years in Southampton Buildings, Chancery Lane. Also the author of
a farce *Founded on Facts*, in which Compton, as Mr. Sceptic, made an
immense success at the Strand in 1849, under the great old Farren's
management. T. P. Wooler also wrote several other dramatic pieces.

[3] This was an operatic extravaganza written for Miss Kate Howard,
lessee of the Olympic, entitled " *The Cricket on Our Own Hearth*,
by Leman Blanchard, a Fairy Tale of Fun." Miss Howard Dot
Spencer Forde (with an Irish brogue) the Stranger ; James Browne
the Carrier, Perrybingle ; Darcie, the Spirit of our Cricket, with
horns and tail ; Romer, Tackleton à la *Freischütz* ; Cockrill, Tilly
Slowboy. The panto. was *Fortunatus and the Magic Wishing Cap :*
Miss Laidlaw, columbine ; Jefferini, clown.

"*Feb.* 1*st.*—All day at home. Went to the Grapes, evening, with Honey.[1] A movement made. 12*th.*—Leave Southampton Street with regret—*much* regret. Stop at N. L. Coffee-house, 121, London Road."

"*March* 5*th.*—Move and take possession of new house, 8, Albion Street, Wandsworth Road. Pretty place, very agreeably situated. 11*th.*—At home all day, dreamy again ; want energy. Strange life mine, very. Wrote a little and thought much. Heigh ho! 15*th.*—Kent came. Good fellow, very. Lent me some cash in the noblest manner imaginable. 23*rd.*—At home all day compiling *Book of Jests* for Cleave. 25*th.*—Spend evening with Scott;[2] gives his imitations. Yates excellent. Arrived two o'clock at home, knocked up. 26*th.*—At home all day. Write short article for *People's Journal,* 'Breakfast and Breakfasting.' 27*th.*—To town, money-hunting. 'Alarming failure !' 28*th.*—Again in town. Meet March. Little chat about ' Saturdays.' Go up to Princess's ; see Collins, but no tin. *Monday,* 30*th.* —Go to town ; get a crown from Cleave on account of *Vivian Vernon.*"

"*April* 1*st.*—To town. *Literary Herald* dies. Meet K. H. Ecstasy ! 9*th.*—At home all day. Began short article, ' Alchemy of Every-day Life.' "

From Monday 20*th* to 24*th* inclusive E. L. B. was engaged in collecting materials, by visiting the district, for " Dover Line Guide Book."

"24*th.*—Went to Tunbridge : very dull. Then to Maidstone : stopped all night. Went to Dover : stopped at the Saracen's Head that night. Fine weather, but cold. Left for Folkestone, and thence to Ramsgate : stopped at Field's.

[1] George Honey, who was afterwards the comedian, was call-boy at the Adelphi in 1843, and sang the verses of the comic duet as the singing mouse in *Harlequin Blue Beard.*

[2] Scott was an obscure actor at the Adelphi, and also, earlier, at the Wells. But his mimetic powers were considerable, and he occasionally gave monologues, introducing imitations of well-known actors of the time—Macready, James Wallack, O. Smith, and Keeley—that were very clever.

All day at Ramsgate, walked to Broadstairs. Met H. Noble. Back to London, got in by 9 p.m. Stopped at Reigate and Staplehurst."

"*May 9th.*—Leave article, ' Romance of Everybody's Life,' with Cunningham for *Home Magazine.* 10*th.*—Write ' An Article from Contributor Extraordinary.' Took it to *Union Magazine. Monday,* 18*th.*—To town in evening. Leave first act of *King Arthur* at Phil Phillips's, of the Bower Saloon. 24*th.*—Go to town. Leave packet with Marriott for *Family Times.* 28*th.*—Finish burlesque, *King Arthur,* but don't much like it. Take it to Phillips, who promises to see what can be done with it. *Nous verrons.*"

"*Monday, June* 1*st.*—Vauxhall opens.[1] Weather like

[1] Vauxhall Gardens opened with concert, in which Messrs. Sinclair, Binge, Hodges, Darcie, J. W. Sharpe, Mrs. John Rowe, and Mrs. Aveling Smith took part ; Tournaire's Equestrian Circus (Tom Barry, of Astley's, as clown ; Widdicomb, master of the circle) ; fireworks before the picture of the Imperial Palace of Pekin. The waiters wore scarlet coats.

E. L. B. in 1870 wrote an excellent history of Vauxhall Gardens for *The Playgoer's Portfolio.* He traces its history back to 1654, when it is mentioned in Evelyn's Diary as " Mulberry Garden ; " and in 1661 the same writer speaks of Vauxhall as the New Spring Gardens at Lambeth. Samuel Pepys makes frequent reference to " Foxhall and the Spring Garden." On June 7th, 1732, one Jonathan Tyer opened the " Spring Gardens " with a *Ridotto al fresco.* When in 1745 Tyer added vocal to his instrumental music, Dr. Arne composed ballads, duets, etc. It is not intended to follow here the fortunes of Vauxhall, as amply set forth in E. L. B.'s account, but names of some of the celebrities that appeared in the programmes may be mentioned. James Hook, father of Theodore Hook, was the organist. Charles Incledon sang there in 1786 and the three following seasons ; he died in 1826. Mrs. Mountain ; Miss Tyer, afterwards married to Liston ; Madame Saqui, the tight-rope walker (1817) ; Miss Taylor ; Miss Povey (1820) ; Miss Tunstall, a celebrated ballad singer. In 1823 Mallinson, a comic vocalist, and the last-named lady made a hit with the duet, " Pretty Polly Hopkins." In 1825 Madame Vestris created her sensation with " Cherry Ripe," and in 1826 Braham was engaged. 1827 Charles Farley produced *The Battle of Waterloo* with great effect. Sir Henry Bishop was musical director in 1830, and there was a strong vaudeville company engaged, including Mrs. Fitzwilliam, Miss Hughes (from Covent Garden), and Messrs. Gattie, T. Cooke, Morley, George Stansbury, W. H. Williams, and Robinson, who made a reputation by

torrid zone.   See St. John.   *2nd.*—Town in evening; call on Mrs. Brodie[1] and borrow playbills.   *6th.*—Experiments with my brother at Vauxhall.   No oxygen, so a failure. Engaged on *The Life* and *The Bell.*[2]   *11th.*—To town with

singing Bishop's "My Pretty Jane."   Herr von Joel, afterwards so well known at Evans's supper rooms, was also engaged.   In 1832 Mrs. Keeley, Mrs. Waylett, Miss Coveney, and Paul Bedford were added to the company; and there was a representation of the Arctic Regions. The price of admission had hitherto been 3*s.* 6*d.* and 4*s.*, but on the first one shilling night 27,137 persons took advantage of the reduction. 1835 was a grand "Fête of Versailles."   Messrs. Bish, Gye, and Hughes became the proprietors for the sum of £28,000, and retained them .till 1839, and in this year Grisi, Rubini, and Tamburini sang in the Gardens. Messrs. Andrews and Mitchell opened Vauxhall for a short season in 1841.   In 1842 there was a sale of "movable property," the pictures by Hogarth and Hayman realizing but small sums.   A celebrated character connected with the Gardens was C. H. Simpson, the master of the ceremonies, with "powdered head and silken-hosed legs, silver-headed stick, cocked hat, and silken breeches.   He was a short man, with large head, a plain face, pitted with the small pox, and a thin thatch of hair, plastered with pomatum and powder. . . . He was continually bowing to everybody he met, and the incessant movement of his arm and the hat at the end of it resembled the motion of a parish pump handle in full play."   He died December 25th, 1835.   Vauxhall was celebrated for its elaborate fireworks, its monster dancing platform, its balloon ascents and parachute descents (Cocking was killed in one of these, July 24th, 1837), for the exorbitance of its charges for refreshment, for its arrack punch, the extraordinary diminitude of its "supper chickens," and the marvellous thinness of its slices of ham.   Vauxhall Gardens closed on July 25th, 1859, and the sale of the effects did not realize much over £800.   The site is now thickly built on.

[1] Brodie, known professionally as George Wild, whose mother, Mrs. Brodie, for many years kept a pastry-cook and confectioner's shop in Great Titchfield Street, Marylebone.   Wild was a clever low comedian, and made a mark in E. L. B.'s farces of *The Artful Dodge*, *Pork Chops*, and *Angels and Lucifers*, all produced at the Olympic when Wild was its lessee and manager.   A lady named Le Batt, a clever vocalist, was a close connection of Wild's, and supported him in the three amusing pieces named.

[2] Blanchard's early days were often passed amidst the most ludicrous impecuniosity and strange adventures, to get a crust by purveying news as a penny-a-liner.   After undergoing romantic vicissitudes as assistant to an itinerant lecturer, as stage property-boy, stage-manager at a long-vanished Chelsea theatre, and a scribe on science, young Blanchard came out as a writer on the staff of *The Town*.   Not long

afterwards the same scribbler used his pen most unmercifully in describing the scenes taking place at the "Copper Hell," in Cranbourne Alley, Leicester Square, where for fourpence any blackguard could spend hours playing hazard with "brown money." The suppression of this sink of iniquity was owing entirely to the publication of Blanchard's articles on the subject in the columns of *The Town*. In its pages, too, he was responsible for theatrical reports. He also described many of the most famous London hostelries, and recorded visits to the numerous tea gardens and suburban taverns, which at the particular period mentioned were favourite resorts of the cockneys. Copy from Bohemian scribes in those days was often written in a very comfortable fashion. All that was necessary consisted in taking a pocket inkstand and a quire of paper and stroll into the suburbs. It was then not very difficult to find solitude in a snug room, or in a garden alcove belonging to those hostelries now fast disappearing, and in one of such places the author sat down and wrote until his article was finished, when it was time to have a smoke. It was with surroundings agreeable as these that the Bohemian Blanchard penned *The Life of a Thimblerigger; Memorials of Tom Spring; The Road of Life; or, The Cabman's Career*, and other works, poetic, humorous, and dramatic.

Journalism, however, was poorly paid for, and Blanchard submitted this fact on a certain occasion to the late Joseph Last, of Crane Court. "I don't dispute it, sir. You send me a great deal of copy for 15s. a week. *It's small pay, but so regular.*" The remark came on Blanchard like a revelation. He bowed and left Last's office. Sauntering one summer day on the pavement before the Edinburgh Castle, in the Strand (a favourite resort—witness Blanchard's genial poem to "John," the friendly waiter there years ago), a year or two later on, the journalist met a small printer and publisher of Holywell Street, a Mr. Olinthus Bostock. "Good-day, Mr. Blanchard." The salutation was returned, and after some conversation the publisher said, "I often wonder you waste so much time on newspapers and sporting prints. Why don't you try a novel, sir—something cutting and moral?" As Bostock averred that by writing a work of this description its author's fortune would be made, Blanchard spent some days in Holywell Street, devising a story, at once thrilling and didactic, on the career of George Barnwell, the London apprentice. On a certain Saturday Bostock entered the room in which the author was hard at work, and with a rueful expression of countenance, said, "I'm going to take a great liberty, but could you lend me a little money? I only want a pound. My paper-merchant wants something on account, and until I pay a trifle he won't send me the ghost of a quire." The historian of Barnwell's perfidious doings informed Mr. Bostock that he was "stumped." "Have mercy on me, Mr. Blanchard! You don't know the straits of mercantile men. You're at work in your shirt-sleeves let me have your coat and waistcoat to raise a few shillings on them Sparks will soon close his warehouse, and if I don't work to-morrow

copy.   Meet Malcolm.[1]   13*th.*—St. John disappoints again.
‘ Horrors of Oakendale Abbey ’ appear.   16*th.*—‘ Bell of

we can't get the novel out next week, and I have no paper at all.
Your things can be taken out a little after six, as my boy, Ezekiel, is
going to bring home some money.” The author took off his waistcoat,
and then Bostock hastily remarked, “ I am ashamed to make such a
request, as you are so kind and affable, but could I beg your boots, too !
With an illustrated Bible upstairs and your things I can easily get the
sovereign.”   “ Have you a pair of slippers ? ”   “ No ; but there's an
old rug in the next room.   Can't you rest your feet on that ?   I'll have
everything out at the time I've named.”   “ Well, don't spoil the ship
for ha'porth of tar,” laughingly exclaimed the author.   “ Mind, boots,
waistcoat, and coat by a quarter-past six, as I have to get up to the
Yorkshire Stingo to hear Bob Glindon and Kitty Tunsfall sing.”

Bostock went away, and some time elapsed before he again appeared.
His demeanour was miserable in the extreme on re-entering the room.
“ Been a long time, Mr. Bostock.   How have you got on ? ”   “ Awful,
sir ; everything seems to go wrong.   Sparks took the sovereign which
I raised, but won't send any paper.   Ezekiel has been disappointed,
and I'm without a shilling.   Is there anybody you know that would
advance a trifle ?   I'll go with pleasure, I want a trifle so bad.”   “ Mr.
Bostock, let us have no trifling.   Go and get some money, and let me
have my clothes.”   “ I could if I had five shillings.   Things are awful
to contemplate.   If Sparks had sent the paper some of it might have
gone for work.   There's a man would lend me half-a-sovereign if I
paid him back a crown I'm in his debt.   He lives in Newcastle Street.
As a last resource, Mr. Blanchard, will you let me have your trousers
for an hour ?   Not longer.   A crown will set me free till Ezekiel comes
back from Cripplegate, where he's gone for £5.   Let me have the
trousers for an hour ? ”   “ Do you think that I am going to be played
with any longer ?   My difficulties have always been great, but I'm not
going to fight this ridiculous situation in a state of semi-nudity.   Go
out and get relief somehow.”

The hours rolled on, but no Bostock appeared, and the end of the
matter was that Blanchard had to pass the hot night in the printer's
stuffy little office.   On Sunday, at noon, he sent up a note to a
friend, Robert Cruikshank, who lodged in Lyon's Inn ; but that
worthy having been at a friendly gathering other than a temperance
one the night before, he did not reach Blanchard until the evening
was far advanced.   He, after an explanation, went back to the Inn,
obtained a watchman's thick great coat, and a pair of huge carpet-
slippers belonging to a laundress, and, arrayed in these articles of dress,
when night enveloped the great city, Blanchard walked to and fro with
Cruikshank on Adelphi Terrace inhaling the fresh air from the river.
After this jaunt, they adjourned to the White Hart, Catherine Street,
and supped, Blanchard sleeping there for the night.

[1] Malcolm, journalist, afterwards a Charterhouse Brother.

St. Paul's' published. 17*th.*—" Life " out; looks very well. *Monday,* 22*nd.*—" Bell of St. Paul's " sung at Vauxhall. 23*rd.*—B. Haydon, the celebrated artist, died yesterday suddenly. 24*th.*—Haydon now known to have committed suicide, poor fellow! His diary intensely interesting.[1] "

" *July* 3*rd.*—Opening dinner at Cremorne.[2] 6*th.*—At English opera. See Keeley, and puts me off a week. At Adams, and arrange to start to-morrow."

7*th* to 11*th* inclusive he was getting materials for guide books.

" Start for Brighton; get there at 4 p.m. Go on to Shoreham, and thence to Worthing. Weather delightful. 8*th.*—Off to Chichester in the morning. See Cathedral, thence come back to Worthing, and go on to Brighton to sleep, Sussex Hotel. 9*th.*—Leave in the afternoon for Lewes and Hastings. Stop at Hastings for the night. Very beautiful place indeed. Thunderstorm. 10*th.*—Stroll over to Fairlight Downs. Meet a Lieutenant of the Coast Guards; jolly fellow, very. View of three hundred miles. One Parkinson my guide. 11*th.*—Leave Hastings and return to town, stopping at Three Bridges for Worth. Beautiful Saxon village. 13*th.*—Go to town in the morning, arrange

---

[1] Benjamin Robert Haydon, a well-known and clever artist, committed suicide in a most determined manner, on Monday, June 22nd, in his studio, situate 14, Burwood Place, Edgware Road. He cut his throat and shot himself through the head. He was sixty years of age, and was born in Plymouth. His body was found stretched before a colossal picture of " Alfred the Great and the First British Jury," one of a series of six which he hoped to get accepted for the walls of the new Houses of Parliament. He had for twenty-six years kept very complete diaries of his daily life and actions, successes and trials ; the last entry was June 22nd, " God forgive me, Amen ! B. R. Haydon. ' Stretch me no longer on the rough world ' (*Lear*). The end of the twenty-sixth volume." Pecuniary troubles and artistic disappointments appear to have unhinged an otherwise sound intellect, for he was a pious and temperate man. The jury returned a verdict that he was in an unsound state of mind when he committed the sad act. Sir Robert Peel had granted him some weeks before a sum of £50.

[2] Mr. Ellis, the proprietor, entertained some four hundred guests ; Mr. W. E. Evans, of the Grand Hotel, Covent Garden, in the chair.

with Last to do *Manly Beauty*.   18*th*.—See Last. Astrological Almanack to be done.   *Monday, 20th.*— Moore's Almanacks to do."

" *Aug. 4th.*—At Museum. Smoke a pipe with E. Wilks ; poor fellow very hard up. Grieving over happier times.[1] 8*th*.—Received £1 from Last for copy of *Manly Beauty*. 11*th*.—Have interview with Keeley. Pay for burlesque. 13*th*.—Strange dream—death caused by loss of gravitation, re-ascend by gradations. Finish *Manly Beauty*. 14*th*.— Busy with farce of *Single Blessedness*. 15*th*.—Disappointed at Lyceum. Keeley ill. No cash anywhere. Meet Alfred Crowquill [2] at Phillips's. 17*th*.—Hear from H. Russell accept-

---

[1] One of Mr. Blanchard's closest chums, and a fellow dramatist, was Thomas Egerton Wilks, author of *The Ruby Ring, or, The Murder at Old Sadler's Wells ; The Old Blue Lion, or, Death on the Seventh Stair; Ben the Boatswain*, and upwards of forty equally exciting pieces. He earned enough by his pen to starve upon, and never harmed a fellow creature by word or deed. The Damon and Pythias of the hour sat in the coffee-room of the Crown in Pentonville, fully described by Boz in one of his sketches entitled "Miss Ivins and the Eagle." Wilks was in luck's way,—a very intermittent circumstance in the playwright's career. He had " gold, bright yellow glittering gold," in his pocket, and the pair had supped luxuriously off Welsh-rabbits and Kennet ale, somewhat extravagantly supplemented by "fours" of gin-and-water. T. E. W. had written a drama in two acts called *Darnley, or, The Keep of the Castle Hill*, and Davidge of the Surrey proved sweet on the play. Finding this to be the case, Wilks, who usually was paid about a pound an act for his dramas, saw an opportunity to get a better price. "I like your piece very much." "Glad to hear it." "What's the price ? " said the parsimonious Surrey manager. "Fifteen pounds." Davidge started as from an electric shock. Wilks remained obdurate. " Come," said Davidge, "don't be hard. Look here," and drawing out a greasy canvas bag he jingled the pieces inside, and laid out one by one in a row before the fascinated eyes of Wilks seven sovereigns and a half-sovereign. " I closed with him," said the playwriter ; " it was the sight of the precious metal. No cheque, not a bank-note, could have produced such an effect." Old John Cooper acted Darnley, and the piece was most successful. Wilks is the Glenalvon Fogg of Albert Smith's *Scattergood Family*, and it was E. L. Blanchard who intro-duced the author to Wilks, who unconsciously was drawn to the very life in the novel. The genial re-union at the Crown on Pentonville Hill occurred more than fifty years ago.

" Alfred Crowquill " was the *nom de plume* adopted by Alfred Henry Forrester, a very clever artist and author, when putting forth his

ing ' Diver's Song.' 18*th.*—Leave farce of *Single Blessedness*
with C. Perkins at the Adelphi. 20*th.*—About town about
loan. Get cash from Last. Arrange new Continental
Guide (*finished* 12*th October*). 21*st.*—Begin *Female Beauty.*
22*nd.*—Last refuses security. Send song of ' Old King Coke '
to H. Russell. *Monday,* 24*th.*—Begin farce of *Bear and Forbear* (*finished on September* 1*st, and was first sent to City
of London Theatre*). 26*th.*—Highly complimentary letter
from H. Russell. 30*th.*—George Mansell (*printer, died
August* 1870, *aged sixty-five*) called ; wants me to write a
new romance of *Jack Sheppard.*"

" *Sept.* 9*th.*—Go out gipsying with Kember, Billing, and
all the boys. Lunch in woods, then go off to Anerley, walk
about twenty miles, and get back tired and knocked up.
10*th.*—Gregory at the Strand, Richard III. *Monday,* 14*th.*
—Begin *Jack Sheppard.* Osbaldiston declines *Bear and
Forbear* for same reason as Honner. 19*th.*—Arrangement
with Phillips on opera (*Rosy Cross*). *Monday,* 21*st.*—Hard
at work on *Jack Sheppard.* 22*nd.*—Send off *Bear and
Forbear* to Greenwood, Sadlers Wells." [1]

books and pictures. They were both of gracefully humorous nature,
attested by the pantomimes written for the Surrey when under the
direction of Dick Shepherd, gentlemanly William Creswick, and by a
smart little book, still readable, *A Bundle of Crowquills,* and hundreds
of woodcuts for books and comic papers like *Puppet Show* and *Puck.*
Forrester was quite a gentleman. He died at Kennington in 1872.

[1] A strange story is told of E. L. B's., search after Greenwood ; E. L. B.
wrote a three-act drama called *The Road of Life;* or, *The Cabman's Career.*
T. L. Greenwood, when lessee of Sadlers Wells (prior to Phelps and
Mrs. Warner joining him), liked the successful piece, and the manager
stipulated with the author to pay a small sum for the right of acting
the play. The author paid a visit to the theatre to obtain his royalty.
" Mr. Greenwood is at his shop," replied an attendant, " and I don't
think he'll be here to-night." Obtaining directions, the playwright hied
away to an apothecary's shop in the St. John's Street Road, and sought
an interview with its proprietor. From a sort of surgery door an arm
holding a jack towel soon protruded, and a rough voice, slightly sug-
gestive of soap and water, exclaimed from the interior, " Don't come
bothering here. This is not the place for any effects dramatic or
otherwise. Call at the ' Wells ' to-morrow night." The mandate was
obeyed. " Please, sir, Mr. Greenwood has just gone down the yard to
get the Clapton 'bus at the Angel," said a boy. " If we make haste we

" *Oct.* 12*th.*—Make up packet for *Mirror.* 18*th.*—Very wretched indeed. No spirits, no dinner, no nothing! 24*th.* —Theatre again. £1 tendered by Osbaldiston and accepted by me. Chat with Laidlaw [1] at Bushel's. *Monday,* 26*th.*—At work on *Jack Sheppard.* Go to Victoria in evening. *Relapse* produced at Olympic. *Cinderella* at former. Both go off well. 28*th.*—Meet Reynolds; his new publication out this day."

" *Monday, Nov.* 2*nd.*—Busy with *Jack Sheppard.* Offer of 30*s.* for six pages. 4*th.*—Still at work for Mansell. Write to *Astrologer* correspondent. Garrick Theatre burnt to ground this morning after *Battle of Waterloo.*[2] 11*th.*—Begin

can catch him." Away the pair scudded out of the theatre and into St. John's Street, towards the famous inn mentioned. " I see him ; there he goes! " But the omnibus was ready to start, and the result of the race was a sight of Mr. Greenwood's back and legs, soon shut out by the door of the vehicle. Two evenings later on, the dramatic author was again in the vestibule of the theatre. " Mr. Greenwood is in the pit pay-place." Through the aperture, sacred to the exchange of shillings for metal " checks," a voice exclaimed, " All right ; brought a receipt ? " " Yes ! " And poor E. L. B. said, " I got the money, but I only beheld a chin, a black velvet waistcoat, and a hand." Subsequently one night at the Hugh Myddelton, Henry Marston said, " My dear Blanchard, let me introduce you to Mr. Greenwood." " We've met before, Mr. Blanchard." " Certainly," was the reply, " but I have only hitherto seen a bit of you. I'm delighted on this occasion to behold the whole of you."

[1] A family of most accomplished dancers and pantomimists. The father was a capital harlequin, and his daughter- Louisa, who was with Madame Vestris (Lyceum, 1847-53), a charming dancer.

[2] Gomersal, when an obscure actor, was out of an engagement, as was too frequently the case with him, and happening to call in at the Tankard, a favourite theatrical tavern in the Kennington Road, he there met with the proprietor of Astley's, who was much struck with his likeness to the first Napoleon. As it happened, the play of *The Battle of Waterloo* was then in rehearsal, and about to be produced the next night ; but the management was in difficulty owing to the very serious illness of the principal actor, who was to play Buonaparte. In this dilemma the manager approached Gomersal, and asked him if he could undertake the part at such a short notice. Gomersal was in very low water, and would have agreed to study any new part by the next night ; he readily embraced the manager's offer, and set to work to study the lines at once. However, when the next evening arrived he was very far from being letter-perfect, and in this difficulty he

Olympic pantomime, *Harlequin King Alfred the Great.* At work on it all day (*finished on the* 13*th*). 16*th.*—Inquest on Alsager.[1] *Life*[2] produced at Olympic, and failed. 20*th.* —Begin and finish *Dakin's Manual.* 27*th.*—Begin article for *Isle of Man,* ' Fancies from the Fireside.' "

" *Dec.* 2*nd.*— Give Jefferini[3] song. Much pleased. 9*th.*— Receive melancholy letter from Fisher. Poor fellow ! (*Died*

bethought himself of a snuff-box which he possessed amongst his properties, which he agreed with the prompter should be the medium for signalling, and that when he required assistance he would tap it and take snuff. The first time that he used this manœuvre it was warmly applauded by the audience, and having to be frequently repeated he found that on each occasion it was good for a round ; hence on the subsequent productions it was always made a prominent feature, and never failed to meet with popular recognition.

[1] This Mr. Alsager was a literary man, engaged as writer of the money article of the *Times.* He cut his throat in three places on Friday morning, November 13th. He was uncle to John Oxenford, and was founder of the Beethoven Quartet Society, and a great supporter of the Philharmonic Society. He was a distinguished musical amateur. He died on Sunday, the 15th, at 2 a.m. The jury returned a verdict that there was no evidence as to the state of his mind. He appears to have been much depressed at the remembrance of the loss of his wife and at his giving up his literary pursuits.

[2] Olympic: G. Bolton, lessee and manager. *Life,* by P. Palmer ; comedy in five acts. Mr. Orston (Archer), Frank Orston (Leigh Murray—good), Emily Orston (Mrs. R. Gordon), Charles Newcombe (J. Howard), Selwood (Maynard), Concord (Wilkinson), Sir Thomas Mentor (Walter Lacy), Fanny Archer (Mrs. Walter Lacy), Mrs. Hookham (Mrs. Griffiths), her daughters Seraphina and Angelina (Miss Charles and Miss Ayres), Sir Jacob Smallwit (Mr. George Bolton), Sir Robert Folair (J. Cowell), Lady Bait (Mrs. C. Jones). A very poor play—a hash-up of *Tom and Jerry, High Life Below Stairs,* and a touch of *George Barnwell.*

[3] A very clever pantomime clown—his real name being Jeffreys— who, in addition to clowning at festive seasons (Christmas, Sadlers Wells, or Olympic, or City of London, or Victoria ; White Conduit Gardens Theatre at Whitsun, or it might be Montpelier Gardens Theatre, Walworth, or Bagnigge Wells), for many years kept a tobacconist's shop known as "The Little Snuff-box," in Garnault Place, Clerkenwell. It was also a gambling-house, and on its floor above the shop E. L. B. has often watched punters and players over French hazard and *écarté.* Jeffreys was a very tall man, and his long

February 15*th*, 1847.)[1] 18*th.*—Busy with pantomime bills. 20*th.*—Finish Olympic bill. 21*st.*—Hear from Leigh Hunt. Leaves *Liverpool Times.* Letter from a Madame Caroline Bontyne for Monopologue. 25*th.*—Miserable, and Christmas Day at home, *solus.* 26*th.*—Pantomimes produced ; both hits, and houses crowded. Olympic: *King Alfred the Great; or, Harlequin History of the Enchanted Raven.* Music by Thirlwall. Victoria: *The Birth of the Steam Engine;* or, *Harlequin Go-a-head and Joe Miller and His Men.* 29*th.*—Busy with rehearsals at Olympic. 31*st.*—Go to Princess's ; bad pantomime. *The Enchanted Beauties of the Golden Castle; or, Harlequin and the One-eyed Giant* —from *Arabian Nights.* " Ten Calendars:" Bologna, harlequin ; Flexmore, clown ; Miss Burbidge, columbine ; Paulo, pantaloon. Old Year out at home. *Sic transit* 1846.

It was during this year that the three little publications, entitled respectively " Bradshaw's

legs made leaps through mimic shop windows exceedingly perilous. On one occasion, when going through this mirth-making performance, the clown missed his mark and fell, whereby an internal injury was sustained, the effects of which he ever felt when exploiting in feats of nimbleness and agility, even to suffering the most intense agony. In later years his facial contortions, which excited roars of laughter from the audience, were only a vent for the tortures the poor fellow in motley suffered from internal pain consequent on his leaping and dancing. Jeffreys sat to a publican's artist, and the sign portraiture, which for a long period (1842 to 1849) adorned externally the Clown Tavern, St. John Street Road, was the face and form of the popular Jefferini. He was clown in E. L. B.'s pantomime, *Harlequin King Alfred,* brought out at the Olympic, Christmas 1846, under George Bolton. He was a pupil of Tom Matthews. He made his *début* before becoming a regular clown at the little Panharmonium at King's Cross in 1837, as Desperetta in *The Dumb Maid of Genoa.*

[1] Charles Fisher was connected with the Fishers of Yorkshire, well known as circuit managers in that county. Clara Fisher, the popular child actress in " Little Pickle " and other parts, was C. Fisher's sister, and David Fisher, original Abbé Latour in *The Dead Heart,* was a relation. C. Fisher was a tall, well-formed man, whose last engagement was under Maddox at the Princess's, and he was a fine Stralenheim at that theatre to Macready's *Werner* : Mrs. Warner being Josephine ; Mrs. Stirling, Ida ; Creswick, Ulric ; Ryder, Gabor ; and Granby, Idenstein. Fisher's death took place soon afterwards.

Descriptive Guide to the South Eastern Railway," etc.,[1] and complete "Guides to Tunbridge Wells, Maidstone, Ashford, Canterbury, Folkestone, Dover, Ramsgate, Margate, etc., Together with their Historical and Local Associations, by E. L. Blanchard," and "Bradshaw's Descriptive Guide to the Great Western Railway, Part II., from Bristol to Plymouth, containing Everything of Importance to the Railway Tourist, and forming a Complete Traveller's Companion to each Town and Station along the Line, and the Attractive Scenery Adjacent, by E. L. Blanchard," were published by W. J. Adams, of Fleet Street.

[1] This work which has now grown to such colossal proportions, and which is our railway guide, not only for Great Britain, but in its continental form all over Europe, and, one might almost say every part of the world—first appeared on October 19th, 1839. Its originator was a Quaker, George Bradshaw, who was an engraver of maps and plans of cities. This brought him into connection with the railways, and he conceived the idea of printing a little manual which would set forth the times of the arrival and departure of trains. A year previous to this, John Gadsby, of Manchester, had published *Gadsby's Monthly Railway Guide*, but he does not appear to have had sufficient energy to have carried on his enterprise. The first number of *Bradshaw* was a little book, just 4½ inches by 2½, bound in violet · cloth, and entitled

"BRADSHAW'S RAILWAY TIME TABLES AND ASSISTANT TO RAILWAY TRAVELLING."

With Illustrated Maps and Plans.

Price Sixpence.

LONDON: SHEPHERD & SUTTON & WYLD.

10 mo. 19, 1839.

There is no copy of it in the British Museum, but it may be found in the Bodleian Library. E. L. B. was early concerned in the venture, and tells us that the companies were, at first, vehemently opposed to the scheme, and, in their niggard way, refused to supply their tables

1847.

FROM the beginning of the year to nearly the end of March the diary appears to have lapsed. On the 29*th* of March he re-commences :—

"At home all day after a ramble in the morning with dog ' Fid.' (This was a pet that had been given him by his mother a few days before.) Write several pieces for the *Curtain*. 30*th*.—Begin Isle of Wight Guide for *Travellers' Miscellany* (*finished on April 2nd*). 31*st*.—Go to town; chat with Barth (printer of *Dramatic Mirror*). Easter pieces announced."

"*April 1st*.—Busy with *Miscellany* copy. Receive letter from Keeley declining *King Arthur*, and one from Spicer[1] announcing engagement of Albert Smith and Angus Reach on *Curtain*. 2*nd*.—Leman Rede[2] dies, aged 45. 5*th*.—*Curtain* comes out in new form, Albert Smith, Reach,

on the odd ground that this would make punctuality a sort of obligation, and that failure would bring penalties. G. Bradshaw, however, was not to be repulsed, and, by various devices, notably by taking many shares, brought over the hostile companies. Bradshaw had as his London agent Mr. Adams, of Fleet Street, with whom E. L. B. was so frequently connected in various literary works.

[1] Henry Spicer, a gentleman of fortune, a dramatist, author of *Honesty, Judge Jeffries, Lords of Ellingham*, and *Cousin Cherry*, and sometime co-lessee (1847-48) of Olympic. He projected and published a theatrical paper, *The Curtain*, its chief feature being a " bill " of all the chief performances of the theatres for the evening. It only had a short existence. Mr. Spicer is living.

[2] Leman Rede died after a very brief illness at his house, 32, Southampton Street, Strand, on April 2nd, at six in the morning. He was born in 1802 at Hamburg, and was the son of T. L. Rede, barrister, and author of *The Laws of England* and *Anecdotes of Eminent Characters* (translation of St. Pierre's work). Leman Rede was the author of numerous plays, *Old and Young Stager*, etc. ; was a writer and journalist ; and married in 1832 Miss Sarah Cooke, daughter of Mr. Cooke, bass singer at D. L. T., and cousin to Mrs. Waylett and Mrs. W. West. He left a widow and one son ten years of age.

and others as contributors. 10*th.* — Usual meeting at
Bushel's: Scales, Pond, De la Motte, Hunt, etc. 13*th.*—
Write for *Curtain* chapter on ' Check-takers: Man at the
Pit Doors.' 16*th.*—Bath publishes a *Dramatic Mirror.*
Laidlaw wants Salt Mines for Vauxhall. Surrey Zoological
bills out. Subject, Gibraltar. 24*th.*—Send ' Distresses of
Management' to Spicer. 27*th.* — Hear from H. Hall,
Glasgow. Wants heading for bill. Write one, and send
it. Send Spicer ' Origin of Applause ' and ' The Love
Chase ' for *Curtain.* 28*th.*—Last day of the fair. Go to
town; meet G. W. M. Reynolds.[1] Arrange for new
periodical. Farce of *Wife for an Hour* produced at
Princess's. Goes off very well indeed."

" *May* 3*rd.*—Send copy to *Curtain,* ' Song of the Stick,'
' Stuttering Contributor,' etc. 4*th.*—Write to Bradshaw about
Handbooks to the Continent. To George Kent (knife
patent). Send Spicer two articles for *Curtain*—' Currency
Committee ' and ' Light Comedians.' *Dramatic Mirror* prints
farce, *Wife for an Hour.* Jenny Lind appears at Italian
Opera at Haymarket. Triumphant success. 5*th.*—Begin
article for *Isle of Man.* George Kent (knife rotary machine)
called; long interview. See Adams about " Watering-

[1] Son of an English admiral, and having been well educated in
Germany settled in London, and became the most successful of penny
dreadfulists. E. L. B. met Reynolds in connection with Stiff, of the
London Journal, in which Reynolds wrote *Faust* (Sir John Gilbert
was its artist), and for whom Stiff published the first and second
series of the *Mysteries of London.* Stiff had rights in their publication, and having quarrelled with Reynolds about money, the latter
left in a huff. Stiff then commissioned E. L. B. to write a third
series of the *Mysteries of London,* for which he had a third less than
the other. E. L. B. used to say his *Mysteries of London* was much
more moral than its predecessors, but it did not sell in anything like
the successful manner the first and second lot did. Thomas Miller
wrote the fourth series. Reynolds was a clever, though a showy,
author, and he was a political humbug all round, though the
denouncer of high people and vice in high places. Dicks bought his
name and copyrights for a splendid annuity. The author of *The
Bronze Statue; or, The Virgin's Kiss,* and *The Loves of the Harem,* died
churchwarden of St. Andrew's, Wells Street, and in the odour of
sanctity.

places of England."[1]   *7th.*—At home, write and send off
' Summer Day's Ramble ' for *People's Press.*[2]   Chapter I. of
Travelling and Travellers for De la Motte.   *Monday, 10th.*
Kent's rotary machine.   Receive from him in payment 15*s.*
Meet Sharp[3] at Vauxhall.   Wants me.   11*th.*—Busy with
articles for *Curtain.*   Send ' Man in Search of Position,'
' Pleasures of Imagination.'   12*th.*—Go to Standard Theatre.
Sup with Nelson Lee.   Long talk about pantomimes.   13*th.*—
Busy at home writing Hastings Guide for *Miscellany.*   16*th.*—
W. Smith[4] (Surrey) died yesterday.   *Monday, 17th.*—Adams
takes house in Albion Street.   Mr. and Mrs. Kember come and
take tea. (*Mrs. Henry Kember died January 2nd, 1866, aged
fifty-eight.*)   18*th.*—At home indisposed.   Got ready copy
for *Miscellany.*   Finish second chapter of *Travelling and
Travellers,* ' Tourists;' send *Babes in the Wood* scene to Wild.
20*th.*—Write ' History of Vauxhall ' in the morning, and
leave it with Wardle [5] in afternoon.   G. Wild severely injured

---

[1] In 1847 England was visited with a severe epidemic, answering to
our influenza of last spring (1890), which was called " La Grippe."
E. L. B. wrote a little book on this, prescribing remedies for it, and
signed " Medicus."   This had a wide circulation, and sold for 1*s.*   No
one suspected it was by the same pen that edited the *London Journal*
and other papers of the day.

[2] *The People's Press* was a monthly publication in the Isle of Man,
price 1½*d,* edited by William Shrimp, which could be posted and
reposted in the United Kingdom free of charge—an old privilege re-
pealed at the close of 1848.

[3] J. W. Sharp, the noted comic singer, died in the workhouse at
Dover, January 1856, aged thirty-eight.

[4] William Cole Smith, aged forty-seven, comedian, had been connected
with Surrey.   Died from general debility, brought on by excessive
drinking.

[5] Robert Wardle was the last proprietor of Vauxhall, died December
29th, 1865.   There might nominally have been another one, but I could
never learn it.   E. L. B. used to purvey news of what went on at
Vauxhall for several newspapers, his first commissioner in that way
having been Mr. Barnes of *The Times.*   Blanchard in early life very
nearly became a member of the *Times* staff.   It appears that he
obtained an introduction to Mr. Barnes, the " Thunderer," so called
from his powerful leaders, and was employed by that gentleman to
catalogue his library in Soho Square.   This was quite a labour of love,
and Mr. Barnes treated him very liberally, so that it was a most
pleasant and congenial occupation.   This employment and intimacy
resulted in Mr. Barnes promising Blanchard a permanent engage-

by his passionate wife, and bruised so much as to render him unable to continue his engagements. *21st.*—Write 'Rouen' article for *Miscellany*, and chapter of *Travelling and Travellers*, 'Stage Coaches.' *Monday, 24th.*—Write 'Electric Clock' for Scales, and two songs for *Curtain*. News of O'Connell's death confirmed (*died at Genoa, May 15th*). *25th.*—Undertake for Mansell 'Theatrical Beauties,' 10s. a week. *26th.*—Meet Spicer, who wants me to be sub-editor of *Daily Advertiser*. *27th.*—At home all day very busy. Write two articles for *Curtain*—'Caleb in Search of the Country,' and 'The Involuntary Demon.' Covent Garden Theatrical Fund Dinner [1] yesterday, £505 subscribed (the last that took place). *28th.*—Give copy to Mansell for No. 6 of 'Theatrical Beauties.' Began chapter of 'Pedestrians' for De la Motte. *Monday, 31st.*—Go to Vauxhall, which opens to-night for the hundred and fifteenth season. Bedouin Arabs the best; ballet very good with W. H. Payne, Tom Matthews, Rosina Wright, Mrs. W. H. Payne, and Miss Annie Payne. Meet E. Laws, FitzJames, T. Lewis, John Ryan (manager), Rogers, Stiff."

"*June 1st.*—Write chapter, 'Commercial Travellers.' *4th.*—Maudsleys' [2] factory burnt down. Take chapters up to De la Motte. Sherry-cobblerize with Baron Nicholson, Rouse, etc. [3] *8th.*—Send Spicer *Comus*, breakfast-table burlesque, and funny encyclopædia. Write Continental chapter for *Travellers*. *10th.*—Send Spicer review, burlesque of Eliza Cook's poems. *11th.*—No. 7 'Theatrical Beauties' out; very bad cut. Talk about change of title. Fine day again. *13th.*—

ment on the paper ; but on the very day that this was to have been carried out, Blanchard, on calling as usual in Soho Square, was informed that Mr. Barnes had died suddenly that very morning, so his hopes were thus abruptly ended.

[1] Duke of Cambridge in chair ; Duke of Beaufort present. Shirley Brooks returned thanks for "Drama and its Patrons."

[2] Maudsleys, the engineers, Westminster Road, Lambeth, nearly totally destroyed, but insured ; no lives lost.

[3] E. L. B. used to frequent White Conduit to enlist the favour of its vocalists, Leffler, Plumpton, Bill Pearce (the "Storm" Pearce), Prynne, and George Jones, to buy a new song. The Richard Rouse here spoken of must in no way be confounded with the "Bravo Rouse," Thomas Rouse, of the Old Eagle, afterwards the Grecian Saloon. For account of Baron Nicholson, see May 1861.

Hall offers me the *Decorator. Monday, 14th.—*Mrs. H. Vining and her two daughters (one of them the present Mrs. John Wood) called to go to Vauxhall. Weather very rainy, miserable evening in consequence. Serenade for Howe. Send article to *Curtain,* the libretto of ' Coming Out.' 15*th.* —Busy with *Travelling and Travellers.* Send ' The Rivals ' to *Curtain.* Letter from Spicer that *Curtain* is to be discontinued. Go in evening to R. Rouse's.[1] 16*th.*—Finish ' Railways ' for *Travelling and Travellers.* Reading *Confessions of Jean Jacques Rousseau.* Extraordinary work of a profound thinker. 17*th.*—Finished ' Steamboats ' for *Travelling and Travellers.* 18*th.*—At home all day, write ' Dover,' ' Watering-places,' for *Miscellany*, and copy for *Travelling and Travellers.* 19*th.*—Busy day in town, cash ¯from

---

[1] R. Rouse, proprietor of Old White Conduit Gardens, just before their demolition in 1849, and also of the Belvidere Tavern at the south-west corner of Penton Street, Pentonville. At the south-western corner of Penton Street, Pentonville, stood an ancient hostelry called " The Belvidere ; " the sign still remains, but the old house has been modernised out of existence, and there is very little trace of it left in the " public " which now occupies the site. The " Belvidere " was celebrated for its racket courts, where all the champion matches were played ; but it attained a still greater celebrity for its discussion society, which held its meetings on Saturday evenings in a large room on the first floor. There was a permanent chairman, and also a secretary ; but in other respects the meetings were open to the world, and were well attended by a very mixed assemblage of Clerkenwell tradesmen, barristers, and literary men ; for this was the nursery of the Senate and the Bar, and men of considerable attainments did not disdain to make use of it as a practising ground. Amongst some of the frequenters may be mentioned Lord Halsbury, the present Chancellor, then a learned junior ; also his gifted brother Harry, now a registrar in bankruptcy ; Serjeants Parry and Tindal Atkinson ; the Hon. Dudley Campbell ; James Hannay, the brilliant essayist ; Wiltshire Austin, a clever but erratic man of letters ; W. E. Church, a well-known Urbanite and critic ; W. A. Holdsworth, the author of a number of recondite works on Jurisprudence ; Walter Tyas, then on the staff of the *Times,* now the Warden of the University of Adelaide ; and many others who have become celebrated in their various professions. Considerable freedom of speech used to prevail at these meetings. On one occasion a gentleman who has since attained a judicial position was making a very strong speech from a Conservative point of view, being most emphatic in his action ; he was followed by a local bootmaker of Radical proclivities, who alluded to him as " the gentleman

Curtain. 20*th.*—Conclude *Travelling and Travellers,* and send Mansell copy. *Curtain* changes hands and printers. Mr. David is to be the editor. *Monday,* 21*st.*—Begin 'Lights and Shadows of Every-day Life'—No. 1, '.Twilight'—for *Isle of Man.* 25*th.*—Busy in town. Abbey Glee Club. James Coward [1] wins prize."

"*July* 6*th.*—Vauxhall, night balloon ascent; narrow escape of Albert Smith,[2] Pridmore. Coxwell aeronaut, 'Gypson,' in the latter's ablest balloon. 12*th.*—An incident possibly for Surrey drama. A man disguised as apple-woman, with stall at corner of street, who at the right moment reveals himself and detects, or prevents, some roguery."

For a considerable portion of the year 1848 E. L. B. appears to have neglected his diary. The first entry was on October 14th, when he writes,

who had combined the sentiments of a demon with the gestures of an ape." On another occasion the subject of debate was, whether a person named Cox, who was a well-known butt in the columns of *Punch,* was a fit person to represent the borough of Finsbury, and a Mr. Shilibeer, an undertaker in a large way of business, and who was also the first to introduce omnibuses to the London streets, made a very eulogistic speech upon the many virtues of Cox ; he was followed by Jack Holdsworth, one of the *Daily News* staff, who perverted Shakespeare, and said that Mr. Shilibeer had come to praise Cox and not to bury him. This made Shilibeer very irate, and he appealed to the chair as to whether gentlemen's occupations were to be alluded to in a flippant manner. This discussion society ceased to exist about five-and-twenty years ago

[1] James Coward, many years a singer at the Foundling, and one who over a long period was associated with " table singing," glees, madrigals, and motets, at civic and other banquets. He enjoyed a pension of £40 from the Governors of the Foundling, and emoluments from teaching singing. E. L. B. picked him up at a glee club that met once a month in the first floor of the Fountain Tavern in Amwell Street, Clerkenwell, a club attended by Pyne (father of Louisa and Susan Pyne), Fielding, King, and other well-known vocalists.

[2] Albert Smith appears to have been fond of balloon ascents, for on Monday, June 7th, of this year he ascended in Green's balloon, the *Nassau,* from Cremorne ; with him were the veteran aeronaut, Shirley Brooks, John Lee of the *Standard,* Mr. Ibbotson, Mr. Thompson, Morris Power, Mr. Davidson, Mr. Drew.

"Returned from York." He took up his London occupation, continued his contributions to the *Magazine of Mysteries and Marvels*, and compiled the "Parlour Songster." The Strand Theatre, of which Mr. Edward Hooper became lessee, and for whom E. L. B. wrote the opening address delivered by Mrs. Hooper, commenced its season on October 30th, with a revival of the musical romance of *Henri-Quatre*, followed by *The British Legion* and *Deaf as a Post*. Mr. Conway, Mr. and Mrs. H. Webb, Miss Rebecca Isaacs, and Mr. and Mrs. Hooper were the most prominent names in the bills. A Miss Decamp made her London *début*, but not a hit, as Florence St. Léon. The address was "well received," and concluded with the following smart lines :—

> "Take up the little bill that's now presented,
> Just back it with your hands, and we're contented."

The *Weekly Times*, 1st Number January 23rd, 1847, then owned by Stiff, was enlarged on December 1st, and in it appeared the first part of E. L. B.'s novel, "Confessions of a Page." (Stiff ultimately became the proprietor of the *Morning Chronicle*, the last number of which was published on Wednesday, March 19th, 1862, after existing ninety-two years.)

About this time begin the references to his looking in at the Wrekin. This was a tavern in Broad Court, Drury Lane, and its site is now occupied by a block of model lodging-houses. Its host for some years was a Mr. Harrold, sometime

a comedian, and an uncle of Blanchard's, who had
an oil portrait of this relation. The Wrekin,
from the early part of the century, had an
interesting history, being the resort of wits and
convivialists. Here met the Mulberries, a club
having a regulation that a paper, or poem, or
conceit bearing upon Shakespeare should be contributed by each member. These contributions
were called " Mulberry Leaves." Hither came
Douglas Jerrold and his great friend Laman
Blanchard (in no way related to our Blanchard),
and then Mr. Godwin, Kenny Meadows (the illus-
trator of Shakespeare), Elton the Shakespearean
actor, E. Chatfield, and others. Jerrold's two
essays, "Shakespeare in China" and "Shakespeare
at Bankside," were originally " Mulberry Leaves,"
and will now be found reprinted in his " Cakes
and Ale." E. L. Blanchard stated that he never
even saw Laman Blanchard, Jerrold's friend. But
from the fact that his uncle was once proprietor,
E. L. B. necessarily took great interest in the
hostelry, and was learnedly posted in its history.
Warner (who married Mary Huddart—the Mrs.
Warner, a handsome tragedienne, of her day under
Macready at Covent Garden and Drury Lane, and
co-manager with Phelps at Old Sadlers Wells)
was host of the Wrekin some time, when a club
called the Rationals, whose members included
Stephen Price, Jerrold, Henry Mayhew, Baylis,
Whitehead, Paul Bedford, Keeley, and Strickland,
used to have a Saturday afternoon dinner. Then
Hemming, a Haymarket and Adelphi actor, became

the host, and he died in 1849.   E. L. B. regularly attended the coffee-room of the tavern from 1837 to about 1846.   During that period he formed the acquaintance of F. G. Tomlins (Jerrold's sub-editor), Howe, Strickland, Walter Lacy, Leman Rede, Mark Lemon, Donald King, Sheridan Knowles, Bayle Bernard, and a large number of other Thespians, authors, and painters, who used to frequent the house.[1]

[1] Under the head of " Licensed Victuallers, their Manners, and their Parlours," E. L. B. wrote the following in *The Town*, April 20th, 1839 :—

" THE WREKIN, BROAD COURT.

"In the very centre of Broad Court, and exactly half-way between Bow Street on the one hand and Drury Lane on the other, standeth that very 'ancient and honourable' hostelrie, yclept the Wrekin, time out of mind the favourite resort of authors, actors, poets, painters, and penny-a-liners. Situated in the immediate vicinity of the theatres, it can excite little wonder that the members of the sock and buskin fraternity should have used this house in preference to others more distant ; but a retrospective glance at the gradual progression it has made from a common alehouse to its present state will serve to show that the reputation of the Wrekin, for being a Thespian 'house of call,' has only been the work of that great architect Time.

"Tradition, we believe, assigns to this house the honour of having been the scene of many an adventure between that amorous monarch Charles the Second and the fascinating orange-girl Nell Gwynne ; whilst it was here also, no doubt, that Charles and his *bon compagnons* caroused 'potations pottle deep' till cock-crow, when his eccentric Majesty, following the example of his opulent landlord, deemed it expedient to retire. Somewhere about the middle of the eighteenth century we find the tavern in the hands of one Sims, a worthy Salopian, who, taking some dislike to its previous name, re-christened it after his native hill, The Wrekin, in Shropshire, and rendered it renowned for Tewkesbury ale and Shrewsbury cakes, at that time the favourite luncheon of the young men about town. Owing to the death of the ale-bibbing proprietor, it shortly afterwards became the property of Mr. Harrold, who, condensing three houses into one, and making several other improvements, raised its estimation greatly ; and it was then opened for the sale of wines and spirits alone. Here it was that the *Catamarans*, a club yet green in the memory of our old stagers, used to assemble, and hence it was that the brightest wit and the readiest pun used to emanate. The nightly conclave generally included the names of Theodore Hook, Tom Sheridan, his father (Richard Brinsley Sheridan), Charles Mathews, the two Kembles, Munden, Jack Morris (the song writer), George Colman, Morton (the dramatist), Reynolds, Monk Lewis, and, in fact, all who had rendered themselves conspicuous in the world of literature, by either the wit in their productions, or otherwise renowned for their talents on the stage. Mr. Harrold resigned the proprietorship of the hotel to his son, having kept possession of it for above five-and-thirty years. It shortly afterwards again changed hands in favour of Mr. Judd, who sold the house to Williams, in whose time it first became a noted house for the Press, which it has continued to be ever since. Mr. Warner, who has since married Miss Huddart, then shared the duties of proprietor with a blithesome widow, bearing the unromantic name of Browne, who established an admirable society there under the quaint title of the *Rationals*, to which most members of the companies of both Covent Garden and Drury Lane then belonged. It again experienced a number of vicissitudes in the different changes that had gradually taken place, when it ultimately fell into the possession of Mr. Hemming, at present a distinguished member of the Haymarket corps, under whose prosperous superintendence we trust it may long continue.

"On turning immediately to the right, after penetrating through the folding doors, theatrically enveloped in green baize, the visitor is inducted to a spacious parlour, which is occupied chiefly by persons connected with either the theatrical or the literary profession, and who may be seen befogging themselves with copious clouds of tobacco, alternately varying the amusement by quaffing deeply the contents of sundry pewter receptacles for half-and-half and stout, or imbibing the contents of a tumbler brimmed with a second edition of gin-and-water, whilst the drinker is discharging from his thirty-six inches of humanity (with true author-like perseverance in continuing the series of his productions) *volumes of smoke.* Having comfortably established the reader in a remote corner of the room, with a reasonable supply of liquids, and an adequate supply of stewed cheese, for which latter the place is especially renowned, we shall take the liberty of introducing him to the company at large, amongst whom he will no doubt recognize some old acquaintances.

"That strange, unearthly-looking individual to the right, with a head of hair resembling a retired shoe-brush, and a sort of oasis in the desert in the shape of an imperial on his chin, is Stirling C—ne, Yates's dramatic factotum, who possesses a peculiar tact for measuring, with all the precision of the tailor's craft, a dwarf or giant with an appropriate character. You think he's engaged in the simple act of lighting his pipe, yonder, do you? Pooh, nonsense! He has just received a note from the immortal Fred, enjoining him to write a piece for the introduction of some polar bears from Greenland, and he is just considering whether the *denouement* can be brought to bear by one of the animals setting fire, with a lighted brand in his mouth, to the mutineers' ship, in the last scene. By the satisfactory whiff that follows the action, you may rest assured that the difficult task is accomplished.

"Next to him, with a dark whisker-covered, and yet, withal, good-humoured, countenance, is Henry M-yh-w, the farce-writer, a most prolific vendor of puns and a clever scholar to boot. At his elbow sits his co-partner (!) in some of his laurels, and this said partner being never seen apart from his distinguished associate, many have come to the conclusion that the Siamese twins were not the only patentees of the indissoluble tie—although the author and his shadow, in this instance, are only similar in their movements, and not in their ideas. The latter individual has lately achieved an eclipse of one of his visual organs ' in an affray with some children ;' this *ocular demonstration* should remind him that bail is not always so easily procured. May you remember this for the future, say we.

"Taking a further sweep on our dexter hand, we arrive at George H-dd-r, a Parliamentary reporter on the *Morning Herald*. He is a gentlemanly young man enough, and, when not engaged in the 'House,' does the debating here with much vigour.

"That parson-looking personage, with a hat apparently striving to guillotine the wearer by meeting longways under his chin, is R—ds-n, the theatrical critic for the *Times* ; a fellow 'of most infinite humour,' who, albeit being eminently sarcastic, never wounds with his satire in consequence of its keenness.

"A noisy collection of human beings in the next box announce at once our immediate vicinity to Messrs. A—ll—n, A—nd—n, T-mk-ns, and a little elderly gentleman with white hair and spectacles, whose name for particular reasons we decline mentioning. The first is a landscape painter and broad comic-song writer of no inconsiderable merit; the second has elevated his *os frontis* at least three inches since he essayed the character of the *Prince of Denmark* ; and the third is the well-known scene-painter, late of the Adelphi and English Opera House, and now of none—the more's the Pitt-y. The little elderly gent seems to drink more than he eats, eat more than he thinks, and talk more than all put together ; his tongue, in short, is a complete illustration of the perpetual motion.

"That pair of awful-looking whiskers and mustachios, which appear at intervals through the smoke yonder, belong unto one Captain G——, whose visage, to our thinking, would be considerably improved by his undergoing a little experiment from the hands of a skilful tonsorial artist.

"Among others who meet here casually to enjoy a social glass are W—e (of the *Herald*), Egerton Wilks, Walter Lacy, Strickland, Hughes, Franks, O'Meara, the two B—ds (brothers), the latter connected with the Press ; L—s, the 'corpulent youth,' and, in short, all who in any way value the comforts of a well-established tavern and good society,"

From December 7th E. L. B. began to write the
"Theatres" for the *Weekly Times.* It is rather
difficult to arrive at what he really received for
these, but it appears to have been from 10*s.* to £1
per week. This season he supplied the following
pantomimes :—For the Olympic : *William the
Conqueror ; or, Harlequin Harold and the Sack of
the Saxons.* Chapino, harlequin ; Mdlle. Vallee,
columbine ; Herr Cole, pantaloon ; W. A. Barnes,
clown. For the re-opening of the Surrey, under
the management of Mr. Richard Shepherd and
Miss Vincent : *Harlequin Lord Lovel ; or, Lady
Nancy Bell and the Fairies of the Silver
Oak.* Tom Matthews, clown ; Deulin, harlequin ;
Mme. Theodore, columbine ; J. B. Johnstone,
pantaloon. For the Victoria : *The Land of Light ;
or, Harlequin Gas and the Four Elements, Earth,
Air, Fire, and Water.* Harlequin, Lupino ; clown,
Sanderson ; pantaloon, White ; columbine, Mdlle.
Zitella. The re-opening of the theatre, which had
been thoroughly renovated, was attended with
fatal consequences. There was a tremendous
crowd seeking admittance to the gallery. Unfortunately the hand-rail of the stairs could not stand
the pressure, and two boys were killed and several
people injured.

Besides writing the pantomimes, E. L. B. supplied
the comic scenes, wrote the bills, etc. His work
was very successful, and he at the same time
appears to have been liberally (for the times) paid
by Flexmore the clown for comic songs he wrote
for him. An occasional odd pound from Kent

(of knife-cleaning fame), subsidies from Adams for additions to "Watering-places," an odd *5s.* from Marryatt for *Chat*, "a halfpenny weekly"—everybody wrote for it, and few got paid ; Robert Brough and G. A. S. doing the illustrations—brought up his earnings so that they averaged from October to the end of the year £4 10*s.* per week ; but he worked hard for it. He was in a better frame of spirits to face the coming year, for the entry of December 31st is : "Brought the Old Year merrily to a close with Sola, R. G. De la Motte, and Howe."

There is nothing specially worthy of notice in the diaries of 1849 till January 31st, when E. L. B. removed to 21, Brunswick Place, Barnsbury Road, where he had engaged a second floor at a yearly rental of £16. For his "Recollections of White Conduit House," which appeared in *Morning Advertiser*, February 5th, he was paid 13*s.*, one hundred and four lines.

"*Feb.* 20*th.*—*Dies* Pancakia, ergo Pancake Diet. 22*nd.*—Shirley Brooks's farce, *Shave you Directly*, was produced at the Lyceum, and was a success. Miss Kathleen Fitzwilliam, Charles Mathews, and Harley had good parts in it."

"*March* 29*th.*—Olympic Theatre burned; began at 5.30, in ruins at 6."

This was, perhaps, one of the most rapid conflagrations known, and originated in the very old green velvet curtain (which drew aside from the centre), catching fire at the gas jet in the prompter's box. Mr. Davidson and Captain Spicer were the lessees, and were uninsured, and they were the more unfortunate in that the house was just about to be occupied for the summer season by Mrs. Nesbit and Mr. Henry Farren. It was also a great blow to Mr. Charles Bender, a valued actor, who was to have taken his benefit that night, and lost everything but a couple of sovereigns he managed to snatch from his dressing-table, and had even then to crawl on his hands and knees to save his life. The scenes that were to have been represented were from *The Rent Day*, *Faint Heart Never Won Fair Lady*, and *Time Tries All*. It will be remembered that the theatre was first opened for equestrian performance by Astley, to whom Lord Dartmouth granted a licence in 1805, through the interest of Queen Charlotte, as an extra return for a pair of very small and well-trained ponies which Astley had sold Her Majesty, and which afforded great pleasure to the royal children. The roof of the original building was in conical and circular form, and the site belonged to the Earl of Craven.

"*May* 10*th*.—Go to Strand ; see W. Farren in new farce. Miserable change from former excellence."

This was Charles Selby's *Taken In and Done For*, in which (old) W. and H. Farren and Mrs. B. Bartlett appeared. William Farren, Senior, was at this time occasionally very indistinct in his utterance.

"21*st*.—Cobbler's holiday as usual. Ball and myself saunter amid green lanes, and dine at Tottenham. Very showery, drenched dismally, but pleasant day nevertheless. Johnny Gilpin's house, Edmonton, The Angel, was the original Bell."

June 25*th*, E. L. B.'s entry : " Rent commences at my new house, 20, Park Place, Barnsbury Park , ' he moved in on July 10*th*.

" *July* 16*th*.—Sent off packet for ' Man in the (Corner),' *Sunday Times*, which appeared on 21*st*. 23*rd*.—Richardson calls for me in phaeton, and away we rattle to Woodford. Stiff, Ball, and other good fellows, dine at Roebuck. 25*th*. —Bought *Chat*, with Mr. Hodge for partner; arrange for contributions to *Chat* 7*s*. 6*d*. per week to run on for garments. 26*th*.—Receive or *Sunday Times* contributions £2." (This must have been four weeks' pay.)

" *Aug*. 1*st*.—Much pained to see in the obituary of *The Times* to-day the death announced of Elizabeth Ockerby, aged thirty. 3*rd*.—Another death among the circle of my friends—William Bradwell. Pierce Egan, aged seventy-seven, died this day. 13*th*.—At British Museum in morning, and at night to supper at Bonner House, where Stiff received the testimonial. C. Ball in chair, Richardson vice, and Miller, Smith, Simnett, and others present. Very pleasant evening, and home at four on following morning. 22*nd*.—Obtain coat from Hodge for *Chat* 30*s*."

" *Sept*. 5*th*.—Arrange for new serial. Fourth series of the *Mysteries of London*."

" *Oct*. 1*st*.—Send *Robinson Crusoe* to Pritchard."

" *Monday, Dec*. 11*th*.—Birthday, *just twenty-nine*. Mother and Malcolm dine and spend day. 31*st*.— Spend the last day of the Old Year over the fireside at home, but not at all jolly. Write to various parties, and so bring the year straight."

The following anecdote will illustrate the difficulties and vicissitudes of a literary career in the first half of the century :—

" At some time in the late ' forties ' Blanchard and another gentleman, who has since attained a foremost position in the world of letters, and whom, for the exigencies of this narrative, I will call Smith, composed the staff of a small weekly periodical, published in the neighbourhood of the Strand. One very hot Saturday evening, in August, Smith and Blanchard were waiting in the office for the arrival of the proprietor with their weekly stipend; but as this gentleman's financial arrangements were of the most uncertain character, and salaries irregular, usually taking the form of a payment on account to one of them, it was agreed that whichever was fortunate enough to obtain the advance should stand a pot of half-and-half to the other.

"At last the proprietor came bustling in, and said, 'I am very sorry, but money is very tight, and I have only half-a-sovereign. You had better have that, Mr. Smith, and I will pay Mr. Blanchard on Monday.' Smith eagerly grasped at the coin, put it in his pocket, and departed with Blanchard in search of the half-and-half; but after a very short distance he was observed apparently following some object down the leg of his trousers, and then stopping short, said, 'Here's a nice go; I have got a hole in my pocket, and the half-sovereign has gone into my boot.'

"Here was a catastrophe! Blanchard suggested that they should go round to Exeter Street, at the back of the Lyceum Theatre, which was then a quiet but disreputable street, and that Smith should take his boot off.

"This was proceeded with, but just as he had extricated his foot from the Wellington boot, the coin was seen for a moment, no doubt from the heat of the weather, adhering to his stocking, and in an instant dropped off, and rolled down a grating in front of a very shady-looking coffee-house. Smith went into the shop, and explained to a dirty-looking woman what had happened; but this lady, instead of assisting him, called out to her lodgers, 'Here's a lark! a bloke has dropped half-a-quid down the airy!' And instantly, to the disgust of Blanchard and Smith, many dirty hands were seen groping amidst the rubbish beneath the grating. At last one of them fastened on to something, the hands were withdrawn, and presently a woman came rushing out of the house; she was at once collared by Smith, and admitted having the coin, but said she should not 'part' unless he accompanied her to her relatives in Westminster, where she was then going.

"Suffering from the pangs of impecuniosity, he accepted this alternative. And here he must take up the narrative, as Blanchard would not pursue the adventure any farther.

"On arriving at a low house in Westminster, they were admitted into a passage dimly lighted by an oil lamp; the lady produced the fated coin, and gave it a spin in the air 'for luck,' but as she did so it slipped, and disappeared between the interstices of the boards. Here was another dilemma! A man was called, who promptly wrenched up the floor, and the coin was discovered amidst the dust. He was then despatched with it to the nearest 'public' to purchase a gallon of beer.

"In a short time this individual returned full of strange oaths, and with the information that the supposed half-sovereign was a bad sixpence; and such was the indignation aroused that Smith was glad to escape with a whole skin.

"On the following Monday the proprietor of the paper was informed of these circumstances, and he explained that having been given a bad sixpence by the conductor of the Brixton omnibus, he had left home with it carefully placed in one pocket and half-a-sovereign in the other; that on alighting he must have given the half-sovereign, with the remark that the conductor had given it to him the evening before, and was not to do it again, and that the conductor, looking at the coin, fervently replied that he never would. Blanchard used to call this 'The Story of the Phantom Half-sovereign.'"

E. L. B.'s receipts for the year were £152 18*s.*; and hardly-enough earned too, for besides his regular contributions to newspapers, which amounted to many columns, entailing hours' attendance at the theatres, he was revising guide books, for which he had to visit various places, taking him from home for days, and writing songs for Phillips and for Flexmore. With all his work he ever found time to visit his mother, as numerous entries in the diary attest; and on most of these visits he took with him some mark of filial affection in the shape of a present. He was an excellent son. He speaks with quite schoolboy glee of long rambles with friends in the country, when, almost playing truant, he rushed off with them for a day in the environs of London; but for these holidays he paid dearly, for they nearly always meant sitting up and working all night afterwards to make up for lost time.

" The last day of the year not spent very merrily, but to make amends for it begin the New Year with a determination to be jollier."

" *Jan. 7th*, 1850.—In evening to Sadlers Wells. See *Henry IV.* and pantomime.[1] Very badly played, and pantomime far from good. A sprite, Thorn, clever, but out of place.. Went to pit, 3*d.*, and crowded much during the evening. 15*th.*—H. Hall comes and spends evening. We arrange for new entertainment to be called *The Railway of Life.* 31*st.*—In evening to Adelphi; see *Willow Copse* (fair), *Frankenstein* (burlesque: bad), and *Mrs. Bunberry's Spoons* (worse)."

" *Feb. 7th.*—Go to Strand. Stirling Coyne's farce, *Unprotected Female*, very good. *Diogenes* burlesque [2] by Frank Talfourd."

---

[1] This was the First Part of *Henry IV.*—Phelps, Falstaff. The pantomime was *Harlequin and the Dragon of Wantley; or, Moore of Moore Hall and Mother Shipton's Black Dog.* Ridgway, clown; C. Fenton, harlequin; Grammani, pantaloon; Thorn, sprite; Miss Kirby, columbine.

[2] This was *Diogenes and His Lantern; or, The Hue and Cry after Honesty;* full of clever satire and good writing, and with a very strong cast: Jupiter, Leigh Murray; Mercury, H. Farren; Mars, W. Farren,

"18*th*.—Write advertisements of Nelson picture for Barratt, and receive from him for so doing £2. 26*th*.—Burne appears at St. James's; mono-polylogue: moderately successful."[1]

"*March* 7*th*.—Olympic Theatre suddenly closed. Watts said to have lost £400 per week. 16*th*.—Town in evening. Arrange with Adams for 'Guide to London' £2 per sheet (Adams's 'Pocket London Guide Book'). 19*th*.—Begin 'Cry from the Courts' for Henry Russell."[2]

"*April* 15*th*.—Receive from William Robert Copeland of T. R. Liverpool for right of playing till the 25*th* March *all my pieces*, £2. 25*th*.—Received from T. O'Keefe the other half £2 10*s*. and give receipt.[3] *Arrange to receive 'Era' in exchange for paragraphs.* 30*th*.—At Wrekin; meet Palser."[4]

"*May* 14*th*.—At home all day. Receive a stray canary that finds its way on to the balcony, and cherish it accordingly. 19*th*.—Start with Sola (the friend so often mentioned) to Gravesend. Lovely day. *Parland* in the offing; visit her. Back over the town; sleep there. 19*th*.—At 7 a.m. visit ship, and then stroll with Sola about Gravesend. Go to Baines's lounge, Terrace Gardens. Tom Matthews, Fox Cooper, Rafter, Laurence, Levy, and fireworks. At night all the voyagers meet at the Falcon; the parting glass taken. 21*st*.—At

Junior; Diogenes, P. Emery; Minerva, Mrs. Stirling; Apollo, Mrs. Leigh Murray; Venus, Miss Rebecca Isaacs; Juno, Mrs. Bartlett; Ceres, Miss Adams.

[1] The entertainment given by Mr. Burne (the manager) was called *A Literary and Dramatic Monologue.* It was descriptive of the progress of the British stage, tracing it from the time of Shakespeare, of whom he had much to say, and was illustrated by various views. It was also anecdotical; something after the manner of the older Mathews.

[2] E. L. B. wrote many of Russell's songs.

[3] This made up £5 for an entertainment E. L. B. wrote for him.

[4] This was a quaint and genial picture-dealer in the Strand. W. H. Smith's premises are on the site of his old shop. It was a gathering-place on Show days, November 9th, or such an occasion as Wellington's funeral, for Palser's Bohemian friends, who found a seat and plenty to eat and drink.

three this morning from my bedroom at the Falcon I see the *Parland* drop down the dark river for the Cape. 30*th.* —Walk at night to Archway Tavern. "

"*June* 11*th.*—All day in. At night to Belvidere. Read in *Sun* notice of an exquisite poem by C. W. Kent, ' Aletheia ; or, The Downfall of Mythology ; ' one of the finest that has appeared since Keats first woke the world to worship his genius. May he produce another soon. 27*th.*—Attack on the Queen.[1] Learned two facts : one that son of Quick the comedian was in Islington Workhouse ; the other that son of Marsden, living in Park Street, has drunk himself insane, and ruined."

"*July* 2*nd.*—Sir Robert Peel, having met with a lamentable accident on Saturday last, dies at eleven this night.[2] 11*th.*—For the evening to Highbury Barn.[3] Heard Albert Smith (passed by his brother Arthur) give his entertainment. Delighted ; the cleverest I have yet seen. 12*th.*— Return books to W. E. Hall, 53½, Westbourne Street, Pimlico, and proceed to friend Kent's at Chelsea. Delightful evening ; Miss Ellen Kent, her lover Mr. Buller, and Mr. Morris, form the party. Chat of old times, literature, and home late ; most agreeable meeting. 17*th.*—David Prince Miller calls, and chat. In evening meet Mr. Bradshaw by appointment. Arrange for Guide to the Manufacturing Districts for £30. To start directly. 18*th.*—At home all day, and write paragraphs about young Hengler, the wonderful rope dancer. 19*th.*—Receive from M. H. Simpson, of Birmingham, for right of playing all my pieces till July 1852, £2 2*s.*" [A like entry appears on 23*rd*, relating to Joseph Clarance.]

[1] This refers to the blow with a light cane received by Her Majesty on the forehead as she was leaving Cambridge House, Piccadilly, when seated in a carriage with three of the royal children. Her Majesty's assailant was Robert Pate, a retired lieutenant from the 10th Hussars, a very gentlemanly-looking and quietly-dressed man.

[2] Sir Robert Peel's death arose from his being thrown from his horse on Saturday afternoon, as he was returning up Constitution Hill, from calling at Buckingham Palace. He was born February 5th, 1788.

[3] Highbury Barn was originally a cook-house on a very small scale, and took its name from a barn attached to an old farmhouse, originally

" *Monday, Aug. 5th.*—All day at home preparing for departure. Willoughby sends large parcel of *People's Journal* to take with me. Early to bed for early train to-morrow. *6th.*—Leave London by 12.15 train at noon, *viâ* London and Birmingham Railway and Trent Valley. Stopped at Stafford for the night, the Vine Inn; but not at all comfortable—wretched place and stupid people. *7th.*—Walk to Stafford Castle, then by rail to Manchester, and of course found it raining. Met Mr. Bradshaw; home with him to his house. Quiet Quaker-like evening. Introduced to wife and family. *8th.*—About Manchester all day going over factories.[1] Great objections raised by many. Meet Darkin, Junior, from London, at railway station. *9th.* —Still in the 'Cottonopolis;' visit engine-makers, umbrella-makers, etc. Pouring in torrents all day. *10th.*—Start for Liverpool. Meet Watkins; pleasant chat with him, having surprised him by a visit. The round of the Concert Rooms. *12th.*—Yesterday (Sunday) went with Watkins, A. Key, Esq., and Ford to village of Hale, ten miles from Liverpool. Child of Hale (with the golden *air*). Delightful drive. To-day visiting the town. Pleasant evening with Whitty (Editor *Liverpool Journal*), Rickards, and others. Songs and supper. *13th.*—Sit for photographic portrait. Start at noon to Kendal; fine scenery. Sleep at Barrow's Commercial Inn. Beginning to feel very cheerless through want of congenial companions. Wrote letters, and then to

part of the property of the Priors of St. John. About 1801 it was quoted as a marvel that eight hundred people could have hot meals here, and that seventy geese would be seen roasting at the fire at one time. It formerly contained some very fine pictures from Zion House. Mr. Edward Giovanelli opened Highbury Barn in 1861, with the grounds greatly improved, and the house much ornamented, and with a large ball and supper room. The Alexandra Theatre, on a portion of the grounds, was opened May 20th, 1865, with W. Broughton's burlesque *Ernani*, and the farce, *Worrybury's Whims*, by Charles Ross and Dominic Murray. Highbury Tavern was a favourite resort of Oliver Goldsmith's.

[1] This was for Bradshaw's handbook to the manufacturing districts of Great Britain, furnishing a very instructive detail of the various branches of art carried on in the counties of Lancaster, Chester, Stafford, and Warwick, by E. L. B., illustrated with well-executed county maps. and published by W. J. Adams, 59, Fleet Street, London.

bed. 14*th*.—Walk at nine to Windermere Lake (fourteen miles). Beautiful prospects all the way. Leave Bowness; miss road, over Troutbeck Hills, and reach Ambleside, knocked up, in evening. Visit Rydal. 15*th*.—Place full of company; charges exorbitant. Walk to Keswick, sixteen miles. Stop at King's Arms. Visit Flintoff's model. Stroll to Grasmere[1] and Wordsworth's grave on my way to Keswick. Beautiful walk. 16*th*.—After visiting church— Southey's exquisite memorial[2]—Derwentwater, and off by coach round Ulleswater and Saddleback Mount to Penrith, and thence to Carlisle, where I sleep at the Commercial Inn.[3] Wretched town and dirty people. 17*th*.—Visit Dixon's cotton manufactory, and back to Kendal for carpet bag. Meet Distin family. 18*th*.—Wet day. Leave at night for Lancaster, and sleep at the Golden Ball. No

[1] In a suburb called Town End resided for some time De Quincey, the "English Opium-eater," and in the church dedicated to St. Oswald Wordsworth was buried, close to the eastern wall. A small dark stone is placed at the foot of the grave, with a taller one at the head, on which is engraved " William Wordsworth." Grasmere is a corruption of Gris, an old Saxon name for the word " swine," which at one time abounded.

[2] Southey lived and died at Greta Hall, on the Cockermouth Road. He was buried in the parish church of Crosthwaite. Southey's tomb is outside the church, and bears the following inscription :—" Here lies the body of Robert Southey, LL.D., Poet Laureate, born August 12th, 1774, died March 21st, 1843 : for forty years a resident of this parish. Also of Edith, his wife, born May 24th, 1774, died November 16th, 1837. ' I am the Resurrection and the Life, saith the Lord.' " Southey's monument within the church exhibits a life-like recumbent figure of the poet, admirably executed by Lough, and Wordsworth has contributed the following lines inscribed on a tablet close by :—

> " Wide were his aims, yet in no human breast
> Could private feelings meet for holier rest.
> His joys, his griefs, have vanished like a cloud
> From Skiddaw's top ; but he to heaven was vowed
> Through his industrious life, and Christian faith
> Calmed in his soul the fear of change and death."

[3] This tour was undertaken for Adams's " Illustrated Guide to the English Lakes " (by E. L. B.), an unpretentious but very useful little work, giving an itinerary of excursions in the Lake District, with the distance so apportioned as to make the excursions possible by people of any moderate walking capacity.

gas, no companionship, 'no nuffin.' 19*th.*—Off to Preston, stopping at Wigan on road. Sleep at Railway Coffee House. Go to Preston Theatre—last night of season. 20*th.*—Back to Liverpool, and slept there. Meet Watkins, Key, etc. Go over Docks and Roscoe Club. 21*st.*—Still at Liverpool. Go to Amphitheatre, Bazil Baker and daughter. Wretched house—saloon promenade; vice and immorality rampant. 22*nd.*—At night to Zoological Gardens. Black Malibran,[1] Cantelow's Hydro-Incubator, etc. In morning among the merchants. 23*rd.*—Bid farewell to Liverpool, reach Newton, go over printing office, then off to Manchester, and sleep there. 24*th.*—Get pass for Leeds, go to Normanton, and meet brother accidentally. Home, York. 25*th.*—At York; very showery. 26*th.* — To Scarborough. Receive from S. Roxby, Esq., for right of playing pieces in his circuit this year, £1. Back at night, and to theatre. Meet Duncan, editor. 27*th.*—On to Newcastle and Berwick, thence to Edinburgh. Sleep at Mrs. Bain's, in Dundee Street; full at Waverley. Delighted with the city and people altogether. 28*th.*—Ramble over Calton Hill, then start to Glasgow. Whisky inauguration. Sleep there, and try Temperance Lodging House. 29*th.*—Back to Edinburgh, and meet Her Majesty, who has just opened Central Station at Newcastle and Border Bridge at Berwick. Slept at Berwick; difficulty in finding bed. Fireworks and festivities. 30*th.*—To Norham Castle, and then back to Berwick and off to Newcastle. Meet brother, and back by mail train to York. Arrive at 3 a.m. 31*st.*—From York to Leeds, and back to York. Stop at Castleford; back by night."

" *Sept.* 1*st.*—At York. Cathedral, short stroll, and early to bed. 2*nd.*—To Hull, and got from Caple for one year's play £1. Send cash home, and return to York in evening. House closed, and sleep at Sun. 3*rd.*—To Leeds; expecting reply from letter to Manchester, but disappointed. About the town, but see very little to please the eye, and nothing to gratify the taste. Back to York in evening. 4*th.*—Stroll with brother along the banks of the Ouse to

---

[1] She created quite a sensation by her singing and performances, in which she was assisted by two clever guitarists.

a tavern called the Marquis; billiards, pipology, songs at the Crown, and home early. *5th.*—To Leeds again; write off another letter; back to York in evening. *6th.*—Walk to Bishopthorpe, ferry across the Ouse; back in evening to York. Heard on banks military band playing some familiar airs and pleasant reminiscences. *7th.*—To Leeds; get letter from Manchester enclosing £5. Return to York, pack up, start by mail train at 2 a.m., and reach home, *viâ* Derby, on Sunday morning. Meet mother, and dine at 2 p.m. Once more at Barnsbury. *16th.*—At work on, and sent, ' Wanderings and Ponderings' to Willoughby as article for *People's Journal*. *17th.*—Jones (artist) calls. W. T. Wood wants ' Electric Telegraph' song. Write in reply. *18th.*— To town. Execution in for three quarters' rent. Man in possession. Vexations and annoyances complete, but having a fervent reliance on Providence for rescue. £28 10*s.* and expenses to pay. *19th.*—Mr. Davis buys twelve ' Songs of the Seasons' (to be written) for £5. Borrow from W. E. Hall £5. Ditto from Moore (7*s.* before) £3 10*s.* All day in town rushing after the means of satisfying the lawyers. Cold terrific. Adams at Paris. *20th.*—Borrow from Willoughby £2. W. T. Wood acceding to terms for song. Pay Rose in cash £15. By deductions, £19 8*s.* 6*d.* Hear of Great Northern pass being at York. *21st.*—Receive from Mr. Wood for song £2 2*s.* From Charles (at Adams's), on account of Bradshaw, £2. Pay Rose up to Michaelmas, £19 12*s.* (with allowance of £7 10*s.*), £28 10*s.*, making with £2 2*s.* 6*d.* expenses the total of £30 12*s.* 6*d.* *23rd.*— Hear from Manchester. By borrowing £2 from Wiseman manage to pay poor's rate, £1 8*s.* *24th.*—Receive from Manchester £5; make purchases, return loan to Wiseman, square accounts, and so ' on we go again.'" [The above are inserted as showing the straits he was put to through his excessive goodness of heart. His brother William was a most unlucky and, it appears, a weak man; he was always in trouble, and ever looked to E. L. B. to get him out of his difficulties; and the latter would perhaps more wisely not have so constantly assisted him, but he never had the heart to refuse.] " *27th.*—See Willoughby, and arrange with him to edit Shakespeare at £2 per month."

" *Oct.* 2*nd.*—In evening, at Wiseman's, meet eccentric undertaker Morgan.   8*th.*—Go to Olympic; see farce of *The Oldest Inhabitant* and the burlesque of *The Princesses in the Tower*—both excellent." [The theatre was under the management of W. Farren, Senior, and in the company were included W. Farren and his sons W. and H. Farren, G. Cooke, Compton, Mrs. Stirling, Mrs. Leigh Murray, Mrs. Bartlett, Isabel and J. Adams, W. Shalders, Norton, Louisa Howard, Ellen Turner, and Mdlle. Adèle.]   "10*th.*— Offer to Mr. Lofts *Stanfield* for £15. 'Confessions of a Page' for £10.   11*th.*—Sell 'Going off at a Sacrifice' and 'Three Perils of Man' for £6, which Shepherd pays me for. 24*th.*—Answer correspondents for *Era,* and that's all (most trying work, requiring unlimited research sometimes, and but very poorly paid).   29*th.*—Flexmore (clown) calls for annual song, and spends afternoon; arrange to write entertainment, *The Emigrant's Voyage;* or, *Scenes and Stories of American Life.*

" *Nov.* 13*th.*—Finish 'Stranger's Guide.'   23*rd.*—Receive from Willoughby (Shakespeare) for *The Tempest,* £2 2*s.*; for 'Wanderings and Ponderings,' chap. iii., £1 7*s.* 6*d.*"

" *Dec.* 7*th.*—See Greenwood, C. Montgomery, Jonas Levy (*for the first time knowing who he is*).   17*th.*—In evening to Queen's; see Kirkland play Hamlet." [25*th.*—Christmas Day evidently spent alone, for he writes only: "Fine clear day. People going about in all directions to enjoy their Christmas Day."]   "30*th.*—Shocked to hear of the death of Osbaldiston at one o'clock yesterday.[2]   31*st.*—Finish the *Winter's Tale* and the Old Year together." [E. L. B. puts

[1] "The Stranger's and Visitor's Conductor through London, giving a full and faithful description of everything that can be seen and how to see it, within the limits of the Metropolis; corrected to the latest period, and arranged in an entirely novel and interesting manner, by E. L. Blanchard."

[2] D. W. Osbaldiston was born in February 1794, and died December 28th, aged fifty-seven, of black jaundice.   He was the son of a Manchester merchant.   Was intended for the Church, but the cassock was distasteful, and so took to the sock and buskin; and, after appearing as Pierre, and Frederick, in *The Poor Gentleman,* at a private theatre, in the year 1817 joined the Exeter and Plymouth circuit, under

down his revenue for the year as £147 14s. 6d. At times he was much driven for money, but appears always to have kept a bold and hopeful front, and only have been too ready to seize on any work, however poorly paid.]

" *Wednesday, Jan. 1st.*—Another year commenced, the eventful '51. 14*th.*—To-night Kent's Theatricals at Miss Kelly's Theatre, Dean Street ; officiate as steward. Bulwer, Ainsworth, and all the most eminent literati present. *Busybody* and *Too Late for Dinner* the pieces. 24*th.*— Preparing *Carpet Bag* for Willoughby."

He appears to have ushered the year in by giving a juvenile party, for he was always fond of children, and he revels in having provided for their entertainment "turkey, two puddings, and snap-dragon." The payment he received from Willoughby for editing the " Shakespeare " was evidently £2 2s. for each play ; and he wrote a good deal for *The*

Mr. Manuel's management. He married a Miss Dawson in 1818. Was well known at the Manchester, Bath, and Norwich theatres. In 1828 he was a member of the Brunswick Theatre company when it met with its destruction. He then joined Mr. Elliston at the Surrey, and became lessee of it at Christmas, 1831. About the year 1836 he was lessee of Covent Garden, and also, at various times, of Sadlers Wells, City of London, and the Victoria. His elopement with Miss Vincent made a great stir at the time ; he died very wealthy. He was a versatile actor, and was good in such characters as Rolla and William Tell. There is an anecdote connected with the Brunswick Theatre which may be interesting. Old Mr. Saker, the comedian, and father of Mrs. R. H. Wyndham, at the time he was engaged for the opening of the New Brunswick Theatre at Poplar, made a virtuous resolution that he would give up drinking of a morning before going to rehearsal ; however, he thought he would have one final glass of ale at a house opposite the theatre before he went in, and be adamant in his resolve ever afterwards. Whilst this last glass was in course of consumption there was a crash and a cloud of dust ; the roof of the theatre opposite had fallen in, and several persons were killed and many wounded. This occurred on April 29th, 1828. Mr. Saker, ever after this unfortunate accident, used to expatiate on the great advantages of taking a glass of ale before rehearsal.

People's Journal. E. L. B. wrote the address for the opening of the Grecian Saloon, which Conquest had then just taken, and which he opened on March 31st.

" *Feb. 7th.*—Write about the *Arabian Nights* for Willoughby ; see him at night with Harrison, of *The Times*, first time for ten years.   Give ' Crystal Palace ' to Adams, £1 (evidently one of the numerous sort of guide-books he was so constantly engaged on).   10*th.*—Meet John Herbert, the comedian.   13*th.*—Went in evening to Princess's with mother.   Saw *Twelfth Night* and pantomime (*Alonzo the Brave*).   Meadows excellent as Malvolio, Addison ditto Sir Toby, Viola Mrs. Charles Kean ; Kerby Sir Andrew, very bad. 24*th.*—Begin burlesque for Conquest.   26*th.*—Macready takes his farewell at Drury Lane ; house crowded ; the benefit realized £906 ; *Macbeth* was played ; Phelps and Miss Warner appeared in it."

" *March 1st.*—Macready dinner.[1]   11*th.*—Finish *Progress of the People* drama.   14*th.*—Hear from George Barker, 56, Brompton Square, concerning lecture.   28*th.*—Finish burlesque of *Nobody in London ;* or, *The Age of Wonders,* and take it to Conquest at the Grecian.   31*st.*—Conquest opens the Grecian."

The new lessee himself delivered the address, written by E. L. B., which was as follows :—

ADDRESS.

New undertakings, old examples teach,
Should have a prologue in an opening speech ;
A few smart lines in rhyming diction dressed,
Wherein all future projects are expressed.
A less ambitious purpose brings me here,
I come to give a welcome most sincere.

[1] This was the farewell dinner given to Macready at the Hall of Commerce, 700 present ; Sir Bulwer Lytton chairman.   E. L. B. wrote an account of the farewell for Willoughby.

If you expect this brief address explains
Why I again hold managerial reins,
Be this my answer:—that I wished to see
Again the stage that yet had charms for me;
To greet an audience as I welcome you,
And meet with *old* friends whilst encountering *new*.

Within these walls, supporters of a house
Where many a brick has echoed " Bravo Rouse,"
I well might think my present project bold,
To take the place he filled so well of old;
But all he did, and ably did, before,
Shall spur me onward to accomplish more.

Shakespeare has told us of the Drama's feature,
" To hold, as 'twere, the mirror up to Nature; "
Whilst such reflections here before you pass,
You see your drama and you have your glass;
Both which I promise with some conscious pride,
Shall be the best that London can provide.

This year all hope to better their condition,
And this is *my* " Industrial Exhibition; "
Although no glass this lofty roof contains,
Who looks for pleasure will not care for *panes*.

The talent of all nations shall be shown,
Especially the talent of our own;
All that is British you shall here find handy,
Excepting one thing British—that is, brandy.

Let, then, the " Eagle " take a higher flight—
It need not soar, remember, out of sight;
Be yours the breath to keep its wings extended,
And give the aid that oft its course befriended.

May crowds attend each night as we progress,
My pinions being the *'pinions of the press;*
And whilst I trust your pleasures to increase,
Hope after *Conquest* you will like a *piece*.

The programme was made up of *A Midsummer
Night's Dream:* Graham, Theseus; C. Horn,

Demetrius ; Miss Julia Harland, Oberon ; Miss Harriet Gordon, Titania.　In the farce of *The Young Widow*, Conquest acted Splash, and there was a ballet entitled *Flora and Zephyr*, arranged by Mrs. Conquest.　The opening night a great success.

"*April 2nd.*—Go to Eagle ; read burlesque to Conquest, and sell it to him for £5.　*12th.*—Hear from Copeland. Farce for Strand, *Taking the Census*.　*19th.*—In afternoon to town ; arrange with Lofts for new publication, 30*s.* per week, to be called *Nobody in London*.　Wrekin : S. Cowell, S. Jones, etc.　*22nd.*—At Wrekin meet Harlstone the comedian first time.　And thence to Wells ; see *Fortunio*, Planché's admirable burlesque ; delighted with it.　*28th.*— Look in at Myddelton ; meet Guerint the old harlequin, Marston, etc.　*29th.*—Write some copy for new publication of ' Everybody.'　*30th.*—Wrekin ; see Copeland first time, Tomlins, Palser, Barratt, comedian."

"*May 5th.*—*Taking the Census* produced at Strand ; goes capitally ; Rogers as Grigg admirable.　*6th.*—Fred Tallis arrived.　Mr. Stanley calls (young Hengler).　*7th.*—Stilt, clown, and John Gardner, comedian, both included in the theatrical obituary.　*12th.*—Receive from Lofts for No. 1 of ' Everybody ' £1.　*13th.*—Receive from Copeland for the entire rights of *The Census* £5.　*19th.*—Write song of 'Youth's First Lesson.'　*20th.*—Hear from Wild as manager of the Marylebone Theatre.　*22nd.*—Hard at work ' being funny' for ' Everybody.'　*26th.*—Obtain at Sadlers Wells MS. of *Shepherd and Shepherdess* drama, not having seen it for thirteen years.　*27th.*—Write to Beal, *Parley's Library for Old and Young*,[1] two guineas weekly.　*28th.*—Arrange with Adams for Lake book, two guineas per sheet."[2]

[1] This was probably a resuscitation of the *New Parley Library*, which was published March 9th, 1844, and which had a large sale.　In it " Vivian Vernon, a Romance of the Reign of Victoria," was the second novel in its pages.　It lived on till the next year.

[2] This was the " Handbook to the Lakes."

" *June 6th.*—See Willoughby.   Biography of Laurence Sterne to do.   13*th.*—Receive a visit from Mr. W. S. Woodin, of 16, Old Bond Street, who offers £5 for an entertainment to be written for him.   (Eventually Mr. Woodin gave £15 for the *Carpet Bag.*)   19*th.*—Idea for lecture, ' Superstitions of All Nations.'   23*rd.*—Fire blazing over London.[1]   Out to Wiseman's at night to know all about it.   At Humphrey's Wharf.   28*th.*—Up by 2 a.m. waiting for daylight to write. Walk at 6 a.m. round Highbury."

" *July 1st.*—I leave copy of ' Absent Friends ' with *Illustrated News.*   3*rd.*—Howe comes in evening; give him first part of ' Alonzo the Brave.'   6*th.*—Walk with W. Fearman to Buckhurst Hill and back to the Roebuck; total distance thirty miles.   9*th.*—The Queen visits the City at half-past 9 p.m.   Very gay scenes, illuminations, and so forth.[2]   23*rd.*—Finish song of ' Alonzo the Brave.'[3]   Finish song ' Good Deeds Never Die,' and send it to Lovell Phillips."

" *Aug. 4th.*—Evening to Sadlers Wells; *Macbeth* admirably played.   Jonas Levy very affable.   Capel. Wooller; see his new farce *Law of the Lips.*   7*th.*—To Sadlers Wells. *Merchant of Venice.*   To Myddelton crib.[4]   Meet Warner,

---

[1] This very destructive fire consumed three huge blocks of buildings, and threatened the beautiful and ancient Ladye Chapel of St. Saviour's Church and the curious old habitations known as Overman's Almshouses. The origin of the fire was not traced, but was suspected to be owing to an incendiary.

[2] Her Majesty accepted the invitation of the Corporation to be present at a grand ball given at the Guildhall in honour of the Exhibition, to which 3,000 guests were asked.   The Queen went in state, her retinue occupying eight carriages.   Supper was served in the Crypt.   Some curious old Amontillado, Steinberg Cabinet vintage 1822, Sherry 105 years old, some of which cost the Emperor Napoleon £600 per butt, and Muscatel and Paxarete were among the wines served at the Royal table, which was circular in form.   Wine glasses, dinner napkins, the dessert plates (Rose du Barri) were specially manufactured for the occasion.

[3] For this E. L. B. got £1 5s. from Howe.

[4] Of this E. L. B. wrote the following, under the heading, " Licensed Victuallers, their Manners," etc. :—

Barton, Stirling, Coyne.   16*th.*—Go to Strand ; see *Lady Godiva* burlesque ; capital, crammed full of puns.   *Shot*

"The Sir Hugh Middleton's Head.

" The ' Sir Hugh Middleton's Head,' or, as it is more generally called, the ' Hugh Middleton,' is situated near to the New River head, close by Sadlers Wells Theatre.   The house is named after the great Sir Hugh Myddelton, to whom the public are so much indebted for wholesome water ; for it was he who projected the New River supply, and from its source at Ware, in Hertfordshire, he conducted the pure and limpid stream into the Metropolis.   ' Mine host ' of the ' Sir Hugh Middleton's Head '—Edward, *alias* Teddy, Wells—is so far from the general appearance of those ' jolly dogs,' landlords, that, unless well acquainted with his habits, you would not expect that he was the ' head ' of the establishment.   He is, however, as good a fellow as could be desired, and abounds with good humour and odd anecdotes, all ' facts,' of his adventures ; of which the ' rats ' and his ' visit to Mount Vesuvius ' are not the least prominent.

" Entering the door on the left, opposite the bar, is the long room ; and farther on, down a step and then to the left, the door of the *sanctum sanctorum* presents itself—to enter which requires an introduction and a fee, which is appropriated to certain regulations connected with this most august body, who have dignified themselves with the cognomen of Cribites.   Teddy, the before-mentioned head of the ' Head,' regularly takes his seat, after nine, in the crib, and is safe to single out strangers and new members to ' tell the tale o'er again ' concerning the odd adventures he has gone through and his glorious deeds of ' olden time.'

" The most prominent character in the crib, passing Teddy himself, is a gentleman in the straw line—not that we mean to insinuate that he is a man of straw, far from it—we believe quite the contrary, but he manufactures and deals in that article.   He is called by some of the Cribites Nancy Brown, and by others the Squire.   If either of these terms is meant to ridicule him, we of the town, who know him right well, can only say that he don't deserve it.   He is a sporting, gentlemanlike man, fond of the chase and the society of brother sportsmen of every description.   We have often met Mr. Brown with poor Bill Sermon—' peace to his manes '—and Bill never associated with a bad fellow, we know ; nor do we think Ben Robinson would, and we have seen Mr. B. in his company.   So altogether, judging from his associations and what we know of him, we shall pop him down excellent. This Cribite enters into conversation with everybody in the room, and may be said to be as good in reply as attack.

" Under the window, generally every night, is seated a portly, aldermanic-looking personage, decorated with a large heavy gold chain. He is quite piquant and up to the mark ; but he has a strange way of

Tower very good.[1] Tom Spring[2] buried at Norwood Cemetery.
26*th.*—See two acts of *Hamlet* at the Wells. Phelps making

making use of the plural of I on all occasions when speaking upon the
affairs of an establishment not one hundred miles from the Surrey
Theatre. He is quite a figure for the part ; a large cloak, with an
immense fur collar, seems to be as indispensable with him over his
coat as the golden appendage is over his waistcoat.

"We cannot help remarking the partiality evinced by 'Q in the
corner' for brandy and water hot. We really think such strong potations are extremely detrimental to his health ; he should abstain from
giving his friends the trouble of sending him home in a coach. Nick,
beware ! By the side of the last-mentioned youth is generally to be
found a little dapper chap, fond of a pipe as long as himself. He is
said to possess great power in his fingers, but he is not one of those
gents who use their digits at a certain 'light genteel business.' He is
by no means a man of that sort ; quite different, or he would not be
allowed to call himself a pal of his lusty neighbour, 'Q in the corner.'

"We now come to the big-whiskered orator of the room. A freer
man we know not in thought or action. 'Tis he who fought the good
fight on Islington Green for that glorious fellow, our old friend,
Finsbury Tom. He argues and maintains his opinions with great
ability. He is generally pitted in juxtaposition with Mr. Brown.

"Our next friend is a person who constantly displays his erudition
by using the W instead of V, and *wisa werse*. He has lately become a
gentleman coper. He is very clever at popping (not the question) ;
and it is said that he is a bit of a billiard sharp. But we doubt this ;
he may have been lucky, and by that means have excited the suspicion
of the flats.

"There are many more (watchmakers, jewellers, etc.), who frequent
this room, but our space will not admit of our noticing them this week ;
perhaps we may give an early look into another room in this house.

"This tavern, though in such a retired situation, has for many years
maintained great celebrity as a theatrical house, from the circumstance
of its being patronized by the- celebrated Joey Grimaldi and other
performers at the Wells. Here poor Joey, when in his prime, was
wont to enliven the merry circle ; his clever but dissipated son, also,
was a frequenter of the ' Hugh Middleton,' almost up to the hour of
his untimely death."

[1] Dramatic bubble by Angus Reach ; J. Reeve, Rogers, and Miss
Polly Marshall.

[2] Thomas Winter Spring, a renowned boxer, born at Witch-end, near
Fawnhope, in Herefordshire, February 22nd, 1795. He was 6 ft. high,
his fighting weight 13 st. 2 lb. He won his first fight when only nineteen years of age ; his second, against Stringer, September 9th, 1817 ;
and his third, against Painter, April 1st, 1818, but was beaten by him

some good points. 28*th.*—In evening go to Grecian Saloon and see J. T. Wooler's piece of *Jason and Medea;* or, *The Golden Fleece at Colchis:* nicely got up, but very vulgar in dialogue.[1] 29*th.*—At home all day. Begin pantomime for Princess's, but making very slow progress. 30*th.*—Richard Jones, comedian, dies, aged seventy-two."

"*Sept.* 2*nd.*—In *Times* account of discovery of gold in Australia. 4*th.*—Barnet Fair. Flexmore and Rogers come in chaise with Mme. Auriol about pantomime. See *Julius Cæsar* (last two acts) at Wells admirably played. To Myddelton;[2] meet Capel, Barton, Greenwood, Jonas Levy, Stirling Coyne. G. Barker calls by appointment. Syllabus for two guineas : lecture proposed, ' Merrie England in Olden Times.' 8*th.*— Busy with pantomime, *The World of Flowers;* or, *Harlequin Warwick, the King Maker, and the Wars of the White and Red Roses.* 9*th.*—Finish above pantomime, and take it to Princess's. 10*th.*—Museum. On reading *Sun* at tavern close by, annoyed by an eccentric reporter, Downes of Islington. Knows everything and everybody. 15*th.*—Write to Shepherd, Barker, Albert Smith, and Sinnett. Take Mr. Moore to Sadlers Wells : Marston, Hoskins, George Bennett, Mrs. Graham. First night of revival of *Timon of Athens* : admirably played.[3] Afterwards to the ' crib :' Barratt, Barton, Coyne, Hoskins, Marston, Warner, Jonas Levy, etc. Long Shakespearean chat, and home. 18*th.*—Hear from Albert Smith, who engages me to write for the *Month.* 20*th.*—Go

in a second encounter in August. This was his only defeat, though he met most of the celebrated pugs. He was presented in 1823 with the Hereford Cup, in 1824 with the Manchester Cup, and in 1845 with a cup as champion of England, for which £500 was subscribed. He was a generous-hearted man, much respected among his class, and had for some years prior to his decease been landlord of the Castle, Holborn. He died August 19th, 1851, of dropsy and heart-disease.

[1] Misses Julia Harland, H. Gordon, Love, M. A. Atkinson, Johnstone ; Messrs. C. Horn, J. W. Collier, Power, Kerridge, E. O'Donnell, P. Corri, and Sam Cowell. Choregraphic artistes, Miss C. Parkes, the Misses Gunness, Mdlle. Luiza, the Misses Amelia, Laura and Isabella Conquest ; Mons. Richarde.

[2] Original name spelt with "*y.*"

[3] Timon, Phelps ; Lucullus, Hoskins ; Apemantus, George Bennett ; Alcibiades, Henry Marston ; Phrynia, Mrs. Graham.

to town and pass Howe in to Strand; see *Figure of Fun*,[1] Bloomer costume. 22*nd.*—At home all day. Send to Albert Smith, 12, Percy Street, sonnet and three pars. for *Month.* 23*rd.*—At work the best part of the day on Shepherd's pantomime, *The King of the Golden Seas; or, Harlequin Prince Bluecap and the Three Kingdoms, Animal, Vegetable, and Mineral.* First lesson on piano. 24*th.*—At work on and finish pantomime for Surrey. 25*th.*—At home till 7 p.m. reading proofs. To town, meet Howe at the York. Pass him to Surrey: see *Linda di Chamouni,* and *Bottle Imp.* Read pantomime to Calcott, the scene-painter; much liked. 26*th.*—Write Flexmore's annual song for him. George Watkins calls; pass him to Wells: *High Life below Stairs.* Meet George Daniel first time. 27*th.*—Sell pantomime to Shepherd (Surrey) for £10; get half."

" *Oct.* 3*rd.*—At Myddelton. George David four years younger than Harley. Write about 'Taking the Census.' 6*th.*—Hard day's practice. In evening begin Marylebone pantomime. *Harlequin XXX, Sir John Barleycorn; or, The Fairies of the Hop and the Vine.* 9*th.*—Hear of Alexander Lee's death.[2] Letter from Smith of Marylebone Theatre accepting pantomime. Through indisposition almost idle day. 27*th.*—See Sala in morning. Pay him 10*s.* on account of sketches for pantomime. Back by three. Leave pantomime with Smith. Go on with Bloomer lecture, and send first part off. 28*th.*—Send off Part II. 'Bloomer.' 31*st.*—Receive sketches from Sala. Write first scene of Sadlers Wells pantomime. Second batch of contributions in the *Month.*"

---

[1] By Edward Stirling; it was a skit on the Bloomer costume. — Miss Polly Marshall (Martha Baily) is a servant out for a holiday, and is induced by a showman (Hudspeth) to appear as one of his figures. While so engaged, her "young man" appears with a rival on his arm, and a "scene ensues." Miss Polly Marshall good in the character. Rogers also as Nobby Nick.

[2] He was a celebrated composer, and died October 8th. He was the son of a great sporting character, and was well known in Dublin society. When he adopted singing as his profession he became a great favourite in the Irish metropolis, and afterwards was joint manager with Captain Polehill of Drury Lane, the Queen's, Strand, etc., and

"*Nov. 1st.*—John Watkins drops in ; take him afterwards to Olympic. See Laura Keene in *Lady of Lyons;* [1] actress of promise, but very artificial. *Azael,* burlesque, very bad. *4th.*—To Strand. See burlesque of *Thetis and Peleus:* [2] very smart. *19th.*—To town in morning, and visit to Albert Smith, who pays me for *Month's* contribution £3 10s. ; pleasant interview."

"*Dec. 2nd.*—At home till night, and then go to Myddelton to meet Greenwood. Afterwards to Grecian, taking Conquest 'Medley Song,' which I wrote during day. *15th.*—At work on Surrey bill. Malcolm in evening. Chat anent marriage, etc. At night to Wiseman's. *16th.*—Rehearsal at Surrey. Comic scenes till 5. At night to Myddelton. Meet Stirling. Coyne, Jonas Levy, etc. Hear of Alexander's death,[3] and George Maynard,[4] who died a few days since at Newcastle. *17th.*—Hard at work; bills and plots of pantomimes all day. At night to Myddelton. Meet Rayner, on the Fund ; £120 a year, aged sixty-five, and subscribed twenty-two years. Barratt, Willyard, artist, his brother-in-law. *24th.*—Call on Conquest and receive for pantomime £2 2s. Chimney on fire varies the Christmas evening amusements. Go to Surrey rehearsal at night; take T. M. Moore. Not in bed till three. *25th.*—Christmas Day, and a glorious sun-shining one. Mother and W. Fearman dine with me. Beef, fowl, plum pudding and mince pies; all very cosy and comfortable. Whist and music in evening.

was a very able musical conductor. He married Mrs. Waylett, the well known ballad-singer, who pre-deceased him some few years.

[1] Miss Laura Keene was a very good-looking actress, and had made some reputation at Richmond under Mrs. Graham's management. She was supported by Mr. Henry Farren as Claude Melnotte, G. Cook was the General Damas, and Mrs. Griffiths Widow Melnotte.

[2] *Thetis and Peleus;* or, *The Chain of Roses.* Peleus, Miss Polly Marshall ; Thetis, Miss Charlotte Saunders. John Reeve was also in the cast.

[3] Mr. Alexander was well known as the manager of the Theatre Royal, Glasgow, and as an excellent comedian. He was born in Edinburgh, and was for a considerable time lessee of the Adelphi Theatre in that city, and also the Carlisle and Dumfries Theatres.

[4] George Maynard was leading tragedian at the Adelphi and Surrey theatres.

26*th.*—Boxing night; busy as usual. Morning to Marylebone. Evening with Watkins to Surrey—private box. All goes off gloriously.[1] Drop in at Wrekin to supper, and hear of a pretty favourable result everywhere. 27*th.*—At home till 4 p.m. Then to town to see the papers. Back to tea. Find Watkins, and with him to Sadlers Wells—private box, *Harlequin and Yellow Dwarf.*[2] Rochet and dogs clever, ditto Thorne Sprite.[3] *Monday,* 29*th.*—Shepherd calls in morning, wants extra comic scene. Go up at night with the brothers Watkins to Marylebone Theatre—private box—and much pleased with pantomime : Pantaloon, Paul Kellino; very good; Tom Matthews, clown, capital; Veroni, harlequin, good. Home late. 30*th.*—Write extra half flat (china shop) for Shepherd. 31*st.*—At home all day. Howe comes in evening. Hot supper; chess—beat him—and grog. Write notice of Marylebone for *Era. Sic transit gloria* 1851. One sigh for the past and a hope for the future."

Total for the year, £139 14s.

1852.

" *Thursday, Jan.* 1*st.*—Begin the new year by writing hosts of letters—Albert Smith, G. Barker, etc. Pop in to Myddelton ; see Greenwood, Jonas Levy, etc., and afterwards to Wiseman's. Capital article by Albert Smith in *Blackwood,* giving his account of Mont Blanc, thrilling account of perils undergone.[4] 7*th.*—To town, and receive from Albert Smith for last account on 'Month ' £2 2s. 8*th.*—Go to 56, Brompton Square to dine with Barker. Meet Captain Bruce of the

[1] *Queen Mab ; or, Harlequin in the Magic Pippin and the Peri in the Pearly Lake.* T. Ridgway, and J. W. Collier, clowns ; Grammani, pantaloon ; Caroline Parkes, columbine.

[2] Milano, harlequin ; Buck, clown ; Bradbury, pantaloon ; Herr Deani, sprite ; Annie Cushnie, columbine.

[3] Rochet, clown ; Naylor, pantaloon ; C. Fenton, harlequin ; De Vere, columbine.

[4] [Few people know that the cultivated entertainment at the Egyptian Hall, Piccadilly, first saw the light in a magazine article.—C.S.]

Grenadier Guards.[1] *9th.*—At home, quite knocked up with the late hours. In evening to Myddelton to see Greenwood, but miss him. Hear from Hoskins a remarkable case of clairvoyance touching the Derby prophecy of last year. Very boisterous night. *17th.*—At night to Surrey. Meet Widdicombe and Charles Dillon. Hear news from Courtney, Miss Vincent; Higgie married Miss Lazenby. *22nd.*—George Herbert Rodwell died this morning. *23rd.*—To town. Pam's. Pass Malcolm into Strand; there meet Stirling, Walter Lacy, W. Brough, Watkins, Ed. Whitty."

"*Monday, Feb.* 2nd.—Receive from W. S. Woodin second instalment, £5, and give him *Carpet Bag* portion. At night look in at Myddelton. Meet Greenwood, Barrett, Shean. *7th.*—At home all the evening, writing song for Woodin, 'The Visit to the Metropolis.' Work till midnight. *Monday 9th.*—At home all the morning writing for Woodin; afterwards dine with him at Brompton, 6, Park Walk, by Goat in Boots. Mr. S. Woodin, Senior, Mrs. Woodin and family present. Evening passed very pleasantly, treated most hospitably, and home by cab to Haymarket, thence walked, half past one. *10th.*—At home till seven, then to Sadlers Wells, where I passed Woodin in to see Phelps's admirable personation of Sir Pertinax MacSycophant in *Man of the World.* Met George Daniel and very interesting confab. with him anent the old writers and Charles Lamb. G.D. tells me he is now sixty-two. *15th.*—Queen's Head old parlour pulled down, 1829. *Monday, 23rd.*—At home till seven, when I go to Walworth Institution, Carter Street, to hear Mr. Toole, son of the Toast Master, give dramatic representation. His Diggory in *The Spectre Bridegroom* very fair indeed.[2] *24th.*—At home all day ; a visitation of the blues. Hear of Miss Vincent having married Crowther of

[1] General Michael Bruce, of the Grenadier Guards, with which he served in the Crimea, died, aged sixty, in October, 1883. He was an excellent actor, and used to play Desdemona in the burlesque of *Othello.*

[2] [This is no other than the celebrated comedian, J. L. Toole, who graduated at the Walworth Institute, and went on the stage, encouraged to do so by Charles Dickens.—C.S.]

Astley's.[1] *25th.*—Ash Wednesday. Very queer. Leave Shakspere volume with Watkins for review. Look in at Wiseman's; see Harrison. *Times* circulation often 40,000; when double supplement lose about £80 a day; part of paper set up in duplicate. *26th.*—Much indisposed, but go to Camden Town, and take mother to Princess's—Flexmore's benefit. See extraordinary piece called *Corsican Brothers*, with strange apparition effects. (This was produced first time February 22nd, 1852.) *27th.*—Write little notices for *Era*, take them to town; don't meet one person I know. *28th.*— At home all day, pushed hard for cash. At night look in at Myddelton; only meet Barrett and Guerint. Hear the former is engaged at Dublin, Queen's Theatre, and that Miss Harriet Gordon has eloped with Pat Corri. Oxberry dies, poor fellow, of disease of lungs. *29th.*—Mother brings old school-boy letters dated 1826."

"*Monday, March* 3rd.—To Marionettes at Adelaide Gallery.[2] Clever piece, *United Service*, well sustained by the puppet actors. Belvidere with Malcolm, and late home. *4th.*—At home. Mother comes in afternoon, and whole day is devoted to the examination of pocket-books ranging over a period of fifty years.[3] *5th.*—Woodin comes in afternoon, and advances third payment of £5. In evening to a Mr. Raven, solicitor, and attest Mr. Maitland's will as witness. *6th.*— To town, and receive from Willoughby for *Henry V.* usual amount, £2 2s. Go to Wells; first night of *James VI.* by Rev. J. White; a failure.[4] *12th.*—Off to Brompton to dine

---

[1] This was an unhappy affair. The marriage took place on Saturday, February 21st, and the bride and bridegroom left for Brighton. On the following Thursday Mr. Crowther, who is represented to have been a handsome man in the prime of life, wa s seized with brain fever. This resulted in melancholy madness, and he had to be confined in a private lunatic asylum. He for some years had played leading business at Astley's.

[2] [The Adelaide Gallery was a part of the site now occupied by Gatti's celebrated restaurant. It was the first home of the Oratorians of the Order of St. Philip Neri, who moved hence to the Oratory at Brompton.—C.S.]

[3] These were his father's (W. Blanchard) pocket-books.

[4] *James VI.;* or, *The Gowrie Plot*, was a five-act tragedy by the Rev. James White, author of several dramas, and turned on the

with the Woodins. Meet on my way Mrs. Hubbard; first time for three years; mutual news. Hear that Carrie B.[1] is in Ireland, flax-farming. On at six to dinner; meet Mr. George Cape; recollections of Ealing, Birkett, etc. Read entertainment, all much pleased; most handsomely treated, and home late. Last paid £5. Meet Malcolm; pass him into Sadlers Wells, *Henry IV.* Barrett's Falstaff admirable. *15th.*—Albert Smith appears for first time at Egyptian Hall with his Ascent of Mont Blanc.[2] *19th.*— Regret deeply to hear this day my friend Cathie died. A worthy man and much missed; my spirits much depressed. *20th.*—Meet Willoughby, and talk of new publication, *The Library of the Seasons. Monday, 22nd.*—To town by eleven to read Surrey Easter piece, burlesque of *King Arthur.* Everybody delighted with it. Afterwards walk to Clapham with Brandon, then back to meet Woodin; go with him to Haymarket, passed in by Buckstone; see Barry Sullivan play Evelyn in *Money;* admirably cast."

"*April 1st.*—Meet Woodin, and take him at night to Strand Theatre. Farce of *Matrimonial Prospectuses;* good. *7th.*— Write Arctic Regions description for Phillips, and send it. Go to town at night; meet at Ashley's Barratt, Pearson, the

endeavour of the king to entrap the Earl of Gowrie and murder him " from motives of jealousy and suspicion." The principals in the cast were as follows :—James VI., Phelps; Earl of Gowrie, H. Marston ; Restlereig, G. Bennett; Alexander Ruthven, Robinson ; Queen, Miss Travers ; Beatrix, Miss Fleet ; Countess Gowrie, Miss Goddard ; Catherine Logan, Miss Cooper. Mr. Phelps and Miss Cooper were excellent. The piece was played for Mr. Phelps' benefit, he also appearing in a farce ; and though only now produced, was written many years before by the author. It lacked dramatic grip.

[1] The future Mrs. Blanchard.

[2] This was the most successful entertainment that Albert Smith produced. His description of the actual ascent (strengthened by the beautiful scenery painted by W. Beverley) actually thrilled his audience. Numerous songs, of which one, "Galignani's Messenger," was a running comment on the events of the day. Countless jokes, and clever imaginary conversations. Original and droll characters— the engineer on the Lake steamer, and Mrs. Seymour, who was ever in search of her black box, particularly—made a novel evening's amusement that filled the Hall for many a long day.

old editor of the *Satirist* (first time); chat, and home very late. *8th.*—Write account for *Era* of Easter novelties. See the Brothers Sala, Wm. Beverley, Fox Cooper (!), at Bushell's. *Monday,* 12*th.*—In evening to town. Go to Surrey, *The Corsicans;* Creswick as the two Dei Franchis; Bateman children (Ellen as Charles de Bionville and Kate as Henrietta de Vigny, in *The Young Couple*), and a new burlesque of mine, *The Three Perils of Man; or, The Three Knights of the Round Table.*[1] All goes off well but the scenery. Receive from *Era* £1. 13*th.*—Capital accounts in all the papers. To town in afternoon; meet T. Alpass at Pam's (Pamphilon's). Hear he is manager of the *Chronicle,* and receive promise of assistance to get thereon. Look in at Strand; see burlesque extravaganza, *Antony and Cleopatra,* Miss Louisa Howard and Walter Lacy. Very thin house. (Also *A Village Tale,* sketched by C. Reade, Esq.: Edward Stirling, Rogers, Attwood, Moore, Moreland, Misses W. R. Copeland, Selby, and Maskell, were in the cast.) 14*th.*— Ascertain that a Mr. Russell wrote the clever Greenwich Fair notice in *Times,* and hear all pay to theatre for admission.[2] 15*th.*—At home till evening; pass Moore into Sadlers Wells. John Saville of Haysted writes theatricals for *Era.* Drury Lane closes till Monday; row with Sims Reeves. 20*th.*—At home till 6 p.m., then to town. Call on Watkins; go to Olympic, see burlesque of the *Camberwell Brothers* (extravaganza by Charles Selby on *Corsican Brothers*). Nicely got up, and admirably played, but bad subject for travestie. Finish at Astley's. Barrett, Pyne, Jolly Gent, and Tancred. Rich man, quaint and curious. 24*th.*—To town at eleven; arrange with F. Tallis to write theatricals for two weekly newspapers. *Monday,* 26*th.*—

---

[1] Magnificent magical extravaganza. King Arthur, Brandon; Sir Lionel of the Silver Shield, Julia Harland; Sir Tristram of the Brazen Mug, H. Widdicomb; Sir Agrovaine of the Rueful Phiz, J. Courtney; Merlyn, Wynn; Penaninkanpapa, Herr Zamiel; Morgana la Faye, Clarissa Doria; La Belle Isonde, Miss Seagrave. The piece was beautifully mounted, and was a great success.

[2] [This must be the celebrated W. H. Russell, otherwise Billy Russell, the *doyen* of special correspondents, whose letters from the Crimea were unexampled at the time, and a distinctly new feature in journalism.—C.S.]

Hear from and write to Barrett offering all pieces for a twelvemonth to J. C. Josephs for two guineas. *27th.*—Go to Surrey; see Bateman children in *The Old Style and the New;* admirably acted, and piece well written by Bayle Bernard.[1] Jonas Levy and Coyne there. Home early."

"*May 2nd.*—Mother comes and brings lamp; a handsome present. *4th.*—To New Road in morning. Meet Thompson Townsend, wondering who he is. Write and send off article to *Leisure Hour* entitled, 'The Cradle, the King, and the Bier.' *5th.*—At home again. Not a penny in the house, and little prospect of immediate supply. Town in evening; see Willoughby. Call on Adams. Walk to Surrey, and walk back again. Tired, and troubled in mind and body. *6th.*— At home brooding all day. Receive from Mrs. Elderton £5 on account of June quarter. Go with Willoughby to Colosseum. See Crystal Palace views, but have all of them. I miss poor Bradwell as the designing hand. *15th.*—First number of Tallis's new paper established and published. Walk home with Marston at midnight. *17th.*—No letters, no nothing. Write song about 'Militia Bill' for Bath. Write to Nelson Lee touching burlesque. *20th.*—Write theatricals for paper. Go to Drury Lane, passed by Lovell Phillips into orchestra; last night of the season. See Bunn first time; a pleasant-looking, portly gentleman. Farewell address, and write an account at Edinburgh Castle, and home. *22nd.*—To town; receive from Tallis £2, for two weeks of theatricals. Go to Reunion Club first time as a member; pleasant evening. Meet Friswell, author of the *New Rosina* (?), and walk home with him, passing Belvidere, seeing for the first time the Flaming and Shilibeer. *25th.*—To town; see Mr. Hutton, new proprietor of the *Weekly Times*, who wants me back again. In evening to Olympic, and see bad farce of Wooller's called *Language of Flowers*. *27th.*—To town with theatricals for L. W. P. Much indisposed all day; back early. *28th.*—Read through the life of Lockington, one of

---

[1] [The Bateman children, Ellen and Kate, were daughters of the late H. L. Bateman, who managed the Lyceum when Henry Irving first appeared there in *The Bells.* Miss Bateman (Kate) was the famous Leah of the Adelphi Theatre.—C.S.]

the pleasantest of biographists. No letters, no visitors, no comfort. In bed at nine. 29*th*.—No better. Chemicals resorted to, to the destruction of the comicals. Tallis £1."

" The Re-Union Club."

At the Bedford Head in Maiden Lane, Covent Garden, many of the Bohemians of E. L. B.'s day were afterwards to be met with as the status of the " Wrekin " diminished. Here a club was formed, denominated the " Bedford," but it was broken up by the dissensions of certain members, the usual fate of Bohemian literary clubs. The rival parties, however, after a time healed their differences, and started anew under the name of " The Re-Union." It met so far back as 1850, and during its existence had many notable followers—men like Blanchard, Marston, Jonas Levy, Stirling Coyne, Leigh Murray and his brother Edward, Carpenter the song-writer, Lowe of *The Critic*, Horace Mayhew, Julian Portch the artist, Cornelius Pearson the artist, Palser, Chard, Paul Bedford, Sala (then quite a young man), Baylis, Horace Green, Deffett Francis the artist, Lazarus, Fred Kingsbury, Leicester Buckingham, Tom Robertson, Horsley, the solicitor who did the " Seasons " by facial expression, and was the butt of the members ; and a host of kindred workers in art and letters. Mr. Jonas Levy many years was Hon. Sec., and continued in that capacity until the club closed its doors finally. The members were only required to pay a nominal subscription of about five shillings a year; and met three nights a week, Monday, Wednesday, and Saturday, in an upstairs room at the Old Bedford Head, not in the present tavern.

"*June 1st.*—At home till evening, when go to Olympic and see Talfourd's clever burlesque of *Ganem; or, The Slave of Love*;[1] crammed full of puns. *Monday, 7th.*—Go early to meet Lovell Phillips at Academy of Music; see Leoni Lee; songs ordered, 'Pearls of the Ocean.' *8th.*—Mother's birthday. G. H. Davidson, music publisher, calls and buys song of 'Militia Mania List! List.' *Monday, 14th.*—At home all day preparing copy for paper. To Wiseman's at night; see in *Sun* excellent notice of 'Jerrold,' said to have been born in 1805, nearly same time as Bulwer and Disraeli were. Also hear of Louisa Pyne's sudden attack of paralysis. *15th.*—Off to Kennington Gate; dine with Mr. and Mrs. Shepherd; magnificently entertained. *17th.*—Write some advertisements for a Mr. Kay Dimsdale, and leave them at Oxford Street. *18th.*—Lovell Phillips calls, and pays for 'Pearls of the Ocean' £1. *23rd.*—Over to Surrey, having finished pantomime. See horrible effect in a piece of strong interest called *Alice May*, by Fitzball. Afterwards the Club. Go to Evans's. See Hine,[2] Edmunds, and other professionals. *29th.*—To British Museum for notes. Write for the paper, and at night to Conquest, selling him the pieces *Bear and Forbear* and *Robinson Crusoe* for £5."

"*Monday, July 12th.*—Go to Highbury Barn Tea Gardens, for the first time. In evening old John Blewitt, the musical composer, pays me an unexpected visit. He will be seventy-two on the 19th of this month; brings songs, and rattles off 'Barney Bralligan' on piano famously. *16th.*—Receive sad intelligence from York.[3] *28th.*—Write theatricals, and off

[1] Miss Louisa Howard, a most beautiful woman, Ganem; Shalders, Clifton, Sanger, Messrs. Fielding, Maskell, E. and J. Turner, and Bartlett in the cast.

[2] A tenor singer who was noted for his rendering of such songs as "Look always on the Sunny Side."

[3] Which necessitated his journeying down there, and was eventually the cause of much trouble to him, and hampered his finances for years, through his burdening himself with his brother's family.

to town.   At Pam's meet Kent; walk home with him; smoke a pipe at Chelsea with his father.   Hear Alastor is 'John Orton.'   S. Phillips, critic of the *Times*, is author of 'Caleb Stukeley.'"

"*Aug. 3rd.*—At home all day preparing contributions for paper.   Little Fred (*his nephew*) my companion all day; filling the young mind with new images through picture medium.   *4th.*—Scribbling in morning.   Willoughby calls with 'Paula Monti' to alter.   In evening to club; introduce Woodin.   Meet Bridgman, old editor of *Puppet Show*, and accomplished journalist, etc.   Now writing for the *Economist* and *Musical World.*[1]   Dr. Richardson, Austins, and usual party present.   *10th.*—Home, and work away on French hodge-podge of 'Paula Monti.'   *11th.*—Complete my copies for the papers, and go to club.   Woodin proposed by me, and elected.   Healy in chair.   Sterling Coyne, aged about forty-eight; Dalton, thirty-one; Jonas Levy, thirty-six; Lucombe, sixty-six.   *16th.*—Poor Frank Hartland killed by beam in Westminster Road, aged seventy.[2]   *25th.*—Meet Woodin; very pleasant evening.   Hear of Forman's death.[3]   *Monday, 30th.*—In evening go to Russell's entertainment at Lyceum, *Emigrants' Progress.*   *31st.*—'Pearls of the Ocean' and the eternal opera to be retouched."

"*Sept. 1st.*—Go to Sadlers Wells—*All's Well that Ends Well*, revived first time.   Very well played and received.[4] Meet Marston, Coyne, Levy, etc., at Knobb's.   *3rd.*—Finish and sent off notes to *King Lear* and *Comedy of Errors*, with notes and introduction complete.   Strolling through

---

[1] [Jack Bridgman was a scholar, dramatist, and journalist of great talent.   He wrote many of the *libretti* for the Pyne and Harrison operas, and was a very genial companion.   He died very recently, in extreme poverty, supported to the last by a few devoted friends.—C.S.]

[2] He was for many years a favourite pantomimist, and played with Grimaldi.   The beam from some buildings in course of erection fell on him, and crushed his skull.

George Forman, for many years a favourite comedian at the Victoria Theatre—about forty years of age—died of pneumonia.

[4] Parolles, Phelps; King, G. Bennett; Bertram, F. Robinson; Lafeu, Barrett; Dumain, Harris; Countess, Mrs. Ternan; Helena, Miss Cooper; Diana, Miss Bassano.

Smithfield see the ghost of Bartholomew Fair. Read ' Bleak House.' Capital ! *5th.*—Walk over to Camden Town to Lovell Phillips, and receive from him £1 for song of ' Youth's First Lesson.' *Monday, 6th.*—Wilson the pianist calls ; have some long gossip. Pressure, long copy for paper. Hear from Leslie, Edinburgh Theatre, wanting a pantomime. Madame Poitevin ascends from Cremorne with parachute, and descends safely on Clapham Common.[1] *7th.*—On ' Paula Monti ;' very tedious work. Stick at it all day till head and heart ache. Look in at Wiseman's, then at Regent, but no company at either place. *8th.*—At home again on French novel ; by ten nearly finish it. To Sadlers Wells at eleven, and see *Young Husbands,* a very clever piece, written, I believe, by Mr. Bingham, who has got the pseudonym of John Daly. *10th.*—To town in afternoon ; see Tallis, and receive from him in advance for paper £1. Chat about novel, to fill one page for £3. *11th.*—To club ; very lively evening ; Woodin in chair. *Age* newspaper gives medals to subscribers. *12th.*—Write song of the ' Gold Fiend ' for Wilson in an evening. *14th.*—Write paper articles. Walk down to Belvidere. Hear death of the Duke of Wellington at 3 p.m. this afternoon. *15th.*—At home till 5 p.m. fixing on titles for pantos. Go to Marylebone ; see Buchanan as Macbeth. Arrange for panto. with Smith for Drury. To club. Woodin gives entertainment extracts. Home with Marston. Hear from Miss Vincent. Wants panto. ; write and decline. *16th.*—Write theatricals. Go to town. See Tallis, and arrange for novel called ' Temple Bar ; or, The Romance of Reality.' *25th.*—Go to Strand Theatre ; meet Woodin. ' Ethiopians ;' Pell and Tamborini good. *Monday, 27th.*—Stroll in morning round by Muswell Hill. Back, and begin panto. of *Harlequin Hudibras ; or, Cavaliers and Roundheads in the Droll Days of the Merry Monarch.* See Greenwood at night, and suggest to him ' Cherry and Fair Star.' Finish at Belvidere. Spencer, an antiquary, present. *28th.*—Proceed with panto., and Wilson leaves songs. *29th.*—Davidson in morning with slave songs. British Museum, and then to Sadlers Wells in the evening. See

The balloon was the " Zodiac," the parachute the " Meteor." The descent was from between three and four thousand feet altitude.

the *City Madam*—first revival.[1] House full of *literati*. Back and write notice. Tallis writes letter of agreement for tale."

" *Oct.* 2.—Tallis's usual £1. See Sterling Coyne's farce of *Wanted, a Thousand Spirited Young Milliners for the Gold Diggings*, produced at Olympic. Moderate success (though a very good cast, including Bender, Hoskins, Compton, etc.) Drury Lane opens for short season with Bolton;[2] bad company and bad arrangements. *5th.*—Wilson calls and pays for 'Gold Fiend' £1. Begin 'Uncle Tom's Cabin,' and delighted with it. Write song of the 'Slave Auction' and divers small matters. Horrible affair at Paris—Bower, correspondent of the *Morning Advertiser*, and Saville Morton, correspondent of the *Daily News*.[3] 8th.—Wilson in morning, W. L. Phillips and Son. Then proofs from Willoughby. See curious Jansen portrait of Shakespeare at Mrs. Jobson's, 11, Wells Row. *9th.*—Receive from Tallis usual £1. Go to Organophonics, St. James's. Much pleased. Afterwards to Haymarket. New farce by J. M. Morton, *The Woman I Adore.* The club, and home. *13th.*—Drury Lane. Read pantomime to Smith and party. All much pleased with it. Afterwards to Davison, and receive £3 for the three songs.[4] Sign assignment. *14th.*—Woodin calls, and tells me he has

[1] Luke, Phelps ; Sir John Frugal, G. Bennett ; Plenty, H. Marston ; Sir M. Lacey, Barrett ; Edmund, F. Robinson ; Lady Frugal, Mrs. Ternan.

[2] G. Bolton opened with *Richelieu.* Cardinal, Robins, from Plymouth Theatre ; De Mauprat, C. Moorhouse, from Broadway Theatre, New York ; Baradas, J. Johnstone ; Joseph, John Dale. Also the Brothers Binslay in a ballet.

[3] Bower appears to have been jealous of Morton, between whom and Mrs. Bower he thought there was undue familiarity. Unfortunately Morton entered the room in No. 22, Rue des Capucins, where Bower was at dinner. The latter seized a knife, and after some altercation on the stairs struck Morton on the neck, severing the carotid artery, and causing his immediate death. It should be added that Mrs. Bower was delirious after the birth of her last child, and in her paroxysms threw doubt on its paternity. Mr. Morton was much respected by the *Daily News*, and had been its correspondent in Constantinople, Athens, Madrid, Vienna, Berlin, and Paris. He was of good family, and a graduate of Cambridge. He was a warm-hearted, talented man.

[4] " Slave Auction," " Uncle Tom's Lament," and " Slave Mother."

engaged the Marionette Theatre, £100 till Christmas. Stops
seven hours with me making out programme. 15*th.*—Moore
and Wilson in morning. Give Wilson 'Woman's Bright
Eye.' Receive dressing-case from Dalton. 20*th.*—Write for
paper all morning. Receive from Willoughby, for *Comedy of
Errors*, £2 2*s*."

" *Monday, Nov.* 1*st.*—Copeland of Liverpool calls for pantomimic contributions. Work hard till ten, then go to Regent.
Read the melancholy suicide of George Anderson, the clown.
Poor fellow ![1] 8*th.*—To town ; leave copy. Dine with Smith
and George Wild at Stadium House, Chelsea. Champagne
again ! Go to Marylebone, Jullien's first night. 9*th.*—See
Woodin, who most generously presents me with a handsome
douceur of £5. 11*th.*—Very busy day. At work on, and
finish by 7 p.m., Sadlers Wells pantomime of *Dick Whittington.*
Then to Greenwood, and leave it for him. 18*th.*—The Duke
of Wellington this day buried with great ceremony, the
streets very full and every shop closed. 25*th.*—See stupid
farce at the Olympic, first night, *Go to Bed, Tom.* Return
to office ; read proofs."

" *Dec.* 3*rd.*—Write and deliver comic scene to Sadlers
Wells — the 'Glenfield Starch' scene. 11*th.*—Attain my
thirty-second year. My conscience ! Trust I may give for
every day some good account at the last. 14*th.*—Lovell
Phillips calls, and grieves me much by telling me of Perry-
man's death — a worthy and kind-hearted man ! 16*th.*—
Go to Drury, meet Smith ; then to Pam's ; off to Olympic,
see fourth act of the *Hunchback.* Edith Heraud's first
appearance as Julia.[2] Look in at Knobb's. 23*rd.*—Write
theatricals, dinner at Drury, rehearsal in the evening. Take
Tallis ; my health proposed, and return speech. 25*th.*—

---

[1] He was only thirty-four years of age, and killed himself by throwing
himself out of window.

[2] [Edith Heraud is the daughter of John A. Heraud, dramatist, and
critic for many years of the *Athenæum* and the *Illustrated London News.*
In his younger days he was a member of the Syncretic Society, and
one of the prime movers in the freedom of the theatres from the old
patent laws. He died in the Charter House, one of the brothers of
that foundation.—C.S.]

Christmas Day. Go to Woodin's to dinner; spend day delightfully, and very hospitably entertained. Stop there all night. *27th.*—Up all night; balcony blown slick away by terrific hurricane. Kept in all morning repairing damage. *28th.*—To Sadlers Wells; see Greenwood, Nicolo Deulin (Daly); very good. Sprites capital; the best pantomime (thought to be) of the season. *30th.*—Greenwood, £10. Go to town with copy; look in at Woodin's; write long account of theatres for papers, and find this week I have only written three columns of the novel."

As he was editing the Shakespeare spoken of he had to spend much time at the Museum; he had his theatricals to write, and, besides, this year E. L. B. wrote the following pantomimes :—

Drury Lane: *Harlequin Hudibras; or, Dame Durden and the Droll Days of the Merry Monarch.* Tom Matthews, clown; Herr Deulin, London Gent; Veroni, harlequin; Louise Blanche, columbine; Halford, pantaloon; Devain, contortionist sprite.

Surrey: *Harlequin and the World of Flowers; or, The Fairy of the Rose and the Sprite of the Silver Star.* Buck, clown; Bradbury, pantaloon; Milano, harlequin; Annie Cheshire, columbine; Molino, sprite.

Marylebone: *Undine, the Spirit of Water; or, Harlequin Teetotum and the Chinese Cup-and-Sorcerer.* Rochez, clown; Harvey, harlequin; Mrs. Harvey, columbine. He also suggested the title and assisted in the Princess's pantomime, wrote the usual song for Flexmore, who this year was at the Adelphi, and wrote the comic business for Copeland of Liverpool pantomime.

Sadlers Wells pantomime : *Whittington and His Cat ;* or, *Dame Fortune and Harlequin Lord Mayor of London*—was to all intents and purposes written by him. Clown, Nicolo Deulin ; Fenton, harlequin ; Caroline Parkes, columbine ; Deani, sprite.

" *31st.*—British Museum for *Coriolanus*. Go to Bertollini's and have macaroni. Look in at Adams's, and come home at six. So ends an eventful year, bringing sad changes upon one branch, and mingling bitters with prosperity. God be thanked for the past, however, and hopeful for the future. Total receipts for this year, £132 10*s*."

His domestic troubles were indeed great—a source of such constant and terrible anxiety as to those whom he felt bound to assist, that it is wonderful he could concentrate his ideas to work at all, much more to write with so much humour. He was most kind and assiduous, as ever, in his attentions to his mother.

1853.

" *Jan. 1st.*—Go to Surrey in evening ; see R. Foreman, and hear of R. Honner's death.[1] Davidson calls. Sell him,

---

[1] Mr. Robert William Honner was born about 1809, and died December 31st, 1852, much respected. He was the son of a solicitor, and a schoolfellow of Joe Grimaldi. Through reverses when his father died, young Honner, having acquired a taste for the stage, was apprenticed to Leclercq, made his *début* at the " Sans Pareil," and travelled the provinces. In 1824 he was at the Surrey ; from thence to the Coburg ; joined Ducrow, and with him got his initiation into stage display and management ; travelled again ; rejoined Ducrow ; thence to Sadlers Wells under Grimaldi. He was under Elliston at the Surrey till Osbaldiston's time, and with Coleman at Sadlers Wells, 1832, and then met and married Miss Macarthy, a talented actress. In 1835 he stage managed for Davidge at the Surrey ; in 1838 became lessee of

and receive payment of £1 for, song of ' Old King Coke.'
Monday, 10th.—At home writing hosts of letters. Review
music for papers. *11th.*—Go to Drury Lane ; see Charles
Reade's piece of *Gold.*[1] *14th.*—To town ; dine at Bertollini's
in hopes of meeting Woodin ; see him afterwards. Receive
from him another £5,[2] and the balance of £10 from E. T.
Smith. Have champagne with him at the Lane; all promising
well. *15th.*—Receive from Copeland £3 by post-office order.
27th.—Drop in at Dormer's. Long chat with Sala ; leave
copy at office, and walk home with Tallis. Hear of Morley's
death. *29th.*—Hear of Hamblin's death, January 8th. *31st.*
—Write prospectus of *Young Englishman's Magazine.*"

" *Feb. 4th.*—Watkins's birthday ; evening with him. Meet
Willis, Barry Sullivan, Paris, and others. Very jolly and
very comfortable. Break up at 2 a.m., and walk home with
the tragedian. *5th.*—Go to Woodin's. Meet Toole's brother
for the first time, and take him to club. *Monday, 7th.*—
Meet Woodin, and receive from him another *douceur* of £5.

Sadlers Wells, part of the time with Greenwood ; from 1841 to 1846
was manager of the Surrey for Mr. Davidge, and after his decease for
his widow. At the close of 1846 Honner became lessee of City of
London Theatre, remaining so until he joined Mr. John Douglass as
stage-manager of the Standard Theatre, which post he retained till his
death.

[1] This was a story of the Australian gold diggings ; its main incidents were interwoven in *Never Too Late to Mend,* produced later.
Mr. Davenport was the hero, George Sandford, and Miss Fanny Vining
the heroine, Susan Merton. Mr. Edward Stirling was excellent as the
kind-hearted, benevolent Hebrew Levi, the good angel of the piece—
a new departure in dramatic writing. *Gold* attracted large audiences.

[2] Woodin's entertainment, *Carpet Bag and Sketch Book,* at the
Polygraphic Hall, now Toole's Theatre, was a great success, but he
worked hard for what he earned. At the end of 72 nights it was
calculated that during that time " he had changed his dress 3,600
times, sung 720 songs, perpetrated 8,062 puns, and entertained
28,000 persons by his own unassisted exertions." Unlike some, he
remembered E. L. B., and that it was to him he owed so much of
his success. [Woodin was a very amiable fellow, but was inclined to
bore some of his companions with accounts of himself and his entertainment. One day, at the Arundel Club, H. J. Byron interrupted
Woodin, who was, as usual, talking about himself and his prospects :—
" I say, Woodin, old fellow, I wish you would go down under the
table, come up somebody else, *and remain so !* "—C.S.]

8*th.*—J. Williams calls first time. Pancakes and fireworks ; all the children come; high jinks. Write in evening song, 'The Whistling of the Wind,' and send it to Lovell Phillips. 12*th.*—Write letter to Empress Eugénie for Mr. Barratt. Shower of proofs in evening. Working hard all day, but very unprofitably, and very unthankfully disturbed by home matters. 13*th.*—Miserable day at home ; prepare copy for *Y. E. Magazine*. *Monday,* 14*th.*—To British Museum preparing *Troilus and Cressida*. See Barratt and give him letter to Empress. 19*th.*—Take little Walter to the Grecian. See pantomime opening ; very good,— *Fairy and the Fawn;* child delighted. *Monday,* 21*st.* —Town with remainder of copy for magazine. Home to dress, and go to Toole's to supper. Perseverance Society at Walworth. Meet the Tooles and Bruton. Home at 6 a.m. after going thence to Somerset House. C. Nicholls's party ; sing 'Guy Fawkes.' *Monday,* 28*th.*—Haymarket in evening, and Bulwer's comedy, *Not so Bad as We Seem.* Delighted with it. Woodin's first night at the Salle Robin. Meet Albert Smith ; pleasant gossip."

"*March* 1*st.*—Begin odd matters for Toole's night at Walworth. Write song for him, 'The Age of Condensation,' and introduction. 8*th.*—To town in evening. From Lee, for March number of *English Magazine*, £4. Go to Drury Lane ; see extraordinary performance of walking head downwards across a flat ceiling by Sands.[1] 11*th.*—Again busy for Toole ; go at night to see him rehearse. Make out programme, and not home till three the following morning. Have remarkable respect paid to me at Walworth Institute.[2] *Monday,* 14*th.*—At night go to see Toole at Walworth, and receive from him, for entertainment, £5. 24*th.*—Write theatres for paper. Toole, who leaves to-night for Dublin at 9 p.m., calls at 8.30 to bid me farewell, and presents me

---

[1] He was an American, and accomplished the feat by having some sort of apparatus attached to his shoes or pattens, which exercised suction on a highly-polished surface. [The feat was done in a different way at the Alhambra by an athlete called Olmar.—C.S.]

[2] E. L. B. was so thoroughly modest and unassuming that any little extra attention impressed him.

with a very handsome ring as a testimonial. Write some things for *Era* at Edinburgh Castle. *25th.*—The three children dine and spend the day. They revel in games of all kinds. Howe and I at chess and cribbage. Received from him 10*s.* on account of song. *28th.*—Go to Drury Lane at night. Brough's burlesque of the *Talisman;* moderately successful. Buckstone's first night of management at the Haymarket.[1] *31st.*—Go to town; dine with Albert Smith and his brother at the Garrick Club. Magnificently entertained. Introduced to Mr. Archdekne and others.[2] Evening with Tallis and party at the Dog. Letter from Buckstone."

"*April 1st.*—To Adelphi; see Webster's *At Home.*[3] To Haymarket, and see Peake's comedy, *Sheriff of the County* (Tilbury in his original character of Mr. Hollylodge, Buckstone his original character, Pansy; poor Bucky but very indifferent), and Planché's admirable burlesque of *Ascent of Mount Parnassus.* Hear of Woodin's being crammed every night. To Wrekin, and hear of poor Boyce's death at Charing Cross Hospital.[4] *2nd.*—Club meeting; agreeable as usual. Afterwards accept Albert Smith's friendly offer and go to the Fielding Club. Met G. H. Lewes, J. W. Davieson of the *Times,* W. Hale, Lee, Murray, Wilkie Collins, etc. First night of the Italian Opera

---

[1] Mr. Buckstone opened with *The Rivals.* Chippendale, Sir Anthony Absolute; Mrs. Poynter, Mrs. Malaprop; Compton, Acres; W. Farren, Junior, Captain Absolute; Miss Ellen Chaplin, Lucy; Messrs. Howe, H. Corri, Rogers, and Clark, and Mmes. Reynolds, L. S. Buckingham, were also in the cast. Mr. Buckstone's *Ascent of Mount Parnassus,* by Planché, in which Buckstone, W. Farren (Fashion), H. Corri and Braid, Mrs. FitzWilliam (Fortune), Miss R. Kewer, Miss E. Chaplin, and Miss Louisa Howard (Castalia), appeared. Mr. Charles Marshall's Panorama was introduced.

[2] [Mr. Archdekne married Miss Elsworthy, a handsome actress, the *grande-dame* at the Lyceum in the Fechter days.—C.S.]

[3] *Mr. Webster At Home in Adelphi Fare of Three Rémoves and a Dessert,* by Mark Lemon. Madame Céleste (the manageress at the time) and Webster, Leigh Murray, Keeley, Parselle, H. Bedford, Mrs. Leigh Murray, Mrs. Keeley, Miss Woolgar, Mr. A. Wigan, Mr. O. Smith, and Paul Bedford took part in it.

[4] Charles Boyce, late of the Adelphi Theatre, only thirty-three years of age, had been ill some time.

opening. Flashing literary gossip. *Monday, 4th.*—Receive from Addison and Hollyer £1. Give receipt for 'Bright Summer Morn.' *6th.*—Write notes to Cervantes, and muddle away an hour at the Belvidere. Spencer, Hodge, an American, and others present. The Rappings[1] talked about. *7th.*—At night go to Haymarket; see new comedy of *Elopements in High Life*, five-act comedy, by R. Sullivan; moderately good.[2] Write half a column about it at the Edinburgh Castle, where I meet Albert Miller. The misunderstanding of nine years ago cleared up. A long chat anent past times. *9th.*—To club. Dalton has gold watch presented to him. John Oxenford of the *Times* is there. *13th.*—Go to Sadlers Wells; last night of the season. See *Henry IV.*, Part II. Delighted with Phelps as the King and Justice Shallow. Read curious review of the Rappists' spiritual manifestation. *14th.*—*Era* pays £1 for Easter amusements. *19th.*—Busy with *Young Englishman* copy. Go to town with copy; to St. James's Theatre. See Houdin; delighted with him, the very best necromancer for 'passing' I ever saw. *20th.*—Busy with copy, and getting circular of Handbook of Isle of Man Districts ready for Adams. Go to club; meet Hemsley, the clever artist. Turns out to have been at the Old Manor House at Chelsea with me fifteen years ago. Curious reminiscences of the olden time. *21st.*—Meet Bradwell, Junior. See Haydon's picture of Napoleon to be sent by Mrs. Barratt to the Empress this week. Look in at Edinburgh Castle, and home. *25th.*—To town, go to Haymarket; first night of Browning's play *Colombe's Birthday*,[3] and re-appearance of Miss Helen Faucit. The play very dull and heavy; elaboration of poetical idea. See Douglas Jerrold, Angus B. Reach, Tomlins, and then to club. Rapid fire of puns and jokes. *28th.*—Drop in at

[1] This is the first actual mention by E. L. B. of the spiritual manifestations in which he afterwards took such interest.

[2] Barry Sullivan, Travers; W. Farren, Charles Perfect; Chippendale, Lord Betterton; Howe, Tom Singlebeart; Compton, Capt. Gawk; Buckstone, Jeremy Tulip; Miss Reynolds, Miss Louisa Lovelock; Mrs. Buckingham, Sybilla; Miss Louisa Howard, Katherina; Mrs. Fitzwilliam, Lady Betterton.

[3] Miss Helen Faucit, Colombe; Barry Sullivan, Valence; Howe, Prince Berthold; W. Farren, Guibert.

Olympic ; see Talfourd's burlesque of *Macbeth*. Robson very clever. Afterwards walk home. On to the Belvidere. Long talk about spiritual rappings and curious letter of Owen's in the *Morning Advertiser* of to-day. Adolphe Didier also promises to find Franklin."

" *May 1st.*—First song of the Superstitions, ' Votive Lamp of the Ganges,' written and sent to W. L. Phillips. *4th.*—Write introduction to Taverns for paper. Go to town and leave it. Go to club. Table-moving the great subject of discussion. *5th.*—Lovely day. Purchase one quart Victoria marrowfat peas, one pint of beans. Write drama. To town. Look in at Strand Theatre. See *Beggar's Opera ;* [1] nicely done. Miss Isabella Featherstone, Lucy Lockit, very clever. *6th.*—Sow peas. Dull and cold. In evening go to Cornelius Pearson's. Mrs. Mole, Wilton, and Mrs. P. and her sister present. Try the table-moving experiments, but only partially successful. Home very late. *12th.*—Belvidereans succeed with the table-moving. Tallis's paper to be enlarged and priced sixpence next Saturday. *14th.*—Club ; meet Sutherland Edwards, and Augustus Mayhew first time. *17th.*—Belvidere ; turn the tables with great success. *18th.*—After going to City spend the evening at Pearson's. Met first time Mrs. Gerald Massey [2] and husband. Extraordinary clairvoyant exhibition by *en rapport*, and the phrenological organ I possess found to be, singularly enough, self-esteem and love of approbation. *19th.*—Write theatricals ; at it all day. In evening take Lofts to Belvidere. Meet Howe and Moore. Try table-moving ; a failure. *20th.* —Dine by appointment with Lovell Phillips. Spin round an insulated table at mother's in a few minutes. Very brilliant experiment."

" *June 2nd.*—Send off to page 29 of copy to Willoughby. Write drama. To town ; meet Tallis, Lofts, and Wright. Try to convince former two of table-moving, but they refuse evidence of their own eyes. *4th.*—Evening to

---

[1] Howard, the Player ; Bernard, the Beggar ; Leffler, Captain Macheath (first time) ; Rogerson, Peachum ; Warren, Lockitt ; Frazer, Filch ; Harrison, Mat o' the Mint ; Rebecca Isaacs, Polly Peachum.

[2] Mrs. Gerald Massey died March, 1866, aged about thirty-eight.

club. Move bandbox very rapidly; nothing more con-clusive. Home with Pearson and Wilton. 10*th.*—Off at two by London and North Western Railway; arrive at Birmingham at 5.50. Tea. See at Shakespeare Rooms Coleman's imposition of *Masks and Faces.* Direct copy of Woodin's *Carpet Bag.* Stop at coffee-house in Union Passage. 11*th.*—Off to Stratford-upon-Avon by coach; arrive at noon. Off to Shakespeare's house, and then to Shottery. See Ann Hathaway's cottage. Delightful walk over the meadows. Stop at the Golden Lion. Harry Hartley landlord; a glorious fellow, and very comfortable. 12*th.*—Long walk of ten miles round by Hampton Lucy and Charlecote. Beautiful scenery, and fine old park. *Monday,* 13*th.*—Such a wet day! Coach to Warwick at four; arrive there at 5.30. Off by Great Western train, and home again at twelve. 14*th.*—Write calendar for paper. Go to Woodin's at night. Long chat with him about the Coleman piracy. 15*th.*—Ward calls from Woodin's. Write short tavern notice of the Wrekin. 21*st.*—To town, and dine with Woodin ; intro-duced to his intended, Miss Sprague. Arrange preliminaries for new entertainment. 23*rd.*—Read some curious articles about the rappings. 24*th.*—Take Walter to Blackwall; first time. Hear from Smith about Drury Lane pantomime. 25*th.*—Write calendar for paper. Town at night. Club; Jopling in chair. Brough and Sidney Blanchard present; first time of seeing them. *Monday,* 27*th.*—Look in at club. Turn Hemsley round by animal magnetism. 28*th.*—Louise Blanche and Madame Louise call in morning. Read in *Times* account of marriage on the 27th inst. of my friend Kent to Miss Ann Young, the eldest daughter, and have cards sent."

One summer day E. L. B. met C. L. Barnett, the author of scores of melodramas, which included *The Dream of Fate;* or, *Sarah the Jewess: The Vow of Silence;* or, *The Old Blacksmith's Hovel,* and pieces of the same class. " How. are you getting on ? " said Barnett — " better than I am, let me hope. I can scarcely get bread.

Writing plays is all very well, but I only wish a widow with a little money would turn up. I'd marry her and open a shop, and sell cooked pork." "Why cooked pork, may I ask, Mr. B.?" remarked Mr. Blanchard, who was not only one of the politest of men, but a student of men and manners, and in addition an earnest enquirer after truth. "Why, because it can be used so many different ways. You can purvey it hot, and then cold, and if it doesn't go off brisk it can be warmed up again. After getting a bit high it does prime for sausages, and when gone like, they can be transmogrified into faggots; which if unfit for human consumption can be dried and converted into seasoning, which does for all the articles before mentioned." The widow never turned up, and Barnett, though, like Dogbriar's father, a man of genius, shared a kindred fate by dying in a workhouse.

"*July 2nd.*—With Wilton to Hanover Square Rooms. Pupils of the Royal Academy's concert; much pleased. To Surrey Theatre; see *Robert the Devil.* Miss Lowe and Drayton very good. *Monday, 4th.*—At eight to Olympic; see Talfourd's new burlesque of *Shylock.* Crammed with puns. Then to club. Chippendale[1] insists upon celebrating the anniversary of American Independence; done accordingly. *5th.*—Home. Find all sorts of annoyances. Patience nearly worn out. *6th.*—To club. Supper celebration. Byrne, of *Sunday Times,* in chair. Drayton sings admirably. I give music toast. Wilton sings 'Alonzo.' All goes off admirably. *13th.*—Finish *Schoolgirl's Life.* Take it to Farren at night. Too late. *16th.*—Club; Mr. Gould, the American, in chair. *19th.*—Call at Woodin's, but don't stop. In at club. Meet

---

[1] "Old Chip" had been for the last seventeen years in America.

John Daly, the author of the clever piece called the *Pines* and *Young Husbands*. 21*st*.—Town early, and dine with my dear friend Woodin, spending day with him. Receive from him £10, making up £20 off account of next entertainment. 22*nd*.—Go to Woodin's. The last night of *Carpet Bag*, given for 266th time. Famous house, crammed to excess, everything going off admirably. 23*rd*.—Up at 5 a.m., and at St. James's Church by ten to see my dear friend Woodin married to Miss Frances Susannah Sprague; then to a grand wedding breakfast in New Moon Street. W. S. W. quite overcome by excitement. Go with his bride, himself, and George Cape to Alford, and leave him there a little recovered. 30*th*.—Go to club. Dr. Darling, the electro-biologist, in chair. Long chat with Daly."

"*Monday, August* 1*st*.—Call on Clark at Electric Telegraph office. All will be done as wished. Go to Chelsea; meet K. Bullen at Don Saltero's. 2*nd*.—Write for paper, and then take little Walter to Astley's for the first time to see the *Battle of Waterloo*, and scenes in the circus. He gets knocked up by the excitement, but reminds me of myself and the eager interest I took in the same matters. 3*rd*.— Home early for peace and quietness, but find very little. All upset as usual. 4*th*.—Take Walter to Gravesend, thinking the steamboat would do him good. Spend an hour at Rosherville, and back by train. Nothing again done all day; expenses increasing, income diminishing. 7*th*.—Leave London at 10.30 with carpet bag; get to Gravesend, walk to Cobham, and thence through Birling to Malling, through cross woods affording pretty scenery. Sleep at Swan Inn; expenses 5*s*. 6*d*., total distance fourteen miles. *Monday*, 8*th*. —Off at nine to walk from Malling to Maidstone, six miles, through woods the whole way, road straight through hop gardens; so good, worth repeating with companion. Stop half-an-hour at Maidstone, and walk on towards Ashford to Parkfield Gate; on for 2*s*. 6*d*. to Ashford; dangerous man in fit on roof. Go on by express, 3*s*. 9*d*., to Folkestone; walk, at half-past seven, six miles across the hills to Dover; stop for night at Flying Horse regularly knocked up. Meet young Hengler. Bill next morning 5*s*. 6*d*. Weather very fine. *9th.*—Smoke a matutinal pipe on shore; waves surging in, and delicious smell of sea-weed all round. Walk about feeling very tired. At seven on to Deal by coach. Arrive at Deal; stroll by starlight round the beach; see Walmer Castle. Take bed at Royal George in Lower Street; small house, jolly landlord, and to bed very tired. *10th.*—Stroll down the Walmer Road to Lord Nelson, pleasant roadside tavern. Write theatricals. Go in afternoon to Sandown Castle, and lounge about the beach. Very much pleased with Deal; pretty types of Kentish beauty, the town remarkably salubrious; gutters through streets might be improved. *14th.*— Walk at 10 a.m. across the sandhills and fields from Deal to old town of Sandwich. Stop there to lunch; grass growing in High Street. Take train on to Ramsgate; stop at the Crown. Look in Refectory; Glover, pianist; Harmonic Meeting. Stroll over the sands and walk about pier. Want a companion very much. Sleep on sofa bedstead, and tired out. *12th.*—Off at ten by steamer; (*The Little Western*) for 4*s.* for London ; estimated distance 98 miles, average rate of steaming 17 knots an hour. Arrive at home 4 p.m. after pleasant passage. *16th.*—At night to Belvidere, and meet Beeston, proprietor of the theatrical journal *Chat*, anent divers matters. *23rd.*—Meet A. Miller, Wandsworth, Kew, and Rail. Receive a letter from poor John Blewitt the composer, who dates from University Hospital. *24th.*—Write theatricals. *30th.*—See Albert Miller off in *Father Thames* to Dover, and give him book of 'Watering-places.' Long read, and to bed. *31st.*—All day writing for papers. Premature death of poor Wilkins, a young and promising author as well as a good actor." [1]

"*Monday, Sept. 5th.*—Dress, and in evening to Drury Lane; see G. V. Brooke as *Othello*. First night of a short season ; burlesque of *Fountain of Beauty;* house very full, performance very queer. *6th.*—Emma, the daughter of poor John

---

[1] John Wilkins, aged only twenty-seven. In six years he had produced at the City of London Theatre upwards of ten dramas. *The Green Hills of the Far West* first brought him into notice. Mr. James Anderson played in his five-act drama *Civilization*, and at the time of his death he had several other pieces written.

Blewitt, calls to tell me of her father's death. I write paragraphs of the event for all the papers in accordance with his dying wish.[1] 9*th.*—Go to Drury; Brooke's *Othello* a mistake altogether.[2] Evening at Bedford, and home. 10*th.*—Private box at Drury; Brooke as Iago, and Davenport as Othello; latter very fine. *Monday, 14th.*—At home all day writing 'Antique Hostelries' for Birmingham paper. 16*th.*—Gray the artist comes at night to arrange about the views of Lake scenery for Woodin's entertainment. Look in at Regent, and see in paper the death of Bradshaw announced, at Christiania, Norway. Deeply and unaffectedly regretted by all, and not least by myself. 17*th.*—Go to town; square accounts with Tallis, three weeks. Come back at six, really very ill, and in bed by eight. Take a composing draught and sleep like a top. *Monday, 19th.*—Town early; see Woodin about Lake Guide. Go to Cremorne; find nobody there I know. Dreary evening. Call at club. New piece, *The Betrothal*, at Drury Lane, coldly received.[3] 21*st.*—All day writing theatricals. 22*nd.*—Farren resigns management, and makes his last appearance at Olympic as Lord Ogleby in *Clandestine Marriage.* 29*th.*—Leave pantomime at theatre; meet Tallis, who has sold his paper, and somebody else the proprietor of the *Illustrated London Magazine.* 30*th.*—Town early; receive from Smith for pantomime £10 on account. Dine with him, Wild, Wilton, J. Rogers, at Coal Hole. Tallis's paper bought by Mr. J. Livesey, the proprietor of the *Preston Guardian.*"

"*Monday, Oct. 3rd.*—Madame Louise and Louise Blanche

[1] John Blewitt died in University Hospital, August 28th, aged seventy-three, and was buried in St. Pancras. But a few weeks before his death he worked for musical publishers, though suffering intense agony from his complaint, and for some years had provided the music for Covent Garden, Drury Lane, Olympic, and other theatres' pantomimes. He was a fertile composer, was noted for his glees, and was for some time musical director of Vauxhall Gardens. But for all this he died poor! He will be remembered for his air to " Barney Brallaghan's Courtship."

[2] [This was not the general impression. In his prime, the *Othello* of G. V. Brooke was said to be a magnificent performance.—C.S.]

[3] Five-act play, by H. Boker. G. V. Brooke, Marsio; Miss Anderton, Costanzia. Piece withdrawn after second performance.

again call. Surrey Theatre re-opens for winter season. Brooke's benefit as Virginius at Drury. Hear he is receiving an average of £200 a week. *7th.*—At home all day trying very hard to be funny, but miserable failure! *8th.*—Go to Torrington Square, and leave pantomime for Charles Kean. Go to Sadlers Wells; see *Midsummer Night's Dream* re-vived for first time. Beautifully got up. *Monday, 10th.*—At night to Adelphi. See *Discarded Son*,[1] new piece; goes off very well. *13th.*—See new farce of Charles Selby's, *Hotel Charges*, at Adelphi. *19th.*—Last night of dramatic season. Brooke, Macbeth, and Smith's benefit. *Monday, 31st.*—Town at two with pantomime. To Drury to see the Horsemanship; very fair. Meet Smith and Wild, and have supper with them at the Albion. Go to club; pleasant party—Carpenter and Levy. Lyceum opens."[2]

" *Nov. 4th.*—The *Empire* first number out. *Monday, 7th.*—Again on pantomime. Go in evening with Miller to Toole's *At Home* in the Southwark Road; afterwards to supper. Meet George Genge, Percy B. St. John, Edward Copping, etc. A pleasant party. All sorts of songs. Not home till 6 a.m. *9th.*—To town. Dine with E. T. Smith and pleasant party in Green Room at Drury Lane. Morning circus per-formance. Take Walter. Evening to club; Frank Matthews there; long chat with him. Meet Pond, Sala, and hosts of people. *Monday, 14th.*—At night to club. To Adelphi. First night of *Whitebait at Greenwich.* Outrageous farce by Maddison Morton. *15th.*—Evans's, Sam Cowell, and home. Cracker for Christmas, and Parlour Song Book pub-lished. *16th.*—To Regent Street, and receive one guinea for words of 'As if you didn't know!' from Addison and Hollier. *17th.*—Writing theatricals. At night to Haymarket. First night of *Love's Alarms*, comic opera by Ed. Fitzwilliam. Goes off only so-so. Write account for it at Edinburgh

---

[1] An adaptation from the French, by B. Webster, in which Leigh Murray was delightful. It was afterwards done as *The Queen's Shilling* for the Kendals at the St. James's.

[2] Vestris management: *A Curious Case, Little Toddlekins,* and, first time, *The Commencement of a Bad Farce, which, however, it is hoped will turn out Wright at Last,*—very poor, and hissed.

Castle. *30th.*—Meet Harrison. *Times* newspaper uses nine tons of paper per day."

"*Dec.* 1*st.*—Write drama. See Adams on return from Manchester, and square £5 old account of 'Handbook to Manchester District.' Olympic; see *Plot and Passion;* very good. *2nd.*—Take Walter with me to Zoological Gardens, Regent's Park; see the hippopotamus, chimpanzee, and ant-eater for the first time; the little one full of ecstasies. Home to tea; tired out with morning walk, and stop at home scribbling for Birmingham pantomime. *3rd.*—Send Hall two comic scenes for pantomime, and remainder of bill. See Stirling Coyne's comedy, in three acts, of the *Hope of the Family* (first time). Very indifferent, but goes off well. *4th.*—Glimpse in evening at Regent of Vincent's extraordinary sermon on table-turning, which he ascribes to satanic influence. *Monday, 5th.*—Write calendar for paper, and annual song for Flexmore. Albert Smith re-opens his *Mont Blanc* this night with new effects. *6th.*—Long letter to Woodin. See at Olympic clever piece of Planché's, *The Camp at the Olympic,* and delighted with it. *7th.*—Write comic scene for Sadlers Wells. Greenwood and club. Chat with Levy. Davidson, music publisher, calls to obtain another portion of 'Villikins and his Dinah.'[1] *8th.*—Meet G. A. Sala. New publication called *London.* Long chat with him at Edinburgh Castle. *11th.*—Birthday. Mother to dinner. Howe looks in during evening. Thirty-three this day! Life's dissolving views— thirty-third slide. *13th.*—Go to Adelphi. See the ice scene in *Thirst for Gold;* wonderful effect. Then to Olympic. Robson is great in 'Villikins.' At Wrekin hear he is about thirty-six, and of weak health, poor fellow! *16th.*—Dine with Mr. Williams, Ledger, Willott, Smith, Scott, and Wild. From Smith £5. Davidson pays for 'Villikins and his Dinah' £1, and gives me a sovereign for tickets to the Wilkins fund. *21st.*—Writing pantomime plots. Arrange

[1] This was sung by F. Robson as Jem Baggs in *The Wandering Minstrel,* then running at the Olympic. It became the popular song of the day. We have seen before how Blanchard wrote it as a boy for private theatricals.

to provide *Era* with them. 24*th.*—Town early. Grand dinner at Drury in Green Room. Health of the 'author' proposed, and have to return thanks. Night rehearsal. Take Albert Miller behind. 25*th.*—Christmas Day. Roast beef and plum pudding, wine and grog, make it as merry as possible, but company very 'slow.' 26*th.*—General holiday. See pantomime at Drury Lane, *Harlequin Hummingtop.* All goes off very well indeed. Sit in stalls, Spicer next to me, and Kent in box above me. 27*th.*—Off to town early. *Era* £2 for pantomimes. Olympic with Albert Miller. *Harlequin Columbus* very slow ; columbine (Miss Wyndham) very good. 29*th.*—Busy with theatres for paper. Moore calls, and take him to Sadlers Wells : *Harlequin Tom Thumb ;* very good for changes, and capital clown, Nicolo Deulin. Afterwards to Belvidere. Fitzjohn calls in morning. Usual overwhelming cavalcade of Christmas accounts. 30*th.*—At home to write *Era* notices, but interrupted for four hours by some one, who wants song, etc., etc. At night to town with copy. 31*st.*—Meet Woodin. See drama, first night, *The Begging Letter.* Not good. To club ; large assemblage. Punch to welcome the New Year in."

This season E. L. B. wrote the following pantomimes : Drury Lane—*King Hummingtop ;* or, *Harlequin and the Land of Toys.* Harlequin, Milano ; columbine, Miss Annie Cushnie ; pantaloon, Halford ; harlequina, Marie Charles ; grotesques, Ethair Family ; clown, Tom Matthews. Sadlers Wells—*Harlequin Tom Thumb ;* or, *Gog and Magog and Mother Goose's Golden Goslings.* Harlequin, Fenton ; columbine, Caroline Parkes ; sprite, Willikind Molino ; pantaloon, Naylor ; clown, Nicholas Deulin. Also a pantomime for Hall of Birmingham, and the usual songs for Flexmore and Tom Matthews.

Rough calculation for year 1853, £146 10*s.*

1854.

"*Sunday, Jan.* 1*st.*—Mother spends New Year's Day with us. Write to Kent and Watkins in reply to pleasant missives. See papers; good accounts. 2*nd.*—See Davidson; give him signatures for 'Old King Cole' and 'Villikins' and 'Pastimes,' for which £2. Dine at Edinburgh, and get cheque from Greenwood, £14, for pantomime. 6*th.*—Write address of 'England Delineated' for Tallis. Receive a very kind and cordial response from my dear friend Kent. 9*th.*— To Drury, seeing new piece of Mark Lemon's called *Paula Lazarro;*[1] not very brilliant. 10*th.*—Grand juvenile party of seventeen little ones given by Master Walter—'Nunky pays for all'—Christmas tree, etc. Mother comes to assist. Lovell Phillips looks in at evening, Howe at night. All goes off pleasantly; a success! 16*th.*—Woodin pays for entertainment £5. At night to Drury. Smith gives me £5 extra for pantomime. 17*th.*—Meet Phelps accidentally at Sadlers Wells in morning, and he compliments me very much upon the Shakespeare I edited for him. Pleasant to feel that he is quite satisfied. 19*th.*—Look into Edinburgh Castle. See account of Smith taking Shadwell Workhouse for a theatre.[2] 23*rd.*—Go to Haymarket; first night of Miss Cushman's engagement. See her as Bianca in *Fazio,*[3] and opening of pantomime of *Three Bears.* Very good. 28*th.* —To Pam's, read papers; then to club—Wilton there; chat with Jonas Levy, and home. Levy called to the Bar. 30*th.* —See Brooke make his first appearance at Drury this season as Brutus."[4]

[1] Or, *The Ladrone's Daughter.* Gideon Lazarro, T. Mead; Juana, Miss Featherstone; Gasper, A. Younge; Mrs. Lewis, Paula; George Bennett, Jose Maria; George Wild, Xenophonte.

[2] E. T. Smith purchased the freehold estate on which the workhouse stood, sold by the Stepney Union, the entire area comprised 17,066 ft., the workhouse stood on 3,800 ft. of ground.

[3] Howe was the Giraldo, Mrs. L. S. Buckingham, Aldabella.

[4] In Howard Payne's tragedy, *Brutus; or, The Fall of Tarquin,* he was supported by G. Bennett, Sextus; Pearson (from Liverpool), Valerius; Kinloch, Aruno; Lee, Claudius; Belton, Titus; Morgan,

"*Feb.* 2*nd.*—Drama for paper; see Adelphi piece of *Number Nip;* [1] very bad. 3*rd.*—Start for Coventry; meet at station Miss Lyon, Howe, Barnsby, and Buckland. Go down with them. 4*th.*—To Birmingham. Stop at Suffield's; at night to theatre, and see *Jack the Giant-killer;* [2] much pleased. Miss Emma Hall very good; all very hospitable. *Monday,* 6*th.*—About Birmingham with Hall. Call on Simpson; arrange for three-act piece, £25, to be called *Aston Hall.* 11*th.*—Go to Haymarket; see Palgrave Simpson's *Ranelagh;* [3] only moderately successful. 13*th.*—Turn tables, etc. 15*th.*—See *First Night* at Olympic; delighted with Wigan's wonderful acting as Achille Talma Dufard. 17*th.*—Cogitating; make an effort to begin Woodin's entertainment, but a failure. Review more books for the *England,* and write *Era* correspondence. To town early, and see Lord Glengall at Drury Lane about new Easter piece. 19*th.*—In evening to Stirling Coyne; arrange with him travestie of *Willikins and Dinah.* 24*th.*—The piano comes, £15; a bargain. Play over all the tunes I know."

"*March* 1*st.*—See in paper death of Thomas Holt, of the *Age.* Vauxhall; see C. May, first paymaster, and the proposer of my health at Drury Lane last Christmas. 2*nd.*—Town with copy; go to crib—Phelps's benefit, *The Miser* and *Wild Oats.* 4*th.*—At night to club, Sala and W. Romer at my side. Met Heath, Bayliss, etc. 5*th.*—Reading Cahagnet's curious clairvoyant revelations. 8*th.*—Look in at Olympic; see charming little piece of *To Oblige Benson.* [4] 16*th.*—Busy

Collatinus; Mrs. Vickery, Tullia; Miss Fanny Cathcart (from Liverpool first appearance), Tarquinia; Miss Lewis, Lucretia.

[1] By Mark Lemon and Shirley Brooks, a burlesque extravaganza. Mrs. Keeley in the title *rôle.* Miss Woolgar, Count Rudolph; Mary Keeley, Ida; Madame Celeste, Cuthbert; Emma Harding, James Rogers and Paul Bedford were in the caste. The scene was laid in the Hartz Mountains.

[2] This was by E. L. B.

[3] The scene was laid at Ranelagh in the time of George II., and the play was in two acts. Sir Robert Rovely, George Vandenhoff; Lady Rovely, Miss Reynolds; Mr. Coddlelove, J. B. Buckstone; Miss Coddlelove, Mrs. Fitzwilliam; Colonel Crawfish, Tilbury.

[4] Adapted by Taylor from *Un Service à Blanchard,* and first played

day in town; opening of the Panopticon.[1]   Haymarket
Theatre; *Willikins and His Dinah,*[2] first night, goes off pretty
well.   18*th.*—Begin *Aston Hall*, but make little progress.
Drop in at Wells; last act of *Town and Country.*   20*th.*—
To Adelphi; *Two Loves and a Life;* very good.[3]   24*th.*—
Stewing over *Aston Hall.*   27*th.*—First night of Chinese
Troupe at Drury Lane;[4] moderately successful.   *Leonce*
opera, by Duggan; Drayton and Miss Lowe very good.   28*th.*
—Work on *Aston Hall*; at night vivid dreams of Elizabeth
Ockerby; never dreamed of her before; curious, on account
of what I have recently read in Cahagnet's book, *Visit from
Soul to Soul.*   29*th.*—Much impressed with dream of last
night.   31*st.*—Howe comes in evening."

"*April* 8*th.*—At night Toole comes, and pays £4 for
assistance.   Go to town; cheque changed by Ward.   12*th.*
—Working at Easter novelties for paper all day, and at
night to hear Toole at the Walworth Institute.[5]   Take
Albert Miller, T. P. Cooke next to us; all goes off admirably.
Club, and home with Mr. Stafford, author of ' History of
Music.'   13*th.* Easter novelties for *Era*, but great scarcity
of information.   17*th.*—Haymarket in evening; see Planché's
clever extravaganza of Mr. Buckstone's *Voyage Round the
Globe* (first night); house capital; piece ditto.   18*th.*—To
town.   *Era* pays £1.   Buy ' Rambles by Rivers.'   24*th.*—
Miserable day; nothing done; upset every way; no money
from anybody; pushed hard for cash.   25*th.*—All day brood-

Monday, March 6th, 1854. Emery, Benson; Mrs. Stirling, Mrs. Trotter
Southdown; Miss Wyndham, Mrs. Benson; Robson, Trotter Southdown.

[1] The Royal Panopticon of Science and Art, Leicester Square, on the
site where now stands the Alhambra.   Leicester Buckingham was appointed the special lecturer on science.

[2] By Stirling Coyne.   Buckstone, Lord Pellemelle; Mrs. Fitzwilliam,
Louisa Howard, H. Corri, also in the caste.

[3] By Tom Taylor and Charles Reade.   Sir Gervase Rokewode
Leigh Murray; Father Radcliffe, Benjamin Webster; Annie Musgrave,
Miss Woolgar; Ruth Ravenscar, Mme. Céleste; Musgrave, O. Smith;
Duke of Cumberland, Charles Selby; John Daw, Keeley.

[4] They were jugglers, and clever.

[5] It was at the Walworth Institute that Charles Dickens saw J. L.
Toole as an attraction, and advised him to go on the stage.

ing over the entertainment. Imagination and inventive powers dormant. No exercise, no enjoyment, no money, ' no nuffin.' 26*th.*—The day of prayer and humiliation for the war; all the shops closed, and London quiet. 27*th.*— John Toole to be married this morning at Stepney; invited, but can't go. Finish the theatricals of the week. Go to town. Look in at Edinburgh Castle; then Ashley's, Marston, Barrett, and party."

" *May* 1*st.*—Begin description of new Crystal Palace for Adams. Write to Hall for cash. 2*nd.*—Woodin calls to tell me about Stacey and Palmer renewing their impositions of last night. Go to lawyer (Abrahams), and thence start to Brentford. Walk to Ealing; a memory of old times vividly reproduced (school days), and thence by G.W.R. to Paddington. 3*rd.*—Writing all day paragraphs for Woodin about the impostors, but it turns out very unsuccessfully, for the newspapers seem afraid. 4*th.*—Writing ' Theatres' for *Empire* ; reduced on Saturday to 4*d.* in price. 5*th.*—Severe pain in my side. All day at home, but nothing done. Very dreary, very weary, and very desponding. Read *Manfred* at night, thirtieth time or thereabouts. 11*th.*—Look in at Drury Lane, *Der Freyschütz* in the German ;[1] magnificently done, incantation scene capital, Caspar good. 12*th.*—Home till eight. Finish accounts of Crystal Palace for Adams. Go into town and leave it, and receive £1 10*s.*, balance of £2 10*s.*, for ' Crystal Palace Guide.' 17*th.*—Wilson calls in morning, and off for long walk round by New River, bowls at Highbury Park Tavern, Hornsey, and Highgate. Walk home after seeing the imposition of *Carpet Bag* at Gate House; very bad and stupid; sixteen persons present. 20*th.*—Off early to British Museum, and work hard on ' England and Wales,' which I begin to find a very unprofitable work. Money hunting, and failure. Provisions all going up, and my ring follows the general example. Correct proofs of ' England and Wales.' Much perplexed by no remittance from Birmingham. 25*th.*—Receive from Hall for piece £15. Get out of debt everywhere as much as possible, and to town with copy for

---

[1] Agatha, Mme. Caradori ; Max, Herr Reichardt ; Caspar, Herr Formes.

paper.   See W. Miller at Edinburgh Castle, Coyne at Nobb's.
26*th.*—To British Museum ; meet Percy St. John.   29*th.*—
Receive one of my dear friend Kent's warm-hearted sunshiny
letters, asking me to become a contributor to a journal,[1] and
to dine with him at Weybridge.   31*st.*—Derby Day.   All
my investments prove unfortunate ; hand over the winner.
Adelphi ; *Marble Heart*,[2] very good.   Look in at club ; Mr.
Copping from Australia, Courtney, Hartley, Tilbury, and
pleasant party present."

"*June 1st.*—Drama for paper.   Go to Haymarket ; see
Knights of the Round Table and burlesque.   2*nd.*—Davidson
pays in full for 'May Heaven Defend the Right,' and for
'Albion's Island Queen ' £2 10*s.*   Flexmore's benefit in
summer season at Wells ; very bad house.   6*th.*—Sadlers
Wells, and see *Black-eyed Susan.*   Devonport.   8*th.*—
Mother's birthday, and she dines with me.   13*th.*—To town
to see *Hush Money*[3] at Olympic ; Robson's acting wonderful,
but piece bad.   Club, and home with Levy.   15*th.*—Drama,
to town, and *Norma* at Drury.   Ascot Gold Cup run for,
Western Australian winning, and for the first time in my
life puts 10*s.* into my pocket.   Toole in City.   16*th.*—
Meet Probert, of *Illustrated London Magazine*, and Lofts.
19*th.*—See Kent at *Sun* office ; long chat with him.   At
Adelphi see *A Moving Tale*[4] and last acts of *Thirst for Gold.*
26*th.*—All day arranging little pars for Tallis's *London
Pictorial.*   27*th.*—Write a little of the drama.   To Princess's ;
see *Faustus* ;[5] very much pleased ; last effect beautiful.
28*th.*—*Era* correspondence, and that's all.   29*th.*—Write

---

[1] *The Sun ?*—ED.

[2] *The Marble Heart ; or, The Sculptor's Dream.*   Drama adapted by
Charles Selby from *Les Filles de Marbre.*   Leigh Murray, Raphael
Duchatlet ; Ben Webster, Volage ; Paul Bedford, Viscount Château-
margaux ; Charles Selby, Mons. Veaudoré ; Mmes. Celeste, Marco ;
Cuthbert, Clementine ; Emma Harding, Mariette ; Sarah Woolgar,
Marie ; Leigh Murray, Mme. Duchatlet.

[3] A revival of a farce by Dance, first played under the Vestris
management here, by Liston, Keeley, Frank Matthews, and Mrs. Orger.
F. Robson now played Jaspar Touchwood ; Mrs. Wigan, Sally ; Emery,
Tom Tillex.

[4] A farce by Mark Lemon, written for the Keeley family.

[5] *Faust and Marguerite.*

theatricals. See lively new piece at Olympic called *Heads or Tails*,[1] by Palgrave Simpson. Sadlers Wells prematurely closes.[2] No pay, no Payne."

"*July 7th.*—Finish, all but song of 'Metropolitan Gossip,' the first part of Woodin's entertainment; take it to him. *20th.*—Receive £1 from Tallis for *Pictorial*, Numbers 1 to 5. *21st.*—Go to Woodin's, and see the *Lake Views;* dine there, and meet Hampton, the aeronaut. *26th.*—Go to Haymarket; see Coyne's piece of *The Old Château*[3] very good, and *Spanish Dancers* ditto. *28th.*—Go to Greenwich, and dine with E. T. Smith, Lord Glengall, Captain Spinner, J. Duncombe, Burgess, etc., at the Trafalgar. Splendid dinner, but upset by the champagne, and out of order altogether."

"*Aug. 5th.*—Last night (549th) of Woodin's *Carpet Bag and Sketch Book.* Sup at Woodin's with large party— Planché, Oxenford, Coyne, the Broughs, etc. Very pleasant evening. *7th.*—Grisi's farewell of Royal Italian Opera.[4] *11th.* —Have a remarkably vivid dream about Caroline. Waking in morning remember that it is exactly ten years since we last saw each other; on one side at least, never forgotten ! *12th.*—To club; meet Gomersal, low comedian, from the North. Chat with Daly. *24th.*—At night J. Toole drops in, and tells me he has engaged with Mrs. Seymour, St. James's. *26th.*—Sadlers Wells re-opens for the season. *28th.*—To Lyceum in evening. Henry Russell as of yore.[5] *31st.*—Home till evening. Drama for paper. Passed by Tully into Strand to see the *Faust and Marguerite*[6] burlesque."

[1] Robson, Quaile; Emery, Wrangleworth; Miss Marston, Rosamond; Alfred Wigan, Harold Dyecaster ; Mrs. Alfred Wigan, Winifred.

[2] It re-opened the following week.

[3] Or, *A Night of Peril.* Drama drawn by Stirling Coyne, suggested by a novel entitled *La Jeune Femme.* Buckstone, Samson ; Howe, General the Marquis de Leyrac ; W. Farren, Armand ; H. Marston, Lalouette ; Miss Reynolds, Julie ; Mrs. Fitzwilliam, Jeannette.

[4] She appeared in *Norma* and *The Huguenots.* First appeared as Ninetta in 1834.

[5] In the *Emigrant's Progress,* and *Negro Life.*

[6] By J. Halford, the author of *Mephistopheles;* Faust, Miss G. Hodson ; Valentine, Miss F. Beaumont ; Marguerite, Miss F. Brunell.

Very bad, and in wretched taste, though Halford's imitation of Charles Kean good. "

" *Sept. 4th.*—Take Walter to Highbury Barn Tavern and Tea Gardens to hear the pantomime. Tired, and back by eight. John Toole calls; chat, and then away to Sadlers Wells; see one scene of *Cymbeline.* See Greenwood. *7th.*—Find John Watkins on return. *9th.*—Visit to Brighton, etc. *26th.*—Leave Southampton at 12.30, and reach London at 5 p.m. Find Walter delighted to see me, and hosts of letters awaiting me. H. Boleno, the new Drury clown, calls. *27th.*—J. L. Toole comes in evening, and reads over his parts to me. *29th.*—Writing all day for *Era* the memoir of poor Mrs. Warner.[1] Go to town with it in evening. See Willoughby about stage edition of *Pericles.* Hear of Wilks's death.[2] *30th.*—Pantomime ordered

---

[1] Mary Amelia Warner, died September 24th, 1854; born at Manchester in 1804. She was the daughter of Huddart the actor ; and, as Miss Huddart, began her dramatic career, when only fifteen years of age, with Brunton, the manager of the Plymouth, Exeter, Bristol, and Birmingham Theatres; made her first notable appearance in London as Belvidera, in *Venice Preserved*, at Drury Lane, November 22nd, 1830, to Macready's *Pierre*, though she had already played at some of the minor theatres in town. Lady Constance, in *King John ;* Olivia, in *Jane Shore ;* Emma, in *William Tell* ; and Queen Elswith, in *Alfred the Great*, or, *The Patriot King*,—were her principal characters that season. In 1836 she was at Drury Lane again, under Bunn's management, and played Lady Macbeth, Emilia, and Marian in *The Wrecker's Daughter.* In 1837, Evadne, in *The Bridal (The Maid's Tragedy)*, at the Haymarket. In the same year married Robert William Warner, landlord of the Wrekin Tavern, in Broad Court. Mrs. Warner was for some four years a member of Macready's company at Covent Garden and Drury Lane, and in 1844 entered into partnership with Phelps at Sadler's Wells, remaining there till 1847, when she became the manageress of the Marylebone, and opened in October as Hermione in *The Winter's Tale.* The management proved most unfortunate, and so Mrs. Warner returned to the Haymarket (having already played there a couple of seasons between 1837 and 1844), and appeared at Sadler's Wells for a limited number of nights, commencing July 28th, 1851, in her most celebrated characters, and made her last bow on the English boards as Mrs. Oakley in *The Jealous Wife.* Mrs. Warner subsequently went twice to America, but returned home in 1853, a confirmed invalid. Mrs. Warner left a son and a daughter.

[2] Thomas Egerton Wilks, dramatic author, died this date in a state

in honour of the Allied Forces gaining victory over Russians. News of the fall of Sebastopol."

From *September 9th* to *26th* E. L. B. was away from London on business for Mr. Woodin principally, as is gathered from the diary, probably to see what success there would be for the entertainment—best rooms, etc. It was also to benefit E. L. B.'s health, which had been anything but good. He started from Brighton, and visited Arundel, Chichester, Portsmouth, Ryde, Newport, Isle of Wight, Southampton, Weymouth, Portland, Dorchester, and Brockenhurst; doing a considerable amount of walking, as was usual with him.

" *Oct. 1st.*—Prepare MS. of *Dodge, Cinderella, Crusoe,* two pantomimes and songs for Coppin to take to Australia. *2nd.*—Work hard on copy of *Dodge.* Tallis calls; arrange to do 10 sheets (5 parts in 2 months) by *1st December.* Go to St. James's; *King's Rival,*[1] first night of opening. Mrs. Seymour lessee, and Toole's first appearance. First piece not over till quarter past eleven, and no chance for farce, so leave. *3rd.*—Copping pays £5 for copy of *Dodge.* Sails to-morrow from Southampton in the *Argo.* Propose his health, and success to him. *5th.*—Write theatres for paper. See Brooke at Drury as Stranger, and Wright in farce of *Young Widow. 6th.*—*Era* for memoir pays £1. *9th.*— Princess's; first night of Jerrold's new play, *The Heart of*

of wretched poverty. His first work was a romantic drama, *The Red Cross,* produced at Sadler's Wells in 1831, and he afterwards wrote some two hundred plays.

[1] By Tom Taylor and Charles Reade, of the time of Charles II. Miss Glyn, Frances Stewart; Mrs. Seymour, Nell Gwynne; Vandenhoff, the King; T. Mead, Duke of Richmond; J. L. Toole, Samuel Pepys; Miss Lydia Thompson was in the cast. *My Friend the Major,* by Charles Selby, was played the same night.

Gold,[1] and first night of the season. Not one of Jerrold's best. House very full, but not very enthusiastic. *12th.*— Worried and flurried by press for copy. To Marylebone Theatre, and see *As You Like It*;[2] well done. Mrs. William Wallack (Ann Waring) looking as well as when I saw her last, twenty-five years ago. Captain Mayne Reid and his young wife and Ben Armstrong present. *13th.*—At night to Sadlers Wells to see grand rehearsal of *Pericles*. Goes very well; a magnificent spectacle. *14th.*—See Tallis, and square with him, Part IV. of 'England and Wales.' See Drury scene painters, and then to Sadlers Wells for first night of *Pericles*.[3] Brilliant triumph. Write notice for *Era.* *17th.*—To Olympic; see F. Robson in wonderful performance of Job Wort in *A Blighted Being*.[4] Mark Lemon and Morris Barnett present. *19th.*—Finish Birmingham at British Museum, then write drama for *Empire*, then to Adelphi, *Summer Storms*, first night, Tom Parry's.[5] *Era* £1 10s. for theatricals. *25th.*—Work late to make up for last night. Idea of *Jack and Jill*. *26th.*—Look in at Strand; Harriet Gordon as Don Giovanni in Dibdin's burlesque. *27th.*—Write Astley's notice for *Era*.[6] See Lovell Phillips about six songs of Mendelssohn's. *28th.*—Take title to Greenwood, *Isaac Walton*. *30th.*—To St. James's; *Honour before Titles*.[7] Bad translation. Adelphi, *Bonâ-fide*

---

[1] Douglas Jerrold's three-act drama. Ryder, John Dymond ; Miss Heath, Maude ; J. F. Cathcart, Pierce Thanet ; Addison, Nutbrown ; Meadows, Yewberry ; David Fisher, Michaelmas ; and Miss Murray, Dolly Dindle. The Comedietta, *Living Too Fast on a Twelvemonth's Honeymoon*, was also played for the first time.

[2] William Wallack, Jacques ; E. F. Edgar, Orlando ; Mrs. Wallack, Rosalind ; Shalders, Touchstone ; Miss Cleveland, Celia.

[3] Phelps, Pericles ; Miss Atkinson, the Queen ; Miss Edith Heraud, Marina. The scenery by Fenton was perfection.

[4] Farce by Tom Taylor. Ellen Turner, Susan Spanker ; Horace Wigan (playing as Mr. Danvers), O'Rafferty.

[5] Keeley, Leigh Murray, and Miss Woolgar appeared in it, but it was a failure.

[6] This was a wonderful representation called *The Battle of the Alma*.

[7] Taken from *La Poissarde*. J. L. Toole, Le Pailleux ; Madeleine his wife, Mrs. Seymour ; Aurélie, Miss Clifford ; Jérôme, Henry Rivers (first appearance here).

Travellers. Write to Woodin and Nicholls about idea for entertainment, *La Belle Alliance.*" [1]

" *Nov.* 1*st.*—Write song for Phillips, ' When Fancy waves her Magic Wand;' first series of six. 6*th.*—Hard at work all day on Drury pantomime of *Jack and Jill*, and finish it at seven; off to Drury with it. All delighted, and all right. 7*th.*—In the obituary of the *Times* to-day John Esdale Widdicomb,[2] sixty-seventh year, and riding-master for thirty-four years at Astley's. At home on ' England and Wales;' write song, ' Fairy Wings,' for Phillips. 13*th.*— Hear of Charles Kemble's death yesterday.[3] 16*th.*—See very bad farce of Mark Lemon's, called *The Slow Man*, at Adelphi. 17*th.*—Off to British Museum for data of memoir of C. Kemble; useless labour, write it at Pam's. 22*nd.*—From *Era* 10*s.* 6*d.* for Kemble memoir. Go to Drury; see props. Adelphi, *Railway Belle*, lively farce, by Mark Lemon. 23*rd.*— Write theatricals for *Empire*, which I hear has changed hands. To Haymarket; first night of clever piece by Bayle Bernard

[1] Farce by William Brough, Mr. and Mrs. Keeley, R. Romer, and Paul Bedford played in it.

[2] Prior to his being at Astley's he had played the " dandy lover " in pantomime to the clown of Grimaldi at the old Coburg Theatre. He was to the last a wonderfully young-looking man, and was an excellent ring-master.

[3] Youngest brother of John Philip Kemble and Mrs. Siddons; and was born at Brecknock, South Wales, in November 1775. Educated at Douai; was in the Post Office, London, twelve months, but left it to appear as Orlando in *As You Like It*, at Sheffield, in 1792. Made his *début* in London as Malcolm in *Macbeth* at Drury Lane, April 21st, 1794. Made his first mark at the Haymarket in 1798, as Wilford in *The Iron Chest.* In 1803 he joined his brother at Covent Garden, and made his first appearance there in September as Henry in *Speed the Plough.* He rapidly rose to be one of the most capable actors in an extensive range of parts, which included *Mirabel, Doricourt, Cassio, Benedick, Charles Surface, Marc Antony, Falconbridge, Pierre*, etc. In 1806 he married Miss Teresa Decamp, by whom he left three children, Mrs. Butler, Mrs. Sartoris, and the Rev. John Kemble. Charles Kemble retired from the stage December 23rd, 1836, as Benedick. He, however, appeared by command of the Queen four years later, and played for twelve nights his principal Shakespearean characters. He held for a time the post of Examiner of Plays, but resigned it to his son J. P. Kemble. In May and July 1844, Charles

called *Balance of Comfort;*[1] well received. 25*th.*—Write song of 'Silver Rills,' and send it to Phillips. The *Empire* ends with Livesey and begins with Thomson. 27*th.* — Write altered opening scene for Sadlers Wells, and go there in evening. Walter goes and spends evening at Phelps's in the Square. 30*th.*—Miss Clifford, *protégée* of Lord G., calls for pantomime. Write drama, and take it; but though going through pouring rain find not wanted, the Empire eschewing fine arts for the future."

"*Dec. 7th.*—Last night of *Pericles* after a seven weeks' run. 8*th.*—Write one comic scene for Smith; go to Wells at night and see *The Rivals,* Phelps playing Sir Anthony Absolute admirably. 11*th.*—Birthday; attain my thirty-fourth year, and already grey and half worried out of my life. *N'importe!* Hard at work all day. Send Birmingham bill off. 18*th.*—To Drury; Gough's oration (Temperance). To Olympic; new piece, *My Wife's Journal;* bad French translation. To club. 19*th.*—Wilson (pianist) and Wilson Ross (essayist) call. 25*th.*—A miserable Christmas Day; not a creature with whom to interchange a pleasant reasonable idea. 26*th.*—Walter, Miller, and self go in private box to Drury Lane to *Jack and Jill;*[2] crowded house, and all goes off admirably. Back in cab, and the dear boy goes gloriously through evening. 27*th.*—Drayton calls in morning and sings hosts of songs; wanting an entertainment done for him. Flaming account of the pantomime in all the papers. Go to town; see *Yellow Dwarf,*[3] a burlesque by Planché, at the Olympic; not his best, but neatly written and carefully got up. Then to club. Hear on my way of

Kemble gave Shakespearean readings at Willis's Rooms. He died November 12th, 1854, aged 79.

[1] Mr. and Mrs. Torrington, Howe and Miss Reynolds; Pollard, Rogers; Sheepshanks, Clark.

[2] E. L. B.'s pantomime, *Jack and Jill;* or, *Harlequin King Mustard and the Four-and-Twenty Blackbirds Baked in a Pie.* Harlequin, Milano columbines, Mlles. Boleno and Ellen Honey; pantaloon, Herr Kohl; sprite, Willikind; clown, Harry Boleno.

[3] F. Robson in the title *rôle,* one of his great parts—Julia St. George, King of the Gold Mines; Miss Marston, Haridan; Miss Bromley, Syrena.

my dear friend Kent's illness. *28th.*—Write notices of Olympic and Sadlers Wells [1] for *Era.* Take Miller to St. James's. *Abon Hassan*,[2] by Talfourd, burlesque; smartly written, but ineffective. *29th.*—Work on 'England and Wales,' completing proofs, and write St. James's notice. Receive from *Era* £1. Drury, first juvenile night; opening at Covent Garden with promenade concerts injuring attendance. Look in at Wells, opening with Payne; by no means realizing the expectations I had formed of it. *30th.*—At home all day poring over newspapers, and wretchedly hipped. Yesterday my friend Woodin was made the papa of a nice little boy. On the same night he opens the *Carpet Bag* at Birmingham. *31st.*—In evening Watkins and his youngest brother come, and we see the Old Year out and the New one in right merrily. All the papers favourable notices."

Total receipts for year, £189.

1855.

" *Monday, Jan. 1st.*—Begin the New Year with a terrible cold. *4th.*—Look in at Wells, and £10 from Greenwood for pantomime. Come home early with purchase of 'Tom Dibdin's Reminiscences.' Read and reflect on the vicissitudes of an author's life. *5th.*—Accident again to the Italian Brothers, and, as I hope, the last of all such exhibitions. *6th.*—Take Walter to Sadlers Wells. *The Rivals* and pantomime of *Forty Thieves.* A very pleasant night; the boy delighted. Great demand for cash in town, and looking anxiously into the future for the prospect of keeping matters square. *8th.*—See Haymarket opening. Stupid, but scenic splendour

---

[1] *Ali Baba and the Forty Thieves*, by W. H. Payne. Nicolo Deulin, Clown; Charles Fenton, Harlequin; Naylor, Pantaloon; Mlle. Nathalie, Columbine.

[2] Or, *The Sleeper Awakened.* The Caliph Haroun Alraschid, J. L. Toole; Miss Marshall, Abon Hassan; Miss Elsworthy doubled the parts of Gulnare and Amine.

great.[1] Entertainment wanted for Miss P. Horton, but decline. *Monday, 15th.*—All day at home on ' England and Wales.' Club. Long chat with Emery, Daly, Lowe, etc. Hear of Angus Reach being mentally paralyzed, poor fellow, and arrange about private theatricals for him. See *Alcestes*,[2] Miss Vandenhoff the heroine. Delighted with the grand old Greek play, Sir Henry Bishop, the composer, presiding.[3] Stop best part of Talfourd's smart burlesque ; then walk home. 18*th.*—Writing theatricals for *Era.* Go to Princess's, but house full and can't get in. Look in at Hopkins's ; meet Cormack, F. Cooke, ' Joe Hayes.' Snowballing the grand amusement outside, and *Louis XI.* the dominant source of attraction within.[4] 19*th.*—De la Motte married again to Miss Caroline Wenlake. *Monday, 22nd.*—All day over ' England and Wales.' At night to Belvidere. See in the *Globe* the death of its Paris correspondent and our old friend Mark Gibbons. 23*rd.*—British Museum for ' England and Wales.' Read *Quarterly Review* at Temple Coffee-house ; capital number. Article on Fire Insurance and Fires (household) very good. At night see Talfourd's smart two-act adapted comedy of *Tit for Tat* at the Olympic.[5] 24*th.*—Club. Happen accidentally to say a good thing ; Tomlins saying À Beckett had a hymn-book before him when writing, remark his wit was to be made a little psalter. 25*th.*—W. Fearman calls in afternoon, acquainting me with the distressing fact of his having been out of a situation for some time. Take him to Sadlers Wells ; give him five shillings

[1] *Little Bo-Peep ; or, Harlequin and the Girl who lost Her Sheep.* Little Bo-Peep, Lydia Thompson ; harlequin, Chapino ; columbine, Mary Brown ; pantaloon, Barnes ; clown, Appleby.

[2] *Alcestes*, adapted from *Euripides* by Henry Spicer, produced at the St. James's. Miss Vandenhoff, Alcestes ; Stuart, Hercules ; Barry Sullivan, Admetus. Glück's music arranged by Mr. Wellington Guernsey. *Abon Hassan* was the Talfourd's burlesque mentioned.

[3] His last public appearance.

[4] Charles Kean, Louis XI. ; Miss Heath, Marie ; Graham, Philip de Comines ; Meadows, Olivier-le-Dain.

[5] From the French *Les Maris me font Rire.* Emery, Frankland ; Robson, Sowerby ; A. Wigan, Thornby ; Clifton, Easy Bolter ; Miss Marshall, Mrs. Frankland ; Miss Bromley, Mrs. Sowerby ; Miss Ellen Turner, Rose.

and a word of hope. 27*th.*—At night to Sadlers Wells ; see last act of *Winter's Tale ;* very well played. Miss Atkinson's Hermione very good.[1] 30*th.*—' England and Wales.' Go to town at night. Amateur performance at St. James's for the Crimean Army Fund.[2] 31*st.*—Arranging old papers, and at night Toole and his brother come to ask me to go to the London Tavern and take the chair on Wednesday next."

" *Feb.* 2*nd.*—Call at *Era* office, and £1 1*s.* paid for past services. Hear of O. Smith's death on Sunday last, his sixty-ninth birthday. Walk back home to write memoir.[3] Again walk into town. Buy Bunn's ' Book of the Stage ' from Lacy for 4*s.* 6*d.*, three vols. 7*th.*—At home till 6 p.m. Then to town, and take the chair at the London Tavern (! ! !), a dinner as a testimonial being given to J. L. Toole. Propose hosts of toasts ; between 100 and 120 present. Sing songs.

[1] Phelps, Leontes ; Barratt, Autolycus ; Ray, Old Shepherd.

[2] *Charles XII., The Honeymoon,* and *The Wandering Minstrel.* The Misses Elsworthy gave their services. House crowded.

[3] Richard John Smith (or O. Smith, as he was generally known, having taken the Christian name after his successful performance of Obi Smith in *Three-fingered Jack*) was born at York in 1786. His mother was a Miss Seracs, an actress of some reputation ; his father treasurer at the Bath Theatre. O. Smith had an adventurous life. He began as a solicitor's clerk, but had a hankering for the stage, of which his parents did not approve, so he shipped himself off to Sierra Leone. In the Gaboon he assisted three slaves to escape, and was severely punished for it. He came back to England ; was pressed for the Navy, but liberated ; and was at last engaged by Mr. Macready at Sheffield as " prompter, painter, and actor of all work, at the liberal salary of 12*s.* a week." Thence he went to Edinburgh for two years, and returned to Bath in 1807, and appeared at the Surrey under Elliston in 1810 ; and it was here he got the name of O. Smith. He was great as Bombastes Furioso, and as Vulcan in *Cupid.* In 1823 he made a great reputation as Zamiel in *Der Freischütz* at Drury Lane. In 1828 he caused the success of *The Bottle Imp* at Covent Garden. He joined Messrs. Yates and Matthews' company soon after they took the Adelphi in 1828, and from that time until his decease remained attached to the fortunes of that theatre. His last original part was in June 1853 in *Geneviève ;* or, *The Reign of Terror.* O. Smith was very tall, had a deep, almost sepulchral voice, and piercing eyes. He was extraordinarily successful in characters of the " uncanny " type. He left behind him a mass of valuable dramatic matters which he had been collecting with a view to publication.

All goes off admirably. Keep it up till after midnight, and then home. *8th.*—Finish *Magazine of Magic*, with W. Fearman's copying, and give him more of the pecuniary. *9th.*—Sell to Lea *Magazine of Magic*, a second copy of book, for two guineas. Go to *Era* office; £1 5*s.* for contributions. *14th.*—Look in at Drury; see two scenes of a farce so bad that it is utterly unendurable—*The Writing on the Shutters.*[1] *16th.*—Bachelorize all day. Pushed hard for cash, and doubtful about the means for the forthcoming spring. *22nd.*—The death of Joseph Hume is announced in paper to have taken place on Tuesday.[2] *24th.*—Last night of the Drury pantomime, and all goes off tremendously. E. T. Smith at Manchester; bought equestrian business. *Monday, 26th.*—Write Toole's song for him. Toole comes at night; arranges matters. Rehearsal of songs with William. Anecdotal evening, and rather late before they retire. Funds at low ebb, and heavy claims on all sides with all my economy. *28th.*—Send off to Toole sketch of song, 'A Norrible Tale.'"[3]

E. L. B. had a great deal of quiet fun in him, and when any one romanced in his presence would often cap his story with something more marvellous. On one occasion some one in the company was descanting on the wonderful instinct of dogs, and cited some ultra-Munchhausen instance. E. L. B. appeared thoroughly to accept the story, and then related one of a dog with which he was

---

[1] George Wild, Corker; Miss Arden, Letty; Miss Love, Fanny Bung.

[2] Joseph Hume, M.P. for Montrose, born 1778, began life as naval surgeon, E. I. Company; was a great Indian scholar, and of great service in Mahratta War, 1803. Left service in 1808; travelled in Spain and Portugal during war, and entered Parliament in 1811 as Member for Weymouth.

[3] [Years after this amusing ditty was introduced by Toole into an Adelphi farce, *The Area Belle*, and became the popular song of the day. It is a great favourite in the provinces to this hour.—C. S.]

intimately acquainted. He was a mongrel terrier of disreputable appearance, but of very knowing air. This canine critic he invariably noticed every Friday scanning the bills of Sadlers Wells (it was during Phelps's *régime*), and noting what was set down for the next night's performance. If it were satisfactory the dog used to wag his very long tail; if he disapproved he turned away expressing his contempt. On the Saturday evening, when so minded, the dog used to contrive to slip by the money and check takers, and secure a position near the front row of the pit. As the play went on, if Toby were satisfied, the tapping of his caudal appendage on the floor could be distinctly heard; a very finely-delivered passage would elicit a low whine of pleasure; at the sallies of a Shakespearean clown he would grin; but should an actor tear his passion to tatters, Toby's resentment and anger would be expressed by a deep and savage growl. Strange to say, the Munchhausen gentleman would scarcely accept E. L. B.'s story as a truthful one.

" *March 2nd.*—Home again all day. The Emperor Nicholas died yesterday morning. *3rd.*—Look in at Drury; see *L'Etoile du Nord;* very much pleased; Bauer good; Drayton admirable. *Monday, 5th.*—To British Museum, and meet Walter and mother in Hall of Antiquities. Adelphi; see admirable drama by Dion Boucicault, *Janet Pride.*[1] *9th.*—Hear from Miller of Charles Perkins having died; another of our early friends gone. *Monday, 12th.*— Scarcity of coin severely felt. *13th.*—On ' England and Wales,' correcting proofs and preparing copy. No cash, no

---

[1] [Was a version of an old French drama, *Marie Jeanne ou la Femme du Peuple.* Ben Webster, Reuben Pride ; Madame Céleste, Selby, and Keeley, all distinguished themselves in the typical Adelphi drama.—C.S.]

health, no nothing.   Last night but three of Sadlers
Wells season.   Want a gladdening gleam of sunshine very
much.   14*th.*—Go to Haymarket; see Coyne's piece of *The
Secret Agent;* not brilliant; Buckstone, Compton, Howe,
W. Farren, *Mrs. C. White (sic), late Mrs. L. S. Buckingham,*
Mrs. Poynter, and Miss E. Chaplin.   Then to club.   Toole
pays £2 for songs.   Phelps' benefit at Sadlers Wells;
Henry VIII. and *Rob Roy;* Phelps the Bailie.   15*th.*—See
Tallis in morning, and receive from him £3 on account.   Go
to British Museum; see Thackeray.   Give copy to printers
Dine at Bedford.   16*th.*—Hear from Lovell Phillips.   Olympic:
Lucky Friday, Alfred Wigan ; and *The Yellow Dwarf and the
King of the Gold Mines;* F. Robson (dwarf, one of his best
characters), Julia St. George, E. Ormonde, Ellen Turner,[1]
Mrs. Bromley, and Mrs. Fitzalan.   Drury Lane : *The Artful
Dodge*[2] goes off wonderfully well.   *Monday,* 19*th.*—Arrange
to let Toole leave his furniture with us while he goes to
Edinburgh.   31*st.*—The amateur performance of pantomime
at Olympic for Angus B. Reach."

" *April* 4*th.*—At British Museum on Part XII. of ' England
and Wales.'   Night to club; take chair.   Interesting system
of mental deduction derived from game of twenty-one
questions; Lowe and Tomlins very clever at it.   Hear of the
death of W. Dunn,[3] the old treasurer of Drury Lane, as having
taken place last night.   *Monday (Easter),* 9*th.*—To Haymarket;
brilliant epigrammatic piece by Planché.   *The New Haymarket
Spring Meeting* 1855.[4]   Afterwards to club.   13*th.*—Write
letters for Barratt to Napoleon and the Empress.   *Monday,*
16*th.*—Great excitement in town ; arrival of the Emperor and

[1] Soon after married Mr. Booth, and retired from the stage.   Her
part, the Desert Fairy, was then played by Miss Fanny Maskell.

[2] E. L. B.'s own.

[3] He was seventy-two years of age, for fifty-six of which he was
officer to the committee of Drury Lane.   He was full of dramatic
anecdote.

[4] Characters : London, Mrs. C. White ; Westminster, Miss Harriet
Gordon ; Belgravia and Tyburnia, Miss Grantham and Mrs. Coe ;
Time, Chippendale ; Lord Mayor's Fool, Buckstone ; City of London
Theatre, Coe ; Standard Theatre, Miss Schott ; Britannia Saloon,
Miss Lavine ; Eagle Tavern, Clark.

Empress of the French. 19*th*.—The Emperor's visit to the City; all London in a ferment. 26*th*.—The treasury exhausted. Thoroughly knocked up with weary walk after the possibles—or, seemingly, the impossibles. The electric telegraph laid down to Balaclava direct, so as to get news from Sebastopol within twenty-four hours! 27*th*.—Scribbling little matters for Woodin all day, and at night to town to appointment with him. He engages Mr. Popham (Dr. Daniel's secretary) for managing man. Give him receipt for *Olio of Oddities* (£50), and receive from him on fresh account £10. Charles Tallis pays £5 on account of Part XI. 28*th*.—To Haymarket; Sims Reeves, *Fra Diavolo*. Club; Sala, Daly, etc.; pay subscription, 5*s*., for the year to June next. 30*th*.—All day on 'England and Wales.' No sleep again at night; vivid memories of the past, and live through-out the night on life embracing the most thrilling fanciful periods of the last fifteen years. Sir Henry Bishop dies, aged seventy-five." [1]

" *May* 1*st*.—May opens with a bright full moon and cloudless sky, blossoming of the buds of nature and of hope. A day of dreamy retrospection and of wonderful romance. C. C. B., after eleven years, from the 10th April, 1844, again encountered, and magical memories of the bygone. Lovely moonlight night, and long walk home. Mystic butterfly expansion and flight. 2*nd*.—Off to town after writing memoir of Bishop. See Barratt; revival of old

[1] Born in London, 1780. Early showed talent for music. Was placed under tuition of Francesco Bianchi, and at fifteen wrote music for several ballets. *The Circassian Bride*, his first opera, was produced at Drury Lane, February 23rd, 1809, the night before the theatre was burnt down and the score destroyed. In 1810 was engaged as musical director of Covent Garden, which position he held till 1824. From 1811 to 1830 he either wrote the operas or the necessary music, additional and arrangement, to operas, etc., of sixty-seven pieces, all produced at Covent Garden; in 1831, *The Romance of a Day;* in 1834, *Manfred;* in 1840, *The Fortunate Isles;* besides other works for various theatres, etc. He was director and conductor of Philharmonic Society, and professor of harmony and composition R.A.M. He was made B.M. Oxford in 1839, and professor there 1848, and was knighted, a then unprecedented honour, in 1842.

memories, and retrospective enjoyment. To club; intensely jovial by force of re-action, songs galore; Leigh Murray and his brothers (Edward and Garstin) there ; both sing very well. I give three songs—the exuberance of spirits—and walk home at 2.30 a.m. *3rd.*—Another delightful day of dreamy retrospection and romance, C. C. B. (Orphan Working School, Hampstead). First visit; association thereafter. Tales of the past and confessions of the heart. Railway to Kingsland ; dreary walk home. Changes and chances. Exquisite lines by convolution; title for drama, *Cadetta ;* or, *The Story of a Life.* Here, if God gives me strength of health and intellect to fulfil my plans, do I solemnly pledge myself to its completion, for the sake of one who is ——. *4th.*—To town ; dreaming more than ever. At night to Haymarket; see new piece, *The Actress of Padua ;*[1] very good, and piece successful. Tomlins with me; house crowded. Hear of romance of Oxenford : loved a fair creature, death, agony of heart, reaction, first that came, equivocal union beneath him, and another story of life's trials. *5th.*—The imagination still in thrall. Dreamy day, and night of dreams. *Monday, 7th.* —On Woodin's business preparatory to the opening ; have dinner with him and Huline the clown (odd association), and at night to Albert Smith's ; delighted with entertainment. Sleep at Haymarket (Woodin's). *12th.*—Off to town ; intensely excited. First night of Woodin's *Olio of Oddities ;* it goes off wonderfully well, under all the disadvantages ; Oxenford and all the press folks there ; place crammed, and £12 in cash taken. *Monday, 14th.*—Capital notices of Woodin's in all the papers. At night to Polygraphic Hall ; assist as much as possible. At club; long chat with Spencer, who had been present at some remarkable manifestations of spiritual presence. Walk home late, pondering over the marvellous experiences of the now thoroughly converted chemist. *15th.*—To Olympic for *Era.* See admirable three-act comedy by Tom Taylor, called *Still Waters Run Deep ;*[2]

---

[1] *The Actress of Padua,* taken from Victor Hugo's "Angelo." Tisbe the actress, Miss Cushman ; Catarina, Miss Reynolds ; Angelo, Howe ; Rodolfo, W. Farren ; Omeida, Rogers ; Tasca, E. Villiers ; Anafesta, Braid. Had been a success in America.

[2] First performance : Alfred Wigan, John Mildmay ; George Vining,

a powerfully constructed piece; highly successful. Dr.
Kirkwood's congratulations; and, though dull, dreary day,
glad to find success procuring notice from the upper ten
thousand. 18*th.*—Shocked by visit from Charles Ball, old
editor of *Weekly Times*, telling me he is utterly destitute.
Monday, 21*st.*—At night to Woodin's; first night of his
imitations of Russell, Smith, clown, etc. To club; Henry
Hartley, of Stratford, in town, and a song or two in consequence.
23*rd.*—Take Walter into town. Find St. Paul's occupied by
Sons of the Clergy. Give Woodin verse naming Derby winner.
Then club; and with Marston look in at Drury; Vauxhall-
like masquerade. All the Sons of the Clergy there. 28*th.*—
Arranging copy for 'England and Wales;' not much done.
A delightfully delirious dream about my dear C——. Wild
and exquisitely dreamy imaginations. 29*th.*—Mrs. Woodin
and Miss Clifford Clifton call; the latter young lady, five
years at Princess's, reads Macbeth, and promising actress."

"*June* 1*st.*—Take boat to Chelsea; wander dreamily round
Barossa Place; see the old house to let. Meet no one I
know. Walk back through park to Warwick Square. At
night to Canterbury Hall, Lambeth, large concert room
holding upwards of 1,200 people.[1] 2*nd.*—Day of great
excitement and strange adventure. Letter from Hastings;
St. Katherine's Docks, European steamer from Limerick.
4*th.*—More troubles! Bothers increasing! Go to town;
dreamy and much perplexed. Poor mother annoyed last
night. 5*th.*—To British Museum for Part XV. of 'England
and Wales.' Correct proofs. 6*th.*—*Era*, and receive 10*s.*
Lounge in balcony; get more dreamy, thinking of many
painful matters and some pleasant ones. 8*th.*—Mother's

Captain Hawksley; S. Emery, Potter; Danvers, Dunbilk; Miss Maskell,
Mrs. Mildmay; Mrs. Melfort, Mrs. Hector Sternhold.

[1] [This was the first of the Music Halls due to the enterprise and
energy of Charles Morton, for many years manager of the Alhambra.
An ordinary sing-song in a tavern parlour developed into a handsome
Music Hall for the people, with a picture gallery that cost thousands
of pounds. Charles Morton's original and excellent idea was frustrated
by the iniquitous theatrical licensing laws. What is being done now
in 1891, viz.: freedom in amusements was conceived by Charles Morton
in 1855.—C. S.]

birthday. Walk in morning to Highbury by New River; home; dreamy and speculative, heart and head enthralled. Look in at Drury, *Barbiere di Siviglia*; see two acts—well done. *9th.*—Day dreamed away. To club, and chat with Talfourd about pieces in prospective. *11th.*—Mrs. Stanley calls, and tearfully entreats me to start her daughter with an entertainment to America. I yield to her persuasive eloquence. At night to Olympic; see *Garrick Fever* revival (F. Robson, Emery, Danvers, White Rivers, Mrs. Fitzalan, Miss Stephens, Miss Ternan). Handsome present from Talfourd of books—extravaganzas. Hear of new play by John Saunders at the Haymarket not being a great success.[1] *12th.* —To Standard (Wright and Paul Bedford there), and to City of London (Charles Mathews, supported by Miss Eliza Arden in his round of characters during engagement in *Game of Speculation, Patter* versus *Clatter, Used Up, Comical Countess, Take that Girl away*, etc. Charles M. has £500 for the month, paid by Johnson and Nelson Lee to E. T. Smith, from whom C. M. was farmed. *18th.*—To Woodin's, Drury Lane; chat with Smith. Wandering through the streets semi-drenched, and unable anywhere to screw my courage to the adhesive point. *19th.*—F. Tallis a bankrupt, Woodin not doing more than paying expenses, and nothing doing anywhere. *20th.*—Off to town with Walter; spend day at Woodin's, and take him to entertainment in evening at Willis's Rooms to hear a Miss Jay—mesmeric trance, speaking medium; nothing in it, all very bad. *21st.*— See stupid slangy burlesque of *Cherry and Fair Star*.[2] *25th.* —Letter from C. C. B., and answer. *27th.*—Woodin calls, and we go to private box at St. James's; French plays; Levassor, clever comedian in the Charles Mathews school,

---

[1] *Love's Martyrdom*, play in five acts, "*quasi*-Elizabethan in tone," and bearing some resemblance to *The Hunchback.* Barry Sullivan, Franklyn; Howe, Laneham; W. Farren, Clarence Franklyn; Leighton, Walter Freelove; Miss Helen Faucit, Margaret; Miss Ada Swanborough, Julia; Miss A. Vining, Hester; Mrs. Poynter, Bertha (an old nurse). Messrs. Cullenford, Rogers, Braid, Coe, Clark, Miss Schott, etc., were also included in the cast.

[2] Author, C. J. Collins. Miss Rebecca Isaacs, Cherry; Miss Fanny Beaumont, Fair Star; Mr. Shalders, Hassenbad; Miss Somers, Pompey. Music, good, by W. H. Montgomery.

supported by Mdlle. Teissière. *28th.*—To British Museum for 'England and Wales.' Not at all well, and far from happy. Oppressed by the surplus population that I have to provide for, and means getting apparently less every day. *30th.*—Household expenditure increasing. To Sadlers Wells; Printers' Dramatic Society plays *School for Scandal.* Walk home with Leslie (age twenty-four); find him an enthusiastic lover of poetry, and improves on acquaintance. Intelligence of Lord Raglan's death in the evening papers of to-night." [1]

" *Monday, July 2nd.*—Remonstrance from C. C. B.; wishes to be fraternal for the future, but nothing more. *14th.*—To town, and see Emma Stanley, and receive on account of entertainment £5. *16th.*—Book hunting for C. C. B. Look in at Strand; bad house; *Wonderful Woman* (Mr. Charles Vincent, Misses Cleveland and Bulwer). Farren's benefit at Haymarket, and last appearance on stage. Played scene from *Lord Ogleby.* [2] *18th.*—Evening dull and dreamy, and myself ditto. Thoughts involuntarily turning towards what might have been. *19th.*—Chat with Meek anent Bacon, Sidney, Marvel, and our choice English spirits. *23rd.*—Heraud's play of *Wife and No Wife* produced this evening at Haymarket.[3] *25th.*—Go to town; disappointed much in cash

[1] He died at 8.35 p.m. June 28th, 1855.

[2] The house was crowded. Miss Helen Faucit appeared as King René's daughter; Mr. and Mrs. and Miss M. Keeley played the leading parts in *A Moving Tale;* Mme. Celeste, Mr. B. Webster, Mr. Selby and Mr. G. Cooke in first act of *Flying Colours;* Sims Reeves sang " Bay of Biscay " and "Death of Nelson;" Perea Nena danced; Albert Smith sang "Galignani's Messenger." The item of the afternoon was the second act of *The Clandestine Marriage,* with Mr. W. Farren as Lord Ogleby (the character in which he first made his name); A. Wigan, Canton; Chippendale, Sir John Sterling; W. Farren, jun., Brush. The curtain fell on a wonderful performance, considering all things, and rose again to show the veteran actor, who was too moved to be able to speak, supported by Buckstone and Harley, who embraced his old companion, and they were surrounded by every actor and actress of note. After this Mrs. Stirling, Leigh Murray, and Compton appeared in *Where there's a Will there's a Way,* and Harley and Buckstone in *Box and Cox,* and the programme concluded with a ballet by the Spanish Dancers.

[3] *Wife and No Wife,* by J. A. Heraud, original play, illustrating the

matters. Look in at Strand with Miller; see execrable piece, *Flitch of Bacon;* or, *The Custom of Dunmow.* The only thing noticeable was a good morris-dance that was introduced, and excellent *danseuse*, Mademoiselle Julie, who imitated in a marvellous manner the style of Perea Nena. 28*th.*—Club, and walk home with Deane the artist."[1]

" *Aug.* 2*nd.*—More dreamy than ever; domestically upset. Write account of Princess's[2] and Olympic, closing for season, and take them to *Era.* Dreamy, very. A double event to-day; C. C. B.'s birthday, and her daughter born on the same day—an old anniversary commemorated in the birthday of my heart. 11*th.*—Take W. F. to concert room, Green Gate; very stupid place, and full and noisy. Suggestion for article. *Monday,* 13*th.*—Having smoked opiumized cigars preceding night experience curious results therefrom. 14*th.*—All day on ' England and Wales,' stirring not from desk till 9 p.m. Hear from nobody, and wrote to ' somebody.' Beautiful weather; like to be by the sea amazingly. 15*th.*—Attend first meeting of contributors to *Comic Times* at the house of Edmund Yates in 43, Doughty Street—Broughs, Sala, Cuthbert Bede, Hale, McConnell, and Bennett. 17*th.*—Go to club; meet Leigh Murray, who leaves Adelphi on 29th Sept. 23*rd.*—Quite upset this week entirely through money matters. Heart broken, and dull and dizzy beyond conception even of thought. *Monday,* 27*th.*—

state of the marriage law in the reign of Queen Anne; a well written and constructed drama. In it Miss Edith Heraud, the daughter of the author, made a most favourable *début* as Olympia; Howe, Pierrepoint (a villain); Barry Sullivan, Lord Osmond (very powerful in a mad scene); W. Farren, Sir Frank Clive (a sort of careless, gay, good-for-nothing City knight); Miss Swanborough, Clarisse; Miss Ellen Chaplin, Dorie.

[1] A delightful and accomplished gentleman, who has been associated with the history of the Arundel Club from its commencement. He has the genuine critical faculty, and a conversation with Deane is in itself an education.—C. S.

[2] Specialities of the season : *Louis XI., Jealous Wife,* and *Henry VIII* The only failure Douglas Jerrold's drama, *The Heart of Gold.* Olympic Specialities : *Yellow Dwarf, Still Waters Run Deep,* revival. of *School for Scandal,* and of *Robert Macaire* for Emery.

All day at *Seven Ages of Woman.*[1] *29th.*—Horribly hard up! Waiting for Tallis. Wrote a little of entertainment. To Drury Lane ; see James Anderson as Rob Roy.[2] Chat with Smith about pantomime. Such lovely seasidish weather ; oh for the south coast ! *30th.*—Send to Tallis again without avail. Lovely weather, too—so provoking. At night to Adelphi : revival of *Victorine ;* or, *I'll Sleep On It.*[3] Mrs. Leigh Murray very good as heroine. Write worse than ever ; old memories revived by it. Meet Ryder, who is off to Paris ; whilst I wish—— Oh ! don't I ? "

" *Sept.* 3rd.—Smith sends cheque for £2 2s. for posters, African twins,[4] and book ; write former. *7th.*—Drury ; see finale of *Slave* and a little bit of the *Mountain Sylph.* *8th.*— Up early, and see my dear mother off to Hastings. *Monday,* 10th.—Mrs. and Miss Stanley call, and pay balance of entertainment ; I give former receipt for £20. Look in at Regent. News arrives of the south side of Sebastopol being in our possession. *11th.*—At night to Sadlers Wells ; see *Rob Roy,* Marston the Rob and Phelps the Bailie ; exceedingly good. Thoughts wandering to the destination of to-morrow, the chance of leaving London for the seaside presenting itself at last. *12th.*—Off for south coast ; London Bridge Station at two. Arrive at five, and go direct to Old Swan Inn in Hastings. Tea, and thence to the heart's Agapemone ; happiness and home beyond my hopes. Thrilling meeting ; stroll by starlight by the beach. Old times and old loves recalled ; the attachment of sixteen years found not to have

[1] For Emma Stanley.

[2] Helen Macgregor, Mrs. J. W. Wallack ; the Bailie, Barratt ; Dougal Halford, Rashleigh ; Osbaldistone, Stuart ; Francis Osbaldistone, Herberte ; Major Galbraith, Hamilton Braham ; Diana Vernon, Miss de Lanza. Sir Henry Bishop's music.

[3] Leigh Murray, Alexandre ; Miss Woolgar, Elise ; Wright, Blaise ; Paul Bedford, Bonassus ; Charles Selby, Chanteloupe.

[4] These were two negro children, Milly and Christina, five years old, " united at lower part of their backs by a fleshy ligature, sixteen inches in circumference." Were first seen at a private exhibition for the satisfaction of the Medical Profession and Press in the Saloon of Drury Lane Theatre. They were very happy and cheerful, and fortunately agreed well together. Were afterwards exhibited at the Egyptian Hall.

abated one jot of warmth; fidelity yet in the world. At
night rest in the Temple of Thought, in her room, which
had been given up for my use. Little sleep in consequence of the delicious reveries indulged in. Awakened
early in the morning by her voice. 13*th.*—Rain, and home
amusements. Clears up in the afternoon; visit St. Clement's
caves lit up; cut out of sandstone rocks; niece, Polly, and
mamma my companions. At night East Cliff and the life-
boat; talking on through the twilight into the starlight;
confessions of the heart; 'Godolphin'—the stars of the past
and of the future. Music; ''Twere vain to tell thee all I
feel,' 'My Fairest, my Fondest.' Domestic enjoyment of the
highest and most refined character. Continual evidence of
attention, and the floodgates of old sympathies pouring forth
all its gushing happiness over the almost crushed heart of
the dreamer. Vivid pictures recalled of the olden times.
14*th.*—Visitors arrive. Morning stroll by the beach; Oliver
the boatman. *Water Lily*, regatta, wins prize. Little Cupid
in the Temple. Afterwards Carina on the Marina, and
delightful walk to St. Leonards. More of the past recalled;
of Chelsea, our first trysting-place; of Richmond of 1842,
and of the fatal year of separation; the history of a heart.
Music again at night—old songs that were wont to be heard
in the days of yore; and the clocks strike 2 a.m. before we
all separate. 15*th.*—To Fairlight by water in Oliver's boat,
the *Lively.* 'Alone, alone on the trysting-stone; alone with
that dearly beloved one.' The Glen, the Lover's Seat; happiness shared; the fullest enjoyment of a bright, cloudless day
on the greensward overlooking the sea for hours entranced.
Back through the old town by dusk. Tea on our return,
and most delightful termination to the most enjoyable day I
ever had in my life; the realization of all that my early youth
dreamed of, and time makes at last a recompense for the
sorrows and sufferings of the past; regrets repaid by atone-
ment, but the separation already dreaded more and more.
Monday, 17*th.*—Morning by beach, and dreamy lounging
along the shore. The Rev. Mr. Wood arrives; we fraternize.
Beautiful cloudless weather. At night long and deeply
emotional *tête-à-tête*—the wedding of the souls. Still in that
shrine of Carina's above; the last look and last touch at

night, and again awakened in the morning by her call. Midst all the happiness of the time the dread of breaking the spell still before me. Delightful dreams all night. 18*th.*—On the Marina; meet Mr. Latimer Clarke, his wife, and father. All go to Fairlight, the marked association of old spots; scamper across the cliffs with Polly. The French coast seen with telescope, the Ulex Europa (? botanical). Ecclesbourne Glen, its fine beach; reminded of old companionship at every step. Nine years ago visited this same spot—coastguard station—thinking solus and solely of one who afterwards shares the prospects with me. Time's changes! 19*th.*—Dip into sea, first time; persuade Mr. Wood to join in the immersion; ludicrous incident. Castle Gardens. At night Louisa B. packs up and leaves for Horncastle. Again, evening of exquisite happiness; Paradise regained, the heart still young as ever. Time has touched but lightly the inner woman, and to me not made change visible in the outer. Late to bed, and awakened early by call from Carina. 20*th.*—At 5 a.m. wander through the footpaths towards Hollington; beautiful green lanes, traversed with the most enchanting and fascinating of companions; then to St. Leonards by 8 a.m., and breakfast. A solitary pilgrimage at noon to the trysting stone, and memories thereof. Rest in boat. Dip again, and catch cold; but afternoon of music, and evening of exquisite happiness renewed. Loathe more and more to tear myself away from the circle of enchantment by which I am surrounded; but duty calls me from Paradise to Purgatory! 21*st.*—About all day by beach and shore, dreamy and smiling blandly like Malvoisin; unable to do more than revel in reveries, and spend the hours of sunshine in fairy-like enjoyment of happy mental visions. At night French games, and much amusement therefrom. More happiness by ourselves in conversation intellectual. Very late again. 22*nd.*—Notwithstanding mutual severity of colds, in afternoon boat on water. Shelley's fugitives one ' boat-cloak did cover.' Sunset glorious. Hearts plighted, united, delighted; ' the world forgetting, by the world forgot; ' the union of thoughts, hearts, and sentiments. In evening album presentation, and lines written therein. 24*th.*—Up at five again to see Mr. Wood off. Day rendered sadder by my own approximate leave-taking. Revisit all the old localities so endeared to me, and bid a silent farewell to the sea for this year. Lonely, desolate feelings stealing over me—the awakening from idealities to realities—'The Icy Veil.' *25th.*—The dream terminates. Will it ever come back again? Tear myself reluctantly away. Presentation Pietas ; thoughtful souvenirs at parting. The adieu ; the sunset vividly radiant over the old town and its beauties. Return by 5 p.m. train ; the dream of happiness over. Vividly moonlight evening, and rapid railway transit. Reaching home, find W. F. at supper, and myself anxiously expected. Dreamy retrospections all the while. *26th.*—Answering hosts of letters. What the future has in store for me is a subject of fearful interest. Worried and flurried by these matters and others beyond measure. Wretchedly sad and unsettled, suffering from the reaction of the pleasant days just passed. *27th.*—'England and Wales' copy gone on with; *Era* notices written. Souvenirs C. C. B. Heart in agitation, and hand and head too. Still dwelling on the past. 'Godolphin' seems at home. Feverish dreams at night, and very far from well in mind or body. *28th.*—At night see, at Sadlers Wells, one act of *Lady of Lyons;* Miss (Mrs.) Eburne, Pauline ; promising actress. Chat with Heraud."

" *Oct.* 2*nd.*—Send off to Woodin, who pays £10. Then to Sadler's Wells with Quillinan. See *Tempest*[1] admirably played ; Barratt excellent as Caliban. *3rd.*—Hear of W. Gaspey, poor fellow, becoming insane. God grant my intellects may remain clear to the last, though they have been severely tried. *4th.*—C. C. B. at Dublin, and undying memories eternally ring in my mind. The past, not the future, are links to bind us. *8th.*—First night of Drury ; opening for the winter season. *Nitocris,*[2] the Egyptian play ;

[1] Phelps, Prospero ; H. Marston, Alonzo ; Lunt, Antonio ; F. Robinson, Ferdinand ; T. C. Harris, Gonzalo ; Lewis Ball, Trinculo ; Ray, Stephan ; Miss Eburne, Miranda ; Miss Hughes, Ariel.

[2] *Nitocris* was written by E. Fitzball. Mesphra, Edgar ; Amenophis, Stuart ; Tihrak, Barry Sullivan ; Kœphed, Miss Anderton ; Cuzar, George Wild ; Ophan, Worrell ; Moscar, Robertson ; Sesostris, Swan; the Dark Warrior, W. Vincent ; Kaphona, Miss Cleveland ; Oran,

theatre crammed to excess. *9th.*—To Lovell Phillips, and arrange for £3 for songs. Dine at Woodin's. *10th.*—Charles Mathews appears at Drury in *Married for Money;*[1] brilliant reception, house crowded. Meet Watkins and Oxenford. *11th.*—At night to Euston Square to meet C. C. B. from Dublin. Etty companion. Chat till late, 10.45 train. Memories, and discussing presentation of the shamrock, and legend of the missing leaf. Struggles between love and duty, and latter victorious after severe contest. *12th.*— Early with Carina in town. Curious articles in *Advertiser* about spiritual manifestations. *13th.*—Town early; see C. C. B. South coast, Croydon, King's Arms, Etty with us. Dreams of the future dark and over-clouded; retrospections vivid and brilliant. Back at eight. See William Beverley at Drury Lane, and chat about pantomime. *20th.*—Call at Lovell Phillips'. Come back with pocket full of toys, souvenirs of Fairlight. Invitation to Doughty Street to see Edmund Yates. Arrange for share in new monthly magazine, *The Planet,* and to subscribe £10 by December. To Olympic, first night of season, *School for Scandal,*[2] and new farce by Coyne called *Catching a Mermaid* (F. Robson, Luffins a Showman). *Monday, 22nd.*—Town early, and see Tallis; £5 on account for Parts XVII. and XVIII. To Willoughby, and very long chat about new work. Home expenses increasing.

Laporte; Grand Hierophant, Younge; Seer of the Pyramids, Templeton; Nitocris, Miss Glyn; Urania, Mrs. Selby; Amanthe, Miss De Vere. Miss Rosina Wright was the dancer. The scenery was something wonderful, and the lavishness of the expenditure on the production had never been equalled. It will be remembered that a play of the same name, written by Miss Clo. Graves, was produced at Drury Lane, Nov. 2nd, 1887, with Miss Sophie Eyre in the title *rôle,* and Mr. J. H. Barnes as Hedaspes—the character most answering to Tihrak, for there was little similarity in the plots.

[1] *Married for Money,* an adaptation of Poole's *The Wealthy Widow,* or, *They're Both to Blame,* first played at Drury Lane, Oct. 27th, 1827. Charles Mathews, Mopus; Mrs. Frank Mathews, Mrs. Mopus; Miss M. Oliver, Matilda; R. Roxby, Rob Royland; A. Younge, Sir Robert Mellowboy. The Lyceum Company had been engaged by E. T. Smith, and played this as a first piece to *Nitocris.*

[2] *Rentrée* of Mrs. Stirling as Lady Teazle; Emery, Sir Peter; G. Vining, Charles Surface; Mrs. Wigan, Mrs. Candour; Alfred Wigan Joseph Surface,

Death of Sir William Molesworth at noon to-day, aged forty-five.[1] 23rd.—*Comical Times* copy. Meet at Round Table, off St. Martin's Lane, Sala, the Broughs, Draper, Yates, Oxenford Hall, Bennett (the Owl), and Bridgeman; then to Woodin's with most of them, being the anniversary of his third year's *début.* Albert Smith proposes Woodin's health, and Brough answers; very merry, and all jolly. Leave at 4 a.m. with Heraud, Yates, and Sala; all perfectly right, and no evil effects therefrom next day. 25th.—Write drama for *Era* and little pars. for *Comic Times.* 26th.—Meet Yates, Sala, and the Broughs at Round Table. Suggest title of the *Train* for first-class magazine. Yates leaving for Brighton. 27th.—Take Walter to Phillips' to spend day, and to Camden Town to spend week with mother. On ' England and Wales; ' much worried about Drury pantomime. At night to town. Frank Matthews at Princess's.[2] New piece at Haymarket;[3] latter, by Mrs. Lovell, unsuccessful. 31st.—Go into Olympic pit to hear Robson sing ' Country Fair,' in *Catching a Mermaid;* wonderful achievement."

" *Nov. 1st.*—Give mother private box for Drury; Walter with her. Write notice of Drury for *Era.* To Adelphi; see farce of *The Hundred Pound Note,*[4] very wretchedly acted. *2nd.*—Write account of Adelphi for *Era,* and receive

[1] Born May 23rd, 1810. Was member for Cornwall and Southwark and Secretary for Colonies. [He was the guardian and patron of Tom Hood the Younger, and was the means of sending him to Pembroke College, Oxford.—C. S.]

[2] Very affectionately received. Appeared as Cropin in *The Wonderful Woman.* David Fisher, the Marquis de Frontignac. *The Critic* was also played. Frank Mathews, Sir Fretful Plagiary; Walter Lacy, Puff; Cooper, Sneer; Mrs. Winstanley, Tilburina; Harley, Meadows. H. J. Turner also in the cast.

[3] *The Beginning of the End,* by Mrs. Lovell, authoress of *Ingomar,* very doleful. Chippendale, Joel Lambert; Howe, Mat Hall; Miss Cushman, Hester Lambert (too rugged). Rogers, Hoffman, Clark, Coe, and Mrs. Poynter also in the cast.

[4] *The Hundred Pound Note* was originally produced at Covent Garden, February 7th, 1827, with the following cast :—Jones, Montmorency; Blanchard (E. L. B.'s father), Morgan; Bartley, Janus; Power (who was lost in the *President*), O'Shaughnessy; Keeley, Billy Black; Mrs. Davenport, Lady Pedigree; Madame Vestris, Miss Harriet

therefrom £1 for contributions. Expenses get awful, and receipts very precarious. *3rd.*—Begin third scene of pantomime. Feel to have lost the power of concentration; thoughts wandering more than ever. Letters from everybody with orders for pieces and articles that I shall be unable to accomplish, I fear. *6th.*—Busy on Drury Lane pantomime; finish it at 9 a.m., and read it to Charles Mathews, who receives me in the most courteous and considerate manner. Roxby, Smith, and Boleno all delighted. Receive from Smith £10 for pantomime. *7th.*—To town at night; Adelphi; revival of *Valentine and Orson*,[1] first time for eleven years. *8th.*—All day writing a little paragraph about Adelphi. At night to Sadler's Wells; see *Comedy of Errors;*[2] very cleverly played. *9th.*—Lord Mayor's day; very quiet procession. From *Era* 18s. Work on ' England and Wales,' and write to C. C. B. Bachelorizing and dreamy as usual. *10th.*—All day at home setting study to rights and reading. At night to Drury; see *Critic;* very well played. *Monday, 12th.*—All day writing song for Phillips, fifth of Mendelssohn's, *The Twilight Hour;* send it. Letter from C. C. B. Meet Daly at club, and talk about ruralities of country life. Earl, the canine painter, and the mysteries of supernaturalism discussed. *16th.*—To Camden Town for carpet bag. Start at 2 p.m. for Hastings. C. C. B. The meeting, the memory, the evening of quiet domestic enjoyment, the night of the

Arlington; Mrs. Faucit, Mrs. Arlington. Keeley's catch phrase, " D'ye give it up? " was caught up by the town ; and Mme. Vestris's " Buy a Broom " song, which she sang as a Bavarian broom-girl, was hummed by every one ; the actress in the character was painted, and modelled in plaster, and sold everywhere. The farce then achieved a run. It did not go at the Adelphi. Keeley resumed his old character, his daughter Mary took Mme. Vestris's, T. G. Shore (his London *débul* favourable) Blanchard's, Hudson Power's, and Bland Bartley's. The " Buy a Broom " song, though excellently sung, was but little applauded

[1] Burlesque by Albert Smith. Mrs. and Mr. Keeley in their original parts; also Eliza Arden as Agatha; Kate Kelly, Oberon Miss Wyndham, Miss Farebrother's part of Princess Eglantine ; Paul Bedford, King Pippin ; James Bland, Henry ; R. Romer, Hanfray; Garden, the Green Knight ; C. J. Smith, the Bear.

[2] Antipholus of Ephesus, F. Robinson ; of Syracuse, H. Marston ; the two Dromios, Lewis Ball and Charles Fenton ; Barratt, Ægeon ; Miss Eburne, Adriana ; Miss Travers, Luciana.

covenant, halcyon hours of happiness, and old dreams realized. Delight of all to see me, and cosy fireside chat about old times and new emotions. The pangs of the past more than atoned for, and all that life can give of the highest happiness experienced. 17*th*.—To the sea in morning with Polly on shore, age nearly sixteen. Thoughtfulness of arrangements as marked as ever. The crisis of my fate apparently approaching. Who would have prognosticated this same, no matter how many years before? Very pleasant party at night; an agreeable Mr. Atkins introduced. An hour by starlight on the beach, and then the dear old songs sung by those dear old lips with eternal youth upon them. 19*th*.— Morning to East Beach; herring-boats coming in and prodigality of fish. Back at noon. Long and happy chat with the never-to-be-forgotten one. Leave the paradise of my present existence at 5 p.m., and seen off by my dear devoted Carina. Arrive in town once again by ten, and write this after midnight in my own old study, with memories of the bygone around me floating fancifully past. 21*st*.—Fetch Walter from Camden Town. Take him to Sadlers Wells; see *Hamilton of Bothwellhaugh*,[1] and pleased with Marston as Cyril Baliol the priest, and delighted with the first and fourth acts. 24*th*.—All day in the midst of this conflicting tumult of feelings; write a comic scene for Sadlers Wells, the first yet done. 26*th*.—Writing introduction scene for Sadler's Wells, second comic scene and scraps for Howe. Letter to C. C. B. How it will all end a source of intense anxiety. Endeavour to drown reflection and feel it hopeless. The past, if it could but be recalled, might change this earth into a heaven for me; and now every day is a scene of mental torture and heartfelt agony. 27*th*.—Write comic scene for Wells, but heart very sad. Consult at night with Greenwood; but my thoughts wandering far hence, and my heart going thither too. *Midsummer Night's Dream* revived at Wells. Rose Edouin a clever Puck. 30*th*.—

---

[1] A five-act historical play by Selous. Phelps, Hamilton; F. Robinson, the Regent Murray; Miss Margaret Eburne, Margaret, wife of Hamilton. Founded on the period between escape of Mary from Lochleven and assassination of Murray. Not a very great success.

King of Sardinia arrives, and illuminations in his honour.
A meteor flashes across London."

" *Dec. 1st.*—To Campbell's, and meet Val Morris ; have
piece to look over, then dine at Campbell's ; Beale, etc.
Home to my study; read ' Little Dorrit.' *4th.*—Montgomery
dies, aged forty-eight ; introduced to him by Maunder in '54·
5th.—To, Drury, and see *Used Up*, and farce by Oxenford from
the French, *Eight Pounds Reward*, at the Olympic. Try
comic scene for *Drury Annual.* *6th.*—Write theatricals
for *Era*, and part of comic scene for Drury. Mystified and
dreamy about the seaside visit. Receive from Hastings for
Mechanics' Institute for lecture, per C. C. B., £1. See Smith
of Drury, and receive balance of £10 for pantomime. Thinking of to-morrow's journey ; see Charles Mathews, and 10*s.*
from *Era.* *8th.*—Off by 5.30 train, and reach St. Leonards
at 9.15. Stroll along beach ; the meeting and the proposal.
Meet Mr. Harry Gee; songs and convivialities. *Monday,*
10th.—Leave by 10 train for Brighton ; 3.30 to town, journey
short, with C. C. B. Camden Town ; the long journey to-
morrow ; domestic evening with mother and C. C. B. Sleep
there, and read ' Ivy Veil.' Emma Stanley comes out at St.
Martin's Hall with *Seven Ages of Women*, afterwards spoken
of as great success. Breach of contract. *11th.*—See C. C. B.
to Dublin. My birthday—thirty-five ! Unusual celebration
long remembered. *12th.*—Write last comic scene for Drury
and Wells. Pass W. Farren into Wells. Write to Toole
about the Stanley affair. Capital notice in *Times* of Emma
Stanley. *13th.*—Receive from Greenwood for Sadler's Wells
pantomime £10. Prepare copy for ' England and Wales ; '
at night to Drury with materials for pantomime. To Drury,
and see *Patter* versus *Clatter*, with Mathews's wonderful
impersonation. Meet Ward, of Bedford Head, about writing
book for Mr. Nicholson, proprietor of Shotley Bridge (Northumberland) Ironworks, and arrange for interview next day·
14th.—Dine with Mr. Nicholson, Sir Charles Fitzpatrick, and
Mr. Weldon, railway contractor, at Reunion. Goes off very
well ; tell him pamphlet, printing and all, will not cost more
than £100. Arrange to go down in February to Shotley, and
stop a month with him. Meet Phillips and Tomlins, who

have been dining with Smith and Mr. Fladgate, the Drury
secretary to committee, Dunn's successor. Hear they have
spoken very kindly and very complimentarily about me. 15*th*.
—Receive £2 19*s*., balance of Part XIX., from Tallis. 17*th*.—
Weather cold, and *plaid* a great comfort—associated with
agreeable memories. Expenses increasing at a frightful rate.
18*th*.—A thorough invalid. Trying to make out Drury playbill.
Give Malcolm some copy for the *Observer*. The poet Rogers
died this morning, aged ninety-six.[1] 21*st*.—Finish pantomime plots for *Era*, and to town ; receive from E. T. S. the
last £5 for pantomime. Spend evening with him at Van
Buren's. 24*th*.—Go to Strand and see first performance of
pantomime, *Black-eyed Susan*, with Talfourd in private
box.[2] Then to club; spend Christmas Eve with Brough
and a few convivial members ; bowls of punch, and con-
viviality and jocularity. Home, and find lamp, a present
from Herbert Watkins. 26*th*.—Mother arrives, and we go
in cab to Drury with Walter. *Hey Diddle Diddle ;* or,
Harlequin King Nonsense and the Seven Ages of Man,
pantomime by E. L. B.[3] Everything in the opening goes
off wonderfully well ; house crammed ; Covent Garden pantomime a comparative failure. 27*th*.—Capital accounts in
all the papers. To town ; see Ledger ; receive £1 10*s*. for
Christmas plots, and 10*s*. on account. At night to Princess's,
and see pantomime of *Maid and Magpie* ;[4] badly written
opening, but beautifully got up, and tricks by Bradwell
admirably and expensively made, but no point about it.
Beautiful letter and Christmas greeting from C. C. B., who,
thirteen years since—heigho ! 28*th*.—At home all day
writing notice of Princess's pantomime for *Era*. Look in at

[1] Samuel Rogers, banker and poet, born July 30th, 1763. Author
of " Pleasures of Memory," 1792 ; " Poems," 1812 ; " Italy," 1822 ; and
" Recollections," printed in 1859.'

[2] Rickett, clown ; French, harlequin ; Priorson, pantaloon ; Mdlle.
Henriade, columbine ; Signor Plimmerini, sprite.

[3] Double harlequinade : clowns, Tom Matthews and Boleno ; pantaloons, Johnson and Tanner ; harlequins, Veroni and Herr Furth ;
columbines, Mddles. Boleno and Marie Charles ; sprites, Brothers
Elliott.

[4] Harlequin, Cormack ; clown, Huline ; pantaloon, Paulo ; columbine, Phœbe Beale.

Drury; see Wild. House crammed to excess. Pantomimists very slow and dreary, and lack of quick action. The new lamp kindling up at home for study with great success. *29th.*— Dear Walter's birthday—six. Goes to Camden Town to celebrate it. I go to British Museum, prepare copy; go to Wells; see opening of *Harlequin and Puss in Boots;* or, *All the World and His Wife and the Ogre of Rats' Castle,* by E. L. B.; very good.[1] Hear of death of Shelton Mackenzie. *31st.*—Go to British Museum in morning, being the last day before the annual closing. Prepare copy, and go to club; few, but jolly. See the Old Year out and the New Year in, and sing an extemporaneous song to do honour to ditto. Home with Spencer, chatting about clairvoyance the whole way. So exits 1855. An *annus mirabilis* of pain and pleasure to me, and God be thanked for the health and happiness I have enjoyed in the course of it. Much of the past atoned for by ——, the wasted life yet made happy by memories, and if no union here, yet a hope of one hereafter. The future a mysterious curtain to be withdrawn."

LIFE'S PROBLEM.

A Metaphysical Madrigal.

I.

" What is Life?" Don't hall and hovel
Share the sunbeam's warm caress?
This reflection, if not novel,
Still is truthful none the less.
Question asked through countless ages,
Muddling mortals more and more,
Puzzling all the greatest sages,
Yet unanswered as before.
Question asked, and oft repeated;
Only answer we can show,
Life commenced must be completed
Somehow, and that's all we know.

[1] Harlequin, Charles Fenton; columbine, Caroline Parkes; pantaloon, Naylor; clown, Nicolo Edouin. *Puss in Boots* in opening capitally played by Miss Rose Edouin, who was so excellent as Puck in *Midsummer Night's Dream.*

II.

In its fleeting glimpse of sunlight,
   In its rain-drops by the way,
Life presents, in more than one light,
   Aspect of an April day ;
But an image, thought the brightest
   When it caught the poet's eye,
Doesn't help us in the slightest
   When we want to make reply.
Still through mental mazes blundering,
   Seeking clues to pain and strife,
Everybody goes on wondering,
   While they have it, " What is Life ? "

III.

What is Time ? To some a minute,
   Others speak of Time as years.
Think of this, you'll find more in it
   Than immediately appears.
Pleasure's straw may lightly tickle
   Idle palms with dainty touch :
Let old age once bring his sickle,
   Harvests don't amount to much.
Each night ends with joy and sorrow,
   Now a profit, now a loss,
Up to-day and down to-morrow,
   What is life ?—Why, " Pitch and Toss."

E. L. BLANCHARD.

Total for year, £198 6s.

1856.

" *Tuesday, Jan.* 1*st.*—The new year opens wild and rainy.
First number of *Train*[1] out; hardly fast enough ! 2*nd.*—In
morning welcome letter from W. B. announcing his return ;
meet him at 5 p.m. Then dine at the Divan ; Lord W. Lennox

---

[1] E. L. B. states that the original staff was composed of the Brothers
Brough, Edward Draper, W. P. Hale, J. V. Bridgeman, Godfrey
Turner, Edmund Yates, G. A. Sala, and C. H. Bennett and McConnell

in chair. Beverley presented with silver claret jug, and Roxby with silver cigar case; healths proposed and responded to. *4th.*—Write *Era* copy; to town with it, receiving from Ledger for week, 10s. *5th.*—Go to Haymarket; *Beaux' Stratagem;*[1] Bella Copeland's *début* as Cherry; inexperienced. Buckstone's Scrub admirable. Drury the acknowledged triumph of the season. *11th.*—Go to Haymarket; see delicious piece of *Little Treasure* and the pantomime;[2] rather slow, though very well appointed. *12th.*—Muddle day away at home. Very dreamy, and reading Reichenbach's work on the 'Odic Forces': very curious. *17th.*—Into town. Account of Russia acceding to propositions; lines about it to pantomime and Woodin. Drury filled to overflowing. Hear of the miserable end of J. W. Sharpe,[3] the comic singer, who died in Dover Union, emaciated and destitute. *19th.*—Home all day. Finish article called 'Five Fridays in a February,' and leave it with Yates for *Train. Monday, 21st.*—Read

the clever artists. "Awakens pleasant yet sad memories; so many have gone. [*The Train*, a first-class magazine, was published by Groombridge & Son, Paternoster Row, and lasted from 1856 to 1858. The first number contained:—Chapter I. of "Marston Lynch," a story by Robert Brough; a poem by William P. Hale; a story, "Mr. Watkins' Apprentice," by William Brough; a poem by Godfrey Turner, "Riding Away;" an essay by John Bridgeman; a story in verse by Robert Brough; the "Parisian Night's Entertainments," by G. A. Sala; a poem by E. Frank Smedley; an article by Edward Draper; an essay on "Boys," by Edmund Yates; and the famous "Nights of the Round Table." In 1858 there was a valedictory address "To Our Readers"—"With this number *The Train* will stop." One sentence in the address is very interesting: "The promoters of the magazine, all working men in journalism, conceived that they would be doing good service by helping to break through the custom of anonymity."—C. S.]

[1] *The Beaux' Stratagem* was compressed into three acts. W. Farren, Aimwell; Howe, Archer; Villiers, Gibbett; Miss Reynolds, Miss Sullen; and Miss Swanborough, Dorinda.

[2] [*The Little Treasure* was Blanche Fane, a lovely actress, who was the talk of the town, and the idol of the *jeunesse dorée* of that time.—C.S.] *The Butterfly's Ball and the Grasshopper's Feast.* Miss Fanny Wright, Lady Silverwing; Coe, Wasp; harlequin, Milano; columbine, Miss Mary Brown; pantaloon, Mackay; clown, Appleby.

[3] Sharpe was at one time quite *the* favourite comic singer, but through dissipation had got thoroughly reduced. He was absolutely penniless and homeless before he was taken into the Union.

Reichenbach and curious tale in *Chambers'*, 'The Dopel-
ganger.' Think, and sing by myself all the evening.
23*rd.*—British Museum for ' England and Wales.' Home to
dinner, W. B. dining with me. Then to club, receiving with
all the honours, through Mr. Levy, *the* pipe.[1] Speeches and
so forth ; large muster ; my old friend Lovell Phillips
present. 26*th.*—In evening Frank Toole comes and brings
some presents from J. Toole, with fine box of toys from him
for Walter."

" *Feb.* 2*nd.*—Write for Phillips duet, 'Bright be our
Guiding Star,' sixth of Mendelssohn's. 5*th.*—Moore comes
and lends me £5 to pay rent. At night we go to Covent
Garden ; private box ; see *Black-eyed Susan*[2] and pantomime.
7*th.*—Woodin calls again, and nothing done in consequence.
At night to Adelphi ; see bagatelle of *Boots at the Holly
Tree Inn.*[3] Then to Emma Stanley's, and delighted with
her entertainment. From *Era* 10*s.* 8*th.*—Write Adelphi
notices ; song for Woodin. Not at all salubrious. Absolutely
without a penny in the world ! 9*th.*—Walk to Addison, and
sell copyright of the 'Twilight Veil' and 'Bright be our
Guiding Star' for £2. Receive a letter from Greenwood with
£10. Pay a number of little debts. I go to Woodin ; his
thousandth night. 12*th.*—At night to Olympic ; the Queen
and Prince Albert there. Second night of French piece,
Stay at Home;[4] smartly adapted from the same source as

[1] Given by E. T. Smith.

[2] Professor Anderson, William ; Miss Harriet Gordon, Susan. The
pantomime was entitled, *Ye Belle Alliance*, or, *Harlequin Good
Humour and the Field of the Cloth of Gold.* Clown, Flexmore ;
pantaloon, Barnes ; columbine, Emma Horn ; harlequin, C. Brown.

[3] Benjamin Webster, Cobbs the Boots ; Parselle and two clever
children (Miss Manning and Miss Craddock), the juvenile hero and
heroine. The piece was a dramatization of the Christmas number of
Household Words.

[4] Both of these pieces mentioned, the latter by Palgrave Simpson,
were taken from *Un Mari qui se Dérange.* George Vining, Frank
Lauriston ; Emery, Dr. Metcalfe ; F. Vining, Sir Charles Letheridge ;
Leslie, Chancit ; Miss Fanny Turner, Mrs. Lauriston ; Mrs. Stirling,
Mrs. Metcalfe. *Stay at Home* was by Slingsby Laurence. [Otherwise
the great philosopher, George Henry Lewes.—C. S.]

Ranelagh. 14*th.*—All day at work on drama, which slowly gets done, and to town with it. Go to Adelphi, and see farce by J. G. Moore, *That Blessed Baby.*[1] See opening of *Jack and the Beanstalk:* very bad. At club; see Mr. Chute, the manager of Bath Theatre, and Addison, manager of York Circuit. 15*th.*—Go to dine at Van Buren's; find myself voted to the chair, E. T. S. on my right, Roxby to my left. Presentation of crown. Make a series of speeches, but suffer from indisposition and low spirits all the time, but not, I think, apparent to the company. 16*th.*—From *Era* 10s. *Monday,* 18*th.*—The veteran Braham dies yesterday.[2] 21*st.*— Mrs. Bradstock removes Toole's things. The last days in the old house, and melancholy thereanent. Mother calls and spends day, taking Walter to Camden Town. Meet *Train* band at Mitre. Club with R. Brough till midnight.

---

[1] Mr. and Mrs. Keeley, Mrs. Leigh Murray and Mr. Shore in the farce. The pantomime was *Jack and the Beanstalk,* or, *Mother Goose at Home Again.* Jack and harlequin, Madame Celeste ; Mother Goose and columbine, Miss Wyndham : clown, Gordon ; pantaloon, C. J. Smith ; Paul Bedford, Bland and Romer, and Misses Mary Keeley, Arden and Kate Kelly, were in the burlesque portion.

[2] Born March 20th, 1777. Made his first appearance as Cupid, in a burletta called *The Birthday,* at the Royalty Theatre in Wellclose Square, in July 1787, as Master Abrahams. He was adopted when eleven years old by Leoni, an excellent vocalist and professor of music, who gave him instruction until he was fifteen, when Braham, as he was then known, actually surpassed his master. He made his *début* as a tenor singer at Bath in 1794, and continued to study under Panzzini. Braham also gave lessons, and in 1795 Lady Nelson, the wife of the hero of Trafalgar, then plain Captain Nelson, was one of his pupils. Braham came to London, and first appeared at Drury Lane in 1796, in Storace's opera of *Mahmoud.* After Storace's death, Braham travelled in Italy with his sister, Signora Storace, and gained the highest honour. He returned to England in 1801, to Covent Garden ; in 1805 joined the Drury Lane company. His last important character was at Drury Lane Theatre in 1839, in Rossini's opera, *William Tell.* He built the St. James's Theatre in 1835, and opened the Coliseum the same year. He married in 1816 Miss Bolton, by whom he had six children ; one afterwards became Frances Countess of Waldegrave, and four sons— Charles and Augustus, tenors ; John Hamilton, basso ; and Ward, who, like Augustus, also was in the army. Braham was a brilliant conversationalist and a composer of great taste. His " Death of Abercrombie " and " Death of Nelson " will live for all time.

22nd.—The miseries of moving commence. *Monday, 25th.*—Moved to 29, Wilmington Square; awful expenditure and bother. 29th.—Hear from E. T. Smith that he has got the *Sunday Times.*"

" *Monday, Mar. 3rd.*—Send title of *Sunday Times* novel of ' Lionel Lee ; or, The Man without a Destiny.' 4th.—Go to Lowe's, Essex Street; pleasant bachelors' party. The masquerade at Covent Garden [1] most fearfully and strangely interrupted at five the following morning by a fire that levels Covent Garden to the ground. 5th.—Go in afternoon to see the ruins : deplorable sight; about the spot all evening. 7th.—Finish account of fire, and to town with it. Evans's; first time I see new room. Then to Hunt's, the ' Feathers,' and from his rooms overlook the still burning ruins of the theatre; sad, melancholy, impressive sight. Meet Albert Smith and Alfred Mellon. 8th.—To City with W. B. Call at Tallis's; no effects. Take mother to Haymarket; first night of Bayle Bernard's comedy of the *Evil Genius.* [2] 12th.—Receive from *Era* £1 10s. for

---

[1] The cause of this fire was never ascertained. It originated somewhere in the flies. The masquerade, given by Professor Anderson (the " Wizard of the North "), the conjuror, was nearly at a close—in fact, " God save the Queen " was being played—when the cry of " Fire ! " was raised. Fortunately only some two hundred people were left in the house. The building was uninsured, and entailed great losses on the principal shareholders—the Kemble family, the family of the late Mr. Harris, Mr. Sermon, Mr. Robinson, Mr. Thomas Grieve, etc.; in addition to the exquisite scenery which had been painted by Grieve, Telbin, and Beverley, the extensive wardrobe and properties, a hundred suits of armour and a host of valuables. Only four pictures by Hogarth, representing the Seasons, were saved. Worst of all, the dramatic library—which was unique, and contained the original manuscripts of *The School for Scandal, The Miller and His Men,* and the opera of *The Slave;* and the original operatic scores of *Elisir d'Amore* of Donizetti and the *Oberon* of Weber—was completely destroyed. Only some furniture and a piano belonging to Mr. Costa, and the " Wizard of the North's " conjuring paraphernalia, were saved.

[2] Chippendale, Hill Cooler ; Buckstone, Tom Ripstone ; Miss Swanborough, Clara Fielding ; Miss Reynolds, Lady Aurora Ringwood ; Compton, Joe Withers. The tendency of the piece was spoken of as excellent, and the literary merit far above the average.

articles in last week's paper. 18*th.*—From Woodin for song, etc., £5. To Drury, and see Emery's *Tale of a Train;* [1] very slow, yet very clever as far as artistic effect is concerned. 19*th.*—To Emma Stanley's *Seven Ages of Woman* at Sadlers Wells. 22*nd.*—First appearance of 'Lionel Lee' in *Sunday Times. Monday,* 24*th.*—Sadler's Wells; first night of the summer season; opened under G. Webster.[2] 25*th.*—All day on tale, and horribly behindhand with everything. Off to Strand; see five minutes of *Queen Bess;* [3] a dreary burlesque. 27*th.*—In morning Miss and Mrs. Stanley look in, first time since the entertainment. Hear they are engaged by Niblo to go to America in June. 28*th.*—At night write a little fragment, 'Covent Garden,' but afraid I am too late with it. My old friend, poor George Wild, died this morning.[4] 29*th.*—Receive from E. T. S., for first number of 'Lionel Lee,' £3."

" *April* 2*nd.*—From *Era* £1 10*s.* 3*rd.*—To town with proofs; see at night first time Robson all through in *Discreet*

---

[1] The speciality of this piece appears to have been a series of tableaux : and in it Mr. Emery assumed, under the general title of *Life in Portraiture,* the characters of Cromwell, Napoleon, Frederick the Great, and Nelson; and realized two of Haydon's pictures—Curtius leaping into the Gulf, and the Field of Battle—besides various characters, [incidental to the Russian War], supposed to be met with in Balaclava Bay.

[2] The piece was *The Marble Heart,* or, *The Sculptor's Dream,* produced two years earlier at the Adelphi, and taken from *La Fille de Marbre.* Leigh Murray, in his original character of Raphael ; E. F. Edgar and Miss Jenny Marston also in the cast. *The Invisible Prince* was the extravaganza, with Miss Harriet Gordon as Don Leander.

[3] *Good Queen Bess,* by C. J. Collins. Queen Bess, Mr. James Rogers; Raleigh, Miss Somers ; Ormond, Miss Weekes.

[4] When lessee of the Olympic, George Wild appears to have been much annoyed with *Punch* for the following criticism it had passed on his theatre :—" The Olympic is to the Adelphi what a Tap is to a Tavern. *The Pieces smack of the Spittoon;* but they are often things of real life, the more especially when a live Horse and a real Cab from St. Clement's Stand are introduced upon the scene." Wild

Princess;[1] wonderful and painfully intense performance. *4th.*—Look in at Sadlers Wells; see *Invisible Prince;* good burlesque, but Harriet Gordon excepted, badly done. *5th.* —W. B. in afternoon, with sad disheartening story of his

accordingly posted up the following bill, giving the extract from *Punch :*—

A COMPLIMENT TO THE OLYMPIC DRAMATIC AUTHORS.

List of Dramatists, whose pieces "Smack of the Spittoon," and who have been kind enough to contribute to that Theatre during the Management of Mr. G. Wild—viz., from April 4, 1841, to the present date :—

Pieces	Author
Charles O'Malley	
Two Jack Sheppards	
Area Sylph	
Maid of Biscay	Mr. SOMERSET.
Young Maids	
The Sea	
A Dey and a Knight	
Cupid	Mr. GRAVES.
Olympic Frailties	
Cousin Peter	
Ladies' Seminary	Mr. WILKS.
My Valet and I	
Bathing	Mr. BRUTON.
Davis and Sally Dear	
The Little Offspring	Mr. RAYMOND.
Spy Seekers	
An Armful of Bliss	Mr. W. MON-CRIEFF.
Peter Priggins	Mr. STERLING.
Bachelors' Buttons	
The April Fool	
The Soldier's Widow	
The Ranger's Daughter	Mr. FITZBALL.
Convent Belles	
Behind the Scenes	Mr. C. SELBY.
24th of May	Mr. REYNOLDSON.
Angels and Lucifers	
The Artful Dodge	
Jack Nokes and Tom Styles	
Pork Chops; or, A Dream of Hope	Mr. E. L. BLANCHARD.
Babes in the Wood	
The Road of Life	
Game and Game	
The Little Gipsy	
Gileso Scroggini	
My Man Tom	
Lost and Won	
Captain Pro. Tem.	
Gwynneth Vaughan	
Self-accusation	
Gentleman in Black	
Ladies' Club	
30, Strand	Mr. MARK LEMON.
Robinson Crusoe	
Whittington and His Cat	
The Demon Gift	
Love and Charity	
Adventures of a Gentleman	
Love and War	
Revolt of Bruges	Mr. ALBERT SMITH.
The Scotch Mist	Mr. H. WILLS.
The Haunted Inn	Mr. PEAKE.
The Evil Eye	
The May Queen	Mr. BUCKSTONE.
My Uncle's Card	Mr. H. P. GRATTAN.
The Rake's Progress	
Sixteen-String Jack	
Jack in the Water	
His First Champagne	
Norval	
Sunshine and Shade	Mr. LEMAN REDE
Life's a Lottery	
Loves of the Devils	
Son of the Desert	
Our Village	
Two Greens	
The Profligate	

Theatre Royal Olympic,
February 26th, 1844.

[1] *The Discreet Princess; or, The Three Glass Distaffs.* Prince Richcraft, F. Robson; Prince Belavoir, Miss Maskell; King Gander, Mr. Emery; Finetta, Babiliarda, and Idelfouga, the three princesses, Misses Julia St. George, Ternan, and Marston; Mother Goose, Miss Stephens.

trouble. From E. T. S., for third chapter of novel, £3. *Monday 7th.*—Intensely horrified by reading the account of the wreck of the *Rutledge*,[1] a Liverpool packet ship, lost at sea on February 20th. *9th.*—From *Era* 15s. for leader and theatricals. Go to Surrey ; see *World of London ;*[2] Monsieur Hanlon, the gymnast, and Shepherd, first time for a long time. *10th.*—Morris Barnett's death at Montreal announced.[3] *11th.*—Emma Stanley and mother in morning. Off to America in a fortnight. Edinburgh Castle. Meet Sala, who is off to St. Petersburg on Monday. *17th.*—W.B. in ; afternoon wasted in chat. From *Era* £1. *19th.*—Receive £3 from E. T. S. for Chapter V. Club at night, and Tomlins in chair. An American comedian, Mr. Florence,[4] introduced. *29th.*— After close work finish tale, and to town with it. Go to Drury ; last act of *Fra Diavolo*, and *Yankee Housekeeper*, the

[1] She struck on an iceberg, and began to fill rapidly. The sole survivor of one of the boats, which, when it left the ship, contained thirteen people, was Thomas W. Nye, who had been exposed for nine days to the inclemency of the weather, and his hands and feet were much frozen.

[2] The drama was called, *How we live in the World of London*, and may almost be said to have been but a threading together of scenes of which Henry Mayhew had written in " London Labour and London Poor." In it were seen Shepherd, H. W. Widdicomb, Miss Sarah Thorne and Miss Marriott.

[3] Morris Barnett was born in 1800, and spent a considerable portion of his early life in France, where he was a musical conductor. He came to London to gain confidence, and entered the chorus of the Adelphi under F. Yates. First appeared at Brighton, and in 1833 appeared at Drury Lane, and was thoroughly successful as Tom Drops in *The School-fellows*. In 1837 he wrote and acted *Monsieur Jacques* at the St. James's Theatre, and saved the fortunes of the house. He then turned his attention principally to literature, but appeared in the *Old Guard* at the Princess's under Mr. Maddox. He was musical critic to the *Morning Post* and *Era* for nearly seven years, and in September, 1854, he gave some farewell performances before going to America. He was not successful in the United States. He wrote a goodly number of plays, of which *The Serious Family* may perhaps be looked upon as the best. [I have often heard my old friend, Mr. J. M. Levy, speak of Morris Barnett as the most delightful of companions and the best of men. He was on affectionate terms of close intimacy with Mr. Levy's gifted and hospitable family.—C. S.]

[4] [The now celebrated " Billy Florence," friend, pal, and cheery boon companion of every good fellow in Bohemian Land, both in England and America.—C.S]

Florences having made their *début* last night; the woman clever, and two songs quaint.[1] *30th.*—At home all day, writing Woodin's song of ' New Budget of Metropolitan Gossip.' "

" *May 1st.*—An anniversary! Dined with Woodin, and received for song, etc., £5. At night to Soho Theatre ; see a Mrs. Newberry as Mrs. Malaprop ;[2] mediocre. *2nd.*— Writing *Era* paragraphs for last week 10*s.* *8th.*—Write Whitsuntide article for *Era*, then to town ; Surrey, Miss Thorne's[3] benefit. See Shepherd, who wants pantomime in a month. *9th.*— Haymarket and Polygraphic Hall. Hear Picco, the blind minstrel, at St. James's. Then night rehearsal, and home. *Monday, 12th.*—Work till late, hindered by W. B. in morning, and pecuniary help asked, and given. Heavy drains on purse from all quarters. *15th.*—Mrs. W. Florence calls and pays £20 plus £5 for piece to be written in a week from this time ! Frightful work to contemplate. See Ledger ; *Era* £1. To St. James's to see Mrs. Purdy as Lady Teazle in *School for Scandal;*[4] amateurish. *23rd.*—At work all day on Florence's piece of *Working the Oracle.* Coyne looks in at night. *24th.*—Receive from E. T. S. £3 for Chapter X. To British Museum with C. C. B. Haymarket ; first night of new piece, *Rights and Wrongs of Woman,*[5] by Maddison Morton. Write account of it, and then to club. *30th.*— Take Albert Miller to Drury : *Cinderella ;* Miss Huddart very good as heroine."

" *Monday, June 4th.*—Get tale done at last somehow, and to town with it. Celeste's benefit at Adelphi, *Flying*

---

[1] The two songs referred to became quite the rage ; they were " Bobbing around " and " Polly, won't you try me, oh ? "

[2] Sir Anthony Absolute, Mr. Shirley ; Captain Absolute, Mr. Charles Lascelles ; Sir Lucius O'Trigger, Mr. Charles Howe ; Lydia Languish, Miss Hemsworth. Mrs. Newbery was a Miss Lucy Bennett.

[3] Miss Thorne played Deschappelles to Creswick's Claude Melnotte and was highly spoken of.

[4] Mrs. Purdy was professionally known as Miss Elphick at the Liverpool and Manchester Theatres. Mr. George Purdy was the Sir Peter.

[5] Mr. and Mrs. Marchmont, Mr. Howe and Miss Talbot, Sir Brian de Beausex, J. B. Buckstone. Miss Bella Copeland played the part of a tiger.

Dutchman; [1] and very bad piece too. Go to club; find myself proposed chairman for the supper night. *5th.*—Glashier on Emma Stanley's business, then A. Burnett, an American poet, with letters of introduction. Write little paragraphs for *Era.* *6th.*—Send off *Alonzo* for Emma Stanley. At night to Polygraphic Hall; saw *Off by Train*—good. See the great Ristori at Lyceum in *Medea;* very great performance. *11th.*—Emma Stanley starts for America in the *Atlantic.* Go to Olympic; see farce, *Fascinating Individual.* [2] Robson in it; not very good piece. Hear of Harry Baxter dying this morning. *13th.*—Receive on account from Tallis £5, from *Era* 15*s.* At night to club, and take the chair—annual club supper—Colonel Addison vice. Presentation of snuff-box to Lovell Phillips. Health proposed by Bridgeman in the neatest speech of the evening. *16th.*—Go in afternoon to *Train* meeting, and pay £3 for expenses. Hear but sad accounts of prospects. *20th.*—Write paragraphs for *Era;* receive therefrom 7*s.* 6*d.* Buy eight volumes of *Literary Gazette* for 12*s.* *21st.*—From E. T. S. £3 for Chapter XIV. of tale. Not well, nothing done. At night to Drury; Lucy Escott's benefit; and Borrani in *Bohemian Girl.* [3] Meet Smith; a long chat. Keeleys engaged, and I to write for them."

"*July* 1*st.*—Write bit of biography of Charlés Young, who

[1] She played Vanderdecken in *The Flying Dutchman,* Miami in the *Green Bushes,* and Harlequin in the pantomime in the same evening. *The Flying Dutchman* was written by Edward Fitzball in 1825, the original cast consisting of T. P. Cook as Vanderdecken; John Reeve, von Brummel; Wrench, Toby Varnish; and Terry, Captain Peppercoal. On this occasion the parts were filled by Wright as Von Brummel; Webster as Varnish; and Selby as Peppercoal; Mary Keeley as Lestille; and Kate Kelly, Lucy.

[2] Robson, Gustavus Adolphus FitzMortimer; Emery, Gaston Murray, Danvers, and Misses Marston and Castleton were included in the cast.

[3] Miss Escott, Arline; Elliott Thaler, Thaddeus; Courtaigne, Devilshoof. On the same night Augustus Braham appeared as Edgardo in *Lucia di Lammermoor,* and Miss Escott sang a new song, "The Crimean Heroes; or, Ladies, Beware!" composed by Tully, which was encored.

died on Sunday.[1]   3rd.—Read 'Little Dorrit,' and delighted.
'England and Wales.'   At night to Olympic; see the *Duo-
logical Farce*, first night; *A Conjugal Lesson*,[2] was very good,
and much more pleased with *Retribution*.   10th.—Off for
walk round by Hornsey; Adelphi in evening; burlesque of
Medea;[3] not particularly good.   Wright as Medea.   11th.—
Town with theatrical notices; from *Era* £1.   12th.—Busy
rewriting pantomime for Surrey.   At night to Drury, and
see Louisa Keeley the youngest daughter; she makes her
début with amateur pantomimists of Fielding Club, as
Gertrude, in *The Loan of a Lover*.   Very good, and much
entertained.   14th.—In afternoon *Train* meeting, and agree
to carry it on; then to Olympic; Brough's burlesque of
Medea;[4] Robson excellent, and piece smart.   Meet Watts
Phillips first time.   15th.—Shepherd returns pantomime.

[1] Charles Mayne Young was born January 10th, 1777, in Fenchurch
Street.   Was educated at Eton and Merchant Taylors'.   Was in a
merchants' house, Longman & Co., for a short time, and first appeared
under the name of Green, as Douglas, at the Theatre Royal, Liverpool.
His success was so marked that the same winter he played lead at
Manchester, and returned to fill the like position at Liverpool the
following summer, from 1800 to 1802.   He was the greatest favourite
in Glasgow.   Married Miss Grimani, of the Theatre Royal, Haymarket, on March 9th, 1805, but lost his wife in her first confinement.
Mr. Young made his London *début* as Hamlet at the Haymarket, June
22nd, 1807; joined the Covent Garden company in 1810, as second to
John Kemble, and lead when he was absent.   He even surpassed
Kemble in many of the characters which were supposed to be the
great tragedian's own.   Young was almost as good in comedy as he
was in tragedy.   He bade adieu to the stage as Hamlet at Covent
Garden, May 30th, 1832.   He was a great favourite in society, was an
accomplished gentleman, and a good sportsman.   Some interesting
memoirs of him were written by his son, the Rev. Julian Charles
Young, rector of Ilmington.

[2] Played by Mrs. Stirling and F. Robson.

[3] *Medea*, or, *The Libel on the Lady of Colchis*, was by Mark Lemon.
James Bland, Creon; Miss Wyndham, Jason; Mary Keeley, Orpheus;
Paul Bedford Glaucé.   Smoothly written.

[4] This was Robert Brough's version of *Medea*, and Robson's impersonation was reckoned one of his very finest.   Julia St. George,
Jason; Fanny Turner, Orpheus; Miss Bromley, Creusa; Clifton and
Miss Stephens also in the cast.   Madame Ristori was present on the
first performance, and appeared to enjoy the fun immensely.

Surrey Gardens opened this day with grand musical inauguration.[1] 19*th.*—More painful worry of W. B. At home all evening. 21*st.*—Begin article for *Train*, 'The Phantoms of the Pavement.' Woodin sends his bust. Worried and unwell all day. *Working the Oracle* produced at Glasgow first time; went off well last Thursday. 22*nd.*—Look in at Adelphi, and see *Born to Good Luck*;[2] Barney Williams very fair. 23*rd.*—Finish article for *Train.* 29*th.*—Go to Carpenter's Mesmerism Lecture at Shaftesbury Hall. See experiments; nothing else done. 30*th.*—Strand at night; see Stuart in good three-act piece *That House in High Street.*[3] 31*st.*—All day writing little paragraphs for *Era;* writing to Smith, agreeing to do Calendar and Comic for Almanack."

"*Monday, Aug. 4th.*—Go to club, P. Phillips present; he tells me he is preparing panorama for Albert Smith, whereat I am glad. 8*th.*—Telescope to be £1 15*s.* Begin almanack, and that's all. Madame Vestris died at midnight.[4]

[1] Jullien was the conductor, and gave a performance of the *Messiah.* Madame Clara Novello, Madame Rudersdorf, Miss Dolby, Miss Weiss and Mr. Sims Reeves were the soloists, supported by a very large band and chorus. In the evening Alboni was the principal vocalist, and Piatti, Bottesini and Savori were the instrumentalists. Southby provided the fireworks, and the back of the lake presented a view of Constantinople and Scutari, painted by Dansen.

[2] Was first produced at Covent Garden in 1842; was founded on *False and True,* produced some thirty years before. Barney Williams played Barney O'Rafferty, and earned great success with his song, "The Flanning O'Flannigans." He was supported by Charles Selby, Mrs. Chatterley, Mary Keeley, and Parselle.

[3] Three-act comedy by Mr. Stuart, who played Colonel Maitland; Mr. Basil Potter, Ensign Maitland; George Cook, Doctor Villiers; Mr. Kinloch, the Major; Miss Isabel Adams, Sophia.

[4] Eliza Lucy Bartolozzi, Madame Vestris, was born January 3rd, 1797, in St. Marylebone, and was the granddaughter of the great engraver Bartolozzi. From her father's teaching, and that of the best masters, she became an excellent musician, as well as perfect in French and Italian. She married Armand Vestris, a dancer at the Italian Opera—a most depraved, dissipated man of only twenty-four, but who had already ruined his constitution—she being only sixteen, on January 28th, 1813, at St. Martin's-in-the-Fields, and made her *début* as Proserpina in Winter's opera of *Il Ratto di Proserpina,* Thursday, July 20th, 1815, and achieved a most complete success, not only by the excellence of her singing, but by her beauty and charm of manner.

11th.—Hard at work all day and night on tale, which finish and post. Order for burlesque from E. T. Smith immediately. Lee Irish comedian, dies.[1] *12th.*—Pay third pound for the loan, W. B. Work all day on 'England and Wales.' Knocked up with overwork.   *13th.*—More 'England and Wales.' *Train*

The young actress next appeared in Paris, both in comedy and tragedy, and returned to London in 1819 to appear as Lilla in *The Siege of Belgrade*, February 19th, 1829. She made a marked success as the Don in *Giovanni in London*, and her portraits in the character were all over the town. She could not, however, with all her popularity, turn *Giovanni in Ireland*, an extravaganza full of grossest improprieties, into a success. It was played December 26th, 1821, and was withdrawn after a very stormy run of four nights. Her husband died in 1825 ; and, having created a most favourable impression in the provinces, she became manageress of the Olympic in 1831, and opened it, January 3rd, with *Mary Queen of Scots*, and *Olympic Revels*, written by Planché and Charles Dance. She brought the theatre up to a pitch of prosperity, and Charles Mathews having made his *début* here December 7th, 1835, in his own farce of *The Hump-backed Lover*, in which he played George Rattleton, won her affections, and they were married July 18th, 1838, at Kensington Church, and immediately sailed for the United States ; but their visit was not a success, and Madame Vestris made her reappearance at her own theatre, which had been managed during her absence by Planché, January 2nd, 1839, as Fatima in *Blue Beard*. Her lesseeship came to an end on May 31st, and she commenced that of Covent Garden Theatre, September 30th, 1839. This only lasted three years, and was unfortunate. She and Charles Mathews for a time joined Macready at Drury Lane, and then Webster at the Haymarket, remaining there till 1845. After a tour they appeared at the Princess's, March 1846. In 1847 Madame Vestris became manageress of the Lyceum till July 26th, 1856, making her last appearance on that date in *Sunshine through the Clouds ;* and it was during this term of years that those exquisite extravaganzas, *The King of the Peacocks*, *The Island of Jewels*, *Theseus and Ariadne*, *The Golden Branch*, etc., were produced. Many hard things, perhaps deservedly, have been said of Madame Vestris ; but great allowances must be made for her. Had her first husband been a different man, she might have proved a very different woman ; for, with all her follies, she was good-hearted, and did many acts of kindness. Her extravagance, however, was unbounded ; she was known to have cut up a three-hundred-guinea Indian shawl merely to use a portion of it for a turban and sash in *Oberon*. She lies buried in Kensal Green Cemetery.

[1] Born in Dublin, December 1st, 1810. First appeared at Sadlers Wells as Remy in *Suil Dhuv ;* or, *The Coiner*, in 1828. Appeared at

band at Fetter Lane ; Masonic Hall copy wanted. Brough to Bruges. Lovely moonlight night ; glorious by the sea. Ah, eh! don't I ? *20th.*—Tired and knocked out. Write paragraph about Irish piece of *Ireland as it is* [1] for *Era.* *21st.*—Home all day, but nothing done ; look over my new purchase (telescope). Arrange little matters. *22nd.*—*Era,* ‘ Madame Vestris,’ £1 1s. *29th.*—Introduced to Little of the *Illustrated News.*”

“ *Monday, Sept. 1st.*—Lovely weather, and I indoors stewing over tale all day, writing sixty lines of it. Knocked up, and very feverish. Hear of G. A. à Beckett's death at Boulogne.[2] Princess's open for the season.[3] *3rd.*—Go to Shepherd, and get the piece of *Three Perils of Man* from him, for which offer him £5. Walk over bridge with Creswick, and write paragraph for *Era.* Election night at club, and everybody elected. Excitement about the British Bank having stopped payment. *4th.*—Begin rewriting burlesque. At night to Haymarket ; see Miss Booth's [4] first appearance as Rosalind ; good, but not great. Meet W. E. Hall and Bayle Bernard. Take them to club to supper, and spend lively agreeable evening. Delighted with Bernard. *6th.*—

most of the London and provincial theatres, and was a member of Mr. Macready's company at Covent Garden during his lesseeship. Was an excellent stage Irishman. Was the proprietor of Beckford's Hotel, Old Street, St. Luke's ; of the Adam and Eve, St. Pancras ; and of the house where he died, the Hoop and Adze, St. John's Street, Clerkenwell.

[1] Or, *The Middleman,* by J. H. Amherst, an actor well known over the water thirty years before, but who died in America—Barney and Mrs. Williams, Ragged Pat and Judy O'Trot. Had been played in the United States seven hundred and sixty-three times. Second title used by H. A. Jones in 1889 at Shaftesbury.

[2] Gilbert Abbott à 'Beckett, called to the Bar, January 1841. Was made magistrate of Greenwich and Woolwich Courts in 1849, and exchanged with Mr. Secker to Southwark, where he administered justice until shortly before his death by typhus fever. He was well known as a dramatic author.

[3] Revival by Charles Kean of Sheridan's *Pizarro.* Mrs. Charles Kean, Elvira ; Charles Kean, Rolla ; Miss Heath, Cora ; John Ryder, Pizarro ; Cooper, Orozembo ; Cathcart, Alonzo.

[4] Niece of the celebrated “ lively Sally Booth.” Compton, Touchstone ; Chippendale, Adam ; Howe, Jacques ; W. Farren, Orlando (first time) ; Patty Oliver, Celia ; Mrs. E. FitzWilliam, Audrey.

All day on burlesque, which find after all no hurry for.
Receive from E. T. S., for Chapter XXIV., £3. Sadlers Wells
opens with *Macbeth*,[1] and write notice. *9th.*—All day on few
lines of tale, and sit up till very late, but hardly anything
done. A Mr. Caldwell, a sporting gentleman, calls about
sporting matter of almanack. Hard pressed, and heart
aching. *10th.*—Work on tale. Smith and Collins call, and
I go through burlesque of *Pizarro*. Finish tale at night.
11th.—At night to Surrey; see new piece of *Half Caste*;[2]
very fair. Carpenter there, and with him to Belvidere. Bad
news from Yarmouth. Pleasant letter from C. C. B. *12th.*
—All day at work for *Era*. For last week £1. Mother's at
night. *13th.*—Night to club. Harlstone and Arkcoll, chat.
Portrait of mother, given by O. C. Watkins. *15th.*—Drury[3]
and Lyceum[4] open for season. Attend both; Mrs. Waller at
former house, and Toole's first appearance at latter. Davidson calls. Pass Miller into Drury; hosts of old faces collect
and re-collect about premises. *16th.*—Begin tale with aching

[1] Thirteenth season of Greenwood and Phelps. Miss Atkinson, Lady
Macbeth ; the witches, J. W. Ray, Lewis Ball, and Charles Fenton ;
Phelps, Macbeth ; and Henry Marston, Macduff ; Rayner, Banquo.

[2] Re-opening by Creswick and Shepherd. House newly decorated.
The Half Caste ; or, *The Fatal Pearl*, adaptation by W. Suter of *Le Sang
Mêlé*, Porte St. Martin drama. The lessees, Miss Marriott, Basil Potter
Widdicomb, Fanny Bland, Kate Percy, Julia Lascelles in the cast,
The same night was played *Mould Hall*, a new Irish drama, in which
Miss Marriott, Potter, and G. Yarnold appeared.

[3] Opened under E. T. Smith's management with *Lady of Lyons ;*
Mrs. Emma Waller, an actress who was considered to have made a
name in Australia and California, as Pauline—she lacked vigour, but
was gentle and graceful. Barry Sullivan, Claude Melnotte ; Patty
Oliver, Helen ; Robert Roxby, Modus. The Keeleys, George Honey,
Mrs. Selby, and Charles Mathews, were also members of the company.

[4] Under the management of Charles Dillon, who appeared in the
title *rôle* in *Belphegor ;* Mrs. Charles Dillon, Madeline. This was a
memorable occasion—for Miss Marie Wilton (Mrs. Bancroft) made her
first appearance in London as Henri ; and J. L. Toole his first appearance as Fanfaronnade, and made a great hit. *Perdita ;* or, *The Royal
Milkmaid*, a burlesque by William Brough on the *Winter's Tale*
was also played, the author appearing as Polixenes, and Mr. S.
Calhaem, Leontes ; Perdita, Marie Wilton ; Miss Woolgar, Florizel ;
Mrs. Buckingham White, Hermione ; Harriet Gordon, Time Chorus ;
Toole, Autolycus.

head, and on it all day. From Ward £1 worth of wine to gladden the heart. Look in at Belvidere; one Alex. Lawrence, a brother of a famous stockbroker, strange being, half cracked, and wholly hard up. Strange reflections thereon. *17th.*—Go to Lyceum and see end of burlesque; very good. Toole funny and Miss Wilton clever. *19th.*—Letter from Woodin, Brighton. Call at *S. T.* office, see Bennett; then going down Thames Street call on Horace Green. Six volumes of *Athenæum* from him; return home with them in cab. *20th.*—Send off copy of almanack to Tonks of Birmingham. Receive from E. T. S., for Chap. XXVI., £3. To club, and hear of the extensive Crystal Palace forgeries of W. J. Robson.[1] *Monday, 22nd.*—All day at tale. Murdoch's[2] first appearance at Haymarket; *Pizarro*[3] burlesque produced at Drury. *24th.*—Books from Jonas Levi, *Theatrical Observer*, and Arcadia. *25th.*—Busy on ' England and Wales.' To Adelphi; a very bad piece called *Lucifer Matches;*[4] Mr. and Mrs. Barney Williams. From *Era* for last week 15s. *26th.*—Town; see Beverley about pantomime."

" *Oct. 1st.*—Go to town and see *Belphegor*[5] burlesque; very fair considering. *2nd.*—Write theatricals for *Era*, and receive therefrom £1. Go to Wells, taking Walter; see *Merry Wives*

---

[1] W. J. Robson was the author of *Love and Loyalty*, and also of *Bianca*. He was a man of very extravagant habits, and it was only surprising that, knowing the amount of his salary, the attention of the directors had not been sooner drawn to his style of living. He forged to an enormous amount.

[2] An American actor of reputation, who appeared as Mirabel in *The Inconstant*, or, *The Way to Win Him*, and was very successful. An excellent delivery and musical voice, and possessed ease and dignity. Chippendale, Old Mirabel; W. Farren, Durctôte; Mrs. E. FitzWilliam Oriana ; Miss Talbot, Bizarre.

[3] Written by Collins. Mr. and Mrs. Keeley, Pizarro and Rolla; George Honey, Alonzo; Mrs. Frank Matthews, Cora ; Miss Cleveland, Elvira; Tilbury and A. Younge, Ataleba and Orozembo.

[4] Or, *The Yankee Girl*, a sort of skit on *Faust*, in which Mrs. Barney Williams represented a Mephistopheles, and Paul Bedford a very ugly gentleman who imagines himself very handsome.

[5] By Leicester Buckingham. Belphegor, Miss Cuthbert ; Madeline, H. J. Turner ; Ikey, the Chevalier de Rollac, J. Clarke ; Fanfaronnade, Master Edouin.

of Windsor; Phelps's Falstaff; much pleased.   8*th.*—Begin
fourteenth chapter of 'Wanderings and Ponderings.'   10*th.*
—*Era* 10*s.*   Look in at Haymarket; *Inconstant* piece going
slowly.   Read report of Robson's apprehension and examination this day.   11*th.*—Sadlers Wells; first night of revival of
Timon of Athens; [1] go, and write account for *Era;* very good.
Meet Mr. Folville, of Hampshire paper, the *Independent.*
14*th.*—Look in at Soho Theatre; French plays.   15*th.*—Hard
at work on 'Wanderings and Ponderings;' burning headache.
W. B. pressing very hard on spirits as well as on purse.
16*th.*—Write column and a half with great difficulty, and to
town; see piece of *The Musketeers* at Lyceum; [2] very fair;
not over till past midnight.   17*th.*—Look in at Lyceum, Drury,
and then to Sadlers Wells; farce, '*I'll write to the* Times;'
very fair; Ray and Belford.   *Monday,* 20*th.*—Meeting of
Train band committee.   Then to Haymarket, and see Murdoch
in *Wild Oats;* Tim, by Buckstone, very well acted.   At club;
all talking of the sad catastrophe last night to Spurgeon's [3]
congregation at Surrey Music Gardens.   23*rd.*—Go at night
to National Dramatic Club, Newman Street; amateurs; highly
respectable.   Meet Bristow, Carlton the mimic (real name
Cooper), in bookseller's shop, Fleet Street.   29*th.*—Dykwynkyn calls, and long chat of six hours about pantomime.
31*st.*—Off by train 2 p.m. St. Leonards.   Nice journey, and
there by 5; pleasant people, and pleasant day accordingly.
The pleasures of the past revived, and all sorts of pleasant-
ries for the future talked about."

[1] Phelps, Timon; Henry Marston, Apemantus; Rayner, Alcibiades;
Ray, Flavius; Robinson, Lucullus; Lucius, Mr. Belford; Flaminius,
Lewis Ball; Cupid, Miss R. Edouin; Timandra, Miss Rawlings.

[2] *The Three Musketeers,* an adaptation of Dumas' story.   Charles
Dillon, d'Artagnan; Mrs. Buckingham White, Anne of Austria; Mrs.
Weston, Lady De Winter; Miss Woolgar, Constance; Mr. Stuart,
Richelieu; J. G. Shore, Buckingham; McLien, Athos; Barratt,
Porthos; Swanborough, Aramis; and Holston, Bonacieux.

[3] This arose from a false alarm of fire.   The hall was densely
crowded.   There were seven people killed and upwards of fifty
injured.   It was a wonder, considering the thousands collected, that
more serious results did not arise.   Mr. Spurgeon was wonderfully
calm and collected throughout the occurrence, and no doubt prevented
even worse arising by his presence of mind.

"*Nov.* 1st.—Lovely morning; boat to Fairlight; friend Lowe of Brentford calls, and joins us. Old places revisited, and sunshine perpetual in future. *Monday, 3rd.*—Strolls and so forth. Woodin to Worthing. Back by five train with Polly. Leave her at Mrs. G.'s. Back home; horrible accumulation of letters to reply to, and everybody in an intense state of pressing for copy. *4th.*—Look in at Adelphi; see *Border Marriage*[1] (bad piece), and Leigh Murray's re-appearance. *13th.*—Go to Strand; see *Little Dorrit*; very slow. *15th.*—At night to Sadlers Wells; *Timon of Athens* and Astley's *Dread*. Write notices for *Era*. *24th.*—Send in to Wells first comic scene. Go to Olympic; *Wives as they were*[2] and Talfourd's *Jones the Avenger*;[3] both slow. *27th.*—See Albert Smith's fourth night of new season. Very smart, and much pleased with it. *29th.*—Go to Drury, see *Il Trovatore* and Grisi."

"*Monday, Dec.* 1st.—Correct proofs, and read 'Dorrit.' Dillon's benefit at Lyceum, and see him play Othello;[4] first night in London. Very fair. A peep at *Giovanni* at Drury. Write notices for *Era* of preceding night; then to St. James's amateur performance; meet Bristow, of the *Theatrical Journal;* tells me he is seventy next February. *4th.*—See bit of *Mysterious Stranger* at Adelphi, and ditto *Elves. 6th.*—To Lyceum, and see the *Cagot;*[5] first night.

[1] An adaptation from the French *Un Mariage à l'Arquebuse*, by Messrs. Langford and Sorel. Leigh Murray played Sir Walter Raeburn.

[2] *Wives as they were, and Maids as they are*, Mrs. Inchbald's comedy. Miss Swanborough's first appearance here as Lady Priory; Mrs. Stirling, Miss Dorillon; Miss Herbert, Lady Mary Raffle; Mr. Addison, Lord Priory; F. Vining, Sir William Dorillon; Gaston Murray, Sir George Evelyn.

[3] Adaptation from *Le Massacre d'un Innocent* by Frank Talfourd. Robson very good as Jones, and J. Rogers made a hit as Shrilly Pipes.

[4] Charles Dillon appeared to have been most succesful in the gentler side of Othello's character, and was, for him, curiously devoid of any rant. Mrs. Charles Dillon was the Desdemona; Stuart, Iago; M'Lien, Cassio; Shore, Roderigo; and Mrs. Weston, Emilia.

[5] *The Cagot;* or, *Heart for Heart*, by E. Falconer. Charles Dillon, Raoul; Miss Woolgar, Lady Eugénie; Stuart, Sir Aymer de Beriot;

Goes off well. 9*th.*—Lyceum, and see *BedouinArabs*—clever, and *Dead Shot*—very well played. Walk home with W. B. 10*th.*—Begin 'Man about Town.' At night to Cowell's den at Surrey, and take my dear Walter as a treat to see *Bombastes Furioso.* Meet Davidson and a friend of Toole's; then home, and write away till five in the morning; knocked up, and still not nearly finished. 11*th.*—Birthday, and thirty-six! Where will the thirty-seventh anniversary be spent? Finish *S. T.* article; to St. James's for Amateurs; home, and write notices for *Era,* for which I get £2 this day; all theatricals for current week. 13*th.*—To Surrey; see *New Juliet,* Miss Clara Leslie;[1] very fair. 17*th.*—At night grand dinner in saloon of Drury Lane. 24*th.*—Christmas Eve spent at night with few but facetious friends—Talfourd, Hale, Leigh Murray, etc. Welcome Christmas, and hope for a pleasant realization therewith expressed. 25*th.*—Christmas Day. From E. T. S. for current week £7. Dine *solus.* Go to rehearsal at Drury at night, and an unpleasant termination of evening. 26*th.*—To Davidson and get copies of panto-mimes. Go to Adelphi and Olympic for *S. T.* and *Era.* Write notices, and not home till 4 a.m. 29*th.*—At night look in at Sadlers Wells; see *Fisherman and Genie;* or, *Harlequin Padmanaba and the Enchanted Fishes of the Silver Lake;*[2] slow, my ideas not carried out—but it goes off well. 31*st.*—Spend the Old Year out at club; divide extemporary song with Hale, who is going to Australia, and after pleasant hour home with Coyne. *Sic transit* 1856."

Total for year £266. N.B.—Of the above gave W. B. over £60.

Mrs. Weston, Astarte. The play was in blank verse. It was thought that Grattan's novel, *The Cagot's Hut,* may have suggested some of the incidents. On the same night J. L. Toole acted Hector Timid in *The Dead Shot.*

[1] This performance gave promise of greater strength in tragic parts.

[2] Miss Olivia Sharp, columbine; C. Fenton, harlequin; Nicolo Deulin, clown; Naylor, pantaloon. Masters R. and N. Deulin as sprites.

E. L. BLANCHARD AS HE APPEARED WHEN AGED ABOUT 37. [*See page* 168.

1857.

"*Jan. 3rd.*—At night to Woodin's, and pleasant dinner party—T. P. Cooke, Yates, Mackery, Oxenford, Kent, etc. Goes off with great success. *9th.*—Write Drama for *Era*, 10s. At night to Pearson's. Amelia B. Edwards, her new novel out, and her departure to Italy next week. *13th.*—Meeting of *Train*, but nothing done. *14th.*—Duggan in morning. All day at home beginning 'Men about Town,' and very far from well; mind and body both out of order. Troubled much with domestic affairs, and the future clouded by dark anticipations; not understood at all at home. *15th.*—Go to Marylebone; see new piece *Ruth Oakley*[1] produced. Emery, Miss F. Clifford very good. *16th.*—Write notice of last night. Go to town, and feel thoroughly upset, mentally and bodily. Back home, and in bed by 9 p.m.!!!!—a thing I have not been guilty of for years. *Era* 10s. *20th.*—Edward Fitzwilliam,[2] composer, died yesterday. *21st.*—Hear of Sam Emery having been smashed going home, *viâ* cab, with Jonas Levy. *22nd.*—Look in at Olympic; see *Young and Handsome;*[3] very neatly written, but not equal to the former

[1] Mr. Emery opened the theatre as lessee. *Ruth Oakley* was a drama in three acts by A. Harris and T. Williams—a very good melodrama, in which Miss Fanny Clifford played Ruth, and Mr. Emery Paul Oakley. Miss Ranoe played the part of a child remarkably well. Messrs. Bailey and Belmore, and Mesdames Robertson, Addison, and Kate Carson, were also included in the cast.

[2] Edward Francis Fitzwilliam, born at Deal, August 2nd, 1824. Educated in England, and finished his education at a good school in Boulogne. Studied under Sir Henry Bishop and John Barnett. When twenty-one years of age he composed his first work, a *Stabat Mater*, which was performed March 15th, 1845, at Hanover Square Rooms. Appointed musical director of the Lyceum under Madame Vestris's management, October 1847. Was musical director of the Haymarket from Easter 1853, remaining at the theatre until the time of his death. He wrote several cantatas; *The Queen of a Day* (a comic opera) and *A Summer Night's Love* (an operetta)—both produced at the Haymarket; besides numerous songs, ballads, and lyric odes; and the music to *The Green Bushes*, *The Flowers of the Forest*, and Perea Nena's ballets. Married Miss Ella Chaplin, December 1st, 1853. He died of consumption, and was buried at Kensal Green.

[3] F. Robson played Zephyr.

extravaganzas of Planché. 23*rd.*—See *Two Heads Better than One* at Drury; usual punishment of tight boots. From *Era* 15s. Chat with Green and Barnett of *Sunday Times.* *Monday, 26th.*—Hear of Bread Riots—the 250,000 builders' labourers out of employ. 27*th.*—Finish 'Man about Town.' Look in at Lyceum; brilliant transformation scene by Fenton.[1] At Corner meet Talfourd, Hale, Green, W. B. Kenney, and Calhaem. Hear of Albert Smith's house, at Walham Green; his failure predicted. 28*th.*—Hear of Harroway's death."

" *Monday, Feb. 2nd.*—*Black Book*[2] produced at Drury. 7*th.*—E. T. S. for paper £2, and presentation of silver snuff-box for pantomime.[3] Meet Palgrave Simpson. 12*th.*—To Haymarket; see a wretched performance by a *soi-disant* Mr. Charles Dawson, of *The Irish Attorney.* *Era* 15s. 17*th.*—Night, St. James's Amateurs: *Othello* and *Wreck Ashore;* very bad. Haymarket, *Wicked Wife*, and very good. 19*th.*—Finish *Sunday Times* copy. Go to Olympic; new piece,[4] and *Sheep in Wolf's Clothing*, by Tom Taylor. Same subject at Haymarket; goes off well. Meet Mr. Kelly, and sup with him at Edinburgh Castle. *Monday, 23rd.*—Heavy day's work at home on 'England and Wales.' Begin the account of London. See farce at Lyceum, *My Friend from Leatherhead,*[5] by Yates and Harrington ; not very good, but goes well, thanks to Toole. To club, and hear of the Webster and Céleste dissolution of partnership. Francis tells me of Charles Sala (Wynne) buried to-day at Kensal Green.[6] 26*th.*—Haymarket;

---

[1] This was in the pantomime *Conrad and Medora*, and was supported by Miss Woolgar, Mrs. Charles Dillon, Mrs. Buckingham White, and Marie Wilton ; Messrs. J. L. Toole, S. Calhaem, Tom Matthews, and H. and J. Marshall.

[2] This was taken from the French, and, as *Les Mémoires du Diable*, was played at the Vaudeville in Paris in 1856. It was chosen as containing a part eminently suited for Charles Mathews. He was supported by Patty Oliver.

[3] Now in the possession of Augustus Harris.

[4] This was *A Splendid Investment*, a farce by Bayle Bernard.

[5] Toole played Loophole ; Marie Wilton, Lemon-drop, a soubrette.

[6] [He was the brother of G. A. Sala, to whom he was deeply attached.—C. S.]

see pantomime.[1] Last week of it, and find it very well done indeed. *27th.*—Go to Surrey and see pantomime of *Winter and Spring*; a mixture of dulness, slang, splendour, and vulgarity. To club, and chat with Tomlins about Thomas Mayhew, who died by prussic acid. The *Literary Times* his projection."

" *Monday, March 2nd.*—Night to Lyceum; Coyne's adaptation of *Une Femme qui déteste son Mari*;[2] very slow, and, with the exception of Toole, badly acted. *12th.*—At Princess's see gorgeous revival of *Richard II.*;[3] first night, episode brilliant. *13th.*—Write notice of *Richard II.* for *Era*, £1 5s. Then to club; meet Tomlins, Mellon, Sydney Foster, Sala, and McConnell; chatting about Rabelais' old books and Dutch booksellers. *14th.*—E. T. S. at Bridport canvassing for M.P.-ship; £2. At night *Virginius*[4] at Lyceum; Dillon very good. Bet Lowe crown bowl of punch that Smith gets in somewhere. *20th.*—See Dillon's *Hamlet*[5] at Lyceum; very good, and well got up. *23rd.*—E. T. S. canvassing for Bedford. *26th.*—See new piece of *Daddy Hardacre*[6] at Olympic, an adaptation by Palgrave Simpson of *La Fille de l'Avare*; Robson very good. Lyceum, ABC Club, Amateurs of Rank and Fashion; very fair. *27th.*—Account of theatres last night for *Era*; paid for same £1 5s.

[1] This was *The Babes in the Wood*, or, *Harlequin and the Cruel Uncle*. Harlequin, Milano; Fanny Wright, columbine; pantaloon, Mackay; clown, W. Driver.

[2] By Madame Girardin, and was entitled *Angel or Devil*.

[3] Mr. and Mrs. Charles Kean, Richard and his Queen; Ryder, Bolingbroke; Walter Lacy, John of Gaunt; Cooper, Duke of York. Mr. Hatton composed the music, and the scenery was by Grieve. [There was a superb scene, in this revival, of the King's entry into London on horseback.—C.S.]

[4] Mrs. Dillon, Virginia; M'Lien, Icilius; Stuart, Appius; Barrett, Siccius Dentatus.

[5] Dacre Baldic, Laertes; Barrett, Polonius; Stuart, the Ghost; Mrs. Weston, Gertrude; Miss Woolgar, Ophelia; J. L. Toole, first gravedigger.

[6] Robson played the title *rôle*, that of a miser. Miss Hughes (afterwards Mrs. Gaston Murray) was excellent as Esther; George Vining, Charles.

31*st.*—To Toole's benefit; crowded house; see *Wonder, Dominique,* and *Good for Nothing.*"[1]

"*April 2nd.*—Finish 'Man about Town' and theatrical paragraphs. To town, and at night to Lyceum; Dillon's benefit, and last night of the season. *Richelieu*[2] and *Belphegor*; good house, and capital speech. 3*rd.*—Toole tells me he had £230 in from his benefit. 4*th.*—Begin Woodin's new entertainment, *Woodin's Looking-glass of Life.* *Easter Monday,* 13*th.*—Look in at Sadler's Wells; first night of Webster's summer season; see *Fair One of Golden Locks* burlesque.[3] 14*th.*—Haymarket; see clever burlesque by Talfourd, *Atalanta.*[4] 16*th.*—*Era* £1 5*s.* for Easter week. 22*nd.* —Finish 'Man about Town.' Leave by train for Hastings; arrive at 9.30; Royal Oak; sleep in quaint old bedroom overlooking sea. Frequenters dull and dense, but full of the influence of the place and pleasures of propinquity. 23*rd.*—About Hastings all day; walk to St. Leonards with C. C. B. The Revels' in the evening; the past, the present, and the future; alternate themes of thought and cogitation; the delight of domesticity, and the explanation of silence. 24*th.*—The day sunny, yet sombre and soft in its shadows

[1] In *The Wonder* Charles Dillon played Don Felix; Mrs. Buckingham White, Donna Violante; Toole, Lissardo, and the title *rôle* of *Dominique the Deserter,* and Tom Dibbles in *Good for Nothing;* Miss Woolgar was the Nan.

[2] This was the first time Dillon had played the Cardinal in London. During his season he had appeared as Belphegor, d'Artagnan, The Cavalier, Fabian, Othello, William Tell, Citizen Sangfroid, The Cagot, Lord Revesdale (in *Life's Ransom*), Virginius, Hamlet, Don Cæsar, Don Felix, and Richelieu.

[3] Mr. George Webster was the lessee. For his opening night he gave *The Death of Eva,* a stage episode from "Uncle Tom's Cabin;" Cordelia Howard as Eva and Mrs. Howard as Topsy. The burlesque by Planché was the same as had been produced at the Haymarket in 1843. Miss Woolgar appeared as Nan in *Good for Nothing,* and the evening wound up with *The Jew of Lübeck,* of which Mr. J. L. Lyon was the hero.

[4] Or, *The Three Golden Apples,* by Francis Talfourd. Patty Oliver in the title *rôle;* Marie Wilton, Cupid, "a great success;" Hippomenes, Miss Ellen Ternan; Paidagogos, Mr. Compton; the King, Mr. Chippendale.

and sunlight. Fairlight unforgotten, and a day never to be unremembered ; the last look at the old spot, and the dream of the future. 25*th.*—Another day delightfully spent by seaside, strolling about among the cliffs so happy, and, like Malvolio, rubbing my hands, smiling and musing meditatively. 27*th.*—Bleak north-east winds, but pleasant, nevertheless ; wanderings and ponderings about among the cliffs. Chat again at night, and quiet social circle ; all peaceful and pleasant, and happy halcyon days. 28*th.*—To Orr Church in afternoon ; new cemetery. Not much better in health, and more vexed at the circumstance from the desire to be better than usual. 29*th.*—Write ' Man about Town ' in *her* sitting-room ; made very comfortable, and as happy as affection can render me ; evidences of tender thoughtfulness in all arrangements, and sense of home made manifest everywhere. 30*th.* —Wet and windy ; up the heights and down in the valleys all day, and at night songs and company. Idea for articles ; ' Man in the Moon ' a possible *sequitur* to the ' Man about Town.' "

" *May* 1*st.*—An anniversary, and spent most happily *dolce far niente* all day, and evening next door at Revels' ; the presentation of the cork stick, and John Chivery sort of situation. 2*nd.*—A day marked with a white stone ; Eastbourne, Beachy Head, Carina, the coastguard station ; back to Eastbourne. Mr. Hardy; the organ at the old church ; the twilight reverie, with the solemn diapason ; moonlight, and so happy. 4*th.*—Cold north-easterly winds. I intend returning, but do not. Evening ramble with Carina ; more dreams of the future, and delicious retrospective memories of the past. About by the sea ; moonlight, minstrelsy, and the last, last evening at the dear old spot. Adieu, or *au revoir*—which ? 5*th.*—Start at 2.30 by South-Eastern ; home by 6 p.m. ; cold, bleak journey, and feel the effects thereof. Find hosts of letters, and my poor boy wretchedly ill ; self not much better. 15*th.*—Scribble paragraphs for *Era*, 17*s.* 6*d.* 27*th.*—Derby Day, fine ; Blink Bonny, a very dark horse, rather startling the knowing ones as the winner. Finish article, and to town. Cross the bridge ; see the return home ; dust and din. Go to Surrey

Gardens,[1] first time ; Madrigals very well sung ; *solus* all evening.   28*th.*—Begin description of Derby for *Era ;* write on late.   Looking in at Corner—Guerint, his early history ; *ætat.* sixty-five.   29*th.*—Peace anniversary.   Town with copy ; correct proofs for *Era ;* see Ledger, and receive last week's 17*s.* 6*d.*   Home ; Guerint comes and spends evening.   30*th.*—Wells suddenly closed ; G. Webster *non est,* and no money."

" *Monday, June* 1*st.*—Begin ' Man about Town.'   Town at night and see Signor Alfred Bosco,[2] a new wizard, at the Strand, the best ' passer ' I have seen since Blitz.   4*th.*—Go to St. James's ; French play *Les Deux Aveugles ;* Pradeau very

[1] The Royal Surrey Gardens were at this time being undertaken by a company, of which Sir W. de Bathe was chairman, and the Mr. Ellis mentioned at times by E. L. B. was secretary.   The working capital was £30,493.   The directors appear to have engaged as good musical talent as was available : Mr. Sims Reeves, Miss Vinning, Mrs. Lockey, and Mrs. Weiss having inaugurated the season by a performance of Mendelssohn's *Elijah.*   Miss Dolby was also engaged, but could not appear. the first night (May 11th) owing to indisposition.   A very capable orchestra was conducted by Jullien, whose programmes, consisting principally of light music, were very attractive to the many. Madrigals and part-songs were sung by the Surrey Gardens Choral Society, under Mr. Land.   The Surrey Music Hall, built in the grounds and opened July 1856, and which cost £18,000 to build, could hold thirteen thousand persons altogether.   There were panoramas, and fireworks always closed the entertainments.   The Guards on their return from the Crimea were publicly feasted here, August 25th, 1856. On May 27th selections from *Il Barbiere di Siviglia,* known as " Opera Recitals," were given ; also *Elijah,* during the week ; and talented vocalists were engaged.

[2] E. L. B. was himself a great proficient in the art of prestidigitation, and was a most admirable sleight-of-hand performer, his long lithe fingers lending themselves to feats of this description.   I remember on one occasion, after a stroll through the leafy glades of Cobham Park, we dined together at the Bull at Rochester : and he frightened a bucolic waiter, whose look of astonishment as he saw shillings rubbed together until they disappeared, and sixpences come out of the performer's eyes, was a thing to be remembered.   Blanchard used to sing a song (of which I fear no copy exists) about three wizards who were holding a quiet *séance,* " and conjuring every one," but who were disturbed by the advent of a fourth wizard, whose feats were of such a remarkable character that the other three quietly rose and departed, agreeing that they had been spending the evening with the evil one. Whilst the song was in progress he illustrated it with a number of feats of legerdemain.   E. L. B. was also a very admirable improvisatore.

clever. *Monday, 8th.*—Dear mother's birthday. Douglas Jerrold [1] died this morning, in his fifty-fifth year; a great loss to the world, as well as to his own social circle. *9th.*—Tremendous fire at Pickford's [2] at 10 at night, and square lit by the flames. *10th.*—Willoughby sends for memoir of Jerrold, and note for 'Heads of People.' No one comes; all solitary and sad—very, very sad. *Monday, 16th*—Am offered an engagement on *The Field*. Tempting, but must decline for reasons of honour. *17th.*—Have interview with Lowe respecting *Field* and *Critic*. Chat with Hale about the

[1] Born in London, January 3rd, 1803. He obtained his dramatic knowledge mostly through his father having been manager of the Southend and Sheerness theatres. Having taken a great predilection for the sea, he became a midshipman in the Royal Navy, in the ship of Captain Austin, brother to Miss Austin the novelist. A year and a half cured him of his love for seafaring, but the knowledge of maritime life that he had gained stood him in good stead afterwards. He was next apprenticed to a printer, where he worked with Leman Blanchard. His first effort in dramatic writing was *The Smoked Miser*, or, *The Benefit of Hanging*, a farce that was very successful in 1823 at Sadlers Wells, when Egerton was manager. He obtained his footing on the Press through an essay which he wrote on *Der Freyschütz*. He was a wonderfully rapid concocter of plays, and for some time supplied a fresh piece of some sort at the Coburg every other week, besides writing for Sadlers Wells and editing the *Weekly Times*. His best-known piece is *Black-eyed Susan*, produced at the Surrey, June 6th, 1829, with P. P. Cooke as William. *The Rent Day*, Drury Lane, January 1832; *Nell Gwynne*, Covent Garden, January 1833; *The Housekeeper*, or, *The White Rose*, Haymarket, July 1834; *The Prisoner of War*, Drury Lane, 1842—were amongst his most famous plays, of which space will not permit giving an entire list. He contributed much to magazines. His "Caudle Lectures" in *Punch* will always be remembered. He started a shilling magazine and *Jerrold's Newspaper*, but these were not successful. About 1852 he became editor of *Lloyd's Newspaper*. He was a brilliant conversationalist and satirist. He died of disease of the heart, and was buried in Norwood Cemetery.

[2] One peculiarity of this fire was the turning loose of upwards of one hundred horses, which galloped over London in the wildest manner, the whole of which were not recovered for some days. Only one, a very savage animal called "The Man-hater," was burned; he would only allow his own particular carman, who drove him, to approach him, and as he was not on the spot no one else could liberate the beast. Forty thousand quarters of corn were destroyed, besides other property of great value.

Rhine. 19*th.*—Into town with copy ; *Era* £1 16*s.* Home sad, and health ditto. 22*nd.*—Finish second song of Woodin's; printer turns up for 'England and Wales,' which is to be resumed. Write to Lowe declining engagement on *Field.* 24*th.*—Slow, sad, and solitary all day. Finish 'Man about Town.' Walk. In bed by 11 ; heart broken and head bewildered, life looking more perplexing in its mysteries than ever."

June 26th to *30th* E. L. B. spent at Margate to endeavour to recruit his health.

" *July 2nd.*—Olympic at night ; Brough's new burlesque of *Masaniello*,[1] first time, very good, and goes off briskly. 4*th.*—Go to Camden Town in evening, and provide mother with a few of the creature comforts. 8*th.*—At night to Newman Street spiritualistic reunion ; a new association, every Thursday. 9*th.*—Town with copy ; night to Haymarket ; see Tom Taylor's new comedy of the *Victims*;[2] admirably written. *Monday*, 13*th.*—At night to Grecian ; chat with Conquest and his son, who, author, actor, artist, shows talent. 16*th.*—Write remainder of 'Man about Town.' *Era* paragraphs, and town with them. 21*st.* —Join the London Archæologists, and go over the whole of the Tower ; a very great treat. 25*th.*—'England and Wales' all day. To club ; take chair. Sala, Burnand, and very pleasant party present. 28*th.*—An event ! After going to mother's, returning to dinner William Douglas Haly, of New York, pays me a visit after fifteen years' absence. Find

[1] Robson in the title *rôle*, in which the author had given him some of the most excruciating puns, but in which character this great actor displayed those tragi-comic powers for which he was so noted. Miss Swanborough, Alphonso ; Miss Hughes, Elvira ; Miss Thirlwall, Lorenzo ; G. Cook as a Neapolitan policeman.

[2] Buckstone, Josh Buttersby ; Mrs. Poynter, Miss Minerva Crane ; Miss Reynolds, Mrs. Merryweather ; Patty Oliver, Mrs. FitzHerbert ; Howe, Mr. Merryweather ; and Rogers, Rowley. Messrs. Clark, Cullenford, and Braid were also in the cast. This was the 1,124th night of the season under Mr. Buckstone's management, during which the theatre had never been closed, except on Sundays. A new ballet called *The Gleaners* was an item of the programme on the same night.

out Hunt for him, and scene at interview. Night with
Coyne and Hinton at Highbury. 29*th.*—Busy on ‘Man
about Town,’ but too much thrilled by the event of yesterday to do much. At night to Adelphi; Jerrold night.
Rent Day and *Black-eyed Susan*.[1] Home at 2 with Deane.
30*th.*—Begin ‘Shall Covent Garden be rebuilt?’ Write
till very late.”

“ *Aug.* 1*st.*—Crystal Palace Water Tower thrown open first
time ; fountains a great treat. 8*th.*—Brough, E. F. B.,
and Watkins’ brother introduced first time. Haly, Sargeant,
and Holt talk about Atlas with Mr. Christie. Photo done, and
bring it home, with general applause. 10*th.*—With C. C. B. to
Olympic, which opens under Robson’s and Emden’s management. 11*th.*—At night to Olympic and see the *Lighthouse ;*[2]
delighted with it ; most effectively got up. Look in at club
afterwards ; Horsley, of Staples Inn, keeps me chatting late.
Monday, 17*th.*—To mother in morning, and give her usual
little present. Hingston, Fred Vizetelly, Holt, etc. ; adjourn
to Red Lion. Ross,[3] the comic singer, home to 13, Wharton

[1] This was the second of the series of the Jerrold remembrance
nights which had been arranged for the benefit of his widow and
family. They included a concert at St. Martin's Hall, readings by
Charles Dickens, an account of his Crimean doings by William Howard
Russell (the *Times* correspondent), and an entertainment by a literary
amateur troop at the Gallery of Illustration. The first dramatic
tribute was given on July 15th at the Haymarket, when *The Housekeeper* and *The Prisoner of War* were played, and only two of the
original cast—Messrs. Webster and Buckstone—appeared.

[2] *The Subterfuge*—an English version of *Livre troisième, Chapitre
premier*, previously adapted at the Haymarket under the title of
A Novel Expedient, and later as *My Aunt's Advice*—was the first piece ;
an address written by Robert Brough was spoken by Mr. Robson ;
and Wilkie Collins's *Lighthouse*, done at Tavistock House two years
previously by amateurs, made up the bill with *Masaniello*. In *The
Lighthouse*, Aaron Gurnock, first played by Charles Dickens, now fell
to Mr. Robson ; Jacob Dale, Mr. Addison ; Martin Gurnock, Walter
Gordon ; Samuel Farley, G. Cooke ; Phœbe Dale, Miss Wyndham ;
Lady Grace, Miss Swanborough. Mr. Vining spoke the original
prologue in front of the act-drop, which was an exact reproduction
of Stanfield's original picture representing the lighthouse.

[3] Ross used to sing at the Cyder Cellars, in Maiden Lane, an underground music-hall that was contemporary with Evans's, but was not

Street, with him. Odd idea of a ' Comic Cyder Cellar ' man singing the worst songs. Passion for dahlias; elegant place and nice garden. Stroll by daylight; the odd idea worth a mem. *22nd.*—From *Sunday Times* £2. Not well in morning, so off by train at 2 p.m. to Epsom, which I see for the first time. Walk on through Leatherhead to Dorking, ten miles, with carpet bag slung over my shoulder; stop at White Horse; Bull Inn better. *Monday, 24th.*—Off early to Leith Hill, a spot long the landmark of my vision. At night to travelling theatre, the *Fire Raiser;* one Montague there, an actor, very good. Moonlight and starlight ramble. Dreamily reposing, with literary chat, refreshing to mental exhaustion. A night and day of pleasant dreams. *25th.*— Up Box Hill, and glorious view from the summit; down hill again, and chat with one of the strollers. Interesting reverie, and pleasant afternoon conversation; then the farewell, the train, and back by 11 to Wilmington Square, and the stern realities. *27th.*—Finish ' Man about Town,' and do a little for *Era,* from which £1. Look in at Lyon's Inn; Lowe and Francis there; early home; long read, and write memoir of poor Thérèse Cushnie.[1] *29th.*—E. T. S. for *Sunday Times* £2. Sorting papers all day. Club, and see George Coppin returned from Australia."

" *Sept.* 11*th.*—Arrange with Mr. Christie, of *Atlas,* to do

so respectably conducted. He sang very powerfully, and with great dramatic effect, a song called " Sam Hall," which would not now be tolerated by decent audiences.

[1] Married in 1849 to Milano, the well-known harlequin and ballet-master. During her whole life Thérèse Cushnie was most highly esteemed for her private worth, and she was celebrated as a dancer. From the first she worked very hard at her profession, having made her *début* at an early age at the Garrick Theatre, followed by engagements at the Grecian Saloon, Surrey, and Astley's. She then studied hard for two years in Paris, of the best masters; her first succeeding English engagement being at the Theatre Royal, Manchester, which was followed by her being engaged as one of the principal dancers at the Royal Italian Opera, Covent Garden. With her sister Annie and her husband, she was for two seasons at Drury Lane, since which time they were at the Haymarket. Thérèse Cushnie last appeared in *The Babes in the Wood,* at Christmas 1856. She died on September 22nd, after giving birth to a still-born child.

a country letter for Birmingham weekly. *12th.*—Sadlers Wells opens for the season with *Hamlet;*[1] write notice, and home early. *Monday, 14th.*—Begin *Sunday Times* almanac; tedious work. Get flurried about winter's approach and work to be done. To Myddelton Hall, and see Seymour Carleton's[2] imitative entertainment; excellent. *15th.*—Much depressed in spirits; indoors, but write little. Go to Wells; Mrs. Charles Young,[3] an Australian actress, appearing as Julia in the *Hunchback.* *17th.*—Try a little more 'Man about Town.' Go to Haymarket; Mrs. Sinclair as Lady Teazle.[4] *Era* £1 10s. *18th.*—Not well. Brown and Coyne at Angel, and proposition to start *viâ* Eastern Counties next day. *19th.*—Off in afternoon to Cambridge: stop for ten minutes at Broxbourne; reach the city of colleges at 7, and stay at Castle, good inn in St. Andrew's Street. Much pleased with Cambridge; go to theatre, in evening at Barnwell; see *Lady of Lyons;* Mrs. Mayland (Miss A.

[1] Reopened the thirteenth year of the Phelps and Greenwood Shakespearian management. Henry Marston again the Ghost; Rayner, Claudius; F. Robinson, Laertes; Lewis Ball, first grave-digger; Miss J. Marston, Ophelia; Miss Atkinson, the Queen.

[2] It was called *Familiar Faces;* or, *Old Friends in New Places,* and was an exact reproduction, alike in voice, manner, and appearance, of Albert Smith, Charles Mathews, Phelps, Henry Marston, Paul Bedford, Wright, Miss Cushman, and Mr. Robson. At the same time Mr. Arthur Young gave, in the costume of the sixteenth century, dramatic readings from *Othello, Merchant of Venice,* and *Richard III.*

[3] [Afterwards Mrs. Hermann Vezin.—C. S.] Mrs. Charles Young was married, when scarcely sixteen, to Charles Young, with whom she was very unhappy, and eventually obtained a divorce from. She was graceful, had a very good, clear delivery, and as yet a not very strong voice; but it was sweet and sympathetic. The fault that was to be found with her at this time was want of power. She was of English birth, but had commenced her career as an actress in Australia. F. Robinson was the Modus; Henry Marston, Sir Thomas Clifford; Lewis Ball, Fathom; and Phelps, Sir Walter.

[4] Mrs. Catherine Sinclair proved herself more capable in the later scenes. She was supported by Miss Talbot as Mrs. Candour; Miss Emma King as Maria; Mrs. Poynter as Lady Sneerwell; Chippendale, Sir Peter; Howe, Joseph Surface; William Farren, Charles Surface, who sang " Here's to the Maiden," usually allotted to Careless; Rogers, Sir Oliver; Compton, Crabtree; and Buckstone, Sir Benjamin Backbite.

Hudson) very good actress. *Monday, 21st.*—To Cathedral in morning at Ely, and shown over it; a very great treat. Back by train; stop at Audley End, and go over Lord Braybrooke's fine place; very pleased indeed; home by nine. *22nd.*—See Greening for almanac. To town; see American tragedian, Roberts, as Sir Giles, at Drury, and find him good. *24th.*— Hear of Sinclair's [1] death on Tuesday, and write memoir for *Era;* to town with it, receiving £1 7s. 6d. for past services. Flexmore calls. Write London letter for *Dudley Express*— the first. *25th.*—To town with copy of letter, which finish, and pipe *solus* in club. *26th.*—E. T. S. £2. See *Cymbeline* [2] at Wells, and Greenwood; one minute at Drury Roberts as Richard III. [3] *29th.*—At night with Coyne at Garrick Theatre,

[1] John Sinclair was born in Edinburgh in 1785. When twenty-five years of age, came to London to take up his commission in a regiment in India, but was asked to sing for the benefit of a lady at the Haymarket in *Lock and Key*, and sang his three songs so well that he was persuaded to give up the idea of a martial career, and he studied for three years under Thomas Welsh. He played for a short time previous to this as Mr. Noble at the Margate Theatre, and made his first appearance as Carlos in *The Duenna*, September 20th, 1811, when actually under articles to his master. He made a great hit as Apollo in the burletta of *Midas*. In 1816 he married, and in 1818 his long engagement with Mr. Harris of Covent Garden terminated. He went to Italy and studied under Rossini, and made his Italian *début* at Pisa in *Torvaldo* in 1821. He then made a most successful Continental tour, and on November 19th, 1824, was engaged by Mr. Charles Kemble at Covent Garden, and appeared as Prince Orlando in *The Cabinet* in 1826. He went to Drury Lane in 1828, to the Adelphi in 1831, again the principal tenor at Drury Lane, and then visited America ; on his return from thence he confined himself to chamber concerts. He became the proprietor of the Tivoli Gardens at Margate, and spent the remainder of his life there. He was a most accomplished singer ; he possessed a wonderful falsetto, and was great in Scotch ballads. He was the father of the Mrs. Catherine Sinclair recently referred to.

[2] Marston, Iachimo ; Rayner, Belarius ; Belford, Guiderius ; F. Robinson, Arviragus ; Lewis Ball, Cloten. Imogen was played by Mrs. Charles Young ; she showed great earnestness of manner and unaffected pathos. Phelps, Leonatus.

[3] Mr. Roberts was an American tragedian, and made his first appearance, Monday, September 21st, as Sir Giles Overreach, in *A New Way to Pay Old Debts*. On Wednesday, 23rd, he played King Lear to Miss Portman's Cordelia. On Thursday he appeared as Richard III. with Mrs. Vickery as the Queen ; Miss Portman as Lady Jane ; Mrs. Selby

music hall, and literary lounges. 30*th.*—See one act of *Love's Labour's Lost,*[1] revived, first night at Sadlers Wells."

" *Oct.* 3*rd.*—Night to Lyceum, *Norma;*[2] write notice for *Era,* and home after club. *Monday, 5th.*—Busy with almanac contributions. Night to Haymarket; see *Lady of Lyons;*[3] Miss Amy Sedgwick's first appearance in London; very successful. 6*th.*—Ought to have dined with Coppin at Craven Hotel, but only got there at the end of the feast, having looked in at Adelphi to see *Poll and My Partner Joe.*[4] 12*th.*—Busy with almanac, and give copy. At night to Strand; James Rogers's farewell benefit,[5] prior to his departure for America. See Robson (*Country Fair*), Keeley's *Blessed Babby,* and then to club; nothing talked about but the horrid murder and mutilation.[6] 15*th.*—Finish ' Man about Town.' Look in at Haymarket; first two acts of *Lovechase;*[7] write notice for *Era.* From *Era* £1 10*s.* 16*th.*—Become member

as the Duchess of York. Mr. Roberts' performances were rather promises of future excellence, when he should have gained more experience.

[1] Marston, Biron ; Miss Fitzpatrick, Rosaline ; F. Robinson, Ferdinand King of Navarre ; J. W. Ray, Lord Chamberlain ; Mr. Williams, Holofernes ; Lewis Ball, Costard ; Miss Rose Williams, Moth. It was noticeable that Dr. Arne's songs of " Spring " and " Winter," generally transferred to *As You Like It,* were introduced and well sung by Miss Eva Brect and Mr. Thompson.

[2] Norma, Madame Caradoro ; Pollio, Augustus Braham ; Oroveso, Hamilton Braham ; Adelgisa, Susan Pyne. The orchestra and chorus under the direction of Alfred Mellon.

[3] Howe, Claude Melnotte : Chippendale, General Damas ; William Farren, Beauseant ; Mr. Rogers and Mrs. Griffiths, Mons. and Madame Deschappelles.

[4] By John Thomas Haines. T. P. Cooke, Harry Halyard ; Miss Arden, Mary Maybud ; Miss Mary Keeley, Abigail Holdforth ; Mr. Wright, Watchful Waxend ; Billington, Joe Tiller ; Charles Selby, Black Brandon.

[5] The bill provided was the comedy, *The Gentleman Opposite :* Miss Herbert, Mrs. Mowbray ; *Phantom Wives, That Blessed Baby,* with Mr. and Mrs. Keeley ; *You are sure to be shot,* with James Rogers as Tom Tipper ; and the burlesque of *Traviata.*

[6] This refers to the finding of a portion of a man's body by two lads in a carpet bag lying on the third buttress of Waterloo Bridge. [Afterwards known as the Waterloo Bridge Mystery.—C. S.]

[7] Amy Sedgwick as Constance ; Chippendale, Sir William Fondlove ;

of the Savage Club,[1] and promise to dine with them to-morrow.   17*th.*—Dine with the Savages at Crown Inn ; Yard in chair.   Afterwards to club, and home by midnight. *Monday,* 19*th.*—Miss very much my poor old dog Fid, who has been with me for eleven years, and has now absented himself for four days; mysterious disappearance.   Go to

Mrs. Marston, Widow Green ; Howe, Wildrake ; William Farren, Master Waller ; Mrs. Caroline White, Lydia ; Rogers, Trueworth ; Clarke, Last.

[1] This club was originated by a choice few of the real " Bohemians," who used to meet at the White Hart, at the corner of Exeter and Catherine Streets, Strand.   Finding that their little social conversations were often intruded upon by strangers the clubbists made a change.   Fred Lawrence, joint author with Halliday in *Kenilworth*, discovered a new habitation for them at the Crown Tavern, Vinegar Yard, kept by one Lawson.   Nine of the original members migrated, and had an upstairs room looking on to Drury Lane ; and the landlord, though he kept a room strictly for their use, charged them only public-house prices—an advantage to men whose pockets at that time were not too well lined.   As far as can be ascertained the names of the nine were Halliday, Strauss, " Professor " Anderson, William Hale, Lawrence, and William, Robert, John and Lionel Brough, of whom the last is the only one surviving.   These thought it would be advisable to recruit their number, and had no difficulty in collecting many really good Bohemians, some of whom are still living and are important members of the club, such as Edward Draper, Tegetmeier, J. Daffit Francis, Dr. Strauss, etc., etc.   The name of the club was suggested by Robert Brough, who thought they might through its assumption either call themselves " Savages " and outside the pale of civilization, or take rank as followers of Richard Savage.   Some months afterwards J. Daffit Francis gave the club some savage weapons, shields etc., and from that time the members have all called themselves " Savages." After a time the club removed to the Nell Gwynne, off the Strand, and it was joined by Sala, Byron, Frank Talfourd, Tom Robertson, Leicester Buckingham, Jeff Prowse (" Nicholas "), William McConnell, Charles Bennett, Harrison Weir, Edmund Falconer, and other well known *literati* and Bohemians.   Thence they moved their quarters to the Lyceum Tavern, and again moved not so very many yards off to " Jessop's "—the building in which the *Echo* office is now situated, and which was once known as a great resort for budding histrions who used to pay for the privilege of acting, and later had an unenviable notoriety as a very late dancing-saloon.   The affections of the Savages appear to have leaned towards the Nell Gwynne, for we once more find them located there ; but after a time they successively pitched their tents at the Gordon Hotel, then under the management of " Doctor

town ; see Smith, Dykwynkyn, and Beverley at Drury, and settle on *Jack Horner,* or, *Harlequin A B C* for pantomime. To Wells at night, and arrange to do *Beauty and the Beast* for his subject. 20*th.*—Find poor dog has been secretly poisoned by a canine Marchioness Brinvilliers. 21*st.*—Write

Strauss ;" at Ashley's Hotel, at Haxell's, and at the Caledonian. This seems to have been their last resting-place on sufferance, for they then took premises of their own in the Savoy, where they dispensed hospitality and good fellowship for a considerable time ; but, becoming cramped for room, they eventually took the lease of their present premises on Adelphi Terrace. It would be impossible to give a list of the really great men known to Art and Literature who have been members. There is scarcely a journalist, artist, or actor of repute but has been enrolled as a "Savage." They have been ever foremost in works of charity, ever ready to assist any of their members in distress, or to aid the families of those who have been left scantily provided for. They have at various times given dramatic performances, which have been invariably of the very best ; and the results of which have succoured those who could not look elsewhere for support. The series of "Savage Club Papers," cleverly written and well illustrated, were issued in the cause of charity. They have a Masonic Lodge, the working of which is wonderfully perfect, and to this day the Savage Club remains a Bohemian Club in the best meaning of the term. It may be mentioned that the Arundel Club, of which E. L. B. was for so many years an esteemed member, was an outcome of the Savages. H. J. Byron, W. P. Hall, and Leicester Buckingham, formed a sub-committee (when the Savages were at the Lyceum Tavern), and were deputed to find a new habitation. In their search they came upon some premises in Arundel Street, and took them in their own names and, on their returning to the Savage Club they announced that if some ultra-Bohemian members were not requested to resign, they should start a club of their own in Arundel Street. As their wishes were not acceded to they became the founders of the Arundel Club. The first Savage Club performance was at the Lyceum in aid of the Lancashire Cotton Famine Fund, and was attended by nearly all the Royal Family (the Queen, Prince Consort, Prince of Wales, Princess Royal, etc., etc.) The burlesque played was *Forty Thieves,* written by seven of the most popular burlesque writers of the day. Mrs. Stirling spoke an address, and all the characters in the burlesque were performed by Savages (including the " 40 "). Miss Louise Laidlaw was the one exception in the cast. It was afterwards played for the same object in Liverpool, and the Club were enabled to hand over nearly £600 to the Fund. [Mr. Lionel Brough, one of the founders of the Savages, kindly supplied some of the above interesting information.]

Olympic notice of *Leading Strings.*[1] 23rd.—Town with more copy. Chat with Christie and Mr. Lawrence at *Atlas* office ; settle with latter £3 for one month's Dudley letter, to last week, No. 5. 24th.—Correcting almanac proofs and arranging them all day. Night to ' Savages ;' then to opening of Adelaide Casino.[2] Club, and give them my picture, and give Doyle 10s. for poor Ball. *Monday, 26th.*—About almanac matter in morning ; in afternoon Christy Minstrels ; then to Olympic ; bad farce of *Deadly Reports.*[3] Then to club ; Chippendale in chair. Hear news of fall of Delhi in evening papers ; excitement everywhere in consequence. 27th.—Not the thing ; try warm bath at 98°. Begin ' Man about Town.' 28th.— E. T. S. calls and pays half for almanac, £10. City of London prize drama, *Lucy Wentworth.*[4] See Nelson Lee.' 29th.—At night look in at St. James's amateurs. At club with Talfourd and Godfrey Turner. 31st.—E. T. S. £2. Visit from Miss Florence Law (a wife separated from a literary husband), who is introduced by Albert Smith. Myself with terrific neuralgic headache. To bed by eight ! ! ! ! ! ! "

" *Monday, Nov. 2nd.*—Frightful headache, and in bed at 7 a.m. 3rd.—Congestion of brain ; pain awful. Flexmore [5] calls, but unable to talk or write. Hear the Leviathan is

[1] This was a three-act comedy of A. C. Troughton, taken from M. Scribe's *Toujours.* Mrs. Stirling, Mrs. Leveson ; George Vining, Frank Leveson ; Miss Swanborough, Edith Belfort ; Binnings the butler, Mr. Addison ; Miss Wyndham, Flora Mackenzie.

[2] This was opened by Bignell, late of the Argyle Rooms, in consequence of his licence for that place of entertainment having been refused. It was a casino, and another Argyle to all intents and purposes.

[3] By Palgrave Simpson, and was taken from the French.

[4] *Lucy Wentworth,* or, *The Village-born Beauty,* by T. P. Prest. The action of the play commences in 1812. One of the features of the scenery was a view of " Frost Fair on the Thames in 1814," with a skating dance on the ice, with Blackfriars Bridge and St. Paul's in the distance. The writing of the drama was said to have been much above the average.

[5] It should be mentioned of Flexmore that when quite a lad he used to work as a warehouseman by day, and as " general utility " at halls, singing-places, and theatres, in order to earn sufficient to enable him to

launched—*Great Eastern;* an accident, and failure. *4th.*
—Still in pain; try a little writing, but process agonising.
At length contrive to be comic! and do a bit of ' Man about
Town.' Go to Wells; *Clandestine Marriage* revived, and
Phelps as Lord Ogleby. *5th.—Era* £1 3s. Lyceum; see
one act of *Rose of Castille;* [1] farce, *A Pair of Pigeons;* very
like *Is he jealous?* *6th.*—A little better, thank God. Finish
Era paragraphs. Try a comic scene, but failure. Go to Sadlers
Wells; two acts of *Clandestine Marriage;* very good.
7th.—Haymarket at night; new comedy by Tom Taylor,
The Unequal Match; [2] very good, and highly successful.
Monday, 9th.—Lord Mayor's Day, and for the first time no
water procession. Begin Drury pantomime of *Jack Horner.*
11th.—To mother's in morning to see the boy, who is re-
covering from a severe cold; take her some old port, etc., to
drink many happy returns of Bill's birthday. *12th.*—To
Hanover Square Rooms; Professor Frickell, wizard, without
apparatus; very neat indeed. *13th.*—Write notice of the
wizard, and to town. From *Era* £1 5s. *Monday, 16th.*—
Musing over pantomime, but little done. At night to
Adelphi; *The Headless Man* [3]—a very bad piece, very well
got up. *17th.*—Busy all day on Drury pantomime; go not
out, and do not much. More annoyances present themselves, so utterly undeserved by me, and so impossible to

support his mother. Though he became one of the most graceful
dancers, he was getting well on in his teens *before he had learnt his first
step-dance from Joseph Cave,* who used often to be employed at the
same houses with him of an evening.

[1] This was done by the Harrison Pyne Company, which included
amongst its members Louise and Susan Pyne, Harrison, Weiss, St.
Albyn, Walworth, and George Honey. *The Pair of Pigeons,* by Edward
Stirling, was acted by George Honey, and Miss Cuthbert, who donned
male attire and played a fop.

[2] Amy Sedgwick, Hester Grazebrook; W. Farren, Harry Arncliffe;
Mrs. Buckingham White, Mrs. Montresor; Buckstone, Doctor Botch-
erby; Compton, Blenkinsop; and Chippendale, Braid. Clark and Mrs.
Fitzwilliam also included in the cast.

[3] An adaptation of *La Légende de l'Homme sans Tête,* by MM. Edouard
Brisebarre and Eugène Nus. It was a ghostly story of a vampire,
specially noticeable for the acting of Webster and Céleste as Carl
Blitzen and Christine. Selby, Doctor Neiden; and Wright, Mary
Keeley, and Marie Wilton were included in the cast.

contend with.   Sit up till 2 a.m. ; sad, nervous, and solitary. *18th.*—Club ;   meet Charles Dillon and Charles Webb, Wilson, and home late.   *19th.*—To Olympic ; Robson's [1] reappearance after provincial engagement. Club ; Levy. *20th.*—All day on Drury Lane pantomime, and by sitting up late I think finish it satisfactorily, as far as the rough draft goes.   Getting careworn and heartsore for want of heart-sympathy.   *Monday, 23rd.*—Olympic ; Coyne's new farce of *What will they say at Brompton ?* [2] Then to Free-masons' Tavern ; *Era* supper—the thousandth number ; meet Crewe (aged 74, a wonderful singer), George, Fidler, Hughes (one of the staff), Herr Lowenthal, etc.   *27th.*—Look in at Strand, and see Bridgeman's farce of *Telegram.*"

" *Dec. 5th.*—From E. T. S. £2. Flexmore and Byrnes in morning.   Owing to more interruption write in eight hours two pages of a comic scene for Sadlers Wells.   Hear of Moncrief's death from Wilton and Tomlins.   *7th.*—Write comic scene for Flexmore, and take it to Drury, where meet everybody.   On account of pantomime £10.   *8th.*—Cold worse, and from domestic causes spirits utterly crushed and broken.   All day at work writing second scene of Sadlers Wells opening, which take, and after sit up till 3, cogitating over remainder.   *11th.*—Thirty-seven this day ! ! !   Have I done enough to be that ?   My life must answer the question. Ride to Turnham Green, and walk back for exercise.   Glass with W. B. at night at the ' Savages ; ' and so ends the end of the thirty-seventh year.   *12th.*—All day over the front comic of Sadlers Wells.   Much indisposed, and greatly upset mentally and domestically ; paying a vast amount for no com-fort, no happiness, or sympathy.   *15th.*—Drury in morning ; see Tully, and watch progress.   Soyer presents me with his book.[3] Home to make out Drury bill. Dear boy and Sola

---

[1] He resumed his old character in *The Lighthouse.*

[2] Robson, Samuel Todd ; Miss Wyndham, Mrs. Todd ; G. Cooke, Croker ; Addison, Harwood Cooper and Miss Marston also in the cast.

[3] This must have been "Soyer's Culinary Campaign," a book which he published after his experiences in the Crimean War. He was sent to reorganize, originally, the hospital kitchens of the British Army, and

to Hudson's entertainment; a painful domestic scene afterwards. *22nd.*—Drury rehearsal in morning; back, and write reviews. At night attend the usual Christmas supper at club. Tomlin in chair, *vice* R. Brough ill; Sala 'vice,' Toole and I next him. Pratton-clarionette, Lazarus flute; very good. Sing 'Guy Fawkes' and Almanac song; all goes off famously. Home at 4 with Marston, Summers, Dr. Brown, and Deane; pleasant evening. *24th.*—Write paragraphs for *Era*, from which £2 10s. for Christmas week. *25th.*—Christmas Day. Miller dines with us, and as jolly as possible under the circumstances. At night to theatre for rehearsal; all goes off well, Back by midnight, and read for an hour. *26th.*—Very busy day for me. In morning

after he had got these into working order on the Bosphorus, he did the same for the Divisional Hospitals at the front. To his efforts and those of Miss Florence Nightingale, with whom he cordially worked, supported by John Milton, Accountant General from the War Office, and the Commissioner sent out by the *Times* newspaper, it is owing that many lives were saved. Years before, in 1846, when *chef* of the Reform Club, he had rendered most useful service during the famine in Ireland. Soyer was a genial, kind-hearted man, and was much liked and esteemed. The semi uniform that he had adopted in the Crimea, and which he used to wear mounted on a white Arab, created then quite a sensation. Our allies, French, Turkish and Sardinian, often wondered what his position in the army could be. His *cortège* was the more noticeable in that he was invariably attended by his secretary, a black gentleman, one Peter de Nully Taylor, who had been well known in the law courts in London, as a very able shorthand reporter. Alexis Soyer was born at Mean, Brie, in France, October 1809, and he was intended for the Church; but not feeling the vocation, he was apprenticed to the celebrated *chef* Dewix of the Palais Royal, Paris, and served with him five years. Soyer's brother was *chef* at Cambridge House, Piccadilly; and when Alexis came over to England to visit him, and liked the country, he determined to remain, and eventually became *chef* to Lord Panmure, Secretary of State for War, and other noble families. He was the author of "The Modern Housewife" (1849), and "Délaissements Culinaires," of the "Gastronomic Regenerator," of "Pantropheon," and "The Shilling Cookery." During the time of the Exhibition of 1851, he had a magnificent species of restaurant, called the "Symposium," at Kensington, by which he lost £4,000, which he honourably paid. He died August 5th, 1858, and was buried at Kensal Green in the vault which he had erected for his wife, who had been an artist of considerable note.

to town; dine at club; write Sadlers Wells[1] and Strand[2] notice for *Era.* Then to Drury;[3] private box for mother and the dear boy. Go to Olympic;[4] write out notices, and do *Sunday Times* and *Era;* all goes off well. E. T. S., as usual, £2. *Monday, 28th.*—Pottering about at home, wretchedly uncomfortable all day. In evening to Drury; see pantomime; goes off very well, but long. Look in at club, and walk home with Marston. *29th.*—Hear from Haly, New York. Pay Dr. Brown for medical attendance for self and boy. At night to Sadlers Wells; see pantomime, *Beauty and the Beast;* scenery good, but wasted thought and energy as usual. *31st.*—Hard at work on ' Man about Town ' all day. Walk into town at night; see the Old Year out with Talfourd, Gould, and Watts at club; slow and sad. And thus 1857 cometh to a close, the year not unproductive of coin, the reward of excessively hard work; but to the heart a blank, chilling void, that has had but one distant glimmer reflected therein. For *all* thank God."

Total for year £260 10*s.*

[1] *Harlequin and Beauty and the Beast,* or, *Little Goody Two Shoes and Mother Bunch's Book-case in Baby-land.* Harlequin, Charles Fenton ; clown, Nicolo Deulin ; columbine, Caroline Parkes ; pantaloon, Mr. Naylor.

[2] *Harlequin Novelty and the Princess who lost Her Heart.* Harlequin, Miss Craven ; W. Dean and J. Howard, clown and pantaloon ; Miss Wyatt and Mdlle. Deulin, columbines.

[3] *Little Jack Horner.* Harlequins, Messrs. Milano and St. Armand ; clowns, Flexmore and Boleno ; pantaloons, Nash, and W. A. Barnes ; columbines, Madame Boleno and Mdlle. Christine.

[4] *The Doge of Duralto,* or, *the Enchanted Eyes,* a fairy extravaganza by Robert Brough, with Miss Hughes, Miss Wyndham, Robson, G. Cooke, and H. Wigan in the cast to be noted.

1858.

" *Jan.* 1*st.*—The year opens with a bright sunny day, but with myself a sad feeling of being thoroughly used up. Town to correct proofs 'Man about Town,' and then to St. John's Gate. Start a new society—the Friday Knights ;[1] Hollingshead, Friswell, Draper, and very pleasant party. Songs, and break up after midnight; the old room over the Gate the scene of the symposium. Pay 5*s.* for annual term of membership. 14*th.*—Home all day on 'Man about Town,' and sit up till 3 a.m. to finish it. The wasted hours, the wasted hopes, warring against, but pressed cruelly hard, yet submissively stoical, and shockingly sensitive withal. Read Emerson, and resolutions strengthened. 15*th.*—At night to the Gate. Appointed chairman for Friday next. Rules

---

[1] Several members of the Re-Union resided in North London, or on its confines—to wit : Jonas Levy (Gray's Inn), Henry Marston (Baker Street, Lloyd Square), E. L. Blanchard (Wilmington Square), Hain Friswell (Holborn), and W. R. Belford (Pentonville). On the off-nights of the Re-Union these worthies used to assemble occasionally at a little ale-house, the Shakespeare Head, at the corner of Myddelton Turning, Arlington Street, Clerkenwell, opposite Sadlers Wells. It was a smoke-pipe and tankard *coterie*, wherein the talk turned on the drama mainly. Friswell became exceedingly anxious that a club should be formed in North London for the convenience of its Re-Union members, and Henry Marston was deputed to beat about for a cosy and comfortable lodge. By an accident the actor strolled into the Old Jerusalem Tavern, attached to that vestige of antique London, St. John's Gate, Clerkenwell, and saw its host—genial, intelligent Benjamin Foster, an excellent antiquary, and no less excellent caterer —explaining his mission. Foster, delighted at the project, said the best room in the old Clerkenwell Gatehouse could be placed at the disposal of Mr. Marston and his friends, free of charge, with every attention to their comfort. They were informed of this proposal, and on a November night, in 1856, Messrs. Hain Friswell, Jonas Levy, Sterling Coyne, and Henry Marston, having sent an invitation to some select spirits, met together and proposed that a club should be formed, inviting every gentleman present to become a member. It was agreed to, and in commemoration of the Knights of St. John of Jerusalem, formerly associated with the Gate, and of their night of the week to assemble, it was resolved to name the new *coterie* " The Friday Knights." E. L. B. became one of its most enthusiastic members.

settled and agreed upon. The Emperor's escape from assassination yesterday the general theme of conversation.[1] *Era* £1 5s. 16th.- Davidson calls, 'Hoop-de-dooden-doo' to do, £2. To Lyceum; burlesque[2] slow and dull. *Monday, 18th.*—Putting papers to rights; hear of Mrs. Nisbett's death on Saturday.[3] 19th.—With Amelia B. Edwards, 'Middy,' and Mrs. Gale to St. John's Gate, whereat nobly entertained by B. Foster; over the battlements, under the crypt of St. John's. Skeletons and signs of wasted mortality, earthy smells, and strange associates. At night to Her Majesty's

[1] This refers to the Orsini conspiracy, when the Emperor and Empress arrived at the opera. A piece of one of the shells cut the Emperor's hat, and General Roquet, who was sitting in the carriage (which was much shattered), was slightly wounded in the back of the head. Sixty people were wounded and three killed.

[2] This was *Lalla Rookh*, supported by Charles Dillon's company, which included J. L. Toole and Miss Woolgar.

[3] Louisa Cranstoune Nisbett, Lady Boothby, died January 16th, 1858, of apoplexy, at her residence, St. Leonard's, near Hastings, Sussex. She was the daughter of Frederick Hayes Macnamara and Jane Williams, and was born April 1st, 1812, at Ball's Pond, near Islington. Her father was a successful actor, and from him she, at an early age, learnt to recite. Her maiden attempt was in private theatricals in 1820, as Adolphine de Courcy in the farce of *Monsieur Tonson*. Her success urged her to appear at the private theatre in Wilmington Square as Juliette, Miss Hardcastle, Jane Shore, even before she was ten years old, for at that age she played Angela in *The Castle Spectre* at the English Opera House; and, having given a wonderful performance of Jane Shore, the infant prodigy determined, as Louisa Mordaunt, to tour the provinces, commencing at Dorking in Surrey. At the age of sixteen she made her *début* at Drury Lane, as the Widow Cheerly in *The Soldier's Daughter*, and by the time she was eighteen she had been acknowledged to be almost perfection in the *rôles* of Juliette, Beatrice, and Rosalind. She married Captain Alexander John Nisbett of the Guards in 1831, but lost her husband seven months later by a fall from his horse, and was thus a widow at nineteen. Pecuniary troubles compelled her to return to the stage, and she reappeared in 1832 at Drury Lane. In 1835 she was manageress of the Queen's Theatre, and here one of her great parts was that of Cornet FitzHerbert FitzHenry in *The Married Rake*. Subsequently she went to the Strand for a time, and to the Surrey; and undertook the management of the Olympic during a temporary absence of Madame Vestris. On October 9th, 1837, she appeared at the Haymarket under Benjamin Webster as Constance, and reached the pinnacle of her fame.

first festival performance,[1] *Macbeth.* Phelps, royal box, fine sight, but otherwise dreary. Meet Ledger, Barney Williams, and other notables. 23*rd.*—E. T. S. £2. At night to third festival performance at Her Majesty's, Piccolomini in *La Sonnambula,* and ballet. House densely packed. *Monday, 25th.*—The marriage-day of the Princess Royal. From Greenwood usual payment of £10 per cheque for Wells pantomime. 28*th.*—All day on 'Man about Town,' and finish at night. 29*th.*—*Err.* copy written. For last week £2 10s.

About this time the property to which she was entitled through her late husband came into her possession, and her first care, as it had been all through her career, was to provide for the whole of her family —grandmother, mother, brothers, and sisters—besides doing many acts of kindness for other relatives. In October 1839, Mrs. Nisbett divided the honours of Covent Garden with Madame Vestris, and it was during this engagement that *London Assurance* was produced, in which she was the original Lady Gay Spanker. At Drury Lane she played with Macready and Anderson, and afterwards returned to the Haymarket. Whilst here Sir William Boothby, Bart., of Ashbourne Hall, Derbyshire, was smitten with her, and married her on October 15th, 1844. Lady Boothby became a widow in 1846, and returned to the stage in 1847. She appeared on March 28th, 1851, and was then suffering from an indisposition from which she may be said to have never really recovered. She was able to appear for Anderson's benefit on April 12th, but was obliged to resign the part of Katina Nelidorf, in *The Queen of Spades,* which she should have acted on the 24th, but Miss Vining was obliged to read her part. Mrs. Nisbett made her final appearance at Drury Lane, May 8th, 1851, as Lady Teazle. From this time her health broke down, and domestic bereavements in her family, to one who was so deeply attached to her relatives, helped to aggravate the evil. The death of Mrs. Macnamara was the final blow, and from its date, December 8th, 1857, till her own death, she never completely rallied. Mrs. Nisbett was one of the most entertaining actresses ever seen on the London stage, and those who were fortunate enough to have heard her laugh always quote it as one of the most rippling, joyous, and musical ever heard.

[1] This was one of a series of four given in honour of the marriage of the Princess Royal to the Prince Frederick William of Prussia. Duncan, T. C. Harris ; Donalbain, Caroline Parkes ; Banquo, A. Rayner ; Macduff, Howe ; Lady Macbeth, Helen Faucit ; the three witches, Messrs. Emery, Ray, and Lewis Ball ; Hecate, Mr. Weiss ; singing witches, Madame Weiss, Mdlle. Sedlatzek, Mr. Montem Smith, Mr. Wynn, and Mr. Bartleman. The National Anthem was sung by those appearing as the singing witches, assisted by Benedict's Vocal Association of three hundred voices ; Benedict conducted. Oxenford's

Then at night to the fourth and final festival performance—
the state visit—*Rivals* [1] and *Spitalfields Weaver*.   30*th*.
—To Haymarket ; see *Sleeping Beauty* [2] pantomime ; very
nicely got up."

"*Monday, Feb.* 1*st.*—British Museum for ' England and
Wales ; ' then at night off to Gravesend by rail to be ready for
the embarkation of the Princess Royal to-morrow.   Stop at
Mitre ; good house.   Then up to the top of Windmill Hill ; old
associations of place revived ; find town in a bustle.   2*nd.*—
The event.   Take up my stand amidst a pitiless snowstorm ;
meet all the Press there—Murphy, Holt, Foster, Collins, Levy,
and so forth.   Afterwards dine with Mayor, and at night to look
at sloshy town illuminated.   Weather very unpropitious.
3*rd.*—Back in evening to town, with nothing got but a severe
cold.   To bed tired.   4*th.*—Elected this day member of
Dramatic Authors' Society.   18*th.*—Helen Faucit's first night
at Lyceum ; [3] six nights' engagement.   22*nd.*—Chat with
Capel and a Mr. Stephen Massett, a new actor.   23*rd.*—Not
well ; only small paragraph written.   Looking out for new
quarters."

"*Monday, March* 1*st.*—At night Miss Goddard [4] at Surrey.
Go to Haymarket ; see Miss Sedgwick Julia in *Hunchback.* [5]
2*nd.*—Scribbling a few *Era* paragraphs all day.   Committee

farce of *Twice Killed* was also given, with the Keeleys, Messrs. Kinloch,
Clark, Tilbury, W. Templeton, and Glendon, Miss Patty Oliver and
Mrs. Leigh Murray, in the cast.

[1] *The Rivals*, by the Haymarket Company ; and *The Spitalfields
Weaver*, by the Adelphi Company.   The National Anthem was sung
by Clara Novello.

[2] *The Sleeping Beauty in the Wood ;* or, *Harlequin and the Spiteful
Fairy.*   Mr. Coe, Miss FitzInman, and Miss Leclercq.

[3] She appeared as Lady Macbeth ; Dillon in the title *rôle ;* J. L. Toole
one of the witches ; and C. Webb Banquo.

[4] After having been absent six years in Australia and California,
Miss Goddard returned, and appeared as Lucretia Borgia, a part she
had played three hundred nights in Australia.   Creswick was the
Gennaro, and Shepherd Gabetta ; Miss E. Webster, the Princess ;
Basil Potter, Duke of Ferrara.

[5] Buckstone as Modus and Miss Swanborough as Helen ; William
Farren, Sir Thomas Clifford.

meeting of club. Byronic deformity mentioned by Trelawney; discussed as affecting his mental character. The assertion of the *Standard* that it has this day sold ten thousand copies also disputed with vehemence. *3rd.*—At night to Lyceum; Yates and Harrington's farce, *Double Dummy.*[1] Practical fun successful. At club elect Toole and three others. *4th.*—All day over 'Man about Town.' Town with it, and spend hour afterwards at Dr. Brown's with Coyne and Levy. Hear of *Sunday Times* already having changed hands, or being about to do so. *5th.*—Copy for *Era*, from which £1. Take Hall to Drury for opening, then to Friday Knights. Meet Toomy, who revives old memories of the *Astrologer.* *6th.*—Take chair at club, and introduce O'Callaghan. Home late, and find more feuds have occurred whilst away: stupid, narrow-minded, and vulgar squabbling about nothing. *Monday, 8th.*—Coyne's comedy of *The Love Knot*[2] produced at Drury with success. I go to Hanover Square Rooms; Stephen Massett[3] not a great success, though a good voice and delivery to aid him. *Monday, 15th.*—Indoors all day. Mrs. Charles Young was a Miss James Thompson, cousin of Mrs. W. West. *19th.*—Hear of *Sunday Times* being sold; Timbs being off the *Illustrated London News.* *20th.*—E. T. S. £2, and one month's notice from this date that the engagement on *Sunday Times* ceases. *24th.*—Begin 'Man about Town,' and at home as before. Belvidere for hour at night; chat with George Ford, the comic singer, and find from *Advertiser* that E. T. S. has got licence for Alhambra, but not for Radnor. Anxious about matters pecuniary. *25th.*—Last night of Sadlers Wells season. Phelps's benefit; *Virginius* and *Young Rapid.* *26th.*—See Printers' Dramatic Association at Sadlers Wells, and then to Friday Knights, whereat find Hollingshead and pleasant company.

---

[1] J. L. Toole and Miss Woolgar as Mr. and Mrs. Priddles; J. G. Shore as Tom Tomkins—very clever.

[2] Marion, Miss Patty Oliver; Wormley, Mr. Kinloch; M. Bernard, Mr. Leigh Murray; Lady Lavender, Mrs. Leigh Murray; Lady Harbottle, Mrs. Frank Matthews; Lord George Lavender, Mr. R. Roxby; Sir Crœsus Harbottle, Mr. Tilbury.

[3] This was an American, who sang various songs, and gave imitations of different people he is supposed to have met with on his travels.

27th.—From E. T. S. £2, or rather from Edward Wilmot Seale, being the first week of new proprietorship. Concert at Sadlers Wells for distressed literary gentleman, believed to be W. Bridgman. To Belvidere, as far as I can do, and wasted and weary day, half worried and half worn. *29th.*—Passion Week. General and Theatrical Fund Dinner, but can't go. Still in limbo. Get out to night to Sadlers Wells;[1] goes off very well."

" *April 1st.*—To town, first time for a month being able to walk. *Era* pays £2 10s. in advance, 30s. for last week. *3rd.*—For *Sunday Times* £2. Go to town in afternoon. Meet Carpenter at the Black Swan, Doctors' Commons. Arrange about doing the music for paper. *6th.*—At night for five minutes to Sadlers Wells opening company.[2] *9th.*—To town with remainder of copy at night, and look in at Alhambra, first time;[3] place crowded. Then see Talfourd's cleverly written burlesque, *Pluto and Proserpine.*[4] *Era* for week 25s. See Ledger. *10th.*—From the *Sunday Times* (ought to be more) £2. Call at Tallis's, but find him out of town, and no cash. Go to look at new bridge at Chelsea, Battersea Park, etc.; get into

[1] This was an entertainment given by Miss Julia St. George, under the title of *Home and Foreign Lyrics*, in which she is supposed to visit Switzerland, Greece, Turkey, Italy, India, America, and her own island, and in which she also imitated various people she had met, dressing them in their national costumes. The arrangement of the music was by G. F. Duggan, and Miss Amelia B. Edwards had written the entertainment.

[2] Opened by Tully—*Maritana* and *The Beggar's Opera.* Henry Haigh as Don Cæsar de Bazan; Miss Stanley as Polly; Russell Grover as Captain Macheath; Mr. and Mrs. Barrett as Mr. and Mrs. Peachum.

[3] This was originally opened as "The Panopticon of Science and Art," and, failing, was purchased by E. T. Smith, and opened on Sundays for sermons and sacred music. It was now taken by Howes and Cushing, American *entrepreneurs*, and was opened as "The Alhambra Palace Circus," with the usual feats of horsemanship, acrobats, and clowns.

[4] Or, *The Belle and the Pomegranate*, by Francis Talfourd, was played at the Haymarket. Pluto, Compton; Proserpine, Miss Louise Leclercq; Minerva, Mrs. Poynter; Ceres, Mrs. Buckingham White; Diana, Miss Fanny Wright. The costumes were designed by Alfred Crowquill. Talfourd punned in Greek, French, and Latin in this piece.

Wandsworth Road with difficulty, and see after ten years the old house in Albion Grove (now called Wilton Street) that I used to occupy. *Monday, 12th.*—Write to Glover, of Glasgow, about pantomime of *Sinbad*, £20 asking for it, but July being the time to think about it. *13th.*—Indoors all day doing very little, and pressed for copy too. At night go to Wells; *Trovatore.* Meet Henry Haigh, Tully, and a few of the old folks at the Corner. *14th.*—Begin ' Man about Town.' At night to London Tavern, Dinner of Friends of the Clergy; Murphy (*Daily News*), Barrow (*Times*), Warren (*Post*), and Carpenter there. Fielding, Montem Smith, Misses Stubbach and Palmer, vocalists. *15th.*—At night to St. Martin's Hall; hear Dickens read 'Christmas Carol,' and delighted. Then to opera, second night of season. See *Huguenots*, and much pleased with *prima donna*, Mdlle. Titiens. *17th.*—At night go to Princess's and see *King Lear*[1] revived (first night). *Monday, 19th.*—Not the thing again; but off early to town; among the artists at the British Institute and the Water Colour Society. Then see Watkins, and meet with Dillon Croker, who accompanies me afterwards to club. Go to Olympic together: Oxenford's *Doubtful Victory*,[2] first night, and then to Re-Union, and Croker's clever imitation pronounced truly wonderful. *21st.*—Busy with ' Man about Town ' copy, but not much done. *22nd.*—To town with ' Man about Town,' then to Surrey. See Henry Phillips; a wreck compared to what he was. Then to Equestrian. Meet Buckstone and Courtney. *23rd.*—Having been up all night, off early in morning, 9.15, *viâ* Great Western. Reach Langton by 11.35; walk over to Stratford (ten miles) by 4 p.m. Attend dinner, Shakespeare's birthday, at Town Hall; Buckstone in chair.[3] Pleasant day and

[1] Lear, Charles Kean; Edgar, Ryder; Edmund, Walter Lacy; Duke of Albany, J. F. Cathcart; Oswald, David Fisher; Fool, Miss Poole; Goneril, Miss Heath; Regan, Miss Bufton; Cordelia, Miss Kate Terry. Music by Hatton.

[2] A version of the French *A la Campagne.* Mrs. Stirling, Mrs. Flowerdale; Miss Hughes, Violet; George Vining, Colonel Olive; W. Gordon, Alfred Cleveland.

[3] Buckstone made a very good speech. In the afternoon the Rev. Julian Charles Young, son of the great Charles Young, gave a Shakespearean reading. In London the day was commemorated by the

late hours at Harry Hartley's hospitable Golden Lion.
24th.—About in morning to Shottery and Bowling Green;
whereat see mulberry tree; then dine with Folkard, Carpenter, and so forth, and take fly to Warwick.   Train at
7.40, and town by 11 p.m.; cab to offices, and then to club,
and tired out.   *Monday, 26th.*—The execution of Lani [1]
(Haymarket murder) this day.   *30th.*—To Royal Academy,
private view; then write about it.   Go to Friday Knights,
whereat pleasant company.   The Exhibition very good this
year; and with some pictures highly delighted."

"*May 1st.*—To town, and from *Sunday Times*, with arrears,
£5. Dine with Coyne and Lowe at Hinton's, Highbury Barn; [2]
then rush off to opera; new ballet; [3] write about it, and home
at 2.30.   *2nd.*—Off to Gravesend.   *Monday, 3rd.*—About
Gravesend all day looking for houses, and pleased with one
in London Road, No. 5, Rosherville; walk over all old localities, and then to town *viâ* Tilbury line.   *4th.*—Try to write:
failure.   Go to Her Majesty's Theatre at night: *Il Trovatore*.   Delighted with Alboni, Titiens, and Giuglini.   *8th.*—
Sunday Times, £5.   Go to morning concert, Willis's Rooms,
then home; dress for opera, then to Lyceum; see 'Joe
Robins' make his first appearance as Simmons in *Spitalfields Weaver* [4] before a London audience; the Keeleys, and

performance at the Haymarket of *Much Ado about Nothing*, and at the
Princess's of *A Midsummer Night's Dream*.

[1] Giovanni Lani, a Sardinian, convicted of the murder of Héloise
Thaubin, a Frenchwoman, at a house of ill-fame in the Haymarket.
Before being executed he confessed that he was guilty and admitted
the justice of his sentence.

[2] Grattan Cooke was the conductor of the band, and there was a
"Leviathan Platform" for dancing. [It was under the management
of Hinton, an amiable and very versatile man. Archibald Hinton was
in turn manager of Anerley Gardens, Sydenham, and of Highbury
Barn, and afterwards the spirited proprietor of hotels at Cherbourg in
France, at Hayling Island, and lastly at Shanklin, where he established
Hinton's Hotel, and where this good old man died.—C. S.]

[3] This was *Fleur des Champs*, with Mdlles. Pocchini and Annétta.

[4] This was a performance almost entirely by amateurs. Joseph
Robins had appeared as clown in an amateur pantomime. He also
played in a version by Mr. Sorrel of *Les Deux Aveugles*, called *Pity the
Poor Blind*, as Horace Tibbs; and T. Knox, jun., as John Moggins,
the other pretended blind man.

so forth. *Monday, 10th.*—At night to St. James's Hall, and Garde Nationale Band. Stop first part, then to club; chat with Hollingshead, Sala, etc. Going to Bedford Chambers, Southampton Street, Strand. *11th.*—So runs the stream of life. Sign agreement with Cox for Bedford Chambers; then back, and dress for opera, *Don Giovanni*—goes off very well. *12th.*—The miseries of moving commence; the rent of chambers, £9 per year, commenced at half-quarter day (last Monday); 3*s.* per week for housekeeper. *13th.*—Hard at work packing up for Bedford Chambers, whereat get most things fixed by night. *14th.*—At my chambers; write 'Man about Town' here, and get through immensity of copy. Knocked up at last. Money pouring out like water for all sorts of expenses. *15th.*—Royal Italian Opera opens. I write notice (one column and a half for *Sunday Times*); get done at 2 a.m. From *Sunday Times* £5 5*s.* *17th.*—Take possession of house, 5, London Road, Rosherville; see mother, etc., all safe, then walk to Northfleet to meet van and boy. All sorts of expenses in every way. *18th.*—Pay Drewell £10 for moving, Mr. Switsur £9 6*s.* 8*d.* for rent in advance. Supply housekeeping expenses, and then back to town very tired, and sleep in chambers first time. Miller calls, and smokes the friendly inaugurative pipe here. *19th.*—Derby Day; ought to have gone. Stop and do a quiet pipe indoors, and write account of the same—a story that takes me all day. *20th.*—Working very hard indeed on the 'Derby Day' article. In a rapid walk to Corner learn that my annual speculations on the event are failures, and lose 10*s.* 6*d.* *21st.*—Up at 6, and to desk again. Write, and finish 'Epsom,' etc., for *Sunday Times.* Paragraph for *Era* from it, 10*s.* Going out stunned by intelligence of W. B. off the paper—old story; more troubles, I fear, in prospective, and heart and hope quite crushed once more. Go to Vocal Association, St. James's Hall, and heavily and sadly home to bed. *22nd.*—From *Sunday Times* £5. Busy all day scribbling paragraphs for it. Go to Adelphi; new piece of Morton's *French Lady's Maid*[1] for

---

[1] Was a broad, eccentric drama adapted by J. Maddison Morton. Madame Celeste, Mdlle. Zephyrine; Mrs. Chatterley, Mrs. Puddifoot; Benjamin Webster, Horatio Sparkins; Charles Selby, Major Folley.

Era.   To Her Majesty's and to the opera. *Monday, 24th.*—
Walk with the boys up Windmill Hill. 26*th.*—After dinner
back by rail to chambers. Lots of letters; copy wanted.
Hear of Charles Dickens's separation from his wife on Saturday! 28*th.*—*Era*, £1. Go to Friday Knights. 29*th.*—
Sunday Times, £5. Long chat at Anderton's, and back to
work. At night to Her Majesty's Theatre; *Nozze de Figaro*
and new ballet."

" *June 2nd.*—Last night of the old Adelphi.[1] Leave Gravesend by boat at 5.30, and off Blackwall find the Jenners on
board; pleasant chat. Home to chambers, and find hosts of
letters. 5*th.*—*Sunday Times*, £5. Busy all day, and fright-
fully overworked at night. To Olympic; see and write about

---

[1] This theatre, more than fifty years old, originally called the
Sans Pareil, was built by Mr. B. John Scott, an oil and colour man in
the Strand, and was opened November 27th, 1806. The brothers
Rodwell purchased it in 1821, and called it the Adelphi. Terry and
Yates became lessees July 1825; later, Yates was joined by Charles
Mathews the elder. His son succeeded with Mr. Yates, who yielded
up his position to Mr. Gladstanes, who, after Frederick Yates' death
in 1842 continued the lesseeship for a year, and then handed it over to
Benjamin Webster, and Madame Céleste became manageress and con-
tinued so up to 1858. Benjamin Webster took his first and last benefit:
Our French Lady's Maid, Welcome Little Stranger, with Wright as Mr.
Osnaburg; Paul Bedford, Mr. Kitely; Mrs. Chatterley, Mrs. Currier;
Miss Laidlaw, Martha; Miss Eliza Arden, Mrs. Kitely. Miss Roden
sang " Waters of Ellè." Next followed the second act of *Black-eyed
Susan.* Benjamin Webster then addressed his patrons on past successes
and future prospects. In his address he mentioned how those inimitable artists—Power, Mr. and Mrs. Yates, the elder Mathews, Terry,
Wrench, John Reeve, O. Smith, Mrs. Nisbett, Mrs. Honey, Mrs. Fitz-
William, Mrs. Waylett, and many others known to fame—had appeared
on the boards. Referred to the theatre having been built on the very
spot on which originally stood the roadside farm of the celebrated
actress Nell Gwynne, and to the well of pure spring water that still
bore her name. He traced the history of the theatre through True
Blue Scott, Rodwell and Jones, Terry, Yates, etc., and concluded with
an expression of his thanks to the public and the press. Then followed
That Blessed Baby, with Mr. and Mrs. Keeley, Messrs. Billington and
Page, Mrs. Chatterley and Miss Laidlaw; after which came a scene
from the musical drama *Mephistopheles*—Mephistopheles, Miss Woolgar; Fiametta, Mary Keeley—and the National Anthem, with the
solo parts by Miss Roden, Miss Eliza Arden, Miss Woolgar, Miss

(for *Era*) Tom Taylor's new comedy, *Going to the Bad*,[1] and then write accounts of two Italian operas. *8th.*—Writing review of ' Rachel's Memoirs.' Mother's birthday, celebrate it by presents and a little impromptu festivity. *12th.*—From *Sunday Times* £5. Finish lots of copy, and go to Princess's in evening to see *Merchant of Venice*.[2] Covent Garden Opera till 5 a.m. next morning. *15th.*—Take the boys by boat to Sheerness, and then for half-hour encounter prize-fighting for championship on the river, and hear Tom Sayers[3] is the victor. Was man destined to be pommelled by another? and for cash too? *17th.*—Very hard-worked as usual, writing all day. Hear Dickens at night read ' Poor Traveller,' 'Boots at the Holly Tree Inn.' *18th.*—Hard at it again from 9 a.m. till 7 p.m. Annoyed by W. B.'s creditors coming as usual to ask me to pay the amounts owing : no end to the vexations. *Era*, 30s. *19th.*—*Sunday Times*, £5. Work hard all day long. Meet E. T. S. and Emden, who wants piece for Lewis Ball, and so forth. At night see *Fra Diavolo* at opera. *22nd.*—Give everybody a treat by having a fly to Cobham Woods and dinner at Ship Inn ; costs me over £1, but hope at least they have enjoyed the day. *23rd.*—Come to chambers by evening, after experiencing the frightful effects of the black and beastly Thames, about which everyone is now talking. *26th.*—At night to three operas—Drury,

Mary Keeley, and Paul Bedford. Madame Céleste and Webster were received with great enthusiasm. The latter was afterwards presented with a valuable gold watch and chain, on the former of which was a suitable inscription, and which was subscribed for by one and all in every department of the theatre.

[1] Peter Potts, F. Robson ; Lucy Johnson, Miss Wyndham ; Captain Horace Hardingham, George Vining ; Miss Isabella Dashwood, Miss Herbert ; Major Steel, Mr. Addison ; Mr. Bevis Marks, G. Cooke ; Smythers (a hairdresser), Horace Wigan ; Moss, H. Cooper ; Charles Rushout, Gaston Murray. F. Robson's benefit.

[2] Antonio, Graham ; Bassanio, Ryder ; Salarino, G. Everitt ; Gratiano, Walter Lacy ; Lorenzo, J. F. Cathcart ; Shylock, Charles Kean ; Launcelot Gobbo, Harley ; Old Gobbo, Meadows ; Portia, Mrs. Charles Kean ; Nerissa, Miss C. Leclercq ; Jessica, Miss Chapman—very successful, first appearance.

[3] This was a fight between Tom Sayers and Thomas Paddock for the championship of England and £200 a side. Twenty-one rounds were fought, occupying an hour and forty minutes ; Sayers won.

Covent Garden, and Her Majesty's; the weather warm, but breeze towards night. *29th.*—Talk of fire at the London Docks this day;[1] immense damage done. *30th.*—Dine at home, and suddenly taken by Lovell Phillips to a dinner of music publishers at Palliser's: Addison, Luff, Duff, Mr. Giddy, Chatterton, Jewson, Simpson, F. Romer, Metzler, etc. Home to chambers."

E. L. B. used to tell with great gusto a story of an American, to whom he acted the hospitable cicerone throughout one day, engaging a cab to drive about in and show him as much of London as could be seen in the time, lunching and refreshing him entirely at E. L. B.'s expense. The American had to return to Southampton that night, and so they had to cross Waterloo Bridge, which was not then free. E. L. B. put his hand in his pocket for the toll, when the American stopped him, saying, "No, sir, allow me; you have been bearing the costs all day, it's my turn now," *and magnanimously paid the penny.*

"*July 3rd.*—From *Sunday Times* £5. Work till night. Then to Drury, *Don Pasquale* and *Trovatore*; Covent Garden, Mario and *Martha*; Her Majesty's, *Sonnambula*; Emden's benefit at Olympic.[2] Back to write all. *10th.*—*Sunday Times* £5. At night to Haymarket; last night of season, and Buckstone's benefit, having kept open five years.[3] Write column for

---

[1] The fire burned for some seven hours, and was fortunately stopped by an explosion which was caused by the contact of some sugar and saltpetre. The damage was reckoned at £100,000.

[2] *A Handsome Husband* and *Hush Money.* Robson, Jaspar Touchwood; and Mrs. Emden, Sally. *The Wandering Minstrel* made up the programme.

[3] *The Married Rake*, and *The Way to keep Him.* Lovemore, Howe; Mrs. Lovemore, Miss Reynolds; Sir Bashful Constant, Mr. Buckstone; Lady Constant, Mrs. Buckingham White; Sir Brilliant Fashion, W. Farren; Widow Belmour, Mrs. Charles Young; Mrs. E. FitzWilliam

Era; Drury and Her Majesty's for *Sunday Times.* 17*th.*—
E. T. Smith's benefit at Drury,[1] and last night of the nine
weeks' operatic season. Opening of Lyceum;[2] benefit at
Olympic.[3] Wrote accounts of all. 18*th.*—To Gravesend.
Toole calls to tell me of his brother's engagement at Adelphi.
22*nd.*—My old friend George Bartley[4] died this afternoon,
aged 74. 23*rd.*—Hear from Haly again. Hard at work on
the Bartley memoir and other matters. Coyne to Ramsgate,
and I undertake the remaining matters. *Era* £1 5*s.*
24*th.*—From *Sunday Times* £5. W. B. turns up sorrowing

and Mr. Clarke were two domestics. The ballet of *Jack's Return from
Canton* made up the programme. Mr. Buckstone made a lengthy
speech, and alluded to the opening of the theatre in September.

[1] Close of the cheap Italian Opera. *Don Giovanni* was played, with
Signor Naudin as the Don, which was followed by *The Waterman.*
Newcombe, Robin ; Rebecca Isaacs, Wilhelmina.

[2] Opened by George Webster with *The Lady of the Camelias.*
Mrs. Charles Young as Violette St. Valérie ; Belton, Armand Duval.
The Burlesque *The Lancashire Witches ;* or, *The Knight and the Giants.*
Mrs. Howard Paul, Sir Launcelot de Lake ; Tilbury, King Arthur ;
Clarke, Wamba. *Why don't She marry?* made up the programme.

[3] George Vining's. He played Colonel Gayton in *The Soldier's
Courtship. Going to the Bad* and *Wandering Minstrel* made up the
bill.

[4] Born at Bath in 1772, was apprenticed to the *chef* at the York
House Hotel in his native city. As soon as he was out of his inden-
tures joined the theatrical profession. At a very early age married
Mrs. Swendall, who, though considerably older than himself, had nursed
him through a dangerous illness in Jersey. Through the influence of
Mrs. Jordan, who discerned his merits, he was engaged by Sheridan
at Drury Lane, and appeared there as Orlando, December 11th, 1802.
During the five years he was a member of the company he often
appeared during Bannister's absences. He joined Incledon at the
Lyceum in giving the entertainment called *A Voyage to India,* and
the seven succeeding years travelled in various capacities throughout
the United Kingdom, and greatly increased his reputation. Married
a Miss Smith in 1814 (his second wife), at Birmingham. She was
a tragic actress of repute, and with her he went to America and
amassed a considerable fortune. On his return joined the Covent
Garden Company, and in 1829 was one of the principals who aided
Mr. Charles Kemble to carry on the theatre. He was then appointed
stage-manager, and the fortunes of the house changed. He remained
stage-manager till 1843, when his son, who was at Oxford, died, and he
withdrew from the stage. He played before Her Majesty at Windsor

and borrowing. I go to Lyceum to see Aldridge [1] as Othello,
and to Covent Garden to see new ballet. 29*th.*—Get through
usual mass of copy, unusually slow. First night of *Don
Giovanni* at Italian Opera; too full to get in."

" *Aug.* 3*rd.*—See in American papers the death announced
of my old friend H. Hall,[2] the comedian. 5*th.*—Writing
but slowly all day. At night dine at Crystal Palace with
directors; all the Press there; S. C. Hall and John Timbs.
Back with Carpenter, etc. Look in at the Red Lion ; hear
of Soyer (see note December 15th, 1857) having just died,
and the American submarine cable just laid. 6*th.*—At night
to Park Lane; see for first time Sir Edward Bulwer Lytton,
who receives me most cordially, and with whom I spend a
delightful hour. *Era* £1. 7*th.*—*Sunday Times* £5. W. B.
in morning. Chair comes, sent by mother. Work till late ;
then go round to all the theatres : Lyceum, Leigh Murray [3]
re-appears. Last night of Her Majesty's, and *Martha* at
Covent Garden. 10*th.*—Queen's embarkation at Gravesend
to see the Princess of Prussia; see the yacht go, also the
fireworks at night with the boys, and back. 14*th.*—Last
night of the Italian Opera; go: *Martha. Monday,* 16*th.*—
With Lovell Phillips and wife to Cobham ; wandering in
the woods, run against Kingsbury, the musical man, and

Castle and Buckingham Palace : Sir John Falstaff being one of his
great characters. His last appearance was at the Princess's, December 18th, 1852. He was for many years the respected treasurer of the
Covent Garden Theatrical Fund.

[1] Ira Aldridge, the African Roscius. *Début* of Annie Ness, as
Desdemona. Mrs. Brougham's first appearance since her return from
Australia as Emilia. Stuart, Iago ; Belton, Cassio.

[2] Born June 4th, 1809. First appearance at the Strand, May 6th,
1836, in Dowling's travesty of *Othello.* Played low comedy parts for
several seasons under the management of W. J. Hammond, and when
he retired Hall became manager. Was great as Creon in burlesque of
Antigone played in 1845. Subsequently joined the Lyceum company
under Vestris from 1850 to 1855. Was stage-manager of the
Birmingham theatre for Mr. Simpson. Left in the latter year for
America.

[3] As John Mildmay in *Still Waters Run Deep.* Mrs. Brougham,
Mrs. Sternhold ; FitzJames, Hawksley ; and George Peel, Potter.
H. Widdicomb also joined the company in *Sarah's Young Man.*

his wife. 20*th.*—Go to Friday Knights, pleasant hour; and walk home with Draper, discursively discussing. Hear of Harley this night being paralyzed. 21*st.*—See Leigh Murray in *Parents and Guardians.*[1] *Monday, 23rd.*—Hear by paper of Harley's death yesterday morning, aged 72.[2] 26*th.*—Go to Lyceum in evening; and am pleased with Falconer's comedy *Extremes :*[3] successful. Look in at Drury, John Douglass in bad piece of *Ben the Boatswain.*"

" *Sept.* 1*st.*—Look in at Lyceum; new farce, *Kicks and Halfpence :*[4] very bad. Club slow, but lively by comparison. 2*nd.*—Ill, and still worried : W. B., etc., wearing out my spirits. *Monday, 6th.*—Do a short review (gratis) for

[1] He played Mons. Tourbillon, and during the same week Claude Melnotte to Mrs. Charles Young's Pauline Deschappelles.

[2] John Pritt Harley, born in February 1786. Began life in a solicitor's office, joined the Southend and Canterbury theatres. He may be said to have made his professional *début* in April 1808, as Doctor Ollapod in *The Poor Gentleman.* He played here and at Worthing and Brighton under Mr. Trotter, the manager of these theatres, as principal comedian till February 1813, when he joined the York Circuit and played Ludovic in *The Peasant Boy,* March 8th, 1813. He appeared in London, for the first time, Saturday, July 15th, 1815, as Marcelli in Arnold's opera of *The Devil's Bridge,* and Peter Fidget in Beazley's farce of *The Boarding House,* and at once leaped into favour. First appeared at Drury Lane, Saturday, September 16th, 1815, as Lissardo in *The Wonder;* and on the 23rd of the same month made a great success as Doctor Pangloss in *The Heir-at-Law.* He was a great favourite of Jack Bannister's, who called him " his theatrical son and successor," and made him several valuable presents. He was for a short time at the Lyceum, and at the St. James's Theatre in 1836. Was with Macready at Covent Garden, 1838, and remained at the theatre with Vestris and Charles Mathews. He joined Braham at Drury Lane in 1840, and in 1850 became a prominent member of Charles Kean's company at the Princess's Theatre. Was one of our best Shakespearean clowns. He had been acting Launcelot Gobbo on Friday, August 20th, 1858, and seemed in unusual health and spirits when he was seized with paralysis of the left side. He was a great favourite both on and off the stage, was of a merry disposition and equable temper, and possessed an extraordinary fund of anecdote.

[3] The author played Frank Hawthorne, and was supported by James Rogers, Mrs. Wallis, Mrs. Charles Young, Miss E. Miller, FitzJames, and Charles.

[4] By W. Brough and Doctor Franck.

Sunday Times.   Little stroll at night, and back to the 'lively' circle. Interruption of communication with the electric cable.   *15th.*—Paid last week's £2 at *Sunday Times.* Write 'Man about Town.' Gossip at club with Godfrey Turner and Hollingshead.   *16th.*—Go to Sadlers Wells (opened last Saturday) ; see *Jealous Wife*[1] admirably played ; meet Jonas Levy.   *21st.*—C. C. B.'s interview with mother, and hear of her change in intentions respecting residence. *22nd.*—Back early to chambers. W. B. on ' check' at Drury. *23rd.*—Go to Lyceum in evening ; see clever ballet by the Lauri family.   *24th.*—Go to Haymarket ; write notice of *Wives as they were, and Maids as they are.*[2] *29th.*—Go to Olympic ; new farce of *A Tale twice told,* by J. P. Wooler."

At one period, during E. L. B.'s residence at Rosherville, he derived much amusement from a contemplation of the shifts used to carry on a neighbouring hotel, which was financially embarrassed.

This establishment had been started as a rival to the glories of the Trafalgar and the other well-known whitebait hostelries at Greenwich ; but its anticipations were not realized : it had to fall back on tea and shrimps for the multitude, and even then its career was not prosperous. Occasionally a traveller of the better class would stop and enquire what he could have for dinner, and would be answered — as if the resources

---

[1] Mrs. Charles Young, Mrs. Oakley ; Phelps, Mr. Oakley ; Miss Mitchell, Harriet Russet ; Miss M. A. Victor, Lady Freelove ; Major Oakley, Henry Marston.

[2] Chippendale and Mrs. Buckingham White, Lord and Lady Priory ; Howe, Sir William Dorillon ; E. Villiers, Sir George Evelyn ; W. Farren, Bronzely ; Mrs. Catherine, Miss Dorillon ; Mrs. Wilkins, Lady Mary Raffle.

of the *cuisine* were on the most lavish scale—that he could have everything in season. When he had ordered his repast, a timepiece, which was one of the few articles of any value which remained, was despatched to a neighbouring pawnbroker's, and out of the proceeds of its hypothecation the comestibles were purchased, the timepiece being ultimately redeemed when the bill was paid.

"*Oct.* 2*nd.*—Princess's opens with *Merchant of Venice.* To Gravesend in afternoon; go on to Northfleet to Leather Bottle for an hour, and splendid view of comet returning. 6*th.*—New ballet at Drury. 13*th.*—At night to Olympic; see Wilkie Collins's extraordinary drama of *Red Vial:*[1] acting of Mrs. Stirling wonderfully fine. 14*th.*—Writing *Era* paragraphs all day, and feel worried and heart-worn more than ever. W. B. in afternoon, and give him my frock-coat as a protection from the cold weather. Dine at Ward's late in the evening with Hart and A. Mellon. Back to Olympic, and write notice. 15*th.*—Anniversary of mother's fiftieth wedding day; go down to Gravesend at night to keep the celebration of the event above recorded; drink my dear mother's health in the best I can afford. 16*th.*—Walk round to Southfleet; beautifully secluded village among hop-grounds, with a fine old church, at which stop and meditate among the tombs; evening spent at the Leather Bottle—no companionship. *Monday,* 18*th.*—All day arranging papers of 'Man about Town' for publication: heavy day. 21*st.*—Leave book with F. Warne at Routledge's, and anxious about issue. See Mr. Seale at Bank, who kindly and complimentarily regrets severance of our connection. Club; Mr. Durham the sculptor, Lowe, etc. 22*nd.*—Write to G. Bell, 186, Fleet Street, executor of Boyne, about my old MS. of 'Dinners and Diners.'

---

[1] This was a very strong melodrama. In it Mrs. Stirling played the part of the Widow Bergmann; Miss Marston, Minna; Walter Gordon, Karl; and Robson was great as a half-witted fellow, Hans Grimm.

W. B. in morning; doing nothing.   At night to Sadlers Wells; first chat with Greenwood about *Harlequin Izaak Walton*.   Then to Friday Knights, now rechristened the Urban Club;[1] punch in honour; take chair, and late festivities. *23rd.*—W. B. and usual upset in morning; cannot write a line after.   Try boat to Chelsea; walk back, and then go

---

[1] The room at the Clerkenwell Gate in which the clubbists assembled was no other than the chamber in which Edward Cave, the famous printer and publisher, set up the type of *The Gentleman's Magazine*, edited it, and gathered about him, not only his contributors, Samuel Johnson, Richard Savage, and Goldsmith, but our Roscius, David Garrick.   Cave, it will be remembered, signed himself in *The Gentleman's Magazine* "Sylvanus *Urban*."   So on the night of November 28th, 1858, Mr. Sterling Coyne rose amongst the Friday Knights, and proposed that they should abandon their original designation and call their Society the Urban Club, a title not only fit but felicitous, holding their gatherings in a room redolent of memories of the old editor and his historic staff of writers.   Coyne's proposition was greeted with acclamation, and the clubbists of to-day retain the name of their *coterie* with peculiar fondness.   Two events in the Urban year are anticipated with great interest, their Shakespeare Commemoration—that of April 23rd, 1890, was the thirty-third—and the Foundation Supper, as near November 28th as possible, each occasion being marked by the services of a member as chairman, who never fails to dilate on the associations of the club.   Amongst the Shakespeare presidents have been H. Marston, Westland Marston, Tomlin, Oxenford, Heraud, Henry Morley, Dr. Doran, Hepworth Dixon, Yates, Sala, Albery, Dr. Richardson, R. H. Horne, Cordy Jeaffreson, Joseph Knight, W. E. Church, J. E. Carpenter, Thomas Woolner, R.A., and Barnett-Smith.   E. L. Blanchard presided at the Foundation Supper in 1863, and at the Shakespeare Dinner in 1867. Among the hon. secs. of the club have been Hain Friswell, H. Thomas (teacher of Elocution in City of London College, where Irving had instruction from him), Carpenter the song-writer, Henry Marston, Daly Besemeres the playwright, Redding Ware, and W. E. Church, the latter holding the office at the present time, having filled it during a period of twelve years.   Members on the roll include the names of Sir Crichton Browne, Thos. Woolner, R. A. ; Dr. Richardson, Maddison Morton, Henry Graves, Thomas Catling, W. Maw Egley, Dr. Evan B. Jones, Dalgety Henderson, Barton Baker, R. Gowing, Rev. H. V. Le Bas, Rev. Astley Cooper, Arthur Lucas, Dr. Noble Smith, George Cockle, Jonas Levy (only surviving founder), and about fifty others The pedigree of the club in reality goes back to the Mulberries.   From the Gate the Urbans had to migrate in 1880, went to Ashley's in Covent Garden, and thence to Anderton's, at which Fleet Street hotel they have found a resort since 1882.

THE URBAN CLUB.

[See page 207.

to Sadlers Wells to see revival of *Henry V.*:[1] very well
done. 24*th*.—Going down to Gravesend in morning, meet

THE URBAN CLUB.

DRAWN BY WARWICK REYNOLDS.

KEY.

1. EDWARD LEMAN BLANCHARD.
2. STERLING COYNE.
3. JAMES HAIN FRISWELL.
4. WILLIAM FARMER.
5. FRED. GUEST TOMLIN.
6. GEORGE LINNÆUS BANKS.
7. JONAS LEVY.
8. HENRY MARSTON.
9. J. W. RAY.
10. WILLIAM R. BELFORD.
11. BENJAMIN FOSTER.
12. EDWARD D. JOHNSON (*science editor.*)
13. HENRY THOMAS (*a clever vocalist and a teacher of elocution.*)
14. JAMES BRUTON.
15. WESTLAND MARSTON.
16. ROBERT BARNABAS BROUGH.
17. THOMAS SPENCER.
18. GEORGE CRUIKSHANK.
19. DR. EDWARDS.
20. JOHN ABRAHAM HERAUD.
21. DR. T. S. BARRINGER.
22. DR. EDWARD BAKER.
23. JOHN HOLLINGSHEAD
24. J. CRAWFORD WILSON.
25. CHARLES HORSLEY.
26. JOHN L. TOOLE.
27. WILLIAM HALE.
28. EDWARD DRAPER.
29. LEICESTER BUCKINGHAM.
30. CHARLES WRIGHT.
31. WILLIAM FIELDING.
32. DR. CANTON.
33. THORP PEDE (*composer.*)
34. BLAGROVE SNELL.
35. CHARLES LOWE.
36. CAPTAIN JACOBS.
37. MR. IZARD (*gentleman.*)
38. LOUIS HERMANN.
39. RENAN.
40. JOSEPH KNIGHT.
41. JOHN OXENFORD.

our old friend Mr. Payne of the Brunswick; we ramble to

[1] F. Robinson, Fluellen; Henry Marston, Chorus; Charles Young,
Pistol; Ray, Williams; C. Fenton, Nym; Mrs. Marston, Dame
Quickly; Grace Egerton, Katherine.

Springhead. Back, and find W. B.; dinner, wine, dessert, and wind up a pleasant but expensive day. 28*th.*—Write a few paragraphs for *Era,* and at night to Canterbury Hall to see new Fine Art Gallery; hospitably entertained by Charles Morton. 30*th.*—Pavilion opens. Mother in morning, and tells that which dissipates all the long dreams indulged in. C. C. B. is lost to me for ever!—a severe shock; but it is but another added to the trials I have passed through, though the barque is now nearly shattered by the violence of the storms."

" *Nov. 4th.*—At night to Pavilion; bad piece, *The Tailor's Home;* and decorations of theatre not finished; walk thence to Sadlers Wells; see clever farce by W. Phelps, *A Tenant for Life. 5th.*—At work for *Era* all day, whence 25*s.* Coyne at night to St. John's Gate, the Urban Club Supper; Coyne in chair, self in vice; meet Farmer, editor of *Weekly News,* and home with a pleasant Dr. Russell of Westminster. 6*th.*— Arranging papers in morning, and at night to Haymarket for *Era,* Charles Mathews's benefit; new piece by W. Brough and Dr. Franck :[1] goes off fairly. Back, write notice, then to club; an hour with Moy Thomas, a highly-gifted and well-educated young author.[2] 10*th.*—Back at 6 to town, and chat a bit about Hudson,[3] Irish comedian, going to Melbourne, Australia; and get through an agreeable hour at club. 18*th.* —Farce of *My Mother's Maid,*[4] at Haymarket, in which Charles Mathews appears : not very good. 19*th.*—All day

---

[1] *Tale of a Coat.* Charles Mathews, Jaques Molinet ; E. Villiers, Baron de Meremont ; Miss FitzInman, Donna Inez ; Mrs. E. Fitz-William, Paquita. It was followed by *The Dowager,* Charles Mathews's comedy, which he produced at the Haymarket in 1843. Mrs. Charles Mathews (formerly Mrs. Lizzie Davenport) appeared for the first time in England as the Dowager Countess of Tresilian.

[2] [This is the William Moy Thomas who has been for many years the dramatic critic of *The Daily News.*—C. S.]

[3] Born in 1811. Made his first appearance at the Nottingham Theatre in 1830. He was an all-round actor, and was considered almost the equal of Tyrone Power. One of his great characters was Gerald Pepper in *The White Horse of the Peppers,* but he was almost equally at home in legitimate drama, comedy, or burlesque.

[4] Another version of the French *Edgar et sa Bonne.*

with *Era* paragraphs, from thence 35s. *24th.*—From E. T. S., for pantomime, cheque of £10. *25th.*—At night to Adelaide Gallery, Ohio Minstrels, under management of Schmidt; meet Card, husband of Georgina Eagle, daughter of Barraud. *27th.*—Busy making fair copy of Wells pantomime; at night to Haymarket, last night of C. Mathews and wife. *Belle's Stratagem*, wretchedly played, and *The Critic*. *28th.*—Go to Gravesend; reach there at 6 p.m., but find grumbling and growling in the ascendant. *Monday, 29th.*—Tremendous row, making the home a most uncomfortable one both for my poor mother and self; I am thoroughly upset in consequence, and become ill once more. *30th.*—My dear mother confined to her bed from the effects of yesterday and causeless and uncomfortable scenes of such frequent recurrence."

"*Dec. 1st.*—More disappointments: Routledge declines to publish ' Man about Town,' and self dreading to incur the expense. No relief from domestic worries; at night seek refuge in club, and chat with Sir William Don. *2nd.*—Go to Olympic; first night of *The Porter's Knot:*[1] a charming piece, exquisitely acted by Robson and the rest. *3rd.*—Write notice of Olympic for *Era*, from which £2; then dine with Talfourd at the Garrick Club, being entertained by him in a most princely style; meet Arcedeckne and Drinkwater Meadows; afterwards to Okey's, and amusing talk with the table. *4th.*—From E. T. S. for pantomime, £10. Astley's for stupid new piece of *Modern Anatomy*. *10th.*—*Era* copy, from which 35s. *11th.*—Another birthday: thirty-eight! and getting very grey. To Wells; see the *Wheel of Fortune,*[2] with Phelps as Penruddock. *Monday, 13th.*—At Gravesend, writing a

---

[1] Only a germ of this remarkably clever scrio-comic drama was taken by John Oxenford from *Les Crochets du Père Martin*, by MM. Cormon and Grangé, produced at the Gymnase, August 18th, 1858. The character of Sampson Burr will always be associated in one's memory as one of F. Robson's greatest performances. He was supported by Mrs. Leigh Murray as Mrs. Burr; H. Wigan, Smoothly Smirk; W. Gordon, Augustus Burr; Miss Hughes, Alice; George Vining, Stephen Scatter; G. Cooke, Captain Oakham.

[2] Mrs. Charles Young, Emily Tempest; J. W. Ray, Tempest; H. Marston, Sydenham; J. Chester, Sir David Daw; Robinson, Henry Woodville: Miss Atkinson, Mrs. Woodville.

few prefaces for Loft's plays.   16*th.*—Attend first rehearsal at Drury; back in haste to write notice of comedy, *The Tide of Time.*[1] Then late to Haymarket; see Don in *Toodles*, an American piece.   17*th.*—*Era*, 30*s.*   To Wells and see Greenwood; and then, though tired out, a very pleasant evening with Amelia B. Edwardes, Duggan, the Coynes, and Miss Philp, a charming vocalist and composer. 18*th.*—Write out plot for *Sunday Times*, and at night to Princess's, for *Jealous Wife.*[2]   24*th.*—All morning at Drury attending rehearsal, and receive from E. T. S. for pantomime settlement £10: in all £30.   Annual banquet; meet all the celebrities, and B. J. Armstrong, Middlesex magistrate.   Then walk with Sala, Green, and Dyson to Midnight Mass at St. George's Cathedral.   25*th* (*Christmas Day*).—Up at 10, and start for Gravesend; rain pouring heavily; go down by North Kent; find Sola returned from Shields; get through the day with a round at whist and a bottle of port.   27*th.*—Up to town again by 4.30.   London swarming with holiday folks. Look in at Drury with Byron; opening goes off famously. Then to Olympic, see *Mazeppa*;[3] write notice for *Daily Telegraph*, and stop with Levy and Albert Feist till 4 a.m. waiting for proofs.   28*th.*—Satisfactory reports of Drury[4] in all the papers.   Very knocked up, but go at night

---

[1] By Bayle Bernard, in three acts. Chippendale, Pendarvis; Miss Reynolds, his daughter Mildred; Compton, Sir Dormer de Brazenby; Howe, Spalding; Rogers, Grainger; Mrs. Poynter, Miss Sabrina Crickhowell; Miss E. Ternan, Alice; and Buckstone, Molehill. Sir William Don played Timothy Toodles, and was a very grotesque and humorous low comedian, and for such a big man proved himself extraordinarily active.

[2] Mr. and Mrs. Charles Kean as Mr. and Mrs. Oakley; Frank Matthews, Squire Russet; Cooper, Major Oakley; Walter Lacy, Lord Trinket; J. F. Cathcart, Charles Oakley; H. Saker, Sir Harry Beagle; Mrs. Winstanley, Lady Freelove; Miss Heath, Harriet Russet.

[3] By H. J. Byron. Mazeppa, F. Robson; Oliuska, Miss Wyndham; Drolinsko, Lewis Ball; Laurinski, G. Cook: Zemila, Mrs. Emden; and Abder Khan, Horace Wigan. It was a piece of the wildest extravagance.

[4] E. L. B.'s pantomime, *Robin Hood*. Harlequins, Signor Milano and M. St. Maine; clowns, Harry Boleno and Signor Delavanti; pantaloons, G. Tanner and another Delavanti; columbines, Madame Boleno and Miss F. Brown.

to Surrey for *Telegraph, Harlequin Father Thames*;[1] see Shepherd; back, and write a column notice for the paper. Houses indifferent through Victoria accident.[2] *29th.*—See morning performance at Drury. Then to Strand; see *Kenilworth*[3] extravaganza: very good, and magnificently placed on the stage. *31st.*—Finish theatricals. Payne calls in afternoon, and we go to Drury in evening. Thence to Sadlers Wells: very well done. Thence to Friday Knights; the loving cup passed briskly round, and we welcome the New Year in with friendly warmth and sociality. Thus ends a year in which I have been more heavily worked and more heavily drained financially than any yet experienced. For all its blessings God be thanked; and its hardships may have had advantages that some time I may learn. *Exit* 1858."

Total for the year, £221.

[1] *Harlequin Father Thames and the River Queen;* or, *Y*^e *Lorde Mayore of London.* Clown, Buck; harlequin, Tapping; columbine, Mdlle. Rosine.

[2] This happened at the afternoon performance of the pantomime on Boxing Day, through the rush of the people who had seen the performance coming out, meeting a number who had collected ready to obtain admission for the evening performance. The casualties occurred on the gallery stairs, a false alarm of fire being raised, when there was a dreadful struggle, in which there were sixteen people killed and upwards of fifty injured, some most seriously.

[3] Or, *Y*^e *Queen, Y*^e *Earl, and Y*^e *Maiden.* Earl of Leicester, Miss Swanborough; Queen Elizabeth, Mrs. Selby; Amy Robsart, Patty Oliver; Sir Walter Raleigh, Marie Wilton; Varney, J. Clarke; Wayland Smith, James Bland; Tresilian, Charlotte Saunders; Mr. Poynter and Mr. Turner as Tony Foster and Michael Lambourne.

1859.

"*Jan.* 1st.—The New Year opens dim and misty. Dine in town with my old friend W. Payne, at The Bedford, meeting Webster and Murray, reporter. Start for Gravesend at 8. Spend the New Year's night filially with my dear mother; very quiet, very tired, and so dozily and dreamily to bed. *7th.*—*Era* for week £2. Look in at Lyceum,[1] clever harlequinade by the Lauri family. *8th.*— At work at memoirs and prefaces for 'British Drama.' *13th.* —Write article for *Era*. Go with Miller, to Adelphi;[2] see comic business; Croueste, Flexmorean clown, very active, but with hardly any purpose. *20th.*—To Lyceum; see *The Sister's Sacrifice,*[3] with Céleste therein : a literal translation. *22nd.*—Go to Wells; see *Macbeth* and the pantomime; latter done in an hour and a quarter. *23rd.*—At night to Red Lion, and attend a spirit meeting : very curious manifestations, and much gratified. *25th.*—Dream away day at home. Hear of Fowler's death (reporter and manager of *The Standard*) announced in papers. *27th.*—*Era*, 30s. Go to Gallery of Illustration, and see good and interesting panorama of American scenery (Brewer's). *28th.*—At night to hear Barnum at

---

[1] *The Siege of Troy*, by Robert Brough, produced on Boxing Day. Hector, Mrs. Keeley ; Ulysses, Ellerton ; Ajax, Charles Young ; Patroclus, James Rogers ; Achilles, Miss Sabot ; Paris, Miss Portman ; Troilus, Miss E. Romer ; Cressida, Miss Kate Saxon ; Minerva, Miss G. Oliver ; Cupid, Miss Julia St. George ; Iris, Miss Rosina Wright ; Homer, Mr. Emery.

[2] This was the new Adelphi Theatre, opened by Mr. Benjamin Webster on December 27th, 1858, with an introductory speech written by Yates and Harrington, and entitled, *Mr. Webster's Company is requested at a Photographic Soirée* ; it introduced all the old Adelphi favourites, and in addition, Mr. J. L. Toole. The well-known farce, *Good for Nothing*, followed, with Toole and Mrs. Mellon as Tom Dibbles and Nan ; and the pantomime was *Mother Red Cap ; or, Harlequin and Johnny Gilpin.* Hildebrand, harlequin ; Miss Jenny Hayman, columbine ; Lupino, pantaloon ; Croueste, clown ; Le Barr, a fop and sprite.

[3] Or, *The Orphans of Valneige.* Geneviève, Madame Céleste ; Josette (a half-sister), Miss St. George ; Cyprian Girard, Emery ; Catherine, Mrs. Keeley.

St. James's Hall, and delighted. Afterwards to club, whereat meet Edgar, Clemow, etc. Begin 'Barnum' life for Willoughby. *29th.*—Delamotte in morning. Go to Willoughby, and receive from him £1 for Barnum article."

"*Feb.* 1*st.*—Letter from Hunt, dated Croydon, asking for loan of 5*s.*, which send. Hear of Charles Farley's death on Friday, aged eighty-eight.[1] 4*th.*—Write a few paragraphs for *Era*, whence £1. Back to chambers; look over old papers, and become sadder than ever. Try to work in evening, but hardly anything done. To Haymarket, and see pantomime of *Undine:* [2] scenery very good, and comic business excellent. 5*th.*—Receive from Lofts £4. Dine at Edinbro'. At night with Talfourd, Green, Holland, and Pearson to spirit *séance*, as before; phantasmagoria and extraordinary effects. 6*th.*—Start at 4 p.m. for Gravesend, and startled by the intelligence of A.'s flight from home—more sorrows. *Monday, 7th.*—Hear the reason why: find tradesmen's bills to the amount (known) of £10 unpaid; settle as many as possible, and order and pay for coals and coke. 8*th.*—All day paying all sorts of bills, for which I find I am liable, and cruelly upset by fresh discoveries; have the greatest difficulty in meeting the expenditure so unexpectedly evolved. 9*th.*—Fit for nothing. No tidings of A. Intend going, but stop through day, and try to enliven the party left behind. No sleep. 10*th.*—Arrive early. Hear from W. B., who calls in afternoon, where A. is, and send her 5*s.* Then afterwards visit from Hannah, and sad story of the woman's foolish and

[1] Charles Farley was born early in 1771, and made his first appearance at Covent Garden as far back as 1782, as a page. He was call boy and assistant prompter, but was so quick that he was soon entrusted with small parts, and then with more important ones. Though he was a clever actor, he rose to greater fame as what we should now call a stage-manager, or producer of plays. He coached Grimaldi to play Orson. He was connected with Covent Garden and Drury Lane during the time of the Kembles, the elder Kean, and from Macklin down to Charles Kean. He retired from the stage in 1834; he also wrote several melodramas.

[2] *Undine;* or, *The Spirit of the Waters.* Harlequin, Arthur Leclercq; pantaloon, Herr Cole; clown, Charles Leclercq; columbine, Fanny Wright. It was notable for the beauty of its scenery, by Beverley. Louisa Leclercq was the Undine.

headstrong way. Send 10s. to her, and thus cleared out of all finances. Go to Adelphi at night; revival of *Invisible Prince*.[1] From *Era* £1. 11*th.*—Trying all day to scribble a few paragraphs, but quite upset for work. Pass Miller in to Adelphi; see burlesque and *Birthplace of Podgers*. 12*th.*—Money all going out, and none coming in! At night attend another spirit *séance* with Talfourd, his mother, etc.; meet Mr. Chinnery, and very interesting manifestations. 15*th.*—A. returns in evening: first of all defiant and insolent, then reticent and repentant; but next time I may not so easily forgive. 16*th.*—Céleste's benefit, new piece by Oxenford, *Lost Hope*:[2] not good. Last night of Wells pantomime; average run. 17*th.*—Busy for *Era*, with Adelphi notice of Wright's return, and Lyceum. Feeling crushed and heartbroken by the persecutions to which I am liable. 18*th.*—Finish *Era* paragraphs £1 5s. Dine at Edinbro'. Looking for Lofts, and find Tallis. To Evans's, hearing a glee or two, and meeting Albert Smith and some old familiar faces. 19*th.*—Mrs. Woodin calls in morning. Leave MS. of ' Journey round St. Paul's' with Smith & Sons. Dine at Bertholini's; at night to Pearson's; Holland, Mole, Spenser and family present; a ' Marshall ' display. Then to club, with Talfourd (born *about* 1827). 24*th.*—Scribble a few paragraphs for *Era*. Reynolds comes, and give him a trifle. Working on Woodin's, but very little done. 26*th.*—Revise Croker's burlesque for him, and put old papers to rights. To Covent Garden,[3] and

---

[1] Or, *The Island of Tranquil Delights*. Originally produced at the Haymarket, Christmas 1846 ; taken from the story of Prince Lutin in the Countess d'Anois' fairy tales. Furibond, J. L. Toole ; Apricotina, Kate Kelly ; Princess Xquisitelittlepet, Mary Keeley ; Gentilla, Eliza Arden. By Planché.

[2] An adaptation by John Oxenford of Dugué's *Les Amours Maudits*, produced at the Ambigu Comique in 1855. Doctor Blangini, Barrett; Madame Antoine, Mrs. Wallis; Alfred Warnford, G. Murray ; Michali, Fitzjames; Mark Momus, James Rogers. *The Child of the Wreck* was also played : Madame Céleste as Maurice, the dumb boy; Mrs. Keeley, Frantz.

[3] *Little Red Riding Hood; or, Harlequin and the Wolf in Granny's Clothing*, by J. V. Bridgeman and H. Sutherland Edwards. Messrs. Mortimer and Raynoe ; Clara Morgan, columbine; Henry Payne, harlequin ; Flexmore, clown ; Barnes, pantaloon. Scenery by Beverley.

see house and pantomime first time ; *Rose of Castille* and *Red Riding Hood :* the Paynes very clever."

"*March 2nd.*—Off by 4.30, and at night see very bad piece at Lyceum, the *Leprachaun,*[1] for Barney Williams ; then Adelphi, *Still Waters* and *Domestic Economy.* 10*th.* —Writing for *Era.* Go to Alhambra Palace, and see the *Rocky Wonders of California :* clever troupe. 11*th.*—*Era* for week £1 10*s.* Toole and Lofts to Edinbro' Castle. Then to see *Infant Magnet,* with Lowe ; experiments curious, but not conclusive. 12*th.*—List of plays for Lofts. Resume ' England and Wales ' after long delay. At night to Hay-market ; see new play by Palgrave Simpson, of *The World and the Stage,*[2] for Miss Amy Sedgwick's benefit. 16*th.*—To Lyceum, *Robert Macaire ;*[3] then Covent Garden ballet, of same piece. 17*th.*—Do *Era* paragraphs ; and whilst dining meet Tully and Reynolds first time at Bedford Head, and wine with them. Adelphi ; see Wigan in *Bengal Tiger ;*[4] first night. 18*th.*—At night see James Bennett, first appearance in London, at Lyceum, as Iago ; good intelligent actor.[5] Club ; meet Bayle Bernard, Charles Kenney (first time), and pleasant party. 26*th.*—' England and Wales ' in the morning. Dine at Bedford Head, sad and *solus.* Cooke's benefit at Astley's ;[6]

---

[1] Or, *Bad Luck's Good Luck with Good Looking After.* By Edmund Falconer, founded on an Irish superstition related by Mr. Crofton Croker. Fitzjames, Gil Perez ; Miss Kate Saxon, Inez ; Gaston Murray, Vicentio ; Barrett, Corregidor ; and Barney Williams, Phelim O'Donnell.

[2] Amy Sedgwick, Kate Robertson ; W. Farren, Hon. Harry Malpas; Compton, Buzzard ; Howe, Leonard Ashton ; Miss E. Ternan, Lady Castlecrag ; **Mr.** Rogers, Sir Norman Castlecrag ; Miss Eliza Weekes, Hephzibah ; and Miss Fanny Wright, the French landlady.

[3] Emery in the title *rôle* ; Charles Young, Jacques Strop. Same night, *Law for Ladies :* Mrs. Barney Williams, Sophia Heartall, in which character she represented a number of different personalities, a sort of American variety show of that date.

[4] He played Sir Paul Pagoda to Mrs. Wigan's Yellowleaf ; J. L. Toole, David.

[5] Clara Weston, Desdemona ; Mrs. Weston, Emilia; Gaston Murray, Cassio ; Fitzjames, Roderigo ; E. Falconer, Othello.

[6] William Cooke, jun., had been laid up for four months. *Guy Mannering* was played, with Miss Rebecca Isaacs as Julia. Marian

his first appearance since his accident—*Guy Mannering.*
30*th.*—To Olympic : revival of *Fashionable Arrivals.* 31*st.*—
Night to Lyceum ; see *Francesca,*[1] a new play by Falconer ;
good, but too long—over four hours ; then farce and ballet :
not over till after 1."

"*April* 1*st.*—Payne calls and joins me in the evening.
We go to Red Lion Street, and enjoy a pleasant two hours'
manifestation.   Payne pleased and astounded.   Club, and late
vigils.   2*nd.*—To Haymarket : Sterling Coyne's new comedy,
Everybody's Friend[2]—goes off well.   Meet Hayden, the old
publisher of *Crown.*   5*th.*—Begin Wyndham's piece, make
little progress.   7*th.*—Phil Phillips, and chat anent Woodin.
Then to see Lola Montès[3] at St. James's Hall ; first night, and

Simpson, Lucy Bertram ; Paul Bedford, Gabriel ; W. H. Eburne,
Henry Bertram; Kate Laidlaw, the Gypsy; Anson, Dominie Sampson;
R. Phillips, Dandie Dinmont; Mrs. Dowton, Meg Merrilies, with scenes
in the circle to make up the programme.

[1] *A Dream of Venice.* Mrs. Charles Young, title *rôle ;* Edmund
Falconer, Signor Gradenigo ; Gaston Murray, Leonardo ; H. Vandenhoff, Antonio Foscarini.   Same night new farce, *Husbands, beware!*
by Edmund Falconer, was played.   It should be stated that the ballet
did not begin till one o'clock.

[2] Felix Featherley, Charles Mathews ; Mrs. Featherley, Mrs. Charles
Mathews : Frank Icebrook, Compton ; Mrs. Swansdown, Miss Rey-
nolds ; Major Wellington de Boots, Mr. Buckstone ; Mrs. de Boots,
Mrs. Wilkins.   This was afterwards known as *The Widow Hunt.*

[3] Lola Montès, Maria Dolores Porris y Montès, was born in Scotland
about the year 1820-21.   She went to India, came to London, married
Captain Thomas James, and led an extraordinary life, wandering about
the world, and eventually captivating Louis I., King of Bavaria, who
made her Countess of Landsfeld, and caused her to be received at court
in 1847.   But she was the cause of his abdication ; for the people re-
belled against the influence she had obtained over him, causing a
scandal.   Soon after her marriage with Captain James she became
a Bohemian ; and, having some knowledge of dancing, in which she
very greatly improved afterwards, she came out as Lola Montès at
Her Majesty's Theatre.   In 1849 she went through the form of
marriage with Lieutenant H——, a wealthy young fellow ; but this
was proved to be illegal, her first husband being then alive.   She then
returned to Paris.   About this time she published her memoirs, but
they were of no great value.   She then went to America and tried
dancing there, but was not a success.   She was very beautiful at one
time, but was very quarrelsome, and full of eccentricities.   She went

home early to write notice. Receive from *Era* £2. 9*th.*—
Send off sketch to Wyndham. Meet Tom Matthews, who
has written his life ; Shepherd, who wants *Pork Chops.* At
night with Frank Talfourd and family to see some more of
the wonderful spiritual manifestations. Message : ' Edward
Blanchard, there is a poor little knot,'—exceedingly curious.
13*th.*—Back to chambers. Look in at Lyceum : *Beau
Brummel,*[1] Emery, short irregular season of six nights. 14*th.*
—Write a few *Era* notices, and receive for week from office
£1 5*s.*, and receive for Part XXXIX., from Tallis, £4 16*s.*
15*th.*—Death of Bozio,[2] the Zerlina of last season's Italian
opera, etc., announced in yesterday's papers. W. B. in
morning ; usual help. Woodin in afternoon, and then to
physical manifestations : curious evidence adduced, but
effects feeble on account of uncongenial influences ; two
sceptics being requested to retire. 16*th.*—Receive from

to California in 1853, and there she is said to have married again, this
time to a journalist named Hull. From thence she went to Australia,
and, returning to the United States, she figured as a lecturer, and did
fairly well ; and so she came to England, and gave her lecture in this
country. The latter portion of her life she was by turns a free-
thinker, a spiritualist, and eventually turned *dévote.* She had returned
to America, and lived very quietly there for a considerable time. In
1860 she had a stroke of paralysis, from which she never completely
recovered, though she was able to get about. She took cold about the
Christmas of 1861, and died of inflammation of the lungs, January 17th
of the following year. Notwithstanding her irritability of temper, she
was often a good friend to many, did numerous kind actions, and,
though she was suspicious of those around her, may be considered to
have been charitable. She was really almost a pauper when she died,
but some of the many friends she had made took care that she wanted
for nothing. Her influence over the King of Bavaria was made the
subject of a clever skit, which was produced at the Haymarket under
the title of the *Pas de Fascination,* in which Mrs. Keeley appeared *à
la* Lola Montès and Keeley as a barber.

[1] *Beau Brummel ; or, The King of Calais*—two-act drama by Blanchard Jerrold. Emery's make-up as the Beau, and his delineation of
this once celebrated character, were very complete. He was supported
by Barrett as Buntley ; Ellerton as Isidore, the Beau's valet ; and James
Rogers as Smalls, a tiger.

[2] Made her first appearance as Adina in Donizetti's *L'Elisir d'Amore.*
Was celebrated as a singer throughout Europe, and died, after a very
brief illness, at St. Petersburg, April 12th, 1859.

Wyndham for piece draft £10. *Monday, 18th.*—To town to attend General Theatrical Fund Dinner; Charles Mathews in chair, and his speech good. Sit with Ledger's party; a feeling of melancholy somewhat induced by recollections of former occasions when present at same place. *19th.*—Over paragraphs about the suppression of German Reed's entertainment at the Olympic by the Lord Chamberlain, till very late. *20th.*—Club, and meet Hermann Vezin; chat about Berlin and mesmerism. Meet R. B. Brough, a sad hypochondriac: in his case see my own reflected. Heaven guard me from it! *21st.*—Hard at work for *Era*, from which 30s. Old memories revived this day by a renewal of the links of the chain that time had severed. *27th.*—At desk work all day. At night to Adelphi; see a wretched burlesque of *Devil on Two Sticks.*[1] *28th.*—Busy all day. Night to Haymarket; see Talfourd's clever punning extravaganza of *Electra.*[2] *29th.* —Finish *Era* paragraphs, from which £1 15s. Leave toys for Coyne's little ones. *30th.*—Mother in town; gives me a call; take her to Bertholini's to dinner; then to Bennett's; meet Buckstone. See *Sonnambula*, Drury Royal Italian Opera; but Victorine Balfe does not sing through indisposition; Mazzini, new tenor, good. Club; meet Sorrel first time."

" *May 5th.*—Write paragraphs for *Era*. Phil Phillips looks in. We go to Princess's; see *Henry V.:*[3] rather disappointed by effects. *6th.*—Night look in at Drury; see last act of *Lucia di Lammermoor*, and Victorine Balfe

---

[1] *Asmodeus, the Devil on Two Sticks; or, The Force of Friendship*, founded on the novel of "Le Sage." Mrs. Alfred Mellon, Don Cleophas; Toole, Asmodeus (very clever in his song and recitation); Kate Kelly, Don Mendoza; Mary Keeley, Leonora; Miss Arden, Fatima (sang very sweetly, "Who shall be fairest?"); Bedford, Don Fernando.

[2] Compton, Ægisthus; Mrs. Wilkins, Clytemnestra; Maria Ternan, Orestes; Eliza Weekes, Electra; Louise Leclercq, Chrysothemis; Fanny Wright, Pylades; Clark, Lycus.

[3] This was produced on March 28th for the benefit of Mr. and Mrs. Charles Kean. On these occasions they generally gave a Shakespearean revival, and this was the first time that *Henry V.* had been done at the Princess's. Mrs. Charles Kean represented with marvellous effect the

very good. *7th.*—Lofts for plays £2, on account of Nos. 16 to 27, £5. *11th.*—Arrive in town early. See Toole at Adelphi in new farce by Mr. Williams, *Ici on parle Français*; then to St. James's and see French plays [1]—private box *12th.*—*Era* £1 5s. Busy all day with *Era* paragraphs. At night to the Marshalls'; interesting spirit manifestations, and talk with them *solus* for hour after. Meet Soames, Monkhouse, etc. The spirits write, 'We do our best, but the conditions are not favourable, Mr. Blanchard,' and more, *vide* pocket book. *16th.*—Meet Mackenzie, nearly blind, beloved uncle of the Murrays. *17th.*—Mother returns. On Woodin's entertainment all day. *18th.*—To Adelphi; see *The House or the Home*;[2] good piece, and Wigans very clever in it. *19th.*—Busy writing for *Era*, from which £1 10s. *21st.*—St. James's in the evening, Amateur Military performance; Miss Wadham's benefit. Write notice for it for *Era*. *25th.*—To town. Olympic and good farce, *Retained for the Defence*.[3] Take Miller to Lyceum, and hear Emery's farewell speech for his benefit. *26th.*—Up at 7; feel very sleepy all day after. Do a little for *Era*; then to Adelphi. Coyne's *Talking Fish*,[4] and failure. Off to Surrey, Flexmore's benefit:[5]

chorus of the play, or muse of history. Her delivery was most excellent, and of rare grace. The revival was one of unexampled grandeur. Kean, Henry V.; Pistole, Frank Matthews; Fleuellen, Meadows; Duke of Exeter, Cooper; Williams, John Ryder; Queen of France, Miss Murray; Princess Catherine, Miss Chapman.

[1] The season was under the direction of M. Jules Samson. Vaudeville called *Monsieur Chapolard; Marie; ou, La Perle de Savoie*, from which the opera, *The Pearl of Savoy*, was taken; and the *Courrier de Lyon*, and *Les Crochets du Père Martin*, from which *The Porter's Knot* was taken; formed the first week's programme, and were played by a troupe selected from the smaller Parisian theatres.

[2] By Tom Taylor; said to have been suggested by *Perile dans la Demeure*. Hon. Horace Chetwynd, M.P., Alfred Wigan.

[3] By John Oxenford, taken from *L'Avocat d'un Grec*. Pawkins, Robson; Whitewash, George Vining; Mottley de Windsor, G. Cooke; Agatha, Miss Cottrell.

[4] This had already been seen at the Olympic, under the title of *Catching a Mermaid*.

[5] *William Tell*, played in three acts; comic ballet, *My Fetch*, with Madame Auriol and Flexmore; *Black-eyed Susan*—Ryder, William; Mrs. R. Honner, Susan—formed the programme.

house crammed.   W. B. calls, and tells me of engagement at Metropolitan Electric Telegraph Company, which relieves me.   Receive from *Era* £1 15s.   28th.—From Tallis on account of Part XL., £3.   Arrange with Lacy for publication of pieces, *Artful Dodge, Road of Life,* etc., the amount, £7, to be deducted out of the takings of the Society.   Meet Carpenter of *Sunday Times,* who leaves paper in dudgeon with Seale.   Gravesend at 8."

" *June 1st.*—Derby Day.   Musjid winning unexpectedly. Come up from Gravesend by boat.   Go to Strand and see very bad farce of *Caught by the Ears,* in which Rogers appears, and bit of burlesque, *Maid and Magpie.*   3rd.— Finish *Era* paragraphs, whence £1 5s.   Dine at Bertholini's ; then walk to Garway Road, Bayswater, to see C. C. B. ; chat for an hour, and walk back.   To club, and hear of Stiff's new paper, *The London Daily Journal,* being stopped by injunction of Ingram.   4th.—Leave copy of 'England and Wales' at printers'. Write a paragraph for Lofts.   Night see a bit of *Trovatore* at Drury.   E. T. S. gives me a douceur of £10 in place of a testimonial.   8th.—Mother's birthday ; make her a present, and Mary Perks comes down to spend the day with her.   9th.—Up at 7 and off by early train.   *Era* £2.   Get Smith's cheque cashed.   Begin Whitsuntide amusements for *Era,* and then with Pearsons and C. C. B. to see some highly interesting manifestations.   A nice party, and a decided success.   Take her back to Bayswater.   To club, rather tired.   10th.—Finish theatricals in morning, and afterwards attend usual meeting at the Mesmeric Infirmary.   Meet and see Dr. Elliotson first time.   Go to Bertholini's.   Meet Byron and friend of his, and take them to Stone's.   11th.—Dine at Opera Colonnade Hotel with Dramatic Authors Society ; Colonel Addison in the chair, and Planché, aged sixty-three, vice.   Maddison Morton, Vincent Wallis, Robert Bell, Palgrave Simpson, Bayle Bernard, Oxenford, Yates, Talfourd, and Byron present. Pleasant evening, dinner 25s. each.   16th.—Very busy with *Era.*   W. B. in afternoon, and—usual money pressure : very heavy and anxious about the future.   At night with Pearson's party to Red Lion Street ; interesting hour with the invisibles and meet Dr. Hales for the first time.   20th.—First of the

Handel Festivals at Crystal Palace.[1] 27*th.* Hear of Toole's odd accident to the eye occurring this day.[2] 29*th.*—Go to Haymarket; first night of Tom Taylor's well written but badly constructed *Contested Election.*[3] Meet Ledger, Povey, Harris, Albert Smith, Walter Lacy, Yates, etc., at Café de l'Europe."

"*July* 1*st.*—Write more paragraphs for *Era,* from which £1 5*s.* 7*th.*—Town by rail, and see Drayton at Adelphi, *Never Judge by Appearances:* not good.[4] 10*th.*—The Tooles come down by boat, dine with us, and we go out afterwards for a fly and a row, back, and a fly and a row out. 11*th.*—Too hot to write; off by train. Go to Olympic, see *Payable on Demand,*[5] Tom Taylor's new piece; clever, but won't be a

[1] *The Messiah.* Sims Reeves, Clara Novello, Miss Dolby, Weiss, and Belletti; Costa, conductor. The *Dettingen Te Deum, Belshazzar, Israel in Egypt,* were the works given. Receipts were about £30,000, and this amount was derived from the 80,000 people who attended, and in whose refreshment the following items of commissariat were consumed:—1,600 dozen sandwiches, 1,200 dozen pork pies, 400 dozen Sydenham pasties, 800 veal and ham pies, 650 pigeon pies, 480 hams, 3,509 chickens, 120 galantines of lamb, 240 fore-quarters of lamb, 150 galantines of chicken, 60 raised game pies, 3,050 lobster salads, 3,825 dishes of salmon mayonnaise, 300 score of lettuce, 40,000 buns at a penny each, 25,000 ditto at twopence each, 32,249 ices, 2,419 dozen beverages, 1,152 ditto ale and stout, 403 Crystal Palace puddings, 400 jellies, *nine tons of roast and boiled beef,* 400 creams, 350 fruit tarts, 3,506 quarts of tea, coffee, and chocolate, and 485 tongues, exclusive of wine swallowed by the visitors.

[2] Toole was playing with his little boy (then three years old), and the child in some manner ran the corner of an envelope with such force into his father's eye as to cut the eyeball. Toole played the same night, but was obliged to absent himself for two nights afterwards.

[3] Charles Mathews, Dodgson; W. Farren, Wapshott; Fanny Wright, Clara Honeybun; Compton, Mr. Honeybun; Mrs. Charles Mathews, Mrs. Honeybun; Buckstone, Peckover; Rogers, Topper; Braid, Gathercole; Clark, Spitchcock.

[4] This was a musical duologue, written by Henri Drayton, and performed by himself and Mrs. Drayton as respectively the Count and Countess de Belleville. The music, which was agreeable, but without any great pretensions, was by E. J. Loder.

[5] Leading incident the same as that in *The Jew of Frankfort.* Action of the play is supposed to take place in 1792, and in its course some

long attraction. 14*th.*—At night *Lady of Lyons* burlesque,[1] by Byron, at Strand ; find it good and amusing. 20*th.*—At night to Adelphi ; see Byron's *Babes in the Wood;*[2] Toole in it. 21*st.*—To Adelphi to see Planché's new (old) piece of *Old Offenders :*[3] success moderate. 23*rd.*—Day wasted going into city for 'England and Wales.' *Monday, 25th.*—The last night of Vauxhall for ever announced.[4] Take short stroll ; but very sad and much pressed by pecuniary emergencies. Try Woodin's, and failure. At night look in at Tom Matthews's entertainment. Literary matter. 29*th.*—C. C. B. in evening ; call with her on Watkins ; pleasant walk through Westminster and elsewhere. Meet at club spiritualistic astrologer, Mr. Kenneth Mackenzie. Curious anecdotes about Thomas Buckley, and sit late telling there-anent. 30*th.*—Mother calls in morning with C. C. B. Take them to dine at club, and thence to coffee and ices to Gatti's at Hungerford. See them into 'bus, and go to Albert Smith's entertainment of *China*; last night of the season,[5] but see it for the first time—much pleased."

twenty-three years are supposed to pass away. Reuben Goldsched, Robson ; the Marquis de St. Cast, W. Gordon ; Lina Goldsched, Miss Wyndham ; Jonadab Manasseh, G. Cooke ; Isaac, J. H. White ; Horatio Cocles Bric-à-brac, H. Wigan ; Marcus Junius Brutus, H. Cooper.

[1] Charlotte Saunders, Claude Melnotte ; Pattie Oliver, Pauline ; J. Clarke, Beauseant ; James Rogers, Widow Melnotte.

[2] *The Babes in the Wood and the Good Little Fairy Birds.* Sir Rowland Macassar, Mrs. Alfred Mellon ; Lady Macassar, Mrs. Billington ; the babes played by Miss Kate Kelly and J. L. Toole ; Smith (a good-natured ruffian), Mr. Paul Bedford.

[3] Another version of *Le Capitaine Voleur*, already done under the title of "£500 *Reward.*" Purefoy, J. L. Toole ; Artimesia, Miss Henrietta Sims.

[4] The entertainment consisted of a ballet by Chapino's pupils ; a concert under the direction of R. Dean, in which Miss Lizzie Harris, Mrs. Mears, Messrs. T. Critchfield, Matz, and Russell Grover distinguished themselves ; an equestrian performance in which Harry Croueste is mentioned ; fireworks with two tableaux, "Thanks, kind friends," and "Farewell, for ever ;" and there was the usual dancing on the platform.

[5] This was also the last time of his appearance as a bachelor, for on Monday, August 1st, Albert Smith was married to Mary Keeley by the Rev. J. C. M. Bellew, and started immediately after the ceremony for his beloved Chamouni.

"*Aug. 4th.*—To Haymarket to see bad new farce of *Out of Sight Out of Mind,*[1] and then to club. *5th.*—From *Era* £1 10s. In evening P. Phillips calls about entertainment, which may be christened *The Cabinet of Curiosities.* At night to Canterbury Hall. Hear fourth act of Verdi's *Macbeth :* first time in England, and not good. *6th.*—At night to Adelphi, Webster's benefit; and see charmingly acted piece of *One Touch of Nature.*[2] *13th.*—Go to Sheerness and back by boat. On board meet Bennett (*The Owl*), Roberts and his friend Shelton, who get off at Southend. *16th.*—Try what town atmosphere will do, and come up by 3 o'clock. Find £3 from Tallis on account of Part XLI. At night to Mr. and Mrs. Reed (Miss Priscilla Horton); first time of my seeing her in any entertainment at all.[3] *19th.*—Come from Gravesend by boat. Dine at Carr's, chambers, and write a few lines. Phillips calls, and engages me till evening in discussion about Woodin's entertainment. Dr. Smethurst's trial over : found guilty, and great excitement over it.[4] Last night of Olympic season.[5] Go for hour to Robson ; hear his speech. *23rd.*—Try to be funny for Woodin. Treat mother and boy to Rosherville, and the sad, sad story on our return : frightful trial to patience. *27th.*—At night Mrs. Charles Mathews's benefit at Haymarket—take Miller; in *Masks and Faces*, Webster, Triplet, and Mrs. C. M. Peg Woffington:

---

[1] This was written specially for Charles Mathews, who played the part of Gatherwool.

[2] This was an adaptation of Mr. Webster's own from the French, and in which he achieved one of his greatest successes, as Holder, a poor copyist, who is in search of the child that his wife had carried off some twenty years before, when she deserted him.

[3] They were then playing at the Royal Gallery of Illustration.

[4] The prisoner was accused of the murder of a lady named Isabella Banks, by the constant administration of small doses of irritant poison. He had committed bigamy in having married the deceased, and had induced her to sign a will leaving him all she possessed, about £18,000. Serjeant Ballantyne prosecuted, and he was defended by Serjeant Parry.

[5] The programme consisted of *A Doubtful Victory, Payable on Demand*, and *Retained for the Defence.* Robson's speech consisted a good deal of a running and punning commentary of the various pieces that had been produced under the joint management of himself and Mr. Emden.

not over till midnight.   30*th.*[1]—At night to Soho Theatre,
Butler's benefit;[2] meet J. Wilton, Hall, Chatterton, Kenney,
Falkner, etc. : performance very bad."

"*Sept.* 1*st.*—Writing all day for *Era*, from which 30*s.*
Dine at Carr's.   Pay Reynolds's weekly black mail.   Night
to Strand ; see brisk farce by Augustus Mayhew, *Goose with
Golden Eggs*[3]—good; and *Victorine* revival and *Lottery Ticket*

---

[1] The evening before, August 29th, was the last night of Mr. Charles
Kean's management of the Princess's Theatre, when *Henry VIII.* was
played, and the lessee recapitulated the events of his nine years'
management, and, among other facts, said that in one season alone he
had expended very nearly £50,000 on productions ; in improvements
and enlargements of the theatre, £3,000 had been expended; and
£10,000 in addition to the general stock which he was compelled
by the terms of his lease, to leave behind him.   Spoke in the most
feeling and graceful manner of the support afforded him by the
"indomitable energy and devoted affection of Mrs. Charles Kean,"
and bore tribute to the consolation she had been to him in his hours of
depression.   He also contradicted the report that had been circulated,
that with his retirement from management he intended to retire from
the stage.   Before the separation of the company Mr. Kean had
presented to almost every member some token of his regard.   The
following is a summary of the history of the theatre during the past
nine years :—1850, Lessees Mr. and Mrs. Kean, and Mr. and Mrs. Keeley.
Opened September 28th with *Twelfth Night.*   The Keeleys retired
with the summer season of 1851, and then Charles Kean became sole
manager, and produced *Merry Wives of Windsor* November 28th, 1851;
King John, February 9th, 1852—the first great Shakespearean revival ;
Corsican Brothers, February 24th ; *Macbeth,* February 16th, 1853 ;
Sardanapalus, June 18th, 1853.   In 1853-4 *Richard III., Faust and
Marguerite, Courier of Lyons,* were produced ; 1854-5, *Henry VIII.* ran
a hundred and fifty nights; April 5th, 1855, *Winter's Tale*—another
great success ; September 1st, 1856, *Pizarro* revival, and October
15th, revival of *Midsummer Night's Dream :* March 12th, 1857, *King
Richard II.*—a success ; July 1st, *The Tempest;* April 7th, 1858,
King Lear, and June 12th, *Merchant of Venice;* March 28th, 1859,
King Henry V.   These were the principal pieces, and those by which
Mr. Charles Kean's reign will be remembered.

[2] Henry Butler was an actor and theatrical agent.   *Delicate Ground,
Monsieur Jacques,* in which Butler filled the name *rôle* ; Miss Raynoe
was the daughter.

[3] Full of bustling fun, turning on the endeavour to recover a goose,
under the wing of which a bank-note for £500 has been concealed, and
sent as a present to the daughter of Bonsor, W. Mowbray ; Turby,

at Adelphi—very bad. *4th.*—Reading Mrs. Winstanley's clever book of 'Shifting Scenes in Theatrical Life.' *7th.*—*Great Eastern* leaves Deptford, and stays off Purfleet, in Long Reach. *8th.*—See the *Great Eastern*[1] pass Rosherville this morning—a great event; she stays an hour opposite town. Write paragraphs for *Era*, for which receive 35*s.* Spend evening at Foster's, with spiritual manifestations, chat, and David Prince Miller, who works wonderful feats of legerdemain, and gives me marionette. *10th.*—To opening of Wells at night; Miss Heath's Juliet good. *15th.*—To town by 12; meet Beverley; talk about pantomime; chop with Smith, who goes off to Gloucester festival. To chambers; correct proofs of *Artful Dodge*. *Era* £1 15*s.* Coffee at Simpson's with Willet, Ledger, etc. To Sadlers Wells; see *John Bull*.[2] *17th.*—On 'England and Wales.' Pay D. P. Miller 7*s.* for two figures. At night to Haymarket, benefit of Charles Mathews: *Road to Ruin* and[3] *Paul Pry* first time; house crowded, Mathews' Goldfinch very good. His Paul Pry less broad than the Listonian rendering. *22nd.*—See Amy Sedgwick as Miss Dorillon in *Wives as they were, and Maids as they are*;[4] and new farce, by J. Bridgeman, called *The Rifle, and How to Use It.* *23rd.*—Finish *Era* paragraphs, and receive £1 15*s.* *24th.*—£5 from Woodin.

Rogers; and Flickster, J. Clarke; Turby's daughter Clara, Miss Ida Wilton.

[1] She was commanded by Captain Harrison, was piloted down the river by Atkinson, and the principal tugs in attendance were the *Victoria, Napoleon, Alliance,* and *True Briton.* There was considerable difficulty in getting her down the Thames, on account of her draught of water—21 feet 10 inches aft and 22 feet 3 inches forward. Though she was very badly trimmed, and yet though her draught of water was so light as not to allow her paddles or screws anything like full force, she was reckoned the then fastest vessel in the world.

[2] *John Bull; or, An Englishman's Fireside.* Job Thornberry (originally played by Fawcett), Phelps; Mary Thornberry, Caroline Heath.

[3] Chippendale, Old Dornton; Howe, Harry Dornton; Buckstone, Silky; Mrs. Charles Mathews, Sophia; Mrs. Wilkins, Widow Warren. In *Paul Pry* Mrs. Charles Mathews highly spoken of as Phœbe.

[4] This was played at the Haymarket. Mrs. Wilkins, Lady Mary Raffle; Chippendale, Lord Priory; and Howe, Sir William Dorillon. In John Bridgman's farce Buckstone played Percival Fluff; Rogers, Sidney Jubkins; Compton, Mutton.

Olympic [1] and Princess's [2] reopen for season. Receive from
Tallis £2 on account of Part XLII. Go to both theatres;
Princess's not over till nearly 1 a.m.; *Ivy Hall*—not good,
and *Love and Fortune*, Planché. *27th.*—Domestic tempers
again burst out like a volcano, and overwhelm the peace of
the valley. Mother and self quite upset, and all things
made uncomfortable, and completely miserable. *28th.*—
At night come up to town; see Adelphi farce of *Love and
Hunger* [3]—very lively; David Fisher very amusing. *29th.*

Busy with *Era* paragraphs all day, from which source
receive £2 10s. At night go to Adelphi; see *Willow Copse* [4]
revival—well played; and afterwards to club, meeting
Charles Hall, leader, and originally in *Arcadia* at Grecian."

"*Oct. 1st.*—Dine at Edinbro' Castle with Bridgeman and
Leslie, meeting Fry and Landels afterwards. At night to
St. James's; [5] *Widow's Wedding*, and travestie of *Virginius*.

[1] The Olympic re-opened again, under the management of Robson
and Emden, with *Payable on Demand; Retained for the Defence;* and
A Morning Call taken from *Il faut qu'une porte soit ouverte ou fermée.*
George Vining, Sir Edward Ardent; Mrs. Stirling, Mrs. Chillingstone.

[2] Princess's opened, under the management of Augustus Harris.
The Theatre had been thoroughly re-decorated in Italian style. The
pieces were *Ivy Hall* by John Oxenford, a piece which resembled
Love in a Village; and a dramatic tableau in " Watteau colours," en-
titled *Love and Fortune,* by J. R. Planché. The company consisted of
Messrs. Harcourt, Bland, F. Widdicombe, Frank Matthews, Meadows,
Graham, Gasden; Mrs. Weston, Newbery, Miss K. Saville, and Mrs.
Charles Young—in *Ivy Hall.* Messrs. Frank Matthews, H. Saker,
R. Cathcart, J. R. Shore, M. Petit; Misses Louisa Keeley, Carlotta
Leclercq; Clifford, G. Darley, E. Wadham, H. Howard, and Mdlle.
Villiers—in *Love and Fortune.* The scenery was painted by Beverley.
[It was in *Ivy Hall* that Henry Irving made his first appearance in
London. Having been tried and found wanting, he went back to
Manchester.—C. S.]

[3] By Maddison Morton. David Fisher, who joined the company,
played Bagster; and Paul Bedford, Stephen Stock.

[4] David Fisher played Hulks—quite out of his line, but very good;
Henrietta Sims, Rose Fielding; J. L. Toole, Augustus de Rosherville;
Paul Bedford and Miss Woolgar resumed their original characters of
Staggers and Meg. Miss Laidlaw, Lucy Vanguard.

[5] The theatre opened, under the management of F. B. Chatterton,
with a shilling pit and a sixpenny gallery, and boxes at three shillings

First night of season, house crammed, pieces queer. 15*th.*—
Look in at Covent Garden; see, first time, two acts of
Meyerbeer's opera of *Dinorah*, and delighted: a wonderfully
effective storm scene in second act. 19*th.*—To Sadlers
Wells; see Tom Taylor's new play of *The Fool's Revenge*;[1]
Foster with me: admirably acted, and a success. 20*th.*—
Very busy in the morning. In afternoon see C. C. B., chat
with her; gleams of sunshine through the clouds. 21*st.*
—At night see Cavalier Poletti, a conjuror, at Gallery
of Illustration: very good. 22*nd.*—To Haymarket, Amy
Sedgwick's benefit; *Plot and Passion*, Amy Sedgwick being
Madame de Fontaine: piece not too well played. *Monday,*
24*th.*—Busy all day on ' England and Wales '—now approaching its termination, after seven years ! ! ! ! 28*th.*—At night
through pouring rain to Pelham Place, Brompton; agreeable
two hours, and then circuitous route in cab home. Have had
this week to chronicle the deaths of two old friends, Didear
and Tom Manders.[2] 29*th.*—At night to St. James's; stupid
piece called *Cupid's Ladder*,[3] by Leicester Buckingham.

and two shillings. *The Widow's Wedding* was by Edward Fitzball, and
in it were Miss Katherine Hickson, Miss Eliza Arden, Miss Murray,
Charles Young, Emery and Barrett. *Virginius; or, The Trials of a
Fond Papa*, was a burlesque by Leicester Buckingham; Charles Young,
Virginius. *The Dead Shot* was also played, with Miss Eliza Arden and
Mr. R. Cockrill.

[1] Adaptation of Victor Hugo's *Le Roi s'amuse.* Duke Galeotto
Manfredi, Henry Marston; Serafino, Frederic Robinson; Fiordelisa,
Miss Heath; Brigitta, Mrs. Henry Marston; Francesca Bentivoglio,
Miss Atkinson; and Bertuccio, Phelps.

[2] Tom Manders, born December 22nd, 1797, was clerk in the Bank
of England from 1814 to 1821, when his office was abolished by the
withdrawal of the one-pound notes. He then turned his attention to
the stage, and began a provincial career with his wife Louisa Powell,
whom he had married in 1820. He became a manager, and then came
to town; played Justice Greedy to the Sir Giles Overreach of Edmund
Kean, at the City Theatre, Milton Street. He was afterwards a member of the Strand and Olympic Theatres, but latterly of the Queen s,
to which theatre he was attached some sixteen years, and was a great
favourite. Was the original Tom Stag in the farce of *Captain Stevens*,
and Sam Slap in *The Rake's Progress*. He became the proprietor of
the Sun Tavern, Long Acre, a favourite theatrical *rendezvous*. He was
much esteemed, and died October 28th.

[3] This was written for Lydia Thompson, and she appeared in it in

Back to write notice. 31*st.*—Bring mother up to town by early train; receive £9; make a little festival for her at Bedford Head, whereat meet Paul Bedford and Webster, who knew her in 1818; take her by cab to Mrs. Hubbard's, at Maida Hill. Back to chambers; six hours' work on 'England and Wales.' Amusing introduction to Miss Grace Darley, our Drury Lane fairy."

" *Nov.* 2*nd.*—Back to town in afternoon; go to Princess's, seeing *The Master Passion,*[1] a new piece by Falconer—not very brilliant. 3*rd.*—At night to Leslie's chambers. *Séance;* Mrs. William Johnson, Pearson, Robt. and Sam Emery present. Afterwards to Hubble's, and chat about it; meet Clark, Leicester Buckingham, etc. Place full, being first night of Halliday's bad burlesque of *Romeo and Juliet.*[2] 5*th.*—Up at 9, and, after reading for an hour, off to British Museum for 'England and Wales.' At night to see Albert Smith's *China;*[3] first night of the season. Write long notice. 9*th.*—Mother calls at chambers, and take her to St. James's; new comedy by late James Kenney, *Living for Appearances :*[4] very fair. 10*th.*—At night to Adelphi; new piece by Watts Phillips,

several characters, and danced extremely well. Miss Nellie Moore was very charming as Winifred; Charles Young, Giles. On the same evening Leigh Murray and Mrs. Frank Matthews appeared in *They're both to blame.*

[1] *The Master Passion;* or, *The Outlaws of the Adriatic*, taken from *Les Noces Vénétiennes* of M. Victor Séjour. Giovanni Orseolo, Ryder; Olympia, Miss Carlotta Leclercq; Morosina, Mrs. Charles Young; Spolatro, Graham; Galieno, George Melville.

[2] Produced at the Strand. Romeo, Charlotte Saunders; Juliet, Marie Wilton; Paris, Miss Bufton. The scenery was painted by W. Broadfoot and A. Callcott, who gave excellent promise of what they would become in the future.

[3] The entertainment opened as usual at the Egyptian Hall, and was very warmly received. A considerable alteration had been made in the first part. The scenery was painted by Beverley and P. Phillips.

[4] *London Pride;* or, *Living for Appearances.* A moral lesson on the folly of a young couple living beyond their means, and, through their extravagance, laying themselves open to the wiles of a designing individual. The young couple brought to their senses by an outspoken, kind-hearted uncle. Harrington, Leigh Murray; Mrs. Harrington, Mrs. Frank Matthews; Toby Veneer, R. Cockrill; Julia Harrington, Nellie Moore; John Warner, Barrett; Frederick Anson, Brazier; Falsetto,

called *The Dead Heart:*[1] lasts more than four hours, but very effective, and well played. 11*th.*—Hard at work on Adelphi notices; by no means well. At night go to Gate; Besemeres resumes his secretaryship. Late vigils, and home with Levy, seeing his remarkable library in Gray's Inn : the most perfect set of chambers, perhaps, in the world. 12*th.*—At night to Princess's; see farce by Williams called *Nursey Chickweed;*[2] take Miller. 16*th.*—Town at night; St. James's ; bad burlesque called *The Swan and Edgar.*[3] 19*th.*—Night to Haymarket ; see bad piece by Tom Taylor, *The Late Lamented;*[4] French flimsiness. 20*th.*—Think of staying in town, but go down to make all happy, and find I should have been much happier in my own company. Sad and ceaseless annoyances, and no comfort. *Monday*, 21*st.*—Worse; frightful scene of domestic trials. 22*nd.*—All day on pantomime, but very little done. At night to Gardens. 23*rd.*—Up to town by 4 p.m. train. To Princess's ; see comedietta, *Gossip :*[5] fair, but not great. 25*th.*—Finish rough copy of *Johannes cum Beanstalk.* 26*th.*—Indoors all day with terrible cold.

W. Carlo ; Darby Colchanen, Charles Young ; Willis, Miss Murray. It was taken from the French, and strongly resembled *Living too Fast.*

[1] This was written in a prologue and three acts. The cast consisted of—Robert Landry, Benjamin Webster; Catherine Duval, Mrs. Alfred Mellon ; Count St. Valérie (father and son), Billington ; Abbé Latour, David Fisher ; Jacques Legrand, Stuart ; Reboul, Paul Bedford ; Toupet, J. L. Toole ; Cerisette, Miss Kelly. The performances of Benjamin Webster and David Fisher will always stand out in dramatic history as perhaps their most successful attempts.

[2] Widdicombe, Jonathan Chickweed ; Barnes, H. Saker ; Nelly, Louisa Keeley. The farce bore considerable resemblance to *Good for Nothing.*

[3] Or, *The Fairy Lake.* It was by Sutherland Edwards and Charles Kenney, and only passed muster through the charming dancing of Lydia Thompson as Cygnetta.

[4] It was taken from the French, and was the same plot as that in *Never Judge by Appearances.* Mr. and Mrs. Charles Mathews, Miss Reynolds and Buckstone were the principals in a small cast. It was only acted three times.

[5] This was an adaptation by Augustus Harris, sen., and Thomas J. Williams of *L'Enfant Terrible.* Alfred Fortescue, Harcourt ; Mrs. Chatterton, Mrs. Charles Young ; Mark Beresford, Ryder ; Mr. Wilmington, Meadows ; Horace Cleveland, J. G. Shore.

Night to Haymarket to see Charles Mathews as Colonel Feignwell (first time) in *Bold Stroke for a Wife :*[1] not very good. *Monday, 28th.*—Gravesend ; indoors all day, a regular invalid. *30th.*—Go to Lyceum, third night of Céleste's opening, and see bad piece of *Paris and Pleasure.*[2]

" *Dec. 3rd.*—Called upon by a poor fellow named M. Dargan, of Bradshaw's, to relieve his distress ; piteous tale of woe. Trying to begin Wells pantomime, but out of spirits for it. At night look in at Drury (promenade concerts) ; go to Princess's ;[3] clever new grotesque dancer, Espinosa. *Monday, 5th.*—Make fair copy (and post it to Wells) of three scenes of opening. Down to Gravesend at night ; Northfleet Volunteer Corps forming ; old *Times* reporter, Dunoon, a character. *11th.*—Thirty-nine this day ! Astonished at it myself. Take Miller to Gravesend, and dine at home for the sake of dear mother. Back in dense fog, and in chambers by 10.30. Afterwards read, smoke, and meditate. *Monday, 12th.*—Read pantomime at Drury, and about theatre all day. Back, and read George Vandenhoff's 'Dramatic Reminiscences.' *14th.*—To Grecian ; Arthur Young[4] in *Shylock :* very queer. *17th.*—Attend rehearsal at Drury, and from E. T. S. receive per cheque £10. Send MS. of pantomime to Davidson's ;

[1] Mrs. Charles Mathews, Ann Lovely ; Chippendale, Periwinkle ; Compton, Obadiah Prim ; Buckstone, Simon Pure ; Tradelove and Philip Modelove, Rogers and Clarke.

[2] Or, *Home and Happiness*, founded by Charles Selby on *Les Enfers de Paris.* Written expressly that the manageress might represent eight different characters, one of them a Mephistopheles. She was supported by F. Villiers, Walter Lacy, Miss Hudspeth, Julia St. George, Kate Saville, James Vining, James Johnstone, F. Morton, S. Lyon, Agnes Burdett, and Misses Neville and Stuart. *A Phenomenon in a Smock-frock* was played at the same time by Rouse and Miss M. A. Hutton.

[3] This was under Augustus Harris's management, and *Home Truths*, an adaptation by Mr. Reynoldson of *Gabriel*, made a hit. It was admirably acted by Mrs. Charles Young, Frank Matthews, J. G. Shore, and Carlotta Leclercq. Espinosa had made a great foreign reputation, and was supported in *Le Grand Pas du Dervish de Faust* by Mdlle. Marequita.

[4] He had made some reputation as a reader of Shakespeare. He was supported by Jane Coveney as Portia and Harriet Coveney as Jessica.

make out plots of Drury and Wells for *Sunday Times;* correct proofs 'England and Wales,' and then deliver them. 23*rd.*—Hard at work, as before. At night, E. T. S.'s annual dinner party (Albion); go, sitting next to Sloman (of Cursitor Street) and opposite Downes (!) of Strand. Mr. Metcalfe, barrister, proposes my health, and I return thanks. Then to club; supper, Lowe in chair, Bates Richards in vice, but only stop a few minutes. Self much upset by severe cold, and equally disinclined for pleasure from hearing of Albert Smith's serious illness.[1] 24*th.*—Woodin in morning, and receive from him for entertainment what makes it £50. Hear of death of Wright.[2] At night to rehearsal at Drury: all looking pretty well, but very tedious in trying over. Finish at club; wish friends a merry Christmas, but self not well, and sad exceedingly. 25*th.*—Take Albert Miller down to Gravesend; roast beef and plum pudding: much as it has been for the last ten years. *Monday, 26th.*—Back to chambers. At night go to Strand to see Talfourd's burlesque of *William Tell;*[3] write notice of it for *Telegraph,* and then to club, and hear all at Drury[4] (whereat passed Miller) went off admirably.

[1] He had a stroke of paralysis.

[2] Edward Wright died at Boulogne on December 21st. He was born in 1813, and was therefore forty-six years of age at the time of his death. Made his *début* at the Queen's in 1834, but was not a great success, and so went into the provinces. His first recognized appearance in London was at the St. James's, under Braham, September 29th, 1837, as Splash in *The Young Widow,* to the Aurelia of Mrs. Stirling, and Fitzcloddy in *Methinks I see my Father.* He was for twenty years a member of the Adelphi company. He was great as Paul Pry, John Grumley and Muster Grinnidge, and was an immense favourite with the public.

[3] It was entitled, *Tell and the Strike of the Cantons; or, The Pair, the Meddler, and the Apple.* It was supported by—Eleanor Bufton and Ada Wilton; J. Clarke as Gesler; Patty Oliver as Lisetta; Miss Lavine as Verner; Sernem the Seneschal, James Rogers; William Tell, Charlotte Saunders; Albert, Marie Wilton; Mrs. Selby and Rosina Wright were also in the cast, and the scenery was painted by Albert Callcott and W. Broadfoot.

[4] This was E. L. B.'s pantomime, *Jack and the Beanstalk.* The harlequins, Milano and St. Maine; columbines, Madame Boleno and Miss Sharpe; pantaloons, Tanner and Buckingham; clowns, Harry Boleno and Flexmore; sprite was Deulin. Misses Mason, Helen Howard, and

Tired out, but satisfied with the reports I have heard, for my good night's rest.   27*th.*—W. B. in afternoon, and give him a Christmas box for the children of 13*s.* Get cheque changed. Very tired, but make up for a wasted day by a busy night. Look in at Drury (crowded); then cab to Wells; see pantomime of *Golden Goose*[1] from private box; back in cab, and write notice of it for *Daily Telegraph.*   28*th.*—Write all day for *Era;* night to club, whereat only business talked of—proposed alterations of rules of election.   29*th.*—More paragraphs for *Era,* and at night to Lyceum;[2] see Spanish Dancers first time—very fair, the burlesque nicely and smartly written, the transformation magnificent.   30*th.*— Hard at work finishing *Era* paragraphs, from which receive £3.   31*st.*—Make up accounts for the year; see burlesque at Adelphi;[3] and then the Old Year out at the club with Toole

Messrs. Templeton and Tom Matthews, appeared in the opening. Robert Roxby was the stage manager.

[1] *Harlequin and the Golden Goose;* or, *The Old Mother Earth, the Little Red Man, and the Princess whom Nobody could make laugh.* It was founded by E. L. B. on one of the Brothers Grimm's legends. Misses Hodson, Hill, Rose Frampton and little Eliza Collier in the cast.   E. L. B. had evidently drawn on his connection with the Friday Knights for one subject, for there was a reproduction of St. John's Gate, Clerkenwell, which Mr. B. Foster, the landlord of the tavern there, had so carefully restored.   Charles Lauri made his first appearance as clown at Sadlers Wells ; H. Lauri was the pantaloon; Charles Fenton, harlequin ; Caroline Parkes, columbine.

[2] The pantomime here was *King Thrush-beard, the Little Pet, and the Great Passion;* or, *Harlequin Hafiz and the Fairy Good Humour.* The opening was written by F. Talfourd.   It was a marvellous transformation scene, worthy of the Vestris productions.   Misses Hudspeth, Julia St. George, Neville, Turner, and Stuart; J. Rouse and Forester were in the opening; J. and H. Marshall, harlequin and clown; Naylor, pantaloon; Miss Rosine, columbine.   The Spanish dancers appeared for a few days in the pantomime.   They were Donna Isabel Cubas and Don Juan Ximenes.

[3] This was H. J. Byron's *The Nymph of the Lurleyberg* ; or, *The Knight and the Naïads,* based on *Lurline,* and was spoken of as one of Byron's happiest efforts.   Mrs. Alfred Mellon, Sir Rupert the Reckless ; Paul Bedford, Baron Witz ; W. Eburne, Count Calimanco ; R. Romer, the Family Herald ; J. L. Toole, the Seneschal—he made a hit in a doleful ditty ; Lurline, Miss Webb ; Wavelet, Miss Laidlaw ; Lady Una, Kate Kelly.

and Talfourd, Byron, Sala, and the Re-Unionists. Thus dies
out 1859 : for all the blessings received during which and
other years, God be thanked.”

Rough estimate for year, £246 10*s.*

1860.

“ *Monday, Jan. 2nd.*—Begin the year with usual settlement of Christmas bills. Reading and pottering in study
all day.   Find town in uproar from the landing of discharged
troops, most of whom appear to be unmitigated blackguards.
5th.—At night look in at Drury ; house crammed in every
part ; see E. T. S., who pays balance of pantomime, £25 ;
see Albert Miller, Tomlins, Talfourd, and Murray. 6*th.*—
Write paragraphs for *Era,* from which £2 5*s. Telegraph*
pays for Christmas article £2.   Finish theatricals, and at
night take Miller to Princess’s : *Jack the Giant Killer ;* [1]
masks and scenic changes the best part of it. 7*th.*—Dykwynkyn calls in afternoon.   Meet Green,[2] and go to Drury ;
overwhelming house ; then to his chambers in Danes Inn ;
very snug. Club ; meet Dillon. Morning, get books from
Davidson ; chat with Paul Bedford, and hear his St. Asaph
story of Incledon and Jack Johnson. 11*th.*—E. T. S. wants
a three-act drama in three weeks, which I promise to do ! !
13*th.*—Finish *Era* paragraphs, for which £1 5*s.* W. B. in
afternoon ; not in good spirits, as himself, so go to St. John’s
Gate, where Brough’s exquisite poem anent the good Samuel
Johnson is read and ordered to be framed. 14*th.*—To
Haymarket ; see pantomime of *Valentine’s Day ;* [3] pretty,

[1] Opening was *King Arthur and the Knights of the Round Table.*
Louise Keeley, Jack ; Rose Leclercq, Queen Bee ; Saker, King Arthur;
Gorgibuster, J. G. Shore ; Sybil, Kate Laidlaw ; Forest, clown ; Cor-
mack, harlequin ; Paulo, pantaloon ; Caroline Adams, columbine.

[2] [This is Horace Green, a member of the Arundel and Re-Union
Clubs, a delightful companion, and a Bohemian of the better kind.
He was the secretary of several benevolent institutions and dabbled in
literature.—C. S.]

[3] Or, *Harlequin, the Fairy and the True Lovers’ Knot.* Misses Henrade, Clara Denville, and Rose Williams were the principals in the

but slow in effect. Pantomimists (Leclercqs) very good. *Monday, 16th.*—To Gravesend, calling as I go upon Davidson, who pays the annual £2 2s. for pantomime printing. Night to Northfleet; chat with a Mr. Hoames, Lecturer at Panopticon, Polytechnic, etc.; experiments in figures and imitative clairvoyance gone through. 18th.—To St. James's; see stupid piece, *My Name is Norval,* by Oxenford; very crude. 19th.—See pantomime with Greenwood,[1] and from him receive £20. 21st.—Dine at Athenian Club, and am put up for member. Much pleased with the place and the people, and meet hosts of old friends. Look in at Lyceum; see comic business. Marshall's fitting as usual very well, and one good transformation scene of house changing round. 26th.—Night to Pearson's; friendly circle; tapping, and message from John Kemble Chapman to me: 'You judge none harshly; love all mankind.' Hope to Heaven I may ever do so. Pleasant evening. 28th.—Mr. Levy sends to me about the *Daily Telegraph.* Have interview with him, and undertake to write articles. All day afterwards over one on the critical clairvoyance case; and at night, with brain overwrought, look in at Club. *Monday, 30th.*— Gravesend. Bring mother up to town; dinner at Bedford Head; see her off to Richmond, as the home she chooses for the future. At night to Lyceum; Tom Taylor's adaptation of *Tale of Two Cities.*[2] Very well done; slow. My article in *Telegraph.*"

" *Feb. 1st.*—Walk; pay for boy's schooling in advance at Gravesend College. Write *Era* copy. 2nd.—To Olympic; see *Alfred the Great* (burlesque),[3] and find it goes very slow;

opening. The Leclercq family were in the harlequinade, with Herr Cole as pantaloon.

[1] This was at Sadlers Wells.

[2] It was done in a prologue and two acts. Collette Dubois; and Madame Defarge, Madame Céleste; the Marquis St. Evremond, Walter Lacy; Lucie Manette, Kate Saville; Jarvis, T. Lyon; Doctor Manette, James Vining; Sidney Carton, Villers; Ernest Defarge, Morton; James Johnstone, Solomon Barsad; Rouse, Jeremiah Cruncher. The dance of the *Carmagnole*, with the original music, formed a very effective tableau, and the trial of Darnay (Forrester) was also a faithful reproduction.

[3] By H. Holt. Carlotta Leclercq, George Melville, Mrs. Weston,

good lines, but dramatic construction queer. Emden wants farce and *Number Nip* done. See Levy of *Telegraph. Era,* £1 10s. 8th.—To Princess's; first night of Hall's comedy, *Caught in a Trap*: slow affair; pointless and plotless. 9th.—Look in at Strand and see pleasant little farce by Wooller, called *Sisterly Service.* 10th.—Finish *Era* copy, whence £1 15s. To St. John's Gate; take a distinguished party (Lady Talfourd and family) over building, crypt of chapel, etc.; then dine with Frank Talfourd at Garrick Club; then with him to Wells. 11th.—Long chat with Adams in morning; dine at Athenian Club. Night, to spirit *séance;* communication: 'Sound the trumpet so that every one may know the glory of God (Soffith),—One that loves you. Do the work of faith; it will be well with you.' Physical manifestations follow, and all very satisfactory. 15th.—To town in evening, to Colonel Addison,[1] Elm Tree Villa, Elm Tree Road, St. John's Wood, after an expensive cab hunt, which may furnish material for paper, 'How I went to the Colonel's Party!' Met the Marshalls and Pearson; and spirit *séance* tried—startling the Colonel; only stop till midnight, and home in cab again. 16th.— At night to Pearson's, returning book. Get communication, 'What you want is your time more at your own disposal,' —very true! 'We like you,'—very complimentary. 'Your time would be useful to us,'—very kind. Afterwards to Club and long chat with Bates Richards.[2] 18th.—Walk, after dining with Woodin, from Richmond through Mortlake to Barnes, and up by train. Go to Drury with him, then to Club, and receive testimonial from E. T. S. of silver claret jug. 21st.—W. Callcott sends me by his father a strikingly effective water-colour sketch, which I get framed directly. 22nd.—To town, and annual dinner of Dramatic and

Miss Clifford, Frank Matthews, and R. Cathcart, principals in the cast.

[1] [An eccentric and genial patron of the play and dramatic author. He wrote several *à propos* farces for the Adelphi in the days of Webster. —C. S.]

[2] [Bates Richards was the author of *Cromwell* and several other fine literary plays. He was for some time editor of the *Morning Advertiser.* —C. S.]

Equestrian Sick Fund Association; Thackeray in chair; Tom Taylor and Russell and celebrities present; wine with Toole. Story told by Rolfe amusing. 23rd.—Few paragraphs for *Era*. Night see Tom Taylor's new comedy of *The Overland Route*[1] at the Haymarket, which is freshly written and constructed, and a success. 24th.—Finish *Era* copy, from which £1 10s. Phil Phillips at night. Pass him in to Drury. Behind the scenes have a chat with Smith, lessee of Her Majesty's!! then sup with him at Albion, where meet Roxby, J. W. Davison, Miller, and hosts of people. 29th.—To Adelphi; see new comedy of *Paper Wings*,[2] by Watts Phillips, with Wigans in it; pretty good. Hear of Phelps being sole lessee of Wells."

"*March* 1st.—Committee of Dramatic Authors, which attend for first time as chairman. 7th.—Amateur performance of Savage Club, which come up to attend: *School for Scandal*,[3] and burlesque of *Forty Thieves*. Lyceum crammed, and pay to amphitheatre 5s. Grieved to hear from Clemow of the serious illness of my old friend Lovell Phillips. 8th.—

---

[1] Tom Dexter, Charles Mathews; Captain Smart, Braid; Mrs. Seabright, Mrs. Charles Mathews; Colepepper, Chippendale; Sir Solomon Fraser, Compton; Miss Colepepper, Miss M. Ternan; Captain Clavering, E. Villiers; Mrs. Lovibond, Mrs. Wilkins; Major Hector MacTurk, Rogers; Lovibond, Buckstone; Moleskin, Clarke. It was subsequently revived under the Bancroft management at the Haymarket.

[2] This was a story of City life. Sir Richard Plinlimmon, Alfred Wigan; his daughter Blanche, Henrietta Sims; Jonathan Garroway, David Fisher; Mrs. Chickane, Mrs. Alfred Wigan; Owen Percival, Billington; William Kite, Esq. ("Accommodation Bill"), J. L. Toole; Tawdry, Kate Kelly; Flimsey, Charles Selby; Peter Pantile, Paul Bedford; Colonel Wiley, Howard; Alderman Fungus, R. Romer.

[3] This was a performance in aid of the widows and families of two literary gentlemen recently deceased. Talfourd, Sir Peter; Robert Brough, Sir Benjamin Backbite; Joseph Surface, J. C. Wilson; Moses, Doctor Strauss. *The Forty Thieves* was written by at least a dozen of the members of the club. Prologue was written by Planché, and was delivered by Leicester Buckingham. H. J. Byron was Ali Baba; Talfourd, Coji Baba; Robert Brough, Morgiana; Lionel Brough Ganem; Francis Brough, Mustapha; Halliday, Cassim Baba; W· Brough, Hassarac; John Holingshead, Mirza; Albert Smith also figured in it; and Her Majesty, the Prince Consort, and Princess Alice were present.

Committee of Dramatic Authors. Meet Colonel Addison. To Lyceum: revival of *Serjeant's Wife*, with Céleste and Mrs. Keeley as Lisette and Margot. Then to Olympic: *Uncle Zachary*[1]—adaptation by Oxenford of old French farce. 14*th.*—Look in at Drury: see Fitzball's new drama of *Christmas Eve; or, The Devil in the Snow.*[2] 15*th.*—Attend Society of Dramatic Authors as chairman, meeting Westland Marston, Selby, Palgrave Simpson, etc. Dine with Bayle Bernard. *Era* £2. 16*th.*—Going to British Museum an atom comes into my eye and causes such excruciating torture that I am scarcely able to make my way home again; after some hours of agony am somewhat relieved by a clever chemist (Wellspring of Chandos Street), but compelled to go to bed at 8, and there sleep and dream for fourteen hours, and the inflammation very painful, and in one instant feel how all my hopes of a living might be destroyed by the loss of sight. *Monday, 19th.*—Supply some scraps that Howe wants for his forthcoming lecture, this being, I hope, the last time of asking on his part. 20*th.*—Finish the lecture memoranda. 21*st.*—To town, and grieved to hear of the death of my old friend Lovell Phillips[3] (on Monday, aged forty-three), with whom many pleasant hours have I spent. To Lyceum at night, and see Colonel Addison's romantic drama of *Abbé Vaudreuil;*[4] write notice, and then club for an hour; all talking of the loss of our dear old

[1] Another version of *L'Oncle Baptiste*, played under the title of *Peter and Paul* at the Haymarket in 1842. Zachary Clench, Robson; his wife Tabitha, Mrs. Leigh Murray; his daughter Amy, Miss Herbert; her lover Frederick Montgomery, Walter Gordon; his uncle Houghton Highbury, Frederick Vining; Reginald Ready, George Vining; Saul Clench, G. Cooke.

[2] This was suggested by Gerome's famous picture, "Tragedy and Comedy," representing the duel in the Bois de Boulogne between men dressed as a Pierrot and an Indian. Emery, Verner; Mrs. Dowton, Miss Page, Roxby, and Helen Howard were in the cast.

[3] William Lovell Phillips died in Oakley Square, Camden Town, of dropsy, aged forty-three. He was an instrumentalist and composer. Was educated at the Royal Academy of Music; was musical conductor of the Olympic, and composed the music of *Gwynneth Vaughan.* He for many years directed the music of the festivals of the General Theatrical Fund.

[4] Or, *The Court of Louis XV.* Madame Céleste in the title *rôle.*

member W. L. Phillips. *22nd.*—To Adelphi : see revival of
Jealous Wife; very badly played. Olympic: new farce by
F. C. Burnand and Montagu Williams, *B. B. (The Benicia
Boy);* very laughable.[1] *23rd.*—Notices for *Era,* and 35*s.*
24th.—Letter of condolence to Mrs. Phillips. Letter from
C. C. B. on important business. To Lyceum : see new farce
by Colonel Addison;[2] write notice. Last night of Drury
season. *29th.*—The miscellaneous benefit night at Covent
Garden for the benefit of Dramatic College goes off well.
30th.—Paragraphs for *Era,* from which £2 2*s.* *31st.* —
Lyceum : last night of season ;[3] Céleste speaks the address ;
write notice."

"*April 3rd.*—To Sadlers Wells and see Julia St. George's
entertainment.[4] *12th.*—Go to Lyceum : see *Next of Kin*[5] and
Forty Thieves burlesque ; Calhaem good. *13th.*—Finish *Era*
paragraphs, whence £2 2*s.* *14th.*—Italian Opera ; first time
this season of Titiens and Giuglini in *Trovatore.*[6] The prospects for E. T. S. looking very good at present. Haymarket:
see *Pilgrim of Love.*[7] *19th.*—Attend spirit *séance* with
Foard, Leslie : results very satisfactory. *20th.*—Finish work
for *Era ;* for last week £2 2*s.* See clever burlesque of *Miller
and His Men*[8] at Strand. *Monday, 23rd.*—The Shakespearean
Festival at St. John's Gate ; Marston in chair: splendid
oration ; Westland Marston, Tomlins, Lowe, Draper, Barnett,

---

[1] [The farce was one of Burnand's first contributions to the stage.
Both authors are alive and well.—C. S.]

[2] It was called "*117, Arundel Street, Strand.*"

[3] The pieces were—*Suzanne ;* or, *The Power of Love,* which had not
been seen in London for twenty-two years ; with *The Abbé Vaudreuil,*
and Colonel Addison's farce. There were also a variety entertainment
and the transformation scene from *King Thrush-beard.*

[4] *Home and Foreign Lyrics ;* and she also appeared as Joan of Arc.

[5] The theatre opened under W. Brough and Falconer's management,
the latter being the author of *The Next of Kin,* which appears to have
been suggested by Warren's "Ten Thousand a Year." *The Forty
Thieves* was a version written by members of the Savage Club.

[6] [Giuglini was a celebrated tenor of the Rubini school, with one of
the sweetest voices ever heard. He subsequently went mad.—C. S.]

[7] *Fairy Romance,* by H. J. Byron, suggested by Washington Irving's
"Tales of the Alhambra."

[8] Written by Henry J. Byron and F. Talfourd.

Foard, Besemeres, and the cream of the Urban Club present;
sing a *réchauffé* of my old song of ‘St. George.’ 24*th.*—
Write a full account of yesterday’s dinner for *Era*. Con-
gratulate French on his new comedy of *A Friend in Need*,
successfully produced at St. James’s. 30*th.*—Meet mother
and C. C. B.; see them back to Notting Hill. Go to Adelphi :
Julia Daly (Mrs. Alwyn),[1] American actress, very good.”

“ *May* 1*st.*—An anniversary, but only mental celebration.
9*th.*—Meet Foard ;[2] take him to Haymarket ; new and bad
comedy of *The Family Secret*, by Falconer. 11*th.*—Benefit
proposed for R. B. Brough, poor fellow, a long, sad invalid, to
get him change of climate. *Monday*, 14*th.*—To Crystal
Palace. Then to Olympic to see *Dear Mamma*, a new version
of *My Wife’s Mother.* 17*th.*—General annual meeting of
Dramatic Authors’ Society ; to Haymarket, and see some bad
amateurs.[3] 18*th.*—Busy with *Era* paragraphs, from which
£1 10*s.* 23*rd.*—Derby Day, and Thormanby wins. Paragraphs for *Era*. Going out for evening papers, deeply grieved
to hear of Albert Smith’s death[4] this morning ; very sudden,
and the result of professional over-exertion. 26*th.*—An

---

[1] She appeared in a two-act comic drama called *Our Female American
Cousin*, written by Charles Galer. She had been seen at Drury Lane
the year before.

[2] [J. T. Foard, a barrister on the Northern Circuit, was the original
projector of the Arundel Club ; at least he kindly advanced the money
to enable them to move from Arundel to Salisbury Street, Strand. He
was for some years dramatic critic to the *Sunday Times*.—C. S.]

[3] These were Miss Ida Sumner, Miss Brennan, and Charles Coghlan,
who appeared in *Somebody Else*. Neither of them were spoken of as
showing much promise.

[4] He died at half-past eight in the morning, in his own home at
Walham Green, of bronchitis. He was born at Chertsey, May 24th,
1816, and was educated at Merchant Taylors. Was intended to follow
his father’s profession as a surgeon, and studied medicine at Middlesex
Hospital and at Paris, and commenced work in 1837 with his father.
He soon turned to literary pursuits, and contributed to *The Mirror*,
Medical Times, etc. Wrote several dramas and burlesques, novels, etc.,—
his “ Wassail Bowl,” “ Adventures of Mr. Ledbury,” “ Scattergood
Family,” “ Marchioness of Brinvilliers,” “ Pottleton Legacy,” and
“ Christopher Tadpole,” were all successes. He also wrote a series of
clever sketches on various classes of London society. In 1850 he pro-
duced his *Overland Route* ; in 1852, March 15th, his *Mont Blanc*, which

inauguration dinner at the Arundel Club ;[1] eleven present ; cost, with wine, 5*s.* 6*d.* per head.   To Haymarket : new farce, *Fitzsmythe of Fitzsmythe Hall,* by Maddison Morton ; write notice.   The mortal remains of Albert Smith this day consigned, in strict privacy, to Brompton Cemetery."

" *June* 1*st.*—Dramatic College fête and fancy fair, laying foundation-stone.   5*th.*—Finish and send off to *The Welcome Guest* poem of ' Grandmother's Caddy.'   6*th.*—All day reading

he ran till 1858 at the Egyptian Hall.   He married Miss Mary Keeley, August 1st, 1859.

[1] In the account of the Savage Club, October 1857, Lionel Brough gives it as his idea that the Arundel Club was an outcome of the " Savage," and that it was founded by H. J. Byron, W. P. Hall, and Leicester Buckingham, in consequence of a little disagreement with the " Savages."   Mr. J. T. Foard's account scarcely tallies with this, and as one of the original members it is probably the more correct. He states : " It was originated by some of the members of the old Re-Union Club, held at the Bedford Head, in Covent Garden, who were dissatisfied with some of the members of that Club and their autocracy on club nights, and was first talked over there, viz., at the Re-Union (identified with ' the Owl's Roost ' in T. W. Robertson's *Society.*)   The original members, so far as I recollect, were—G. F. Torrelino, the Shakespearean critic, and author of a small book on the English stage, and one of the council of the Camden Society ; Frank Talfourd ; Blanchard ; Hollinshead, who seceded, however, at the first meeting or very soon after ; Crawford Wilson, myself, and two or three others : among these *being H. J. Byron, who joined us in a few months,* and Tom Robertson, introduced by Byron, about or within a year after, if my memory serve me.   The premises we first took were at the bottom of Arundel Street, Strand—hence the name of the Club— on the site of the present Arundel Hotel, and we occupied two or three rooms.   Leicester Buckingham and Belford, the actor, were among the members during the years 1859-60.   Crawford Wilson, Byron, Horace Green, D. W. Deane, Robertson, Belford, and Buckingham, were among the regular attenders at the Club during the first year." The Arundel Club removed to 12, Salisbury Street, Strand, in June of 1861, and remained there till the month of September, 1888, when the excellent premises in which it is now located, 1, Adelphi Terrace, Strand, were occupied.   The Salisbury Street house (now pulled down) was celebrated for its large upstairs room, in which the members met, and in which, perhaps, more thoroughly jovial suppers were eaten than in any other club in London.   The ceiling was a particularly handsome one, and the old copper kettle for hot grog a standing institution. The Arundel was, and remains, a thoroughly Bohemian club.   In the

Professor Hare's wonderful book on spiritualism ; riveted to its pages, and convinced of the truth of the statements therein recorded. *7th.*—Ascot Cup day. *8th.*—Dear mother's birthday, her seventy-third. Go with Payne to spirit *séance* with the Marshalls at Leslie's chambers ; Boosey, Jackson, and Leigh Murray present ; strong manifestations. *9th.*—Meet Barry Sullivan (just returned from American tour), Foard, Talfourd, and Hogarth, who have been to spiritual manifestations, and are convinced of the truth thereof. 13th.—At Astley's : *Fair Rosamond;* not good. 14*th.*—At night to spiritual *séance:* large party present ; the spirit hand promised to be seen ; I am asked to change places, and the bell

list of members for the year 1868—the earliest that is procurable—we find the following names : *Committee*—J. V. Bridgeman, Henry J. Byron, Charles J. Coleman, D. W. Deane, James T. Foard, Horace Green, A. S. Hart, Samuel Joyce, Frederick Lawrence, Jonas Levy, W. H. Maitland, G. A. Sala, J. Palgrave Simpson, Frederick G. Tomlins, J. Crawford Wilson. *Members*—W. R. Belford, John Billington, E. L. Blanchard, John Boosey, Leicester Buckingham, F. C. Burnand, Edwin Canton, J. H. Chute, John Clarke, J. Sterling Coyne, Edward Dicey, Charles Dickens, jun., Andrew Halliday, Tom Hood, Henry Howe, Horace Mayhew, Julian J. Portch, W. J. Prowse, W. Winwood Reade, T. W. Robertson, George Rose (Arthur Sketchley), Clement W. Scott, E. A. Sothern, Barry Sullivan, Francis Talfourd, J. L. Toole, Hermann Vezin, F. Wallenstein, Harrison Weir, W. S. Woodin. To this illustrious roll in after years were added :—James Albery, Sydney B. Bancroft, Maurice Barrymore, Ernest Bendall, Edward T. E. Besley, Arthur Cecil Blunt, Henry G. Bohn, Stanislaus Calhaem, d'Arcy Chaytor, Frederick Clay, C. F. Coghlan, Henry B. Coulson (Conway), Earle L. Douglas, A. W. Dubourg, Charles Dunphie, T. H. S. Escott, Sebastian Evans, W. Schwenck Gilbert, Bernard J. Hall, John Hare, Sir John Holker, Bronson Howard, Cecil Howard, Henry Irving, David James, J. Cordy Jeaffreson, W. H. Kendal, John Kershaw, W. Beattie Kingston, Joseph Knight, Frederic Lablache, Luigi Lablache, W. Meyer Lutz, Viscount Macduff (now Duke of Fife), F. H. Macklin, Dr. Westland Marston, Herman C. Merivale, W. Cosmo Monkhouse, H. J. Montague, Albert Moore, Dominick Murray, H. Nairn, Captain Power, Robert Reece, Wybert Reeve, Thomas Wemyss Reid, Frederick Robson, Dante G. Rosetti, Sir Charles Russell, Frederick Sandys, Captain Hawley Smart, George Clarkson Stanfield, Joseph Ashby Sterry, Charles J. Stone, Thomas Thorne, H. F. Turle, Charles Warner, James A. M. Whistler, Horace Wigan, W. G. Wills, Hon. Lewis Wingfield, Thomas Woolner, Charles Wyndham, William Yardley, Sir Charles L. Young. (See Appendix.)

is then rung in the air and placed on my knee—a thrilling touch. *23rd.*—*Era* £1 5s. All London in an uproar with grand review of Volunteers; I go up the Duke of York's column, and get splendid view of the effects of the masses; cab to Hyde Park; have good position. To Haymarket in evening : Miss Sedgwick's benefit; new comedy by Falconer, *Does He Love Me?*—middling; write notice. Read Fitzball's ' Thirty-five Years of Dramatic Author's Life.' *Monday, 25th.* —Send lyric ' Leaf from Author's Note Book ' to *Welcome Guest*, which contains this week the Caddy poem. Much pleased with the simple-mindedness of Fitzball's narrative and the evident sincerity of his style. *26th.*—Odd and strange dream of my own death; afterwards hear that at that moment R. B. Brough [1] died, at the age of thirty-two, at Manchester. *27th.*—Try to arrange a drawing-room opera for Alfred Mellon ; complete it at night—*Red Rufus.* *28th.* —Write a few paragraphs. Look in at Arundel Club and pay £2 2s. for year's subscription; poor Bob Brough's death universally talked about and regretted. *29th.*—Writing memoir of Robert Brough for *Era*, from which £1 15s. To Coyne's party; meet Mr. Allum, the architect,[2] Mr. and

[1] Robert B. Brough was born in London, April 10th, 1828, went to Manchester in 1843, and in 1847 conducted a very bright periodical, called *The Liverpool Lion*, which he enlivened both with his pen and pencil for many a year. His first dramatic work was a burlesque, called *The Enchanted Isle*, written in collaboration with his brother William, and was brought out at the Amphitheatre, and was soon reproduced at the Adelphi in London. He married Miss E. Romer in 1851. He became well known as a contributor to all sorts of periodicals. Among them may be mentioned *The Man in the Moon, Diogenes, The Comic Times, The Welcome Guest, Train,* and *National Magazine.* Some of his poems bear the stamp of genius. He wrote two novels, " Marston Lynch " and " Which is Which ? " and a remarkable set of Radical poems, called " Songs of the Governing Classes," and he was the author of several burlesques. He was no mean actor. His health completely broke down, and he was on his journey to Wales to recruit it, when he was taken ill at Manchester, where he died of atrophy, and left a widow and three young children, one of whom, Miss Fanny Brough (Mrs. Boleyn), is one of the brightest ornaments of the modern stage. He was loved by all who knew him, and was the most generous of men.

[2] [Mr. Allum designed the Grand Stand at Lord's Cricket Ground, and promised on his plans to make a little box on the staircase from

Mrs. Storr and Amelia B. Edwardes, about twenty others, and a most pleasant evening. 30*th.*—Callcott calls from Madame Céleste about Lyceum pantomime; decline, but give her *Chaucer* manuscript as available. See Beverley, at Covent Garden, and arrange to do *Peter Wilkins and Tom Thumb* at Her Majesty's. To Arundel Club, but find the dinners discontinued. With Archer, Barry Sullivan, and Mr. Morris to Athenians, whereat have cold fish to make up. Reunion, and give Mellon drawing-room opera MS. to consider."

"*July* 13*th.*—Meet Mr. Home, the celebrated American medium, at Lawler's, the artist's : at night go to his house in Sloane Street ; a large party assembled, Mrs. Milner Gibson, S. C. Hall and wife, Barratt, Robert Dale Owen, Miss Howard, Miss Andrews, Wilkinson, Waterhouse (of pamphlet reminis-cences), Squires, and above fifty others, including Hogarth and Talfourd. 14*th.*—Go to see Mr. Bathurst Burch give his entertainment called *Odds and Ends* at Willis's Rooms : his sleight-of-hand very good. *Monday,* 16*th.*—Arrange copy of pantomime for Astley's, *Harlequin Chaucer and Grim John of Gaunt.* 19*th.*—To Adelphi and Strand : *Harvest Home* revival at former, and bad farce, *Volunteers' Ball,*[1] at latter. Busy on Brough's benefit. 20*th.*—The Brough con-cert wretchedly attended. 21*st.*—Dramatic College fête at Crystal Palace :[2] go, of course, but expensive affair ; all goes

which several of us could see the matches of the year. Robert Reece, Frank Marshall, etc., were among the first visitors, and I have seen every cricket match of importance from that box for the last twenty years.—C. S.]

[1] By Williams and Burnand.

[2] The various actors held different stalls. J. L. Toole was a " Cheap Jack," James Rogers looked after a " Temple of Mystery," Clarke of the Haymarket had a " Punch and Judy Show." Benjamin Webster delivered an address written by Robert Bell. There was an excellent concert, to which the best-known vocalists contributed. Miss Marshall, Miss Hudspeth, and Miss E. Johnstone looked after a fairy post-office. Buckstone and Compton had the Aunt Sally. All the favourite actresses had stalls of some sort ; 8,409 people were admitted by pay-ment of half-a-crown. [The Dramatic College Fétes were the most degrading exhibitions ever patronized by the dramatic profession. They did not save the Dramatic College from bankruptcy.—C.S.]

off admirably; back, and write account for *Era*. Chat with Toole, who worked wonderfully all day, and Hermann Vezin, who tells me is engaged at Sadlers Wells. *25th.*—Brough Benefit.[1] *26th.*—Look in at Strand; new piece of *Observation and Flirtation.*[2] *28th.*—To Gravesend in Mr. John Clarke's beautiful yacht, *The Glimpse*, with Mr. Wheaton, a yacht artist; no wind, but get caught in a sharp thunderstorm; do not arrive till midnight, at which time make the Terrace pier; rather slow, but hospitably entertained."

"*Aug.* 1*st.*—Hear of Alfred Dickens's death. 2*nd.*—*Era* copy all day, whence £2 2*s.* Go to Marshall's for Maitland to come to *séance;* meet Lady Dinorben, Lady Ann Sherson, Captain Sherson, Mr. Halse, mother, C. C. B., who stays till midnight. Many happy returns. See them home in cab. Manifestations very interesting and convincing. 3*rd.*—Delighted by a visit from Emma and Mrs. Stanley, after their four years' wandering in all parts of the world. *Monday,* 6*th.*—All day writing an account of my view of the spiritual *séance* notice in *All the Year Round.* 9*th.*—Go to the Stanleys' to dinner: all sorts of reminiscences of travel. Fancy Mrs. Stanley with box of lucifer matches in jungle keeping off lions and tigers on journey from Madras to Bombay! 16*th.*—Arrange *Era* paragraphs. Go to Astley's, seeing *Mazeppa* and W. West and Batty for first time:

---

[1] This was held at Drury Lane, and the artists were the principals from the Haymarket, Adelphi, Princess's, and Strand Theatres, assisted by members of the Savage Club. House was well filled. Burlesque and the comedietta, *Cruel to be Kind; The Last of the Pigtails;* a scene from *The Willow Copse*, and *Fitzsmythe of Fitzsmythe Hall*—formed the programme. G. A. Sala spoke an excellent address. Mrs. Stirling spoke a prologue written by Shirley Brooks to the burlesque, *The Enchanted Isle*, which was the earliest work in which Robert Brough took part in writing with his brother; and the characters were taken by members of the Savage Club. George Cruikshank, Alonzo; Leicester Buckingham, Prospero; Francis Talfourd, Caliban; J. Hollingshead and J. D. Francis were also in the cast; Kate Terry, Ariel; and Fanny Stirling, daughter of Mrs. Stirling, made her *début* as Miranda.

[2] Written by Horace Wigan. It was acted by Misses Bufton, H. J. Turner, M. Oliver, Lavine, and Swanborough.

greatly disappointed by the interview. *Era* £1. 17*th.*—At night to *séance*, meeting Mr. Atkinson and Mr. Chinnery, Halse, and Colonel Addison : the spiritual manifestations interesting. The hand shown, and a message to me, ' Blanchard, do not fear ; we will not injure you by our touch ; you have much power. God bless you ! you will lose your nervousness.' 20*th.*—Hear from Pilsner of the death of poor Flexmore,[1] in his thirty-sixth year. ' Where be thy quips and thy jibes now ? ' 21*st.*—Write memoirs of three clowns—Paul Herring, Flexmore, and Nelson [2]—and sad memories of the past. 25*th.*—Emma Stanley calls and pays for song £3 ; we then go to Egyptian Hall, and settle for rooms for her for £400 a year. Go to Floral Hall afterwards for Mendelssohn night. 31*st.*—*Séance* in Duke Street : the ' man in the cloak ; ' singular movements of furniture, chairs going about in all directions ; very wonderful and convincing ; present, Halse, Trench, Belford, and Buckingham."

" *Sept.* 1*st.*—Write memoirs both of Mrs. Yates [3] and

[1] Richard Flexmore was the son of a comic dancer of the same name, and was born at Kennington, September 15th, 1824. Began his career at the Victoria ; first appeared as clown at the Grecian 1844. In his first season he broke the small bone of his leg, which incapacitated him for some time ; but he appeared the following year at the Olympic as clown. He was for several seasons at the Princess's, and one of his greatest successes was his graceful imitation of the principal opera dancers ; the dance he used to accompany by a very clever song. He was seen at most of the theatres in London, and last appeared as clown in *Jack and the Beanstalk*, at Drury Lane, in 1859. He married in 1852 Mdlle. Auriol, and performed with her a great deal on the Continent. He was most generous, and supported his mother up to the time of his death. He was buried at Kensal Green.

[2] Arthur Marsh Nelson was born in 1811, and died at Burnley. He began his connection with the stage, playing leading parts in the legitimate drama in the provincial and minor theatres. He subsequently adopted the talking clown as his vocation ; he was a clever musician and a great favourite. His last appearance in London was at the Alhambra.

[3] Mrs. Yates was the daughter of Brunton, a respectable actor of old Covent Garden Theatre, and afterwards a provincial manager. She was born at Norwich, January 21st, 1799, and made her first appearance at Lynn, March 15th, 1815, as Desdemona to Charles

Countess of Craven [1] (Louisa Brunton), who both died this week. A poor ' super ' calls on me to-day for aid, and makes me very sad to hear his history. *4th.*—Write paragraphs for *Era*. See ballet of *Don Juan* at Rosherville : very effective. Look in at theatre, and see G. Smythson, a good low comedian. *6th.*—Polygraphic Hall, and see Lauri family; three children. [2] *8th.*—Sadlers Wells opening night under Phelps' sole management : *As You Like It; * Mrs. C. Young (afterwards Mrs. Hermann Vezin) plays charmingly, Hermann Vezin very good. [3] Write paragraphs for *Sunday Times*, Coyne being off for his tour, and long notice for *Era*. *12th.*—More *Era* copy.

Kemble's Othello. Her next success was at Birmingham, as Letitia Hardy to the Doricourt of Elliston. She then gained experience in the provinces, and came to Covent Garden and played Letitia Hardy for the first time in London, September 12th, 1817. She was equally successful in Shakespearean characters. Was leading lady in her father's theatre, the West London (afterwards the Queen's, and Prince of Wales's of Tottenham Court Road) at the time of his opening it, September 9th, 1822. She married Mr. Frederick Yates in 1824, and when he joined Terry as proprietor of the Adelphi, she became one of the principal attractions of the theatre. After her husband's death Mrs. Yates only played for one season at the Lyceum, and then retired to Brighton, where she died. Her connection with the Countess of Craven, and her own agreeable manners, attracted round her a large circle of friends. She was the mother of Edmond Hodson Yates, who, even whilst he was in the post office, devoted considerable attention to literature, and made his name, as an author, journalist, and critic, as the " Lounger at the Clubs " in the *Illustrated Times*, and later became proprietor of *The World.*

[1] This was the once celebrated Louisa Brunton, of Covent Garden and Drury Lane Theatres. Her father was Brunton, the well-known manager of the Norwich circuit, who had been appreciated at Covent Garden as far back as 1774. Louisa Brunton was born in February 1782; and made her first appearance at Covent Garden, October 5th, 1803, as Lady Townley in *The Provoked Husband.* The mantle of Miss Farren, afterwards Countess of Derby, fell on her shoulders in 1796, and she became the favourite actress in genteel comedy. She was very handsome, and retired from her profession on her marriage with Lord Craven, which took place about 1807.

[2] Jenny, Fanny, and Septimus Lauri appeared in a sketch by James Bruton called *Going on Anyhow*, and assumed a variety of characters. Fanny appears to have shown most promise.

[3] Phelps, Jaques ; Mrs. Charles Young, Rosalind ; Hermann Vezin, Orlando ; Lewis Ball, Touchstone ; Barrett, Adam ; Kate Saxon,

See capital piece called *Colleen Bawn*,[1] by Boucicault : effects at end of second act extremely good.   13*th.*—Haymarket at night ; see Miss Florence Haydon [2] make her *début* in *Naval Engagements*—very fair.   To Wells : interview with Phelps about pantomime ; settle on *Sinbad the Sailor*, and £1 per night.   28*th.*—Meet Thompson, who wants articles written for *London Review*, and Stiff, who gives me copyright of 'Confessions.'   Getting oppressed by heavy work in prospect.   29*th.*—Bennett (the *Owl*) to spiritual *séance.*   'You will not yet get in this house ; the house is surrounded by its circle.'   'Gentlemen, this is my house.'   'Cromwell, did you not see him ?'   'This is my dwelling-house.'"

"*Monday, Oct.* 1*st.*—Prepare 'Confessions' for publication : ready at night.   Take Walter to Rosherville Gardens, and see monkey ballet of *Savoyard and His Monkey* ; Willikins Molino very good.   3*rd.*—Boat to town : see bad piece at Lyceum of *Brigand and His Banker.*[3] 4*th.*—Give 10*s.*

Audrey ; Fanny Josephs, Celia. *The Welsh Girl* was played afterwards, with Fanny Josephs as Julia.   E. L. B. wrote of Hermann Vezin :—"There was an evidence of intelligence which gives us great hopes of his future career on these boards.   His voice and figure are greatly in his favour, and his action is unexceptionally easy and graceful."

[1] *Colleen Bawn ;* or, *The Bride of Garryowen*, taken from Gerald Griffin's novel, "The Collegians."   Dion Bourcicault (at this time he used to spell his name Bourcicault), Miles-na-Coppaleen ; Billington, Hardress Cregan ; C. J. Smith, Corrigan ; Mrs. Billington, Mrs. Cregan ; Mrs. Alfred Mellon, Anne Chute ; David Fisher, Kyrle Daly ; Mrs. Bourcicault (Agnes Robertson), Eily O'Connor ; Falconer, Danny Mann ; and Father Tom, C. H. Stephenson.   The piece was celebrated for the cave scene, where Miles jumps into the water and saves the "Colleen Bawn."   It was followed by an extravaganza, *She would be an Actress*, in which Mrs. Bourcicault personated several characters.

[2] She appeared in Madame Vestris's original character, Miss Mortimer.

[3] This was by Tom Taylor, and was founded by him on M. Edmond About's *Le Roi des Montagnes.*   It was in two acts.   Miss Porcupine, Mrs. Keeley ; Miss Melton, Miss M. Ternan ; Photini, Madame Céleste ; Captain Obadiah Harris, H. Watkins ; Doctor Schultz, Villiers ; John Joseph Jerrams, John Rouse ; Hadji Stavros, George Vining ; and Captain Perikles, Forrester.   It was a failure, and was withdrawn within a week.

towards Flexmore monument. Finish *Era* copy. *5th.*—Cooper
calls, and receives for revision of 'Dinners and Diners' £5;
take him round to Delamotte's, and arrange for £15 for use
of 'Confessions' in penny numbers and a five-shilling
volume. *10th.*—To Lyceum—Josephine Gougenheim;[1] then
to Haymarket—John Brougham.[2] *11th.*—Go to Olympic to
see a supposed new farce by Morton, called *A Regular Fix*,[3]
but which I recognize as *Couche du Soleil* of thirty years ago.
12th.—Hear of the Alhambra licence being granted. Then
to Strand : see burlesque of *Fra Diavolo*. *17th.*—Gravesend
very gay ; Queen disembarks here from her Continental tour.
Work away at my pantomime and correspondence in *Morning
Star* touching spiritual manifestations. *18th.*—From *Era*
for concert rooms £2 2s. Lyceum, *Love Chase*,[4] with Miss
Gougenheim as Constance. Miss Rose Howe's first appearance in *Grist to the Mill :*[5] not much. *24th.*—All day on
Drury pantomime of *Peter Wilkins*, and complete a fair
copy by sitting at my desk from 4 p.m. to 4 p.m.—24 hours ;
quite knocked up. *27th.*—Interruptions again ! People apparently take me for a rich relieving officer.[6] *Monday, 29th.*
—Busy on Tom Taylor's opening at St. James's,[7] under

[1] This actress had appeared in London some nine years before, and
in the meantime had made some reputation in America and Australia.
She re-appeared in *The Irish Heiress*, by Dion Bourcicault, which was
originally produced at Covent Garden in 1842 ; as Norah Merrion she
made a very favourable impression. Henry Neville made his first
appearance in London as Percy Arden, and he also made a hit ; he had
come from the Theatre Royal, Liverpool.

[2] After eighteen years' absence in America (during which he had
made a reputation as author and actor), previous to which he had
been a member of Madame Vestris's company at Covent Garden, he
re-appeared in England in *Romance and Reality*, a two-act farce.
Himself as Jack Swift, an Irish under-servant, to the Rosabelle of
Florence Arden, and the Oliver and Jasper of Rogers and Chippendale.

[3] Robson appeared as Mr. Hugh de Brass.

[4] Mrs. Keeley played the Widow Green ; Henry Neville, Master
Waller ; and George Vining, Wildrake.

[5] She appeared as Francine. Sang nicely. She was married to
Mr. H. Watkins, an American comedian.

[6] [How true this is ! It happens to every literary man who lives in
chambers. People think your time is theirs.—C. S.]

[7] The theatre was opened by Alfred Wigan with the drama entitled

Wigan's management. 30*th.*—To meet mother and C. C. B., and take them to dine at Bertholini's; then with C. C. B. and Mrs. Green to Gatti's, and after to Emma Stanley's entertainment; see *Seven Ages :* the outlines rather worn, but a triumph of head-work. Oysters at Rule's after, and see them home. 31*st.*—Walk in morning round by Chelsea, Barossa Place, and then back to town musing. To Strand; see clever piece of *The Postboy,* with James Rogers excellent."[1]

"*Nov.* 5*th.*—All day on *Tom Thumb* for Her Majesty's; but in no spirits to be funny. 8*th.*—Princess's; see Byron's new farce of *Garibaldi Excursionists;*[2] odd effect of gas going out and piece played in the dark. 10*th.*—To Haymarket; see Tom Taylor's *Babes in the Wood;*[3] a very long and dull comedy. *Monday,* 12*th.*—New piece by Watts Phillips, *The Story of the* '45,[4] produced at Drury this evening, with Webster, Toole and Paul Bedford from Adelphi. Drama too long, and not well constructed. 15*th.*—With Ledger in morning to St. James's, to see new French *soubrette danseuse.*[5] From *Era* £2. 17*th.*—Made ill by an uncalled-for aspersion on my literary honesty in *Athenæum* of this week; whence source as the text for an article on plagiary; write reply. 21*st.*—Stick to the Wells pantomime and sit up till 3 a.m. making rough

Up at the Hills, which told of Indian life. Alfred Wigan, Major Stonyhurst; Miss Herbert, Mrs. Eversley; Charles Young, Captain Slack; Ashley, Lieutenant Greenway; Terry, Nabichull. Mrs. A. Wigan, Mrs. Colonel M'Cann; Monee, Kate Terry; Dewar, Tunstall; Emery, Dr. M'Kivett; Miss Nelly Moore, Margaret Lovell; Miss Mason, Kate Neil. It was a success. At this time, Miss Kate Terry was appearing in a modernized version of *The King of the Peacocks* at this theatre.

[1] This drama was by J. T. Craven. Rogers played Joe Spurrit; Patty Oliver, Maria Bingley; Parselle, Mr. Bingley; J. Bland, Sir John Bingley; Miss Bufton, Miss Wharton. The piece was a tremendous success."

[2] All the gas in the front of the house and the footlights went out suddenly; some water had got in the metre. Some few of the audience left the theatre.

[3] The piece was in four acts, and played four hours. Miss Amy Sedgwick was Lady Blanche; and W. Farren, Frank Rushton.

[4] Webster played Sir Andrew Silverton; Toole, Enoch Flicker; Bedford, Guffoy; and Miss Henrietta Sims, Isabel.

[5] This was a Mdlle. Albina de Rhona.

sketch of the introductory scenes. 22*nd.*—Wells; see Edmund Phelps as Ulrick in *Werner*. To Her Majesty's to see *Robin Hood*.[1] 24*th.*—*Athenæum* prints vindication. 29*th.* —To Lyceum : see Drew in *Handy Andy;*[2] good Irishman in bad piece. *Era* copy, £1 10*s.*"

"*Dec.* 1*st.*—Drury closes through bad business to-night. Carlton Cooper about ' Confessions : ' £15 to pay. 7*th.*—*Era* £1 10*s.* Tullis pays balance £4 8*s.*, thus closing the long-standing account of ' England and Wales' account. Go to Alhambra inaugural banquet.[3] Sit next to Sala, and pleasant chat about old times. 8*th.*—To Princess's to see Fechter in *Corsican Brothers ;*[4] not so good a version as before. 11*th.*— My birthday : forty ; not spent very agreeably. 14*th.*—Paragraphs for *Era*, receive £2 2*s.* ; then arrange with Mr. Levy of *Telegraph* to write articles for Christmas. 15*th.*—Call on E. T. Smith and first instalment of pantomimes £20. *Monday,* 17*th.*—Write Woodin's last song ; see him go through rehearsal. Poor Deulin[5] dies very suddenly. 18*th.*—Make out Woodin's programme of *Cabinet of Curiosities,* and see him go through in costume all the parts. 21*st.*—*Era*

---

[1] Sims Reeves having been taken ill, his part was sung by Mr. Swift.

[2] It was by Sterling Coyne, with John Drew in the title *rôle.* Miss Hudspeth was Oonah Rooney.

[3] The banquet was by E. T. Smith, who was the proprietor. The designs were under the superintendence of William Beverley. The paintings in the dome were Moorish, representing the Court of Lions in the Alhambra, and incidents relative to the last invasion of Spain by the Moors ; these were carried out throughout the proscenium. James Ellis, once of Cremorne Gardens, was the director of the refreshment department ; James Tully, musical director. The building cost £120,000, and was calculated to hold with comfort 3,500 people. E. T. Smith presided at the banquet and George Augustus Sala replied for the Press.

[4] Miss Murray was the Emilie de Lesparre ; Rose Leclercq, Folichone ; Meadows, Colonna ; Augustus Harris, Château Rénaud.

[5] His real name was Isaac Dowling. He had made a reputation as Harlequin at the Grecian Saloon. He was about forty-eight years of age. Had been at rehearsal in the afternoon and was quitting the theatre when he found he was spitting blood ; and, almost immediately after, in Wilson's tavern, Drury Lane, he vomited a large quantity of blood, and in a few minutes expired. His lungs were found to be extensively diseased.

£1 10*s.* Sadlers Wells; see Phelps and bit of rehearsal. Engage to put the ' Noctes Ambrosianæ' into shape for him; he tells me he was the tenor with the Woods. Go to Drury, see scenery searched after by Ledger. Write paragraphs of the death of Alfred Bunn.[1] To Polygraphic Hall; W. Woodin's *Cabinet of Curiosities*, first night. *24th.*—Write letters to mother wishing her the compliments of the season. Write articles for *Telegraph*, to introduce the Christmas notices. *25th.*—Christmas Day. A large family dinner; evening passed in various ways; chat and song, and conjuring tricks. *26th.*—Private box at Drury[2] for mother, Horace Greene, Talfourd and Miller. Go to Strand, *Cinderella.*[3] Write notices; take them to office; finish at Arundel. *27th.* —Go to Wells; see *Sindbad the Sailor;*[4] sit with Phelps in front of house. Afterwards to *Telegraph* office and write notice. *28th.*—Writing from morning till night *Era* copy. Receive £2 5*s.* Take Byron to Drury; see *Peter Wilkins* first time, and very much pleased with the way in which it is acted. *29th.*—At Her Majesty's[5] first morning performance,

[1] Mr. Alfred Bunn died at Boulogne, December 20th, of apoplexy. He had been connected with the stage ever since the year 1826 at the Birmingham Theatre. In 1833 he was manager of Drury Lane and Covent Garden Theatres, and continued to manage Drury Lane until 1848. He was noted for the strong companies that he got together. He was the author of the libretto of *The Bohemian Girl*, and of several other works, and had latterly been correspondent to two or three London papers.

[2] E. L. B.'s pantomime, *Peter Wilkins; or, Harlequin and the Flying Women of the Loadstone Island.* Harlequins, Cormack and St. Maine; pantaloons, Naylor and Martin; the Misses Gunniss, columbines. The Lavater Lee Family, sprites. Clowns, the Hulines and Power. Tom Matthews played Jack Robinson; Templeton, Peter Wilkins.

[3] Or, *The Lover, the Lackey, and the Little Glass Slipper*, by H. J. Byron. Patty Oliver, the Prince; Charlotte Saunders, the Valet Dandini; J. Clarke, Baron Balderdash; Rogers, Clorinda; Miss Simpson, Cinderella; Miss Lavine, Thisbe.

[4] E. L. B.'s pantomime, *Harlequin Sindbad the Sailor; or, The Fairy of the Diamond Valley and the Little Old Man of the Sea.* Miss Fanny Josephs, Undine; Kate Saxon, Gulbeyaz; Miss Caroline Parkes was the *prima ballerina;* Martin, harlequin; Phœbe Lauri, columbine; Frederic Lauri, clown; Edward Lauri, pantaloon.

[5] At this theatre under E. T. Smith's management comic opera, *Queen Topaze*, was being given, and, for the first time on record here

which goes off very well, but a very indifferent house.   Little
Lilia Ross very good.   31*st.*—With general wishes for everybody's Happy New Year, go out to post my letters, and sit up
to see the Old Year out at chambers alone ; reading my own
novel of twelve years ago, 'Confessions of a Page,' just re-issued
in numbers ; and so goes out the year, for the mercies received during which, and the strength given me to bear up
against almost unparalleled annoyances and depressing
domestic anxieties, God be thanked with the most profound
and heartfelt gratitude ! [1]   And so exits Old 1860, that has
flashed past with the rapidity of a dream."

Rough revenue for year £289.

a pantomime written by E. L. B., entitled *Harlequin and Tom Thumb ;
or, Merlin the Magician and the good Fairies of the Court of King
Arthur.*   J. Lauri was the harlequin ; Jenny Lauri, columbine ;
C. Lauri, clown ; H. Lauri, pantaloon.   Lilia Ross played Tom
Thumb.

[1] Mr. James T. Foard in a most interesting letter referring to E. L. B.
and the Arundel Club relates the following :—"I had an introduction
to Leman Blanchard as far back, I think, as 1850 or '51, at any rate
while he was writing 'The Wanderings and Ponderings of an Autumnal
Excursionist' [*referred to by E. L. B. in his diary for* 1850] as he was
then journeying in the northern counties, the Lake District, etc., etc.
We met at Liverpool, and he stayed with me for two or three days
there.   I recollect accompanying him to a social gathering at Liverpool,
at which Mr. Spencer the chemist, and discoverer of the electrotype,
was present, when Blanchard favoured us with some of his improvised
verses on the company present.   [*This is evidently the* pleasant evening
referred to by E. L. B., songs and supper, *Aug. 12th,* 1850.] . . . I can
recall at this instant, one anecdote of Blanchard which places his
gentle and considerate character before the mind as well as any other
I might be able to remember : One night, it was in the sixties, he asked
me to acompany him to Sadlers Wells.   I was going on a 'first night'
to Drury Lane, and could not, and so he left the Club in a great hurry
to take a cab to drive to the Wells.   Some few minutes after, I walked
leisurely to the theatre in Drury Lane, and found him standing ner-
vously restless, as was usual with him, in front of the house and with
one solitary cab on the stand.   I asked him what he was doing there,
as he said he was in a hurry.   He replied, 'Well, there's only this
horse on the rank, and he is just getting his evening meal' (the horse
had a nose-bag on), 'and I don't like disturbing him, as it is perhaps
his first comfortable meal to day.'   This no doubt was whimsical, but
it was thoroughly characteristic."

1861.

"*Jan. 1st.*—The year opens with much anxiety about the future. Shall I ever have any happiness? *3rd.*—Cheered by New Year's congratulations in letter-box. Take Talfourd and Hogarth to Drury; pantomime goes off very well, and house good. *4th.*—From *Era* £1 15s. Look in at Alhambra, and afterwards at Her Majesty's; *Queen Topaz* very bad, *Tom Thumb* good. *11th.*—Take boy to Sadlers Wells; see *Sindbad;* chat with Phelps, and from him £15 on account of pantomime. Arrange to do the German play, and 'Noctes,' etc., for him. *12th.*—Take the boy to morning performance at Her Majesty's; house good. Evening to Lyceum;[1] see Callcott's charming scene. *16th.*—Read for Phelps a translation by Hermann Vezin of German play called *Reinhard and Leonora*, from which Tom Taylor evidently derived the basis of his *Unequal Match;* present version won't do. Look over my dear father's old pocket-book diaries. *17th.*—Paragraphs for *Era*, whence £1 10s. After hearing of poor Mr. Stirling's death, have to take chair at Athenian supper, but out of spirits. *24th.*—Get for pantomime copyrights £5; write for *Era* and receive £1 10s. At night to Strand; see Wooller's drama of *Silver Wedding*,[2] a pretty piece, and successful. Then to Whittington Club; see a Mr. Bland give a conjuring entertainment. *26th.*—Go to Leader and Wick, get for copyright of *Starlight* and chorus, £2 2s. Go to Home's, Sloane Street, to *séance;* meet Lawler, Sargood, Mr. Boyd, and Madam. Very interesting; get permission to bring Buckingham, Talfourd, and Hogarth. Off in a cab to town and fetch them. Accordion played, bell rung, and

---

[1] The extravaganza of *Chrysabelle;* or, *The Rose without a Thorn*, was being played here by Edmund Falconer, and in it appeared John Rouse, Forrester, J. Morris, Clifford; Misses Lydia Thompson, Neville, Ternan, Hudspeth, Marie and Annie Colinson, Turner, Stuart, and Clara Denville.

[2] Two-act drama by J. P. Wooler. Max Altmann, Parselle; Gertrude Altmann, Mrs. Selby; Adeline, Fanny Hughes; Wilhelm Leonhardt, W. Mowbray; Judas Braitkopf, H. J. Turner; Rosa Morgenroth, Charlotte Saunders.

handkerchief passed across table, etc. : much pleased.　Supply Woodin with his book, for which £10.　*29th.*—Begin notice of Charles Kean's appearance with his wife [1] last evening at Drury, when the house was crammed from floor to roof. *30th.*—Go to Richmond ; take mother her pension, dining with C. C. B. and mother ; seventy-four last birthday, and finding her in good health and spirits."

"*Feb. 1st.*—Finish quantity of *Era* work, whence £1 15*s.* Chat with Byron about a new entertainment for Wooller and Beale, 'the British Serenaders.'　In evening to Drury with C. C. B., and see *Hamlet:* the play scene best ; house crammed.　*21st.*—To Olympic ; see charming piece by Craven, called *Chimney Corner.*[2]　*22nd.*—To Grecian ; much pleased with pantomime of *Blue Bird of Paradise.*[3]　*23rd.* —To Drury, seeing *Gamester,*[4] a dreary piece ; but Kean good.　*27th.*—Astley's[5] put up for auction by Batty, and bought in, no bidding being high enough.　*28th.*—To Drury ; Kean's benefit, *Richard III.*[6]　To Sadlers Wells, and see *Julius Cæsar ;*[7] chat with Phelps."

[1] They had been absent from London some eight months, and re-appeared as Hamlet and Gertrude.　Miss Chapman, Ophelia ; Cathcart, Laertes ; Lambert, Polonius ; M'Lien, the Ghost ; Belford, the King ; and Tilbury, First Gravedigger.

[2] Peter Probity, F. Robson ; Patty, Mrs. Leigh Murray ; John, Walter Gordon ; Solomon Probity, Horace Wigan ; Charles Chetty, Gaston Murray ; Grace Emery, Miss Hughes ; Sifter, H. Cooper.

[3] This was by Conquest and Spry.　King Charming, Harriet Covency ; Princess Florina, Miss Conquest ; Prince Pigmy, G. Conquest ; who distinguished himself greatly by his acting of the part, and by his extraordinary aerial flights, jumps through traps, etc.　Clown, Rowella ; pantaloon, Harry Power ; Harlequin, Osmond ; columbine, Miss Davies.

[4] By Edward Moore, originally produced in 1753.　Mrs. Siddons and John Kemble were great as Mr. and Mrs. Beverley, now played by Mr. and Mrs. Charles Kean.　Cathcart, Stukely ; Lambert, Jarvis ; Everett, Lawson ; and Miss Chapman, Charlotte.

[5] It was held on lease from Mr. Cobbold at a ground rent of £500 per annum, forty-four years unexpired.　The bidding rose to £15,000, but £17,000 was the reserved price.

[6] Mrs. Kean as the Queen ; Miss Chapman, Lady Anne ; Cathcart, Richmond.

[7] Phelps, Brutus ; Henry Marston, Cassius ; Hermann Vezin, Mark Antony ; Barrett, Casca ; Miss Atkinson, Portia.

" *Mar.* 1st.—For Sadlers Wells pantomime £30 from Phelps. *Era* £2. 6th.—Haymarket Theatre; see new comedy by Tom Taylor—*A Duke in Difficulties*[1]—not well constructed at all. Busy on Woodin's article. *Monday,* 11th.—To Assembly Rooms, where see Le Moiski, a Polish duke, who performs some wonderful feats in mesmerism. Experiments most extraordinary, and I think most convincing; the power explanatory of some supposed miracles. 14th.—To Strand, and see bad farce of *Change for a Sovereign*, by Horace Wigan. 15th.—The death of the Duchess of Kent this morning. 20th.—To Princess's; see Fechter play Hamlet[2] first time, and the first time I ever sat through the five acts of this play, and saw the Closet Hamlet of Shakespeare presented on the stage; very good indeed, and very successful. Read Kent's charming memoir of Bulwer in the volume of the ' Derby Ministry,' and look over old letters from him, expressing the warm friendship that has existed over twenty years unbroken. 21st.—Slowly writing review of Fechter's Hamlet. 22nd.— Go to masquerade at Her Majesty's; E. T. Smith's benefit. Have a rapid chat with him; tells me he has lost £21,000 there. 23rd.—Letter from C. C. B. Last night of Drury dramatic season. 26th.—Writing notice of yesterday's Theatrical Fund Dinner. E. T. Smith in chair."

" *Monday, April* 1st.—With Oxenford to Strand, to see Byron's burlesque of *Aladdin;* very fair, and write notice for *Telegraph* of it. 2nd.—Go to Haymarket; see *Miller and His Men* revival; fairly written, but badly acted. 4th. —*Era* copy, £1 15s. Hear of poor Saker's[1] death, of

---

[1] This was a piece written specially for Miss Fanny Stirling, who appeared in it as Colombe, with her mother Mrs. Stirling as Joconde.

[2] This was the first time that *Hamlet* had been played in England with a flaxen wig. Fechter also made considerable alterations in the dress and "business." Miss Elsworthy, the Queen ; Miss Heath, Ophelia ; Graham, Claudius ; Basil Potter, Ghost ; J. G. Shore, Laertes; Meadows, Polonius ; L. J. Sefton, Horatio ; Widdicombe, First Gravedigger.

[1] He had only a few days before played the Second Gravedigger in *Hamlet.* He died from a virulent attack of small-pox, while quite in the prime of life. He was well-known in the provinces and Dublin, and was a great favourite at the Princess's.

Princess's.   11*th.*—On Grand Jury at Maidstone, Easter Sessions; find the affair very dreary, and brother Grand Jurymen very stupid.   A lovely day; but stop over the indictment some seven hours.   Sleep at Bell; Landlord Epps a character.   12*th.*—Correspondence for *Era*, whence £2 10*s.* for last heavy week.   17*th.*—From *Telegraph* for Easter, £1. See Brough and Halliday *àpropos* sketch of *The Census*— amusing.   Hear of Edwin James and his fraud of some forty thousand pounds on the Earl of Yarborough and son.   Hear also of Renton Nicholson's serious illness.   19*th.* — *Era* paragraphs done, whence £1.   Go to Lyceum; see Miss Matilda Heron as Medea — very bad.[1]   Last night of Lyceum.   23*rd.*—Attend the annual celebration of Shake- speare's birthday at St. John's Gate; Westland Marston in chair; sit next him, with Tomlins, and Morgan John O'Connell, and George Daniell, aged seventy-two; sing ' St. George ' with improvised verse; all a great success."

" *May 9th.*—Up to town with Harrison Weir; copy for *Era*, and £1 5*s.*   Then to Oxford Concert Hall, and after- wards to Weston's; back to dress and go to Italian Opera at Covent Garden for Dramatic College benefit.[2]   Begin at 7; not over till 1.35 a.m., after which write a column notice; finish at 3 a.m.; meet there Copping, Charles J. Dunphie, of the *Morning Post*, a very congenial companion.   18*th.* --Hear this day of the death of Renton Nicholson.[3]

---

[1] This was an American actress, and she appeared in a version of Legouvé's tragedy which closely followed the original text, and was in prose. She was artificial in her acting and over elaborated. Forrester was Jason.

[2] Scenes from seven different pieces were played. Celebrated vocalists also gave their assistance ; there was a vocal association of two hundred voices. Mrs. Stirling and Miss Fanny Stirling spoke an address, written by Tom Taylor, entitled, "Past and Present," a dialogue between the ghost of Anne Bracegirdle and Miss Thalia. Almost every actor and actress of note took part in the evening.

[3] When E. L. B. was but a boy of seventeen, and looking anywhere to earn an honest penny, circumstances almost compelled him to write for *The Town*, a scurrilous and infamous paper, with which, but for his necessities, E. L. B. would not have been associated. His contributions to it were harmless enough ; they were theatrical reports and tavern sketches, one of which " The Wrekin," embodies some curious and

23rd.—At night go to Princess's; see Phelps as King

interesting accounts of its most celebrated *habitués*. It was the property of Renton Nicholson, better known as the Lord Chief Baron Nicholson, who had a strange, chequered, and, it must be said, not too reputable a career. He was born early in the century, in a then pretty suburban thoroughfare of East London, Hackney Road. But when a mere child he was brought to Islington, near which a couple of sisters opened what then fell under the name of "a young ladies' seminary." By this means they supported themselves with comfort and in respectability, and carefully looked after their little brother Renton, early deprived of parents—a serious deprivation, for the lad never had a firm moral hand laid on his proclivities. When a boy at home with the hard-working, kindly sisters, he became a nightly visitor at old Sadlers Wells, hard by the sisters' *domus;* and, in after years, Nicholson used to tell capital stories of the famous clown, Joe Grimaldi, on and off the stage. At sixteen Nicholson became a pawnbroker's assistant in High Street, Shadwell, where he grew intimate with all the plebeian pugs, rooks, and sports of that essentially blackguard and unsavoury parish. Amongst other companions he found a good friend in Jem Ward, originally a coal-whipper, but subsequently a great expert in the fistic art. When Nicholson's articles of apprenticeship ended, he migrated due west to a Kensington shop, kept by Wells, a successful pawnbroker and silversmith. Other situations in the same capacity, about various quarters of London, brought Nicholson in contact with all the representatives of Bohemian and flash life— journalists, players, tavern vocalists, soiled doves, rooks of all shades, from the turf welsher to the skittle sharp; Bow Street runners, magsmen, and bruisers—with which remarkable fraternity the help to " mine uncle " had a fast tie to the end of his days. About 1830, Nicholson opened a jeweller's shop in Cranbourne Alley, his chief customers being sixty-years-ago " mashers " and members of the *demi-monde.* It soon ended in insolvency and the King's Bench. From that time to his death, in May 1861, at the age of fifty-two, Nicholson was always in the hands of money-lending sweaters, "friendly " attorneys, and sheriffs' officers. Nicholson himself almost boasted, in the Gordon Hotel, under Covent Garden Piazza, that his practical knowledge of London bagnios and debtors' " stone jugs " was not to be matched by any " flash cove," living or dead. Let it be said that Nicholson, who got hold of plenty of money, always paid pounds for the shillings he might, for the time being, have in his possession. He was literally the Robin Hood of forty-years-gone Bohemia; barefacedly a freebooter among the aristocratic pigeons, but literally a Good Samaritan to the impecunious and fallen of both sexes. Association with him led one to arrive at the conclusion that he might have been a splendid fellow but for striking his flag to a sense of duty and simply going on the down-grade of inclination—that mode of conduct that may be called

Lear;[1] to Alhambra, and thrilled by Leotard's[2] wonderful feats of throwing himself across the building."

"*June 5th.*—Maitland's amateur performance at Campden House; meet Dunphie, Levy, Oxenford, Mr. and Mrs. Milner Gibson, Lord Raynham, Boucicault; large and brilliant party, grand supper afterwards. *6th.*—Paragraphs for *Era*, thence £1 17*s.* 6*d.*; see Blondin at Crystal Palace; second performance—appalling; meet Dicey, just returned from Rome. *8th.*—Dear mother's birthday; seventy-six this day. *20th.*—See new comedy of *A Charming Woman*[3] at Olympic; write notice; go on with ' Noctes Ambrosianæ.' *22nd.*—Princess's; see a stupid comic drama called *A Homestead Story*;[4] write

the "I-shall-do-as-I-like method." Nicholson became notorious, after keeping " brown money " gambling houses, cigar-shops, betting resorts, and bagnios, by projecting a weekly publication called *The Town.* It ante-dated our society journals, but chiefly dealt with the phenomena of flash life. The first number appeared on Saturday, June 3rd, 1837; Last, the printer, finding capital, Archibald Henning, who drew the first *Punch* cartoon, furnishing the pictures, while Nicholson sat in the editor's chair. The paper was published by a Mr. Forrester—not to be confounded with the artist who playfully called himself "Alfred Crowquill "—at 310, Strand. Amongst the writers were Dalrymple (burlesque author), a clever Bohemian; Henry Pellott, once clerk and solicitor of the Ironmongers' Company; J. G. Canning ("Theophilus Pole "); Dr. Maginn, scholar, wit, and free liver; and Hemming, of old Adelphi memory. Nicholson subsequently attained immense notoriety as Chief Baron of the judge and jury at the Garrick's Head, Bow Street, and the Coal Hole Tavern, whose site is occupied by a part of Terry's Theatre. Nicholson used to have a refreshment booth on all the big race-courses, and, for a time, was proprietor of Cremorne Gardens. He may be described as a plebeian Falstaff turned tapster; humorous, handsome, obese, sensual, impudent; a rooker of the rich and the soul of good nature to the poor.

[1] Edmund Phelps, Edgar; Miss Atkinson, Goneril; Miss Heath, Cordelia; Ryder, Kent; Maria Harris, the Fool.

[2] He had made a wonderful Continental reputation, and may be said to have almost introduced the trapèze performances into England. His feats were so gracefully performed as to take from them any thought of accident or danger arising to himself.

[3] An adaptation by Horace Wigan from Rosier's comedy *A Trente Ans*, produced at the Vaudeville Theatre, Paris, in 1840. Amy Sedgwick, Mrs. Bloomly; Horace Wigan, Sympton, an imaginary invalid.

[4] Taken from a French piece called *Geneviève.*

notice, and then to Waterloo Bridge to see the dreadful conflagration in which Braidwood was killed.[1] 29*th.*—Olympic; see bad farce of *Peace and Quiet*;[2] write notice."

"*July* 4*th.*—First paragraph I read records the death of my old friend Harry Hartley. Go to meeting of Arundel Club, at their new premises in Salisbury Street; meet Toole, Woodin, etc., there. 12*th.*—To Haymarket Theatre; Buckstone's annual benefit.[3] 25*th.*—Go to *séance* to Marshall's; communication to me: 'Edward, you will have good news, the Lord will help you; Edward, you are quite safe.' 26*th.* Writing for *Era* all day, £2 10*s.* Great excitement of the Northumberland Street tragedy of Roberts and Murray.[4]"

" *Aug.* 1*st.*—Go to Red Lion *séance*; a large party, Foster, Murray, Buckingham, Marston, etc. Communication to me: 'My dear friend, the Lord will give you power.' 2*nd.* —Finish *Era* paragraphs, £2 5*s.*, which includes Southend article. 8*th.*—To Gore Lodge to see Charles Mathews and the

[1] This was a fire at the Loftus Alum Works, known as the Tooley Street conflagration. The wall fell into the roadway and buried Mr. Braidwood and a Mr. Scott under the ruins. The oil, tallow, and tar floated on to the Thames and absolutely set it on fire. Several lives were also lost on the river. The funeral of James Braidwood, the respected Superintendent of the London Fire Brigade, who was much lamented, was one of the most impressive scenes witnessed in London. Nearly 2,000 people took part in the procession. There were fourteen mourning coaches, and several private carriages. The body was interred at Abney Park Cemetery.

[2] By F. J. Williams.

[3] For the occasion a new comedy in five acts, founded by J. R. Planché on Alexander Dumas' *Un Mariage sous Louis XV.*, entitled *My Lord and My Lady; or, It Might have been Worse*, was played. Mr. and Mrs. Charles Mathews as Lord and Lady Fitzpatrick. A Mr. Andrews, an American actor from the Park Theatre, New York, made his *début* as a French servant Louis. It is supposed to have been the first comedy ever produced on a Friday night.

[4] Roberts was a solicitor in Northumberland Street. Major Murray occupied himself with finance. Roberts appears to have had some grievance against the Major, and fired at him in his (the lawyer's) chambers. Major Murray in self-defence took up first the tongs and then a champagne bottle, which he broke on Roberts's head. Roberts died from the effects, and a verdict of justifiable homicide was returned.

Court of Uncommon Pleas party. 22*nd.*—At Lyceum ; see Falconer's comedy of *Woman*; or, *Love against the World*;[1] very slow and wordy. 30*th.*—Call at Dramatic Authors' Society ; square accounts; find £15 17*s.* recorded in my favour; paying for my contracts £7 5*s.*, receive balance £8 12*s.* 31*st.*—To Gallery of Illustration in afternoon. Close of Reed's season, and much pleased with John Parry.[2] Then to Haymarket ; first night of the new comedy (said to be by Charles Mathews), called *The Soft Sex*;[3] not good— a satire on strong-minded women."

" *Sept.* 4*th.*—Find my article on the ' Grand Jury ' is in *All the Year Round*; writing another one for ' Robin Good- fellow,' which send home ; title, ' Twenty-one Miles from London Bridge.' 6*th.*—Byron asks me to write for new publication, called *Fun.* 7*th.*—To Sadlers Wells, first night of season ; Mrs. D. P. Bowers, American actress, as Julia in the *Hunchback*; moderate. *Monday*, 16*th.*—Byron's new publication of *Fun* comes out this week ; a close copy of *Punch* in all its arrangements. 21*st.*—First night of *Louis XI.*; Phelps very nervous, but in some parts very good. 24*th.* William Farren died this day.[4] 26*th.*—Receive

[1] Miss Murray, Mrs. Weston, and Lydia Thompson, with Hermann Vezin, Walter Lacy, and Addison, were the principals in the cast.

[2] Mr. and Mrs. Reed and John Parry were appearing as Mr. and Mrs. Candytuft and Mr. Babbleton in a triologue called *The Card Basket,* written for them by Shirley Brooks.

[3] Charles Mathews acknowledged this as his. It was not well received.

[4] Born, May 15th, 1786 ; died, September 24th, at his house, 23, Brompton Square, from paralysis, from which he had long been suffering, in his seventy-sixth year. His father was an actor, who had played with Garrick at Drury Lane, and he died in 1795. He was educated in Soho, and had Liston for a schoolfellow, and made literally his first appearance as Sir Archy MacSarcasm at Plymouth; played for a considerable time in Ireland, and made his London *début* at Covent Garden, September 10th, 1818, as Sir Peter Teazle. He remained at this theatre till 1828, playing at the Haymarket during the summer seasons ; and he then went to Drury Lane, remaining there till 1837, when he returned to Covent Garden under Osbaldiston's management. He then joined Benjamin Webster at the Haymarket as stage-manager. Had his first paralytic attack in 1845, while playing Old Parr. He afterwards became lessee of the Strand and Olympic Theatres. Took

for *All the Year Round* article £3 3s. 28*th*.—Go to Strand, and sit in orchestra by the leader, Frank Musgrave, the house being so full, to see Byron's new burlesque of *Esmeralda;* [1] full of puns, words that sound like puns, but are not; very successful."

" *Oct.* 2*nd.*—See bad piece of *Midsummer's Eve* at Lyceum; [2] and Edwin Booth; good actor, second night as Shylock [3] at Haymarket. 3*rd.*—Write obituary notice of Arthur Smith [4] for *Era*. Go to Olympic; see bad piece of *Jack of All Trades.* [5] To Haymarket, and behold a worse one, of *Paul Pry Married and Settled.* [6] 4*th.*—Vandenhoff [7] dies this day, aged seventy-one. 10*th.*—To Strand, and see

his farewell of the stage at the Haymarket, July 16th, 1855, in one scene, as Lord Ogleby in *The Clandestine Marriage*. This character, Sir Peter Teazle, Squire Broadlands, Michael Perren, Uncle John Nicholas Flam, Uncle Foozle, Grandfather Whitehead, and Old Parr were his most celebrated parts, and in them he was surpassed by none. He was married to Mrs. Saville Faucit.

[1] *Esmeralda;* or, *The "Sensation" Goat,* founded on *Notre Dame*. Marie Wilton appeared as Gringoire; Fanny Josephs, Esmeralda; Eleanor Bufton, Captain Phœbus; Kate Carson, Fleur de Lys; James Rogers, Claude Frollo; Danvers, the Goat; H. J. Turner, King Clopin. The music was arranged by Frank Musgrave.

[2] In this Miss Ellen Terry played Puck. It was written by W. H. Yelland.

[3] Mrs. Charles Young was the Portia.

[4] Brother of Albert Smith. Died October 1st, in his thirty-seventh year. He was business manager at the Egyptian Hall for his brother, and arranged Charles Dickens's readings. Was one of the committee of the "Thames Fisheries Society," and wrote the little *brochure*. He was also almoner of the Fielding Club, a benevolent association to assist actors in distress.

[5] A serio-comic drama adapted from the French *Le Ramoneur*, by H. Neville and Florence Haydon, who, with J. W. Ray, made their first appearance at the Olympic. Horace Wigan was also in the cast.

[6] Written by Charles Mathews for himself.

[7] John Vandenhoff, born at Salisbury in February 1790, and being intended for the Priesthood in the Romish Church, was educated at the Jesuits' College, Stoneyhurst. Made his first appearance as Osmond in *The Castle Spectre* at Salisbury, in 1808. Worked steadily in the provinces till 1813, when he played Rolla at Liverpool. Appeared at Covent Garden, December 9th, 1820, as King Lear; but, finding the best parts were occupied at that theatre, he returned to Liverpool and

farce *Short and Sweet :*[1] another version of *How do you Manage?* Agree with Mr. Simpkin for £6 to write almanack. 11*th.—Era* copy, whence £2. Dine with the *Fun* folks at the London Tavern : our inaugurative dinner ; present Mr. Maclean, his son, Burnand, Brough, Byron (in chair), Ince, artist, and Urquhart, the commercial director ; a very pleasant gathering and liberal spread.[2] 12*th.—* Receive from Mr. Phelps for 'Noctes Ambrosianæ,' £12. 14*th.* Send article 'Rhyming Ramble up and down the Thames' to Simpkin, and copy to *Fun.* 19*th.—*Byron pays for *Fun,* £1 10*s.* Go to Wells ; see the revival (first night) of *Midsummer Night's Dream.* Then to Princess's, and see outrageous burlesque by John Brougham, called *Po-ca-hon-tas,*[3] a wild absurdity. 23*rd.—*Send copy to *Fun,* and see Fechter as Othello, first time at Princess's : a curious performance, with some considerably good points ; Ryder as Iago, and Carlotta Leclercq as Desdemona very good. 26*th.* —To Haymarket in evening ; Charles Mathews's benefit : *Old and Young Stager,* and *One Hour,* or, *The Carnival Ball.* Startled by his saying, in a sort of farewell address, that he was going to give an entertainment and take his leave of the stage. 31*st.—*To Haymarket, and see Booth as Richelieu."

brought about the "Salter riots," so called from its being thought he was going to oust an actor of that name who was a great favourite with the Liverpudlians. The difficulty was got over by both Salter and Vandenhoff being engaged, and alternating the principal tragic characters. In June 1834 Vandenhoff played lead at the Haymarket, and then went to Covent Garden and Drury Lane. At the former theatre he appeared frequently with Macready and Charles Kemble. Took his farewell of the stage October 29th, 1858, at the Theatre Royal, Liverpool, as Brutus in *Julius Cæsar,* and Wolsey in the third act of *Henry VIII.* He died of paralysis.

[1] By A. C. Troughton. *How do you Manage?* was adapted by Haynes Bayley for the Adelphi, and was acted there in February 1835.

[2] [Maclean, the first proprietor of *Fun,* was a picture-frame dealer in the Strand. I think Tom Hood must have been at the dinner, for he wrote for the first number of *Fun,* and was afterwards the editor. —C. S.]

[3] Or, *The Gentle Savage.* Miss Helen Howard in the title *rôle,* Augustus Harris burlesqued an operatic tenor, and John Brougham gave imitations of leading tragedians.

"*Nov. 7th.*—Do *Era* copy; then to Wells with second scene; to Drury—see Avonia Jones as Medea, her second performance—very good; then to Lyceum, Falconer's[1] benefit; then to Alhambra; see Leotard; hear of Talfourd's[2] marriage and all sorts of interesting news. *9th.*—To Lyceum: *Peep of Day;*[3] begins at 7, and not over till midnight. *13th.*—See Greenwood's piece of *Is it the King?*[4] in which Ada Swanborough makes a successful first appearance. *16th.*—To Haymarket, and see Sothern, from America, play a foppish lord very funnily.[5] *18th.*—*Octoroon*[6] produced at the Adelphi, but no great hit; the *Colleen Bawn* reached its 278th night on Saturday. *23rd.*—To Her Majesty's concert-room, and Charles Mathews's inauguration supper for his 'At Home.'[7] *28th.*—To Strand, and see Byron's *àpropos* sketch of *Rival Othellos*[8]—very slight; then'

[1] This was distinguished by the *bénéficiare* reciting a poem of his own composition on the early courtship and marriage of Shakespeare and Ann Hathaway.

[2] Francis Talfourd was married, on November 5th, to Miss Frances Louisa Towne.

[3] Or, *Savourneen Dheelish*, by E. Falconer. It was taken from one of the "Tales by the O'Hara Family." Harry Kavanagh, Hermann Vezin; Mary Grace, Clara Weston; Barney O'Toole, Edmund Falconer; Captain Howard, Walter Lacy; Father O'Clery (priest), Addison; Kathleen Kavanagh, Mrs. D. P. Bowers. There was a great quarry scene in this.

[4] At the Strand, in the character of Christian of Denmark; really a girl, but brought up to the age of sixteen years, and known to the world, as a boy.

[5] This was in *Our American Cousin*, in which Sothern appeared as Lord Dundreary, which was afterwards to secure for him a world-wide fame. The part as originally written, when the piece was played at Laura Keene's, in New York, consisted of about twenty lines. As a Trenchard, Buckstone; Florence, Mrs. Charles Young; Abel Murcott (a broken-down, hard-drinking clerk), Chippendale; and Mary Meredith, Patty Oliver. The play was by Tom Taylor.

[6] Or, *Life in Louisiana*, was by Dion Boucicault. The author, Salem Scudder; Agnes Robertson, Zoe (the octoroon); Emery, Jacob M'Closkey. Salem Scudder was afterwards played by Mr. Delmon Grace.

[7] This was an autobiographical account of Charles Mathews' life, interspersed with songs.

[8] These two characters—Theophilus White and Augustus Brown, J. Clarke and James Rogers—burlesqued the methods of Brooke and Fechter.

to Drury Lane, and see his burlesque of *Miss Eily O'Connor.*[1]
29*th.*—*Era* copy, and receive from paper £2 2s.; to Her
Majesty's Concert Room to see Mr. and Mrs. Mathews at
home; very entertaining to me, from its suggestiveness and
associations of the past, but not likely to be a permanent
success. 30*th.*—To Myddelton Hall to Maclagan's concert;
very versatile and clever; then to Bayswater Athenæum, to
hear Yates deliver a lecture on Modern Society; very fair,
and Albert Smith-like."

" *Dec. 5th.*—Chat with Smith about Louise Keeley playing
the part in the pantomime. 11*th.*—Close my forty-first
year, a day of solemn retrospection. Have at least the
satisfaction of knowing that during that time I have never
injured a living creature. Get up a little festivity for the
juveniles. 12*th.*—To Sadlers Wells; see Mrs. Conway as
Ion[2]—very good. Then to Myddelton, and see Conway
very violent; George Daniel (seventy-two) very amusing.
14*th.*—The whole town in excitement about Prince Albert's
illness; hear in evening that he died at eleven; all deeply
impressed with the significance of this event. 16*th.*—
Papers all in mourning—*Morning Star* excepted, through
machine difficulties. *Telegraph* admirable; 141,622 copies
officially announced to have been sold this day. 23*rd.*—
Funeral of the good and deeply lamented Prince Albert;
to Strand for *Telegraph;* write notice, finished by 1 a.m.
27*th.*—Busy with *Era* work, and £2 5s. Sadlers Wells at
night; see *Cherry and Fair Star.*[3] See Fenton—funny,

---

[1] Atkins appeared in the title *rôle;* Louise Keeley, Miles-na-Coppaleen; Eliza Arden, Hardress Cregan; Robert Roxby, Danny Mann.
Tom Matthews appeared in the piece as Serjeant Tooralrooral. It was
interspersed with parodies of the current songs of the day.

[2] Mrs. Conway was a younger sister of Mrs. Bowers. Possessed an
intelligent face, good figure, and a rich and melodious voice, and was
devoid of the exaggeration for which the American school had then
rather a bad character.

[3] This was E. L. B.'s pantomime, *Cherry and Fair Star,* or, *Harle-
quin and the Singing Apple, the Talking Bird, and the Dancing Waters.*
Charles Lauri, clown; Chapman, pantaloon; Duprez, harlequin;
Mdlle. Nathalie, columbine. Miss Hudspeth was the Princess Fair
Star; and Charles Fenton, Prince Cherry.

and transformation scene good ; write at *Telegraph* office accounts thereof. 28*th.*—From E. T. S. £20.[1] *Monday,* 30*th.*—Wishing everybody 'A Happy New Year!'—feeling myself intensely miserable and wretched. 31*st.*—See the last of the year, the sun sink eclipsed beneath the horizon. Look in at Gardiner's ; see bowls of punch preparing, but hasten away back to melancholy musings ; read Byron, and, whilst turning over the pages of 'Manfred' hear the bells ringing in the New Year. I open the window and look seaward, out into the cold winter air, and breathe a fervent prayer for the peace that I hope the New Year will bring to my spirit, with a hearty thanksgiving for the blessings I have received throughout my life."

Rough estimate of revenue for year, £284 10*s.*

1862.

" *Wednesday, Jan.* 1*st.*—The year dawns upon me as usual very tired, and much perplexed to guess what the future has in store. 4*th.*—Paid for almanack from *Fun* office for matter, £1 15*s.* To Haymarket ; see Miss Jane Coombes [2] appear as Constance in *Love Chase :* a failure ; write about it. 10*th.*— On *Era* paragraphs, for week, £2. From *Daily Telegraph* for Christmas week, £2 2*s.* 11*th.*—Dicey calls, and arrange to write letter for *Northampton Mercury,*[3] beginning from next week. Attend an interesting *séance :* communications from my father and D. W. Haly—all very singular and convincing. Messages from my father, January 11th, 1862 :— 'There are many spirits which have assembled to greet you

[1] This was for E. L. B.'s pantomime, *Harlequin and the House that Jack built ; or, Old Mother Hubbard and Her Wonderful Dog.* The dog was represented by Signor Lorenzo. Harlequins, Cormack and St. Maine ; columbines, Misses Gunniss ; pantaloon, G. Tanner ; clowns, Forrest and Huline ; sprites, the Ridgway and Summerell families.

[2] This was a young lady who was supposed to have made her professional reputation in Canada and America. She wanted brightness.

[3] [This was the property of the mother of Edward Dicey.—C. S.]

here to-day; I am glad to make you sensible of my presence. I am often with my friends on earth; yes, my son, I am delighted to speak and say to you, I am with you often when you are not aware of my presence. You have much medium power, and you will be sensible of that presence.' 'I wish you to bear a message to mother: say to her, I am often with her in spirit, and stand at Heaven's portals ready to greet her when we shall be reunited never more to separate: William, for Sarah his wife.' 16*th.*—To Haymarket: morning performance of pantomime, *Little Boy Blue;*[1] then to Sadlers Wells, and hear of the death of Raymond.[2] 18*th.*— St. James's; see a new piece,[3] which turns out old adaptation of *Chevalier de St. George;* write notice. 22*nd.*—Write the first London letter for *Northampton Mercury;* post it. 30*th.* —From *Fun,* £2 6*s.*; *Era,* £1 5*s.* To Sadlers Wells to see *Romeo and Juliet,* with Mrs. Conway as Romeo."[4]

"*Feb.* 6*th.*—From *Fun,* 15*s.*; write 'Summer Shadow' song; *Era,* £1 15*s.* 8*th.*—From Phelps, Sadlers Wells, £34 for forty-eight nights; up to date. 15*th.*—Go to Princess's; see an appalling piece, *The Angel of Midnight.*[5]

[1] The title of this was *Little Miss Muffet and Little Boy Blue;* or, *Harlequin and Old Daddy Long Legs.* Miss Muffet, Louise Leclercq; Little Boy Blue, Henrietta Lindley; The Queen Bee, Miss Henrade; Harlequin, G. Becket; Columbine, Miss Rosine; Clown, Charles Leclercq; Pantaloon, Herr Cole.

[2] Malone Raymond, or more properly Richard Malone, was born in Dublin in 1800, and came of a very good family. Made his first appearance in Londonderry as Collooney in *The Irishman in London.* Performed in Ireland for a considerable time, then came to Liverpool, where he made a hit in the character of O'Slash in *The Invincibles,* and from that time adopted Irish characters exclusively. Made his first appearance at the Haymarket, April 14th, 1842, as Major O'Flaherty in *The West Indian.* After giving entertainments for some years, in 1860, he became acting manager of Sadlers Wells, remaining there till the time of his death.

[3] *Self-Made,* three-act drama adapted by George Vining, who played the principal male character; Miss Herbert, the Countess de Presle.

[4] Mrs. Rogers was the Juliet. They both were successes. Phelps was the Mercutio. [Romeo has also been played by Miss Cushman, and Madame Vestvali.—C. S.]

[5] An adaptation by John Brougham from the French of MM. Barrière and Plouvier, *L'Ange de Minuit.* Miss Marriott was the

Monday, 17th.—Write memoir of Mrs. Bradshaw[1] (Miss M. Tree), who died this day at noon. *20th.*—Last night of *Cherry and Fair Star* at Wells. Get cheque for London letter, £5. *21st.*—Paragraphs for *Era,* and receive £2. From E. T. S., £10; in all, £50. To Princess's; see last night of pantomime, *Dick Whittington.*[2] *25th.*—The long looked-for case, Ledger *versus* Webster,[3] this day decided before Cockburn at Court of Queen's Bench: verdict for plaintiff, 1s. *28th.*—*Era* paragraphs and notices, £1 15s. To Surrey, and see *Adam Bede.*"[4]

"*March 1st.*—To Wells in evening, and see *Pizarro.*[5] Receive from Phelps balance due from pantomime, £11,

Midnight Angel; George Jordan, the Student; Ryder, Colonel Lambeth. Spoken of as a sensation drama conceived in the very worst taste.

[1] Maria Tree, sister to Mrs. Charles Kean, began life as a vocalist, was instructed by Signor Lanza and Tom Cooke. First appeared as Polly in *The Beggar's Opera* at Bath, November 13th, 1813. Appeared at Covent Garden, September 10th, 1819, as Rosina in *The Barber of Seville*—made a great success; also as Ophelia, Viola, Juliet, Rosalind, Imogen, and appeared with Miss Stephens in *The Comedy of Errors.* Was an exquisite figure, had very expressive features; made her last appearance at Covent Garden, June 16th, 1825, as Mary Copp in *Charles II.,* and Clari in the opera of that name, of which character she was the original. She married Mr. James Bradshaw, some years M.P. for Canterbury, who died, leaving her a widow with one daughter who married Mr. H. Langley of the 2nd Life Guards.

[2] This was *Whittington and His Cat,* or, *Harlequin King Kollywobbol,* and was by Byron. Princess Popsi-wopsi, Rose Leclercq; John Haslem made a hit as the little Bacchus, and imitated Leotard on the trapèze; Hildyard, Clown; Paulo, Pantaloon; John Lauri, Harlequin; Caroline Adams, Columbine.

[3] This was a libel case, brought by Frederick Ledger, proprietor of the *Era* as plaintiff, against Benjamin Webster, manager of the New Adelphi Theatre, as defendant. It had arisen out of certain strictures which the plaintiff had passed on certain systems and tricks made use of at benefits in aid of dramatic charities. [Notably the Crystal Palace Fancy Fair, which was most justly condemned in the *Era* as a disgrace to the dramatic profession.—C. S.]

[4] This was by J. E. Carpenter. Creswick made his reappearance, and was supported by Vollaire, Maclean, Miss Pauncefort, Miss E. Webster, Miss E. Johnstone, and Charles Rice.

[5] Revival. Phelps, Rolla; Edmund Phelps, Alonzo; F. Villiers, Pizarro; T. Lyon, Orozembo; Miss Atkinson, Elvira; Mrs. James Rogers, Cora.

making £49. 3*rd.*—Fechter appears at Princess's as Iago:
a decided success. 6*th.*—To Princess's, and see *Working the
Oracle* produced first time in London—a farce I wrote six
years ago: goes off pretty well. 8*th.*—Go to St. James's;
see a good comedy, adapted from the French by Horace
Wigan, called *Friends or Foes.*[1] 11*th.*—Deeply grieved to
hear of my friend Frank Talfourd's[2] death, which took place
on Sunday at Mentone. Have to prepare *Fun* copy, but not
in the humour for it, feeling very sad. 13*th.*—From *Fun*
office, £1 6*s.* 6*d.* Another American medium arrived, and
pronounced satisfactory; he answers my writing with Francesco F. on the arm. 15*th.*—Write for *Era* notice of Sadlers
Wells[3] and Harrison's benefit, and Phelps', the last night of
the season. Then go to Marshall's, sit at circle, and have communications purporting to be from my dear friend Talfourd:
' My old friend, this is a happy change into everlasting life.'
Question : ' Can you write ?' Answer : ' I will try.' Then
the name written. ' The truth of heaven is revealed, thanks
to the knowledge of spiritualism.' Question : ' Whom did
you meet ?' Answer : ' Alfred, Elizabeth, and all my friends :
William Talfourd, in the fifth sphere.' 18*th.*—29,701, the
last number of *The Morning Chronicle*, published this day,
and announced to be re-named on Monday. 22*nd.*—Attend
the presentation by Gladstone (then Chancellor of the

---

[1] Taken from Victorien Sardou's *Nos Intimes.* Mr. and Mrs.
Union, George Vining and Miss Herbert ; Mr. and Mrs. Meanley,
W. H. Stephens and Mrs. Frank Matthews ; Doctor Bland, F. Dewar :
Frederick Fervid, F. Charles ; was a great hit. [It was in this play that
Miss Kate Terry (Mrs. Arthur Lewis), made her first great hit. She
was the under-study for Miss Herbert, and once she took the character
Miss Herbert never played it again. Another version of the same play,
called *Peril*, by Savile and Bolton Rowe, was produced years after at the
Prince of Wales's under the management of the Bancrofts.—C. S.]

[2] Francis Talfourd was the son of Justice Talfourd, and was in his
thirty-fifth year when he expired, on March 9th ; was educated at
Eton, and intended for the bar. His first travestie was *Alcestis*, but
the burlesques he wrote after this were almost innumerable. He had
only been married five months. He was a most genial, warm-hearted
companion, of brilliant literary powers, and was always ready to help
in any good work.

[3] *The City Madam* was played, followed by *Doing for the Best*, with
Phelps as Dick Stubbs.

Exchequer), of the Kean testimonial at St. James's Hall.[1] Last night of the season at Drury, and Smith's benefit.[2] *27th.*—Receive from Davidson for copyright of pantomime, Drury, £2 2s. Look in at Strand : G. W. Jamieson,[3] an American actor, as Grandfather Whitehead."

"*April* 24*th.*—Copy for Woodin's entertainment to be done, £20. Look in at Strand ; see burlesque of *Pizarro :*[4] not very brilliant. See diorama and ballet at Lyceum, and hear of Lord Westbury's haunted house. 25*th.*—On *Era* work, £1 10s. 29*th.*—Chronicle the death of *The Literary Gazette*, after forty-five years' existence, on Saturday last. 30*th.*—Mother comes up for her quarterly treat. Take her and C. C. B. to St. Clement's,[5] but not a good dinner ; then to Adelphi, *Dot and the Phantom ;*[6] Toole's Caleb Plummer very good."

"*May* 1*st.*—Great International Exhibition opens : all day writing account of it. At New Royalty see a bagatelle called *The Spirit Medium.* 13*th.*—Hear with regret of Sir William Don's[7] death. 16*th.*—Walk to Wells : write account of new piece called *Family Pride*, adaptation from the

---

[1] This was a service of plate valued at 2,000 guineas. Several of Charles Kean's old co-Etonians took part in the presentation.

[2] *The Wonder* was played, compressed into three acts. Mr. and Mrs. Charles Kean were Don Felix and Violante ; Miss Chapman, Donna Isabella.

[3] He had made his mark in *The Octoroon* at the Adelphi. Grandfather Whitehead was a stock character of his in America, and his performance in England justified his having played it upwards of three hundred times in the States.

[4] Or, *The Leotard of Peru* by Leicester Buckingham. Rogers, Cora ; J. Clarke, Pizarro ; Ada Swanborough, Alonzo ; Eleanor Bufton, Elvira ; Fanny Hughes, Orozembo ; Fanny Josephs, Ataliba.

[5] [This must have been Carr's Restaurant in the Strand.—C. S.]

[6] This was another version by Boucicault of *The Vampire*, which had been seen in England originally in 1820, and revived in 1829, both at the English Opera House. T. P. Cooke was great as Ruthven.

[7] Died at Hobart Town, Tasmania, March 19th, 1862. Was the son of Sir Alexander Don, a Scotch baronet. Was originally in the 5th Dragoon Guards, but ran through his property and was obliged to sell his estate, Newton Don, which fetched £85,000. Being accounted a good amateur actor, he determined to take to the stage as a profession, and so played in the North of England, and went to America

French of *The Poor Nobleman.*[1]   24*th.*—Off to Crystal Palace to see Flower Show; then to Princess's; return of Kean: see *Louis XI.*   30*th.*—Hear that sale of the *Athenæum* is about 10,000; of *Critic,* about 2,500."

"*June* 4*th.*—Derby Day: Caractacus winner.[2]   All day over London letter.   5*th.*—Write Derby article for *Era.* Hear of John Drew's[3] (comedian) death.   6*th.*—Win 15*s.* by Oaks stake.   21*st.*—Great excitement about the Boucicault and Webster dispute, and what they will do on Monday.   To St. James's, and see comedy by Watts Phillips, called *His Last Victory.*"

"*July* 3*rd.*—Bad piece at Strand.[4]   5*th.*—Go to Arthur Sketchley's[5] entertainment at Bijou Theatre, and to Lyceum, and see bad farce called *Colleen Bawn.*[6]   19*th.*—Dramatic College Fancy Fair at Crystal Palace.   21*st.*—Grieve to see in the *Times* obituary for to-day the death of Freeman Gage

in 1851, and was successful in New York and Philadelphia, remaining there five years. Then came to England, played in the provinces, and eventually at the Haymarket. Was over six feet in height, and was only thirty-six years of age, when he died of consumption, leaving a widow.

[1] These were both taken from *Le Pauvre Gentilhomme.*

[2] [A rank outsider, which belonged to a London publisher. He had won at Bath a few days before.—C. S.]

[3] Born in Dublin, September 3rd, 1825. Was taken to America when he was but six years old; began life as a sailor. Made his first appearance at the Richmond Hill Theatre, New York, and his first hit in 1845 at the Bowery as Dr. O'Toole. In 1853 was lessee of the Arch Street Theatre in Philadelphia, and from that time was looked upon as a star actor. About 1858-9 visited San Francisco and Australia with great success; came to Dublin, October 1860, and from thence to London, where he appeared in *The Irish Emigrant.*

[4] This was a piece called *The Silent System,* by T. J. Williams, brought out to introduce Miss Tungate.

[5] [Arthur Sketchley was the *nom de plume* of George Rose, most amusing and charming companion. He was an Oxford man (Magdalen Hall), and was for some years a clergyman in the Church of England. On his conversion to the Church of Rome he became private tutor to the present Duke of Norfolk. He was an able dramatist and *littérateur,* and is buried at St. Thomas's Catholic Church near Fulham.—C. S.]

[6] By William Brough and Halliday. It was a farcical extravaganza, called, *The Colleen Bawn Settled at Last.* It was a piece of topsy-turveydom.

Delamotte, aged forty-eight: another of my old friends gone !
24*th.*—A visit from Mr. Bonner (engraver of Cumberland's
plays) respecting my old drama, *Road of Life,* the manuscript of which he has lost, and arranging advertisement
offering reward for its recovery.[1] 26*th.*—To see Josephine
Woodin and Madame Mortimer in new entertainment. This
is in opposition to Woodin, to whom she is sister : very
indifferent."

" *Aug.* 22*nd.*—To *séance* at Marshall's ; communication
from Talfourd : ' I will be with you in your room, and
impress you with holy thoughts. You must keep up your
spirits, for I can see plenty of luck in store for you, my old
friend. Give my regards to the King of the Gate, Leicester
Buckingham. I will be with him at his table. All spiritual
powers will be great on earth. I will give you a piece ; use
it. " Cock Robin "—" Francis." ' Began at 9 ; over at 10.30."

" *Sept.* 12*th.*—Look in at Strand, and see Belford's Dundreary in *Sam's Arrival:*[2] he good, piece bad. 13*th.*—Receive
letter from C. C. B. announcing her intended departure to
Otago, New Zealand. Meet Falconer, and settle pantomime
subject as *Goody Two Shoes and Harlequin Cock Robin*
(Talfourd). Walk to Ealing, reviving old memories of school
and boyhood. Call on C. C. B. at her brother's : coming of
age of her nephew. 19*th.*—*Era* £1 15*s.* Drury Lane: see
Boucicault's spectacle, *Relief of Lucknow;* very effective in
parts. C. C. B. getting ready for starting, and the last
interview: feel very, very sad. 20*th.*—Pack up parcel of
literature for New Zealand, and off to Blackwall to visit the
ship. A memorable day, making another change, and
indicating an approaching loss : severely felt, and terribly
depressing my spirits. 24*th.*—To Gravesend, and find the
ship has only just arrived. A dark night, but take boat and
go on board. The first page of a new chapter in life's sad
experiences. 25*th.*—Again on board, taking things essential
to voyage. The last adieu, or *au revoir*—which ? Back,
and twilight stroll : meet a sympathetic friend, and the story

---

[1] [Why did he not go to the Lord Chamberlain's office, where he
would have found a copy ?—C. S.]

[2] This was an " absurdity " by Oxenford.

told of the secrets of the heart. 26*th.*—This day, at 11.30, sails the ship for Otago, New Zealand, bearing the one who has been so long loved. Sadly to town, and plunge into work, and finish at Arundel amidst the light-hearted, feeling silently the heavy blow I have just sustained. 27*th.*—Sadlers Wells, reopening for winter season under management of Lucette and Phillips."[1]

" *Oct.* 3*rd.*—Find letter from C. C. B. on her voyage. 4*th.*—To Surrey : reopening with *Medal of Bronze,*[2] and looking-glass curtain. 9*th.*—Sadlers Wells for new piece of *Willow Marsh :*[3] not good."

" *Nov.* 6*th.*—See *John Duncan,* ship, off to Otago, with Miss Rye and female emigrants, and feel to envy her, as she will see my loved one if she has safely arrived. My domestic tranquillity much upset ; but what is the use of grieving ? I have made my bed—I must lie on it. 7*th.*—To Wells : very bad piece, *Charity ;* or, *My Lord Welcome,* founded on *Les Misérables.*[4] 8*th.*—To Drury Lane : *Othello ;*[5] Swinbourne the Moor : write notice. 11*th.*—

> Again *Fun,* and little done ;
>   Though up to 1, yet scarce a pun ;
> What pleasure ?—None,
>   Frost—begun.

---

[1] A new drama in three acts, *Clouds and Sunshine in a Life,* by Adolphe Faucquez, was played. Henry Forrester, E. F. Edgar, A Montague, Sophie Miles, W. H. Stephens, Lewis Ball, Charles Crook, Emily Dowton, and Miss M. Ball, a child, appeared in it. Catherine Lucette and Morton Price (Captain Horton Rhys) gave a musical entertainment, called, *A Double Courtship ;* and *Two Heads are Better than One* made up the bill.

[2] Or, *The Queen of the Innocents,* adapted from *La Bouquetière des Innocents,* by Vollaire and H. G. Plunkett. Under the sole lesseeship of Mr. Shepherd, who played Jacques Bonhomme. Mr. E. Price from Liverpool, made a successful *début* in London as King Louis ; Miss Fanny Clifford, Margot ; Miss G. Pauncefort, the Marchioness. The looking-glass curtain was a new arrangement of plate-glass in eight compartments, and was said to comprise upwards of one thousand feet of mirrors.

[3] This was also by Adolphe Faucquez.

[4] Adapted by Hazlewood, and compressed into two acts.

[5] Mr. Swinbourne had made a good professional reputation, which

14th.—To Olympic ; see *Camilla's Husband :*[1] a good piece. *20th.*—Make a fair copy of pantomime for Drury. Send off a short poem to Tom Hood, called 'Phantasmagoria.'[2] *28th.*—To Drury, and see *Bohemian Girl :* Miss Hills the *débutante.*"

" *Dec. 4th.*—Make complete copy of Princess's pantomime of *Riquet with the Tuft, or, Harlequin and Mother Shipton.*[3] *10th.*—Sit up till past midnight for the sake of drinking my own health, having none else to care about me, on having attained my forty-second year, which at one time I never expected to see. God be thanked for all, and hope for peace at some date. Find letter from C. C. B., dated the Tropics, October 22nd. *26th.*—Go to Strand ; see *Ivanhoe*[4] for *Daily Telegraph*, and write nearly three columns. *27th.*—Kindly notices in all the papers of my pantomimes. At night to Dion Boucicault's new Westminster Theatre :[5] beautiful and commodious building, but the pantomime of *Lord Dundreary* dull and pointless. *31st.*—The Old Year goes out on one of

was confirmed by a London success. Ryder, Iago ; Charles Vandenhoff, Cassio ; Fanny Clifford, Desdemona ; Miss Atkinson, Emilia.

[1] This was a three-act drama by Watts Phillips. Dogbriar, F. Robson ; Lady Camilla Hailstone, Miss Kate Saville ; Fusell, Horace Wigan ; and Maurice Warner, H. Neville. [This was the last play in which Robson appeared.—C. S.]

[2] A lovely little poem was printed in a periodical called *Saturday Night.* Among the contributors were Arthur Prowse, Gilbert Robertson. Rands, Byron, Sketchley, and C. S.

[3] *Prince Riquet with the Tuft ;* or, *Harlequin and Old Mother Shipton,* E. L. B.'s pantomime. Milano, Harlequin ; Annie Collinson, Columbine ; Holford, Pantaloon ; R. Power, Clown. The scenery was by Beverley.

[4] *Ivanhoe, in Accordance with the Spirit of the Times.* Burlesque extravaganza by H. J. Byron. Cedric, Turner ; Wamba, Miss Marshall ; Wilfred of Ivanhoe, Charlotte Saunders ; Sir Brian de Bois Guilbert, C. Rice ; Isaac of York, J. Clarke ; Rowena, Ada Swanborough ; Rebecca, J. Rogers ; Black Knight, Eleanor Bufton ; Prince John, Fanny Josephs.

[5] This had hitherto been known as Astley's, and had been thoroughly rebuilt. The pantomime was called *Ladybird ;* or, *Harlequin Lord Dundreary.* Miss Edith Stuart was charming as Buttercup ; Dupré, Harlequin ; Miss A. Cushnie, Columbine ; Huline, Clown ; Silvester, Pantaloon.

the brightest of days.   I see it out quietly by myself over a solitary pipe, recalling many memories of yore."

Approximate revenue for year, £311 2*s.*

1863.

" *Jan. 2nd.*—To Princess's, taking Crawford Wilson; well pleased with pantomime; well played, and beautifully put on the stage.   But, with the exception of Drury, very bad business going at all the theatres.   Look in at St. James's and see *Carte de Visite.*[1]   Hear of the death of Mrs. William Barrymore,[2] and add another to the list of the records of the lives I have known; feel very sad.   Go to St. James's: see Arthur Sketchley's new drama of *The Dark Cloud:*[3] a success ! 10*th.*—Lyceum opens under Fechter's management: sketch of *Sudden Attack* and *Duke's Motto;* house full, theatre looking very elegant, ' everybody ' there.   13th.—Receive from Falconer for Drury Lane pantomime[4] £25, first instalment.   16*th.*—Startling proposal for directorship of the

[1] This was a farce by F. C. Burnand and Montagu Williams, and introduced a new comedian in Mr. Johnson of Edinburgh, and a pretty, lively *soubrette* in Miss Nisbett.

[2] Known some fifty years previously as Miss Adams, one of the best of English dancers ; was always an attraction at the Old Circus, now the Surrey, in the grand ballets there.   Her husband, William Barrymore, was for many years stage-manager and inventor of pantomimes at Drury Lane, at which theatre she appeared with great success, particularly as Fenella in *Masaniello.*   In 1831 she and her husband went to America, made a great reputation, and settled at Boston ; and when Mr. Barrymore died, in 1846, his widow returned to this country, where she resided up to the time of her death, having reached nearly her eightieth year.   She was a clever linguist, artist, and musician.

[3] An original play, Miss Herbert, Arthur Stirling (excellent), Mr. and Mrs. Frank Matthews, Adeline Cottrell, and Miss Nisbett were in the cast.

[4] The theatre was opened under the management of Edmund Falconer, who had completely restored it after the Louis XIV. style, introduced a new chandelier, and thoroughly re-upholstered the house. The pantomime was E. L. B.'s, *Little Goody Two Shoes,* or, *Harlequin Cock Robin.*   Lydia Thompson, Helen Howard, Miss Wentworth, and Messrs. Robins and Tom Matthews, were in the cast.   Harlequins, Cormack and St. Maine ; columbines, Madame Boleno and the Misses

Globe Printing Company.[1] 17*th.*—In morning to day performance of Adelphi pantomime, *George de Barnwell*,[2] the French clowns being very good. At night write to C. C. B., and go after to Olympic and see *Robin Hood.*[3] 23*rd.*—Fire at Princess's ; poor little ballet girls burnt in pantomime.[4] *Monday, 26th.*—To New Westminster, to see Boucicault's new piece of the *Trial of Effie Deans.*[5] 31*st.*—See clever adaptation from the French by Leicester Buckingham at St. James's, called *The Merry Widow,*[6] with a good situation of reading an imaginary letter, an idea I have had long years in view."

"*Feb. 5th.*—Write a lyric for St. Valentine. This day

Gunniss ; pantaloons, G. Tanner and Deulin Johnson ; clowns, Harry Boleno and Charles Lauri.

[1] [This was the company that started *The Glow-worm* of which Frank Burnard and Arthur À. Beckett were editor. On the death of the paper the offices became a Sporting Club, it became the Vaudeville Theatre.—C. S.]

[2] Or, *Harlequin Folly in the Realms of Fancy*, by H. J. Byron. The burlesque portion included Fancy, Miss Seaman ; Romance, Miss Wright ; Claptrap, Miss Vining; Folly, Miss Woolgar, who afterwards burlesqued the part of Millward to the George Barnwell of J. L. Toole, in which he was inimitable. Miss Kate Kelly was admirable as Maria ; Paul Bedford and Miss Stoker were also in the cast. John Lauri, harlequin; Hildyard, clown; Paulo, pantaloon; Caroline Adams, columbine. The French clowns were Arthur and Bertrand.

[3] This was by F. C. Burnand.

[4] The girls' names were Hunt and Smith, who died from their hurts. Robert Roxby, stage-manager, was seriously injured in endeavouring to put out the flames. It was fortunate, with such a number of people on the stage, that the accident did not result in more evil consequences.

[5] Miss Atkinson, Meg Murdochson ; Rose Leclercq, Madge Wildfire ; Ryder, David Deans ; Leeson, Laird of Dumbiedikes ; Swinbourne, Geordie Robinson ; Dewar, Ratcliffe ; Henry Vandenhoff, Duke of Argyll ; Charles Vandenhoff, Reuben Butler ; Dion Boucicault, Counsel for the Defence.

[6] Taken from the French *Jeanne qui Pleure et Jeanne qui Rit* of MM. Dumanoir and A de Keranion ; done at the Gymnase Dramatique, April 4th, 1860. Mrs. Charles Mildmay, Miss Herbert ; Florence, Patti Josephs ; Niobe, Adeline Cottrell ; an army surgeon, Arthur Stirling ; Mrs. Frank Matthews was old Mrs. Mildmay ; and Frank Matthews, Decimus Dockett. [I used the same situation in my little play, *The Cape Mail.*—C. S.]

Parliament is opened with much excitement, the public looking forward to the marriage of the Prince of Wales with Princess Alexandra. Write account of the funeral of the poor little ballet girls, and contribute my mite towards the subscription. 7*th.*—Surrey, to see Shepherd's version of ' Heart of Midlothian ; '[1] well got up, but not remarkable for construction. 13*th.*—*Fun* office £3. *Era* £1 15*s.* Second instalment from Falconer for Drury pantomime, £25. 19*th.* —A glance at New Royalty, *Effie Deans.*[2] Princess's, *Winning Suit,*[3] not bad. Then to Alhambra : see Verrick, another horrible acrobat, bending his neck back—sickening sight! 23*rd.*—Arrange for first deposit of £50 in London and Westminster Bank as a nest egg. *Bonnie Dundee,*[4] a Scotch spectacle, produced at Drury Lane by Falconer : a failure. 27*th.*—Mr. Edward Levy calls, and I agree to write the Gravesend account for the *Daily Telegraph* of the Princess's landing. 28*th.*—To St. James's, and see adaptation of ' Lady Audley's Secret ' :[5] not badly done ; scenery, by Beverley, very good indeed."

" *March 7th.*—The Princess Alexandra of Denmark arrives ; see the landing from Terrace pier, with Press celebrities and Prince of Wales ; write *Era* account, and up all night over

---

[1] This was called *Effie Deans, the Lily of St. Leonard's.* Mrs. Eburne, Jeanie ; Mrs. Emma Robberds, Effie ; Miss G. Pauncefort, Madge Wildfire ; Mr. Gourlay, the Scotch comedian, was the Laird of Dumbiedikes, and sang " The Laird o' Cockpen " well.

[2] This piece was called *The Scotch Sisters ;* or, *The Trials of Jeanie and Effie Deans.* Fanny Clifford, Jeanie ; Julia Walmisley, Effie ; H. Fraser, David Deans ; Russell, Laird of Dumbiedikes ; Miss Plucknett and Mrs. Russell, Madge Wildfire and Meg Murdochson.

[3] By Lewis Filmore, known as the translator of Goethe's *Faust.* Amy Sedgwick, Orelia ; Herman Vezin, Roderic ; Henry Marston, Pedro ; W. H. Stephens, King of Castille.

[4] Or, *The Gathering of the Clans.* Edmund Phelps, Graham of Claverhouse ; Mrs. E. Falconer, Janet ; Henry Loraine, Alastor McDonald ; Charles Selby, M'Ian ; Miss Hudson, Elspat ; Miss Wentworth, Jessie. It was principally spectacular.

[5] Mr. George Roberts, George Walters, adapted Miss Braddon's novel. Miss Herbert was excellent as Lady Audley ; Frank Matthews was the Luke Marks ; Arthur Stirling, Robert Audley ; Gaston Murray, George Talboys ; Simpson, Sir Michael Audley ; Miss Cottrell, Alice Audley ; Ada Dyas, Phœbe,

four columns for *Daily Telegraph* ; begin at midnight, and at 10 next morning deliver copy. *9th.—Daily Telegraph* comes out with supplement, which, 1*d.* with paper, find sells the amount of 205,884 copies! Unprecedented. At night bonfires all over the place. *13th.*—From *Telegraph* office £6 6*s.* for the hard week's work past. *Era* paragraphs £2 5*s.* *19th.* —From Sketchley £1, *Era* £1 10*s.*, and *Fun* £4. To Olympic and see clever adaptation by Horace Wigan of *Taming a Truant.*[1] To Haymarket: Wild's benefit, and see *début* of Ellen Terry in *Little Treasure*!!![2] *21st.*—Record the death of Charles Selby, who died this morning.[3] Balance from Falconer for Drury £26, pantomime having gone seventy-six nights. Settle on story, *The White Cat,* for next year."

"*April 4th.*—Attend General Theatrical Fund Dinner: Charles Dickens in chair; about two hundred present; goes off well; write notice. *Monday, 6th.*—Attend Strand: Byron's burlesque of *Ali Baba,* or, *The Thirty-nine Thieves;* goes off well. *10th.*—*Fun* £2, and *Era* copy £2. At night

---

[1] Taken from *La Papillone* by Sardou. Miss Hughes, Aurelia Howard; Miss Latimer, Florence Flutter; Henry Neville, Flutter; W. Gordon, Captain Pertinax; Horace Wigan, Blush.

[2] This was a memorable night, for Miss Ellen Terry made her adult London *début* as Gertrude, having come from the Theatres Royal, Bristol and Bath. This is what E. L. B. said of her :—" Is very young, but shows no trace of immaturity either in her style or figure. Tall for her age, of prepossessing appearance, and with expressive features full of vivacity and intelligence, she secured at once the sympathies of her audience, and retained them by the joyous spirit and deep feeling with which she imbued the personation. In the girlish playfulness exhibited through the first act Miss Ellen Terry was especially happy, and in characters illustrative of a frank and impulsive temperament the young actress will prove a most desirable addition to the feminine strength of the dramatic corps." [It was not her *début,* for she had played as a child, as Mamillius in the *Winter's Tale* at the Princess's, under Charles Kean.—O. S.]

[3] He was in his sixty-second year, and was as favourably known as a light dramatist as he was as an actor. He joined Mr. Macready at Drury Lane in 1842. Was for a considerable time a member of the Adelphi and Lyceum companies, and shone most in character parts. His farces were favourably received at almost every theatre. His last appearance was as M'Ian in *Bonnie Dundee,* at Drury Lane.

to Yates's entertainment; spirit-rapping skit a failure, rest good.[1] To Princess's and see Byron's *Haidee*,[2] a prettily got up but confusedly constructed extravaganza. *16th.*—Go to Haymarket: Telbin's panorama; very good, prefaced by Coyne's sketch[3]—average. Sorry to hear of the death of James Rogers;[4] write memoir. *17th.*—Shown by night the *Telegraph* at full work; ten feeders to each machine, 270 a minute; see the casting operation, all done by Italians; very interesting. *23rd.*—At St. John's Gate: Shakespeare dinner, John Oxenford in chair, Coyne in vice; about forty-five sit down; I give the old song of 'St. George,' and respond to the toast of 'Literature and the Press.'"

"*May 1st.*—Write letter to Mr. Levy, accepting engagement offered on *Daily Telegraph*. *6th.*—At night to Haymarket: Countess of Gifford's (Lady Dufferin's) comedy *Finesse*; or, *Spy and Counterspy*; not very brilliant, but successful.[5] *22nd.*—Description of dreary Derby Day for *Era*

---

[1] [This was at the Egyptian Hall, in conjunction with his friend Harold Power.—C. S.]

[2] This was called *Beautiful Haidee*. Miss Patty Oliver in the title *rôle*; Miss Murray, Lord Bateman.

[3] This was a holiday piece called *Buckstone at Home; or, The Manager and His Friends*. It was a sketch after the manner of Planché's *The New Haymarket Spring Meeting*. The panorama that was introduced represented the principal points in the Prince of Wales's Eastern tour, and an illustration of the marriage scene at Windsor.

[4] James Rogers was born in 1821, and was intended for an engraver, but joined Mr. George Wild at the Olympic in 1841. He made a hit in E. L. B.'s drama, *The Road of Life*. He soon made his mark as a burlesque actor, and had parts specially written for him. One of his great characters was the Post Boy, in Craven's drama of that name. He visited America for a short time in 1857, and then joined the Lyceum company. He was best known perhaps as a favourite at the Strand, in all the burlesques produced there. Was buried in Brompton Cemetery.

[5] On the 18th of this month a benefit in aid of the widow of the late James Rogers was given at Drury Lane. The application for seats was so great that the whole of the space generally occupied by the orchestra and half of the pit were converted into stalls. The programme consisted of *Retained for the Defence*, played by members of the Savage Club. Lionel Brough, Pawkins; Leicester Buckingham, Whitewash; W. H. Prowse, Thwaites; H. J. Byron, Fergusson.

£3 5s., and *Fun* £1 15s.   To Olympic: Neville's benefit

Augusta Wilton made her *début* in this.   Arthur Sketchley gave *Mrs. Brown at the Play.*   Webster appeared in *One Touch of Nature*; J. L. Toole and Paul Bedford in a scene from *The Green Bushes*; Creswick in a scene from *Hamlet.*   The Strand company in the farce of *My Preserver*; and Widdicombe and J. G. Shore in the farce of *The Two Poults.*   During the evening Miss Patty Oliver delivered the following address written by E. L. B :—

> " Ere yet more pleaders in this cause appear,
> I, for a moment, ask a listening ear.
> As one who often held that Actor's hand,
> Who sent the roar of laughter through the Strand ;
> And watched the kindling of the light of mirth
> From eyes that now have looked their last on earth ;
> I, too,—a sister of the art—would crave
> Your leaves to throw a wreath upon his grave. -

> " You have heard—some know—the story of his life,
> That brief existence with afflictions rife ;
> How to the last he struggled with the foe,
> Whose shadow darker nightly seemed to grow ;—
> Still smiling through his sufferings, and though wrung
> By quivering pain, a jest still on his tongue.
> *He* had cause indeed to wish the play had power
> To ' ease the anguish of the torturing hour.'
> Shall it be said, the man who bravely fought
> Life's battle out, no noble lesson taught ?
> No ! 'twas a hero's sermon for the age,
> Preached from the Players' pulpit of the Stage.

> " This fortitude in bearing sorrows shown
> Enabled others to forget their own ;
> How many a care he banished from their mind,
> How many hearts he gladdened, left behind ;
> He from the saddest laughter could beguile,
> The dullest left his presence with a smile.
> Though broad Burlesque his later path attended,
> To gross extravagance he ne'er descended—
> The proper range of humour well he knew,
> Kept strict decorum constantly in view.
> Quaint and original in each design,
> The truthful artist filled up every line.

> " You have felt, like us, 'twere idle tears to shed,
> To help the living is to mourn the dead ;
> Those whom he laboured for demand our care,
> In our remembrance of to-night they share.

—Claude Melnotte ;[1] write notice. *25th.*—Take Walter to pay his first deposit into savings bank, 10*s.* Record death of General Stonewall Jackson—a heavy Confederate loss, and deeply to be regretted. *27th.*—Hear of Swanborough's[2] sudden death ; Strand Theatre closed. Go to Olympic : see first night of clever piece by Tom Taylor called *The Ticket-of-Leave Man* ;[3] goes off well, and admirably acted. *29th.*—*Era* copy £3, and *Fun* £2. *Daily Telegraph* £2 2*s.*, and arrange to begin regularly ; complimented by Mr. Levy on the past. Go to Cremorne with Belford and see my piece *Bridal of Beauty*, and receive for balance £15."

" *June 4th.*—Night to Haymarket : slow farce, *Unlucky Mortal.* *6th.*—From *Daily Telegraph*, for first week on staff, £3 3*s.* *8th.*—Dear mother's birthday, aged seventy-nine. Attend Princess's,[4] Adelphi, and Strand, writing notices afterwards of each. *11th.*—To Haymarket, and see indifferent

> If we cannot recall the one so gifted
> To raise our spirits, *theirs* can be uplifted ;
> Your presence here will give those hearts relief,
> Your sympathy assuage their bitter grief.
> For service to a woman thus bereaved
> From woman's lips be gratitude received.
> So take for one missed sadly from our ranks
> The Actors' tribute, and the Widow's thanks."

The benefit realized £350.

[1] Henry Neville was much admired as Claude Melnotte ; Pauline, Kate Saville ; the *bénéficiaire's* father, General Damas ; Mrs. Stephens, Madame Deschappelles ; Mrs. Leigh Murray, Widow Melnotte.

[2] H. V. Swanborough, sen., who committed suicide while suffering from mental depression.

[3] It was in this that Henry Neville was the original and best Bob Brierly that has been seen, frequently as it has been acted by others. Atkins, James Dalton ; G. Vincent, Melter Moss ; Kate Saville, May Edwards ; Horace Wigan, Hawkshaw the detective ; Maclean, Mr. Gibson ; Fanny Hughes, Emily St. Evremond ; R. Soutar, Green Jones ; Mrs. Stephens, Mrs. Willoughby ; Miss Raynham, Sam Willoughby ; Harwood Cooper, Maltby. [The play was adapted by Tom Taylor, from a French play by Brisbarre, called *Leonard.*—C. S.]

[4] At the Princess's, *Court and Camp*, an adaptation by G. Roberts of *Les Premiers Amours.* At the Adelphi *The Willow Copse* was revived ; J. L. Toole, Augustus de Rosherville. At the Strand *Aladdin* was revived ; Miss Jenny White made her first appearance in London in it.

adaptation by Burnand and Williams called *Easy Shaving.*
18*th.*—Hear from C. C. B. from Otago, dated April 18th. To
Princess's and see Walter Montgomery make his first appearance in London as Othello:[1] not at all striking. 24*th.*—
Princess's, seeing Mademoiselle Stella Colas[2] make a London
début as Juliet—decided success. 26*th.*—From Lindus,
Princess's pantomime, £10 on account. To St. James's
Hall : the first and only reading of the Keans, prior to their
departure for Australia.[3] Meet dear friends Kent, father and
son."

" *July* 1*st.*—Licensed Victuallers' School Dinner at
Cremorne ; hear my address indifferently spoken by the
boys. Write introduction, etc., for paper. See mediocre
comedy drama by John Brougham, *While there's Life there's
Hope,* produced at the Strand. 10*th.*—To Adelphi ; see
Haunted Man and burlesque of *Il Trovatore;* Toole in
both excellent. 11*th.*—Record death of Distin.[4] 16*th.*—To
Strand, seeing new burlesque of the motto, *I am ' All there,'*
by Byron ; very good."

" *Aug.* 1*st.*—Dine at Anerley with *Telegraph* people
(eighth anniversary) ; Edward Levy in chair ; 115 present ;
back by eleven in waggonette, having proposed chairman's
health and sung ' Honourable Ted.' 7*th.*—Appalled by
intelligence about the Globe Printing Company, which

[1] Ellen Terry was the Desdemona ; Henry Marston, Iago ; Miss
Atkinson, Emilia ; C. Verner, Cassio : Robert Roxby, Roderigo.

[2] Stella Colas came from the Théâtre Français, and had made her
name in St. Petersburg as well. She played with comparatively little
French accent, and she had all the advantages of youth, a pretty, expressive face, graceful figure, and a very rich voice. She had studied
under Ryder. Whether in the balcony or the tragic scenes, she was
equally graceful. Walter Montgomery was the Romeo; George Vining,
Mercutio.

[3] This was in aid of the Shakespeare Fund, which was established in
1861 for the purchase of various interesting relics relating to Shakespeare at Stratford-on-Avon. The Keans read scenes from *King John;*
Charles Kean recited the " Execution of Montrose " and Macaulay's
" Horatius Cocles," and Mrs. Charles Kean, Hood's " Bridge of Sighs."

[4] John Distin, sen., died July 8th, aged sixty-nine. Was a celebrated
cornet player, and also manufacturer of brass instruments.

quite upsets me.   17*th.*—Go to Strand to see farce by T. J. Williams, called *Turn Him Out;* practical fun. 22*nd.*—Go to Princess's; the theatre opens to Walter Montgomery's Shylock in *Merchant of Venice;* his management not good.   24*th.*—Go to Adelphi; Mrs. Stirling's return in new drama of *Hen and Chickens.*   31*st.*—To Olympic; first appearance here of Miss Lydia Foote[1] (real name Legge), niece of Mrs. Keeley; and to New Royalty opening, under Mrs. Selby's management; a French adaptation of one of Selby's singularly bad farces."[2]

"*Sept. 4th.—Seeing Wright.*   Sadlers Wells reopens for winter season, under Miss Marriott's management, with *Love's Sacrifice;* very fairly played.   *Monday, 7th.*—Go to Olympic; Tom Taylor's *Awful Rise in Spirits;* an exceedingly bad piece, that elsewhere would have been hooted. 10*th.*—Settle with Greenwood about pantomime for Princess's.   Find a letter from Nelson Lee, requesting an address for his opening at City.—12*th.*—Woodin and his wife come about entertainment.   To Drury; opening of season; new comedy, *Nature's above Art;*[3] very foggy and feeble. *Monday,* 14*th.*—To Adelphi and Surrey; new comedian (Wood)—not great—at former, and (Wallace)[4] *The Scottish Chief,* a repolished play, at latter.   21*st.*—Go to see new piece at Strand by Bridgeman, called *Where's your Wife?* the

---

[1] She appeared as May Edwards in the *Ticket-of-Leave Man* and made a great success.   She had previously appeared at Sadlers Wells and the Victoria.

[2] This was a piece called *Court Gallants.*   There was also a *ballet divertissement* in which Rosina Wright danced well, and concluded with a burletta called *The Pirates of Putney.*   In this Jenny Wilmore and Ada Cavendish made their *débuts* in London.   The company was composed of a number of new people, and was spoken of as a nursery for promising talent.

[3] Or, *A Romance of the Nursery;* a three-act comedy by E. Falconer. The theatre was re-opened under his management in conjunction with F. B. Chatterton.   The company included Ryder, G. Belmore, Walter Lacy, Addison, Miss Murray, Rose Leclercq, Charlotte Saunders, Mrs. E. Falconer, Barrett, F. Charles, and Kate Harfleur.

[4] This was played by Anderson with Fernandez as Douglass, and on the same evening Thomas Thorne appeared as Peter Spyke with Miss Esther Jacobs as Gertrude in *A Loan of a Lover.*

re-opening of the Haymarket—much improved ; [1] then new drama at Drury by Burnand—*The Deal Boatman.*[2] 25th.— Greenwood, arranging pantomime ; then Dykwynkyn ; then Woodin and worry—so the morning goes. To Adelphi ; Webster's annual benefit ; *Masks and Faces* ; Mrs. Stirling playing admirably. 28th.—At Princess's ; and see new burlesque at New Royalty, by Burnand, called *Ixion.*[3] Have to look in at Haymarket besides."

"*Oct. 1st.*—To Adelphi ; Miss Bateman [4] as Leah ; house crowded. Find the child has grown up a fine young woman. *2nd.*—Go to Marylebone Theatre, meeting Sefton Parry. See there *The Ghost*, without glass illusion. *3rd.*—Dine at Arundel. Look in at City of London,[5] opening night of season ; hear my address fairly spoken, and see a bit of *Peep of Day*, and hosts of people. *5th.*—Woke at 3 a.m. by a shock of earthquake, which was felt all through England. *9th.*—Strand in evening ; new piece ; good : H. T. Craven's *Miriam's Crime.* *12th.*—Opening of Royal English Opera ; Wallace's *Desert Flower* ; a very mild affair, but well received. *26th.*—To Haymarket. Charles Mathews's reappearance, in *Cool as a Cucumber* ; after Parisian triumphs plays admirably, and looks wonderfully fresh. *31st.*—To Lyceum. First night of Fechter's second season ; *Bel Demonio.*[6] "

[1] Re-opened with *Charles XII.*; *The Bengal Tiger*; and *Founded on Facts.*

[2] This was spoken of as creditable to Mr. Burnand, it being his first attempt at serious dramatic composition. George Belmore excellent as Jacob Vance, a Robsonian character ; Rose Leclercq, Mary Vance.

[3] Or, *The Man at the Wheel.* Jenny Wilmore in the title *rôle.* Ada Cavendish, Venus ; David James, Mercury ; Joseph Robins, Ganymede ; Felix Rogers, Minerva. It was a great success.

[4] This was the elder of the Bateman children who had made a sensation as child-actors here. Miss Bateman had returned to America and there gained experience. Her performance of Leah was universally considered great. Her delivery of the curse was actually blood-curdling.

[5] It was opened by Nelson Lee. J. F. Young spoke the address.

[6] Fechter had introduced fresh mechanical appliances to the stage, and some patented improvements, and generally bettered the arrangements behind the footlights. *Bel Demonio, a Love Story* was a new version, by John Brougham, of the French drama *L'Abbaye de Castro,*

" *Nov. 2nd.*—To Drury; new farce by Oxenford, after 'Manfred;' *Beauty or the Beast*[1] a wild adaptation of an outrageous French farce, but goes off well. *6th.*—*The Singing Goat*—a new piece at Haymarket—and *Bull in China Shop;* go, and find it exceedingly bad. *10th.*—To Sadlers Wells; Westland Marston's new play, *Pure Gold;*[2] nicely written, but with few exceptions execrably acted. *13th.*—Write pantomime for Princess's, *Old Woman who lived in a Shoe;* or, *Harlequin Tom Tucker. 14th.*—Evening, Haymarket; translation by Leicester Buckingham *Silken Fetters;*[3] success moderate. *Monday, 16th.*—Surrey, *Game of Life;* or, *Swallows of Paris.* Hear from New Zealand. *25th.*—Hear of the death of Robson, 'the old playgoer.'[4] Then to Strand; burlesque by Burnand, *Patient Penelope;* or, *The Return of Ulysses;*[5] short, but a success."

" *Dec. 4th.*—Read pantomime to Falconer, Chatterton, and

which had already been dramatized under the title of *The Broken Vow,* and was played at the Olympic Feb. 17th, 1851. Fechter played Angelo ; Miss Kate Terry, Lena; G. Jordan, Count Campéreali ; Emery, Ranuccio ; F. Charles, Fabio ; Miss Elsworthy, the Countess. *Bel Demonio* was preceded by *Uncle Baby,* a comedietta by W. Gilbert, in which H. Widdicomb, Carlotta and P. Leclercq, J. G. Shore, and F. Charles appeared.

[1] Taken from *Ma Nièce et Mon Ours.*

[2] Henry Marston, Frank Rochford ; Miss Mandlebert, Mrs. Rochford ; Mrs. Buckingham White, Miss Fortescue ; Edmund Phelps, Sir Gerard Fane ; Miss Marriott, Evelyn.

[3] This was taken from Scribe's *La Chaine* played at the Théâtre Français in 1841, and also had been previously done at the Adelphi in 1842, under the title of *The Breach of Promise of Marriage.* Mr. and Mrs. Charles Mathews, W. Farren, Howe, Maria Harris, and Chippendale were in the cast. Maria Harris had been playing very charmingly in this as Clara Hazelton, and in the title *rôle* of T. J. Williams's comedietta *Little Daisy.*

[4] He obtained this *sobriquet* from having written an interesting book called "The Old Playgoer" in which he stood up for the Kemble school of acting. He was originally a schoolmaster, and wrote several educational works, and also contributed to periodical literature. His great companion was Mr. Caulfield, the author of "Wonderful and Eccentric Characters."

[5] Suggested by *Le Retour d'Ulysse.* Eurymachus, Maria Simpson ; Medron, Charles Fenton ; Penelope, Ada Swanborough ; Ulysses, G. Honey.

Roxby, of *Sindbad the Sailor*.[1] All seem satisfied. 15*th.*—From E. T. S. on account £20, for *Chaucer; or, John of Gaunt.* 28*th.*—Good notices in all the papers. 29*th.*—Write to my old friend Kent, now proprietor of the *Sun* newspaper, giving him my annual New Year's greetings. 31*st.*—Write column for *Era,* then a host of New Year congratulations to everybody. Then a sad hour of *solus* meditation, recalling the memories of the few, very few pleasures I have had in my life, and reading old articles of the season I wrote in *Chambers' London Journal* twenty years ago. Thus see out the Old Year, which, bringing me a larger income than yet recorded, has brought me more work to earn it and more to support out of it. But for the health therein enjoyed, and for the fortitude that has enabled me to bear up against troubles almost unparalleled,. I here give the Great Ruler over our destinies heartfelt thanks."

Estimated revenue for year £370 18*s.*

1864.

" *Friday, Jan.* 1*st.*—Go to Astley's with Clement Scott; opening fair, but not carried out.[2] To *Daily Telegraph* for arrears, £6 6*s.*, when proposition is made for permanent engagement on leader staff,—to consider. 8*th.*—The Princess of Wales has a son at 9 p.m. *Era,* £1 5*s.*, and Lindus,

---

[1] *Sindbad the Sailor; or, The Great Roc of the Diamond Valley, and the Seven Wonders of the World.* Young England, Miss Rose Leclercq; Ali Ben Rumfiz, Tom Matthews; El'Eb-Nee, Mr. Fitz James; Sindbad, Lizzie Wilmore. Clowns, Harry Boleno and C. Lauri; pantaloons, J. Morris and Mr. Barnes; harlequins, Cormack and Saville; columbines, Madame Boleno and the Misses Gunniss. In the opening, the scenery of which was painted by W. Beverley, there were no less than nine magnificent tableaux, and in the harlequinade, so different to modern pantomime, there were nine different scenes, winding up with another grand tableaux.

[2] *Harlequin and Friar Bacon ; or, Great Grim John of Gaunt and the Enchanted Lance of Robin Goodfellow,* by "Francisco Frost."—E. L. B. Oberon, Miss Nisbett; Chaucer, Miss Craven ; Harlequin, W. Driver; Columbine, Miss Newham ; Harlequina, Miss Nelly Davis; Pantaloon,

balance of pantomime, £16 ; *Daily Telegraph*, £3 3*s.*, and
Fun office, £1. Meet T. W. Robertson,—his birthday, thirty-
five,—and afterwards read his graphic theatrical sketches.[1]
Go to Drury, and see a dreary piece, three acts, by Falconer,
called *Night and Morning;* very bad,—say so.[2] *Monday,*
11*th.*—Second deposit in Westminster Bank of £50. Attend
St. James's ; appearance of Charles Mathews in *Love Letter.*[3]
To Strand, and see bad farce of *Margate Sands.*[4] 22*nd.*—
From Greenwood, £50. Go to Doughty Street, and meet
Mr. and Mrs. Byron, Price, Mr. and Miss Levy, etc.[5] Most
agreeably entertained ; an evening to be remembered. 26*th.*
—During a walk to Gad's Hill meet Charles Dickens on my
way, pedestrianizing like myself, and mutual recognitions."

" *Feb.* 1*st.*—At night to the Strand : new comedietta of
Unlimited Confidence; very good.[6] 4*th.*—To Egyptian Hall ;
see Arthur Sketchley make his appearance in *Paris*, which

Stilt ; Clown, Edwin Edwards, well known on the Continent and at
Olympic, some years previously. Music arranged by Tully. [I was
appointed dramatic critic to the *Sunday Times* on July 20th, 1863.
This was one of my first professional visits to the play with E. L. B.—
C. S.]

[1] Probably on the *Illustrated Times.*—C. S.

[2] No similarity to Bulwer Lytton's novel. Julian di Vivaldi, Phelps ;
Princess Olympia, Miss Heath (afterwards Mrs. Wilson Barrett);
Ninetta, Miss Murray (afterwards Mrs. Samuel Brandram) ; Santoni,
a monk, John Ryder ; Duchess of Ferrara, Miss Atkinson ; scene laid
i n Italy. Phelps poor in his part.

[3] *Adventures of a Love Letter.* Charles Mathews's adaptation of
Sardou's *Pattes de Mouche,* was done at Drury Lane in 1860, by Mr.
and Mrs. Charles Mathews, as Major Blunt and Catherine Bright ;
Mrs. Frank Matthews, Mr. Wagstaffe ; Misses Fanny Josephs, Emma
Waterpark and Cottrell, H. J. Montague, Arthur Clinton and J. John-
stone also in the cast.

[4] By W. Hancock. Adolphus Pilkington, Belford ; Carnation
Curleycrop, A. Wood—plot turns on exchange of clothes after bathing ; better done by George Wild and James Rogers in James
Brunton's farce, *Bathing*, at the Olympic twenty years before. The
same idea occurs in the modern French play, *Niniche.*

[5] [The Levys, Byrons, and Yateses, all lived in Doughty Street.—C. S.]

[6] By A. C. Troughton. Miss Jefferson, Miss L. Thorne ; Florence,
Marie Wilton (excellent as a reputed young widow) ; Lieut. Hilliard,
Parselle ; Col. Dacres, Belford.

is likely to be popular.[1] 11*th.*—Hear of Sothern's accident—thrown from horse—and write paragraph for *Era* about it, very sorrowfully.[2] 15*th.*—To Princess's: new comedy by Watts Phillips, called *Paul's Return*, which is a success.[3] To Surrey ; see drama called *Ashore and Afloat*, with very strong effects.[4] From Drury, second cheque of £25. Go to Polygraphic Hall and see Grace Egerton (Mrs. Case).[5] 25*th.*[6]—Go to Royalty, and delighted with Theresa Furtado, representative of Ixion ;[7] then look in at Her Majesty's, and see the last act of *Faust* in English.[8] 27*th.*—To Princess's, and see the brothers Henry and Charles Webb appear as the two Dromios in *Comedy of Errors :* a decided success."

"*Monday, March 7th.*—Go to Drury : fresh bill, *Manfred* revived, and *The Alabama*, by J. M. Morton, altered from his

[1] This was a sketch of an excursion to Paris, in which the Griggs's and Mrs. Brown are prominent. The panoramic illustrations by Matthew Morgan, hitherto only known as a designer of cartoons, were specially commended.

[2] Sothern would ride all sorts of horses ; this accident happened on the 9th in Hyde Park—he injured his shoulder very much. The Haymarket was closed that night in consequence of his being unable to appear.

[3] Richard Goldsworthy, George Vining ; Abel Honeydew, David Fisher ; Beatrice Goldsworthy, Kate Saville ; Lieut. Herbert, H. Forester ; a domestic comedy.

[4] The effects were a sea-fight, and the descent into a mine. Hal Oakford, Shepherd ; Newton Barnard, J. Fernandez ; Ruth Ringrose, Miss G. Pauncefort ; Abel Ringrose, C. Foster ; Joshua Boynton, J. W. Ray (first appearance here) ; Algerine Pirate, C. Butler. [Thomas Thorne highly spoken of for his humour in a mariner's part. He chaffed " Dick Shepherd " dreadfully throughout the play, but got all the laughs.—C. S.]

[5] She appeared in two sketches entitled *A Drawing-room Floor*, and *The Wizard of the East*, and assumed a number of characters, male and female.

[6] On this date Ellen Alice Terry (Miss Ellen Terry) married G. F. Watts, the celebrated R.A.

[7] Burnand's burlesque, *Ixion ;* or, *The Man at the Wheel*, had reached its 130th performance.

[8] Santley, Mephistopheles ; Lyall, Valentine ; Swift, Faust (Sims Reeves indisposed) ; Mdme. Lemmens-Sherington, Margaret ; Florence Lancia, Siebel ; Mdme. Jaccani, Martha ; Dussek, Wagner.

own farce, *The Spitfire.*[1] *8th.*—A visit from Toole, who sings for
the first time in London my old song of 'A Norrible Tale,'
in farce of *Area Belle*, last night: a success 11th![2] *21st.*—
Look in at Adelphi: Webster in *Dead Heart*; then to
Montgomery's readings at St. James' Hall.[3] To Woodin's: his
first night of *Elopement Extraordinary*[4] and *Bachelor's Box:*[5]
a decided success—the best thing he has yet done. *24th.*—
Theatrical Fund Dinner, nineteenth anniversary; hear Miss
Poole sing 'Wapping Old Stairs' again: a great treat.[6] *28th.*
—To Drury, and see the revival of *Henry IV.* (first part);
Phelps good as Falstaff, but, beyond the rush of supers at
the end, not very expensively produced. *29th.*—To Haymarket; see Burnand's new burlesque of *Venus and Adonis:*
cleverly written, but ineffective in representation."[7]

[1] The caste was the same as already seen at the theatre, including
Phelps, Poole, Ryder, Misses Cicely Nott, Rose Leclercq, Heath, etc.
Percy Roselle appeared in *The Four Mowbrays*, in which he played
four characters and sang some songs. This play was seen at the
Adelphi in 1831, under the title of *Young and Old.* Miss Poole, as a
child, made a hit in a similar character to that little Roselle now played.
In *Alabama* Lydia Thompson played Phœbe; G. Belmore, Christo-
pher Clipper. *The Spitfire* was originally played at the English Opera
House, September, 1837. Miss P. Horton as Phœbe.

[2] After a long illness at Blandford, in Dorsetshire, surrounded by
his wife and family, on Friday, March 11th, 1864, died Sam Cowell, a
descendant of the Siddons and Kemble families. Began life as a singer
and member of Theatre Royal, Edinburgh. Then joined Adelphi and
Princess's, sang with Sims Reeves under Bunn's management at Covent
Garden, and before Her Majesty at Windsor. Gave concerts in the
United Kingdom. He bore the reputation of being the originator of
Music Halls, and certainly first drew attention to the Canterbury,
where he was a great favourite. He was afterwards, for a long time,
at Evans's, where he made large sums. He had been a bankrupt, and
died in distress, leaving his family totally unprovided for.

[3] Walter Montgomery, the actor, gave selections from Shakespeare,
Hood, Tennyson, Macaulay, and the " Ingoldsby Legends."

[4] By John Oxenford.

[5] By Tom W. Robertson.

[6] Shirley Brooks in the chair. Buckstone spoke for the General
Theatrical Fund; Mark Lemon for the Drama and Dramatic Literature. B. Webster proposed chairman's health.

[7] Miss Snowden, Jupiter; Coe, Pluto; H. Compton, Vulcan; W.
Farren, Mercury; Caroline Hill, Apollo; Fanny Wright, Bacchus;
Henrietta Lindley, Proserpine; Clark, Até; Nelly Moore (from

"*April 1st.*—Write obituary account of my respected friend George Daniel, who died on Wednesday, aged seventy-four, whose memoir I never expected to write.[1] *Monday, 4th.*—This day dies the veteran T. P. Cooke, aged seventy-eight.[2] Garibaldi at Southampton ; great reception and excitement. *8th.*—Write memoir of T. P. Cooke, and hear afterwards of the death of Charles James, the bright scenic artist, and my friend : delighted to hear this is a false report. *9th.*—Find myself booked for the Garibaldi business for the *D. T.* 11*th.*

Theatre Royal, Manchester, and from St. James's), Venus ; Louise Keeley, Adonis ; James Rogers (from Strand), Aurora. Oscar Byrne arranged a wonderful *sabot* and other ballets for it. Miss Snowden afterwards became Mrs. Chippendale.

[1] George Daniel, the Director-General of Cumberland's *British Theatre*, was born in London, September 16th, 1789, and died at his son's house, The Grove, Stoke Newington, March 30th, 1864. As early as the year 1805 he published " Stanzas on Lord Nelson's Victory and Death." In 1812 endeavours were made to suppress his " Royal Stripes ; or, A Kick from Yarmouth to Wales," it being very telling against the Prince Regent, and £10 was offered for a single copy. He was the author of several works—a three-volume novel, " The Adventures of Dick Distich " (written before he was eighteen). His burlesque, *Doctor Bolus*, was produced at the Lyceum in 1818 ; his musical farce; *The Disagreeable Surprise*, Drury Lane, 1819; and *Sworn at Highgate*, in 1833. He became editor of Cumberland's *Minor and British Theatre* in 1825, and edited the entire sixty-four volumes. He contributed largely to magazines. Used for years to dine at the Sir Hugh Myddelton, and was a prominent member of the Urban Club.

[2] Thomas Potter Cooke was the son of a surgeon, and born in Titchfield Street, Marylebone, April 23rd, 1786. Joined the Royal Navy in H.M.S. *Raven*, in 1796 ; was a sharer in Earl St. Vincent's victory ; was wrecked off Cuxhaven, and afterwards joined *The Prince of Wales*. He left the navy after the Peace of Amiens, and joined the dramatic profession in January 1804, at the Royalty Theatre, and subsequently was a member of Astley's, the Lyceum (under Laurent, the clown) ; and then went to Dublin. In 1809 he was at the Surrey, and made his first appearance at Drury Lane, October 19th, 1816, as Diego in *The Watchword ; or, The Quito Gate ;* went to Covent Garden, October 1822. He first played Long Tom Coffin in *The Pilot*, at the Adelphi, October 1825, and William in *Black-eyed Susan*, June 6th, 1829. His last appearance was on March 29th, 1860, as William, at Covent Garden, for the Dramatic College Benefit. His most celebrated characters he acted the following number of times :—William, 785 ; Long Tom Coffin, 562 ; the Monster in *Frankenstein* and the Vampire (this character he also played in 1826, at the Porte St. Martin,

—Up early, and off to Nine Elms, in carriage arranged for by Macdermott of the *Morning Post*, to write the triumphant entry of Garibaldi into London: Woods, *Times;* Murphy, *Daily News.* Narrow escape on return,—post-chaise upset, and self scarred and shaken. Five hours on the road from Vauxhall to Stafford House, amidst millions of people the whole way: emphatically the greatest sight ever witnessed. Write notice with difficulty at office; not in bed till the morning. *12th.*—Find myself severely strained and sprained; receive a flattering recognition of the satisfactory result from the *Daily Telegraph.* Go to Drury after, and see a bad farce called *An April Fool.*[1] *21st.*—The Stratford Festival; off by 4.30 train, reach Stratford at 9. Rest at Red Horse, in next room to that of Washington Irving. Stroll to the Pavilion—magnificent building. Meet John O'Connor, of Haymarket, and Alfred Mellon. *22nd.*—Dine with Mr. Flower, the mayor,—very hospitably treated; then to Pavilion, write despatch for town; then home to Red Horse. *23rd.*—The Tercentenary Festival begins. Banquet at Pavilion; meet Edward Ledger with Massey; stop to see fireworks, which are very bad. Parkinson of *Daily News,* Macdermott of *Post,* Williams of *Standard.* See Shakespeare's house, meet Halliday, and general reunion. Write copy and send off parcel by train. *Monday, 25th.*—In for a busy week; *Messiah* in morning, concert at night. *26th.*—Off to Charlecote; see the old hall of the Lucys', and its park and pictures; send off a column about it, and then to see *Twelfth Night* at Pavilion.[2] *27th.*—Send copy for *Daily Telegraph;* then to

Paris), 365; Roderick Dhu, 250; Aubrey (*Dog of Montargis*), 250; Vanderdecken, 165; the Red Rover, 120; Poor Jack, 140; Luke, the Labourer, 181; My Poll and My Partner Joe, 269. He was the best representative of the British sailor ever seen on the stage; was a noble, kind-hearted man, and had the interest of the dramatic profession sincerely at heart. He was buried in Brompton Cemetery.

[1] By Brough and Halliday. Lydia Thompson, Robert Roxby, G. Belmore, and G. Weston in the cast.

[2] *Twelfth Night* was done by the members of the Haymarket company. Louisa Angel, Viola; Henrietta Lindley, Olivia; *My Aunt's Advice*—Sothern's version of "Pierron and Laferriere" (Livre II., Chapitre iii.)—followed: Sothern as Captain Howard Leslie. In *Comedy of Errors* H. and C. Webb were the two Dromios, and

Pavilion : *Comedy of Errors* and *Romeo and Juliet.* Back to Red Horse ; a strange tramp, Patrick O'Keith,—songs from Lover, and songs and recitations very good ; give him a line or two in *Daily Telegraph* afterwards, and hope to make him a subject for a special article. 28*th.*—To Pavilion, and *As You Like It.*[1] Take chair at our final supper to the Stratfordians. Off to town, going up with Compton, Gruneison, Robert Keeley. Go to Strand Theatre for Byron's burlesque of *Mazourka.*[2] Write Stratford copy at office ; to *Era*, and do ditto. 30*th.—Daily Telegraph*, two weeks, £6 6s. In evening to Haymarket: new three-act piece called *David Garrick*, by T. W. Robertson, from the French ; goes off well.[3] Stratford expenses paid, £10."

"*May 2nd.*—To St. James's: *Silver Lining*, and revived farce, *Out of Sight out of Mind ;* see Mathews playing Mr. Gatherwool. 11*th.*—To St. James's : new comedy called *The Fox Chase*,[4] by Boucicault, which proves to be a five-act farce, —diverting, but decidedly not an ' original ' comedy. 13*th.* Am sorry to record the death of William Searle, an excellent actor, who twenty-two years ago played admirably in my *Road of Life* and *Pork Chops.*[5] 16*th.*—Go to Strand ; new piece,

J. Nelson and Vining the Antipholi ; in *Romeo and Juliet* Stella Colas, Juliet ; J. Nelson, Romeo.

[1] Mrs. Charles Young, Rosalind ; Charlotte Saunders, Audrey ; Creswick, Jaques ; W. Farren, Orlando ; Chippendale, Adam.

[2] *Mazourka ;* or, *The Stick, the Pole, and the Tartar*, taken from *Le Diable à Quatre.* Maria Simpson, Mazourki ; Marie Wilton, Mazourka ; Eliza Johnstone, Count Tiddlewinki ; George Honey, the Countess ; David James, Turner, and C. Fenton also in the cast.

[3] The original cast was David Garrick, Sothern (in this he made his greatest success next to Dundreary) ; Simon Ingot, Chippendale ; Ada Ingot, Nelly Moore ; Squire Chevy, Buckstone ; Mrs. Smith. Mrs. Chippendale ; Araminta Brown, Mrs. E. Fitzwilliam. Rogers and Clarke were also in the cast.

[4] The idea was taken from the French *Sullivan.* Charles Mathews and Frank Matthews appeared in it.

[5] William Searle, born January 1816, first appeared at the Surrey under Osbaldiston ; from thence went to the Adelphi, and then joined the York and Norwich circuits. Made his first hit in London at the Strand, as Bats in Douglas Jerrold's *Perils of Pippins.* He then went to the Olympic, where he remained till 1844, and subsequently became

Maid of Honour, by J. P. Wooller: slight, but successful. Then to Olympic; Tom Taylor's "morality," *Sense and Sensation:* very dreary.[1] *17th.*—At night to Princess's; Dominic Murray, an Australian actor, in *Born to Good Luck:* fair, but nothing particular.[2] *18th.*—Go *solus* to Cremorne; find it dreary enough by one's self, but pleased with entertainment. See E. T. S., and from him receive £10, which I accept as payment in full for Astley's pantomime, as he has had severe losses this year. *20th.*—*Era*, £2, *Daily Telegraph*, £3 3s.; then to Freemasons' Tavern; Newspaper Press Dinner, inaugural festival; Lord Houghton in chair; meet hosts of Press people I know. Off at 8 o'clock to Lyceum to see Fechter's Hamlet;[3] not over till past midnight; then write notice for *Era*. *25th.*—Derby Day fine, and Blair Athol wins. Go down in landau with Gilbert, Howe, Church, King, and Montgomery; first time by the road, about which I have written for more than twenty years (!). Very fatiguing day's work; back by rail at 6, and at 9 get to *Telegraph*, where work till 2.30, getting about two columns done."

"*June 1st.*—In *Era* record with a sad heart the death of my old friend Phil Phillips.[4] *8th.*—Mother's birthday; after clearing up papers, go to Kensington, and celebrate her

stage-manager of the City of London and Astley's Theatres. Was an admirable "character" actor.

[1] Or, *The Seven Sisters of Thule*. It was a peculiar production, in which the seven cardinal virtues were supposed to combat the seven vices. It had a very strong cast, and C. Coghlan and Rignold made their first appearance in this theatre in it.

[2] He played Waverley Brown, and the next night Taddy O'Rafferty in *Born to Good Luck*.

[3] Kate Terry was the Ophelia; Miss Elsworthy, Queen Gertrude; Miss M. Henrade, the Actress; G. Jordan, the Ghost; G. F. Neville, Laertes; H. W. Widdicombe, First Gravedigger; Emery, Claudius. The scenery was magnificent.

[4] He died May 29th, 1864, aged sixty-two. Studied contemporarily with Clarkson Stanfield, and painted dioramas for the Surrey, when Davidge was manager. In 1839 he built and opened the Bower Saloon, in the grounds of the Duke's Arms Tavern, Stangate Street, Westminster, which he had purchased, for musical and pictorial entertainments; but they did not succeed. He subsequently became scenic artist to the Lyceum, Haymarket, and Adelphi Theatres. He accompanied the Queen to Ireland in 1849, and under Her Majesty's patronage took

attainment of an eightieth birthday by taking her (and Mrs. and Miss Hall) to Cremorne. *Monday*, 13*th.*—Pay Church my share (£3 8*s.*) of Derby Day expenses. Haymarket, new farce, *Lord Dundreary Married and Done for :* very slight affair ;[1] Adelphi, *Dead Heart ;* revival same cast. 19*th.*—Off to attend dinner of Dramatic Authors' Society at Gravesend (Ship) ; John Oxenford in chair, grouped with Stone, Buckingham, Webster, Wigan and Walter Gordon, Palgrave Simpson, Planché, Bernard, Burnand, Byron, etc. : a pleasant day. 20*th.*—To Olympic ; see revival of *Masaniello*, with Miss Raynham[2] as the hero, the piece suggesting a host of painful memories. 25*th.*—Attend piece by Oxenford from Casimir Delavigne, *The Monastery of St. Just*, at Princess's.[3] Have letter from *Stage*. To Princess's ; house crammed, and have to stand at back of boxes ; piece not over till 11.30. Then to chambers and write notice. 28*th.*—Shocked this morning to see the sudden death recorded of Washington Wilks, who died last night at public meeting."

" *July 6th.*—Buckstone's benefit at Haymarket, and last night of the season. Go to see old comic opera of *The Castle of Andalusia,* which goes off pretty well, but has a very old-fashioned look. 7*th.*—With Draper stroll through Covent Garden market, tasting bananas for first time, a vegetable

the " Chinese Gallery " at Hyde Park Corner, where he exhibited a panorama illustrative of the Irish tour. Mr. Phillips married the daughter of T. Rouse, of the Royal Grecian, in 1837 ; she was also a celebrated artist. Their pictures were hung at the Royal Academy and other exhibitions. He was much esteemed.

[1] By H. J. Byron, and had been done at Liverpool in the beginning of the year. My Lord is snubbed by every one of the characters except Asa Trenchard, and most of the characters of the original reappear—Abel Murcott as a reformed man.

[2] [Miss Raynham was a very remarkable impersonator of boys' characters. Her Sam Willoughby, in *The Ticket-of-Leave Man*, was unequalled.—C. S.]

[3] Produced in Paris in 1835 as *Don Juan d'Autriche ;* at Covent Garden, April 23rd, 1836, as *Don Juan of Austria*. John Dale and Helen Faucit principals. At Princess's Stella Colas doubled the parts of Donna Florinda de Sandoval, and Peblo, a boy-novice ; G. Vining, Philip II. ; Henry Marston, Charles V.; John Nelson, Juan ; J. W. Ray, Quexada ; Mrs. Henry Marston, the Duenna Dorothea.

sausage tasting like marrow flavoured with pine-apple. *9th.* —To *Daily Telegraph* office, and thence for two weeks and extras, £6 6*s.* In evening to St. James's : bad burlesque by Burnand, *Faust and Marguerite.*[1] *16th.*—Fifth Dramatic College Festival at Crystal Palace ; write account for *Daily Telegraph.*[2] *26th.*—Look out materials for life of Mrs. Wood (Miss Paton). Mother meets with serious fall, which keeps her in bed."

"*Monday, Aug. 1st.*—To Princess's, where see Dion Boucicault's drama (or adaptation) of *Streets of London :* not brilliant.[3] *2nd.*—Meet E. Ledger, and lose bet about T. P. Cooke's legacy. *3rd.*—Letter from Gus Harris about doing Covent Garden pantomime. Smoke a solitary pipe at midnight, musing, and ' sitting on the carpet of circumstances, wagging the beard of bewilderment.' *6th.*—Attend ninth dinner of *Daily Telegraph* at Old Manor House (Toomer's) in Green Lanes ; E. Levy in chair, Ellis vice : I give two toasts. Back with Prowse, Wright, Dicey, and Shenton to Doughty Street, where champagne supper winds up. *8th.*—To Adelphi : new farce by T. F. Williams, called *My Wife's Maid ;* a translation, but goes off well, thanks to Toole.[4]

[1] Mr. and Mrs. Charles Mathews, Mephistophcles and Marguerite, the latter imitating Stella Colas and Miss Bateman in " the curse ; " John Clarke, Martha ; Walton Chamberlayne, Wagner ; H. Ashley, Faust ; H. J. Montague, Valentine. Wallerstein arranged the music, Oscar Byrne the ballets.

[2] A fancy fair was held, with a Richardson's Show, a Wombwell's Menagerie, and such-like affairs. Toole and Paul Bedford had a " Temple of Magic," and Mr. and Mrs. Howard Paul a " Fan-tastic Fan-like Fan-ny Edifice," in which they sold fans.

[3] Taken from Brissebarre and Nus' *Les Pauvres de Paris,* produced at the Ambigu Comique in 1856 ; also adapted by Stirling Coyne for the Surrey, as *Fraud and its Victims,* March 2nd, 1857 ; also by Benjamin Barnett and J. B. Johnstone, as *Pride and Poverty,* at the Strand ; and in America as *The Poor of New York,* by Dion Boucicault. G. Vining was great as Badger ; Jonas Puffy, David Fisher ; Dan, Dominick Murray ; Gideon Crawley, J. W. Ray ; Captain Fairweather, H. Mellon ; Lucy Fairweather, Fanny Gwynne (first appearance in London) ; Paul Fairweather, H. Forrester. The sensation scenes were the proposed suffocation by charcoal of Lucy and her brother, and the house on fire, when real engine, etc., were introduced.

[4] Mrs. Mellon played Barbara Perkins ; and Paul Bedford, Tootles Senior. Toole, Lysimachus Tootles.

9th.—Dine at Arundel, meeting Toole, and amused by his legerdemain proclivities. *11th.*—New farce at Adelphi, by Brough and Halliday, called *The Actor's Retreat*, which is very far from good.[1] *12th.*—Hear of F. Robson's death as having occurred late last night: write the memoir.[2] *13th.*—Interview with Committee Royal English Opera to do pantomime, as Brothers Grinn, for £100; Harris to have £20, and publishing rights to go with sale. *22nd.*—Grieved to hear of the death of my old associate James Howe, who, had he lived till October 23rd, would have been forty-four. Another gone of a group that I little thought I should have outlived.[3] *27th.*—Meet Greenwood by appointment at Covent Garden, and arrange pantomime scene with Harris. Meet Toole, who tells me has renewed engagement with Webster on advantageous terms—£30 per week and two months' *congé* a·season.[4] *29th.*—See new piece at Adelphi (a translation, I believe, by Webster), called *A Woman of Business :* Toole and Mrs. Stirling very good."[5]

[1] Toole is supposed to have a horrible dream, in which old actors, etc., in their several parts, pass before him.

[2] Born at Margate in 1821 ; was apprenticed to a copper-plate engraver, but chose the stage, and first appeared at the Amateur Theatre, Catherine Street, as Simon Mealbag in *Grace Huntley*. He then went to Whitstable, Uxbridge, etc., and then joined the Grecian in 1844, and remained there five years; in 1850 he went to the Queen's Theatre, Dublin, and stayed there, and at the other principal house, three years. At Easter 1853 he succeeded Mr. Compton at the Olympic, where he made his first appearance, March 28th, in *Catching an Heiress*. His Jem Baggs, Macbeth, Shylock, Fouché, Medea, Yellow Dwarf, will always be spoken of as extraordinary performances. He was joint lessee with W. S. Emden of the Olympic from 1857 to the time of his (Robson's) death. He was, without doubt, the actor who could alternate extravagance of farce with the most powerful tragedy, and be equally successful in both. He had been ill for a considerable time before his death.

[3] This is the James Howe so often mentioned in the earlier pages of E. L. B.'s diary. He was a first chorister at Westminster, and later at the Temple, and was a good buffo singer; many of his songs he arranged himself. E. L. B. was a kind friend to him.

[4] [This was considered, at the time, a marvellous salary. Actors not nearly so popular now demand as much if not more.—C. S.]

[5] Toole, Simon Foxcraft ; Billington, Mr. Hall ; Mrs. Stirling, Mrs. Hall; Mrs. Billington, the Hon. Shrimpton Smallpiece; C. II. Stephenson, Wylie.

" *Sept.* 14*th.*—Up for Toole's benefit at Adelphi: house crammed. New piece, *Stephen Digges*, is admirable.[1] Write notice, and cab to office, but crowded out by press of matter. 16*th.*—Olympic closes under Emden's management, and with farewell address in very bad taste. *Ticket-of-Leave Man* performed to-morrow night for 407th time, this having been a continuous run. 17*th.*—Heavy thunder showers, in midst of which off to Surrey; new four-part drama, *A Fight with Fate*—not good piece, but ship on fire and earthquake effects striking.[2] 18*th.*—To Haymarket: opening night of season, *Castle of Andalusia.*[3] 21*st.*—Off at 11 by special train to Woking—Dramatic College picnic: very slow affair, Toole the life of the party. See Starmer, Frimley, Campbell, H. Bedford, and Mrs. Rivers among the inmates; the latter formerly Miss Smith, who played Duke of York to Kean's Richard at Drury.[4] 24*th.*—Drury opens for season; first part of *Henry IV.;* look in.[5] Then to Adelphi: Webster's benefit, and last night.[6] Write notices of all. 28*th.*—To Strand, and see charming piece by Craven, called *Milky White,*[7] in which the author plays the hero admirably.

[1] Suggested by Balzac's *Le Père Goriot* to John Oxenford. In this Toole played the name-part, and exhibited that pathos with humour for which he is now so famous. Mrs. Alfred Mellon was excellent as an old servant, Betsy.

[2] Fernandez, highly spoken of as Henry Martindale.

[3] Weiss, Compton, Chippendale, W. Farren, Buckstone, Louise Keeley, and Nelly Moore were in the cast.

[4] [When the Dramatic College finally collapsed, all the remaining pensioners were solaced with a fund started by Edward Ledger, Editor of *The Era,* who had protested from the outset against the worthless scheme.—C. S.]

[5] Phelps, Falstaff; Walter Montgomery, Hotspur; Henry Marston, Henry IV.; Helen Howard, Lady Percy; H. Raymond, Bardolph.

[6] *Stephen Digges* and *Who's Your Friend?*—with Webster as Giles Fairland, written for him, but originally played by Charles Mathews— with *Babes in the Wood,* formed the bill.

[7] H. T. Craven wrote the piece for Robson, who was to play Daniel (Milky) White, a saturnine, disagreeable, deaf man, who recovers his hearing sufficiently to lead him to imagine that he has learnt that his daughter is hoping for his death, and turns her out of doors. Ada Swanborough played the daughter, Annie; David James, Archibald Goode (her lover); Stoyle, Dick Dugge; Mrs. Manders, Mrs. Suddrip.

James Stoyle, a new comedian, makes his first appearance in same drama."

"*Oct.* 1*st.*—Terrific explosion of the powder mills near Belvidere at 7 this morning, startling London and the country for miles round.[1] 3*rd.*—Writing for *Daily Telegraph* all day, and after dining go to Astley's—Ada L. Isaacs Menken[2] as Mazeppa; then to Haymarket—new French actress;[3] then to Adelphi—John Collins, Irish comedian,[4] good. 6*th.*—Attend Dramatic Authors' Society: clear up for entire year, and give receipt for £42 2*s.* 10*d.*   To St. James's: see *Woodcock's Little Game*, stupid adaptation by M. Morton.[5] 8*th.*—To Drury:

[1] These were the Messrs. Hall's powder-mills at Low-wood, and those of Messrs. Daye, Barker, & Co.; 104,000 lbs. of powder exploded; the river embankment was blown up, and fatigue parties of soldiers were employed to construct a fresh one. Panes of glass were broken in Erith and Gravesend, and not one was left in Woolwich. The shock was felt in London, and the report heard even as far off as Aylesbury. Two barges were blown to pieces, several houses destroyed, and some lives lost, while numerous people were injured. The loss to the mills alone was £200,000.

[2] [This extraordinary and gifted woman was the wife of J. C. Heenan, a prizefighter, who fought with Tom Sayers the memorable battle. Her sympathetic and poetic talent was acknowledged by Charles Dickens, Algernon Swinburne, and many others.—C. S.]

[3] Mdlle. Beatrice (Lucchedini), from the Odéon and Vaudeville, an Italian, appeared in the title-*rôle* in Fanny Kemble's English version of Dumas's *Mademoiselle de Belle Isle*, originally played by Mdlle. Mars at the Français. Other versions of the play are *A Night in the Bastille*, played, December 1839, at Drury Lane. Mrs. Stirling, Gabrielle; Vining, Richelieu; Elton, D'Aubigny. Mr. and Mrs. Charles Kean produced A. R. Storr's version, *The Duke's Wager*, at the Princess's, June 4th, 1851. The cast now was—the Duc de Richelieu, Howe; Duc d'Aumont, Walter Gordon; D'Auvray, Weathersby; D'Aubigny, W. Farren; Marchioness de Valcour, Louise Angel.

[4] John Collins was the original Paul Clifford, and had been well known at the Covent Garden and Haymarket Theatres; returned after eighteen years' absence in America. He appeared as Sir Patrick O'Plenipo in *The Irish Ambassador*, and Teddy Malowney in *Teddy the Tiler*, and was highly successful in both.

[5] Taken from *La Terre Promise*, produced at the Vaudeville-Félix. Principal character—Mrs. Frank Matthews, Mrs. Colonel Carver. Charles Mathews, Woodcock; Miss Wentworth, Mrs. Larkins; Fanny Hunt (first appearance here), Mrs. Woodcock; H. J. Montague, Christopher Larkins; J. Johnstone, Swansdown.

Othello.[1] Then to Sadlers Wells: new play by Buchanan, called *The Witch Finder;* success moderate.[2] 10*th.*—Go to New Royalty, seeing an indifferent piece by John Brougham, called *The Demon Lover.* Then look in at Adelphi: *Rory O'More.*[3] 15*th.*—Opening of Strand Music Hall (now the Gaiety Theatre), and the New English Opera Company, Limited, at Covent Garden, with *Masaniello.* 17*th.*—At night go to Drury: Helen Faucit's reappearance in *Cymbeline.* Falconer's new farce, *O'Flahertys,* very bad: the play well acted, but heavy.[4] 18*th.*—To Hanover Square Rooms to see the Davenport Brothers:[5] a very puzzling performance, but, owing to the noise of a 'press meeting of seventy of the leaders of opinion,' not so complete as expected. 22*nd.*—Reopening of Lyceum with *The King's Butterfly.* Go to Lyceum: house full, piece long, scenery by Callcott good.[6] 24*th.*—At night see two wretched farces at Adelphi and Haymarket, *Doing Banting* and *On the Sly.*[7] 27*th.*

[1] Phelps, Othello ; Creswick, Iago ; Mrs. Hermann Vezin, Desdemona (first appearance here) ; G. F. Neville, Cassio ; Walter Lacy, Roderigo.

[2] Action of play took place in 1693, at Salem, New England. Miss Marriott, Elijah Brogden, an imbecile youth—very good ; George Melville, Martin Holt ; Charles Horsman, Walter Vane ; W. H. Drayton, Josiah Jones, the villain ; Miss E. Beaufort, Ruth Holt ; Miss L. Harrison, Hester Holdenough.

[3] Rory, John Collins (originally played by Power, who sang the "Cruiskeen Lawn ") ; Mrs. Alfred Mellon, Kathleen ; Paul Bedford, Scrubs ; Billington, De Lacy.

[4] Miss Faucit first played in it at Sadlers Wells in 1854. The cast was—Leonatus Posthumus, Phelps ; Creswick, Iachimo; Miss Atkinson, the Queen ; A. Rayner, Cymbeline ; Walter Lacy, Cloten. The second title of *The O'Flahertys* was *The Difficulty of Identifying an Irishman.* Falconer's reappearance, after his two years' illness, as Thaddeus O'Flaherty ; G. Belmore, Gammon ; Miss Hudspeth, the Chambermaid ; Miss E. Falconer, Mary Constant.

[5] [These swindlers, led by an American adventurer named Fry, were subsequently exposed and routed out at Liverpool, through the instrumentality of Henry Irving and Philip Day, both actors.—C. S.]

[6] New version of Paul Meurice's *Fanfan la Tulipe;* another adaptation was *Court and Camp,* produced at Princess's in May 1863. Miss M. Henrade, Alice de Rosel ; Fechter, Fanfan; Ryder, Baron d'Alvare; Widdicombe, Ramponneau ; F. Charles, Gabriel ; Carlotta Leclercq, Mdme. de Pompadour.

[7] The first by Brough and Halliday; the second, Maddison Morton's adaptation of *J'invite le Colonel.*

—Off to Haymarket: see *The Stranger*, and good perform-
ance of Mrs. Haller by Mdlle. Beatrice. Then to Drury:
Othello, Creswick; Iago, Marston. *28th.*—To Surrey, and see
Leslie's clever drama of *The Orange Girl*. *29th.*—St. James's
at night: new comedy by Palgrave Simpson, called *Step by
Step*,[1] goes off very well."

" *Nov. 1st.*—To Olympic; first night of Horace Wigan's
management; *The Hidden Hand*, and two new farces, all
French adaptations.[2] *7th.*—To Strand, to see a Miss 'Milly'
Palmer (*fiancée*, it is said, of Liverpool Joe Nightingale)
make her *début* as Pauline in *Delicate Ground*.[3] Then to
Adelphi, and see *Colleen Bawn*, with Collins as Myles.[4]
15th.—MS. for Covent Garden; chat with Harris, and dine
with him and Santley (going to Barcelona), J. L. Hatton,
Jarvis, A. Miller, and others at Albion; a notable affair.
21st.—Leave first scene with Roxby. Then Drury farce,
A Young Lad from the Country, by Oxenford: very queer.
Then Burnand's burlesque, *Snowdrop*, at Royalty, which
goes off well.[5] *22nd.*—Go to London Pavilion: see Redwood,
the tight-rope dancer; hear Vance, a wretched singer; see

[1] This was the second title, the first being *Sybilla;* scene in Den-
mark. Mr. and Mrs. Charles Mathews, Nilo Fleming and Sybilla;
Frank Matthews, Joachim; H. Ashley, Count Wolfenstein; Fred.
Robinson, King Christian.

[2] *The Hidden Hand* was an adaptation of Dennery and Edmond's
L'Aïeule, produced at the Ambigu Comique, October 17th, 1863. Motive
traced to Lytton's *Lucretia*. Lord and Lady Penarvon, Henry Neville,
and Kate Terry: Muriel, Louisa Moore; Enid, Lydia Foote; Sir
Caradoc ap Ithel, H. Coghlan; Lady Gryffyd, Miss Bowering; G.
Vincent, Madoc; his niece, Nelly Farren. The farces were: *The Girl
I left behind me*, by John Oxenford, an adaptation previously done by
Palgrave Simpson as *First Affections*; and J. M. Morton's adaptation
of *Les Trois Chapeaux*, entitled *My Wife's Bonnet*. Amy Sheridan
and Nelly Farren played in them.

[3] Afterwards married Herr Bandmann, the German tragedian.

[4] Henrietta Sims, Eily O'Connor; Mrs. Alfred Mellon, Anne
Chute; R. Phillips, the Danny Mann.

[5] Or, *The Seven Mannikins and the Magic Mirror;* recalled the fate
of the Sleeping Beauty. Fanny Clifford, Queen Narcissa; Lydia
Maitland, Prince Candid; Joseph Robins, Frizzle; W. H. Stephens,
King Bonbon; Rosina Wright, the Elf King; and Nelly Burton,
Snowdrop.

Lauri family (with whom chat) do a clever ballet ; the Drury
clown very good indeed, and very like Wieland.[1] A muscular
woman in the ballet he tells me is Miss Kathleen, a Sadlers

---

[1] "A little more than forty years ago—or, for the satisfaction of those
who insist on chronological accuracy, on the evening of Saturday,
September 15th, 1838—I was waiting at the wing of the Royal English Opera, as the Lyceum was then called, to accompany my early
friend, George Wieland, to the City of London Theatre. The famous
pantomimist, who was here filling up his time before the recommence-
ment of the Drury Lane season, had promised to give his services that
night for the benefit of a well-known clown at the East End, who
stood sadly in need of some substantial help through sudden pressure
on his pecuniary resources, caused by the afflictions that had befallen
his family. It was well known in the profession that the purse and
personal services of George Wieland were ever at the disposal of his
more unfortunate brethren ; but in this case he had taken especial
interest, as the poor wearer of the motley supplicating his aid was a
man of acknowledged worth and ability, though his talents had never
enabled him to secure more than a scanty subsistence for a family
increasing out of all proportion to his reputation.

"Old playgoers need not be told that Wieland was an artist in his
peculiar line, excelling all who had come before him, and who has never
been equalled since. He was about twenty-eight years of age at this
time, but had been upon the stage since a child : and his marvellous
embodiment of the droll imp in the ballet of *The Daughter of the
Danube* had then placed him at the highest point of his particular
branch of the profession. In the dangerous department of the art to
which he had devoted himself with so much zeal he had suffered the
usual penalties of popularity ; and after being shot up traps and sent
flying off on wires at perilous heights for nearly a quarter of a century,
the reflection that so many of his limbs were left unbroken used to
astonish him in his frequent moments of serious meditation. He was,
however, no mere acrobat or gymnast. His powers of expressing
purpose by action were of an extraordinary kind ; and when Edmund
Kean, after witnessing some of his remarkable pantomimic performances, used to say ‘that boy could convey, by gestures alone, the
significance of every line of *Hamlet,*' the compliment conveyed was
felt to be only a fair tribute to the cleverness of an exponent of what
is now almost a lost art.

"On the Saturday night referred to, Wieland was playing, for the
twenty-eighth time, his popular character of Diavoletto, in Alexander
Macfarren's now almost forgotten dramatic composition, known as
The Devil's Opera, in which Miss Priscilla Horton as Pepino, the page,
and Miss Poole as Signora Giovannina, the *gouvernante,* rendered with
such admirable effect the best songs of the composer. In the last
scene, Wieland had to rapidly run down to the footlights on his knees,

Wells child the other day, but now twice married !   28*th*.—To Haymarket: Bridgman's version of Mosenthal's play *Sunny Vale Farm*, for Mdlle. Beatrice ; very dull, and by no means a great success.   29*th*.—To Oxford Music Hall : hear *Orphée aux Enfers :* very well done, but the comic singing so

a feat of physical dexterity on which he had always prided himself. The carelessness of a stage-carpenter had left the trap by which the pantomimist had ascended a few moments before, above the level, and the result was a severe injury to the knee-cap of the performer, that compelled the immediate descent of the curtain. Borne to the wing in an insensible condition, Wieland was placed on a couch, while the nearest surgeon was sent for. When he attended, the painful nature of the accident suggested the ready opinion that many days, if not weeks, must elapse before the pantomimist could appear in public again. Wieland, suffering most acute tortures, feebly murmured that he had promised, in the course of the next hour, to appear at the City of London, in his character of the imp in the ballet of *The Daughter of the Danube*, and that if disappointed, the audience would probably resent their displeasure by hooting at the poor clown who was taking a benefit that night, and injure, in many ways, the prospect of providing for the poor sick family depending on the extra attraction that had been offered. Medical remonstrance was of no avail, and the coach, coming to the stage-door of the Lyceum at the appointed time, Wieland was helped into the vehicle, and I accompanied him, in his state of acute suffering from the injured limb, to the theatre then recently opened in Norton Folgate. The house was full to overflowing, and relying on the unfailing punctuality of the prominent 'star,' the overture to *The Daughter of the Danube* was, at the instigation of the prompter, proceeding at the appointed hour. There was but a short time left for assuming the needful costume, during which brief period Wieland fainted three times from the extreme physical agony he was enduring, but the promise he had so generously given had been faithfully kept, and though the weird antics of the amusing goblin never created more merriment than on that occasion, and tears, wrung by pain, streamed frequently from under the mask during the memorable combat with Gilbert, the good-natured, self-sacrificing representative of the German goblin exerted himself more than usual, and even complied with the earnest demand of the audience for a repetition of the principal movement. 'This will lay me up for another month,' said Wieland feebly to me as we parted after midnight at the door of his house in a street near Bedford Square ; 'but, thank Heaven ! I have helped to put into the pockets of the poor fellow a good hundred pounds, for the benefit of the sick children he is working so hard to support.'"—E. L. B.

It was E. L. B.'s opinion that Wieland was the greatest exponent of the now almost lost art of pantomime whom he had ever witnessed

dreary! 30*th.*—To Adelphi to see produced the great French drama of *The Workmen of Paris:*[1] begins at 7, and not over till 12 ; delighted with it."

" *Dec. 5th.*—Take MS. to Roxby. *Ruy Blas,* with Fechter, at Lyceum.[2] 10*th.*—Make out Drury pantomime bill, on which all day. Sit up *solus* till after midnight, and, as nobody else seems to think about it or care about it, wish myself the usual happy returns on the occasion of it being —11*th*—my birthday: attain my forty-fourth year: a letter from mother received this morning assuring me it is not forgotten. Make the household as lively as I can, but not merry myself. 22*nd.*—Off to St. James's for new comedy, *A Lesson in Love.*[3] 25*th.*—Oh! what a sad, dull day for me! Don't see a creature to say to, or receive from, a genial word ; and after striving over a few lines of notice for *Daily Telegraph,* attempt a dinner at the Divan, which costs me 4*s.*, and is execrable. 26*th.*—Very busy day. Write introduction, New Royalty, Adelphi, and Strand notices for *Daily Telegraph.* See *Grin Bushes* of Byron at Strand, and no

in the course of his lengthened experience ; this was high praise from one who had been a worshipper of the great Joey Grimaldi, and who had seen Ella, Bologna, and all the most famous pantomimists of his time. He used to relate an anecdote of meeting Wieland at a supper-party on one occasion. Wieland, upon being asked to give a specimen of his art, said it was difficult for him to do so without the aid of a definite story, and costume and scenery. He, however, threw a sofa cushion on to the hearthrug, which was supposed to represent a dead child, whilst he, as its father, portrayed such grief and sorrow, by his action alone, that he moved his little audience to tears. Wieland first appeared as harlequin, in *Harlequin Blue Beard,* at the Adelphi in 1843.

[1] Or, *The Dramas of the Wine Shop,* taken from the Porte St. Martin play, *Les Drames du Cabaret.* Benjamin Webster, Van Gratz ; Mrs. Stirling, Marguerite ; Mrs. Alfred Mellon, Blanche ; Henrietta Sims, Josepha ; A. Seaman, Rosetta, Mr. and Mrs. Billington, R. Phillips, J. Clarke, C. H. Stephenson, and C. J. Smith were also in the cast.

[2] Ryder, Don Salluste ; Carlotta Leclercq, Princess Neuborg ; Mrs. Winstanley, Duchess of Albaquerque ; Fitzpatrick, Don Cæsar.

[3] Three-act comedy adapted by Mr. Cheltnam from the French. Mr. and Mrs. Charles Mathews, Orlando Middlemark and Mrs. Sutherland ; Mrs. and Mr. Frank Matthews, Anastasia Winterberry and Mr. Babblebrook ; Miss Wentworth, Edith Leslie.

great success. 27*th.*—Glad to find good notices in all the papers. Rise early, very tired, and see morning performance at Drury:[1] as usual, not half the effects carried out. To Covent Garden; transformation scene capital.[2] 29*th.*—Walter's birthday, completing his fifteenth year to-day; and may he have a bright career before him! At Adelphi: farce by Coyne on Davenport subject, *Dark Days in a Cupboard,* which turns out very indifferent. 31*st.*—Dine with the usual large Christmas party at the Levys', 2, Russell Square. All the leader-writers and staff of *Telegraph* present, with Charles Braham (son of the B. whose style he resembles), Sothern, Byron, and others. Magnificent dinner: songs (I sing 'Honourable Ted' and 'Almanack and St. George'), and with gin punch see the Old Year out and the New Year in. Thus ends a very busy, prosperous year, for health during which I give God thanks."

Estimated revenue for year £491 2*s.* 6*d.*

1865.

"*Monday, Jan. 2nd.*—Reappearance of Miss Bateman at Adelphi as Leah. 8*th.*—Hear by American mail that James Wallack[3] died at New York; write memoir. 13*th.*—

---

[1] E. L. B.'s pantomime *Hop o' My Thumb and His Eleven Brothers; or, Harlequin and the Ogre of the Seven-League Boots.* Lydia Thompson, Sungleam; Helen Howard, Man in the Moon; Miss Hudspeth, Actinia; Tom Matthews, Daddy Thumb; clowns, Harry Boleno and C. Lauri; pantaloons, W. A. Barnes and J. Morris; harlequins, Cormack and S. Saville; columbines, Madame Boleno and the two Misses Gunniss.

[2] E. L. B.'s pantomime, *Cinderella; or, Harlequin and the Magic Pumpkin and the Great Fairy of the Little Glass Slipper.* Clara Denvil, Cinderella; E. Danvers, Prince Ugolino. The Payne family were great in the opening, and Donato the one-legged dancer made a great hit on this his first appearance. In the harlequinade F. and H. Payne appeared as harlequin and clown; Mdlle. Esther, columbine; Paul Herring, pantaloon.

[3] James Wallack was born in Hercules Buildings, Lambeth, August 17th, 1794. His father, William Wallack, belonged to Astley's company, and married Mary Johannot, who became one of the favourite actresses on the minor boards. James Wallack made his first appearance as

Destruction by fire of Theatre Royal,[1] Edinburgh, Wyndham being at the Surrey Theatre the same evening. 14*th*.—To Drury, and receive from Falconer and Chatterton £50 on account. Receive from Mr. F. for prologue £3 3*s*. *Monday*, 16*th*. —See *Billing and Cooing*[2] at New Royalty, by Oxenford, and

a child actor in 1804 at the German Theatre in Leicester Square, and, at twelve years of age was engaged at Drury Lane. He played the Negro-boy in the pantomime of *Furibond; or, Harlequin Negro*, in 1807. October 10th, 1812, on the opening of the New Theatre, though only eighteen he played Laertes to Elliston's *Hamlet*, and from that time was a prominent member of the company, appearing with Edmund Kean. In 1817 he married the daughter of John Johnstone, the Irish comedian, and took his new-made wife to America. Made his *début* at the Park Theatre, New York, in September 1818, as Macbeth. Lester Wallack, his eldest son, was born in 1819. James Wallack only stayed a year in America, then returned to Drury Lane to appear as Hamlet, and made his great success as Rolla. Re-visited America in 1821, and on the journey to Philadelphia the stage carriage broke down and he received a compound fracture of the leg, from which he never thoroughly recovered. He returned to England in about two years' time, and was received with acclamation. July 14th, 1823, he played Roderick Dhu in *The Knight of Snowdon*, at the Opera House. On the 28th of the same month he played Faust in *Presumption; or, The Fate of Frankenstein*, and in the autumn of that year became stage-manager at Drury Lane, appearing as Doricourt, Lovemore, and Harry Dornton. His great parts were: Allessandro Massaroni in Planché's *The Brigands*, Drury Lane, 1829; Martin Heywood in Douglas Jerrold's *The Rent Day*, January 25th, 1832. Soon after this he went to America again, became manager of the National Theatre, New York, in 1837. August 31st, 1840, he played Don Felix, in *The Wonder*, at the Haymarket in London. In 1841 again went to New York, and on May 21st of that year the National Theatre was burnt down, by which he suffered considerably. He then starred in the States, and, returning to England first appeared at the Princess's, October 8th, 1844, as Don Cæsar, also made a name in *The Rent Day* and *Wild Oats*. He then returned in 1845, and re-appeared at the Park Theatre, New York, and in September became associated with the Arch Street Theatre, Philadelphia. Made a success throughout the States, and in May 1852, opened what had been Brougham's Lyceum as Wallack's Theatre, remaining in America until his death, and appearing frequently in Shakespearean parts.

[1] This was built on the site of the Adelphi Theatre, which was also burnt down, May 1853, and was situated at the head of Leith Walk. Several lives were lost.

[2] Taken from *Gli Inamorati* of Goldoni.

Mrs. Green's Snug Little Business,[1] at Strand; the first piece quaint but badly acted generally, the last very bad. *18th.*— To Covent Garden; receive cheque from Company *viâ* Mr. Russell, my share being £65. Deposit in London and Westminster another £100, making total of £305. *19th.*—Pay Harris his £20; settle on *Aladdin* for next Easter subject. *21st.*—At Lyceum see Fechter playing Robert Macaire in piece called *The Roadside Inn.*[2] House full of fog and famous folks. Have Kent with me in stalls, and greatly grieved to hear his father has been struck with paralysis. Drama goes off fairly—not greatly. *28th.*—Hear a local legend of the Ship, Southfleet, when mendicant arrives and leaves the old landlord Drew some thousands in his will; occurred some years ago. *30th.*—At Drury see Phelps as Cardinal Wolsey in *Henry VIII.* (three acts); Miss Bateman as Julia in *Hunchback*—a moderate success; near midnight begin copy. Hear Surrey Theatre is being burned down; rush back to chambers for dates of history.[3] *31st.*—My opinion is, the Surrey, with no loss of life, is not a thing to be deplored."

"*Feb.* *1st.*—Go and look at the ruins of the poor old Surrey; meet Chaplins and Vokes, who appear quite distracted. *2nd.*—Paul Bedford's complimentary benefit at

[1] This was by Charles Smith Cheltnam.

[2] [Taken from *L'Auberge des Adrets*. H. Widdicombe, Jacques Strop. Fechter made some ingenious alterations, particularly in the death scene of Robert Macaire, in which he tumbled down the staircase, and into his son's arms.—C. S.]

[3] The fire occurred at twenty minutes to twelve on the night of Monday. By twelve o'clock the theatre and its contents were nearly burnt out, so rapid was the spread of the conflagration. The ballet girls, children, and those employed on the stage, could only escape in the light costumes in which they had been appearing, there not being even time to procure a cloak, and had to turn out in the snow. Messrs. Shepherd and Anderson were the lessees; they suffered to the extent of some £10,000. Numerous benefits were given in aid of the sufferers. The proprietors of the *Daily Telegraph* gave £50, and opened a list; William Batty, £20; George Vining, £10 10s.; and a subscription list was opened at *The Era* Office. Much more loss of life would have occurred but for the coolness and presence of mind of Rowella the clown, Evans the pantaloon, Vivian the sprite, and Green the stage-manager.

Drury;[1] an immense house, and the whole of the theatrical profession on stage; a really extraordinary and gratifying sight. Having written for *Era*[2] a history of the Surrey Theatre, get for week and last £3. To Bedford Head; invitation to dine with Paul Bedford, J. L. Toole, Watson (Williams in theatrical matters), and pleasant little festival. All sorts of songs and speeches, and gratifying compliments to everybody. 13*th.*—Morning performance of *Money* at Drury for General Theatrical Fund. 15*th.*—Find I have to record the death of poor Gustavus Dunning (E. T. Smith's manager), aged 44. Cardinal Wiseman dies this day. 16*th.*—Benefit at Drury[3] for the Surrey Company; house crowded. 20*th.*—Rush off to Haymarket to see a Miss ' Blanche Aylmer ' make a *début* as Lady Elizabeth Freelove.[4] Then to Drury to see *Richelieu*—Phelps very good. 25*th.* —At night to St. James's; new (adapted) comedy by Leicester Buckingham called *Faces in the Fire*,[5] which goes off very well. To Princess's; see a wretched farce of David Fisher's, *Heartstrings and Fiddlestrings.*"

" *March* 4*th.*—At Olympic see Tom Taylor's five-act drama of *Settling Day*;[6] a long four-hours' piece, smartly written, but an ineffective drama. 6*th.*—To Drury; see wretched

---

[1] *The Area Belle, My Aunt's Advice*, and *Box and Cox* constituted the programme.

[2] This was a most truthful and concise history, occupying two and a quarter columns of the *Era* of February 5th.

[3] *School for Scandal* and first act of *Black-eyed Susan* were played. Phelps was the Sir Peter, and James Anderson the Charles. Creswick the Joseph, Amy Sedgwick Lady Teazle, in the first piece. In the second Mr. Shepherd, William; J. L. Toole, Gnatbrain; and Miss Woolgar, Susan.

[4] This was in *A Day after the Wedding*. W. Farren played Colonel Freelove. Miss Blanche Aylmer proved a very novice, but was nicelooking.

[5] Taken from *Mathilde; or, La Jalousie*, by M.M. Bayard and Laurencin, produced at the Vaudeville, Paris, June 1835. Mrs. Hargrave, Mrs. Charles Mathews; Mrs. Glanvil, Miss Herbert; Philip Hargrave, Mr. Arthur Stirling; Mr. Glanvil, Frederic Robinson; Cecil Vane, Charles Mathews.

[6] This was an original play and the following were in the cast. H. Wigan, H. Cooper, D. Evans, Mrs. Leigh Murray, Miss Kate Terry, Miss Lydia Foote, Maclean, R. Soutar.

farce, *Going to the Dogs*, by Brough and Halliday, and Helen Faucit reappears as Imogen in *Cymbeline*.[1] Look in at Adelphi. *7th.*—To Astley's; see a very clever piece by Henry Leslie called *The Mariner's Compass*.[2] *13th.*—Fechter ill, Mdlle. Beatrice plays Mrs. Haller as an attraction at the Lyceum. *14th.*—To Astley's, private box, to see *Jack Sprat*, with Lawson; goes off very well. *17th.*—Find Coyne's cheque for Dramatic Authors' Society, £25 6s. 6d., paying all up to this date and defraying my annual subscription for benevolent fund. Take the chair at dinner; and though severe cold, the usual two songs and make lots of speeches, to my own astonishment. Barnett proposes the chairman's health, and Tomlins the 'Drama and Stage.' Buchanan and hosts of old Urbans present. *18th.*—To Haymarket and see Watts Phillips' piece of *Woman in Mauve;*[3] much disappointed. *20th.*—To Drury Lane; see a bit of *Romeo and Juliet*: Helen Faucit playing Juliet charmingly. *22nd.*—To Princess's; see an admirable drama by Dion Boucicault called *Arrah-na-Pogue;* goes off with great *éclat*. The *Daily Telegraph* this day published extra half-sheet, the largest size it has yet attained. *23rd.*—Dramatic Authors' Society meeting; resolving authors shall reserve for a twelvemonth any piece they please and then place it on the books. Fees increased for first twelvemonth. Then to Adelphi; see bad farce by Morton called *Steeplechase*.[4] Hear from C. C. B., date of 17th January. *25th.*—Ninety-ninth and last night of Drury Lane pantomime. Destruction of Surrey Theatre at Sheffield. *27th.*—See comedietta from the French called *Cross Purposes;*[5] piece very slight."

[1] James Anderson was the Iachimo. Walter Montgomery, Leonatus Posthumus.

[2] This was the author of *The Trail of Sin* and *The Orange Girl*. Fernandez excellent as Ruby Dayrell. E. T. Smith was the lessee at this time.

[3] This was a piece of which Sothern had great opinion, though his character, that of Frank Jocelyn, was not a very great one. [It had been advertised for weeks before, all over London, in a novel manner: "Watch this Frame" (a blank one.) When filled in the words were *The Woman in Mauve.*—C. S.]

[4] [It proved to be one of the greatest of Toole's Successes.—C. S.]

[5] This was an adaptation by Mr. Parselle, and was played at the

" *April 2nd.*—Richard Cobden dies this day, aged 61 ; and thus goes a great man. *3rd.*—To Olympic, comedietta *Always Intended;* adapted by Horace Wigan—more bright. *7th.*—Look out material for a sketch of the Queen's, now to be called the Prince of Wales's, Theatre ; and to open next week with Marie Wilton for directress. *10th.*—Byron's pastoral extravaganza at Adelphi *Pan,* or, *The Loves of Echo and Narcissus;* not so much done with subject as might have been—well played by Toole as Pan. *12th.*— General Theatrical Fund dinner. Wilkie Collins in chair ; good chairman and excellent speech, but not a very good dinner nor a very enjoyable evening : the Freemasons' Tavern Company pronounced inferior to the old time of the land-lord. *13th.*—New burlesque at Royalty called *Pirithous,* by Burnand. Well got up and neatly written, but no story. *14th.*—Write anticipatory notice of new Prince of Wales's Theatre, then go up and see it. Meet Charles James, Mrs. James and her daughter. Old times gossip with Tomlins, Leigh[1] (grand-nephew of old Mrs. Charles Mathews). *15th.* —To Prince of Wales's Theatre[2]; first night of season. Byron's burlesque of *Sonnambula;* good, house crowded, and all

Strand, the author appearing as Edward Hartwright. Miss M. Palmer, Laura Goodman.

[1] [There is nothing like hereditary genius. Mr. Denny, the admirable artist at the Savoy, is the son of Mrs. Leigh, long known as the best of old women on the stage.—C. S.]

[2] The following account of the Prince of Wales's Theatre in Tottenham Street, Tottenham Court Road, is taken from the anticipatory notice which he wrote, and which gives a history of the theatre. It was origin-ally established in 1810, when a license was given to one Paul, a retired pawnbroker, persuaded thereto by his wife, who was anxious to go on the stage, and was opened on Easter Monday, April 23rd, 1810, as the King's Ancient Concert Rooms, with a burletta called *The Village Fête,* founded on *Love in a Village,* really the opera itself ; Mrs. Paul the Rosetta. The speculation was not successful, Paul lost all his money, and in 1821 Mr. Brunton became manager. He was a fair actor, and his daughter, afterwards Mrs. Yates, played the leading *rôles.* S. Beverley then followed as manager. Frédéric Lemaître made his *début* in this country here, the theatre being then known as the Regency, and was afterwards again entitled the West London Theatre, the name Brunton gave it when he opened the house in 1829. It was called the Queen's, in compliment to Queen Adelaide, on the accession of William IV. Messrs. Chapman and Melrose were

goes off well. 17*th.*—To Strand, *One Tree Hill,*[1] and Drury, *Comus.*[2] 26*th.*—Startled by American mail bringing the intelligence of Abraham Lincoln's assassination by Junius W. Booth, the actor; can think of nothing else. 29*th.*—To Her Majesty's Theatre; first night of season; see *Sonnambula* :

managers in 1830, Macfarren in 1831, and a noticeable performance of *Acis and Galatea* was given with E. Seguin, Mrs. Glover, Mrs. Humby, T. Green, and Mr. Tilbury. In December 1833 the theatre was called the Fitzroy, and was run by some members of the Mayhew family. Gilbert Abbot à Beckett and Henry Mayhew (under the title of " Ralph Rigmarole,") being the two authors to the theatre. It came under Mrs. Nisbett's management in 1835, who called it the Queen's again. Then Colonel Addison, with Mrs. Waylett as directress, and George Wild tried to make the house pay, but without success. In 1839 Charles James, the well-known scenic artist, took up the management, and contrived for twenty-six years, up to the time of its passing into the hands of the Bancrofts to obtain some income from it. Under the new *régime* of Marie Wilton and H. J. Byron, the appearance of the house had been thoroughly altered. It was made a perfect little bijou of a theatre, not only by the taste displayed in the ornamentation and upholstery, but in the introduction of flowers and ferns, and, as a matter of record it will be well perhaps to give the programme and cast of the opening night. The first piece was J. P. Wooler's *The Winning Hazard.* Miss Lilian Hastings (from the Bath and Bristol Theatres), and Miss Bella Goodall from Theatre Royal, Liverpool, as Aurora and Coralie, Sidney Bancroft (from Prince of Wales, Liverpool), Jack Crawley, all made favourable impressions, as did F. Dewar as Dudley Croker, and E. Dyas as Colonel Croker. Then followed Byron's new burlesque extravaganza *La Sonnambula,* or, *The Supper, the Sleeper, and the Merry Swiss Boy.* Marie Wilton, Alessio ; Lilian Hastings, Teresa ; Bella Goodall, Lisa ; F. Dewar, the Count ; J. Clarke, Amina ; Harry Cox, " A Virtuous Peasant ; " and Fanny Josephs as Elvino. It was followed by Troughton's farce, *Vandyke Brown.*

[1] A two-act drama by H. T. Craven. Mr. and Mrs. Bubble, Mr. Belford and Miss Milly Palmer ; Tom Foxer, D. James ; Cecilia Weston, Ada Swanborough ; Jack Salt, H. T. Craven ; Dick White, James Stoyle.

[2] Milton's masque. Miss Augusta Thompson made her *début* as Sabrina. Henri Drayton, First Bacchanal ; Mrs. Hermann Vezin, the Lady ; Walter Lacy, Comus ; Elder Brother, Edmund Phelps ; Younger Brother, Miss E. Falconer. Wilbye Cooper was also in the cast. The masque was first performed in 1834. The adaptation for the stage was first made by John Dalton, and was brought out in three acts, with music by Doctor Arne, in 1738—Quin as Comus, and Mrs. Cibber as the Lady. Mrs. Clive, Mrs. Arne, and John Beard were in the cast. In 1772 it was done by George Colman at Covent Garden,

a Miss Harris[1] very bad; the new tenor, Elvino, not much better."

"*May* 1*st.*—New Royalty: a trifle by Wooler called *Squire of Ringwood Chase.* Egyptian Hall, Colonel Stoddart's illusions; young man expert practitioner. Then Victoria, Céleste's reappearance.[2] 3*rd.*—To Drury: Falconer's long play of *Love's Ordeal,* or, *The Old and New Régime*[3]— very long (four hours) and very dull. 4*th.*—Attend Charles Salaman's concert lectures at Grosvenor Street, 'Music and History of Italian Opera.' At Olympic; see *Ticket-of-Leave Man* revived. 10*th.*—To Prince of Wales's; see comic drama *The Fair Pretender,* by Palgrave Simpson[4]—not very good. 11*th.*—Look in at Drury: *King Lear.*[5] 12*th.*—Hear of Hood having *Fun,* and my payment problematical.[6] 13*th.*—Edward Ledger comes down, and take him (*viâ* Singlewell), long ten-miles walk through Cobham Wood; tea at Falstaff. Picked up on road by an unknown but courteous friend, and drive

and afterwards at the Haymarket, Mrs. Siddons having appeared as the Lady. It was revived at Drury Lane in 1833 by Bunn; by Madame Vestris at Covent Garden in 1842; and by Macready in 1843; but it appears that it was never more splendidly mounted than by Messrs. Falconer and Chatterton.

[1] This was Miss Laura Harris, Elvino was M. Carrion; the Count was Mr. Santley; Mdlle. Redi, Lisa; Signor Bossi, Alessio; Signor Casaboni was the Notary.

[2] This was in *The Woman in Red.*

[3] In this play the author endeavoured to give a larger and more truthful picture in action than has hitherto been presented on the stage, of the pre-existing social antagonisms and rival class characteristics which in ferment produced the great French Revolution of 1782." Comte d'Ostanges, J. Neville; his wife, Mrs. H. Vandenhoff; Hortense, Mrs. Hermann Vezin; Duc de Chartreux, Walter Lacy; Vicomte Lauzan, H. Sinclair; Mdlle. de Meranie, Rose Leclercq; Eugene de Morny, Edmund Phelps; Mons. Robespierre, Edmund Falconer. The play was of considerable literary merit.

[4] An original two-act drama.

[5] Phelps, Lear; Miss Atkinson, Goneril; Mrs. Hermann Vezin, Cordelia; Miss Corbet Weston, Regan.

[6] [On the contrary *Fun,* under Tom Hood's management, was a brilliant success. On the staff were Gilbert, Prowse (Nicholas), Archer, Brough, Harry Leigh, Tom Robertson, Arthur Sketchley, Savile Clarke. —C. S.]

back to Rosherville; the day a success. *15th.*—Operetta at Haymarket called *The Miller's Daughter*,[1] by Langton Williams—slight. Then to Lyceum, *Don Cæsar de Bazan:* Fechter as usual. *16th.*—Opening of the new Alexandra Theatre, Highbury Barn;[2] see a burlesque of W. Brough on *Ernani.* *17th.*—See at Olympic Coyne's comedy of *Everybody's Friend*, and a Mr. Charles Walcot, an old American actor,[3] make his appearance as Major de Boots—not good, *18th.*—Upset by letter about the confounded *Globe* Company. that I thought I had long heard the last of. *20th.*—Second annual festival of Newspaper Press Fund : Charles Dickens in chair. Arrange to become a life subscriber. *24th.*—Haymarket; see new comedy by Oxenford, called *Brother Sam ;* not a very brilliant affair, produced for Sothern. Pay to Newspaper Press Fund three guineas, making me a life subscriber. *29th.*—At night to St. James's ; drama of *Eleanor's Victory*, adapted from novel by Oxenford ; Miss Herbert very good.[4] *31st.*—Derby Day ; off to course per South Western Railway. Go all over Downs. Meet Clark and Halliday, with whom lunch ; then Toole and Billington in Mr. Thorpe's wagonette, with whom stop and go back to town ; Gladiateur, the French horse, winning, amid great excitement ; the road very crowded returning."

"*June 5th.*—To Strand ; Burnand's extravaganza of *Windsor Castle*,[5] with new music by Frank Musgrave : the

---

[1] Book by W. Suter. Miss Louise Keeley was the Diana, and sang very charmingly ; Mr. Whiffen, John Digby.

[2] Edward Giovannelli had been for some five years proprietor. The burlesque was *Ernani, or, Horns of a Dilemma.* The music by B. Isaacson. Don Carlos, Josephine Ruth ; Ernani, Rachel Sanger ; Scampa, Mr. Danvers. Rachel Sanger made a great hit, as did Mr. Danvers.

[3] He was an Englishman by birth and was supported by Kate Terry as Mrs. Swansdown ; and H. Neville as Felix Featherley ; Lydia Foote, Mrs. Featherley ; R. Soutar, Icebrook ; Mrs. Leigh Murray, Mrs. Major de Boots.

[4] Miss Herbert, Eleanor Vane ; Gaston Murray, Mr. Monkton ; H. J. Montague, Launcelot Darrell ; Arthur Stirling, Dick Thornton ; Frederic Robinson, Bourdon ; Mr. and Mrs. Frank Matthews, Major and Mrs. Lennard ; J. Johnstone, Vandaleur Vane ; Miss Weber, Laura Mason.

[5] Messrs. J. Stoyle, D. James, C. Fenton, H. Turner, Collier, Edge,

first opera-burlesque in this country—a success.   7*th.*—
Attend Olympic, *Twelfth Night* [1]—not very brilliantly played.
8*th.*—Mother's birthday; take her some wine, and with her
to Cremorne; see all the amusements, even to the fireworks at eleven—a great success.   10*th.*—Attend Prince of
Wales's: new drama by Byron, *War to the Knife;* [2] written
with much smartness, and goes off very well.   12*th.*—To
Adelphi; see tragedy called *Geraldine,* [3] written by Mrs.
Bateman, and with Bateman and his daughter in the cast.
19*th.*—New farce called *Pouter's Wedding* [4] at St. James's;
turns out to be a very bad adaptation by Maddison Morton
of a French comedy.   20*th.*—Attend meeting at Drury with
Beverley to settle pantomime; to be entitled *Fortunatus.*
24*th.*—Attend *Lady of Lyons* at Adelphi; Miss Bateman's
benefit; piece goes off pretty well, but nothing particular.
26*th.*—See a very weak adaptation of French piece, *The
Better Half,* [5] at Strand.   27*th.*—Leigh Murray's benefit at
Drury.[6]   28*th.*—Off to Apsley House and hear the dreary
readings of Mr. and Mrs. Alfred Coyne.   29*th.*—Off to

and Thomas Thorne; Mesdames Ada Swanborough, M. Simpson,
Fanny Hughes, L. Weston, Elise Holt, Raynham, and the Misses H.
and E. Gunniss were in the cast.

[1] The cast included Messrs. H. Wigan, G. Vincent, R. Soutar,
Coghlan, Edgar, Maclean, Evans, Rivers, and H. Cooper; Mesdames
Kate Terry, Lydia Foote, and A. Bowering.

[2] Mr. and Mrs. Harcourt, Mr. Montgomery and Fanny Josephs;
Mrs. Delacour, Marie Wilton; John Blunt, E. Dewar; Mr. Rubbly,
J. Clarke; Captain Thistleton, Sidney Bancroft; Jane Trimmer,
Blanche Wilton.

[3] [Or, *The Master Passion.* Geraldine de Lacey, Miss Bateman;
Hubert de Burgh, G. Jordan; David Ruthin, Mr. Bateman. He was
an old Welsh Harper, and cut a ridiculous figure.—C. S.]

[4] Taken from *Les Noches de Maluchet.* Simon Pouter, F. Robson;
Alderman and Mrs. Marrowfat, Mr. and Mrs. Frank Matthews.

[5] Taken by T. J. Williams from *Madame André,* and already known
at the Adelphi as *The Woman of Business.*

Second act of *Masks and Faces,* two scenes from *Twelfth Night;*
selection from *A Regular Fix;* W. H. Weiss, Louisa Pyne, Santley
and Madame Sainton Dolby sang; an address written by Shirley
Brooks and delivered by Mr. and Mrs. Leigh Murray; scene from
The Willow Copse; Robson sang, for first time in London, "Villikins
and his Dinah," and Mr. and Mrs. Howard Paul gave a portion of
their entertainment.

Adelphi; Toole's benefit; new piece called *Through Fire
and Water* [1]—good idea, but piece too long. 30*th*.—Meet
Toole; and at night to Olympic, Kate Terry's benefit, and
new drama *The Serf*,[2] by Tom Taylor—not very brilliant."

"*July* 4*th*.—A visit from Tallis about my old work
'Temple Bar.' 5*th*.—Off to Hanover Square Rooms:
Charles Hugo Hind, tragedy from memory—very dreary.
Walk back with Dunphie to Olympic, Neville's benefit; and
see a very bad burlesque by a Mr. Trail, called *Glaucus*.
16*th*.—To Dramatic College fête for *Daily Telegraph*.
29*th*.—To Haymarket; first night of Walter Montgomery's
season, and he as Hamlet [3]—not a bad performance."

"*Aug.* 6*th*.—Vivid dreams at night about C. C. B. and
mother curiously commingled. 10*th*.—The Prince and
Princess of Wales depart in *Osborne* Royal yacht for
Germany. I go in boat on river with 'Gentleman Joe
Martin,' the pilot. 12*th*.—To Olympic, and see a wretched
burlesque *Prince Camaralzaman*,[4] by Messrs. Best and
Bellingham—very bad indeed. 17*th*.—Off in Barker's
steam tug (*The Nelson*) with party from London; meet
Bates, Spencer, Hunt, Carpenter, etc. Go round the Nore
and have a pleasant day. Look in at Rosherville Gardens,
leaving them there. 21*st*.—See Aldridge as Othello at
Haymarket;[5] performance tol-lol in some parts and in-tol-er-

[1] This was by Walter Gordon. Principal characters played by
J. L. Toole, Henrietta Simms, and Mrs. Alfred Mellon.

[2] Or, *Love Levels All*, an original drama. Ivan, H. Neville;
Countess de Mauléon, Kate Terry; Khor, Horace Wigan; Count
Karstaff, G. Vincent. Miss Kate Terry delivered an address written
for her by Tom Taylor, and in it he referred to her having been an
old stager when she closed her teens, and to her having doubled
the parts in *Twelfth Night*, and various other characters she had
appeared in.

[3] Madge Robertson made her first appearance in London as Ophelia,
and obtained a conspicuous share of the honours of the evening.
Fernandez was heartily welcomed to the West End as Laertes.

[4] Or, *The Fairies' Revenge*. The music was by J. H. Tully. Nelly
Farren, Prince Camaralzaman; Miss H. Lindley, Badoura.

[5] Montgomery was the Iago; Fernandez, Cassio; Hon. Lewis
Wingfield, Roderigo; Madge Robertson, Desdemona.

able in others.   30*th.*—To Haymarket; see an extraordinary play in five acts, seven tableaux, called *Fra Angelo*,[1] written by W. C. Russell, son of Henry Russell, composer; laughter more than applause."

"*Sept.* 2*nd.*—Very unwell; come up for opening of New Royalty under new management.   Have to stew in a hot theatre on the loveliest of moonlight nights; *Castle Grim*,[2] a new operetta—very grim affair.   4*th.*—First night of *Rip van Winkle*[3] at Adelphi, with Jefferson—a decided hit; meet Dicey and Sala.   23*rd.*—Drury re-opens for season: *Macbeth* and *Comus.*   25*th.*—Re-opening of Prince of Wales's Theatre; burlesque of *Lucia di Lammermoor*—not good."

"*Oct.* 4*th.*—To Princess's, first night : *Never Too Late to Mend* ;[4] house very full; all the celebrities there; piece begins at 7 p.m., and over by midnight; great excitement in theatre about the prison discipline in second act.   9*th.*—Go to Astley's (*Child of the Sun*)[5]—a failure; and Haymarket, *School for Scandal*, reopening for season; piece seemed long

[1] Period of the thirteenth century.   Vollaire as the Hunchback in the title *rôle*.   Marina, Louisa Moore ; Leonora, Katherine Rodgers ; Marquis de Volenza, Fernandez.   [The author is the now celebrated writer of nautical novels, and the son of "Cheer, boys, cheer" Russell, happily alive and well.—C.S.].

[2] Music by G. Allen, book by R. Reece.   Elliot Galer, G. Honey, Fanny Reeves, Susan Galton, and Lydia Maitland were the principal members of the company.

[3] Or, *The Sleep of Twenty Years.*   Drama by Dion Boucicault.   Mrs. Billington as Gretchen ;   Henrietta Simms and Billington, Paul Bedford, Felix Rogers, were included in the cast.

[4] By Charles Reade, in which the author closely followed his own drama, *Gold*, produced at Drury Lane, January 1853.   Tom Robinson, Vining ; Susan Merton, Katherine Rodgers ; Louisa Moore, the boy Josephs ; George Fielding, G. Melville ; William Fielding, Gaston Murray ; Meadows, F. Villiers ; Isaac Levi, T. Mead ; Peter Crawley, Dominick Murray; Rev. Mr. Eden, J. G. Shore; Hawes, the Governor, Charles Seyton ; Jacky, S. Calhaem.   There was almost a riot in the house about the death of Josephs in the prison scene, and Mr. Vining had to come forward and make a speech to quiet the audience.   [F. Guest Tomlins, the dramatic critic of *The Morning Advertiser*, got up in the stalls and made a speech protesting against the brutal realism —C.S.]

[5] This was by John Brougham.   Ada Isaacs Menken as Leon ;

and dreary. 14*th.*—St. James's reopens; though a wretched wet night, go; see *Caught in the Toils*, Brougham's weak adaptation of 'Only a Clod'[1]—very dreary, and only Miss Herbert effective. 19*th.*—The great domestic difficulty pressing heavily at the present time; three nephews more to keep. 23*rd.*—Royal English Opera season opened on Saturday, and good accounts of it in papers. Edward Ledger married Miss Tayler this day. 28*th.*—*Aladdin* pantomime at Covent Garden; then to Coyne, and per cheque Dramatic Authors' Society, £36 3*s.* St. James's Hall, to see French giant, Anak the Anakim.[2] Take McDonell to Drury: Falconer's farce of *Husbands, Beware!* and *Julius Cæsar.* 30*th.*—To St. James's, for revival of *The Ladies' Club.* Hear of the death of James Lowe, editor of the *Critic*, who expired on Sunday at 10, Lancaster Place, Strand, where he had chambers: another link snapped in the Re-Union chain."

" *Nov.* 4*th.*—To Drury; revival of *King John*[3]—not brilliantly played. 6*th.*—To Lyceum; meeting Kent in stalls; pleasant chat between the acts of a dull piece, *The Watch Cry*,[4] under Fechter's management. 8*th.*—To Olympic:

Kate Carson, Juanita. The music was by J. H. Tully. The theatre was under the management of E. T. Smith.

[1] This was Miss Braddon's novel. Miss Herbert played Julia Desmond; Walter Lacy, Francis Tredethlyn; Belton, Roderick Lowther.

[2] This was a Frenchman, named Jean Joseph Brice, who was born on January 26th, 1840. Was 8 feet high, weighed 30 stone, 54 inches round chest, 25 inches across shoulders. He appeared as a Brobdingnagian, supposed to have been overcome by some Lilliputians.

[3] Phelps, King John; James Anderson, Faulconbridge; Swinbourne, Hubert; Master Percy Roselle, Prince Arthur; Miss Atkinson, Constance; Rose Leclercq, Blanche of Castille; and Mrs. H. Vandenhoff, Elinor.

[4] An adaptation by Palgrave Simpson of *Lazare le Pâtre*, originally produced at the Ambigu in 1839. Another version of it, done at the Grecian, was called *Roland the Reaper.* Fechter, Leone Salviati; Bianca d'Albizzi, Miss Elsworthy; Judael di Medici, S. Emery; Mosca Caponi, H. Widdicomb; Messrs. Raymond, C. Horsman, Clifford, and Fitzpatrick were also in the cast. [Emery recovered damages in an action for libel against Arthur à Beckett, who said he did not know his part; which was perfectly true!—C. S.].

new (adapted) comedy by Oxenford called *A Cleft Stick*[1]—very farcical, but very funny.   11*th.*—Go to Prince of Wales's Theatre ; new comedy of *Society*[2]—brisk, and well received.   13*th.*—To Haymarket; see wretched piece, *Who killed Cock Robin?*[3] adaptation by Charles Mathews.   16*th.*—All day sketching a history of the Strand Theatre,[4] and writing a lyric for Tom Hood's next Christmas number.   18*th.*—Go to Strand re-opening ; entirely reconstructed ; Burnand's burlesque of *L'Africaine*[5]—not very brilliant.   21*st.*—At first scene of Drury pantomime, *Little King Pippin ; or, Harlequin Fortunatus,* which is only now being thought seriously

[1] Taken from *Le Supplice d'un Homme,* by Grangier and Thiboust. F. Younge made his first appearance after his return from Australia as Timothy Tickleback ; Carnaby Fix, Horace Wigan ; Mrs. Carnaby Fix, Miss Beauclerc ; Mrs. Strombelow, Mrs. Stephens ; Sybilla, Mrs. St. Henry.

[2] By T. W. Robertson.   Sydney Daryl, Sydney Bancroft ; Tom Stylus, F. Dewar; Chodd Senior, J. W. Ray; Chodd Junior, J. Clarke; Maud Hetherington, Marie Wilton ; Lord and Lady Ptarmigant, Mr. Hare and Miss S. Larkin ; Olinthus O'Sullivan, H. W. Montgomery. [This was the stepping stone to Robertson's success.—C. S.]

[3] From *Le Meurtrier de Théodore.*

[4] Fifty years previous to this the building was known as " Reinagle and Barker's New Panorama, near the New Church in the Strand," and there was presented a view of the Bay of Naples.   Then Burford had a panorama there, and for a short time it was used as a chapel.   In 1832 it was opened by Benjamin Lionel Rayner as " Rayner's New Subscription Room " in the Strand, with two new burlettas entitled *Professionals Puzzled* and *Mystification,* in which Mrs. Waylett was the chief star.   The larger theatres had the Lord Chamberlain on their side in their endeavour to crush the smaller houses, and so it was declared illegal to take money at the doors.   An adjoining sweetmeat establishment was annexed to the premises, and visitors paid four shillings an ounce for lozenges, and had an admission for the Strand boxes given them; or bought half an ounce of peppermint drops and had a gratuitous ticket for the pit thrown into the bargain.   At last W. J. Hammond became manager, and produced *Othello according to Act of Parliament,* the first attempt to give the theatre a reputation for burlesque.   Harry Hall was manager from 1842 to 1845, then Roberts, then William Farren in 1850, and about 1858 the Swanboroughs.

[5] J. D. Stoyle, Vasco di Gama ; David James, Nelusco ; Thomas Thorne, Selika ; Inez, Ada Swanborough; Don Pedro, Miss Raynham; Don Alva, Elise Holt ; Grand Inquisitor, Charles Fenton ; Don Diego, H. J. Turner.

about. *25th.*—Leave MS. of three scenes at Drury, going over them with Dykwynkyn; then to Haymarket, *Overland Route* revived; meet George Coppin, who departs for Australia this night. Then to Drury; see a bad adaptation by Falconer, called *Galway go Bragh.*" [1]

"*Dec. 9th.*—Dykwynkyn calls: his birthday, fifty-four, comparisons and congratulations; then to work on *Henry Dunbar,*[2] which piece comes out at Olympic; not over till midnight, and write a column notice for *Era.* *11th.*—This day am forty-five!!! Can hardly realize the fact, and God be thanked for all. *16th.*—Off to St. James's: *School for Scandal;* Miss Herbert, Lady Teazle[3]—very good, rest queer. *22nd.*—All day preparing a notice of Miss Bateman,[4] who this evening takes a farewell of the stage at Her Majesty's —house crowded. *23rd.*—Look in at Alhambra to see Callcott's transformation scene; go to Astley's.[5] *25th.*— Oh! such a doleful, dreary Christmas Day for me! Stop in chambers over article for *Daily Telegraph,* which deliver at night; then back, and at other articles till 4 a.m. *26th.*— Another rushing day. Greatly grieved to hear at Arundel of death of Hart, whose next birthday I had hoped to celebrate.

[1] Or, *Love, Fun, and Fighting.* It was taken from Lever's "Charles O'Malley." Falconer, Mickey Free; Miss Hazlewood, Frank Webber; Rose Leclercq, Lucy Dashwood.

[2] Or, *The Outcast,* adapted by Tom Taylor in a great measure from *L'Ouvrière de Londres,* by M. Hippolyte Hostein, done at the Ambigu Comique, November 1864. Kate Terry, Margaret Wentworth; Henry Neville, Joseph Wilmot; H. J. Montague, Clement Austin; Helen Leigh made her *début* as Laura Dunbar, and Nelly Farren played a *soubrette.*

[3] Frank Matthews, Sir Peter; Mrs. Frank Matthews, for first time, Mrs. Candour; Walter Lacy, Charles Surface; and Belton, Joseph.

[4] She appeared as Juliet to the Romeo of J. C. Cowper; Howe was the Mercutio. On the same evening Miss Bateman's two little sisters made their appearance as Diggory Dawdlegrass and Daisy, in T. Williams's farce, *Little Daisy.*

[5] *Harlequin Tom Tom the Piper's Son, Pope Joan, and Little Bo-Peep;* or, *Old Daddy Long Legs and the Pig that went to Market and the Pig that stayed at Home.* Caroline Parkes and Milano in opening scenes; Rowella, clown; Vestris and Esther Austin, harlequin and harlequina; Misses Emma Carle and Grosvenor, columbines.

Go to Adelphi[5]; look in at Drury; rush off to Prince of Wales's;[6] and write notices. *27th.*—Go to stalls at Drury Lane; see *Little King Pippin;*[7] delighted with Percy Roselle; the other little things not done so well as they might have been. *28th.*—Take Horace Green to Covent Garden to see *Aladdin*[8]—splendidly got up. *29th.*—Look in at Haymarket: *Orpheus and Eurydice,*[9] by Planché—very neat. *30th.*—Dress, and then to grand annual banquet at 2, Russell Square, given by J. M. Levy to the *Telegraph* staff; meet the Lord Mayor (Mr. Phillips), Chas. Braham, Edwin Arnold, Byron, and all the strength of the staff. Sing 'Norrible Tale' (*bis*), 'Rotunda,' and 'Guy Fawkes,' which I had no notion I could recollect, and 'Almanack' song; pleasant evening. *31st.*—The last day of the old year—awake very tired. 'Family' reunion. Send books of pantomimes, etc., wanted for Australian copyright to Coyne. Quiet evening, and welcome the New Year in by reading Tennyson's poem and keeping open doors. Thus closes the busy, chequered year 1865; and God be heartily thanked for all the blessings vouchsafed to me. Welcome 1866, and may peace and happiness come with it."

Estimated revenue for year, £441 8*s.*

[1] *Behind Time.* Toole very funny as Jeremiah Fluke.

[2] *Little Don Giovanni;* or, *Leporello and the Stone Statue,* by H. J. Byron. The Don, Marie Wilton; Leporello, J. Clarke; Ottavio, H. Collier; Donna Anna, Miss Hughes; Masetto, Fanny Josephs; Zerlina, J. Hare.

[3] Or, *Harlequin Fortunatus and the Magic Purse and Wishing Cap,* by E. L. B. Augusta Thompson, Fortunatus; Master Percy Roselle, Little King Pippin; Henri Drayton, Mammon; Boleno and E. Lauri, clowns; Cormack and S. Saville, harlequins; Barnes and J. Norris, pantaloons; Madame Boleno and Miss C. Morgan, columbines.

[4] Or, *Harlequin and the Flying Palace,* E. L. B.'s pantomime. Aladdin, Rachel Sanger; Abanazar, W. H. Payne, afterwards Clown; Kazrac, Fred Payne, afterwards Harlequin; Widow Chin Chin, Charles Steyne; Princess Badroulbadour, Blanche Elliston; Genius of the Lamp, Miss Dacre; Columbine, Mdlle. Esta; Pantaloon, Paul Herring.

[5] This was called *Orpheus in the Haymarket.* David Fisher, Orpheus; Eurydice, Louise Keeley; Pluto, Bartleman; Juno, Miss Snowden; Jove, W. Farren; Minerva, Miss Coleman; Diana, Henrietta Lindley; Cupid, Ellen Woolgar; Venus, Nelly Moore; Mercury, Fanny Wright.

1866.

"*Jan. 8th.*—To Strand : see John Brougham's very bad three-act drama called *Nellie's Trials* (same piece as *Might of Right*).[1]   10*th.*—Take Walter to morning performance at Astley's: *Tom, Tom, the Piper's Son.*[2]   11*th.*—Get private box for Lyceum ; see for first time *Master of Ravenswood*,[3] strongest impression being that Carlotta Leclerq is very good, and that last act is the best.   13*th.*—Dine with the Lord Mayor!! (Phillips) at the Mansion House at 6 ; about eighty there ; magnificent spread ; meet George Phillips and brother, old acquaintances ; sing 'St. George,' 'A Norrible Tale,' 'Almanacks.'   Mr. J. M. Levy touchingly spoke of his fifty years' friendship with the Lord Mayor, and how they climbed the hill of life together.   To E. Levy's, where Albert C. Wright and Byron.   15*th.*—Receive from Drury £25, first instalment of pantomime account.   See burlesque of *Princess Primrose* (produced on Saturday), or, *The Four Pretty Princes*;[4] prettily put on the stage, but very coarsely written.   18*th.*—

[1] Or, *The Soul of Honour*, produced at Astley's, January 30th, 1864. Ada Swanborough in the title *rôle*.   Tom Thorne as Jacob Tinsel.

[2] It was by T. L. Greenwood.

[3] Palgrave Simpson's adaptation of *The Bride of Lammermoor*.   The most popular version of this novel was a three-act drama by John William Calcraft, in which Messrs. Murray, Mackay, and Mrs. Siddons appeared in Edinburgh.   E. L. Davenport and Mrs. Mowatt played in it at the Marylebone in 1848.   Frédéric Lemaître was great in the French version, *La Fiancée de Lammermoor*, as Edgar Ravenswood, at the Porte St. Martin, March 28th, 1828.   In the Lyceum version, Lucy Ashton, played by Carlotta Leclercq dies in the arms of Ravenswood (Charles Fechter), as they are swallowed up by the quicksand. This was a marvellous moonlit scene, and the rest of the scenery, by T. Grieve, was looked upon as some of the best that he had ever painted.   Hermann Vezin was the Hayston of Bucklaw ; Miss Elsworthy, Lady Ashton ; G. Jordan, Sir William Ashton ; Mrs. Ternan, Alice ; Widdicombe, Captain Craigengelt ; J. H. Fitzpatrick, Colonel Douglas Ashton ; Miss E. Lavenu, Henry Ashton ; and Sam Emery, Caleb Balderstone.

[4] By Best and Bellingham.   The four Princes were—Amrus, Lydia Foote ; Turfi, Amy Sheridan ; Hasard, Ellen Leigh ; and Pecki, Miss H. Everard.   Miss Wilson was Princess Primrose ; R. Soutar was the Demon Uglee.

See new farce at Adelphi, *Pipkin's Rural Retreat*,[1] by T. J. Williams; goes off well; Toole very good. 19*th*.—All day writing with a sad heart the memoir of poor G. V. Brooke, drowned in the *London* steamer, on the 11th instant![2] Story of Toole's success on his first trip. 21*st*.—Meet Kingston and Avonia Jones (widow of poor G. V. Brooke), and with her fruitlessly go in search of E. Gardner, that she might hear poor Brooke's last words."

[1] Toole played Brittle Pipkins; Miss A. Seaman, Betsy Perks; Paul Bedford was Shandy Gaff.

[2] E. L. B. states that Gustavus Vaughan Brooke was born on April 25th, 1819, at Hardwick Place, Dublin, and as a child was a great favourite of the novelist, Maria Edgeworth, by whose brother Lovell he was educated; and was noted for his love of, and skill in, athletic sports. He was then placed under the tuition of the Rev. William Jones, to be prepared for college, with a view of his joining the Irish Bar. He went to see Macready when he was fourteen years of age, and this decided his future career. He called the next day on the great actor, and told him that he wished to join the profession, and Macready pointed out to him all its perils, dangers, and hardships. This did not alter Brooke's determination, for he soon after called upon J. W. Calcraft, manager of the Theatre Royal, Dublin, and requested to appear in the character of William Tell, and recited to him one or two pieces.   Calcraft and his wife were very much struck with his recitation, but told him that they could do nothing at present. Almost immediately afterwards, Edmund Kean, who had been engaged to appear, was unable to do so through illness. The manager was in a fix, and thought of Gustavus Brooke, and allowed him to appear on Easter Tuesday, 1833, as William Tell. The result was sufficiently satisfactory to obtain for him an engagement, and he appeared as Virginius, Frederic in *Lover's Vows*, Douglas and Rolla. He then went to Limerick and Londonderry, and was engaged for twelve nights for Glasgow. From thence to Edinburgh, where he was engaged for the rest of the season, and earned the title of "The Hibernian Roscius." He then came to London to the Victoria and joined the Kent circuit. After considerable work in the provinces he appeared as Othello at the Olympic Theatre, January 2nd, 1848, and was at once acknowledged as one of the greatest tragedians of the age, and had the most liberal offers, but he returned to the provinces, and after a tour went to America, and made his *début* at the Broadway Theatre, New York, December 15th, 1851, as Othello. His first appearance in Philadelphia was on January 5th, 1852, as Sir Giles Overreach. He had made a considerable sum of money, but he invested it in taking the Astor Place Opera House, New York, which he opened in 1852, but lost everything, and became deeply involved in debt; but, to his honour

"*Feb. 5th.*—See dismal comedy at Strand of *Fly and the Web*,[1] by Troughton. *6th.*—Drury Lane second payment of £25. *10th.*—At Drury see *Stranger;* Phelps, and Mrs. Hermann Vezin as Mrs. Haller. Hear from Edward Murray doubts of Covent Garden, but find it open after all ; hear the money is very doubtful indeed there. *15th.*—To Haymarket : *A Romantic Attachment,* and Ada Cavendish's first appearance.[2] *27th.*—Go to St. James's ; *She Stoops,* very indifferently acted ; Calthrop, under name of Clayton Hastings, not a light comedian. *28th.*—Try a desperate remedy for the 'blues :' go in evening to first supper of 'The Vagrants,' held at what used to be Hubble's ; James Bruton in chair, and some fifty present ; I take McConnell, the barrister, who returns thanks for visitors ; I return for Literature, proposed by Carpenter ; a very pleasant evening."

"*March 3rd.*—Go to Drury, and by cheque from Chatterton

be it remembered, he paid every shilling afterwards. On September 6th, 1852, he recommenced touring through the States as a star, and his progress was triumphant. He returned to England and reappeared at Drury Lane, September 5th, 1853. In 1854 he took his farewell of the London public, and sailed for Australia. He became lessee of the Theatre Royal, Melbourne, but the speculation was unsuccessful, so after seven years' absence he returned to Drury Lane, October 28th, 1861, appearing as Othello. G. V. Brooke was tall, dignified, and graceful ; his features were eminently expressive, and on the stage his walk and presence were majestic. As a tragic artist he stood at one time in the highest rank. His style was perfectly natural, from no school, but fresh from the hand of Nature. He possessed a voice of great power, which he used effectively. He was almost absurdly generous. The unfortunate steamer, *London,* had left Plymouth on January 6th, and had been battling with fearful weather until the 11th, when she went down with two hundred and twenty souls. Only sixteen of the crew and three passengers survived. Gustavus V. Brooke set an example of courage and fortitude to all on board—working at the pumps ; and appears to have accepted his coming doom with resignation. The last words he was known to have uttered were, " If you succeed in saving yourselves, give my farewell to the people at Melbourne."

[1] Suggested by Scribe's *Le Gardien.* Scene transformed to England and to epoch 1760.

[2] This was her first appearance in comedy *rôles,* she had hitherto appeared in burlesque and extravaganza. W. Farren, Compton, and Mrs. E. Fitzwilliam were in the cast.

£25. To Standard; see piece of *A Patriot Spy.*[1] 10*th.*—
Write to R. Banner Oakley, to ask him for something for
Covent Garden pantomime: not had a sixpence yet, and
greatly concerned thereby.   10*th.*—Dine at Freemasons'
Tavern, Newsvendors' Benevolent Institution; McCullogh
Torrens, M.P., in chair; I respond to the Press toast,
giving a hint about the unstamped prize and subscription boxes; go to Masham, 80, Fleet Street, and get
two guineas, for which I give up all further claim on
Covent Garden. 24*th.*—To Adelphi, and see 172nd and last
night of *Rip van Winkle*, Jefferson's benefit. A fire at
Daily Telegraph office; suspicion of incendiarism. 28th.—
General and Theatrical Fund dinner, Lord Mayor (Phillips)
in chair; attend dinner, the *Telegraph* Levys all present, but
my severe cold completely destroys the pleasures of the day.
31*st.*—Then to New Royalty: new burlesque by Reece called
Ulf the Minstrel;[2] and Olympic *Ticket-of-Leave Man* revived
(419th representation)."

" *April 2nd.*—Off to Haymarket: *Favourite of Fortune,*[3]
Westland Marston's new comedy, charmingly written and
goes off well. 7*th.*—Chatterton pays per cheque £20,
balance due for Drury. 9*th.*—First night at Surrey of
Theodora:[4] Avonia Jones (Mrs. G. V. Brooke); no great

---

[1] Originally produced at the Surrey Theatre, November 1859;
Creswick and Sarah Thorne in their original characters.

[2] The theatre was opened under the management of Patty Oliver.
R. B. Brough had a share in the writing of the piece. Patty Oliver
played the Princess Diamonduck; Lydia Maitland appeared as Ulf;
Annie Bourke as Bimbo.

[3] Caroline Hill appeared as Euphemia; Henrietta Lindley, Camilla;
Sothern, Frank Annerley; Mrs. Chippendale, Mrs. Lorrington; Buck-
stone, Tom Sutherland; Kate Saville and Nelly Moore, Hester and
Lucy Lorrington.

[4] *Theodora, Actress and Empress*, by Watts Phillips. In this drama,
showing an episode in the career of the celebrated actress and courtesan,
the main interest turned upon her condemning to death her son Philip
the issue of her marriage, some twenty years before she became
empress, with Creon, whom she has won from Miriam, a young Jewess
that Creon had deserted, and who from that time forward devotes
herself to vengeance on Theodora. Avonia Jones, Theodora; James
Bennett, Creon; Miss G. Pauncefort, Miriam; James Fernandez,
Philip; C. Butler, Justinian.

success. As I sit in the stalls, a thumping bundle of bread and cheese plumps down from gallery nearly on my head —a narrow escape."

"*May 5th.*—See Byron's new drama of *A Hundred Thousand Pounds*[1] at the Prince of Wales's Theatre : first act very good, and the piece a success ; meet hosts of people I know. Back to write notice, and then to Woburn Lodge and sup at Edward Levy's ; Robertson, Sloper, Albert Levy, and Byron and Prowse present. *7th.*—To Adelphi : see *La Famille Benoiton*, called *The Fast Family*, and don't like it.[2] *16th.*—Derby Day, and Lord Lyon, the favourite, comes in the winner ; go down by S. W. R. ; weather cloudy but fine ; spend on the course four dreary wretched hours, all alone ; then meet Mr. Lawson and the Phillipses (sons of Lord Mayor), and kindly provided with sitting room and refreshments. Back to town at 6, and then work away for *Daily Telegraph*, producing a two-column article. All my speculations, as usual, in ' sweeps ' awful failures. *17th.*—To Princess's : a tremendous house, and brilliant reception of the Keans,[3] this being their first appearance in England after their return from their famous tour round the world. Go to Lyceum ; *Corsican Brothers* being played here for the first time with Fechter.[4] Then to Prince of Wales's.[5] *23rd.*—Death of Miss Cottrell[6] of Olympic, who died on Monday, aged only twenty-five."

[1] The first act of this was considered to be the best. Marie Wilton, Alice ; Sydney Bancroft, Gerald Goodwin ; J. W. Ray, Joe Barlow ; J. Clarke, Pennythorne ; John Hare, Fluker ; F. Dewar, Major Blackshaw. Miss Goodall, Blanche Wilton, and Montgomery were also in the cast.

[2] It was by Ben Webster, Junior.

[3] They appeared in *Henry VIII.* Mr. and Mrs. Charles Kean as the Cardinal and Queen Catherine ; Miss Chapman, Anne Boleyn.

[4] English version of Alexandre Dumas' novel, dramatized by MM. Grangé and X. de Montepier, first played at the Théâtre Historique, August 10th, 1850. Fechter ; the brothers Dei Franchi ; G. Jordan, Château Rénaud ; Hermann Vezin, S. Emery, H. Widdicombe, Mrs. Ternan, Mesdames Henrade and E. Lavenu were also in the cast.

[5] Louisa Moore made her first appearance here as Miss Thistledown in *The Bonnie Fishwife*.

[6] At a very early age she had appeared as an actress at the Olympic

"*June 2nd.*—See Offenbach's *Bluebeard*,[1] a preposterous piece of nonsense. *4th.*—Go to Lyceum: *Dr. Davy*,[2] Vezin's piece. Then to Princess's: *Louis the Eleventh*.[3] *6th.*—Send mother hamper of wine and spirits as a birthday present. *20th.*—Go to Haymarket: *Dundreary Married and Done For* revived; to Princess's: last night of Kean's *Merchant of Venice* and *Jealous Wife;* and Olympic (Kate Terry's benefit),[4] *The Hunchback.* *30th.*—See *La Belle Hélène*[5] at Adelphi: Offenbach's music very pretty and sparkling; and Burnand's libretto in rhyme very neat."

"*July 2nd.*—To Princess's: *The Huguenot Captain;*[6] Watts Phillips. *6th.*—At Arundel, and meet Barry Sullivan, just returned after four and a half years' absence in Australia. *14th.*—Opening of the Hall at Margate-by-the-Sea (Spiers and Pond); meet Brown, Leigh, and everybody. *25th.*— This day poor Robert Roxby dies,[7] the stage-manager of

and St. James's Theatres, and had made her mark; but possessing a considerable knowledge of music, she thought it advisable to turn it to account on the operatic stage, and only the week before her death was appearing at Her Majesty's Theatre, as Mdlle. Edi.　She married John Haines, the violoncellist.

[1] An adaptation by Bellingham of Offenbach's *Barbe-Bleu.* Libretto by Henri Meilhac and Halévy, music arranged by J. H. Tully.　Robert, Ellen Farren; King Earlypurl, W. H. Stephens; Prince Sapphire, Amy Sheridan; Mopsa, Susan Galton.

[2] E. L. B. evidently means by this that Hermann Vezin excelled as David Garrick in *Doctor Davy*, for the piece was really an adaptation by James Albery of *Docteur Robin.*　Miss Henrade was the Mary.

[3] Charles Kean, J. F. Cathcart, Miss Chapman, Mrs. Charles Kean, and Vollaire were in the cast.

[4] Kate Terry played Julia, for the first time; Miss Ellen Terry (Mrs. G. F. Watts) played Helen, also for the first time, with great spirit and animation; Henry Neville was the Master Walter; Horace Wigan, Modus.　Kate Terry delivered an address written by Tom Taylor.

[5] E. L. B. means by this *Helen; or, Taken from the Greek*, Burnand's free version.　Mrs. Alfred Mellon, Paris; Paul Bedford, Calchas; Miss Furtado, Helen; J. L. Toole, Menelaus; Miss A. Seaman, Orestes.

[6] Mrs. Stirling, George Honey, George Vining, Augusta Thompson were in the cast.　Miss Neilson played Gabrielle.

[7] Son of William Roxby Beverley, and brother to William Beverley, the scenic artist.　After considerable experience in the provinces he

Drury, after a long illness; I should think he was about fifty-seven."

" *Aug.* 4*th.*—Poor Charles Ball, the original editor of *Illustrated London News,* *Lloyd's Weekly News,* 'Censorius' of the *Dispatch,* died, aged, I should think, over seventy. 6*th.*—First night of Amy Sedgwick's opening Haymarket: *The Unequal Match.* 11*th.*—Astley's opens under the management of a Miss Sophie Young, with *The Mysteries of Audley Court,*[1] dramatized by John Brougham; piece very bad, actress middling: take Jonas Levy. 27*th.*—To Strand: *Waiting for the Underground;* trashy fun by L. H. du Terreaux. 29*th.*—Busy with *Era* copy. To Adelphi (Toole's benefit), and see *Paul Pry* and stupid farce, *Keep Your Door Locked.*[2] Write notices *Daily Telegraph.* A son of Mrs. Warner[3] tries Hamlet to-night at Wells for his father's benefit: not great. 30*th.*—For three weeks' hard work for *Era* £3 10*s.,* being my own modest estimate : ought to be ashamed of myself."

" *Sept.* 8*th.*—*Era* £2. Surrey Theatre reopens: prize drama, *True to the Core,*[4] by A. Slous; good subject, drama indifferent, acting capital. Write column and a half notice

appeared at the St. James's Theatre in 1839, when Hooper was the lessee. From that time he remained in London, and was for a long time a member of the Lyceum and Drury Lane Companies; at the latter theatre he had been stage-manager for eleven years.

[1] Robert Audley, George Jordan ; George Talboys, Henry Sinclair; Alicia Audley, Maud Shelley ; Phœbe Marks, Miss Marian ; Lady Audley, Sophie Young.

[2] This was the first time that Toole had attempted the character of Paul Pry ; he dressed it exactly after the manner of Liston. Mrs. Alfred Mellon was the Phœbe, and gave the song of " Cherry Ripe," Robert Herrick's words, so charmingly set to music by Charles Horn. Harry Stanley, originally played by Mrs. Waylett, fell to the lot of John Billington. The farce was by Arthur Matthieson. On the same night Toole played Menelaus in *Helen.*

[3] This was John Lawrence Warner. He was described as having a tall, graceful figure, fine forehead, and most expressive features. His performance was considered highly creditable. Miss Neville was the Ophelia ; W. Roberts, the King ; Mr. Jaques, Laertes ; and W. Brunton, the Gravedigger.

[4] The action of the play takes place in July 1588, and had to do with the coming of the Spanish Armada. Creswick, Martin Truegold ;

for *Era.* 10*th.*—To New Royalty (second night of season); burlesque by Reece, *The Lady of the Lake.*[1] 13*th.*—To Sadlers Wells (first night of season) : see *Othello ;* Salter[2] the Moor, young Lawrence Warner Iago ; both very fair. 14*th.*—To Haymarket : see Amy Sedgwick in *Love Chase* (her benefit, and last night but one of her summer season). 15*th.*—To Lyceum, opening with Boucicault's new drama of *A Long Strike,*[3] which I think very highly of. Write long notice for *Era.* Go to Arundel, and hear of Robertson's comedy of *Ours*[4] being a success at Prince of Wales's, opening also this evening. 22*nd.*—Drury opens : *King John* and *Comedy of Errors.*[5] Have Palgrave Simpson, Stone, Clayton, and Leigh in private box. 26*th.*—See dress rehearsal of a bad piece by Tom Taylor, *The Whiteboy,* at Olympic, which

Mabel, the " Rose of Devon," Kate Saville ; Marah, Georgina Pauncefort ; Master Wallet, the Pedlar, Mr. Shepherd ; and Geoffery Danger, Henry Marston. The Admiral, E. F. Edgar.

[1] The full name of this was *The Lady of the Lake, plaid in a New Tartan.* James V. of Scotland, Rosina Ranoe ; Malcolm Græme, Henrietta Lindley ; M'Howler, W. H. Stephens. The theatre was under the management of Miss M. Oliver.

[2] This was J. H. Salter, from the Theatre Royal, Liverpool. Miss Leigh was the Desdemona, and Mrs. J. F. Saville, from the Nottingham Theatre, Emilia ; Cassio, Mr. Collier, late of the Strand. Later in this same week Salter and Warner reversed the parts.

[3] This play was in four acts, and was suggested by Mrs. Gaskell's stories, " Mary Barton " and " Lizzie Leigh." Mrs. Boucicault, Jane Learoyd ; Dion Boucicault, Johnny Reilly ; S. Emery, Noah Learoyd ; J. C. Cowper, who had been for a long time a favourite at Liverpool ; Jem Starkie ; H. Widdicombe, Moneypenny.

[4] It had its trial trip at the Prince of Wales's, Liverpool. Sir Alexander Shendryn, J. W. Ray ; Blanche Haye, Louisa Moore ; Mary Netley, Marie Wilton ; Lady Shendryn, Miss Larkin ; Angus M'Allister, S. Bancroft ; Prince Perovsky, Mr. Hare ; Hugh Chalcot, Mr. Clarke ; Sergeant Jones, F. Younge. One of the scenes which produced the greatest enthusiasm was the departure of the troops for the Crimea, and in the third act was shown the interior of a Crimean hut with Chalcot, the hitherto useless man about town, doing the cooking.

[5] Phelps, King John ; Barry Sullivan, Falconbridge ; Percy Roselle, Prince Arthur ; F. Barsby, Louis the Dauphin ; Barrett, Cardinal Pandulph ; Miss F. Bennett, Prince Henry ; Mrs. Hermann Vezin, Constance—her first appearance in the character, very highly spoken of ; Mrs. H. Vandenhoff, Queen Elinor ; Adelaide Golier, Lady

opens for season to-morrow.[1] My old friend ' Bob Souter ' of the *Advertiser*, the oldest leader of the 'Gallery,' died this week, aged seventy. 29*th*.—Meet Billington and Hare (the young actor of Prince of Wales's) for the first time in private."

" *Oct.* 1*st*.—To Haymarket : *Heir-at-Law*,[2] first night of season. 2*nd*.—Look in at Drury : *Macbeth*, Barry Sullivan ; and Lady Macbeth, Amy Sedgwick. 4*th*.—To Haymarket : return of Mr. and Mrs. Charles Mathews.[3] 6*th*.—New Holborn Theatre[4] opened with Boucicault's drama, *The*

Blanche. In the *Comedy of Errors*, the brothers Webb were the two Dromios ; and H. Sinclair and F. Barsby respectively Antipholus of Ephesus, and Antipholus of Syracuse.

[1] This was supposed to have been written many years before it was produced, and E. L. B. seems to have thought it founded on one of the " Tales by the O'Hara Family." The scenery was laid in Ireland, in 1795, about three years before the great Irish rebellion. Captain Trevor, H. J. Montague ; Grace Moriarty, Miss E. Wilson ; Grace Dwyer, Milly Palmer ; Redmond O'Hara, Henry Neville ; Paddy M'Kew, George Vincent. In this, too, Miss E. Farren played the part of Pandreen, an "innocent," who is dumb. Jerrold Reeves, Sergeant Sidebottom.

[2] With one exception, when it was played for Harley's Benefit at the Princess's about twelve years before, *The Heir-at-Law* had not been seen since 1835. On this occasion J. B. Buckstone was the 'Zekiel Homespun ; Chippendale, Daniel Dowlas ; Mrs. Chippendale, Lady Duberly ; Nelly Moore, Cicely Homespun ; Caroline Hill, Caroline Dormer ; W. Farren, Dick Dowlas ; and Compton, Doctor Pangloss.

[3] They appeared in *Used Up*, and in W. Brough's adaptation, *The Comical Countess*. Under another title, *A Decided Hit*, a translation by Howard Paul. It had been played at the Lyceum some fifteen years before.

[4] Built by Sefton Parry, and named by him Holborn Theatre Royal, was situated on the north side of Holborn, not very far from the opening of Chancery Lane. The gallery entrance in Brownlow Street, was built on the site in which Charles Mohun died in 1684. The theatre had three entrances, from Holborn, Brownlow Street, and Jockey's Fields. The act drop was painted by Charles S. James, and was a Watteau theme. The bill of the play for the night was a new farce by T. J. Williams, called *Larkins's Love Letters*, very similar to *Waiting for the Underground*. The second title to the *Flying Scud* was *A Four-legged Fortune*, and the cast in it was certainly excellent. Captain Grindley Goodge, G. Neville ; Colonel Mulligan, E. Garden ; Mr. Chouser, Westland ; Mo Davis, Vollaire ; Tom Meredith,

Flying Scud, with which delighted; it makes a decided hit. Write notice which runs to three columns. *8th.*— To Haymarket and St. James's: write notice of former (*Overland Route* and *Critic*), and leave latter (*Belle's Stratagem*)[1] for another occasion. Meet Harrison of the *Daily Telegraph.* *9th.*—To Strand; see a burlesque by Burnand on *Der Freischütz.*[2] *10th.*—To Prince of Wales's: see very bad burlesque by Byron, *Der Freischütz.*[3] *15th.*— To Drury, taking Stone, to see *Macbeth;* a new tragedian, named Talbot, not good.[4] *16th.*—Strand: see a slight adaptation by W. H. Swanborough, *In the Wrong Box*, and sit through the burlesque. *17th.*—See at New Royalty a clever piece by H. T. Craven, called *Meg's Diversions.*[5] *20th.*—Go to Drury: *Faust* carefully got up, but a very heavy

G. Blake; Katey Rideout, Bessie Foote; Nat Gosling, G. Belmore; Ned Compo, Miss M. Fawsitt; Julia Latimer, Miss J. Fiddes; Lord Woodbie, Fanny Josephs. The part of Nat Gosling was one of the best that G. Belmore ever played, and but little behind him was Charlotte Saunders, as Bob Buckskin, another jockey who will put on too much flesh. Vollaire's Mo Davis may almost be said to have been the original from which so many stage Hebrews have been copied.

[1] This was for the re-opening of the theatre under Miss Herbert's management. She appeared as Letitia Hardy to Henry Irving's Doricourt. Walter Lacy, Flutter; Mr. and Mrs. Frank Matthews, Hardy and Widow Racket; Gaston Murray, Sir George Touchwood; Mr. Burleigh, Saville; F. Charles, Courtley; E. Dyas, Villers; Carlotta Addison (first appearance here), Lady Frances Touchwood; Eleanor Bufton, Miss Ogle. On the same night a new farce by John Oxenford, entitled *Professor of What?*—and in it J. D. Stoyle made his first appearance here as Job, and created a most favourable impression. Henry Irving was the stage-manager.

[2] Or, *A Good Cast for a Piece.* Zamiel, Miss Raynham; Caspar, Charles Fenton; Rudolph, David James; Agnes, Ada Swanborough; Madame von Stuckup, T. Thorne; William, Miss E. Johnstone; Anne, Fanny Hughes; Catspaw, F. Robson.

[3] Or, *The Bell, the Bill, and the Ball.* Lydia Thompson, Max; J. Clarke, Caspar; F. Younge, Zamiel; Louisa Moore, Agatha; Lydia Maitland, William; H. W. Montgomery, Kusno; F. Glover (first appearance here), Hugo.

[4] This was H. Talbot, an actor who had made a considerable name in the provinces. Miss Amy Sedgwick was the Lady Macbeth.

[5] Miss Oliver in the title *rôle*, the author as Jaspar Pidgeon; Roland, F. Dewar. In this was introduced a realization of Calderon's picture, " Broken Vows."

play in representation.[1] 22*nd.*—Standard Theatre burnt down yesterday morning.[2] 24*th.*—Begin first scene of Drury pantomime, *Number Nip; or, Harlequin and the Gnome King of the Giant Mountain.* 27*th.*—*Daily Telegraph* arrears £3 3*s.* Olympic: first night here of Wilkie Collins's piece of *The Frozen Deep;*[3] goes slowly. 31*st.*—To Haymarket: *A Dangerous Friend,* adaptation by Oxenford of *La Tentation;* not good, though with C. Mathews and wife in it."[4]

"*Nov.* 1*st.*—Reece, like Albert Smith and Byron, has 'walked' the hospitals. 2*nd.*—Dine at Arundel, and then to St. James's, seeing a stupid farce by Norton, called

[1] Bayle Bernard's version of Lewis Filmore's translation of *Faust.* Phelps, Mephistopheles; Mrs. Hermann Vezin, Marguerite; W. Harrison, Valentine; O. Harcourt, Siebel; F. Barsby, Wagner. Lisa was played by Miss Poole, who sang "Dews from the Heaven descending." The arrangement of Spohr's music was by J. H. Tully, who had also taken some of the best numbers from Bishop, Mendelssohn, Haydn, and Weber. The piece was most elaborate in scenic effects, the whole stage-management being entrusted to Mr. Edward Stirling. This was the first season of Chatterton being the sole manager of Drury Lane.

[2] It was situated in High Street, Shoreditch, and built some twelve years previously by Mr. Douglas. On the same ground had been a theatre originally built by Mr. Gibson, who was succeeded in management by Nelson Lee, and then by Mr. Douglas. This building was erected on the site of the little Curtain Theatre, in which Grimaldi once performed. The theatre, now burnt down, was calculated to hold some four thousand people. The evening before, *Der Freischütz,* a burlesque by John Douglas, son of the proprietor, had been performed, and the house had been crammed. The place was entirely gutted, and not a shred of scenery, dresses, or anything else was recovered, except a carroty wig belonging to Brittain Wright, the comedian. The fire began at 6 a.m. on Sunday morning.

[3] First played on Twelfth Night, 1857, at Tavistock House, Charles Dickens's London residence, with scenery by Stanfield and Telbin, and in it Charles Dickens's family appeared, he himself playing Richard Wardour; Wilkie Collins, Frank Aldersléy; Mark Lemon, Lieutenant Crayford. At the Olympic, Lydia Foote was the Clara Vernon; Henry Neville, Richard Wardour; H. J. Montague, Frank Aldersley; Horace Wigan, Lieutenant Crayford; Dominick Murray, John Want; Mrs. St. Henry, Lucy Crayford; Amy Sheridan, Mrs. Steventon; Miss Alliston, Rose Ebsworth. Hawes Craven painted the scenery.

[4] Another version of this, called *The House or the Home,* by Tom Taylor, was done at the Adelphi.

Newington Butts.   *5th.*—Leave first scene of pantomime at Drury.   To St. James's : *Hunted Down ;* or, *Two Lives of Mary Leigh,* three-act drama, rather heavy, but of ingenious construction, by Boucicault.[1]   *10th.*—To Strand ; see adaptation from Charles Goldoni's comedy by Oxenford, called *Neighbours.*   *12th.*—Scarcely able to write a line through the terrible mental worry I am enduring.   To Princess's : see *Barnaby Rudge*[2]—a failure, Miss Miggs by Mrs. John Wood (daughter of Mrs. H. Vining).   Write notice by 2.   *13th.* —To Artemus Ward's first night at Egyptian Hall, *Among the Mormons ;* get a hearty laugh.   All the notabilities there : meet Home the medium, now Lyon, in possession of large property.   *14th.*—Hard at work ; see Dykwynkyn about pantomime ; much behind-hand.   Then to Alhambra dinner : Cossett in chair ; Oxenford, Dunphie, Hollingshead, etc.

[1] John Leigh, Walter Lacy ; Rawdon Scudamore, Henry Irving ; Mary Leigh, Miss Herbert (originally played at the Prince's Theatre, Manchester, in August, by Miss Kate Terry) ; Clara, Miss Ada Dyas (originally played by Lydia Foote) ; Lady Glencarrig, Miss Guillon Le Thière ; Mrs. Bolton Jones, Mrs. Frank Matthews.   It made a most favourable impression on the audience.

[2] This was not the first version of Dickens's novel, Charles Selby having already arranged one, which was produced at the English Opera House, afterwards named the Lyceum, June 28th, 1841 : The author played Chester ; Miss Fortescue, Barnaby Rudge ; Mrs. Harris, Miss Miggs.   In the December following another version was brought out at the Adelphi : Mrs. Yates as Mrs. Rudge ; Miss Chaplin, Barnaby ; Wilkinson, John Willett ; Paul Bedford, Gabriel Varden ; O. Smith, Hugh ; Edward Wright, Tappertit ; and Yates, Sir John Chester, and doubled the character with that of Miss Miggs.   In a few weeks Yates resigned both characters—Mr. Cullenford then playing Chester, and Miss Gower Miss Miggs.   The play was most probably produced to introduce Mrs. John Wood to the London stage.   She was for some time a member of the Theatre Royal, Manchester, where she married Mr. John Wood the comedian, and accompanied him to America in 1854. Made her *début* there, in September, at the New Boston Theatre.   Five years later she was manageress of the American Theatre, San Francisco ; and, returning to New York, became an immense favourite.   Miss Miggs was made a "Yankee girl," and as such was a success so far as the acting was concerned.   Mrs. Henry Vining was Mrs. Rudge ; Katherine Rodgers, Barnaby ; Augusta Thomson, Dolly Varden ; Mr. and Mrs. Charles Horsman, Maypole Hugh and Mrs. Varden ; S. Calhaem, Simon ; C. H. Fenton, J. Willett.

15th.—Record death of Mrs. Chatterly.[1] *17th.*—Hear from C. C. B., dated September. *19th.*—To Drury : Helen Faucit's reappearance ;[2] and then to Her Majesty's : *Oonagh*, long-winded five-act drama by Falconer.[3] *21st.*—To wretched burlesque at Haymarket, by Burnand, on *Antony and Cleopatra :* well got up, but so dull ![4] *23rd.*—To St. James's Hall, Miss Glyn's readings ; Helen Faucit as Pauline at Drury. Write notices of both. *26th.*—At Adelphi new drama by Tom Taylor and Dubourg, called *A Sister's Penance ;* good acting by Kate Terry.[5] *29th.*—To New Royalty : latest edition of *Black-eyed Susan*, indifferent burlesque by

[1] Maiden name, Louisa Simeon. Born October 16th, 1797 ; made her first appearance at the old Lyceum, July 1816, as Harriet in *Is He Jealous ?* Soon after married William Chatterly, a favourite comedian at that theatre. In July 1821 she played Julia, in *The Rivals*, at the opening of the Haymarket Theatre. First appeared at Covent Garden as Miss Hardcastle in *She Stoops to Conquer ;* in the November following also played there—Letitia Hardy, Edmund in *The Blind Boy* and Lady Teazle. She was afterwards married to Mr. Place, February 13th, 1830, and left the stage ; but, again being left a widow, joined Mr. Alfred Wigan's company when he was manager of the Olympic. Her last engagement was at the Adelphi Theatre. She died Sunday, November 4th.

[2] As Rosalind in *As You Like It.* Walter Montgomery, Orlando ; H. Webb, Touchstone.

[3] He opened the theatre as manager with his play, the second title of which was *The Lovers of Lisnamona*, founded on Maria Edgeworth's novel and Carlton's " Fardouroughra the Miser." The author played the Miser. Oonagh was played by Miss Fanny Addison. The play dragged its weary length along till past two in the morning, when the carpenters took the law into their own hands, pulled the carpet from under the actors' feet, and lowered the curtain. *The play was never finished*, for it was not seen again.

[4] It was called "*An Eccentric View of the Well-known Tale of Antony and Cleopatra :* Her Story and His Story related in a Modern Nilo-metre." Compton, Lepidus ; Caroline Hill, Eros ; Mrs. Charles Mathews, Cleopatra ; Charles Mathews, Antony ; Rogers, Pompey the Great ; Fanny Wright, Octavius Cæsar ; Clark, Octavia.

[5] Into this was introduced a scene of the Indian Mutiny, and John Billington as Ammedoolah figured conspicuously in the play, he having fallen desperately in love with Alice Vernon (Kate Terry). Fanny Hughes was the Marion Vernon, the sister who was betrayed; Hermann Vezin, Markham, the hero.

Burnand.[1] Write notice of that and Haymarket revival of *Game of Speculation*."

"*Dec.* 10*th.*—The ' good Mary ' returns with ' Joey ' after a week's stay in Essex. Stop up till about 2 a.m., and drink my own health, sadly *solus.* 11*th.*—Complete my forty-sixth birthday ! ! ! Read pantomime of *Number Nip* in green-room of Drury, and usual delay in theatre. Sorry to hear of my old friend Palser's (the printseller) death ; about fifty-seven, I think. According to my old custom, spend the evening with my mother, taking her a little present, and receiving one (book) in exchange. This week have about as serious an attack of illness as ever I had in my life. Beautiful day. Ledger's daughter married ; invited, but can't attend.[2] 25*th.*—Christmas Day. I spend my Christmas Day, as usual, *solus* in my chambers, working for *Daily Telegraph.* The housekeeper sends me up a slice of goose for my dinner, and I work on till 3 next morning to get ready with the heavy pressure of ' light ' articles wanted ; awfully tired. 26*th.*—In morning to Haymarket : see clever troupe of performing children.[3] Then to Olympic ;[4] then,

---

[1] The title of this was, *The Latest Edition of Black-eyed Susan,* or, *The Little Bill that was Taken Up.* Patty Oliver in the title *rôle*; Rosina Ranoe, William ; Danvers, Dame Hatley ; Fanny Heath (from the York circuit), Gnatbrain ; Miss Bromley (a *débutante* in London), Dolly Mayflower ; Charles Wyndham, Hatchett ; Dewar, Crosstree ; Russell, Doggrass.

[2] Eliza Ledger, elder daughter of Frederic Ledger, married John McCabe.

[3] They were called " The Living Miniatures," were trained by Mr. Coe, of the Haymarket Theatre, and appeared in a sketch called *Littletop's Christmas Party,* and in a burlesque written by Reginald Moore, entitled *Sylvius ;* or, *The Peril ! the Pelf ! ! and the Pearl ! ! !* The names of these children appear to have been mostly *noms de guerre.*

[4] Benjamin Webster, lessee ; Horace Wigan, manager. *London Assurance* was played. Charles Mathews returned to the theatre, in which he made his first appearance in 1835, to play Dazzle ; Lady Gay Spanker, Mrs. Charles Mathews ; Grace Harkaway, Milly Palmer ; Ellen Farren, Pert ; Horace Wigan, Sir Harcourt Courtly ; Addison, Max Harkaway ; Henry Neville, Charles Courtly ; Dominick Murray, Dolly Spanker ; G. Vincent, Mark Meddle ; H. Cooper, Cool.

after a hurried peep at Drury, which appears to be going on all right,[1] to Prince of Wales's: Byron's *Prometheus and Pandora's Box*—very slight.[2] *27th.*—Very tired, but cheered by the good accounts of Drury in papers. Writing hard for *Era*. Then to Haymarket: *Lesson for Life;*[3] very dull. *29th.*—With Stone to Drury to see *Number Nip*, and I am disappointed, as usual. Then to St. James's: see Gilbert's first piece, a burlesque called *Dulcamara*, which goes off well.[4] *Era* £1 15s. *31st.*—See at Drury morning performance Duke of York's boys in attendance; and usher in the New Year at midnight after a very dull hour, which I do my best to turn into a lively one. Thus goes out a year of (to me) almost unprecedented hard work and domestic worry. God be thanked!—though I had few happy hours in it, I have done much, I believe, to make others happy; and again I hope the severe trials to which my life has been subjected will soon end, and that at last the peace I have so long

[1] E. L. B.'s pantomime, *Number Nip*, or, *Harlequin and the Gnome of the Giant Mountain*. Nymphalin, Miss Hudspeth; Pipalee, Lydia Thompson; Percy Roselle, Number Nip; Tom Matthews, Hans Hansell; Harry Boleno, clown; Barnes, pantaloon; Cormack and Madame Boleno, harlequin and columbine. There was a double set in the harlequinade: C. Lauri, clown; S. Saville, harlequin; J. Morris, pantaloon; Adéle Marion, columbine.

[2] This was called, in the bills, *Pandora's Box* or, *The Young Spark and the Old Flame*. F. Younge, Jupiter; Henrietta Hodson, Prometheus; Lydia Maitland, Venus; Lydia Foote, Minerva; Mr. Trafford, Phœbus; Mr. Tindall, Vulcan; Nelly Thompson, Pandora; J. Clarke, Juno; Bella Goodall, Hebe; W. H. Montgomery, Epimetheus.

[3] Tom Taylor's play, originally done by amateurs at the Lyceum, and produced in Manchester, October 4th, 1866. Sothern played Vivian; Nelly Moore, Mary; Chippendale, Doctor Vivian; Howe, Lord Greystone; H. Compton, Raggett, the Cambridge "Leg;" Clark, Topham.

[4] This was the piece, in the writing of which the now celebrity, W. S. Gilbert, was to commence his career as dramatic author. He called it an "eccentricity," and its second title was, *The Little Duck and the Great Quack*, founded on *L'Elisir d'Amore*. Frank Matthews in the title *rôle;* Carlotta Addison, Adina; Miss E. M'Donnell, Memorino; J. D. Stoyle, Beppo; F. Charles, Belcore; Gaston Murray, Tomaso; Eleanor Bufton, Gïanetta.

prayed for will be mine. So, 1867, do all that you can for me, please."

Estimated revenue for the year, £289.

"*Memorandum.*—Have this year lost £100 by Covent Garden, and been heavily drained by domestic troubles and ceaseless claims of my brother and his family."

1867.

"*Tuesday, Jan. 1st.*—Begin year by paying taxes. Fine frosty day. 12*th.*—To this date nothing to record but domestic grievances, which had better be left unwritten. Now nine in family to support—belonging to other people. 13*th.*—To Princess's, revival of *Streets of London ;* and to Haymarket, revival of *Serious Family.* 15*th.*—Sad accident on the ice at Regent's Park ; hear of thirty lives lost.[1] 16*th.* —Hear of death of Harry Webb, the actor and manager of Mr. T. L. Greenwood.[2] 18*th.*—Go to St. James's ; hear Miss Glyn read *Othello.* Clever, but dreary. 21*st.*—See *John Bull* at Drury ; very badly done.[3] 25*th.*—*Era* £1 10*s.* Dramatic Authors' Society £18 4*s.* 9*d.* 28*th.*—To Covent

[1] Some fifteen hundred people were on the ice formed on the ornamental water opposite Sussex Terrace, when it suddenly gave way, and all the people were precipitated in the water. It happened about four o'clock in the afternoon. Nearly fifty lives were lost.

[2] Henry Berry Webb, born in London, November 22nd, 1814. After playing as an amateur in London, appeared at the Chichester Theatre, June 1833. Then went the Devon circuit in 1838. Succeeded Wright, of Adelphi fame, at Birmingham, and remained with Mr. Simpson eight years. Made his *début* in London at the Surrey, September 7th, 1846, as Gravedigger to Macready's *Hamlet.* Remained there until Mrs. Warner took the Marylebone, when he joined her, and then subsequently became lessee of the Queen's Theatre, Dublin. With his brother Charles Webb constantly played the Two Dromios His last engagement was at Drury Lane, under Chatterton's management, when he played First Witch in *Macbeth.* Was buried in the cemetery, Gravesend, on January 18th.

[3] Phelps, Job Thornberry ; Mrs. Hermann Vezin, Mary Thornberry ; Mrs. H. Vandenhoff, Mrs. Brulgruddery ; Edmund Phelps, Tom Shuffleton.

Garden; see *Forty Thieves*; coarsely treated—all legs and limelight—but splendidly got up."

"*Feb.* 4*th*.—Drury: Phelps as Sir Pertinax MacSycophant; then to Hanover Square Rooms: Captain Mayne Reid's readings very bad. After feverish night have odd dream about C. C. B. and mother, utterly unsuggested. 5*th*.— Have heard of dear mother's illness, which is curious in connection with the dream recorded above. 6*th*.—To Princess's: T. W. Robertson's drama of *Shadow Tree Shaft*;[1] not a great success. 12*th*.—To the Grecian, and much pleased with George Conquest's *Devil on Two Sticks*. Vampire and twenty-eight traps employed."

"*March* 4*th*.—Look in at Drury: *School for Scandal*[2]; then Haymarket: Gilbert à Becket Junior's version of Victorien Sardou's *Nos Bons Villageois*, here called *Diamonds and Hearts*.[3] Record death of James Bruton; died this day, aged about sixty.[4] 6*th*.—Charles Browne (Artemus Ward) died this day at Southampton, aged thirty-three. Saddened by having the usual luck of writing memoirs of those I have known.[5] 11*th*.—Drury, *Wanted Husbands for Six*, by Charles Kenny, from the French. 16*th*.—Adelphi; and see Watts Phillips's

---

[1] The scene was laid in Staffordshire in the time of the Young Pretender, but what success did attend the piece was principally owing to the scenery. The cast was not an extraordinary one.

[2] Phelps as Sir Peter; Mrs. Hermann Vezin, Lady Teazle; Barry Sullivan, Charles Surface; T. Swinbourne, Joseph Surface.

[3] Wellbourne, Chippendale; Sir Charles Claverton, Howe; Frank Wellbourne, W. Farren; Maud, Nelly Moore; Lady Claverton, Ione Bourke; Growler, Rogers; Pennybrass, Clark.

[4] Born at Stratford-upon-Avon in 1815, was apprenticed to a silversmith, but turned his attention to literature, and became celebrated as a comic lyrist. Though self-educated, his work was excellent, and he turned out several charming ballads. He was a great humourist and punster.

[5] Born at Waterford in America in 1836, was a printer by trade, and travelled throughout New England until he settled down in Boston, and eventually became writer. His forte consisted in comic stories and essays. He afterwards turned his attention to lecturing, and from the quaintness of his delivery he became a great favourite, and earned considerable sums of money. He lectured in all sorts of extraordinary places, and before some very extraordinary audiences.

Lost in London—well written, but not a great go.[1] *25th.*—
Look in at Lyceum : revival of *Duke's Motto*, which ran 174
nights the first season.   See Swinbourne play Rob Roy, very
well done, at Drury."

" *April 2nd.*—Alfred Mellon buried this day at Brompton
Cemetery ; nearly a thousand people attend.[2] *2nd.*—Go·to
New Royalty ; one hundredth night of *Black-eyed Susan ;* a
supper in celebration, and Miss Oliver in chair.   I return
thanks for Press.   *4th.*—*Era* £1 15*s.*   Sorry to see announced the death of Charles H. Bennett, a clever young
artist (*The Owl*), aged thirty-seven. *6th.*—To Prince of
Wales's ; see Robertson's new comedy of *Caste ;* a brilliant
success, and one of the best pieces I have ever seen.[3] *8th.*—
To Haymarket, and see Mrs. Scott Siddons make her

amongst the miners, Mr. Hingston, his agent, having piloted him well.
He was once captured by Indians, and in crossing the Rocky Mountains he and his agent were attacked by wolves.   After travelling in
America, from about 1863, he returned to New York in 1864.   He
came to London in 1866, wrote for *Punch*, and then lectured in the
Egyptian Hall.   He will always be remembered at least by one work :
" Artemus Ward, his Book."   T. W. Robertson was a great friend of
his, and with E. P. Hingston was appointed his executor.   After pro
viding for his mother he left a considerable number of legacies to
children, and at his mother's death her legacy to be devoted to the
foundation of an asylum for aged and incapacitated printers.

[1] Job Armroyd, Henry Neville ; Nelly Armroyd, Miss Neilson ;
Benjamin Blinker, J. L. Toole ; Tiddy Dragglethorp, Mrs. Alfred
Mellon ; Gilbert Featherstone, Ashley. 1t was a play with a very
sad ending, but with great capabilities for any actress who undertook
the part of Nelly Armroyd.

[2] Was born at Birmingham in 1822, the youngest of fifteen children,
and was the only one who showed an inclination for music, and by the
time he was fifteen had acquired such proficiency on the violin as to
be admitted a member of the orchestra at the Birmingham Theatre,
where he soon rose to be leader, which post he held for seven years.
He was also possessed of an excellent voice.   His Figaro, Dulcamara,
and Count Rodolpho were most efficient.   Became conductor of the
Adelphi in 1844.   In 1847 appointed leader of the ballet music at the
Royal Italian Opera, and was also conductor of the Italian Opera in
the provinces.   In 1857 conducted the Pyne-Harrison English Opera
Company at Covent Garden, where was produced his opera of *Victorine.*
His Promenade Concerts were the best, perhaps, that were ever given.
He married Miss Woolgar.   Died March 27th, 1867.

[3] The Hon. George d'Alroy, Frederick Younge ; Captain Hawtree,

metropolitan *début* as Rosalind; only a promising actress.'
11*th.*—Copy out and send off the Nuptial Ode, which I call
' Cupid's Rose Leaves,' to H. B. Ffarington, Mansion House.
12*th.*—Robert Bell, journalist and dramatist, died this day,
aged sixty-four.[2] 13*th.*—See the Oxford and Cambridge boat
race. Oxford again the winner—seventh time in succession.
Finish extra lines for H. B. Ffarington, from whom letter of
thanks and £5 5*s.* 20*th.*—See Clarke make his first appearance at Adelphi in bad piece of *A Fretful Porcupine;*[3] then
to Strand, and see indifferent burlesque by W. Brough, of
Pygmalion.[4] 22*nd.*—Finger-weary; go to six theatres and
write something about each of them; finish about half-past
one. 23*rd.*—Meet Arthur Sketchley, with whom to Drury :
Great City—great rubbish.[5] Olympic, burlesque equally bad.[6]
25*th.*—*Era* £1 10*s.* for Easter theatricals. To St. James's; see

Bancroft; Eccles, George Honey; Sam Gerridge, Hare; Marquise de
Saint Maur, Miss Larkin; Esther Eccles, Lydia Foote; Polly Eccles,
Marie Wilton.

[1] W. Farren, Orlando; Howe, Jaques; Chippendale, Adam; Compton, Touchstone; Nelly Moore, Celia; Mrs. E. Fitzwilliam, Audrey;
Caroline Hill and Miss Sydney, Silvius and Phœbe.

[2] Well known on the *Atlas* newspaper, and by his novel, " The Ladder
of Gold," also by a remarkable article which appeared in the *Cornhill
Magazine* on modern spiritualism, entitled " Stranger than Fiction."
He wrote two good comedies, *Marriage* and *Temper*, played at the
Haymarket Theatre.

[3] He played Tracey Toogood. The piece was taken from the French,
and was very like *Chesterfield Thinskin.* On the same evening J. Clarke
played Blinker in *Lost in London*, in the absence of J. L. Toole.

[4] Or, *The Statue Fair.* Ada Harland, Galatea; Ada Swanborough,
Venus; Elise Holt, Cupid; Miss A. Newton, Psyche; Eliza Johnstone,
Mopsa; David James, Cambyses; Miss Raynham, Pygmalion; Thomas
Thorne, Princess Mandane. The music was arranged by Frank
Musgrave.

[5] By Andrew Halliday. Madge Robertson, Edith Fairlam; C. Harcourt, Arthur Carrington; W. M'Intyre, Mogg; Miss R. G. Le Thiére,
Mrs. Mauvray; C. Warner, Lord Churchmouse; F. Villiers, Mendez,
a Jew; J. C. Cowper, Blount. The final scene was a realization of
Frith's picture of " The Railway Station."

[6] A mythological burlesque by F. C. Burnand, entitled *Olympic
Games.* Amy Sheridan, Aurora; Maria Harris, Mercury; Nelly
Harris, Hebe; Louisa Moore, Venus; Mrs. St. Henry, Juno;
Dominick Murray, Minerva; H. J. Montague, Mars. Ellen Farren,
described as the life and soul of the burlesque, played Alectryon.

Idalia—not good.[1] 29*th*.—New Haymarket piece in five acts called *A Wild Goose Chase*, for Sothern; long rambling affair.[2] 30*th*.—Find mother better. Hear of Young's marriage, and taste the wedding cake. Bless us! how time has passed! And I?"

"*May* 6*th*.—*The Day* newspaper dies, after short seven-weeks' struggle. 7*th*.—Forage for memoir of my old friend John Povey,[3] who died last Thursday, aged sixty-nine ; and Madame Persiani, whose death is recorded.[4] 13*th*.—To Adelphi: *Henry Dunbar*, first time there. See John Parry's new sketch called *Merry Making*. 14*th*.—Poor William

---

[1] Founded by Mr. Roberts on Ouida's novel, and partly perhaps on Miss Edwards's " Half a Million of Money." Miss Herbert in the title *rôle* ; Henry Irving, Count Falcon ; F. Charles, Victor Vane ; J. D. Stoyle, Volpone Vitello ; Gaston Murray, Baron Lintz ; Charles Wyndham, Hugh Stoneleigh ; Mrs. Frank Mathews, Madame Paravent.

[2] A version by Boucicault of a story by Major Edward Bruce Hamley, entitled " Lady Lee's Widowhood," on which John Lester Wallack had previously founded a play, entitled *Rosedale*, which was really an Adelphi drama, but Sothern took a great fancy to it since it would enable him as Captain Robert Devlin to impersonate one or two characters. Caroline Hill played Lady Merivale ; Howe, Colonel Higham Ferrers ; Rogers, Mike Walsh, the gipsy ; Buckstone, Squire Bubb ; Walter Gordon, Doctor Vane ; Ione Bourke, Aurelia ; Miss Sydney, Neena ; Mrs. Chippendale, Lady Frances Devlin.

[3] John Povey was born at Birmingham in 1799 ; was the son of James Povey, known as the "Warwickshire Incledon." John Povey appeared at Drury Lane in 1817, with Edmund Kean, Elliston, Munden, Tom Cooke, Fanny Kelly, etc. In 1821 was at the English Opera House. He went with his sister, the well-known ballad-singer, to America, and appeared at the Park Theatre, New York, as Hawthorne, in *Love in a Village*. Remained in America for twenty years. He was manager and agent to Mrs. Fitzwilliam, Miss Philips (formerly of Drury Lane Theatre), Charles Mathews, and Buckstone ; and from his straightforward conduct was known as " Honest John Povey." Was buried by the side of his sister, who died in 1861.

[4] Fanny Persiani was the daughter of the distinguished tenor Tacchinardi, and was born at Rome, October 4th, 1818. First appeared as Francesca at Leghorn in 1832 ; soon after married the composer Persiani. First great success was in the title *rôle* of *Lucia di Lammermoor* at Naples, in 1835. Was great in *La Sonnambula*. Came to London in 1837, and was an operatic star here for ten years. Retired from professional life in 1849.

McConnell, the young and clever artist, dies this day. 15*th.*
—To Princess's, first night of summer season ; see *Antony
and Cleopatra;* Miss Glyn good.[1] 16*th.*—To Olympic ; see
Patter versus Clatter ; Charles Mathews very good. 18*th.*—
Clarkson Stanfield dies this day, aged seventy-four.[2] 21*st.*
—Call on Coyne. From Dramatic Authors' Society £6 14*s.*
22*nd.*—Derby Day. Prepare to go, but driven back by storm ;
so take to writing instead all day, memoir of Stanfield, etc.
Hermit won. Meet Harry Reeves, the always unfortunate
light comedian, whose request for small loan is responded to
for sake of old memories. 24*th.*—Birthday of Joseph Knight
of *Sunday Times.* 25*th.*—Attend opening of New Royal
Amphitheatre, Holborn ; the horsemanship very good indeed.[3]

[1] Henry Loraine, Mark Antony ; Charles Verner, Enobarbus ; H.
Forrester, Octavius Cæsar ; E. F. Edgar, Pompey ; Walter Joyce.
Lepidus ; James Johnstone, Eros. The first recorded performance of
Antony and Cleopatra was at Drury Lane in 1759 : Garrick, Antony ;
Mrs. Yates, Cleopatra. In 1813, at Covent Garden, Kemble's version,
which contained much of Dryden's *All for Love,* was performed with
Young as Mark Antony ; Mrs. Faucit, Cleopatra. At Drury Lane,
again, a revival took place in November 1833 : Macready, Antony ;
Miss Philips, Cleopatra. The best revival was that under the Phelps
and Greenwood management at Sadlers Wells, in 1849, with Miss Glyn
as the Cleopatra.

[2] Born at Sunderland in 1793, and died at 6, Belsize Park Road,
Hampstead, after a few weeks' illness. Was the son of James Field
Stanfield, who in early life had been a sailor, which probably led to
the son following the same profession for a time ; but in 1822 he first
appeared as a painter, and exhibited at the Society of British Artists,
and was engaged as scene-painter at the Coburg in 1824. Went to
Drury Lane, and from that time his scene-painting became celebrated,
He particularly enriched the pantomimes. For *Harlequin and the
Queen Bee,* in 1828, he painted a diorama of Spithead, Portsmouth, the
Isle of Wight, etc. ; in 1829, for *Jack in the Box,* a diorama of Windsor
and its neighbourhood ; in 1830, a diorama illustrative of Swiss and
Italian scenery ; in 1832, *Harlequin Traveller,* of American scenery ;
in 1833, *St. George and the Dragon,* of Egyptian, with the cataracts
and pyramids ; in 1837, *Peeping Tom,* of Coventry, of Italy, Savoy and
French Flanders. This was his last pantomime scene-painting. In
1839, out of friendship for Macready, he painted the scenery for the
revival of *Henry V.,* and in 1842, for the same reason, some Sicilian
views for the production of *Acis and Galatea.* He was elected an
Associate of the Royal Academy in 1832, and was celebrated for his
seascapes.

[3] This was opened by Thomas M'Collum and William Charmion, and

29*th.*—Hear of W. R. Copeland's death, of Liverpool, aged sixty-seven." [1]

"*June* 1*st.*—At Adelphi see new piece by Charles Reade called *Dora,* for Kate Terry ; first act good.[2] 8*th.*—Mother's birthday—write to her.   Holborn theatre ; Tom Taylor's new drama, *The Antipodes,* or, *Ups and Downs of Life ;* not good.[3] 15*th.*—Interview with Chatterton, and settle on *Jack the Giant-killer.*   New piece at Strand, *Our Domestics*—translation ; good.[4] Princess's, *True to the Core.*[5] 17*th.*—Chat with

was built on the site of what had been a metropolitan horse bazaar. It would contain about two thousand spectators.   The drop-curtain was by Julian Hicks.   Thomas Fillis, " Charlie " Keith and the brothers Daniel were the clowns ; John, Joseph and Henri Delevanti were the acrobats and jugglers.   A new farce called *Grim Griffin Hotel;* or, *The Best Room in the House,* by Professor Pepper and John Oxenford, was played; in it Sallie Turner appeared as Pertzer the chambermaid, and sang, " The Bailiff's Daughter of Islington."   It was a vehicle for introducing Pepper's " Cabinet of Proteus," from which all sorts of extraordinary people came forth.

[1] Lessee and manager of the Theatre Royal and Royal Amphitheatre, Liverpool.   Was apprenticed to a chemist ; but, through his father having become possessed of the lease of a theatre, and carrying it on, he became interested in stage life, and took to it altogether.   He married a sister of Douglas Jerrold, and a sister of his was the celebrated Mrs. Fitzwilliam.   He was well known on the western and northern circuits.   About 1842 he succeeded Mr. Hammond as lessee of the Liver Theatre, and, in 1843, of the Theatre Royal and Royal Amphitheatre, which he let to H. J. Byron in September 1866.   In 1851 he was manager of the Strand Theatre, London, which he rechristened " Punch's Playhouse."   His oldest friend was J. Baldwin Buckstone.

[2] Founded on Alfred Tennyson's poem.   Luke Blomfield, Billington ; Farmer Allen, Henry Neville; William Allen, Ashley; Mary Morrison, Miss Hughes ; and Dora, Kate Terry.   Henry Neville's disguise was excellent, and he and Miss Kate Terry were highly commended.

[3] Had in it some of the racing element in England and the digging element in Australia.   Ellen Terry, Madeline ; Vollaire, Murray Seymour ; Emery, Duck-fingered Joe ; Westland, Mowbray Darcus; Mrs. Raymond, Mrs. Seymour ; E. Price, Sam Strangeways ; G. Blake, Dingo ; Charlotte Saunders, Miskin.

[4] Adapted from *Nos Domestiques* by Frederick Hay ; very much resembled *High Life Below Stairs.*   Tom Thorne and David James excellent as Joseph and Francis.

[5] Transferred from the Surrey : Creswick in his old part, Martin Truegold ; Nelly Moore as Mabel.

Toole, who has given more than £200 for a piece by Byron. To Adelphi, and see a new farce by T. M. Morton, called *A Slice of Luck*. 21*st*.—The longest and the saddest day to me ; the house a den of misery—no sunbeam even in the sky. 24*th*.—At night to French plays; opening of season with Ravel and Deschamps as the principal attractions. House very full; pieces very uninteresting. Raphael Felix was the director."

" *July* 1*st*.—To Haymarket; Sothern revives *Lord Dundreary;* crowded house, but think less of assumption than ever. Write long notice for *Daily Telegraph*. 3*rd*.—Dress and sally forth for 103, Lancaster Gate, Hyde Park, which reach by eleven. Brilliant affair—Mr. Levy's party. Meet Titiens, Lemmens-Sherrington and husband, Boucicault, Sothern, Raymond, Edmund Yates, Mapleson, A. Wigan and wife, John Parry, Arnold, Robertson, Wright, George Moss and his wife, etc. Leave soon after midnight. 4*th*.— Attend Buckstone's annual benefit—*Peter Smink*, and *Who wants a Guinea?* Write notice.[1] 18*th*.—Saddened by seeing in the *Times* obituary the death of Leicester Buckingham, who died at Margate on Monday, aged forty-two.[2] 20*th*.—To Princess's ; first night of *Man o' Airlie*, with Hermann

[1] Peter Smink also played under the title of *The Armistice* at the Surrey, in 1824. It was by Howard Payne. The original Peter was John Reeve, and Ninette Madame Vestris. *Who wants a Guinea?* by George Colman the Younger, was originally produced at Covent Garden, April 1805 ; was revived at Drury Lane, 1828—the respective representatives of Solomon Grundy being Fawcett and Liston, now played by Buckstone ; Barford by John Kemble and Cooper, now played by Howe ; Andrew Bary by Emery and Harley, and now by Compton ; and Henry by Charles Kemble and Wallack, now by W. Gordon. The originals of Fanny were Mrs. Gibbs and Miss Love, now played by Miss Ione Bourke.

[2] Was the son of James Silk Buckingham, the traveller and journalist, and at one time Member for Sheffield. He had travelled a great deal with his father, and was well known as a lecturer. He delivered the explanatory description at the Panopticon, later the Alhambra, when it was a scientific institution, and also described the places of interest in Hamilton's *Tour in Europe*. A great many of Leicester Buckingham's farces, and indeed comedies, were taken from the French. He was a dramatic and musical critic of the *Morning Star*, as well as a writer on general subjects.

Vezin's management for summer season.[1] 22*nd.*—Chat with Russell at Covent Garden about pantomime, and *Valentine and Orson* chosen. To Spectroscope at St. James's Hall,[2] and the *Love Chase* at Haymarket.[3] 25*th.*—The 'distinguished amateurs' at Holborn, Marquis Townshend,[4] etc. Go to see them in *King O'Neil* and *Miller and His Men.*"

"*Aug.* 10*th.*—Death of Ira Aldridge this day recorded.[5] 12*th.*—Write article in reply to John Hollingshead's injudicious one in *Broadway.* 16*th.*—Walter busy for his departure on Sunday. I shall miss him very much here. He has accepted

[1] Suggested to W. G. Wills, the author, by a German drama by Carl von Hoëlt. It will be remembered that the hero, James Harebell, is a poet who entrusts all his savings to a scamp, in order that his work may be published. The man to whom he sends the money uses it for his own purposes, which drives the " Man o' Airlie " mad for a time. Hermann Vezin gave a very powerful rendering of the title *role.*

[2] This was an invention by M. Gompertz, and by its means extraordinary optical illusions were produced, such as the sudden appearance of ghosts, etc.

[3] The cast was almost the same as when played here seven years before. Miss Amy Sedgwick, Constance ; Mr. and Mrs. Chippendale, Sir William Fondlove and Widow Green ; Howe, Wildrake ; Kendal, Master Walter ; Ione Bourke, Lydia ; Rogers, Trueworth ; Clark, Last.

[4] This was in aid of the Universal Beneficent Society. *King O'Neil ;* or, *The Irish Brigade.* Marquis Townsend played Louis XV ; Sir R. Roberts, General Count Dillon ; W. L. Maitland, Sir Henry Arundle ; Lord Arthur Pelham Clinton, Major de Burgh ; and Sir John Sebright, Rafe. These also appeared in *The Miller and His Men,* and in *Turn Him Out.* They were supported in the evening by Eleanor Bufton, Ada Swanborough, Mrs. Leigh Murray, Patti Josephs and Louisa Eden.

[5] He died on August 7th, at Lodz, in Poland ; having been born in 1804. Was the son of a chief in Senegal, and was intended for the pulpit. He was not allowed to appear in New York for long, on account of his colour, as his appearance produced disapprobation ; but in 1833 he made his *début* in London under the name of Keene, at the Victoria Theatre, and subsequently at Covent Garden on April 10th 1833, as Othello to Warde's Iago and Ellen Tree's Desdemona. He made a splendid continental reputation, and was well liked in the provinces. Was decorated by the Emperor of Russia. His last appearance in London was in August, 1865, at the Haymarket, as Othello, to the Iago of Walter Montgomery.

post as tutor in a school. 18*th.*—Walter starts on his expedition to Mr. Kinshaw's school at Brixton. I give him a sovereign for pocket money, and Mr. Gilley half a sovereign ; so he goes off well stocked and in good spirits. 21*st.*—To Adelphi ; see Kate Terry's Julia in *Hunchback.* 22*nd.*—My old friend George Cockerell, of *The Sunday Times,* dies, aged forty-eight. 31*st.*—Kate Terry's last appearance on the London stage as Juliet—at Adelphi, in *Romeo and Juliet.*"[1]

"*Sept.* 2*nd.*—Go to Haymarket (Mrs. Scott Siddons)[2] ; Egyptian Hall (Frederic Maccabe) ;[3] and Strand (Mr. and Mrs. Howard Paul).[4] 5*th.*—Write a few lines about Oscar Byrne, who died yesterday, aged seventy-one.[5] 11*th.*—To Haymarket : Mrs. Scott Siddons as Juliet—weak, but with some good points.[6] 14*th.*—First night of Surrey season, new farce by T. J. Williams,[7] and piece by Watts Phillips, *Nobody's Child ;* house crowded ; the drama pretty, but

[1] Henry Neville was the Romeo ; Billington, Mercutio ; Miss Terry shortly afterwards married Mr. Lewis.

[2] She appeared as Rosalind in *As You Like It,* to the Orlando of Mr. Kendal.

[3] His entertainment was called *Begone, Dull Care!* in which he assumed various characters.

[4] They appeared in two little sketches. The first, *Ripples on the Lake,* as Mr. and Mrs. Dove. Mrs. Howard Paul represented Selina Ann, and gave her famous imitations of Sims Reeves, Thérèsa, the Parisian singer, and Henry Russell. Howard Paul impersonated Napoleon III., sang H. S. Leigh's "Life of Julius Cæsar," and appeared as Mephistopheles in his vocal version of *Faust.* He appeared as Staley Myldew, and sang the song of "The Twins," and also as "Major Greenback, the Stage Yankee."

[5] Appeared at a very early age in a ballet called *Oscar,* arranged by his father, a well-known dancer, a contemporary of Garrick, at Drury Lane, where for some years he remained the stock "Cupid." He then travelled in the United Kingdom and on the Continent. In 1850 joined the Princess's, under Charles Kean's management, for whom he arranged all the ballets and dances introduced into the Shakespearean revivals and the pantomimes. Subsequently was at Drury Lane under Falconer and Chatterton, and his last engagement was at Her Majesty's, November 1866.

[6] Kendal was the Romeo.

[7] *A Cure for the Fidgets.* Edward Terry played Finnikin Fussleton ; his *début* in London.

better written than constructed.[1] 16*th.*—To Lyceum; first night, and Fechter as Claude in *Lady of Lyons;* house crammed. Charles Dickens and Wilkie Collins in box beside me, and the usual notables present; much struck with the excellence of Carlotta Leclercq's Pauline; piece not over till midnight.[2] 17*th.*—Hear from C. C. B., dated June 19th, and from mother; old memories refreshed, but *not* re-awakened, for they have never slumbered!! 21*st.*—Drury reopens with *Faust* and *Miller and His Men.*[3] Take Courtney—private box—and saddened much by hearing of the death of my old friend F. G. Tomlins, aged sixty-three; I shall greatly miss him. 23*rd.*—Very sad, writing a tributary paragraph in memory of dear old Tomlins.[4] 28*th.*—Prince of Wales's reopens for season with *Caste,* which see again with real pleasure. 30*th.*—Revival of *Arrah-na-Pogue* at Princess's."

"*Oct.* 11*th.*—Meet Kent, chat, and hear he is working *The Globe* with *The Sun,* and a dozen provincial papers.

---

[1] There was a very strong part in this for Mr. Creswick as Joe, a poor miserable waif, almost an idiot. Georgina Pauncefort, Patty Lavrock; E. F. Edgar, the villain, Capt. Lazonby; Vollaire, Peter Grice, the miser; Edward Terry, Limping Dick. Some wonderful scenic effects in this piece.

[2] Fechter made a great success. Miss Elsworthy, Widow Melnotte; Mrs. H. Marston, Madame Deschappelles; G. Jordan, Beauseant.

[3] Phelps and Mrs. Hermann Vezin again the Mephistopheles and Margaret. It was the first time *The Miller and His Men* had been done at Drury Lane, though it was produced at Covent Garden so far back as October 1813. In the present production, Edith Stuart, Claudine; Miss Stafford, Ravina; C. Harcourt, Count Frederick Friberg; E. Phelps, Lothair.

[4] Frederick Guest Tomlins had been for many years connected with journalism, for, in January 1814, he criticised Edmund Kean's Shylock at Drury Lane. Was for some time acting editor and afterwards proprietor of Douglas Jerrold's *Weekly Newspaper.* Was political editor of *The Weekly Times,* and wrote under the name of "Littlejohn." Was dramatic and then art critic to the *Morning Advertiser,* and was the author of the tragedy, "*Garcia; or, The Noble Error,*" produced at Sadlers Wells, December, 1849. He was clerk to the Painter-Stainers Company, and died at his town residence, Painters Hall, Little Trinity Lane, City. He was buried at St. Peter's Church, Croydon.

14th.—Attend Adelphi, Drury, Haymarket, and Gallery of Illustrations; back by midnight, and write copy.[1] *16th.*—To St. James's; see J. S. Clarke, a new American actor, as Major de Boots in *A Widow Hunt*—funny, very.[2] *19th.*—This week record the deaths of Avonia Jones[3] and Madame Boleno.[4] *21st.*—To Olympic; see one of Maddison Morton's adaptations, *If I Had a Thousand a Year.*[5] *23rd.*—To Adelphi: *Maud's Peril*, by Watts Phillips;[6] effective drama, Belmore and Miss Herbert capital. *24th.*—Opening night of the New Queen's Theatre: Charles Reade's piece of *The*

[1] *Man is not Perfect, nor Woman Neither*, adapted by Benjamin Webster Junior, from *L'Homme N'est Pas Parfait*, by E. Thiboust, played at the Variétés; also adapted by Clement Scott in his *Off the Line*. Harry Mallet, G. Belmore; his wife Jane, Mrs. Alfred Mellon; Mike Chizzle, C. H. Stephenson. At Drury Lane, *Macbeth*. Mrs. Hermann Vezin and Barry Sullivan principals. At Haymarket, Amy Sedgwick, Hester Grazebrook in *An Unequal Match*. For first time *The Winning Card*, adapted by an actor, W. A. Wood, from the French. Mr. and Mrs. German Reed and John Parry at Gallery.

[2] Stirling Coyne's comedy had been previously played as *Everybody's Friend*. Was first brought out at the Haymarket in 1859. It was also played at the Olympic May 17th, 1865, with Mr. C. Walcot, an American actor, in the principal part. Henry Irving and Ada Cavendish, Mr. and Mrs. Featherley; Eleanor Bufton, Mrs. Swansdown; Miss Larkins' first appearance at the St. James's as Mrs. Major de Boots; G. W. Blake, Icebrook. From this date almost may be traced the life-long friendship which was struck up between E. L. B. and J. S. Clarke.

[3] Avonia Jones, Mrs. G. V. Brooke, was born at Richmond, Virginia, U.S.A., in 1836. Was the daughter of George Jones, well known at the Bowery Theatre from the year 1831. Avonia Jones made her *début* in London at Drury Lane, November 5th, 1861, as Medea, and also played at the Adelphi and Surrey Theatres; she had made a good reputation in Australia. She died October 4th, 1867, in New York, of rapid consumption. She never completely recovered the sad loss of her husband in the *London*.

[4] Celebrated as a columbine.

[5] Charles Mathews, Paddington Green; Horace Wigan, Percy Chaffington. It was in two acts. Mrs. St. Henry and Louisa Moore also in the cast.

[6] Suggested by Dr. Bernard's *L'Innocence d'un Forçat*. Miss Herbert played Maud Sefton; Ashley, Gerald Gwyn; Billington, Sir Ralph Challoner; G. Belmore, Toby Taperly; Mrs. Billington, Susan Taperly. Belmore showed much of the genius and versatility of Robson in this part.

Double Marriage.[1] *25th.*—After recording the death of W. H. Weiss, the vocalist,[2] hear that another Arundel member, poor Frederick Lawrence, the barrister, died to-day, aged forty-seven."

In *Echoes from the Clubs*, of October 30th, 1867, we find the following description of E. L. B. under " First Night " notice :—

"Do you see that pale-faced, long-fingered man in the second row of stalls? It is impossible to tell his age. He looks thirty, but may be over a hundred—indeed, must be somewhere thereabouts, if his experiences are to be believed. He has done more earnest, slave-driving work in literature than any man in the house, and yet he is comparatively unknown. We all love him, for he has made us laugh every Christmas since we were in petticoats, and we all turn to him for information, for he is a walking encyclopædia. He writes to order for the Israelites just now. Why turn up your nose? If he doesn't do it, some one else will. He must live."

"*Nov. 2nd.*—To *Doge of Venice* at Drury Lane ; good adaptation by Bayle Bernard.[3] *4th.*—To Arundel, and then

[1] The New Queen's Theatre was built from the designs of C. J. Phipps, on the site of St. Martin's Hall, Long Acre, and was opened under the management of Alfred Wigan. A new comedietta, by Felix Dale, *He's a Lunatic*, was the first piece, and John Clayton appeared as Colney Hatch ; Sanger, Sir March Hare ; Ellen Turner, Mrs. Hanwell ; Fanny Heath, a maidservant, Hatter ; Charles Seyton, Bedlam, a burglar. *The Double Marriage* was a dramatization by Charles Reade of his novel, " White Lies," which in its turn was founded on a play by Auguste Maquet, entitled *Le Château de Grantier*, produced at the Gaieté, Paris, 1852. Baroness de Baurepaire, Mrs. E. F. Saville ; her daughters Josephine and Rose, Fanny Addison and Ellen Terry ; Edouard Rivière, F. Charles ; Captain Raynal, Alfred Wigan ; Colonel Dugardin, C. Wyndham ; Doctor Aubertin, W. H. Stevens. Lionel Brough made his *début* in London as David.

[2] Willoughby Hunter Weiss was born April 2nd, 1820. Made his first appearance as Count Rodolpho in *La Sonnambula* at the Princess's Theatre, January 1843.

[3] Of Lord Byron's play, *Marino Faliero*, first acted at Drury Lane,

to Prince of Wales's; see bad farce by W. S. Gilbert, *Allow Me to Explain.*[1] *6th.*—Pay 10*s.* 6*d.* for Burton memorial, and £1 1*s.* for Tomlins testimonial; pay also one guinea for preliminary fee for installation in Urban Lodge *in re* Freemasonry. *11th.*—See new piece at Strand, *Kind to a Fault*—very good.[2] *Hamlet* at Lyceum; hear Fechter is unable to play after second act.[3] Write article after midnight. Meet Murray returned from Scarborough. *12th.*—To Olympic: a revival of Marston's comedy of *The Way to get married.* *14th.*—At night to Queen's: *Still Waters run Deep.*[4] *15th.*—Expenses for some weeks past exceeding income. *18th.*—To Lyceum: Miss Vestvali, Romeo—not great, but far from bad.[5] *20th.*—Go to St. James's; see J. S. Clarke as Tyke in *School of Reform.*"[6]

April 25th, 1821. Lord Byron's drama was revived by Macready at Drury Lane in 1842, he appearing as Marino; Hudson, Bertuccio; Anderson, Lioni; Phelps, Israel Bertuccio, and Helen Faucit, Angiolina; Miss Turpin, Mariana. It was only played for three nights. On this occasion the cast was as follows: Israel Bertuccio, J. C. Cowper; Marino Faliero, Phelps; Angiolina, Mrs. Hermann Vezin; Fernando, Edmund Phelps; Leoni, Barrett; Bertram, C. Harcourt; Calendaro, Charles Warner; Strozzi, W. M'Intyre; Steno, H. Sinclair. Edward Stirling was the stage-manager of this piece, which was produced on a very lavish scale, and with a carnival scene in which was a great ballet arranged by Cormack.

[1] George Honey, Cadderby; Bancroft, John Smith; H. W. Montgomery, Ferdinand Baker; Rose Massey, Mrs. Cadderby.

[2] By William Brough; reminiscent of *Is He Jealous?* It was in two acts.

[3] John Ryder finished the performance as Hamlet, and H. Mellon played the Ghost.

[4] First produced at Olympic May 14th, 1855, with Mrs. Melfort as Mrs. Sternhold, and Miss Maskell as Mrs. Mildmay. Mrs. Wigan, who now appeared as Mrs. Sternhold, took up Mrs. Melfort's part after a few nights at the Olympic, but was not the original. Alfred Wigan resumed his old character; Ellen Terry was Mrs. Mildmay; Charles Wyndham, Captain Hawkesley; W. H. Stephens, Potter.

[5] Felicita Vestvali had been a singer, and was a native of Westphalia. Had made a reputation in America, and had been seen at the Surrey some years previously. Milly Palmer, Juliet; Ryder, Friar Lawrence; Walter Lacy, Mercutio.

[6] Originally produced at Covent Garden, January 15th, 1805. The original Tyke was Emery, also played by Lionel Raynor in 1824 at Covent Garden, and by Lysander Thompson at the Olympic in

" *Dec. 2nd.*—To Olympic : *From Grave to Gay*, comedy adapted by young Ben Webster.[1] *5th.*—See farce of W. S. Gilbert's at Royalty, called *Highly Improbable*, and which is very queer. *6th.*—Hear of Her Majesty's Theatre being burned down; write history for *Daily Telegraph*. *7th.*—See ruins of Her Majesty's.[2] See farce at Adelphi called *Up for the Cattle Show*, by Harry Lemon. *10th.*—All morning preparing complete history for (*Era*) Almanack of Her Majesty's. To club to be brightened up; and Green is the only one to remember that on the 11th I turn forty-seven—much to my own surprise ; and thank God, with all the singularly unceasing family trouble I have had, apparently am ' getting on ' still. *13th.*—More almanack work, and finish *Era* copy, £1 15s. Obliged to draw £25 more from my little deposit account to

February 1848. He went to America, and Clarke, who was very clever in the character, appears to have taken him as his model. Henry Irving played Ferment ; Eleanor Bufton, Mrs. Ferment ; Miss Larkin, Mrs. Nicely ; Ada Cavendish, Lady Avondale.

[1] Taken from *Feu Lionel*, by Scribe and Charles Potron, first produced at the Français, January 23rd, 1858. Richard Wise, Charles Mathews ; Lady Diver Kidd, Mrs. Stirling ; Colburn, Addison ; his daughter Constance, Louisa Moore ; Edward Armitage, Henry Neville ; Cornelius Tattenham, Horace Wigan.

[2] The fire was discovered at five minutes to eleven ; by one o'clock the theatre was gutted, and the whole of the Arcade at the back was burned—nothing was saved. Mr. Mapleson, who then had the theatre, was not insured for a single farthing ; and Lord Dudley, who held the ground lease, only insured for £40,000. Madame Titiens, Mdlle. Kellogg, Mr. Hohler, and Santley were the principals engaged, and were to have appeared in *Fidelio* the following night. The theatre which originally stood on this site was erected by John Vanbrugh ; thirty people subscribed £100 each, and it was opened with opera 1705. This theatre was burnt down June 17th, 1789, the Italian Opera being transferred first to the Haymarket, and then to the Pantheon in Oxford Street. The house was re-built and re-opened in 1791 as the King's Theatre. Taylor, Goold, Waters, Ebers, Benelli, Laporte, and Lumley, were among the earlier managers, and the greatest singers who had appeared here were Mesdames Fodor and Pasta, McCrevell, Begrer, Naldi, Ambrogetti, etc. Lumley revived the fortunes of the house in 1842, and had a splendid season in 1847 with Jenny Lind. E. T. Smith held the lease for five years, from 1861, when it came into Mapleson's hands. La Scala excepted, it was the largest theatre in Europe. It changed its name from the King's to Her Majesty's in 1837.

CHATTERTON, HALLIDAY AND BLANCHARD. [*See page* 349.

meet expenses—doubled by recent hard work. Terrible account of Fenian explosion at House of Correction in evening papers.[1] 21*st*.—Rush to Prince of Wales's : new comedy by Boucicault, *How she loves him;* farcical affair.[2] 24*th*.—To Haymarket; see bad burlesque of *The Brigand*,[3] by Gilbert à Becket. 26*th*.—I think, with all the terrible hard work of yesterday, this has been the very hardest day I ever had; copy all day from daybreak. Peep at Drury, meeting a young Phelps; then to Strand, in dense fog : see Brough's *Caliph of Bagdad*[4]—very slight. Copy down to *Daily Telegraph;* and at *Era* copy till 4 a.m. 27*th*.—A visit from Walter, who yesterday was, and to-day is, going through his Civil Service examination. Jonas Levy and I look in at Drury;[5] stop to see a bit of comic business—well done. Hear of Lyceum pantomime being all in a state of confusion with alarm of fire.[6] Miss Foote (Dowager Countess of

[1] Deaths and injuries to fifty-seven people occurred through this wanton act, which it was imagined was perpetrated with a view to freeing Colonel Burke and Casey, members of the brotherhood, who were detained there. Timothy Desmond, Jeremiah Allen, and Ann Justice were first charged with being concerned. Dr. Kenealy defended.

[2] S. Bancroft, who made a hit as Beecher Sprawley in this, says in his book that the piece went well up to the end of the third act, when a situation went all wrong, and the rest of the play was not allowed to redeem the mistake ; he appears to have regretted it. W. Blakeley played Sir Abel Hotspur ; Hare, Nettletop ; H. J. Montague, Dick Heartley ; H. W. Montgomery, Doctor Minimum ; E. Dyas, Sir Jericho Maximum ; Mrs. Leigh Murray, Lady Selina Raffleticket ; Lydia Foote, Mrs. Nettletop ; Marie Wilton, Atalanta Cruiser.

[3] Or, *New Lines to an Old Ban-Ditty.* Compton, Massaroni ; Ione Bourke, Marie Grazia ; Kendal, Albert ; Fanny Wright, Theodore ; W. Rogers, Prince Bianchi ; Clark, Fabio ; Miss Dalton, Ottavia.

[4] The Caliph, Ada Swanborough ; Mahoud, Tom Thorne ; Darina, Miss Newton ; Chibib, Mr. Turner ; Cadi, David James ; Lady Camira, Miss Harland ; Hazib, Charles Fenton ; Hassan, Elise Holt.

[5] At Drury, E. L. B.'s 18th pantomime, *Faw, Fee, Fo, Fum;* or, *Harlequin Jack the Giant-killer.* Ondine, Miss Poole ; Jack, Joseph Irving ; Adelgitha, Edith Stuart ; Pigwiggin, Percy Roselle ; Nectarine, Kate Harfleur ; Harry Boleno, C. Lauri and Little Tom Dot, clowns ; Fanny Lauri, Adèle Marian and E. Valckenaere, columbines ; W. Barnes, J. Morris, and J. Russell, pantaloons ; S. Saville, Olger, and Cormack, harlequins. Tully arranged the music, and Chatterton was the manager.

[6] At the Lyceum, E. T. Smith was manager. The evening opened with a farce by T. J. Williams, entitled *Cabman No.* 93. The pantomime

Harrington) dies, aged sixty-nine.[1]   28*th.*—Edward Ledger rushes up with copy of *Era* 'Almanack,' which looks very well.[2]   To Adelphi, and see *No Thoroughfare*, with which much pleased.[3]   Look in at Re-union, and receive congratulations; then to Arundel, meeting Horace Mayhew.   29*th.*—Pack up, and off; reach Rosherville by 6 p.m.; the turkey cooked; find a 'family party' ready to partake of it.   30*th.*—Leave again; come up for Haymarket drama, *A Wife Well Won*, founded by Falconer on Paul de Kock's *Man with the Three Pairs of Breeches.*[4]   New Year wishes interchanged with old friends.   31*st.*—The last day of the eventful Old Year, and send off greeting to mother, as the only one left with a memory of the past.   Miss Sally Booth dies, aged seventy-six.[5]   'Nothing is so wonderful as to-morrow,' Arab

was Harlequin Cock Robin and Jenny Wren; or, Fortunatus, The Three Bears, The Three Gifts, The Three Wishes, and the Little Man who woo'd the Little Maid, by W. S. Gilbert.   Among the principals were Henry Thompson, Kate Blandford, Bella Goodall, Espinosa, Nellie Burton, Lizzie Grosvenor, Caroline Parkes, Miss Furtado, and Miss Roselle.   Harlequin, N. Waite; harlequina, Esther Austin; columbines, Misses Page and Lizzie Grosvenor; clowns, A. Forest, E. Lauri, F. and J. Forest; pantaloons, J. Beckenham and T. Lovell; sprites, the Dusoni family.

[1] Maria Foote was descended from Samuel Foote the dramatist, and was born at Plymouth, June 1798.   Her father originally in the army, became manager of the Plymouth Theatre, where she made her *début* as Juliet, July 1810, and in 1814 as Amanthis in *The Child of Nature* at Covent Garden.   Her parts were Maria Darlington in *A Roland for an Oliver*, Rebecca in *Ivanhoe*, Virginia and Miranda, and Letitia Hardy in the *Belle's Strategem.*   Her only son Charles, Viscount Petersham, predeceased her; her daughter, Lady Jane St. Maur Blanche, married the Earl of Mount Charles.   She married Charles, fourth Earl of Harrington, April 1831.

[2] This was the first issue (1868).

[3] This was Wilkie Collins's dramatization of his story of the same name, written in collaboration with Charles Dickens for the Christmas number of *All the Year Round.*   Joey Ladle, Benjamin Webster; Walter Wilding, Billington; Bintrey, Belmore; George Vendale, Neville; Obenreiser, Fechter; Marguerite, Carlotta Leclercq; Sally Goldstraw, Mrs. Alfred Mellon.

[4] Sothern, Albert Bressange; Madge Robertson, Marguerite de Launay; Rogers, Goulard; Buckstone, Alexandre; Kendal, Marquis de Chamont; Howe, the Count; Braid, Citizen Latour.

[5] Was born at Birmingham in 1793, appeared when only eleven years old, at the Manchester Theatre under the elder Macready's

proverb. ' After all, these years, which we get to look upon as definite periods of time marked off by a sort of temporal park fence, are nothing of the kind ; there is no break in the sweep of that planetary motion which we thus set off into hours, days, and years. " Time " itself is an incident of sense and circumstance, as strictly non-essential to existence as night, which is nothing but the poor little penumbra cast over its space by our own little world.' Thank God for all ! and ' bless everybody,' as Tiny Tim says."

Estimated revenue for year £283, including salary from *Daily Telegraph*, £150.

management as Duke of York and Prince Arthur. From thence she went to the Surrey under Elliston, and made her *début* at Covent Garden, November 23rd, 1810, as Amanthus in *The Child of Nature*. Was the original Claudine in *The Miller and His Men*. Played Juliet and Cordelia. Was a member of most of the better London theatrical companies. Made her last appearance at the Marylebone in 1841 for the benefit of Mr. Attwood, when she played Kate O'Brien in *Perfection*, and Lisette in *The Sergeant's Wife*.

END OF VOL. I.

Printed by Hazell, Watson, & Viney, Ld., London and Aylesbury.